I0603481

Pelsaert's
Nightmare

Pelsaert's Nightmare

-A novel-

Gregory Warwick Hansen

THE GRAYSON PRESS

First published by The Grayson Press

Copyright © 2020 Gregory Warwick Hansen

All rights reserved. No part of this publication may be reproduced, distributed, or transmitted in any form or by any means, including photocopying, recording, or other electronic or mechanical methods, without the prior written permission of the author, except in the case of brief quotations embodied in critical reviews and certain other noncommercial uses permitted by copyright law.

For permission requests, write to the publisher at
The Grayson Press
23 Albert Street
Port Melbourne, Victoria 3207
Australia

www.gregoryhansenwriter.com
Ordering Information:
Special discounts are available on quantity purchases by corporations, associations, and others. For details, contact the publisher at the address above.

Printed in the Australia

A catalogue record for this book is available from the National Library of Australia

ISBN 978-0-6486881-0-5 (hardback)
ISBN 978-0-6486881-1-2 (paperback)
ISBN 978-0-6486881-2-9 (ebook)

Cover art: Dusk Bruny Island – Christine Gibbs
Cover design: Jennifer Bullock
Maps: Jennifer Bullock
Author photograph: Sherrie Antonio
Interior Layout: Pickawoowoo Publishing Group

For Sherrie,
whose provisioning of this voyage ensured a smoother passage
and more welcome outcome.

In the antipodean winter of 1629, the Dutch East Indiaman *Batavia* was wrecked on the desolate cays of the Houtman Abrolhos, an island chain lying beyond the sea horizon of what is now Western Australia.

Her merchant commander was Francisco Pelsaert.

A man's life is larger and more complex than the representation of any one event, yet a single incident is enough to disfigure the past and contest the moment.

At times he was a prey to agonies of morbid uneasiness, amounting sometimes to panic. But he remembered, too, moments, hours – perhaps whole days – of complete apathy which came upon him as a reaction to his previous terror and might be compared with the abnormal insensibility sometimes seen in the dying.

Crime and Punishment, Fyodor Dostoyevsky

Manifest of Those Met and Those Mentioned

Of Pelsaert and his family

Francisco Pelsaert, Uppermerchant, *Batavia*'s Commandeur and member-elect to the Council of the Indies
Barbara, his mother
Anna and **Oeyken**, his younger sisters
Maria, Barbara's maid and family nurse
Opa (Dirick), Francisco's grandfather
Hans, his grandfather's cousin
Marta van Luyck, a Flemish widow

Of the Dutch and VOC at home and abroad

VOC (*Verenigde Oost-indische Compagnie*), the Dutch East India Company (the "Company")
The High and Mighty or **Gentlemen Seventeen**, the VOC Directors at Amsterdam
Council of the Indies, the VOC's governing body at Batavia

VOC associates

Cornelis and **Frederick de Houtman**, VOC pioneers in the East Indies

Henrik Brouwer, a member of "The High and Mighty"

Jan Coen, VOC-appointed Governor General of the Dutch East Indies (Batavia)

Jacques Specx, his successor (and daughter, **Sara**)

Antonio van Diemen, a Councillor of the Indies

Pieter Vlack, a Councillor and Coen's brother-in-law

Pieter van den Broecke, a Councillor and leader of the trade mission to India

Walter van Heuten, Van den Broecke's lieutenant

Hendrick Vapoer, a VOC emissary dispatched to India

Grijph, VOC "supercargo" aboard the *Dordrecht* bound for Amsterdam

Adriaan Bok, a VOC official (Amsterdam)

Meyer, a VOC archipelago-based agent

Gillis, a VOC inter-island official

Pieter Cortenhoeff, a standard-bearer at Batavia

Other residents of the Netherlands

Abraham Cortenhoeff, Amsterdam's Town Clerk (uncle of **Pieter Cortenhoeff**)

Belijtgen, wife of Jeronimus Cornelisz (and their **baby**)

Rubens, Flemish painter and collector of antiquities

Torrentius, Dutch painter, atheist and libertine

Other residents at Batavia

Maartens, a sick-visitor and church layman

Croock (and unnamed **woman**)

Sambrix (and unnamed **woman**)

Pieterge, wife of **Willem Jansz** (away in Ambon)

Hartanti, carer-servant of Pelsaert

Of *Batavia*, the Abrolhos and Great South Land

VOC officials
> **Jeronimus Cornelisz**, Undermerchant reporting to Pelsaert
> **Salomon Deschamps**, Senior Assistant to Pelsaert
> **David Zevanck**, a clerical assistant

Sailors
> **Ariaen Jacobsz**, Skipper of *Batavia*
> **Jan Evertsz**, High Boatswain of *Batavia*
> **Claas Gerritsz**, Uppersteersman of *Batavia* and later the *Sardam*
> **Gillis Fransz**, Understeersman of *Batavia*
> **Jan Pelgrom**, cabin servant aboard *Batavia*
> **Jacob Jacobsz**, Skipper of the *Sardam*

Soldiery aboard *Batavia*
> **Mattys Beer**, soldier
> **Wiebbe Hayes**, soldier
> **Jan Hendricxsz**, soldier
> **Coenraat van Huyssen**, cadet
> **Allert Jansz**, gunner
> **Wouter Loos**, soldier
> **Stone-Cutter Pietersz**, lance-corporal

Passengers
> **Gijsbert Bastiaensz**, Predikant aboard *Batavia*
> **Maria**, his wife
> **Gijsbert Bastiaen**, their eldest son
> **Judith**, their eldest daughter
> **Wybrecht Claasen**, their servant-girl
> **Lucretia Jansz**, passenger aboard *Batavia* and wife of **Boudewijn van der Mijlen** (at Arakan)

Zwaantie Hendricx, Lucretia's maid
Mayken Cardoes and **baby**, passengers aboard *Batavia*
Unnamed mother and **baby**, passengers aboard *Batavia* and its longboat

Of India (Hindustan)

The Imperial household
 Jahangir, Mogul emperor of India (son of **Akbar** the Great)
 Nur Jahan, his wife
 Itimad-ud-daulah, her father (and Jahangir's vizier)
 Asaf Khan, her brother
 Khusrav, Jahangir's eldest son
 Shah Jahan ('The Wretch'), Jahangir's middle son
 Shahryar, Jahangir's youngest son
 Mahabat Khan, Jahangir's childhood friend and chief general
 Abul Fazl, friend and vizier to Akbar

Khanin's household
 Wasim Khanin, a Mogul courtier
 Hussain, his cousin (and **Farida**, Hussain's wife)
 Asmat Khanin, Wasim's wife (and her **eunuch**)
 Waheeda, Wasim's most recent wife
 Muzaffir, Asmat's brother

Merchants, camp followers and one dying man
 Medari, a Muslim merchant and indigo buyer
 Mirza Sadiq and **Ghazi Fazil**, Muslim indigo growers at Bayana
 Pagoo Singh and **Nagar Bai**, Hindu indigo brokers at Bayana
 Randasingh, a camp follower on the march to Kashmir
 Fakkad Khan, a camp follower on the march to Kashmir
 Inayat Khan, a dying resident of Agra

Christian missionaries
Antonio Andrade, a Jesuit priest and first European to enter Tibet
Manuel, a Jesuit brother accompanying Andrade

English emissaries
William Hawkins, an early English emissary to the Mogul court
Thomas Roe, the subsequent English ambassador

Also

John Calvin, French theologian and proponent of predestination
Gerhardus Mercator, Flemish geographer and cartographer
Prester John, legendary priest-king said to rule over a lost Christian people in "the Indies"
Ernst von Mansfeld, German military commander during the Thirty Years War
Constantine, 4th century Roman emperor

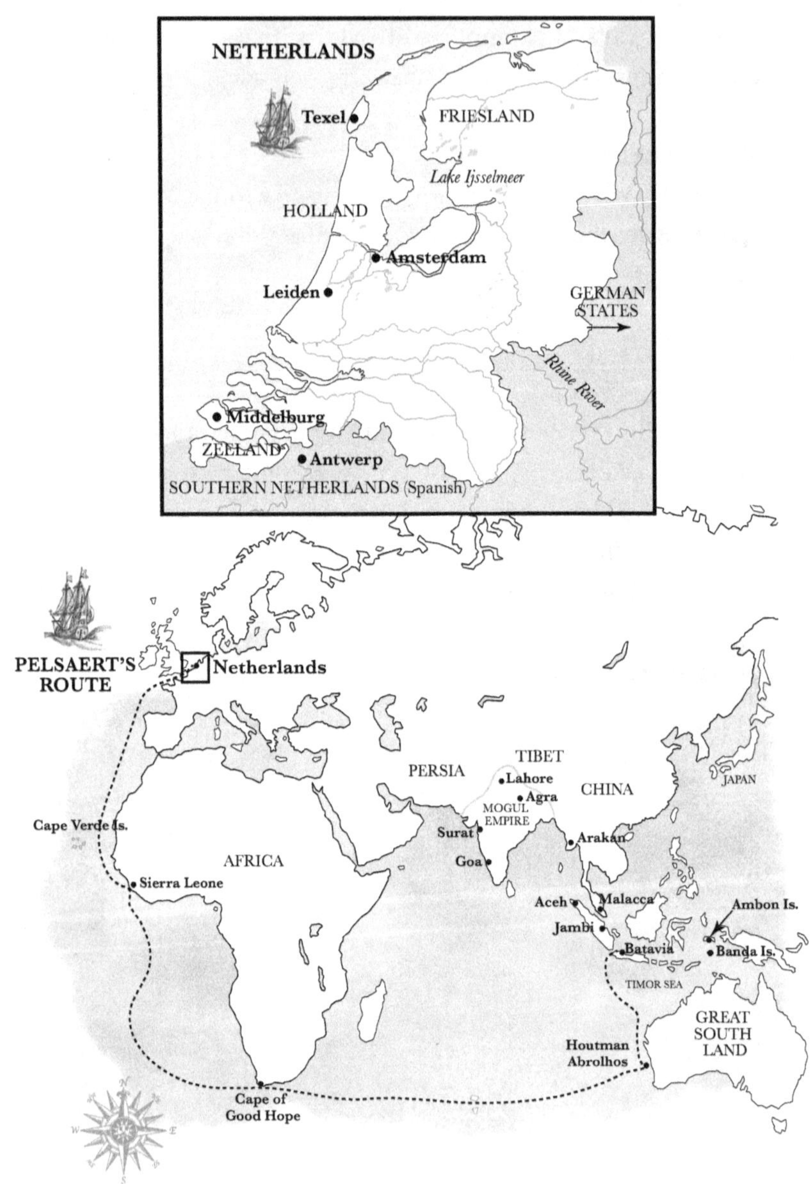

NETHERLANDS
Texel
FRIESLAND
Lake Ijsselmeer
HOLLAND
Amsterdam
Leiden
GERMAN STATES
Rhine River
Middelburg
ZEELAND
Antwerp
SOUTHERN NETHERLANDS (Spanish)
PELSAERT'S ROUTE
Netherlands
Cape Verde Is.
AFRICA
Sierra Leone
PERSIA
TIBET
Lahore
Agra
MOGUL EMPIRE
CHINA
JAPAN
Surat
Arakan
Goa
Aceh
Malacca
Ambon Is.
Jambi
Batavia
Banda Is.
TIMOR SEA
GREAT SOUTH LAND
Houtman Abrolhos
Cape of Good Hope
N
W
E
S

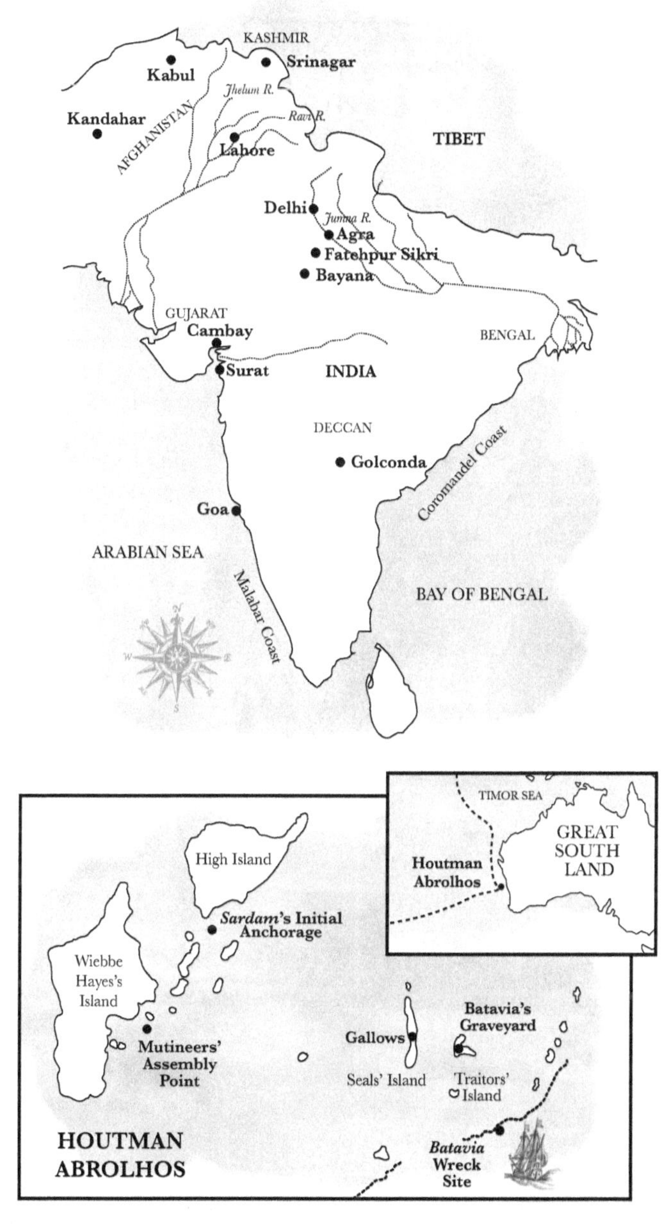

KASHMIR
Srinagar
Kabul
Jhelum R.
Ravi R.
Kandahar
TIBET
AFGHANISTAN
Lahore
Delhi
Jumna R.
Agra
Fatehpur Sikri
Bayana
GUJARAT
Cambay
BENGAL
Surat
INDIA
DECCAN
Golconda
Coromandel Coast
Goa
ARABIAN SEA
Malabar Coast
BAY OF BENGAL
N
W   E
S
TIMOR SEA
GREAT
SOUTH
LAND
Houtman
Abrolhos
High Island
Sardam's Initial
Anchorage
Wiebbe
Hayes's
Island
Batavia's
Graveyard
Gallows
Mutineers'
Assembly
Point
Seals' Island
Traitors'
Island
HOUTMAN
ABROLHOS
Batavia
Wreck
Site

PELSAERT'S NIGHTMARE

"Francisco, wake up! Come Maria, the child must be dressed and breakfasted and ready for his grandfather. Quick now, Francisco – out of bed!"

"But surely, ma'am, a fever is upon him."

"Nonsense," and scoring her own flushed cheek with shell-like nails. "Hurry, there's much he must attend to."

"Ma'am I beg, look how the child stews! He's barely mindful and of such a sweat as it bleeds from his skin!"

In another part of the house, the spectre of a baby's mewling.

Francisco please, a hand upon his sleeve, the panelled ceiling dark like the underdeck of a ship, that saline stomach roll – *ugh*. His eyes recoil as he startles to a dream no less pressing, their burning faces a smudge without feature, the sun a cinder of light so intense that the sky appears green, the colour of unhealthy stucco.

"Commandeur, please..."

He tries to focus, to remember where he is, the rocking ceaseless. A small box rests upon his knees: ink and paper, the worded binding of a life. Except that he has no energy, and there isn't the luxury to stretch and rid himself of cramp. The baby is crying incessantly now. Otherwise the longboat is a silence of frayed inertia, of forbearance spun from exhaustion. Except for Evertsz. "In the name of God shut that carping brat up or so help me I'll toss it to the waves."

"Quiet," growls Jacobsz, the tiller stained with the juice of his armpit. Pelsaert hates the skipper but hate is scarcely of service here. The baby is the thing most alive, the resentment most struggling to assert itself. It goads its mother, has her scrabbling at her bodice, her florid teat unremarked. Zwaantie, the skipper's concubine, is seated shoulder hard, the only other woman in this cram of almost fifty. The young mother is frightened; frightened for her child, frightened by the isolation it provokes. She's heard the tales, of horrors on the open sea. She plugs the infant's mouth with her ungiving nipple.

Francisco stares at her and Zwaantie through pews of expressionless seamen, the baby a mere two months old, the tiny emissary of a distant republic. And he wonders how the other children fare, trying to sort out in his mind the number and ages of those left behind. Not to mention the grown folk — God, how many? — their faces an anonymous coinage. Easily his greatest trial is among this lot, this self-saving ark of talent and latent treachery. It's been, now, how many days? He opens the box to consult the last entry in his journal and finds that he has written little; just the skipper's daily reckoning and a note on the weather. It's astonishing to observe how so little might substitute for so much. It's as if he lives in dust, the sweet draught of language all but dried in the ironic desert of the sea. Something is upon them, something huge and unfolding, and there are not the words.

S HE STANDS THERE staring at me, her eel-dark hair a cable of insolence. She's
   waiting, her caution not above contempt; waiting to see whether I might
die. Today. Tomorrow. The day after...

I've survived long enough to appreciate the casualness of disappointment.
If for nothing else I'll live to defeat her, to cast back in her face *my* contempt for
her sullen forbearance. Yes, I am more than I appear – no ordinary sufferer.
An appointee to the Council of the Indies, no less! If only that whore's shit
Van Diemen would stop trying to eclipse my sun. No, I will not be watched
to wither by a mere serving girl no better than a slave!

Don't excite yourself, Francisco – the woman's little more than you allege.

Silence.

Might she read my thoughts as I read hers? It stinks in here yet I feel
unequal to the task of asking that a window be opened. Having ventured to
the hearth of lands unknown, I can scarcely credit that everything is now
dwindled to this lurid space, the next too shuddersome to contemplate. If I
could raise myself, I would seek the bracing sunlight. How often have I stood
of a morning – here, and in India – in greedy contemplation of a day at its
ablution, the light moist on limbs rinsed of night and for one brief moment
unadorned by worry or account? Yes, before the hours turned into something
shrill and without clarity...

No, the humour of this accursed place is strangling, the air charged with
a sweet heaviness that torpors the will. I close my eyes and ask – surprised to
hear my voice rasping, whisper-like – for some water.

Hartanti hesitates, her wariness teetering on respect for the menace of
illness. The water tastes of pewter – *blah* – and I watch as she moves beyond
my reach, her slender vertebrae and that womanly backside stirring a flicker
of muscle. Ha, a good sign, no?

"Heer Maartens is here," she turns on me.

"Who?"

"A visitor."

"Not some churchman!" I huff, and thinking of Bastiaensz.

"Not quite," replies the stranger as he pokes his head through the doorway, his knock a pointless courtesy. "Governor Specx has asked me to call."

One look at him and my suspicion is confirmed. "Ah, a sick-visitor." I fall back on my pillow. *Clownish and uncircumcised idiots*, that's what Coen had thought of them, may his soul rest in peace.

Maartens and Hartanti stand side by side, watching me through a screen of thought like women from a harem balcony. I'm jealous of their relative youth, their guarded health. I gesture to a chair beside the bed, its architecture cool and upright as I sometimes dream of Antwerp – that chair remembered, almost throne-like, in the study of my grandfather. And his globe of the world, the known and the speculative encircled within an equatorial brace of sandalwood.

Maartens fits himself to the unyielding seat, his arse uncomfortable.

"What news from the Castle?" I ask.

"There is little I might tell."

"Come, Jacques Specx is a friend."

Maartens says nothing. It's as if he's unsure of what he's been asked to attend.

"What, will no one speak with me – tell me how my confirmation to the Council fares?"

"I'm sure I wouldn't know about such things," and his eyes are elusive. I saw that look among those on the island, a withholding that left them all diminished – even Salomon. Ordinary men turned cowards.

"Hartanti, you may leave us," I wave.

My wick is as shrivelled as my appetite, and I feel a steepening lethargy. I'm unequal, even, to this watery fool they've placed 'twixt me and all that I've laboured for. Batavia has become a judgement of polite avoidance. *Look at you: an invalid unable to account for your wreckage, to give us anything which might restore our estimation.*

"None of this was my fault!" I shout, and startled by my outburst.

Silence. Nothing to suggest that another may have heard. I scrutinise Maartens' physiognomy.

"The Governor trusts you'll soon be well enough to resume your duties," he says.

And with that, a glimmer of hope. My honour, my service to the Company – surely this lifetime's sweat must count for something! *Francisco, and*

Brouwer calling me aside, *that report of yours has greatly impressed the Directors. They're not averse to risk so long as men of calibre campaign wholly for success. You go back to India and its heathen Mogul, enrich us as you say you can, and with you will travel a letter commending your appointment to the Council of the Indies.* The canals beyond the Guildhall reeked in the August heat, Amsterdam not unlike Surat on days when the wharves mix spice and vice in equal measure.

I stare at Maartens, his face as harmless as a bun, and don't trust him. "What's your position in the colony?" I ask, knowing that his answer will loiter short of truth.

"I'm a lay-reader, little else. Under direction of the Church Council. I was aboard the Governor's ship last year when…"

I'm watching him closely, his halting delicacy. Batavia is a small town and they all fear contamination. I am lodged beyond the Castle walls. "'Tis a long way to come for so lean a post," I say.

He fingers his collar, its starch turning to glue with perspiration. "I seek no more than to serve the Company and my God."

Hmph. "Are you married?"

His skin mottles as he studies his knuckles. A proper little self-abuser, I should think, and a party to that witch hunt which doubtless sought to ruin me at the beginning of the year. Moral guardians, my arse! Predikants and their apprentices – all interfering and stern counsel and of no salvation to anyone, least of all their own.

"I hope to find a wife," I hear him say.

"You'd better source yourself a native," I reply unkindly. "The only Dutch women are those who come married, and the competition for widows is fierce."

"I hear even those who are married are not safe from opportunists." It's then that I see him smile, a subtle weighing derived less from common gossip than some intelligence he has on me. I am right not to trust him.

"There's scarcely a husband who can secure his wife in this faraway place," I feebly rejoin.

You would know, Francisco. How many married women? Women whose husbands were away, engaged in the honourable pursuits of the Company?

No, that's not true! Van der Mijlen was dead. I never ventured against Lucretia. I – I tried to protect her after the assault. She was distraught. None already knew that her husband had perished.

So many dead. It's rather a lot to answer for.

I was not to blame!

"Heer Pelsaert?" Maartens is leaning close, his visage squeezed and distant as if peering from above into the obscurity of a deep shaft. And it is me who lies at the bottom, panting. "Sir, can I get you some water, a little wine?"

I shiver involuntarily. "I feel chill, Maartens, even though I see you sweat. I fear I am forgotten."

They would *all* like to forget; have the sea rise up and smother the innocent with the guilty, rinse the stain of what happened clean away. The evil ones already punished, the survivors yet to disappear.

And waving him away, "Even if you are a spy, Maartens, you must come again."

One does not sleep. One does not waken either. My body is a cornered nation in pained revolt against that which invades. Yet it is not the flesh alone that suffers. I am soul sick, hounded by demons whose faces resolve into something startlingly familiar, much as if I were standing before a transparent glass in whose reflection I nonetheless trace outlines of my imprecise phantom. Lord, how did I arrive at this?

I am not an old man yet illness now occludes my youth. I am trapped before my time, curtailed in all my prime. Well do I remember that first tremor, the aching desertion of outward care which was inseparable from the chills. And a lethargy such as I had never experienced but have subsequently learned to live with in unequal truce. The rainy season had arrived, the land cooled to an anger of impotence and opportunity. I did not stir for days. I did not know for days. It is said that in birth a man embarks upon his journey towards death. If so, then at Agra I arrived at its first great metropolis.

My life has been industrious, its habits attuned to detail. My apprentice-ship was a rapid and adventurous schooling in the ways of the Company, and I proved an exemplary second to my superiors.

It was at Agra, at the seat of Jahangir, that Mahometan monarch of all Hin-dustan, that I attained an elevation which ought permanently to have fostered my standing. Yet I found lacking in others the very support that should have pearled my oyster. Surat, a dirty city full of trade and the shipboard shuffle of pilgrims bound for Mecca, was at least washed by distant sea breezes that came swallowing up river from the west. At low tide the sandbanks provided a platform upon which to load and unload all manner of traffic, the overseeing fort constructed of white coral. When I first arrived, none from Europe had long been in residence, but a cemetery was already formed. The English and ourselves lived in the town and without defence, for such was the legacy of the great Akbar – not to mention the preoccupation of every man with trade – that we were protected by the universal talisman of commerce. I was not long in Surat before adventure ushered me across its portal and I, under Wal-ter van Heuten and with several assistants in tow (Salomon among them), journeyed to the interior, to the fabled capital at Agra. I was brimming like a florid youth to meet the opulently rumoured Jahangir. I well remember the loaded wagons, the porters clothed in ivoried tunics and colourful scarves, the cattle straining on roads a-slush with mud and dung, and the intemperate sun a liquid fire. It was to be my last sighting of the sea for several years and I was moved, in departing, by the daring of our race. To have reached half-way around the globe, to have landed at the tasselling surf of the great Mogul kingdom itself, all this filled me with a sense of imminent destiny, of pride at finding myself numbered among that select and wandering caste. As we turned from the Arabian Sea, from the spars and sail of our unfolding great-ness, I felt a sense of transfer, a conveyed responsibility to complete a mission, the watching eyes of those who had ferried us to these opportune shores now assessing our calibre and the probability of success. In those innocent days I sorely loved the concept of our fleet: the shipwright's palette and carpenter's sculpting, the science of the astrolabe and the bluff and trusted competence of our men. Company men, all. Yes, those ships and their skippers were the long and stalwart line of our communication, the floating bastions from which we sallied. How cruel then, how ironic to reflect that from that very harbour, after everything that would colour and embolden my career, I should return one day – in transit to an even more important destination – and meet Ariaen Jacobsz. By that time my health had become, shall we say, unreliable. But worse was to come.

$\backsim$

"Salomon – quick, there isn't a moment to spare! We must pen a message to Governor Coen."

But you have spoken to him already.

"We must apprise him of what's happened. We must hastily arrange our return to the islands. Who knows how many…"

Heer Commandeur, I too have been abandoned there.

"Salomon?"

We all await your promise.

"I – I can redeem all of this. Salomon. I – I can save myself. Salomon?"

"Tuan?"

Hartanti stands there, her brow creased in alarmed unknowing. Her eyes wondrously dark, her cloth stainfully green, she holds a pewter chalice in which a little wine is poured. Her forearm is slender and unblemished, its colour a warmth of lacquered health. Yes, colour is everything in this accursed climate.

"Where are they, Hartanti?"

"Tuan?"

$\backsim$

Each man seeks to expand upon his grade – each man, that is, who is covetous of his worth and contemptuous of that which would confine him to his origins. I was born into a state of orphanage. No, that's not strictly true. Both my parents survived the advent of my birth, and my mother still lives as far as I know. But I am of a nation forged in the testament of fire, a race denied its birthright by the Catholic injustices of a foreign prince. Like the Hebrews of old, we were galvanised in God's covenant to oppose the cruel excesses of the idolater.

My family were from Flanders – still are – but events would play their part in shifting the locus of opportunity from south to north, from Antwerp to Amsterdam, a city suddenly burgeoning with refugees of wealth and talent, its promise farthest from the reach of Spanish troops. No Pharaoh of old was more tyrannical, no Caesar more overbearing than the popish Spanish crown. In the generation before my birth, its presumption to rule not only the pastures of our tending but the very conscience of our people purported an arrogance that could not go unresisted. It was an age when the true light of reform shone in stellar contrast to the robes and incense of a sinister priesthood, when under that alien tongue alone the inquiry of what a man might reason might likewise consign him to the flames. The enslaving and unspeakable cruelties that Spain visited upon the Indians, smelting their idols to cast in golden ostentation the impiety of their own, now sought fresh and violent practice upon a true and Christian people. Their villainy against us would invoke the sword of Gideon and sling of David, would marshal our heritage in defiance of their oppression. If ever there was proof that the Almighty favoured the righteous, such was the prospering of our cause – even to this day. While the Spanish menace falters, its empire depleted through savagery and extortion, we extend the imprint of Batavia, our ships the envy of the world, our arms a shield of Godly virtue. Never was there an enterprise so great, so civil in the sanctity of its mission, as the Dutch –

Oh for God's sake!

Silence.

"Who's there?"

I detect a snigger – a sigh, perhaps, of impatience? *You were born into a Catholic household.*

"But not the house of Spain!" and piqued by this dream of presence.

You're very swift to declaim what you're not. "Never me, never me." It begs a truth that might one day leave you empty.

I feel, as I have increasingly of late, the unbelonging of my life, my bath turned cold.

You've opted for very little when all is said and done.

"How do you mean?"

The Company or nothing — that was a narrow horizon, surely.

"Narrow? When I have ventured more than most men, crossed seas and continents? The Honourable Company has been my making. It has been my family —"

You have a family.

"Yes — but no. To get on in this world I've had to journey far, to live apart, to..."

Follow your dreams?

I hear but cannot accept. To accept is to confess that I have been a refugee on the make my entire life.

Tell me Francisco, what sort of dreams do you thrive on?

"Lately my thoughts have been full of brooding."

I shouldn't wonder. Still, it shall soon be over.

"How do you mean?"

You're dying, Francisco. Surely you can read the signs this time: the absence of all recovery, those little interludes of respite which favour the illusion your body has hardened to the necessity of what you're yet to accomplish. So much to do, so little time.

"You mock me!"

You mock yourself to think that you have any future after all that has happened.

"I want only that my name," and gasping now, "be recalled with honour. That my reward of office be honoured, too."

Honour was abandoned at the Abrolhos, your reputation weathered in your absence on the Timor Sea.

"I did what I thought best!"

Silence.

"Are you listening? Jacobsz couldn't be trusted!"

The night is very dark, and I can smell my hair, my feet. I need water, not this salt that steams from my limbs but something clean, something rushing and pure. We came ashore the day after making landfall, the perilous balance of our journey in the longboat now mercifully resolved, and to our luck found a waterfall. God be praised, we could quench our thirst and replenish the casks. After weeks in fragile company with the sea, its element too vast and inscrutable to engage with any affection, I now plunged my face into the quivering pool, the brine rinsed from the sores encrusting my lips. So cool and prayed for, this salvation, the dancing voices of those survived leaping like birdsong in the shaded gully. Not like the desolate coastline of that place we'd parted from ten days earlier, a land utterly without promise, its vast shelf rebutting all civility. Even the natives glimpsed had seemed tentative, apparitional.

Yet here, too, somewhere on the southern shores of Java and finding refreshment, danger continued to lurk within the tortoiseshell jungle, and I prevailed on discipline to post sentries. My beard was cool on my throat, and having slaked my thirst I locked eyes with Jacobsz...

We each stand amidst the excited peals of those who had little thought to survive the crossing – the tearful mother bathing her infant whose cries no longer offend, and Zwaantie, farther off, attending her toilet – and are calculating *what next?* Ever since the wreck – and may God forgive him his culpability – we have lived a game of goad and chance. Even now his insolent eyes are in no hurry to look away, sampling my position and his predicament. With a sailor's eye for the wind, he turns and shouts for Evertsz, the high boatswain. The two of them have been in collusive disagreement ever since we left the Great South Land – their pact, I suspect, has begun to unravel. I must hold my tongue and preserve my command to the conclusion not only of our safe arrival in Batavia but the rescue of those left behind at the wreck. The skipper is doing his best to appear without fault and inspire confidence – to impress me, I should think, for he hates me and I feel nothing in return but scorn. The braggart has brought us to this, his intemperance the very stink of mutiny. As for Evertsz, he's simply a criminal with rank. There's no doubting he led the assault on Lucretia, cornering her on deck that night, leaving her to shiver in a filth of excrement. And Jacobsz knew. They all knew. Each would have me presently grateful for what is an unwarranted and exaggerated worth. But it's Evertsz I'll nail first. When we arrive at Batavia

I'll let the authorities literally drag the truth out of him. You see, this is what I've had to contend with.

—⁂—

"Francisco, my child, hurry along. Your grandfather has arrived. Oh Maria, help him with that buckle on his shoe. Here, let me fix your collar."

"Mama?"

"It's not every young boy who is given this opportunity."

"Will I be coming back?"

"You go, now, to live with Opa."

"But Anna – and Oeyken?"

"Oeyken's a baby. Your sisters will remain here with your stepfather and myself." Then squatting before me, an irreducible distance preserved by the volume of her skirts, she adds, "Opa is thinking of you."

I'm mistrustful of what she means and ask, "Will I be able to see you?"

"Of course, you silly dumpling! Doesn't Opa visit regularly?"

Maria is standing in a corner, her hands folded across her apron in a way that leaves me less than convinced. My trunk is packed and, outside, voices are raised in salutation. I hear the wagon turn around. There is laughter, then a brisk clop of footsteps in the hallway.

"Ah, there you are, my boy. And looking a damned sight better!"

"Father, please..."

"Oh, one shouldn't coddle the lad. He'll soon find himself among men, eh?" And fastening a hand on each shoulder, he gives me a vigorous shake. "Just remember, there's no wealth without your health."

"I've no money either, Opa."

He laughs as mother looks away. Then squatting as she did, his knees creaking and his smell peppery, "Well then, we'll need to school you in the ways of a proper little Hollander."

"Are we not Flemish?" I reply, attuned to a former pride of difference.

Opa's eyes grow pragmatic. "These days it's best if we all become a little more Dutch." Then smiling, "Come, you'll live with me and I'll teach you many things."

I am helped into the wagon, its smell of horsehair, and a loud thud behind me signifies the fellow exile of my trunk. Mother is on the front step, smiling. Strange, she seems less certain than I of what awaits, for I know nothing. Maria is perched behind her, my stepfather and sisters nowhere to be seen. As the wagon jerks forward, I know that my life will never be the same, that I must absorb new ways. It is the beginning of my odyssey, one that will never lead me home.

If, in this shiftless torpor, I might revisit any of my dreams, perhaps it would be of India. Its unlovely plains were the making of me, its teeming discourse the theatre of my maturity, its siren beauty the realm and anguish of my heart.

Having sailed for the East in the *Weapon of Zeeland*, I'd already served time travelling to the Moluccas, Ambon and Banda – islands rich in clove, pepper and nutmeg; yes, exotic frontiers yielding camphor, gold and opium. Oh, and slaves. In Banda the native population had all but been eliminated, so it was essential that others be found to harvest the plantations and work the mines. I confess it took some getting used to – the frequent necessity for chains, the floggings and exemplary deaths that served as warning to all that a new order had arrived in the islands. Governor Coen was quite adamant: *We must ride the natives with a sharp spur.*

Thus I learned the ways of the Company, visiting the limp and woven villages which so much river wash had snared at the mouth of each estuary, the sun striking fiercely through a copper haze. Life shuffled and squatted and bellowed aloud in a wilt enforcement of traditions, the fume of incense vying with the call to prayer in jealous antipathies of superstition. Each backwater was its own dog-infested republic, each republic the chattel of some greater despot. And these we dealt with gingerly.

Throughout the archipelago the reek of decay was always mitigated by the appearance of so much growth. Indeed, it was impossible to drop a seed without it instantly germinating into the mortality of its cycle. The face of Death, like the shrivelled visage of some whore, bore a disguise of potions, spice and perfume.

Such was my proclivity in acquiring the trade that within a few short years I was sanctioned to join our mission in India. Oft had I boarded a local jacht beneath the guns of Batavia Castle, but only to such island destinations as was routine to this part of the world. A venture to India, on the other hand – that most rumoured of continents – appealed to my adventurous curiosity, and I jumped at the opportunity. The Company was bent on expansion and, thus, to the Western Quarters – those lands which fringed the Arabian Sea – was I dispatched, newly promoted to the rank of undermerchant and with instructions to report to Pieter van den Broecke at Surat. The journey was arduous inasmuch as we were landed on the Coromandel Coast, then forced to haul ourselves across the treacherous Deccan to that distant port. It was evident by this journey alone that the cause of trade might be better served by simply sailing around the vast peninsula that is India. Yet, in another sense, this transit was invaluable to my understanding of the regions in which I would reside for the next seven years.

Never had I come across such a superfluity of people, nor had I witnessed such extremes of wealth and want. In our Fatherland there is a sense of commonwealth – of master and servant, to be sure, of artisan and labourer, certainly, but all subservient to a unified purpose and the justice of God. In my formative travels across Hindustan, however, I learned that the country was ruled by an accepted malaise of inequity, that the rich were absolute and self-serving in their power while the common folk were domiciled in bitter want and servitude. Of the latter, scarce any make the effort to advance their lot because a workman's line can follow none other than that of the father, nor can they intermarry with any other class or kind. Thus did I learn that while a local prince may intoxicate himself with the abundance of his table and the flesh of his zenana, so is the populace resigned under its marred and idolatrous gods to an immovable fate.

I close my eyes having caught myself in essay. But what did I really learn, what did I really take away from that place? The smell of it, perhaps. Yes, more than anything else it was the smell that clung to me, an odour not of anything in particular but an exudation that was composite, whose ingredient was complex and difficult to dissect. The heat, too, made a man sweat, and the burden of it had a taste as well. When I close my eyes to conjure India, it is its smell and taste, not the shapes and sounds, that first stir a particular affection and revulsion in me. India would single me out, raise my capital in the eyes of others yet breed politics and envy, uncertainty and ill health. I dream of India not out of love – although it was my home for all those years, and there is one for whom I momentarily cannot bear to think. No, I dream out of jealous respect for the investment I made within its borders. God knows I could hate the place for what it daily was. But we enter into strange partnerships, especially when far from our beginnings, and in that temperamental environment I saw a way for the Company – and myself as its loyal servant – to marry fortune.

⤚ᴓ

"You could do worse than marry Marta van Luyck."

I don't know whether Opa is addressing me or himself. We are rocking side by side in the wagon and he turns to me, as if in afterthought, to wink.

"Such a young widow," he muses, then patting the back of my hand. "Your mother would have it you're still a child. I tell you, Francisco, it's never too early to be schooled in the ways of the world." His hand now rests on his knee like a crabbed tree root, his ruby ring a beetle. I am dressed in a grey suit, my collar freshly starched. My grandfather, like most men of true or feigned distinction, dresses in black, his silver buckles and cloak studs little rapiers of light. Despite a vaguely ecclesiastical whiff, there is more of the alderman about him, something firm and self-sufficient. He has this habit of smiling without warning, something I rarely see a churchman do, and I never know whether to feel comforted or afraid.

"A border runs through our lives," he gestures. "It's not only nations that bear with enmity or uneasy truce. A man, too, can be in conflict with what he is, with what he must become. Here, in the south, we have learned to accommodate history, to live with the Spanish and traditions of our faith. But I'll let you in on a little secret," and leaning forward to capture a more sweeping view of the passing landscape, "Antwerp is dying, our Protestant neighbours – good people, clever people – all fled to Amsterdam. I am old," he glances at me, "and have witnessed things no one should see."

He pauses and I know, even though it occurred long before I was born, that he's referring to the Fury, its memory a taste of bile, its atrocity rewarding no one.

"Our family is Catholic," he continues, "and you were *born* a Catholic. I live, now, to manage the estates of widows and monasteries. Can you see what I'm saying?"

For want of comprehension I stare at him dutifully.

"We are a province without a future, a part of something that was once important but has now moved elsewhere. The Hollanders and their confederates, they're on the cusp of something."

My grandfather is working his mouth, pinching the tongue between teeth that are healthy still. "You could do worse than marry Marta van Luyck," he repeats, looking straight ahead, "but if you're really clever, you'll head north and make of yourself a Protestant."

I marvel, now, that I ever considered life so purposeful, that I imagined my choices so clear and warranted and attracted to righteous outcome. In the harm done me by those who would take advantage of any stumble, I have mostly harmed myself. I gave up everything to become what others would accept, little realising that my accomplishments for the Honourable Company would breed a less than honourable envy. You teeter and the smiles become sneers, the whispers smearing. Hands that once clasped yours in friendship or raised a glass now rudely handle you in your helplessness, unclothe and expose you to improper malice. I am tired, possibly just short of death but determined not to die. Yet I do not know how to live. I am surrounded by enemies, voices out of earshot, rivalries deaf to all telling of how it really was. I am confined in my frailty – Hartanti the turnkey – by the ascendant opportunism of others.

How I now long for the skies that freshly baked me, a careering wind that gathers force from the farthest pockets of the earth; the sheer borderlessness of those days, weeks – nay, months at sea. Anything but this prison, these whitewashed walls that have developed lesions of mould and whose plaster stinks. And this cot, too, in which I sweat, its bedding soaked with an inescapable odour of ash that defines my transformation into something spent. God, why did I ever return to the East! I was already with fever, its recurrent embrace. I knew with each self-promise to abandon India, to turn from this malady which would surely increase its grip if I stayed, that time was running out. But to return to Amsterdam incomplete? I was only half-finished and intuitive enough to know that my reputation was being tested, my abilities misrepresented by others less friendly to my advancement. To be sure, I had acquired one of those tropical illnesses so mortal to our countrymen. But death may maggot more than flesh, and to be buried before I'd had the chance to erect my memorial was to be denied my legacy.

If only it could have been experienced as some great discovery, this scent of place unlike our shores north of the equator. But the crisis coloured everything, turned to obstacle every hour and minute disclosure.

India and the Indies, these destinations would blister my blood, but the Great South Land, its chill and windswept salts and those unflinching cliffs that defied all landing – I wonder, now, what I would make of it were I released from impotence and permitted to retrace my experience, to revisit the near past with a reclaimed sense of freedom. I wonder now, almost a year later, what has become of Loos and Pelgrom?

Pelgrom. I despised the boy. Was repulsed by his adolescent, almost hysterical thirst for blood. But I had seen more than enough death for one day, the hands a tidy heap beside the block, the carpenter's mallet and chisel still to be rinsed. On his knees and bellowing to be spared, the twitching feet of the others, their bloodstained thighs revolving in the breeze, curdling my stomach if not a sense of justice. I had had enough. I loathed Pelgrom and found my disgust conducive to an exercise of mercy. The mercy

I had in mind, however, was of a kind to make one pause in the calculation of its blessing. Yes, to dwell in exile – not in some known and familiar land, befuddled by drink and living off tavern-talk – but at the edge of such desolation that anyone worthy of the descriptor human must surely quake at the prospect of his abandonment there. And yet it was a favour when I think of what was to happen to the others, those I'd spared or punished with a relaxation that corresponded to their degree of culpability. Besides – and for reasons I can't quite answer for, even today – I respected Loos. Certainly enough to spare him the grisly mutilation and death visited upon the others. While Pelgrom was a cabin boy (and strange, is it not, that I shouldn't much remember him from the voyage?), there was something manly and contingent in the aspect of Loos, an admissiveness to appalling behaviour summoned in the devilry of others. Despicable though his actions were, he was a soldier in whom I might otherwise have placed my trust, a man not unlike Wiebbe Hayes but on the wrong side of the mutiny. I liked him for no other reason, perhaps, than that he didn't unduly plead his case. The elected leader of an unholy cause, even *he* deduced the unholiness of it. It seemed appropriate then that I should shackle that hysteric Pelgrom to the resourceful but damned Loos, and maroon the two of them upon a sparsely inhabited wafer of chance.

Yes, it is almost a year now and here I lie, prone with weakness and wondering whether, after the initial shock of abandonment, they mightn't have prospered on the margin of that forbidding continent. Or at the beckon of those black apparitions, perhaps ventured into the interior. Might they, even now, be sitting in health around some glittering fire and feasting on their day's event? Might they number among some larger gathering, the unhumid stars vast overhead, having surrendered themselves to the unintelligible lore of some other dreaming?

I dream – whether awake or asleep – and it is a nightmare to me.

It is a cool and darkened room, the floors polished. I can hear my grandfather's voice. It echoes off the tiles, lurks behind the furniture. "Where are you, Opa?" I call. There is a flutter of laughter, the timbre of a woman's voice, and although I cannot see my grandfather I can clearly see the lady – young and quite beautiful, I think, for something stirs in me, a sensual discomfort not unmixed with fear. She is standing in profile, pearls sewn to the clinging of her shape. Her hands are lightly clasped, the fingertips in playful mirror, and it is then that she notices me, half turns as if to attend or fend an importunate child. I know I am in love with her but my grandfather's speech, himself unseen, continues to murmur its attentions, to covet her ear, and I feel the adolescent signature of my grey suit, find myself cornered by his dark shoes, their silver buckles. I hear him speak the name *Lucretia* and I look, afresh, into her face, the eyes blue and her skin as lustrous as the underbelly of a fish. It is and isn't the Lucretia I know, her flaxen hair unrestrained by the bonnet that serves no other purpose than to ornament her beauty. "What about our grandmother?" I shout, ashamed and flushed, but Opa is now talking to someone else, Lucretia's image displaced by the presence of another. He's stocky and crude, his ginger beard broad like the collar it partially obscures. "You're saying you'd pay me to take him off your hands?" and not looking in my direction, my grandfather now clearly visible and leaning close to whisper in his ear. "Jacobsz, is that you?" I venture. My grandfather pauses, a finger raised to his lips, the ruby ring a drop of blood. Once again that flutter of laughter before a sudden shriek. The eyes of the two men fix on one another. Lucretia, where is she? The dusk is deep and sanguine.

"You *did* do worse than marry Marta van Luyck."

I startle, and call out, "Who's there?"

"One might presume a man to know himself. But then again you always were a boy, Francisco."

"Step from the shadows, whoever you are!"

"Oh come now, it's only your conscience at play."

"I have no need of conscience!"

A sardonic laugh – guttural, devilish, womanly. Peering now, I hoist myself upon rag-shrouded elbows: "I *know* that voice."

"More than a voice. I was an entire system of belief."

I sense its disembodied presence drifting nearer.

"Oh Francisco," and caressing, "you weary yourself. You wearied us all."

And I now discern a silhouette.

"A bit too sure of your own dignity to feel certain about it. A straw man dressed in finery and frills."

It's moving towards me.

"You weren't a patch on those you looked up to, those you wanted to please but feared. Coen – ah – now *there* was a man, make no bones about it. Never hesitated for an instant to impose himself, to embrace what was unpopular but necessary, his ambition pure and absolute. A bit like myself."

And colour, now, is beginning to catch the folds of whatever garment – yes, a red jacket, its buttons mine, and trimmed with a neckerchief all too familiar. Can this be me, an aspect of self I do not recognise? But as the mirror draws nearer, my grey costume traded for this brocaded attire of rank, I see the light creep higher to reveal a closely shaven jaw unlike my own, and from within the remaining shadow the lurid incandescence of two amber eyes.

"Greetings, Francisco."

Ah! And I know him – *it!* – the very lynchpin of all my disasters, the world upturned and soured by his vengeful appetite. The fiend! The tiger!

I could not have imagined anything more lethal or perverse than the bizarre horror of what I returned to. I could not have imagined there were such creatures in the world, men who dressed like us but whose substance was without the very soul of compassion.

I had thought the lesions of criminality attended to, Jacobsz and Evertsz – men whose corruption, though shattering in its consequence, was of common stock – now seized and dealt with. But I had yet to reckon with he who, in all outward appearance, played the relative to what I, myself, purported. Although I was late to recognise the implication of his feigned demeanour, I had never come across a man so absent from what a man should be. Yes, I had never thought to come face to face with the Devil.

I FIRST JOURNEYED TO Batavia at a time when our banner needed reasserting. Believe me, an Englishman will never prove an honest friend, despite our Protestant cause and occasional alliance. Together we had already disposed of the island interests of Portugal, that diminished and tired old man of Europe. But the English have always possessed an inflated sense of their due, their Company one in name only and quite unlike ours which is an instrument of national destiny. They tried to meddle in our business, to assert themselves on the very ground ceded us by the local ruler. When we destroyed their factory they little took the hint, instead mustering a fleet and forcing us to abandon our settlement. Indeed, they even persuaded that foolish chieftain to side with them.

It was during this period that I found myself introduced to the steeliness and resolve of Jan Coen. The newly appointed Governor rallied our refugee camp — or more to the point, set the women and children to one side and secured the Company baggage, then prepared for war. I rarely saw him beyond the privacy of his apartment or Council chamber without his breastplate.

As in the Netherlands when pressed by the Spanish foe, our displacement would be short-lived, our reappointment wrathful. The little town of Jacatra, within whose Chinese quarter we had established ourselves, breakfasted tensely in anticipation, the English ships now driven off, the guns of our fleet trained on the palisades thrown up by its defenders. Not for an instant was there any doubt in Coen's heart, his mineral eye as impervious to failure as the polish of his armour. "Should we call on the town to surrender?" enquired one of our party. "Corporal, arrest that man," the Governor's reply. The machinery was of a motion too ponderous to recall. Already the boats were filled with troops, a falconet fitted to the bow of each and with wicks smouldering, the pikemen a veritable forest of needles. As they pushed off from beneath the fortress walls of our armada, flags of the Fatherland (inseparable from those of the Company) billowed in enormous sheets from the stern of each steadfastly rowed craft. From shore a desultory fire was commenced, little puffs of smoke adding to the tropical haze. I could see the occasional flare as the enemy anxiously steadied their defences. And then our men were landed, each boat spilling its content to form a dark and continuous band, our banners punctuating the phalanx of pikes, the beating drums almost drowning out the musket fire and wedded to the roar of soldiers. Spurts of orange flame and a blue-grey drift swiftly recomposed the moment, the entire spectacle visibly bruising as our two thousand men advanced upon the town and disappeared into whatever horror awaited. It is difficult to convey the tugging of emotion I felt whilst watching from the deck of our flagship, the smoke now rising in columns from the town. The sound of battle carried across the water like a drone of bees in spring, the buzzing imperishable amidst the fall of petals. I knew that the English — cowards that they are — would have abandoned the Javanese to do their fighting. I knew, too, that there would be cornered innocents: women with babes who had inexplicably failed to flee before the assault, families who, if not unhappily killed, would presently have their sensitivities turned to ash. There would be little place for too feeling a heart in the furnace of battle, and I imagined the arquebusiers forming up to exterminate pockets of resistance, the flash and puff of powder adding to the sulphur of this burning day swift turning into night. I suffered a fierce longing to be there, to rally with men who by their energy and swordplay were reinstating our advantage, and was thankful, too, that I stood apart and didn't have to kill. The images of Antwerp, long before my time, were etched into books and the conscience of our generation: the ungovernable riot of the Spanish, women stripped and strung up on meat hooks, the defenders diced in body parts. Remnant of that salacious carnival, there were trees my grandfather pointed out which, even now, I shudder to think of. Thus any excitement I might have felt at the martial panorama before me was quenched by a shiver for what was doubtless happening in the detail.

At length a trumpet sounded from the shore and a distant cheer went up. This acclamation suddenly resounded throughout the fleet, the ships' trumpeters responding and our guns firing a salute. It was one of those rare occasions when I saw Coen smile. "Now we shall rebuild it to our satisfaction."

And so Batavia arose from the ashes of Jacatra, and dominating its seafront the new white coral walls of Batavia Castle. *Diamond City*, the locals dubbed it because of the four gun-studded bastions named Diamond, Ruby, Sapphire and Pearl. But it was less in gems and more in spice that the wealth of the city multiplied. And with that wealth grew the fair civility of our capital, *Queen of the Eastern Seas.* The retourships from the Fatherland with their cargoes of soldiery and colonists were ballasted, too, with bricks out of which a more familiar streetscape steadily emerged, the avenues straight and planted with Suriya trees, the canals a reminder of home. Because we couldn't trust them to stand with us in a moment of crisis, the natives themselves were not permitted within the gates of the town, although some of us had servants from other climes. All in all – and but for the accursed heat and humidity – it was a model city, the heart of Jan Coen's empire.

Deep in the forests of the ocean where fish weave like bubbles and slow-moving serpents covet the gloom, there in the remnant of *Batavia* and arranged as if, in fact, the vertebrae of that ship now spent, sandstone blocks intended as a portico for the Castle have settled like the ruined coinage of Atlantis, the watery medium now sealing of their purpose and drowning all memory. Except that I remember – leastways whilst I still draw breath. Yet just when you think you've apprehended the character of your fate, a second and more subtle injury confounds you – steps from the shadows, as it were, of that emergency you've steeled yourself to bear.

It wasn't enough to have lost the ship. No.

I had carried with me that gate from the other side of the world but had failed, in my misadventured passage, to deliver the very thing at which to present myself. I too, like those lost knuckles of stone, was left behind, caught in the tendrils of the sea, watching myself vanish, an arm outstretched, while another who should have drowned – whose mother, likewise, ought to have been slain for ignoring the astrology of fate – was salvaged from the waves, the last to come ashore, the first of all such monsters.

"Do you really imagine that under the circumstances you should remain worthy of our affection?"

Van Diemen has a sly, sour little countenance. He doubtless knows I come here commended for advancement by the Directors back home.

"It's a misfortune, to be sure, but no fault of mine."

He looks at me incredulous, his expression baiting me to answer more. "To become a Councillor is to be indefatigable in the duties one performs, the responsibilities one assumes."

"I have reported the skipper to His Excellency."

"Yes yes, we know of your accusation and Jacobsz is in custody. But your misfortune leans heavily upon the rest of us. The Mataramese laid siege to us last season, withdrawing only when their supplies were exhausted. The sultan, though, needs to preserve his confederacy, and in coming weeks we expect him to arrive with his entire army."

He pauses to assess my understanding.

"There are not that many of us, Heer Pelsaert. Powerful though our guns may be, we are a pocket, after all, and the natives bear us no love. Your vessel is wrecked, abandoned hundreds of leagues distant, and quite apart from its cargo, you have left the soldiers and their arms behind."

I want to escape his presence, to depart Batavia this very instant. I know my responsibilities. I don't need this vain and anxious booby to tell me how dire the situation is. I have presented myself to the Governor, apprised him of what I know, and received his instructions. Yes, I've seen the guttered quarters beyond the walls, the scars of siege, but others – Van Diemen included – will have to deal with this. I have my own people to rescue. "If you will excuse me," I brush him aside, "I've urgent preparations to make."

"The Governor treats you indulgently, Heer Pelsaert. Despite all that has happened, your luck still holds. Make sure you don't fail us further."

I turn briefly to size his threat and say nothing. Batavia stinks of Dutchmen.

❧

It is curious to reflect how weak I was, yet in my anger I overlooked this depredation. I must have appeared to Van Diemen like something shrivelled, my lips cracked and weeping, my eyes alight yet trapped within a flesh that was all too scored and listless, the contrast hinting at imbalance. In his well-fed hauteur he must have been repulsed by my reduced showing. We were all reduced, we who had teetered at the edge of existence upon that boundless sea, our bowels cramped, our gums green and our skulls hollowed out. The infected blood of India still trickled within me. When at last we were sighted and struggled, dazed, to come aboard the *Sardam*, my body forgot itself in the urgency of what conscience demanded. The expressions of compassionate horror upon the faces of our rescuers, these were the only mirror that afforded me a glimpse of my condition. I had no wish to hide behind my frailty – there was another rescue to organise – but our suffering did soften judgement. I saw it in Coen's attitude when summoned. Whatever censure he had in mind was stayed at the very sight of me. In spite of the food and grooming I received, I was a grey thing, a tortured vessel of unfinished business. It struck me, too, that the Governor perhaps read some unwelcome message of self in my wretchedness. Such, however, was his grip on our Eastern affairs – indeed, his purchase over all our lives – that I little imagined he would die before I returned again.

Had I lost a friend? He was friend to none. In any case the likes of Van Diemen would have poisoned him against me in the shock of what was to follow.

I turn on my pillow and try to block it all out, my eyes squeezed shut, my breath shallow and rasping. And still these visitants – the living and the dead – parade through my mind, call to me like inadmissible acquaintances. I am ever tethered to their fairground intemperance. The mattress crawls with the prickle of my skin, the pillow stained with drool. If only to sleep awhile and dream of something else.

Mountains. Yes, so high the sky seems pressed for space, its blue all the more vivid for this clarity which will have nought to do with the dusty plains. The snows hang in brittle splendour, the stillness balancing these heaven-touching confections. In the unfiltered sunshine I feel an emptiness of care, a delight in having come this far and of being privileged to see all this. An invisible breath tingles my ear and I adjust the shawl around my neck. In the valley before me, everything is green and fertile. Fragment sounds float up: the lowing of cattle, a thread of music, the shout of boys. All rises to dissolve in the trackless ether as if not to distract the mind from so wondrous a contemplation. It is a landscape fresh and previously unknown to me. It is Kashmir.

When I awaken to how things stew in this airless prison, I forget how sharp the difficulty in having aspired to that destination. Indeed, I forget altogether the challenges attendant upon having travelled to India in the first place.

—♭—

"Pelsaert! Excellent, you've arrived."

"Heer van den Broecke —"

"Ah, we'll have none of that. Call me Pieter."

I nod shyly, grateful.

"This is Walter van Heuten, one of our staunchest." (Walter nods curtly.) "And over here, Salomon Deschamps, the best scribbler in Surat. If you've anything important to commit to paper, have Salomon copy it down."

The assistant rises from behind his desk and smiles. He's perhaps not much younger than myself but his face, clean shaven, has not outgrown its youth. I shake each man's hand in turn and glean from the weightlessness of Deschamps' that he is a person of modest ambition.

"So the journey," continues Pieter, "how was it?"

"Long and insightful."

"Did you meet the King of Golconda?"

"I was well advised to keep out of harm's way."

"Ha ha! Quite right. There is nothing but intrigue and treachery among this lot."

I smile as if to convey an awareness greater than I possess.

Pieter continues: "It's no secret the Great Mogul thinks his southern neighbour a notch or two above his station. You don't need to be a soothsayer to foretell that one day they'll come to blows."

"The country I passed through would burden any expedition," I reply. "The Deccan is tortuous to the point of hostility itself; it would surely swallow the ambition of any ruler."

Van den Broecke raises an eyebrow. "Great or small, the despots of Hindustan are swift to take offence." He shifts to peer through the window. "They'll risk their fortune – and drain a nation's blood into the bargain – just to secure themselves an honour. They're only cautious where their harems are concerned." Then turning to me with a wry expression, "And a word of advice: don't even look in *that* direction."

Walter clears his throat.

"No," concludes his superior, "it's tricky, here, simply keeping above the politics."

"We wield no settling influence?"

"Nothing to speak of."

"No respect, even, for our maritime?"

"India is an entirely different kettle of fish," snatches Walter. "These are powerful if skittish kingdoms. You can't just bang a few heads together and get away with it as Coen does in the islands –"

"The centres of power are all inland –"

"Removed from the persuasion of our ships –"

"And the population teeming –"

"The number of their levees alone would exhaust our arm in the act of butchering."

"No," advises Pieter, "the best we can do is whore ourselves more effectively than our rivals."

It seems a pallid form of campaigning after the reduction of Jacatra. "Are our interests in jeopardy?" I venture, not wishing to sound impertinent.

Van den Broecke and Van Heuten look at one another and heave a sigh. Salomon Deschamps strikes me as deaf or impervious to what is being said.

"The English have the jump on us," begins Walter.

"I thought we were established at Surat first."

"That's true," nods Pieter. "We had an agent here nearly fifteen years ago. But the loneliness of the post and intrigues of the Portuguese took their toll."

"Opened his throat with a razor," adds Walter, his eye dark and not unmocking. I steal a glance at Deschamps and find him now attending.

"Anyway," continues Pieter, "the English then moved in. Sent a pirate, as far as I'm concerned, by the name of Hawkins. The bugger managed to thread a path to the Great Mogul himself. Turned out he could speak the lingo and this mightily delighted Jahangir, Persian and the like being the idiom of his court."

"Jahangir even presented him with a white woman from the harem. To live with him as his wife!" Walter slaps his thigh, and it occurs to me that I should acquire something of the language.

"However, the Portuguese were up to their old tricks and had the pirate's concession revoked."

"Can they still exert an influence in these parts?" I ask, aware that Surat is no longer their patch.

"The Moguls are masters at pretending a modest interest," replies Walter, "but like a harlot withholding her promise, they play each European suitor one against the other."

"It's always been something of a race," adds Pieter, "ever since Akbar's day when we all started turning up on his doorstep. The Moguls have been slow to apprehend that we might be anything other than a curiosity." He fingers his beard. "The old emperor had a mystical side to him, an openness that was doubtless intended to win over his subjects. As a Mahometan, he dealt fairly with Hindus and was interested, in turn, to learn about *our* beliefs as we started arriving at the fringes of his realm."

"That's where those fucker priests got in first! Hm – your pardon."

"Quite," says Pieter, raising a hand. "Jesuits from Goa. One has to admit that the zealotry of these people baulks at neither espionage nor martyrdom. The conversion of a king means the conversion of a kingdom. It's an aberration of religious commonsense I'll never understand, but as this land is truly spiced with a love of idolatry, we can expect them to succeed where the purity of our own creed fails to impress."

Van den Broecke pauses a moment. "In any case, the salvation of souls is none of our concern. Nor are the Portuguese above making a pact with the Devil. Surat is the chief port in these parts because of the pilgrims who embark for Mecca. Before our arrival, Portuguese ships controlled such freight and the Great Mogul, possessing no maritime of his own, was content to avail himself of their dubious service. Since then, we – and the English –"

"There's another lot we'll have to deal with one day," mutters Walter.

"– yes, we and the English," continues Pieter, "have swept most Portuguese traffic from the Arabian Sea."

"Akbar is now dead," adds Walter, "and the Jesuits largely limited to Goa."

"His son and heir who, as you know, goes by the title Jahangir – *Seizer of the World* – now rules from Agra."

"And even that's a moot point. The wife, Nur Jahan –"

"Meaning *Light of the World* –"

"Is said to be the power behind the throne. Her father is her husband's prime minister, and her brother, Asaf Khan, a trusted adviser."

So many names so confusingly linked; there's much I need to quickly learn.

"Our opportunity and future in Hindustan depends on our access to the court – in particular, this ruling clique. That brings me back to the English."

A silence ensues in which we four all stare at the empty centre of the Company's accounting room. At length Van den Broecke expands:

"Five years ago they sent out another emissary, this time, one, Thomas Roe. A blustery sort of fellow, full of his own dignity and not afraid to match it with Jahangir. He's gone now, no doubt worn out by the games he had to play to get ahead, but not before obtaining licences for the English. To be sure, Roe was sorely tested – the Directors of their company share neither the imagination nor diligence of our venerable Gentlemen – but I think Jahangir quietly favoured him, especially as he represented an English king. The Great Mogul kept the conceited fellow ever in the corner of his eye like some gruff but indulgent uncle his brother's son."

"So, put quite simply, we've re-established our presence here –"

"But haven't ventured as far as the English nor profitably appealed, as yet, to the cupidity of one who would style himself *Seizer of the World*."

"Must we trade with him direct?" I ask.

Pieter wrinkles his nose. "Not exactly, but our activities require his protection. Good relations mean good trade."

"His queen and her brother manage firmans for the English —"

"It's an advantage we must presently debunk."

"And the prize?"

"Indigo."

I look around and everyone looks at me, including Salomon.

"Its extract is turning Europe blue," shrugs Walter. "There isn't any border to this appetite."

"And as Coen has done in the Spiceries — but with greater need for subtlety here since we can't displace the Moguls — the Company must secure an exclusive right to those regions in which the plant is cultivated."

"We need to lock up the trade and lock out the competition!"

"Quite. The English may have ventured a start in this direction but they bring with them nothing that local rulers want. Little wonder Roe was apoplectic at the poverty of his countrymen's bribes: peeling mirrors, faded velvets. Theirs are pawnbrokers' gifts, tokens of unreliable specie. We, on the other hand, intend serious business."

An air of determined self-satisfaction absorbs the afternoon heat.

"Francisco, you come as one chosen to abet this enterprise —"

"We can set about loading the Indian palate with a measure of the spices we harvest in the islands —"

"You're experienced in the inter-island trade —"

"And can purchase, here, the calico needed in Java —"

"To clothe — at a sale advantageous to ourselves, of course — those communities tied to the production of spices —"

"Which we in turn monopolise —"

"To the exclusion of English and Portuguese interests, and by force of arms if need be."

"Whatever we might derive from Europe — laken, wine, glass or lead — these exports alone won't drive the trade in Hindustan. But our reach is now such that we can shop in one part of the globe for that which will purchase advantage in another."

"We've spent the past few months establishing our credentials —"

"Putting our native agents and informants to work —"

"I must say, that Medari is a crafty bugger! There's something altogether repulsive about him."

"I agree. In any case, we're ready to move on Agra, not only Jahangir's capital but close to the indigo growing districts. Walter will head the mission. Francisco, you'll go as his second."

Van Heuten and I more openly size one another up.

"This is a great opportunity," continues Van den Broecke. "You'll be accompanied by a team of assistants. I'll even relinquish my favourite scribbler — eh, Salomon? A man might go far in the right company."

"The Jan Company," quips Deschamps, presumably happy to join us.

"Ha ha, right you are!"

And as Van den Broecke turns, I observe now what I didn't all those years ago: a laughing expressionlessness of eye, a slap on the back that doesn't necessarily confirm me in his interests.

I achieved more, I believe, than any Company official so tasked, especially after Walter's death. As distant as any Netherlanders from the hearth of their upbringing, I, Salomon, and a handful of others dwelled deep in the interior of an alien domain, our communication with Surat stretched over hundreds of miles, our health shadowed by a robber climate. And in those seven years I built up the local trade on behalf of the Company, made our factory at Agra a citadel of commerce, learned the native tongues and compiled a chronicle of Mogul India. And then, as I sensed the jealous ingratitude of those who would cheat me of my worth, and with an eye to the future, I drafted my report to the Honourable Directors back home, a treatise whose recommendations, if pursued, would bind our destiny even more closely to the riches of Hindustan.

—6

You learn things then know, in the stagnancy of your knowledge, that you hunger for more. Not additional learning; no, rather the wherewithal to turn that cumulative intelligence to account. Only an unambitious man lives with repetition for more than a year or so.

My ascent, I suppose, has been rapid; it is little more than a decade since I first set sail for the East and in that time I have risen from clerk to appointee to the Council of the Indies, a delegate of the very High and Mighty in Amsterdam. I would have been seated at the right hand of Coen himself. Except that Coen is dead and Specx, though kindly towards me, is now the power in a world that has been shaken of its former certainties. Between who I was and who I might have been, the dead are piled high, their faces leering like those severed heads mortised into victory towers celebrating Jahangir's triumphs, dire milestones to turn the stomach and make one clutch at the fabric of existence, no aspect of it too worn before the prospect of extinction.

I might have been a thinker except that the energies of our age have been focused more on deeds. Our nation has had little time to contemplate anything other than the necessity for action. Yes ours has been a nation on the make and I, in its costume, have been similarly engaged, too busy crafting my public image to imagine that it might one day count for little. Have I gotten it all wrong? Did I try too hard? And if I was once spelled for success, why could my record not insure me against a loss that was surely the provenance of others?

I think in metaphors. How else to keep the disaster at arm's length? I thought I had a sense of humour but no one dares now laugh with me. I thought I could address myself with familiarity to anyone, but no one visits except that sick-sitter whose name I can't presently remember. I no longer enjoy the comfort of friendly colleagues. And as for women, to think that I once possessed a vigour for them, my bed now anything but a couch for pleasure, my teeth weakened and my breath stinking. God, what was it I wrote in that report about the three grades of indigo? Oh yes: the *nauti* is like a growing lad who is yet to attain his prime, the *ziarie* more a man in full possession of his potency, and the *katel* – ah, the *katel* – he's an old and decrepit figure who has had to cross many valleys of sadness and mountains of misery, who is not only changed and wrinkled in the face but also falling into helpless senility. God, what was I thinking? Has my life, in similes, been as empty and as wandering as this? How trite the mind of inexperience, how assumptive its clichés before a visage of true calamity!

⌐ᴐ

You might, you know, have shown a little sympathy for me — now that you, too, are dying.

I'm not. I can't — not yet. I have my name to —

Resurrect?

I've warranted nothing to sacrifice my honour.

Van Diemen doesn't think so.

Van Diemen is a crocodile.

The Company little fosters camaraderie, just one-upmanship. Surely you've partaken of the game — prospered, even.

Who are you?

How easy you forget yourself in the focus of your woes. But I understand this. I, too, was summoned before my time, deprived of the opportunity to shine in ambition.

Van Heuten?

You were rarely personal towards me.

You rarely showed me any affection.

And what might you know of that? You were too absorbed in giving good account of yourself to notice that I, like you now, was fending off the flux. I'd needed the assurance of a Company man, someone I could turn to to ease the cheerlessness of extinction. You've seen how we die out here, our graves eroded by neglect in some ruinous corner forever foreign. What was once my heart is now pissed on by dogs.

I looked in on you every day.

Only to see if I still breathed.

There was much to do, much that was expected of us.

You were waiting for me to die, anxious lest the opportunity to replace me be given to another.

There was no other. All the more reason, don't you think, to have attended you in friendship.

I tutored you, took you up to Agra.

Van den Broecke assigned me to the mission.

Christ, you were always an unsharing sort! Clever, to be sure, but constantly with an eye to your own advantage.

We all were.

What I presently recall of Walter van Heuten was how afraid he looked, lying there on his cot. Despite the heat, those unseasonable shivers were a sign – increasingly understood by all whose complexion wasn't burnished – that time was mortal, our lives singly detachable.

Lake Ijsselmeer shimmers like a silver desert beneath the winter grey, the haze curtaining the sun, the skaters stretched in column for a mile upon its frozen expanse. Like strange insects in silhouette, they bob from side to side, and I am taken by a vision of exodus. What passes as sport strikes me as something grander, an exposed but determined escape across the ice, its bridge too fragile to be anything other than briefly opportune. In a distant embankment of cloud I half expect some wrathfulness to sweep forth with staves of lightning. In these atmospherics my fancy sides with the children of Israel as they flee Egypt, the Lord turning the elements on their head to shepherd them to an improbable salvation. A sight, too, of such intimate grace, it seems more like a dream than any spectacle of fact. Whether here, in Friesland, or further south in the manifest reaches of the Maas or Rhine, water has always been the agent of our tribal wager.

Prior to setting up as an apothecary in Haarlem, Cornelisz had come from Friesland, a province of marshes and lakes, the sparsity of its people and the foreignness of their speech further dissolving any kinship. I should have known him for the alien that he was.

It is told by Mahometans themselves that Jesus said: The world is a bridge, pass over but build no house upon it.

I gleaned this in an inlay of such beauty that I could scarce believe the rulers of that land were without our love of God. Nothing seemed forsaken in the brimming oneness which moved me to believe that the lady was essential to my spirit. In the necessary concealment of our love we, too, were like those flightful Israelites, and sensitive to omens which abetted our licence, I was readily given to the surmise that he who hopes for an hour might hope for eternity.

I didn't anticipate the world to be so brief a vanity, that the summons to life might best be served in prayerful preparation for what, unseen, was yet to come.

❧

"Tuan, the sick-visitor has returned."

My eyes focus on Hartanti, someone I will never know, much less care about. I only seem to register her when she hovers before me. "What does he want?" I challenge.

"Sir, I've come again," intrudes this other, pushing past her.

"Who the devil?"

"Maartens, Heer Pelsaert. I called on you yesterday."

In a mood of petulant ungenerosity, I see someone sent to ensure that I discreetly relinquish my tenure in this world. "Yesterday?" I muse. "Where the devil did the night disappear to?"

"You slept perhaps better than you imagined."

"You can't begin to *imagine* what I imagine…"

The corners of his mouth crease in a barely repressed smile, and I know he isn't as ingenuous as he pretends. "Hartanti, leave us," I say, but gesture nothing to make Maartens welcome.

"Governor Specx expresses the hope that you are feeling a little more recovered," and he reaches again for the chair by my cot.

"Why doesn't he come himself?" I ask indelicately.

Maartens studies his hands, the answer surely obvious. "You requested that *I* return."

"Did I?"

"Even if I were a spy."

"And are you?"

"My answer is straightforward inasmuch as I'm not certain of what my task consists."

It's my turn to smile. I choose to be reassured, knowing that even if he is Van Diemen's ear, I can nonetheless school my own biography. It's not his fault he's turned up in the colony like a maid at a whorehouse. They've had to find him something to do, I suppose, and I can draw on his uselessness.

"Apart from visiting me, Maartens, what else have they got you doing in Batavia?"

"The Church Council employs me as a copyist. I minute their meetings and compile their resolutions." He looks away, self-conscious. Of course he knows that I received a warning at the commencement of the year. What of it? The lady was more than willing, her supple opportunity restoring me to a vigour I'd been sorely denied.

"Is that it?" and sinking back on my pillow, staring at the ceiling, the shapes and hues – continents and seas – which stain its whitewash.

"I also assist with minute-taking at the Castle, and the interrogations..."

My eyes flicker. Scrabbling to raise myself, I ask, "You're privy to what takes place in the dungeons?"

His own eyes have become as lightless as Van den Broecke's in the concealment of his agenda. Am I part of the interrogation – and overlooking the fact that all of them have been dealt with except the skipper? "Jacobsz, is he still held?"

"The Fiscaal Advocate has not yet reached a conclusion."

"Would they persist with the word of a drunkard and liar, as incontinent a miscreant as ever betrayed the great responsibility entrusted him?"

And still those fish-flat eyes. "He has not submitted under torture," the calm reply.

"Can I never be free of this until someone believes me?" and ashamed of my weakened outburst.

Maartens assesses me with a duty that's the warrant of another, any pity precluded by an untouched sense of neutrality. The silence is condemning.

"I must write to the Governor. Salomon!" I shout. "Salomon. Here, man, and take this down!"

"Heer Pelsaert." And I look into his eyes. "Heer Pelsaert, Deschamps is no more."

"Salomon?"

Maartens? Yes, this is who – unknown and unloved by me – now attends my suffering.

"Oh Salomon," I shrivel, "that I couldn't protect you." And I see a countenance of such anxious self-betrayal that I curse a thousandfold the very germ of that tiger who snatched the innocence of all. "He was as loyal a soul as ever a man might want in a younger brother!" And weeping, now.

"Heer Pelsaert, I beseech you," and wetting my lips with a hastily decanted cup.

I glimpse Hartanti at the door. "Tuan?"

"Get out!" shouts Maarten. Then returning to me, "He strangled an infant with a shoelace. Surely it is time to forgive yourself."

"If – if only I'd been there to protect him, to protect the others…"

My sick-sitter resumes his seat, the proxied vigilance of Van Diemen seeking evidence.

"Maartens, for God's sake have pity on a dying man."

"Should I summon a predikant?"

"Ha!" and startling stillness into the room. I would sooner have Hartanti inflict on me her dutiful indifference. Maartens attends closely, is trimmed by his unwisdom and anxious not to let me slip from his hook. I see him plainly now: the uncertain eye, the tumbling intelligence. I despise his false clericalism. "What good was a predikant," I challenge, "when the scripture of those marooned was so readily abandoned, when that very predikant failed to solace those who daily faced destruction?"

"Sir, you overweary yourself."

I laugh aloud and dribble with infirmity. "Bastiaensz is no better than I. We each betrayed our flocks. Oh don't concern yourself with the niceties of faith," and reckless now. "Do you want to know why the Portuguese — and the Spanish, for that matter — succeed where we obtain nothing? Come Maartens, it's more than just the incense and dress-play. By the love of Christ, man, what have we to gain when everything is already mapped to the exclusion of most, when Heaven's gate is locked to all but a chosen few among whose ranks we can never be sure of finding our place? No wonder Cornelisz and his butchers paraded themselves with an angry pride of probable exile!"

"That is blasphemy, sir. I beseech you."

"Know, Maartens, what it is to abide within a system that doesn't measure trust, which doesn't cherish hope. Bastiaensz: all of his family — save Judith — consumed. I hated him. I hated him his passive endurance."

"What might he have otherwise done? The cutthroats were all around him."

"He could have prayed for the strength to raise his voice against evil."

"Prayed for death, you mean." And again I see him smile, a humour ill-tailored to something that cannot be joked of. "He is a man, after all, like any other man. You, sir, of all people, should understand that."

"There are degrees of humanness, degrees of degradation. He swore an oath to the Devil when he had already sworn one to God."

"Heer Pelsaert, Bastiaensz has not been above the suspicion of authorities here. Indeed, Governor Specx detains him in Batavia whilst we come to our conclusions regarding this whole sorry affair."

"We?" I pick him up.

Maartens looks sheepish, as if having bitten on something disagreeable and determined not to show it. "As mentioned, the role of skipper is still being investigated."

And me, by the feel of it. "Can there be any doubt as to his guilt?" I flatly ask.

"Concerning the allegation he was going to commandeer the ship and turn pirate?"

"That he was in it with Cornelisz from the very beginning."

Maartens leans away from me to stare at the wall above my cot. Hanging there is a tattily framed painting of several East Indiamen at Texel. If that distant sea runs cold, the humidity here nonetheless foxes it with mildew. 'Tis a fanciful rather than factual image of where it all began.

"Cornelisz is gone," he says. "Despite the testimonies you recorded, it would have been better had you brought him back to Batavia." He sighs, his eyes now studying the backs of his hands. "We might have put one before the other, to have witnessed honour among thieves fall out." He then fixes me with an accusative stare and says, "The only name linked to Jacobsz's is yours."

"Mine?" I cry.

A shrug, a circumstance, a fact from where he is seated. "Predikant Bastiaensz has written a letter to his surviving family in the Fatherland."

I wait patiently for more like the patient that I am.

"In it he states certain things, makes certain – shall we say – recommendations."

It's my turn to stare.

"Let me see if I have it right: *After sailing from the Cape, there arose some trouble between the skipper and the Commandeur due to two women, one of whom was mishandled on the ship. As a result, many troubles and disasters followed.*"

I am struck almost dumb. "He infers that I was in part to blame?"

"He concludes by warning the Honourable High and Mighty Lords to have, at all times, good and God-fearing persons in the Company's employ –"

"Not for an instant would I argue with that!"

"– especially skippers *and* merchants."

The room feels heavy on my chest as if the first tablets of torture were being applied. Behind Maartens' boyish visage lurks a cruelty of advantage. I've become well-schooled in the ways of sinister youth. "How come you by Bastiaensz's correspondence?"

There's a slight hesitation – a boy, nonetheless, sent on a man's errand. "We pressed the predikant on what he could tell us. He was an important witness."

"You confiscated the letter?"

"We examined its content." Maartens seems on the verge of abandoning all pretence. "The predikant was weary. He had suffered greatly. Another man of the cloth – even a lay clergyman like myself – was deemed a comfort, a balm to whatever his conscience might answer for."

"Can I see this letter?"

"It has been sent."

Now it's my turn to grimace a smile. "What, no copy made?"

Maartens shakes his head as if not having heard. "It troubles everyone that the skipper won't break."

And if he won't, am I next in line for their rough and sporting justice? Good Lord, am I to be ever shackled to Jacobsz, to be never released from his animosity and crimes?

⟿

"**Francisco**, are you certain I can't persuade you to remain?"

At another time I might easily have defected from my chosen course. But too much had ebbed between us to allow any lessening of my resolve. Van den Broecke was not the friend I'd thought. "Goodbye Pieter," I clasped his hand, "and thank you. I'm sure Vapoer can adequately attend to business here."

Van den Broecke appeared less confident. "These are testing times. Jahangir is rumoured to be dead one moment, alive the next. Whichever, the omens are clouded and his hour upon the throne can only be in its last grains."

"Despotism will ensue if nothing else," I replied, thinking of Europe's crowns, perhaps, but more so that unfairness which had slighted my diligence and hard work. "The gang of four have fallen out with one another now that the emperor – like Akbar, before him – has grown impotent. They'll recruit armies and torture this country in their thirst for power." And shrugging for the unsavoury fact. "The queen's brother has betrayed her and is thinking of his future by siding with her stepson. Mark me, Shah Jahan shall reap what others have sown."

Van den Broecke's comradely disposition faltered just long enough to register an imputation.

"In any case," I continued, "we each know enough to understand that our opportunities are only half-secured. We also know that this place can snatch at a man's health. I'm returning to the Netherlands because I need to ease myself of an infirmity which thrives here. I need to see my family," and wondering what awaited me, the loved ones I'd not seen in ten years. Indeed, was 'loved' a proper descriptor?

I knew my true mission. Recovery, yes; a visit to my mother, of course. But always before my mind were the Lords High and Mighty, the Gentlemen Seventeen who presided over the Company in Amsterdam. Van den Broecke and I may have collaborated in a variety of written matters but in my luggage was a report I'd been working on, a missive filled not only with insights into the customs of Hindustan but describing, for the venerable Directors back home, the precise nature of the indigo trade and the opportunity to be gained by shifting the weight of our operations from the Coromandel to the Malabar Coast. In seven years, too, I had witnessed enough of courtly life to know that further profit might be had in the sale of curios and toys to those who never wearied of extravagance. Thus was the paper I kept close to my person, not letting on to Pieter that through it I planned a personal coup. Keeping a firm rein on my aggrieved pride and courteous in farewell, the ship at Surat was about to convey me to Amsterdam where I would state my case and open a new chapter in my life.

"Farewell then," relinquished Pieter. "Whatever the misunderstanding, let us part as friends. Repair your health and return some day."

It was then that he pressed on me that letter of reference – his commendation of my services, to use to the advantage of whatever I might purpose. Despite my bitterness at having been passed over for promotion, I was momentarily taken aback and, swallowing to recover, smiled glumly with the determination of one preparing to campaign at an altogether higher level. "Come, Salomon," I turned to Deschamps. "A long overdue visit to the Fatherland awaits."

The *Dordrecht* lay at anchor near the mouth of the river. It was strange, after so long a time ashore, to feel the self-correcting balance of the lighter and inhale a sea that stretched to the very kingdoms of the setting sun. Somewhere in that orange-fingered west an afternoon bore snow, perhaps, on streets and canals and the bookcase houses I was presently at a loss to reconfigure. I felt a prosperous calm in this alteration to my affairs, this opportunity to replenish myself in the climate of my birth. The imminent adventure of returning home made me wistful, and when I climbed the side of the ship to board its tightly knitted planking, my eyes were borne aloft into the enclosure of rigging, its open sinew, and I felt myself comforted as if within a church. Looking back to shore, the raisin light coloured everything with a warmth that fairly glowed upon the skin, the boats of the fishermen hauled up on the beach, their nets spread on the sand. Boys played in the fulcrum of day, their bodies like little beans, their modest garments patches of pure colour, the hastening syllables of their speech floating clear across the water. I might have reached out and stirred my fingers in their life – indeed, I could smell the cooking, its savour fresh and briny and unlike the concocted perfumes of dishes served at Agra. For a moment I was touched by the simplicity of life as it could be, the huts mingling with palms and seeming as one with the textures of nature. Indeed, Surat tapered without formality, the centrepiece of what was deemed most civilised – the Mogul fort so inexpertly constructed – soon giving way to a raggedness characteristic of the country.

"Heer Pelsaert!" And turning, I saw Grijph issue from a hatch beneath the sterncastle. "Welcome aboard."

"My dear Commandeur…"

Waving aside any formality, he embraced me; would have me escorted immediately to my quarters; turned to the officer of the watch as I turned to Salomon.

"She's not a new vessel," cautioned my host, "but she *is* illustrious."

"Of course," I answered. "The *Dordrecht* was our flagship when I first sailed to the East."

Long before that, in the year of my birth, Cornelis de Houtman had journeyed in her to the Indies in quest of spices. And a short generation later, his brother Frederick – at a time when I was learning the Company's business – had sailed in this very same and ageing ark from the known world to the increasingly opportune. And chancing upon those islets that would unhinge my reputation, he christened them in self-styling honour the Houtman Abrolhos. Thus in the year of my birth did a scion of the family Houtman initiate our great overseas adventure; so was the year of my undoing brought on by the very corals named in that family's honour. My life in its hounding has been cursed with their name. Much better would it have been for the *Dordrecht* to have come to grief upon the Abrolhos and have spared me that premiership of disaster. Yet misfortune of another kind would presently accompany my boarding of this ship.

"Heer Pelsaert, let me introduce you to the skipper."

A man somewhat older than I stepped into a stillness surrounded by the busy theatre of provisioning. I can't remember if he spoke to me or whether the acknowledgement was grunted. What I *do* recall is that he looked me up and down as if it were already settled in his mind that my rank warranted little and my clothes were an insult to what he deemed the proper engagement of a man. Yet each of us had served a decade in the East – I'm sure his name wasn't unfamiliar to me for there is no smaller community abroad than those charged with the distant manipulation of empire. The skipper's own appearance was less than freshly laundered, his face weather-eaten, his beard as unruly as I imagined his hygiene to be. Bareheaded yet sheathed in a leather corselet, he looked more like the sergeant of a company of pikemen than the maritime authority aboard a Company ship. In any case, and like a servant bound in unloved discipline, there doubtless lurked a vicious precocity for drink. There was little to distinguish between Heer Grijph and myself, yet my host for this voyage was treated with utmost deference by the ship's master. I can only say that from the moment I set eyes on Ariaen Jacobsz, I disliked him his apparent dislike of me. My God, as if I were some thief, come to steal of his place and honour! Hadn't I already had enough taken from me to rule any concern of his invisible? I was aboard this ship with one mind and purpose only, armed with ideas and a paper that would reveal me for the expert I had become, my thoughts trained purely on the Directors at Amsterdam, this voyage merely a prelude to the prime assault. Yes, I was fighting for my professional life and this man – Jacobsz – dared to sneer!

I turned to Salomon and found him, likewise, staring at me in a way that unsettled my sense of priority. Even as I habitually dictated memoranda, he would occasionally pause to look up, as if implying I might like to reconsider the accuracy of what I'd said. It was unnerving to be queried by subordinates. And in the aftermath of everything about to transpire, it was of little comfort to consider them morally polluted, to imagine myself free of their unspoken assessment. They are all ghosts to me now, the living as well as the dead. They haunt me with the impression that I might be less than what I supposed, that I have always lived a lie.

My luggage was stowed aft and I found myself in Grijph's cabin, a tray of wine poured, the conversation reaching and permissible behind closed doors. Yet aboard that ship, as I recall it now, I felt constrained within a sort of purgatory (ha, once a Catholic, eh?) and distracted in having retired one long-time commission for the promise of a gambler's throw. Despite what passed as parting goodwill, I was angry with Van den Broecke and stewed resentfully in what I would now use to spur my career. There was a proper way to handle things, and I had been less than properly dealt with. As for Asmat, my wincing regrets were repressed by what I allowed myself publicly (which was nothing) and fraught with what Pieter might have known and made quiet use of.

I wonder, now, to what degree my resentment interrupted the cordial lines of conversation. I overheard the skipper one evening pass a remark that sounded less than innocuous, and was surprised to find myself leaked abroad in such a manner. I was determined from that moment to guard my tongue, to watch for insult. I had not come this far to have my position further undermined. As for the rumour that I was not up to my job...

I couldn't give a whore's snatch if he was Jesus Christ himself! The turd is scarcely worth a sniff of my backside, pretending he's all proper and mighty –
Careful Ariaen, he's one of the Company's pampered princes –
Pampered prince, my arse! He's being recalled to the Fatherland.
No – I heard they were loath to let him go.
Me too...
I'm telling you, the only thing precious about him is his conceit. He's a woman with a cunt's beard, his hand on so tiny a muscle a fisherman would snip it for bait.
That's not what I hear –

What would either of you know?

They say there was a princess at Agra –

Christ, there you go again with your fucking princes!

No, a prin*cess*. Listen up, they say there was this noblewoman, if you like, who was partial to a little Dutch courage.

It'd take more than a drink to firm up that prick!

Listen, will you! Apparently the husband was away at court, and our honourable Factor was inclined to trade in wares other than indigo.

A noblewoman, for chrissakes! There's none but black and heathen slaves.

I've not travelled to the interior but I hear that some are great beauties –

That they have great charms of manipulation, if you know what I mean –

They're all whores!

Ariaen, come. When have you ever ventured further than the first brothel you've stumbled across?

I thought he had a wife?

Oh don't be so milky –

There's only black cunts in these regions, and trumped-up Factors who imagine their turds don't stink!

Jeronimus later testified that he caught Zwaantie and Jacobsz together in the ship's privy. I can imagine, with disgust, his breeches pulled down around his ankles, her skirts pushed up; the rotund shapelessness of an unlicensed and licentious passion, the two of them grunting like pigs where, nearby, pigs duly grunted.

There are places warm and end-of-day, places whose territory is a state of mind ambitioned by the heart. Shadows gather like promises beneath the trees while overhead, in a peach and turquoise gloaming, the sky loiters, full of birds unobserved at noon.

Her skin was a varnish of honey, each bead of perspiration shaped like some translucent ladybird to magnify the perfection of her chemistry. Her scent contained a humour of unpowdered liberty, the freedom to startle and intoxicate, to recover some childish moment of discovery. Her eyes, too, were those of a maiden, her jewellery fringes of gold which danced about her face and jingled on her wrists and ankles. These she removed and set aside as if she thought the dusk were listening. And equally enchanting were her teeth, their coral beauty luminous between the dark pouter of her lips, the taste of cinnamon rising on her breath.

In the declining warmth of that lingering sky, the birds I most remember were the vultures that landed out of sight beyond the shadow of the trees.

Everyone was silent in the boat. An immensity of unbitten hardship opened before us like some parched and unspeakable phantom in whom we preferred not to believe. There was no telling how our ordeal might end. Indeed, no man can properly savour what is yet to be eaten.

I would later hear of many who were in that boat — seamen, mostly — that they expected nothing but death. Such boasting isn't true. In constant peril, yes, we hugged that alien coast. And when the search for water proved arid and we contended with the awful necessity of crossing the sea, we were as a chip of hope, determined to out-swell ill fortune. The urgent and unfriendly humanness which had prevailed now turned from haplessness to discipline as we committed ourselves to chance. I don't care how they spice their tavern talk — a malicious fate may have shimmered in those burning skies or lurked in the amethyst prisms of the deep, but everyone in that boat wrapped their trust in a belief that we might negotiate an outcome short of death. Wherefore would any man embrace the desert if not certain of defeating his thirst? Despite our fears and fatigues, we were too preoccupied with wriggling life itself to surrender exclusively to death. Jacobsz knew. I knew. Others of varying integrity and worth knew. And the silence was compelling as each debated with himself the extremity to which we might be put. All silent save one who thought to lance the tension with words that snatched at reassurance: "They say that them as are adrift — well, that they cast lots when things get desperate."

"No one's to so much as scratch his arse unless I give the order," growled Jacobsz, the tufts of his unkempt beard making me think of Moses. He glanced at me, perhaps contending in his own mind that I was as good as useless but that my favourable witness might yet bring him salvation. We were in this together.

The only one who unsettled me in our shared resolve to reach Batavia was Evertsz, the boatswain – he who had led the assault on Lucretia, although she could vouch for little but the sound of his voice. He glared at Jacobsz – the skipper, too, in my judgement, having sponsored that odious insult – but the latter refused to hold his stare. First the disaster, then this protracted crisis, had bred a falling out among thieves. I didn't trust the skipper but we all had a claim on him. Evertsz, on the other hand… Irrespective of whether there might be any drawing of lots, I knew that he would eat me. All weapons had been collected in the stern of the boat. They rested between Jacobsz and myself. I needed the skipper, he needed me. And Evertsz was beginning to realise that neither of us needed him.

I beheld Zwaantie, shoulder-pressed to that young mother. Despite her debauchery since leaving the Cape, her flagrant conceit and plotting against Lucretia, I presently gleaned in her forbearance a support for the woman beside her, and understood why Jacobsz had numbered her among those to be saved. And in this gesture of deliverance I experienced a momentary affection for the skipper.

But when I thought of those abandoned on the islets – Salomon and Lucretia; perhaps Jeronimus among them – I shuddered to think any more.

When their ruler went out riding it was with a great troop of courtiers and soldiers, the cavalcade a saddled embroidery of silks and brocades of the most whimsical sash and preening. The procession was designed to impress on the mind the manifest inequities that might gorgeously attire one man and stimulate his spite whilst leaving others numbed and subservient. There were wayside lines in silent prostration outside houses which, in sum, did not amount to so much as the imperial privy. Strange, now to think of it: Jahangir perhaps needing to stop at any of these unadorned quarters, the happy insult of a moment's overlap where, indeed, both emperor and peasant might squat with their breeches down, their robes tugged up. A man does a lot of thinking in the contemplation of his arse, and to give him credit, Jahangir was a thinker. He would have understood in so cornered a privacy that Lord Bowel was master over all, and been tickled by that democracy which regularly linked king and commoner. The necessities of life were a reminder that even high station could be degraded to the lowliest of functions, and the lowliest of men momentarily exalted to shit as the emperor himself.

But if costume be a seal of rank, then nakedness can be a spur to cruelty. When Jahangir's son rebelled against the father and was brought to heel at Lahore, there were tears of reconciliation, a kind of titular forgiveness for those in the family business of feeding on one another. Still, there was a price to be paid, a demonstration shocking in its spectacle. Raised from his knees, the misdemeanant prince – he whom his brother, Shah Jahan, would one day finish off – was placed atop a regaliaed elephant and led between the flanks of a grisly honour guard: three hundred of his fellow rebels, naked and impaled whilst yet breathing, the stakes rising through the fundament to protrude in a rupture of flesh about the neck and shoulders. It seems the emperor was very pleased with the effect. He had an eye for violent symmetries, an imaginative flair for punishment, and in this land of vicious opulence a lord is very much its statute. There are cautionary decrees, to be sure, and the custom of the marketplace will remove a thief's hand as swiftly as any eye or tooth in the barbarous redress of a wrong. But wherein would a Dutchman resort to such calculated acts of cruelty?

I can see him smiling – even now. Brought before our bench, dirty and dishevelled, his wrists manacled. Was it pride or simply the ambiguous and untutored innocence of a child who pulls legs from insects, the wings from flies?

⸻

You cannot be serious.

It's true. We're better schooled in manners appropriate to civilised discourse.

I think you rather overstate your advantage.

Not at all. Our republic embodies the zeal of reformed Christian charity. We have learned harshly at the hands of others what it is to battle degradation. We have fought beneath the banner of Providence to secure our way of dealing with things, the right to define our decency.

You're just defending yourself. It must have come as quite a shock –

What took place was an aberration. Be there evil men, they do not detract from the conscience of a nation such as we present.

Tell me, what was going through your mind as their wrists were being forced down on the block?

Don't.

Wasn't death sufficient?

They were tigers, outside the law.

And by what code did you exact those sentences?

Their punishment, before God, was no more than they deserved.

And Salomon?

I – I cannot speak of it. I – I thought to have spared him in the very sparing of him. I wish to God I'd marooned him, instead, with Loos and Pelgrom. At least his fate might have been terrible rather than squalid.

That brings me to Stone-Cutter Pietersz. You were there. You watched him mount those steps; you and those who remained, now safe in the embrace of Batavia – as safe as such a hell of sickness might permit. Though Jahangir and Coen were dead, it was a moment the judicial scientist in each might have savoured. So what might Stone-Cutter, do you think, have made of his final contribution to this story?

He was with those who forced Salomon to strangle the baby. He wiped out Bastiaensz's brood!

You think you had problems, your reputation being picked apart by jealous rivals, your carousing with yet another man's wife chided by those busybodies of the Church Council. Think of Stone-Cutter, oaf that he was, and of the hours ahead – the trestle waiting, the butcher standing in the corner with a crowbar, and the cartwheel itself. The mutiny's lieutenant-general must have prayed for the light of consciousness to be brief.

I – I was not responsible!

He was the last to die.

And in that crushing moment – the knuckling thud of iron on bone, the unfairness of my attachment to those who had wilfully put themselves at risk – I cry out: No, I am the last to die!

✑

"Hartanti!"

All the world is night.

"Hartanti?"

And the night is silent. Save for the desperation of my breathing, my rampant heart. Holland's *Lion Rampant* – ha! Nothing gains but the graveyard. Nothing. I fear I may float from my anchor, that the fever which sorely rages now rages to leave, taking me with it. I have become the unreliable fibre of my storm-strained ship. The very cradle of life threatens to unravel. And there I stand, above this crisis, yet knowing that at any moment I might be plunged into ungovernable oblivion.

The darkness remains uninterrupted. Hartanti does not come. She has hidden herself from her unchosen duty to me; has turned a deaf ear, so to speak. Some place other – perhaps nearby, perhaps the other side of the canal, for her comings and goings are not strictly in keeping with the exclusion of natives. Ah, but then servants have always been privileged… Where is she? "Hartanti?" My echo sounds childlike and frightened. "Mama? Opa?"

In the lane beyond my grandfather's gate, beggars of cunning watchfulness await – the so-called honest poor, starched of soul, their outstretched palms an invocation to others to fulfil a duty. I knew I was lucky, privileged to have had a benefactor though little fêted with childhood. I think I spent too much time alone, my grandfather forever in the ear of some monk or heiress, their smiles corpulent or wary. A boy in a tunic, secured in so many ways, my sisters now distant relatives, my mother my aunt. Yes, a privileged servant, tethered to a world that was never rightfully mine, a burden on the family. Yet my grandfather never grumbled; indeed, he was committed to doing his best by preparing, when the time came, to apprentice me north. *We will have to school you in the ways of the Dutch.*

Hartanti!

No, she has slipped my mooring in these unfixed hours. Somewhere soft and scented, her thighs stained, perhaps, with the crust of another's seed, she listens to the heartbeat of her own miracle and knows nothing. Nothing of me. God, how I long to be wanted by one as indifferent as her! How I long to be attractive to another, to be worthy of the merest, meanest touch. I hate what I've become. It's not just the shivers and the shit. I already disgust myself to a point of indifference. No, it's more the mirrored fact that I've become something fouled and shrivelled in the casual eye of others. There's the smell of a corpse about me. But until they know I'm securely buried, there's that nose-plugging commerce of polite distaste.

Hartanti? No, I shan't call again. She will doubtless be here when I awake. *If* I awake.

⌀

"Come, put your backs to it!"

Everyone in the boat felt the sudden urgency, the altered circumstance. The sea had risen with a gusty wind out of the northwest. Having drawn close to the breakers in our search for a landing place, we now found ourselves like a craft snared in the current above a waterfall, pinned close to the violence of the surf as the weather deteriorated towards dusk.

Jacobsz didn't need to curse. In the terror and discomfort that bound us we were already cursed.

The oars dipped in a ragged line like the legs of an insect feeling its way across uncertain territory. And vast indeed was the angry pallor of the sea, the sun banished by an onset of cloud and squally rain which, though an ordeal to us in our little ark, may have proven a salvation elsewhere. All of us – we who were searching for water, and the others, island-trapped and parched – had fervent cause to pray in this universe turned upside down. In prayer was God, and in the extremity of our peril it seemed that should we only strive to do His work, He would watch over us. How might we otherwise have had the courage to endure, to have not been overwhelmed by that which threatened momentarily to drown us? All eyes shone white in the closing light, every fibre of our being alert and gripping. Only the infant bawled in oblivious demand, reminding us of how far we had travelled. Shipwreck is not a destination, and there are some cargoes more personal than indigo or nutmeg.

Every time the boat lurched there was a stifled cry, an adjustment of stomach and the senses. But speech remained the instrument of those in balancing command.

"She's about to blow up ugly," shouted Evertsz from the bow. "We've not the planking to keep her out all night!"

Jacobsz's eyes were fixed on the disintegrating horizon. He had *Batavia*'s three steersmen with him, surely insurance enough to risk a watch throughout the hours of darkness.

"Skipper?" challenged Evertsz.

"Stow your noise, we'll take her offshore. We daren't run the surf." Then addressing the cramped machination of the oarsmen, "Come on, put your backs into it you worthless sons of bitches!"

Peak and trough, up and down. Behind us that comfortless land, its cliffs as high as Dover's but tainted with a russetness that bespoke of nothing living. All day we had tried our luck, tacking northerly along its uninterrupted seawall in the hope of finding a cleavage that might offer shelter. And just when our prayers seemed on the verge of being answered, a wildness of breakers like those that had snatched our ship to its doom amidst the island reefs precluded any attempt to land.

Denied, I could only look on, thinking of the others left behind and of the hours now thickening into days between us. In the gathering gloom I stared at that repudiating shore as we prepared for another hazardous night, and knew it to be an evil and demolished looking land, a fortress continent.

I can scarce recall a moment where I've not been attended by the creak or trickle of water. Not even in Hindustan's withering summers where the gardens of our native hosts ran with sculpted watercourses, their courtyards layered around ponds filled with waterlily and coloured fish. The palace itself was magnificently irrigated, the liquid clarity of its streams – for not one grain of impurity was tolerated – diverted along beds of black and white marble. And even in the yard of the Dutch factory I had a pool constructed in the local style, its waters infused with a fellowship of ruby-dyed fish. In the presence of these and their measured transits of the tank, I would often work of an afternoon, my pipe on a dish. I found that writing came to me with the scent of water, a tidy sum of pages, as time allowed, satisfying my whim to become an author of these lands. Even Company ledgers qualified as a literary pursuit in such pleasurable surrounds.

Only in the reception yard where oxen and donkeys were watered did we suffer a pestilence of mosquitoes. They hovered in the absence of fish and plagued me in the evenings, often awaking me with their whining. From the canals and ditches, too, where cattle wallow during the hottest part of the day and frogs bleat by night, that selfsame zinging arose with the mist that crept from the Jumna's banks to swaddle the guarded hours of Agra's nocturne. The itching of my skin in those early days was a torment, but soon my flesh grew hardened and unfeeling. By then I had concerns of a more irritant complexion: recurring weaknesses and a fever that I never managed to shake entirely. I believe there is a miasma which steals abroad at night from the stagnant pools in less cultivated parts of the city. I, like others, had learned to avoid questionable drink. At the factory there was an assured quantity of wine and other spirits.

—❦—

"No no!"

She looks at me like a child who is determined to pop a sweet.

"'Tis not what you think!" I cry.

She raises the Venetian glass, my brief absence from the room unwitting of this advent, my medicines neatly decanted on a chest in the corner. Her smile is enhanced by the sapphires which glitter from her ears. It is a face whose eyes and mouth I have come to know well, whose lips will have never tasted such bitterness.

Too late! She swallows the potion in a single draught.

—❦—

It's a comfort to me, now, to see you dying — and not just of body. The sea cleansed everything of its pretence and illusion. It stripped you of your wooden palace in the haemorrhaging of Batavia, usurped you of a wooden power in the exposure of your hide. And as the sea smoothed away those sandcastles of your fondling expectation, so too would it float me to my destiny. And mine was to deny you yours.

You've often neglected to arrest a thing before it breeds calamitous. Yes, you will go down in history as the man who failed to divine me soon enough, the man who looked away as the inundation began.

I swallow, dry of throat, and would will myself to sleep were I not afraid of what sleep might bring, the inescapable presence of his fiendish ghost. My thirst remains unslaked. I turn on my side, my flesh dampened as if puddled.

—❦—

The sea. The sea is something we well know, a sibling whose harsh character must be carefully handled. We may aspire to pastures, hoarding our guilders in the promise of a house and plot of earth, but it is from the sea that we have raised ourselves, scouring the waterways and pumping the mire, our streets paved with a liquidness that connects us to the uninterrupted oceans of the world.

The Spaniards – and the Portuguese before them – imagine themselves the very priests of sail and presume a precedence to transgress all borders of the globe. But they merely ply between what they plunder, their interests vested in the soils they enslave. What discourse, they, with any ocean other than to negotiate its crossing in order to appropriate the gold of others? It is a means to an end, nothing more. At home they fish in little boats and roam the cliff-tops with their goats, but their land, I hear tell, is arid and rocky and craves the blood of others to fertilise its desert. Their affinity is one of conquest.

Ours, by contrast, has been more a quest attuned to the exigencies of survival. In the Low Countries one didn't need to go to sea to inhale its brine or be exposed to the globe's true highway. No, it came to us, our lives barely risen above the possibility of inundation. The wind and tides of the North Sea; the windmills perched like sentries and executing their four-armed ceremonial upon low and ever extending earthworks; the entire landscape bearing the appearance of a carefully constructed encampment – yes these were the coordinates of our upbringing. We lived with the sea as one lives with the necessities of each season.

The Fatherland was stretched so fragile, its fields so crucially drained that it seemed scarcely possible we should harbour any thought of ventures abroad. Certainly the Spaniard – he who once held sway over our watery lands, and whose Christian tongue and patronage was once thought proper – grew abusive as we assumed some majority in what we might think. In struggling to our feet we were destined to strike back. And in what resistance wrought, so too was our right to commerce amplified, the geography of what constrained us challenged. Were we not, after all, descended from those proud Batavians who in ancient times had fought Caesar's legions to a standstill? And as a result, did we not become citizens in a great family of nations, respected for daring to be ourselves? The kings of Spain showed none of the old Roman's sense, thus those who should have loved us became our enemy.

We knew what to make of the sea because the sea, in turn, had made us. And we harkened, too, when God called for some sacrifice, knowing, like Abraham before us, that to perish something of ourselves was the inescapable fealty of salvation. Thus in the time of my grandfather, when Alva's troops camped in legion beyond the walls of Leiden and battered the city with their great siege guns, the starved defenders shoring their thinning ranks amidst the rubble and rising smoke, never did the citizens during those terrible months forsake the covenant of their faith, their stomachs desperate, their rations reduced to rat meat and boiled hide, roots and bark. When the breasts of nursing mothers ran dry and women lay dead in the streets, they knew then what they had to do to compel their deliverance. And I can see them now, even though it occurred long before I was born: the rags and banners of their defiance as they proceeded, contrary to the toil of everything that had taken generations to build, open the dikes as if taking a knife to their own veins, to flood the very gardens of their creation. No surrender, the waters slowly rising around the beleaguered Spanish battalions, their helmets and their armour, their guns and war-soiled tents little buoyant in the drowning fields. And as if God approved the venture of such self-mutilation, a wind blew out of the north to hasten the rout of the invader.

Despite that passing loss of land, the survivors of Leiden knew that the sea, too, was their element, that we were an amphibian nation, nourished on bread and herring. Even as a child, those commemorative feasts of such simple fair – every October third – loaded the palate with their garnish of self-belief. Although my grandfather was cautious in the expression of his opinions, I recall him examining me with a measured eye as if weighing my future course. As an indignant schoolboy I used to think that one could never burn enough Spanish ships. Then later, as I grew busy in the business of the Company, the great patriotic struggle felt like a summons to church, a mindedness reserved for the ritual of fresh clothes and prayer. Still, it was part of a catechism I was expected to know, and I remembered that memorial day down the years. Indeed, despite a life abroad and the responsibilities which have consumed my energy, I've managed to remember various dates and retain an imaginative taste for chronicle. Every October, for example – except that October last.

By then my life had fractured into its own desperate struggle. Only the day before, as I now recall, had we rowed across to Seals' Island with Jeronimus and the others – impossible to remove the stain with their lives. After the boatswain (not Evertsz but, rather, he of the *Sardam*) had washed his arms in the sea and the carpenter his chisel and mallet, we rowed back to where the others – the survivors – stood at the water's edge in a silence of unforgiveness. Like Leiden I was under siege, but in whatever sacrifice was called for I saw no happy relief.

"**H**urry, hurry – in God's name!"

She has to be carried down the stairs that flank our apartments and across the reception court to the adjoining garden. Lord, how has it come to this? Our moonlit fervour makes the dogs suspicious. They leap at their chains, not quite barking but growling nonetheless to have us state our business. *Sssh*, the reprimand of an unseen handler.

Salomon struggles and staggers in the darkness, his heart aflutter as much as mine. Men become bound to one another in dubious ways, and I can tell he feels cornered, condemned by his inferior status to abet what is distasteful to him. In making him an accomplice I have commandeered more than his loyalty. I have purchased his alarmed soul.

A lamp is lit in the corner of the garden. I have him fetch a pick and a shovel.

"**O**f course I wanted you to stay."

Van den Broecke sits at the edge of my cot, yet even in my fevered state I can tell that things aren't what they seem. There's an absence of colour, a kind of bloodlessness which makes memory so poor a substitute. And despite the twinkle in his eye, the familiarity of his chin-coned beard and winged moustache, I cannot *taste* the scent of him.

"You allowed Vapoer to travel to Lahore in my place," I say.

Pieter draws a breath I do not hear and shrugs. There's a certain resignation in his smile. My smiling assassin. "I can read those thoughts of yours, you know," and he reaches for the back of my hand.

I'm momentarily startled by the incongruity of this meeting.

"Francisco, don't plague yourself with enemies any more than is necessary."

"How am I to trust you?"

"I could well turn the question about. Boarding that ship with a document crafted to enhance your standing in the eyes of the Directors. You quite fancied yourself an expert in matters pertaining to Hindustan."

"Wasn't I?" and swallowing, ashamed to admit to a doubt that has always shadowed my proficiency.

Pieter resumes his smile, his eyes crisping in affection. They were blue, I remember – like mine – but just now they're merely a suggestion of engagement, leached of tone as I am of strength. He leans closer. "Didn't we collaborate on a great history of these lands and their rulers? Were we not among the most literate of the Company's honourable sons?"

"What became of our words?"

Pieter doesn't look at me. He has arrived, perhaps, at a truth that still eludes. "I *did* write," he begins, addressing a space between us. "Just as you smuggled your paper aboard the *Dordrecht*, I entrusted you, also, with correspondence addressed to the Directors. We had long worked in tandem – you at Agra, I at Surat. I observed what you did, was impressed by your grasp of heathen tongues. You were a real asset; your value to me needed impressing on the Company."

"Then why was Vapoer promoted in my stead?"

Pieter now studies me closely as if I were a child. "It was time your talents were employed elsewhere."

"Meaning?"

"Come Francisco, you know you were fomenting plans of your own."

"They were secret."

"And so too, I suppose, was Asmat Khanin?"

I stare at him, incredulous, and note that the twinkle has disappeared from his colourless eyes.

"As if we haven't had enough of our own to bury in this wretched place," he adds, perhaps alluding to Van Heuten.

"What does Wasim Khanin's wife have to do with it?"

"Oh come now, Francisco, we're both sons of Antwerp. Even as newly minted Dutchmen, you and I were always going to be that little further from home. My father knew your grandfather. My mother was heavy with me at the time of the Spanish Fury; your family had a small estate outside the city. In that season when thousands perished, we fled and found sanctuary to the north, my mother's womb spared the butcher's hook." He shifts closer. "We've tried to look out for one another, to remember where we come from in the administration of a simple kindness. Heaven knows there's more than enough envy going around and few, in these forgotten parts, to share enough of home to be able to share anything at all. The Company is filled with mercenary spirits."

"I don't understand."

"Most would cut you adrift without a moment's hesitation. Indeed, most conspire in your downfall already."

"I'm not yet done!"

"We're all done in the end." And he looks above my bed to assess the painted coinage of the Company, the stylised ships at anchor off Texel. "You joined us at a good time, the preliminary groundwork laid. You were the youngest in an ambitious band of brothers. But now Coen's dead, and I – well, I've been preoccupied, myself, of late." And I perceive a sweet sadness in his expression. "You think I slighted you with Vapoer but no, Francisco, you wronged yourself. Slave girls, servants – fair enough. But the wife of a courtier?"

"I was discreet."

"You buried her in the grounds of the Dutch factory."

"I didn't know what else to do."

"The misadventure was desperate, I'll admit. But surely you didn't imagine that things might continue as if she'd never existed?"

"I remained discreet."

"But others weren't nearly so liberal with their silence."

"You mean —"

"I mean it was time to reassess a situation that wasn't about to heal itself. You – or, more precisely, the Company was being discomforted."

I'd known but couldn't bring myself to admit it. It was like being branded, of always arranging one's clothing to cover a scar. "Who?" I ask, and already singling out the culprit from at least a dozen faces.

Medari.

The too-well-nourished broker, his rounded cheeks and that insufferable clamminess with which he always caressed my hand. "I have a most excellent consignment from the villages around Bayana."

"I will go there myself, shortly, to see," and trying to release myself from his grasp.

"You are travelling to Bayana?"

"Within a few days."

"I think this is not profitable of your time." And he wipes the sweat from his neck, preparing to dissemble from merchant to manipulator. "The sun, I think, is rather hot for a Hollander."

"Medari, I need to see for myself what this year has been capable of producing." Indeed, I needed to ease myself, in excursion, of that pain which troubled my waking hours and sleep alike.

"Ah, indigo is very scarce. If it's not the rain one season, it's locust the next. I know. I have travelled the villages. I have paid a fair price to the farmers. Everyone knows me as a fair man."

"I thought you said you had an excellent consignment."

"A most excellent consignment, Allah be praised!"

"What then of the rain and locusts?"

He observes my mirthless smile; is briefly expressionless in the permutation of his thoughts. "You will buy from me since I have already bought from the farmers," he says sulkily.

"Medari, you're quite as ravenous as those pushy Armenians who deny everyone in their haste to come first. All they do is unsettle the market with their greedy eyes."

"You must buy from someone," he insists.

"I've not yet spoken with Mirza Sadiq or Ghazi Fazil at Bayana." These respected merchants have always been gimbals of stability in a volatile environment. Coffee is served in Venetian glass, and at the patterned borders of carpets whose symmetries are the eternal signature of this country, I cannot help but feel an overwhelming affinity for the calm and conversant civility of such households. Amsterdam's cold and tiled checkerboards have seemed more than their literal world away, and were it not for the depredations of climate and the complicated aspect of more recent times, how might I argue that I am not at home among these courteous peers whose language I now speak? Of course I must avoid Fazil this time around.

"Why do you deal with these men when they charge you more?" intrudes Medari upon my musings.

"They sow most of the indigo there and are locally honoured. In some seasons they have sold to no one but ourselves."

"It is not the same at Ghanowa."

"I'm quite capable of assessing the situation myself."

"You will need a buyer, and I have already settled with the farmers there."

"What about the other brokers? Pagoo Singh, Nagar Bai?"

"They are thieves and infidels."

"I've always found them firm in their bargains and modest of manner."

"They are idolaters who worship painted whores. They refuse all knowledge of Allah, may He be glorified and exalted."

Dealing with Medari is like dealing with a truculent youth. My smile – never warm towards him – is beginning to tarnish with impatience. "Tell me Medari, how is it you, a Mahometan, are alone a broker when your Mahometan masters usually entrust such work to Hindus?"

"How is it you, of all people, might continue to trust a Hindu?"

Medari takes advantage of my mild wonder to add, "You have many servants at the factory. They are alert to the security of your property, day and night."

"So?"

"Perhaps there are too many of these. Perhaps there is not enough for them to do. Ah, I understand, servants are cheap and plentiful in this country.

But idle hands give leisure to idle tongues, and the bazaar trades in more than silver, silks and indigo."

"What are you saying?"

"I whisper no more than what I hear, my dear and honourable Factor," and pawing at my hand once more. "I speak less from knowledge and refute even more. After all, what are rumours but the chaff of envy? For such things as I hear, there would be a terrible price to pay were they true." He gives my fingers a squeeze. "But then talk is full of mischief, no?"

I am sufficiently unnerved to want to imagine that Salomon or another has committed some embarrassment. But Medari doesn't shift his eyes from mine. Petty though he's always been, and harmless but for that tedious manner of insinuation, nevertheless I wish him dead. "In any case," I compose myself, "I must travel to Ghanowa and Bayana to see the crop for myself."

"You see. You satisfy yourself. Then you buy from me."

Can it be that I was undone by my concealed and buried past?

Come Francisco, martyrdom doesn't fit you.

But I only wanted what was most advantageous for the Company.

What about your private business dealings, that little on the side?

Most of what I risked has amounted to nothing.

Listen closely: to live is to blemish one's infancy. We're none immune to the conscience of our deviations. What was it you said about those grades of indigo? *Nauti*, the growing lad; *ziarie*, a man in vigorous prime. But *katel* – ah yes: like an old and decrepit man who has journeyed many valleys of sadness and mountains of misery, who is fast falling into helpless senility. Ah, I like that. You're quite metaphorical, Francisco; quite the man of your times.

But I'm not old.

How many of us get to become so?

But there's so much yet to be done.

You started as a humble Company assistant. You arrived at Surat an undermerchant, ready to embark on greater things. Look at what you achieved! In the space of ten years you've risen from a nobody to become member-elect to the Council of the Indies. If it doesn't profane the secret intent of He who rules in Heaven, I might have thought you were shaping up to be one of God's elect!

What became of us, Pieter? What became of our hopes?

1629. It wasn't favourable. You lost your ship.

Is it *Batavia*, then? Does nothing else count?

Of course it's *Batavia*. You don't come away from something like that with your reputation intact. Honestly, we've all had occasion to stick the knife into someone at one time or another. You imagine yourself either spotless in intent or excluded from such abuse?

But I was not to blame!

Silence.

Pieter?

⁓

"**H**eer Pelsaert, let me introduce you to Jeronimus Cornelisz. He's new to the Company. It'll be his first voyage to the Indies, and he's to accompany you as undermerchant." Adriaan Bok steers the two of us together.

"Your advancement is rapid," I joke, extending my hand in a display of the renewed esteem I enjoy. "I was a mere clerk when I first shipped for the East."

Cornelisz is clean-shaven and hungry of eye. Neither old nor young, he responds with an unsettling smile that momentarily strips me of my bluster. I have always been at my most assured in the company of slaves and superiors. Cornelisz's near rank, his undoubted virginity in the ways of the Company and the unknown folio of his character, somehow expose me.

I hear him say, "A man might make a great thing of himself, given diligence and the opportunity." It's a cultured voice, and I find myself jealous of my station.

"Where do you hail from?"

"Haarlem," he looks away.

I feel that I suddenly know this man – not like Brouwer, Van den Broecke or the great Coen himself, men I've seasoned with and looked up to, men who've curried my advancement. No, this is someone from a different walk, someone for whom I'm responsible, to be sure, but I do not need to favour. Despite the fact that we both serve the Company and he's answerable to me, I readily discern that I need not know him much at all.

"Heer Cornelisz has studied as an apothecary," prompts Adriaan. "His knowledge of drugs and potions will prove an asset to the spice trade."

I suspect his skills will be diverted more to the sick and dying.

"You are most fortunate, Jeronimus, to be sailing under the tutelage of Heer Pelsaert. If I may be so bold, there is no finer Company son."

"Adriaan, you endow me with an honour too equally shared among others."

"Nonsense, the Company has had its eyes further opened. Your Indian report is the talk of the Amsterdam Chamber." Then turning again to Cornelisz, Adriaan adds, "Heer Pelsaert has been highly appointed for this voyage to Java. Mark you follow in his ways."

Again I witness that smile, its subtlety conveying not so much his gratitude as wry amusement. It's as if he doesn't believe what he hears, or is keeping his purpose close to his chest.

"Have you seen *Batavia* yet?"

The question stirs me from an unaccountable unease. "No," I reply.

"She's the most beautiful of ships, her paint and varnish scarcely dry." And at this we each nod for the renowned genius of our shipwrights.

Perhaps I am not sufficiently returned to Holland, having lately voyaged several months in the *Dordrecht*, to feel an abundant enthusiasm for the imminent journey back East. Yet here is my destiny, a privilege bestowed by those I was anxious to engage. I am appointed Commandeur of the new flagship named in honour of our illustrious ancestors, a labelling as proud as when Coen similarly rechristened Jacatra's smouldering ruins.

"How quickly might we sail?" asks Jeronimus.

"Your eagerness is almost fugitive!" laughs Adriaan.

Cornelisz colours slightly, more bashful I think than captured. But indeed, how many of us might not be running from something? The waterfront is a-throng with characters of desperate description, all alleging their ability to sail and citing their experience before the mast — so much so that one would think the entire manhood of the Netherlands to have existed at no other place than at sea, their present shore life a miserable and marooned interlude. I wonder at their wives and children. I wonder at the level of degradation that would willingly exchange one form of hardship for another. I wonder of Cornelisz.

"Within the fortnight," I answer. "The autumn fleet assembles off Texel." Cornelisz and I attend one another closely. He is dressed as a gentleman but his coat scarcely disguises its patches of wear. His collar, too, whilst modest and of the usual business cut, could do with the attention of a laundry maid. To my surprise I realise that he, likewise, is observing my appearance, his eyes focused on the silver clasps of my scarlet vest and the turquoise sash I wear in concession to sensitivities acquired abroad. I am to visit my younger sister, Oeyken, after this appointment and thought to dress for the occasion.

"Are your personal affairs in order?" I enquire.

"Quite." Nothing of his person moves. Just the eyes. They lock with mine.

"We will need to go over your duties. To ensure that all is understood and in readiness. Once at sea there is no turning back."

And again that shrewd expression. Were Cornelisz a youth, I should have taken it for enthusiasm. To the contrary I feel as if I'm abetting his deliverance from a set of circumstances he would rather not confront. The suspicion makes me brusque. "You're new to the Company. Usually only those who have proven themselves are promoted to the rank of undermerchant. I trust you will honour the work ahead."

"Heer Uppermerchant, I fully intend to impress on others the integrity I most value in myself."

I search now — and in the aftermath of what transpired — for portents, signs. I hear a rustling behind every silence, spot an insolence in every gesture. Thus in Jeronimus's words do I detect, too late, the latency of his menace.

Turning to Adriaan I ask, "Has a skipper been appointed to *Batavia*?" This is of no small importance since I will have to share the Great Cabin with whomever, and the voyage from Surat had gotten off to a less than auspicious start, Jacobsz's insolence towards me being brought before the ship's council.

Adriaan smiles. "The Chamber has been anxious to assign just the right man. Your voyage home to the Fatherland proved both prosperous and uneventful. The Directors like that sort of combination."

True. The *Dordrecht* was an old ship, but once clear of India she had made a tidy passage home.

"Indeed, so impressed were they," he continues, "that I think you'll find yourself unsurprised at their choice."

Thus I learn, in the presence of Cornelisz, that *Batavia*'s newly appointed skipper will be none other than Ariaen Jacobsz.

Why did I go back? To the East? After all, I'd departed in a pique, angered at my treatment by those I'd served too well. It mattered little that soothing voices attempted to stay my departure. I would have only subsided into a routine determined by others.

Still, at Agra I had matured to become my own man, immersed in a life which, though tied to the commercial necessities of the Company, stood at some distance from its cultural regulation. In companionship with a handful of Netherlanders — and of course our English rivals who, out of working hours, were good for the occasional drink and, yes, as fellow travellers far from home were likewise forging, here, its surrogate — we trod a path of balanced assimilation, cautious to remain who we were but anxious not to be forever alien amidst the teeming energies of that place. I have heard the expression "going native" and can safely declare that there was nothing in the existence of any native met that required a closer acquaintance with his habits, yet it is impossible to live long among a foreign people without wishing to diminish that foreignness. By nature and example, we who ventured East and travelled up country were bound to be curious and adaptive. Like fishes in the sea, we had to breathe and eat and partake of our environment. The Company may have projected its bottom line in indigo, calico and spices, but its servants, those of us recruited to its farthest outposts, were required to shape an existence from the circumstances in which we found ourselves.

I've always had an aptitude for languages. As a Fleming migrating to Amsterdam, I found the beating heart of the United Provinces anything but united when it came to the jostling of provincial tongues, not to mention its waterfront additions of German, Norwegian, French, English and countless other sounds initially foreign to my ears. There were men of a dozen races and a thousand places, each with a story as desperate or demeaning as his neighbour's — the detritus, all, of a crumbling experiment, its reduced hope now funnelling itself into Europe's premier market. And as with markets everywhere, such are the environments in which to listen and learn and become a citizen in the citizenry of others. In the course of my Indian sojourn, just as I glimpsed things which delighted and informed, so too did I acquire a knowledge of the lexis spoken by Hindus and Mahometans. In this way I felt gradually more at home in my billeted country, less afraid of the hours outside work, and more savouring of what its opportunities afforded. Yes, I made a life in India.

I didn't realise this until I returned to my fatherless Fatherland. My grandfather, too, was long since gone, and of kin in whom there remained any unaffected tie, that left only my twice-widowed mother, both my sisters having married well. Yet when I visited mama I saw how separately we'd seasoned, the vitality of our mirror now tarnished. We had lived too long apart — I in circumstances of partial orphanage and then abroad; she a dependent in a second marriage and with my sisters to bring up — to experience any unselfconscious felicity in meeting. It was as if that worst of things to befall any Dutch household had unwittingly occurred, that *dust* had been permitted to settle across the years which distanced us. Seeing my mother, seeing the lines etched into her face — and knowing that I, too, had wrinkled, my beard grown grey and my health loosened — I realised that we each were reaching from a depth of past towards a present wherein there scarce existed any reason to think we should recognise one another. The fact of our relationship no longer stood up to its meaning. "My child, how you have changed…"

My meeting with my sisters and their families reminded me that I had none of my own. They had done well. Their marriages were prosperous and they lived in gabled terraces along the Herengracht, their husbands engaged in happy speculations which strike the silver-chiming music of this city. I was welcomed, had extraordinary tales to tell, ate and drank the fare of the comfortable burgher class – indeed, had as good a time as any well-mannered guest at the table of a gracious yet distantly acquainted host. I no longer knew these people well enough – even little Oeyken in whom I might have been expected to take a proprietary interest as is customary in an older brother. Their marriages had taken place without me, just as the men in mother's life (my father notwithstanding) were alliances forged that bore little reference to my calendar. Without any such intent or malice, I found myself cut adrift. Not excluded, no. Simply absent, unable to feel for them as I might have had I settled in Amsterdam and possessed a wife. A Dutch wife of my own. Then I might have been more attuned to what it was that defined their private lives.

Despite their marriages – and I speak nothing in deficit of their husbands' characters – Anna and Oeyken were to furnish fewer living children than those conceived. Indeed, it seems to me we've always been a family in constant struggle, our considered and not inconsiderable gains marred by random impediment and subtraction. In the unknown faces of all those little deaths, to think that life can be such a gamble!

My mother had fulfilled her purpose and my grandfather had safeguarded a portion of the family ark throughout the unsteady years. Now she was old, he was dead, my sisters of no material concern, and I… where was I now placed? Indeed, did I have a place here in the Fatherland? Despite my standing in the Company, my salary as an uppermerchant was scarcely equal to the booming prices favoured by Amsterdam's more prestigious quarters. As a bachelor, too, I questioned my readiness to acquire a house. As for a wife, who indeed might have proven a candidate? What European women, let alone Netherlanders, had I been exposed to in the past ten years other than strumpets who wriggled in the bilge of the Company's service or others whose jaded flirtation bespoke of boredom in their married lives? Our practice out East was with Easterners themselves, their dark or sallow skins bejewelled, their wardrobes hued and cut in ways deemed most unchristian yet never, for all the temptation I felt, in the least immodest. Slaves were the currency of lesser men, and in my early days I'll admit to the taking of servants who never smiled, who never looked at you as they gathered up their dignity and left your presence. It left me feeling empty, my privacy which yearned for an affectionate domesticity yielding little but a sense of transgression. It was sometimes easier and freer to venture into the muskier, more flickering shadows of the settlement. No names – simply coinage and laughter, the bite of a nipple and sweet fog of tobacco. The Church Council – Maartens and his ilk – they were always of a mind to censure such pleasures. But then they made a virtue of bringing their wives and children with them, their piety a huddling preoccupation in places that had no interest in their selectivity of salvation.

Death by climate and boredom, that was the obstruction and spur to any intercourse. The cemeteries were, at first, like some tiny upper shelf in a large cabinet. Soon they comprised an entire hall within the Company's house of affairs. It is grim enough for a man to endure these tropical seasons; why you would bring your family here is beyond me, especially if it be the hope of a parent to bequeath something to his children. The young with the old, the promising with the scarcely missed, they all end up in these exiled necropolises whose monuments are as mortal under the monsoon as their occupants were to the flux. Remarriage among survivors is a reminder that nothing lasts forever in these parts, although children of mixed couplings are proven to stand a better chance. If those parents are of good esteem, there is little stigma attached to their Eurasian offspring. Already there are such families in Batavia who elicit the utmost respect and who contribute to its administration with a more resident understanding.

Still, it is a hard thing to concede that home may no longer reference the scent and temperate light of one's weaning. There are many, too – and I found this conceit more practised in the Fatherland – who consider the issue of mixed marriages to combine the worst traits of either race and nothing of the good. In any case it's against Company governance to take an Asian wife back to the Netherlands. To become too fond of such a wife is to exile oneself to the colonies forever.

I am a man, of course, and my loins have entertained an expressive vigour, but there's been little permanence attached to any object of desire.

A servant is a servant after all, and because I spent much of my time at Agra, far from Surat and infinitely removed from the larger community of my kind at Batavia, the only women of quality were the wives and daughters of India's lords and merchants. I am a man, of course, yet a man among such people might remain an oddity. As for she of whom I cannot bear to think, the opportunity to pretend to something else was ultimately doomed in what accidentally transpired, my difference both confirmed and condemned in what flared and faltered. Thus in spasms of desire and discontent I grew to love India until I also grew utterly sick of it. I loved the panoply of this strange and outlandish land until, revealingly, it proved too foreign to my over-jaded senses. I loved the excitement and freedom of venturing into the unknown until, likewise, I knew only weariness and disappointment. I cherished the opportunity of responsibility until that responsibility was suddenly withdrawn. And the sheer improbability of my one true romance appealed until its probability grew problematic and withered at the outstretch of my hand. It was an omen that stood to preclude any marriage of East and West, a talisman which augured that one death should surely be followed by others. Why did I choose to go back to the Indies? Ever restless, a man has never arrived at where he needs to be while there is yet breath to draw.

Lucretia. Ah. There was a time, before the onset of all our disasters, when confined to the nocturnal cradle of the ship, rocked by a tempered silence that clawed at the buttons of my slumber, I would dream of you and, in the privilege of my aloneness, stroke myself. Ah, the swallowing pleasure…

"Hartanti," I call out. "Hartanti!"

"You have made a good impression, Francisco. It merely remains for you to demonstrate your suit and consolidate your position."

I'm visualising what needs to be done, can see the mechanics of my theory, but have not arrived at the moment wherein I present the Directors' instructions – *my* recommendations – to Governor Coen. Batavia is literally a world away, and there is another aspect of my commission that will transport me back to India. I am imagining, perhaps, my next meeting with Pieter van den Broecke. I turn to Brouwer and say, "It will take at least two years to determine whether I'm right."

"Your argument had all the force of one who has served to manipulate our advantage. Those of us who have ventured East understand one another. The Company's impetus to profit, however, has attracted the weight of some who have never so much as stepped aboard a coal barge. Still, if counting houses are the climate of the many who rule over us, your arguments added up."

I smile weakly, the victor of my own good sense and revested with the unanimous confidence of the Directors. I had argued that things should be done differently, had meditated on a plan (spurred to ingenuity in the rancour of being passed over) and now found myself at the end of these labours, my protestation answered. But was I ready to return to India? Could I withstand its heat and humidity and the intrigue of another two years? "I should like to have spent a little more time in the Fatherland," I say. "Four months in ten years is not such a homecoming," and knowing that a conventional sense of home eludes me.

"We all have work to do, work that will earn us our respite in the end." Brouwer's collar is sewn with pearls. Neither of us allude to the chequered condition of my health. During these past couple of weeks, Amsterdam has been damp and clammy, and my bones have ached of an evening with a familiar grinding, even as my skin shivered. I am grateful to Brouwer and can't afford to let him down. As if intuiting my misgivings, he adds, "I too must allow the Company to decide my whereabouts. And like Jacques Specx, under whom you'll sail with your portion of the fleet, I know it won't be long before I'm sent once more to Batavia. Specx is a good man; he'll advance your cause. And I regularly correspond with Coen."

Despite the recent suspicion that people and circumstances had turned against me, the future appears rosy, my credentials assured. And somehow it all seems a lie. I know I'm privileged and that a man — a man with ideas and gumption — is readily the commander of his fate. Yet there's presently no refusing the opportunity imposed. I must return to the East, even though it isn't without serious risk.

Specx is a good man; he'll advance your cause…

Of all those alive and near to me in death, he is the one I wish most to hear from. Governor Specx, now that Coen is dead and useless. Strange, is it not, to think that one who was so feared, whose mineral eye distilled the terror of a basilisk and whose power was absolute, should now moulder in a graveyard outside the Castle walls. Did his end square up to the reputation of his life? I think not. Too many disappear here, boxed and shuttered away in whitewashed rooms and visited, if at all, by the likes of Maartens — ha, those clownish idiots as Coen labelled them. I wonder who steadied him as he shat himself to death? The indignity of it, the very levelling which brings into question the value we place on precedent and honour. The flux is no respecter of rank. I have seen all manner of men reduced to a common fear, their eyes an intelligence of incomprehension. Walter, when you died I could not, at the time, have inhabited the loneliness of your vanishing world. I saw in your face only that recognition — nameless — which we all strive to avoid. I saw it, too, in the eyes of the men we rowed across to Seals' Island — that expression, almost, of mild wonder that it should have come to this. Our separate stories remain just that — stories bearing little commonwealth other than we each must share in death.

But what of the hereafter, here on earth? What of one's legacy? Lord knows my work remains unfinished. Lord knows the retrieval of my reputation is incomplete. That bastard Van Diemen would have me buried more than once. I have little to bequeath other than I did my best. Whatever gain I set aside for myself followed strictly in the wake of my responsibilities to the Company. I have been an honourable man; shouldn't that count for something?

When Coen died, almost a year ago now, I heard speak of a splendid funeral with a great troop of soldiers – the Governor's plumed helmet, gauntlets and spurs carried by the very highest officials, Van den Broecke among them. The dead man's horse, draped in black velvet, was led by his groom and valet. And the coffin itself, borne by four uppermerchants (and surely I would have been among those chosen), was beheld by all the captains of the fleet anchored before the Castle. They said there were tears, but in the death of others we each weep for what is self-intended, for the mortality of our barely tutored dreams. When even the great must so demonstrably perish, what purchase is there for any of us to cheat disappointment? *The katel is like an old and decrepit man who, in the course of his journey, has had to cross many valleys of sadness and mountains of misery...* Except that we were not old, Coen little more than my elder brother in years, each of us merely compromised by this miserable steam-bath climate. There may have been ritual lamentations at his funeral but there was scarce a tear shed afterwards, and I heard no one speak of love. Coen desired only one thing: the armament of his ambition and this kingdom of his making. A bamboo kingdom tempered by the amount of stone we could import for its defence. Even as his interment proceeded, Batavia was once more under siege by the Mataramese. The arrival of Specx would shortly put an end to this feeble charade, but the fact is of no comfort to me when I keep hearing Van Diemen hiss: *We are not many, Pelsaert, and the natives bear us no love. Your ship is wrecked hundreds of leagues distant, and you have abandoned all the soldiers and their arms...*

Jacques Specx – oh how I wish I'd never been detached from you as the fleet divided at Texel! You would arrive at Batavia to discover smoke rising from the enemy camp, the commander-in-chief dead and the settlement in mourning. You'd scarcely a moment in which to recover your land legs before the Council appointed you Governor in Coen's place. It must have come as a shock to find yourself suddenly elevated to the highest office outside the Netherlands. But then you were a man of long years and respected standing in the Company. You were perhaps the successor we required in the wake of your Old Testament predecessor, that man of brimstone and scant mercy where malfeasance was discerned. You had come into an inheritance which little formed you until informed of a chapter in Coen's administration that had ill-handled your name and family. Between the time of my ruined arrival in Batavia and my equally ruined return four months later with that pitiful troop of Abrolhos survivors, your daughter Sara suffered grievously at the hands of your predecessor. We all defer to a love of power, but not of a kind that would martyr innocents as in the days of old Rome. I scarce understand the world anymore, having seen and heard things to a cumulation that leaves me withered. And what I thought was merited in law has been so soaked in blood as to be no longer deserving of the name Justice. She was of your flesh — that half, at least, which wouldn't incur the curious stares and sneers of those in Holland. There is no place, after all, for the taking of Asian wives except in quarters remote from the hearth of our nation. Sara's Japanese mother precluded her, by birth, from accompanying you on your pilgrimage to the Fatherland. Much better, would it, had she been permitted to travel to the land of your infancy, to the city of her young suitor. In God's truth I even met his uncle — Amsterdam's Town Clerk — prior to joining the fleet at Texel. We come too far to do such violence to one another, and discipline can become a searching sport in punishments for those bereft of affection and kin. They no more than sought to liaise in one another — like Romeo and Juliet in the English play I hear of — but Coen, never a man of unguided love, despite a wife, nor compassion where mere children were concerned, was not prepared to relax that code under which he considered all Batavia should be schooled. You can easily lose a sense of perspective in these parts, the sun too hot, the air too close. And as you undertake that great work which is to the acknowledged profit and glory of the Fatherland, it is easy, also, to deny this truth and imagine oneself as far removed from matters commonplace as a night star from the crowded land at noon. They had little to preoccupy them other than their youth, little in experience to warn them of the consequence. And in an act of love what dreaded consequence might any of us anticipate? I think now not of my own misadventure but of something, here, that continues to appal me in the savagery with which such naturalness was suppressed. "Not under my roof!" Coen was supposed to have roared. Did he feel responsible for her, her guardian while you were away? I doubt it. It would have been more in the character of controlling troops, the punishment meted more of the parade ground variety. Before the town hall at Batavia, your twelve-year old daughter was tied to a post and soundly flogged. It little mattered that her coupling with the lad, scarcely fifteen, had been consensual. I picture Jacobsz with Zwaantie rutting near the ship-caged pigs and shudder at the sweat of their crude and goading pleasure. Sara and her lover, by contrast, were captured in the hygiene of the Governor's apartment, the sheets fresh but a little moist in the tropical afternoon, her virgin blood a tell-tale stain, her skin only that once broken yet now to be flayed before a gawking multitude. But worse would be the fate of young Cortenhoeff. Yes, the flag-bearer whose taste she had experienced, whose loins had probed the cavity of her own sweet youth, was led, like Pelgrom, to the appointed moment wherein a blindfold was secured to screen the shadow of the sword, and he who was a nephew of the Town Clerk of Amsterdam, who had sailed to the East in the expectation of blooming in the enterprise of the honourable Company, was decapitated at a single blow. For the life of me I don't understand what their crime was other than to offend the Governor's etiquette. Lord knows much worse – and among those of equally tender years – would take place on the Abrolhos, that narrow universe of murder.

They say that Coen was worn out with years of empire building, that his judgement was impaired by too long a service in the belief of his own infallibility, and that the flux merely finished off a withered shell. Weary he may have been but he breathed nothing other than command and continued to exercise a keen appreciation of things contingent. *You shall sail in the name of God and hasten with all possible diligence to the place where you have lost the ship and left the survivors.* These were his final words to me, firm but not unfair. Then while I was absent in my trial of recovery and redemption, he set about crucifying children.

All this time, Jacques, you sailed in my wake. Not steered from the usual route, of course, but delayed in departure and unknowing of the circumstances that accrued with explosive rapidity beyond the watery horizons ahead. I wasn't there to witness your transition to the highest office, to throw my energies into helping break the Mataramese siege, to benefit from your counsel in crises of the most personal disruption. What must you have made of it all, your journeying with one purpose supplanted by the commission to something altogether unexpected and elevated?

Rumour has it that Jan Coen died of anguish at the prospect of your arrival in Batavia, of having to answer to you as a man for the mistreatment of your daughter. It is a fanciful conceit. In the portrait I keep of him he never showed remorse, nor was he the type to betray fear. The timing of things can be limitless in its irony. It might have fared better for me had he lived to receive me a second time, the salvage almost entirely successful, only the human cost inexplicable. He had instructed me in July, knew well I was eager to redress the situation, and might have received me that November (had he lived) with the curiosity of one for another who had been to hell and back, whose unprovoked difficulties betrayed a strain never felt by him or admitted to. Instead, Jacques, my vanguard became the limping straggler of your fleet, and in those delaying months there had played itself a story of such posture and brutality that none who watched the *Sardam* sail in and hurried to hear its news could afford to tolerate that these, too, were men worthy of the name or meriting of mercy. It was just another thing you had to deal with on top of everything else, your daughter still recovering from her wounds in the very chamber wherein that first impetus to life had been chastened by the thorn of death.

I spend a great deal of time projecting my thoughts at the ceiling, its limewashed sky, taunted in memory by episodes I would rather forget. Even cheerful thoughts become infected by the calamity that overwhelmed me. What good a moment's grace or the perception of felicity when all is perception only or a siren's endangering music. Whenever I conjure Van den Broecke's laughing camaraderie or feel, as if he were present, the firm hand of Brouwer's approbation, I suffer, too, the calculating censure of Coen's eyeful silence, the grubby tugging of Medari, and the inconsequence of all those pleasures whose risk now ridicules any pretension I might have had to becoming a great man. Even to catch myself dreaming of Lucretia, to recall the flirtatious chivalry I practised aboard *Batavia*, is to invite such painful dismissiveness that I wince to think how derelict I was in the discipline expected of me. Yes, I quite forgot myself and my shortcomings in the ripening of my station, in the ease with which I'd learned to command respect. Even setbacks, those professional embarrassments which saw me manoeuvring to sidestep one authority for a higher bench, were easily absorbed in the eventual recognition of my talents. Nothing seriously deflected my calculating progress, my steady rise. Nothing crippling stood in my path to besmirch my standing or outlaw me in the affection of others. Until that night when, hurled from my bunk by the violent concussion, I was cast into sickness of a different tarnish, an unanticipated mortality of spirit from which I would not recover. It was as if the sun had suddenly withdrawn from my prosperous polders, the shadows creeping like water across the fields and I, too, as one with the drowning Spanish legions. Scrambling from the coffin of my quarters, a black pandemonium in my ears and illness clinging to my breath, I appeared on deck, ludicrous in my nightclothes, my eyes searching for news, for answers. Throughout the shocked confusion a thick and chilling salt spray gave the impression we were caught amidst the breaching of a thousand whales. The ship had been snared by some unseeable presence, and just as I feared the waters to be rising in the hold, so too did I feel a mounting accusation. From a fever of unsound sleep I had awoken to this nightmare, to my regained but lone responsibility.

For weeks (and when sufficiently convalescent) I had sensed betrayal, had overheard the whispers and sniggers whilst ministering to Lucretia in the aftermath of her assault. I had tried to understand the nature of this provocation against me, to picture the faces involved and their possible number. During my confinement I was impotent to know that dislike and indiscipline might feed an appetite for mutiny. What most shocked me, as I regained a little focus, was the realisation that my fears sprang not from thieves and wastrels on the lower decks but from among those nearest me in authority, that the challenge, were such an act to manifest itself, might arise from among my very lieutenants! I had, as it were, stepped from health into ill health only to return a short time later to the hushed staring of those who'd had the run of things in my absence. Evertsz, even more so than Jacobsz, was insolent enough not to conceal his malice. And now this dire emergency.

In the shouting and screaming and rude fixture of the ship, I knew that everything had come apart, that the intent of even the most vicious and unruly had been overwhelmed by this greater peril, that the uncertainty of others was now submerged in the uncertainty of all. Throughout the darkness of that disastrous pre-dawn, I felt a subtle equalling of the scales, my authority somewhat restored in the appeal to universal victimhood. "Skipper," I shouted, "what have you done? You've run a noose around our necks!" Jacobsz's eyes were shining in circumstances unaccustomed. He might have struck me to the deck but for the confounding wisdom that we were all imperilled by something harsher than personal animosity. He may have hated me for the judgement I asserted, but were we not to perish that very morning he needed me to help save himself from hanging.

Had the disaster only stopped at shipwreck, I should have been grateful. Jacobsz, he who had been the loudest and most insulting of my enemies, was forced into an alliance of sorts, and in the murkiness of daybreak, as we attempted to forestall doom, there prevailed a fitful cooperation. Throughout the weeks to come we would share a testy but resolved adventure, our mutual contempt no less diminished but our energies twinned in exculpating leadership. In those daily struggles that lured us further from the wreck, I could see his mind working like a Nuremburg clock, his seamanship shortening sail to follow in the wake of my rescued authority. If Evertsz would have me dead for what I knew of him, the skipper appeared no longer of a mind to allow that outrage. And in the withholding of violence, Evertsz succumbed to an angry despair, the longboat unexpectedly his prison, just as the *Sardam* would become one in the months ahead for those whose crimes remained vague and allusive. The watery path to salvation, like the torture we applied in the extraction of free confessions, brought some men closer to a moment of judgement. Despite its prayed-for necessity, we were all in varying degree afraid of what arrival in Java might mean. The privilege of having escaped those barren crumbs where others had been left was no escape at all.

"Francisco, I tire of Agra."

I close my eyes.

"I think you tire of Agra, also."

Am I in Agra? "I'm unwell," I say aloud.

"Ah yes, you don't look the best. More the *katel* than the *ziarie*, is that right?"

Something stirs in the periphery: tones which seem more a lightness of sound than light itself, the echo of an imagined past. I reach out as if to seek my mother's hand or, like someone blind, describe the profile of a father I scarce remember.

"You more than match Inayat Khan in the shrivelled aspect he presented."

"Inayat Khan?"

"He lived – or should I say, was dying – in the precinct of the Red Fort. I chanced upon him one day and was so astounded by death's visage, that grisly endurance of the body when life has already dimmed from the eyes, that I had him borne to the palace and propped on cushions for the painters to record. And not before time, either. He expired the following day."

"You recorded his death?"

"I wanted to dissect the precise humour of his end."

"Surely that's the behaviour of a ghoul," I struggle.

"I could have you spitted for that!" And he laughs a woman's confident laugh. "But think of it, Francisco; think of the favour I conferred on him – to expire in the presence of such luxury, to be harnessed in observation to an eminence such as mine. Yes, a lofty and bejewelled emperor may ride a stallion, the hooves of which secure him above the common earth, yet a particle of dust is always privileged to stick to his shoes. Even though Inayat Khan was scarce aware of the honour I did him, he would share a page in my narrative. I might have had you painted, too, had I lived to glimpse this moment."

I stare at the thought, at the unpretty sight of myself as subject. Some things become death. In heroism they lend themselves to chronicle. I simply stink and feel unbathed, my body an insult to my mind. "Could I see the picture?" I ask.

The phantasm seems to shift, uncertain at this turn. "I'm afraid it's with the rest of my papers, and I no longer command the services of a librarian."

"Never mind. I feel more than equal to its mirror."

"I think you need cheering. We all need cheering in the waver of extremities."

"You're not Maartens, are you? Not another accursed sick-visitor?"

"I'll ignore that. You're not yourself."

"But —"

"Come, Francisco, let's stop beating around the bush. You're a cultured man, your hands are delicate. I like a person who embodies an expressive harmony of interests. And I *know* you've brought me something."

I'm trying to focus, to summon my residual energy to bear on this presence which is full of light and colour yet insensitive to recognition. "Do I know you?" I ask.

The laugh becomes spurting. "Do you not perceive the world into which you were born?" he answers. "It should offend my esteem — and fare for you very badly were you not already close to death — *not* to know me."

Even though a comprehension of his features eludes me, I observe numerous details: a body shirt of the finest, almost translucent muslin — something that strikes me as lewd — and a green and gold turban which, unlike the perfect mushrooms that adorn other heathen lords, is more cavalierly knotted and inclined to one side. "After all," he continues, "what an insult to have written dismissively of my character yet to have known me so little as to have known me not at all."

"You?"

"It perturbs me that small men persist in harbouring such lofty opinions."

"I set out nothing but the truth."

"You tell nothing but those truths you want to hear."

I notice, now, the pearls: a great string of them, each as large as my thumbnail. And earrings of like sumptuousness. If his shirt be almost invisible, not so those golden bracelets which manacle his wrists, the sapphires and rubies that ornament his person. "Have I wronged you?" I lamely ask.

"It's no skin off my nose. Incidentally, have you ever watched a man being flayed?"

His presence is unnerving, tempting. The face begins to resolve itself around eyes that are liquid, like those of a horse. The moustache, I see, is little more than a brush of down, the hair before his ears mere ringlets. I sense the humour of a power almost Roman. "So, Francisco, when so many others have fallen over themselves to please me, what have you managed to bring?"

"A cameo, a jewel of great antiquity. It once belonged to the Emperor Constantine himself."

"What, the hand-me-down of someone long vanished? Nothing else?"

"There are gold chains and silver plate, tapestries and sea-horse teeth —"

"Unbelievable! I casually express the desire for a fine Arabian horse and you send me sea-horse teeth? Even that Englander, Roe, struggled to impress. Your lands must be impoverished to present like beggars at my court."

"How might we presume to know your wishes?"

"Ha! You took it upon yourself to become an authority on my family, never having so much as dreamed of India during the life of my father (may his memory be cherished) yet scripting him in gold whilst I, who reigned over the territories of your ambition, was portrayed as a villain of cruel satisfactions. I think it well we never met," and all amusement now sliding from his tone. "There was little need — oh, a huge need on your part, I'll admit, but absolutely none on mine. Thomas Roe may have been a pompous sort but I did enjoy the game-playing we traded. You, Francisco, strike me as something altogether more servile."

"But we never met — I viewed you only at a distance. How might you know this of me?"

"My noble Pelsaert, you were always a shimmering hypocrite at the fringes of greatness."

"You are unjust, sir!"

"The English have a king, someone with whom I might play the cousin. A little king, to be sure, but we sovereign rulers understand one another. You Dutch, on the other hand, are a greedy piracy, full of your own lordlessness, seduced by the polity of what: some company? Tell me, how might I be given to understand the nature of your republic? How might I admire it?"

"It's a nation of free men," I pipe, "a brotherhood under one God to the exclusion of tyrants."

"Yet do you not make war and enslave others?"

"Only against those who would limit our right to survive and prosper."

"I'll tell you something, Francisco," and settling himself at the edge of my cot. "I never lie to myself. What need? You've seen the paintings of me, surely? And that's another thing: you ought to have known that I've quite an eye and maintain a studio of over a hundred artists. Do you honestly imagine that beyond gold, silver and the power to deprive another man of his life I intuit little else? I have fathered an entire style of seeing in this country! You Dutch are fond of pictures. Even above your bed in this shabby room – and let me tell you, Francisco, I wouldn't be caught dead *or* dying in such a squalid enclosure as this – yes, even above your bed I see an illustration of something I have no need of seeing for myself: your ships and, beyond them, only the merest suggestion of land. Yes, that's the difference; you have not at home what I have here in abundance. Mine is an empire of such territory that there is little leisure in which to hypothesise what lies beyond such seas as I have not seen. You see, Francisco, everyone of a will to advance his station in this world comes to India. India *is* the world. And I in name am its Seizer!"

I perceive his boast to be not as self-satisfied as he might wish it.

"You don't believe me?" he shakes his head, his pendulous jewels rudely startled. "Upon this globe I slipper stand, with bow and arrow lethal in the dispatch of my enemies. Or regally couched am I in generous receipt of those who rule over lands in which I am little interested. Paintings are my geography. From the Shah of Persia and Sultan of Turkey to a lowly English king, the world is arranged beneath my throne; cherub, beast and empire in my service!"

"Your throne, like my cot, is but an hourglass."

"True, but just think how fabulous and tapestried was the life I led, how to the core of a human universe. And you, a mere observer – a diarist like myself, to be sure, but without audience." He anticipates my objection by declaring, "You only summon me to your thoughts because of an aggrieved sense of injustice."

"Don't flatter yourself that your dying was any the more gracious for having died an emperor."

"See, you're bitter."

"Even in this world you were not entirely what you wanted to be."

"And now you're being petty."

"The Englishman, Roe, he presented you with Mercator's atlas. As Seizer of the World you discovered you had a lot to learn, that there is much of this earth which exists in supreme indifference to who we are."

"I sent the maps back to him. They were of little import."

I study him a moment as he similarly studies that aspect of himself he wishes to project. It strikes me that power is a blindness, that only those who have had their opportunity robbed of them are granted, Cassandra-like, an unavailing prophecy of insight. In his manipulation of expression I read the complacency of a kingdom ignorant of its territorial myopia. And I read his displeasure. "I think it was a mistake," he says, "to have imagined that you might bear me anything I valued."

"I went to great trouble to argue for and accrue the treasure I brought back East."

"Trinkets and toys, Francisco. You aimed to seduce me as if I were a child."

"The cameo itself was worth an emperor's ransom."

"Not valuable enough to prevent it from falling into the hands of Cornelisz."

"None could have predicted the disaster. We were lucky to have brought the people and stores ashore."

The silence is begging.

"When on campaign," he explains, "my baggage was entrusted to ten thousand men. A commander's head would compensate for any mishap. Yet your lieutenant openly paraded his insolence and fawned upon the very treasures you would have me grateful for. It was a contaminated dream, Francisco, a dream no longer worthy of the life that had passed from me."

"Are you really dead?"

"Safely so," he smiles, like one admitting to an embarrassing misdemeanour. "Did you not know this prior to your departure from Surat?"

I can't remember what I knew or when. To whom, then, did I intend my precious cargo? "Was it Shah Jahan?"

"Who succeeded me? Yes, after a fashion of murder. You were lucky, Francisco, not to have married — although my wife was the light of my palace — nor to have sired children. Those born to great account are jealous of what they scarce have any fondness to lose. In our family we eat our own, and my rebellious son set to work with an appetite upon his brothers and nephews. That I did not live to see it — despite the cruelties you accuse me of — is one small respite. As for the punishments I ordered, these were never unwarranted, nor were they out of proportion to the crimes committed. I often cosseted a humour which amounted to little less than clemency, as when that miserable idiot broke a precious dish of mine. I had the wretch flogged, of course, then tidied up and sent off to China with five thousand rupees to procure another." And he chuckles at the lesson of that barefoot journey.

"No, like you, Francisco, I grew old. Old before my hour. I might have wished for nothing other than a peaceful twilight, the affection of a servant. But do you know what it is for the weather to tremble at a distance, for the skies to darken before a tent can be pitched? The clouds whisper and there is little prospect of precluding the discomfort. We each have suffered the intrigue of others, we each have contended with the ravages of ill health. It is a prerogative of kings to be able to silence vicissitude with opium and wine. Perhaps it is a prerogative of merchants also? I was out hunting when one of the bearers fell from a precipice. There is a moment in every man's life when the omens are not propitious and what has been forestalled can be forestalled no longer."

"Do you believe in the angel of death?"

I hear his woman's laughter burble without comfort.

"Did it come for you?" I press.

"He was in the act of chasing a deer. The sun was hot…"

"And?"

Jahangir shrivels into the frailty he observed of Inayat Khan, the colour draining from his features, his torso ashen beneath that almost invisible muslin. "A man can disappear from view," he murmurs. "Three days later, the world I circumferenced like the diurnal motion of the sun itself suddenly detached me from its necessity." He turns to me with an expression that still harbours puzzlement. "You know of what you wither."

And I see the charter of my decline, the prolonged fuse burning as had the slow matches of our guns that noontide when, almost a year gone now, we cleared the *Sardam*'s deck for action, our numbers few but our outrage focused on the boat that drew near, their entire race costumed in pilfered laken, its scarlet like the blood that perfumed those waters, their viciousness trimmed in gold and silver passementerie. If surprised by Mercator's maps, how might Jahangir have known of or reacted to even lesser kingdoms and their tyrants?

"Wherefore would you come aboard armed?" I shouted. The glint of steel was scarce concealed.

One, Hendricxsz, as ferocious a scoundrel as Cornelisz, answered defiantly, "We'll answer when we're on the ship."

"If I no longer know you for *who* you are," I answered back, "I presently know you for *what* you are," and all the while feeling the excited tension of our party to open fire on this disease of men in whose company we had ventured forth upon this disastrous voyage.

Their boat now bobbed beneath the *Sardam*'s cannon, and the empire of their brief winter began to splinter at the arrival of our determined force. But it was too late. Unrecognised at first, the angel had placed a withered carnation at my table. And though I lacked nothing of the vigour required to rescue my sensibilities, the story I breathed was now polluted, my future chronicle mortally imprisoned in the saline glare of that September day. Yes, just weeks after the initial fracture of her keel, *Batavia* would spawn a horror beyond any power of mine to redeem.

I FEEL ALMOST WELL today. The light is noiseless through the sieve of shutters, and if not for an absence of church bells I might think it Sunday. If so, I might enjoy an unanticipated peace, its leisure free of hope or expectation. Far better than fretting for news that doesn't come. Or when it does, dishevels the stability of what one has chosen to think. In fact, so pleasurable is this sudden and well-felt inertia that I find I'm hungry. Yes, bread and eggs — something not too spiced or troubled over — that's what I want.

"Hartanti!" I call, and scarce daring to hope that the worst may be behind me. "Hartanti!" I call again, my voice thin but even. Throughout the building nothing stirs. I listen for activity in the garden but not so much as a bird disturbs the silence. I imagine everyone at a little distance, attending their chores — laundering, scrubbing floors, bartering at the market which is situated outside the walls. My room is an oasis of filtered sunlight, a place wherein I'm securely harboured, safe and well-tended — a space in the minds of others, never far from their concern. I am Francisco Pelsaert, after all — member-elect to the Council of the Indies. There's no denying who I am, and I want two eggs!

"Hartanti — where are you, girl? It's morning and I hunger for some breakfast."

And still the silence persists as if the hour has been abandoned. Surely I missed nothing in my sleep? Surely I would have heard?

When Jahangir gave the order to resume the march and the vastness of his army milled in slow procession like a festival of bickering pilgrims, the haze of dust was intensified by smoke from the burning camp. Where the emperor was, so must everyone attend, and the destruction of whatever moulded the disposition to stay put ensured that traders and camp-followers, likewise, now took to the road. I never saw such a multitude, nor was the desolation of the abandoned camp dissimilar to the ashes of any warlike anarchy. When I finally sailed from the Abrolhos I was careful not to leave so much as a nail behind. Only the dead: most of them vanished in its uncertain geography, some deliberately exhibited.

Damn it all, the very memory interferes with my appetite! *Hartanti*, I think instead of bellow. Has all of Batavia similarly disappeared?

That uncomfortable dread, of remaining a prisoner to my weakness, readmits itself. It is my illness — this unmannered visitor, never constant, always arriving at the least propitious of times — which separates me from the affection of others, rules me into their past.

Hartanti?

I feel deeply, morally, this inability to leave my bed, to venture out in search. I am no supernaturalist. I know that beyond these shutters the world I've experienced continues to trickle and converse in all the steady meter of its variety. I know that were I to die tomorrow — as indeed each of us must die, the death of others a companion sight and lesson — yes, I know that the very engine of this planet would not for one second stall upon its axis. But to die before one's proper death, to feel, as I do now, a space or vacuity insert itself between who I am and the receding consciousness of those who know me, this stokes such an anguish that I read in it the conspiracy of abandonment. Their eyes converse, fingers drawn to lips. It is an eavesdropping sort of denial. I'm sure Hartanti serves at the table of Governor Specx; is waylaid and imposed on for information by that bastard upstart Van Diemen!

My appetite is gone.

The coastal fringe lies green and dormant in the sun. The sea, too, is colour-fast, its tropical palette deepened as if with a drop of indigo. Things always look more favoursome at a distance.

Nearer home and when a breeze was up, the skies seemed haunted by memories of winter, their blue soon indistinguishable from the toneless greys that characterised the shrunken light of Christmas. At sea, too, upon my first voyage to the Indies, a familiar vestment of atmospherics was tethered to our early passage like a persistent yet endurable discomfort. Only in the tropics — first, south of the Cape Verde Islands as we approached the stupefying latitudes of Sierra Leone, then later as we threaded the archipelago that defined the Spiceries — only then did I become acquainted with the glare of something altogether indifferent to the dazzled instrument of my eyes. This was not a circumstance limited to we Netherlanders. The English, too, were hard put adjusting to so unlike and intemperate a place. Indeed, it was not difficult at times to imagine oneself adrift in the exotic Eden of scripture, so prompting was the inclination to become other than one's schooled demeanour in this humid and sun-slashed quarter. And like Eden, paradise harboured a serpency that could readily bring a Christian into mortal crisis. In the broth-like accumulation of days, it wasn't difficult for a man's soul to become as disfigured as the corrosion of his strength. If the Portuguese and Spaniard fared any better, it was because of the tireless sunshine of their native shores and their blood-tainted affiliation with Africa and its Moors.

At first I was among those who confirmed in me an identity fostered out to the honourable Company. I was a Netherlander in protracted journey with my kind, our voyage in the *Weapon of Zeeland* an extended charter of what I was (or had been, until now), the ghost of my grandfather — and even the bosom of my mother — redolent in the enterprise that guided our ship. Yes, the maritime command of the Company both muted and prolonged a sense of leave-taking.

Then suddenly, after months at sea, here we were in a foreign place, our insistent familiarities — the sable tunics, in spite of the heat — now discordant in this all-too-real dream. In the crossroads before Batavia we were released into a different perfume, the lighters rowed by Java men whose scent was like an airing of vegetables compared with we whose long confinement stirred an aroma more akin to the privy. It was also the babble of unknown tongues; it drew startling attention to the fact that we were no longer where we had started. This, in fact, was the new beginning. Not our joining of the Company. Not our embarkation at Amsterdam or departure from Texel. Not even the slow cure of our meditations during the long voyage out. No, our ferrying from the ship to this shore-littered settlement by men whose skins were moist with exertion and the oils of their diet represented our arrival at a moment of definitive rupture. The Fatherland was now another country, removed by half a year and half a world, and this — this busy place of transplant, this little Holland which was no Holland at all — this was our new and curiously tailored reality.

I was anxious to learn, to accommodate the demands now upon me. The token familiarities of Batavia might otherwise have occasioned a terrible sickness for home and I was here to work, to make something of myself. I was eager to explore what was foreign, to manoeuvre among experiences that would refine my merit. And so, early on, I coasted the archipelago's outposts, drew close to those far perspectives to enter less open worlds, their rivers brown and serpentine and a worry to pilots whose jabber was translated in hand signals to straining helmsmen. Tortuous navigation was in our blood, and our jachts were ideally suited to the slow but profitable adventure of commerce. The *Sardam* was one such craft, a vessel that would become all too familiar as it hovered on the lagoon in the lee of High Island… That events such as occurred that day should have complicated our mission, those ragged men on the beach and the costumed delinquency of their enemies construing the very see-saw of an unimaginable story, this chilling advent damaged my appreciation for that diligent little workhorse of the fleet. The *Sardam* was too long in locating the survivors, too long a makeshift prison and, like *Batavia* herself, too long my couch in illness to leave it unpolluted in my affections.

I heard Jacques Specx once remark that, now and again, persons of strange opinion come here. And so it was that in my initiation into the coastal trade I swiftly learned to limit my surprise, to accept without question (though not necessarily without judgement) the many compromises effected to sustain the work of the Company. If I knew myself already far from home, imagine my feelings when greeted by agents who ought to have been Dutchmen but who had largely discarded the appearance and custom of their race. As the river wharves came into view, a veritable sing-song of children's voices flittered along the bank, the shadows fluid with the motion of their running. The stockades, such as they were, exhibited a blend of what was unthinkable of Batavia itself, our agents and village headmen sharing the privilege of these squalid forts, the smoke of cooking fires rising from the yards amidst a crude accumulation of stores.

"Gillis, my friend! I was beginning to think myself forgotten."

The voice was clear and certainly European, but of the crowd assembled on the wharf I could discern none of such appearance.

"Meyer," shouted our merchant, "you'll soon forget your*self* in this idle place!"

"Idle?" A burnished face appeared, its beard unkempt, the head a good head higher than the rest. "It's all a man can do just to keep afoot of his survival. Did you bring me any contraband?"

"You know the Company frowns on personal trade. There might just be three firkins of gin," and Gillis caught my eye, winking.

"Who's this then?"

"Francisco Pelsaert. A junior under my charge."

"His first tour?"

"'Tis rumoured I've travelled half a world to meet you," I boasted.

"Ha ha. Well said, young toad! Come ashore and share a drink — if Gillis, that is, has lived up to his promise and smuggled me that which inspirits all!"

And then Meyer was suddenly revealed in all his improbability, barechested and with what, at first, I took to be some kind of amulet but which proved itself a tattoo. Instead of breeches he was wrapped in a long skirt such as the natives wear, and for a belt he boasted the halter of a Spanish sword. He was entirely barefoot, the soles of his feet the colour of ashes, and as we followed him through the crowd, his odour, in sharp contrast to those among whom he lived, betrayed a musk of indolent compromise. At Gillis's side (and trailed by porters who carried, among other things, the three firkins) I allowed my eyes to sample the curious expressions of those who jostled in carnival procession about us — cheeky children and young women whose modesty was as comely as any invitation to pay closer scrutiny.

"Careful, young man, you're not seduced from your forbearing," laughed Meyer.

I must have coloured, for the girls giggled their understanding.

"He's new to the routine," reiterated Gillis. "Batavia teaches little of what to expect in the islands."

"Quite." Meyer shook his head as he led us into the stockade: part fort, part factory, part petty-royal enclosure, bantam roosters scratching the dust in their competing claim to the site. The throng stopped at an invisible line and Meyer turned to yell something with remarkable facility for the native tongue. Several old women sat, as if blind, upon mats that formed a precinct of preliminary kitchen chores – shelling nuts, stripping roots, pummelling grain into a paste, all within near reach of a cooking fire. It wasn't easy to tell whom these venerable matriarchs devoted their almost somnambulistic labours to – Meyer or the village headmen who sat on a slightly raised platform towards the rear of the enclosure. In all likelihood there existed some arrangement which fitted the machinery of our trade to the niceties of custom and pre-rogative. If Meyer felt at all marginal, he didn't show it. Over the entry to a nearby hut, the VOC flag was suspended like a curtain. Meyer directed us to a little patch where a bench and several remarkably crafted chairs awaited. Seating himself with his back to what I supposed was his residence, he tossed a command over his shoulder in that dialect which was becoming familiar to my ears. The Company banner was deftly drawn aside and a woman emerged, wrapped in cloth more preciously trimmed than the apparel I observed of others, her youth – that unblemished clarity of face – arresting my admiration before I noted, too, her swollen belly.

"Pelsaert, you've certainly an eye for the ladies," remarked Meyer as his concubine, I assumed, settled three cups upon the bench. "You could do worse than Company work in the fields, here, of the Lord."

"Mind you don't corrupt him," said Gillis, tugging at his collar beneath the hot sun.

"Ha! A lady and a life in the tropics might prove his recompense."

"I've come here to learn," I said.

"Well, first, you need to understand there are no Ten Commandments south of the equator." And in his smile I observed that his teeth were stained by betel, making them appear as if of some predator that had bitten into the carcass of its prey. A firkin was breached and the jacht's crew took advan-tage of this moment to dissolve into the village in pursuit of whatever sated desire.

"Tell me, Meyer," drilled Gillis, "how travels our prestige in these parts?"

"The Acehnese are watching. They detest the Portuguese but eye us with a steady mistrust. We're all kafirs to them."

"Kafirs?" I queried.

"Unbelievers. Whether you're a good Calvinist or a Popish prick, it makes no difference. The Portuguese have been around a long time, long enough to demonstrate that they can achieve no more than what they've managed already. Their priests are their own worst enemies, if you ask me. Good health, gentlemen." Meyer took a swig, weighing the taste in his mouth. "The local lords are beginning to look to India and beyond," he continued.

"How so?" asked Gillis.

"There are ties with the Mogul court; they have holy men from Mecca. It would be best to keep our lips sealed and our consciences blank in the matter of religion."

Gillis grinned with a relaxation uncommon to him. "There's little chance of transgression on the part of our predikants unless ignorance intrudes."

"That's true," rejoined Meyer, laughing. "When a man is conceited enough to have numbered himself, already, in God's lifeboat, his relief doesn't garner much by way of compassion for the drowning of others. Unions, funerals and frownings – they're good for little else."

And in their mockery I would come to recognise an easy mark in Gijsbert Bastiaensz, a man whose chief crime was his ineffectuality, whose family – but for a daughter – would be butchered, a man who shared my table throughout the long months aboard *Batavia*, who was unquestioningly civil yet gallingly usurped at every turn of the imagination as ever any man I was so goaded to strike. Indeed, I might have punched myself for having surrounded my person with such sorry sheep. If God truly died and was buried on Batavia's Graveyard, more's the pity its only minister did not make of himself a worthier sacrifice.

"You heard that Van den Broecke has been sent to India," gossiped Gillis.

"Doesn't surprise me," and Meyer drained his cup.

"Coen wants to lock out the English –"

"He wants to be careful he doesn't overreach himself."

"– and is sure to build up the mission there."

They each paused to reflect on the implication of this, staring at me as if I were an instrument of the Company's designs. It occurred to me that Meyer was less an agent than a spy. Certainly the collected produce in the yard appeared ill-kept and haphazard to the point of token. It was not an appointment I envied.

"What's the latest folly, then, at Batavia Castle?"

"You want to choose your words with care, my friend," answered Gillis, alluding to my presence.

"Come, I'll wager young Pelsaert, here, is eager to learn the intricacies of survival. Isn't that right?" At a snap of his fingers, Meyer's woman decanted another measure of gin.

"I aim to get ahead," I responded, more out of politeness than insinuation.

"Then let me give you some advice —"

"Meyer, look at you; look at how you live! You're hardly in a position to dispense advice."

This was not unkindly said, nor did Meyer take offence. Leaning close to me, he continued by asking, "How much do you earn? Twenty-four guilders a month?"

I swallowed. It seemed a long way from the top, and even the likes of Gillis were far from handsomely rewarded.

"If not advice, then, consider this: you can breathe the world's hypocrisies and learn to cultivate an unblinking heedlessness, or you can step away from that fawning dance in which others so belittle their time."

"Meaning?"

"You shall surely rise; I see it in your eyes — the hunger of a man unsure of what's on offer but determined to get a slice of it."

I was about to protest but, still short of his meaning, was uncertain, myself, of what I protested.

"You're ambitious," he continued. "You have an eye for the ladies, too," and hocking his head in the direction of his hut, its pennant stripes of red, white and blue strangely incongruous in this jaundiced atmosphere. "Your salary will increase but never enough to satisfy your craving. Merchants of whatever rank don't earn enough to keep with the illusion of their worth. And that illusion is a fever which bewitches all who think they've made a proper decision in coming to Batavia."

"Meyer, I protest!"

I was now intrigued and wanted Gillis to be still.

"He's hardly a boy, Gillis. Mark me, he may even become your supercargo one day. And good luck to you, Heer Pelsaert. But just remember what you might be called upon to do in your scramble to the top. Ambition, like war, is endlessly tactical, and a wearied man often seeks shelter at the threshold of an opportune but unspelled evil. As for me – and in spite of what *you* might think or my friend Gillis, here, protest – I'm a good and loyal servant of the Company. I simply know my place – my prospects, if you like – and care nothing for the foppery that would play me for a lesser man were I to jostle with the burghers at Batavia. You, Gillis – you imagine me lonely? I'll tell you, Pelsaert, loneliness is the unremitting battle for recognition. I would be one in a dormitory of rivals at Batavia, a kind of orphan. Here I am a man, a man who has struck out for himself on ground of his choosing."

I stole another glance at Meyer's woman, her small hand resting on the curvature of her stomach. I wanted to linger awhile, to go on observing the curious making of a man in this domestic tributary of the Company's adventure. His tattoos and sarong, his chatter in a tongue whose meaning was as yet unripe but which clearly shaped some influence, these were the ingredients of a seductive fascination. In the displacement of such surroundings I realised that I, too, was willing to experience a sort of premeditated vagabondage, a subsidised apprenticeship that would round me out as I, in turn, rounded on the prize that was yet to state itself this early in my career. I knew that Meyer was right, that Batavia was no proper goal in itself. Yet it was difficult not to hanker for the kind of rank that afforded ready access to the most privileged of its doors. A place at the Governor's table, perhaps even the position itself (ha, did I dare imagine that?) – yes, that was the distant effect of a cause yet to fight its campaign. There was one thing I was certain of: should I be assigned to the Indian mission, I would most readily go.

Now and then, persons of strange opinion come here. Those words and the ferocity of their truth are not lost on me. Yet Meyer seemed no stranger to decency, leastways not the glimpse I had of him. He appeared to survive in a state of precarious grace, the ructions of a wider world finding little quarrel with his backwater.

I re-picture him and his girl-wife, the promised baby and the roosters, the shadows gathering as they had, back then, when I returned to the jacht, the river brown and sweetly noxious, the children scampering along its bank in defiance of their parents' summons to end-of-day chores, this dishevelled but not unkindly pocket now yielding in the softening light to a dusky anonymity. In a blink it is gone, swallowed in a lapse of memory, in my preoccupation with colours of a different hue, the water blue and crystal, the *Sardam* as fine a jacht as ever put to sea, its mission as purposeful as ever hope with prayer conspired. At a distance the land is flat but not unsullied. A favourable wisp of smoke rises to the south. But in spite of everything I'd learned through witness down the years, I was not prepared for what that distance carefully concealed. Persons of strange opinion… Why did you come here, Cornelisz? What was the reason for your advent?

I remember it was always windy. From the moment we first struck to the day, almost six months later, when, departing that unknowable continent a second time, we abandoned those two delinquents to the mercies of fate. Of the islands themselves a less hospitable place could scarcely be imagined. They were mere stubbles of discard, rubble cays denied the love of land. Beyond the horizon to the east, their sinister parent would reveal itself devoid of sanctuary. It was as if our stranding had occurred in some unfinished place, the comfortless fragments of our choiceless hope mocked by boundless sea. There was no drinking water to be had, nothing of shade. I gazed upon these island platforms, these calcified lily-pads, for what they were: Death's barely buoyant antechamber. We couldn't all stay there, not indefinitely. Across this desolate spectacle the wind, so blustery that to speak was to shout, maintained a scalding that was as abrasive to the spirit as the unfamiliar coral was to the delicacy of our shoes. Even as the initial crisis settled, the breeze did not. At night it moaned about our fires and stoked our darkest thoughts; at dawn it breathed a pallor that was distinctly grey. Where the broken ship was cradled, it misted a fine spray from breakers that stretched as far as the eye could see. It added to our thirst with the parching of our lips. And it pick-pocketed the resolve of all whose cloaks were far from deeply lined. It was the never ending companion to our nightmare.

The first of the winter gales was soon upon us. In the search we under-took of the predicted and nearby coast, the rain was as welcome as the storm was not. In the longboat, sopping, men could at least suck the moisture from their beards as they pondered whether they might presently drown. The wind sped us northwards, further from all consideration of return. We had come too far to go back empty-handed, and in any case the adverse distance dimin-ished its advisability. To continue, driven on by wind and sail, this seemed a better course. Despite the shoreless formidability of the Timor Sea, to attain Batavia seemed a bold and obvious solution to all our miseries. How more sturdy, then, would be our commission to rescue.

But the wind was then to prove itself as detrimental as flustered con-science to the execution of our cause. That which had sped us to the annun-ciation of disaster now fostered a state of purgatory so beloved of papists. If two weeks had been more than sufficient to bring us – the first survivors – to a place of succour, how galling then to suffer, in our well-equipped return, an obstructing and wind-tricked lapse of more than two months! If I could sniff the familiarity of place, I certainly could not see it. "In God's name," I shouted at the skipper and helmsman, both, "are you not mariners? Do we not pay you to cipher this?" And flinging my arm at the empty horizon, vexed beyond endurance.

Jacob, the *Sardam*'s skipper, eyed me cautiously and responded nothing. Gerritsz, the helmsman, likewise held his tongue and glanced up at the sun. We had all served long months together, the daily ocean scouring the timbers of our ritualised existence. All were aware of the great heat of my distress. After a time the skipper remarked, "*Batavia* was lost in an uncharted moment. The bearings taken at the wreck have been faithfully traced."

"Are you telling me it doesn't exist, that the isles are spectral?"

"Commandeur, we have followed the line of latitude as determined from the beach –"

"May I remind you that on that beach await more than two hundred souls!"

The entire crew paused to stare at me, whether to query, now, the probable number or to insinuate by their silence that it was not of their fault that we were here to make good what was scarcely of their making in the first place. If only Jacobsz were with us, I could focus all my anger, ride his culpability with a sharp spur. If Jacobsz were here, we might even find *Batavia*. Instead, I've left him at Batavia Castle, detained in a dungeon within sound of the sea.

I turned to go below, to intimate that this unpalatable annoyance was beyond further warrant of debate, that only in the satisfaction of our search might I find the peace that gloomily eluded me. I don't think any on board lived without great anxiety as each day slipped away, the inextinguishable ocean to the west a sanguine flood. And still those flattened cays remained incorporeal, the substance of a fairy dream or nightmare.

When discovery came there was only a tolerable joy among us, the wind, that constant miser of good fortune, now blowing from the south and southwest, skewing and delaying our approach. As forestalling night once more cloaked the mystery of what we might find, the mash and hiss of broken water hinted at reefs and dirty ground, a world of intricate terrors beneath the flat mantle of appearance.

Looking back on it now, I'm sure I must have imagined much, that the revelation of what had taken place tempted me to hear or witness what I could not have known. Before noon, as the *Sardam* inched its way close, smoke rose from the High Island. Nearer the stricken *Batavia* itself, an uneven smudge also climbed the sky. There were survivors, God be praised, but it was difficult to discern whether any had noted our arrival. I recalled the deserted campfires we had come across in our search for water on the shores of the continent, the natives vanished, their absence no less unsettling than had we actually met to barter. It was in the hour before Wiebbe Hayes revealed himself that I thought I heard a crack, perhaps two. Knowing now (and uncomprehending, then) of that which would appal us, our advent at this critical juncture in the island war had weighed against the mutineers. Despite the crackle of their weapons, Batavia's Graveyard would never conquer High Island. Again and again I hear and see this drama played out in my dreams: the invaders floundering comically in the shallows, those still aboard their homemade sloops resorting to the instrumental cowardice of calculating execution — yes, a musket pops and one of Hayes's defenders crumples. At my imaginary distance they resemble schoolboys in a kind of snowless snowball fight, and in this miniature of perspective I'm reminded of the spectacle of Coen's grand assault on Jacatra, and find myself astonished that life can be done away with so childishly.

It was an ill wind for them that ended all their hopes — and mine. I had thought to come across thirst and starvation, the bodily depredations of a desolate wait. Not for a moment had I conceived of murder, and on such a stupendous scale.

The wind remained the defining element, our chorus throughout the weeks ahead. It haunted the evenings with its echo of lives now silent, their bodies nowhere to be found. Within the canvas shelters, those who remained lived with the perplexity of their survival, stained by the experience of their witness. There was not a woman breathing who had not been forced against her will. I rarely slept on Batavia's Graveyard and was anxious to be aboard the *Sardam* before nightfall. Out by the wreck, the breakers maintained an incessant din which, in the small hours, and as I tossed and was sponged by fevers that resided still, steadily frayed my optimism concerning salvage. I would count the prisoners in my mind, the number of those whose fate was still to be decided, and tremble at the thought of how few we were, notwithstanding the gallows that had already been put to use. Even on the day we rowed Cornelisz and his principals across to Seals' Island, their howls of execration were pathetically reduced, the wind snatching at the final breath of those who, like gulls squabbling over titbits of blame, screamed "Revenge! Revenge!"

The following morning, and every morning thereafter, the wreck loomed to ballast our residual community, to affix our purpose to the reclamation of its precious entrails. At first light the campfire smoke on Batavia's Graveyard stirred white against the saline chill. It was all we could do not to think of what had taken place here, not to seek some audience or clue amidst the relics we continued to live amongst. We passed over, through and around these with dull minds, scarcely acknowledging the ghosts who roamed in the breakfast silence, the business to hand our armour — yes, another day supervising the Gujarati divers at the edge of the reef.

Yet in spite of our success in recovering the money chests, the operation progressed but slowly, compelling us to live for one thing whilst billeted in the ruins of another. The liberation of the islands had simply complicated a mood of forbearance in which, during the detaining weeks ahead, none were released from what had happened or, depending on their culpability, were free of what was to come. Indeed, it was almost impossible to separate the wicked from the fair, so coercive the threat of death that the weak and guileless had consented to have their names added to the rollcall of those already damned. In the stillness that reclaimed some sanity of conscience, it seemed as if few – Wiebbe and his followers notwithstanding – hadn't directly or indirectly participated in the orgies of this puppet state. Even the predikant was besmirched in the contradictions of his suffering, an accessory not clearly worthy of the pity inspired by the slaughter of his family, he and his daughter, Judith, supping at the table of their chief tormenter whilst Cornelisz's henchmen set about exterminating the others. What was going through their minds during and after that meal? How could Bastiaensz allow himself to live and follow orders, to suffer his eldest daughter to become the whore (for I won't say wife) of that violent youth, and curry longevity in a nightmare it would best to have woken from? Bastiaensz, after all, was supposed to be the castaways' spiritual shepherd, his daughter the inviolate article of a clergyman's respectability. But in the suppression of the mutiny the predikant seemed less mindful of his martyred wife and children and more attuned to the persuasions of his own misfortune. He had been forbidden to preach; had been forced to work, launching and hauling in the murderers' craft although alleging himself so starved he could scarce get up; had listened to the menacing banter concerning his fate, then become the emissary of Cornelisz himself, sent to persuade the loyalists with Hayes that the volumed slaughter they'd heard of was, in truth, none other than a misunderstanding! Then with the other women parcelled out to lesser villains, these, too, found themselves jealous of Judith. What business hers to besot so handsome a braggart as Coenraat van Huyssen? And, indeed, she needn't open her legs to any but him. When he died that morning on the shore of High Island, run through like the others upon the concealed pikes of Hayes's invention, it was said her face betrayed no emotion, that she remained impassive in what was doubtless a hurried assessment of her situation, the prospect of being demoted to the common whoredom. In that event she might have joined the rest in their dislike of anyone unduly merited — even one privileged to the most unnatural and least appetising of advantages! Thus they all hated Lucretia as they might have hated themselves, ashamed of the surrender that had permitted them to live, and jealous of the fact that she was exclusive to Cornelisz, the consort of this self-styled Captain-General — yes, Queen of Batavia's Graveyard.

I found the southerlies and the salvage work consoling. It diminished the chance of spending any time among those of whom it was difficult to meet without their silence invoking a judgement of sorts, as if I were being dared to contribute an understanding more sympathetic to their unspecified anger. Was I to blame for what had taken place? Had I not mounted their rescue? What more could I have done? It had been a complexity of two tales, of separate necessities. And in the aftermath of their brief but cruel vignette, my world now took pre-eminence, the Company my compass in the re-establishment of a former faith. Only it was not the same. The modestly laughing Lucretia of our early voyage, that feminine jewel at table and seductress of my stroking dreams, she now haunted me during that antipodean spring as we scoured the Abrolhos for every peg and nail, gathering up the evidence of our occupation as if determined to expunge the stain of what had occurred. There had to be some profit from the loss, some separation. But it proved a fragile and begrudged redemption, one that wasn't earned without further loss of life, and in our return to Batavia I commanded more a convict ship than any pride of the Fatherland. Indeed, I had become the custodian of a freak show, and the now taciturn Lucretia, she whose eyes condensed the injuries she bore, even she appeared to number me among the damned.

"**M**y husband thinks it strange you serve no prince. He imagines your loyalties must divide themselves without a sovereign."

"Your husband imagines, perhaps, not enough what it is to be a sovereign people. Indeed, we share a prince but govern ourselves more openly than most."

"Your pride sounds like a compensation."

I'm about to bite back, all too familiar with the arrogance of those accustomed to privilege, when I see that she is smiling.

"Admit it, Francisco —"

"You dare utter my name?" and smiling, myself, at the shape her accent gives it.

"You crave the luxury, the confirmation of a title."

"I'm already respected."

"Yes, but not enough. Are there none but merchants among you?"

"You mock me," I laugh, my Persian more than serviceable.

And this time she is halting. "I perhaps envy you a little."

"Envy?"

"As men you lead such varied lives." And she offers me her profile, her head completely uncovered.

"Beyond Hindustan, you mean?"

"No, beyond what is tolerated of a woman."

"Is your life not already rewarded?"

She bears me a quizzical expression. "My husband is a powerful man and quite at ease in the certainty of his authority. He permits a licence quite unheard of, even in the zenana of the emperor."

"You mean in relation to you — and his other wives?"

She regards me now as if searching for a genuine insult, and I suspect I possess the key to something she desires. It fills me momentarily with confidence.

"You are without a wife," she stabs, "even in your native land?"

"Yes," I hesitate, and knowing she knows this to be the case.

"Are you always without a woman?" She can't look at me now, the squared beauty of her shoulders supporting a proud vulnerability. While it can't be edifying to be one among many, my lack of all estate in the matter of matrimony leaves me feeling naked before her rank. I think carefully before replying. "Agra is a large city."

She weighs this as if vindicated. "Hindus or slaves, it isn't much to pick from."

"I've not been as fortunate as your husband," I reply.

Asmat now stares at me, and I'm not inclined to read offence. "You Dutch," she pouts, "you're quick to seize what doesn't belong to you. Your eyes are as sampling as your hands. You're like thieves."

"We pay for what we venture," and cautious, now, humbled by my procured privacies.

"You wouldn't be so profitable if you didn't rob the villages around Bayana."

This strikes me as unduly pious given the unblinking burden of the court and its courtiers. "We deal honourably enough," I answer. "Besides, the plantations wouldn't prosper as they have were it not for our enterprise."

"Tell me, is indigo so important a thing?"

"It is for the dyers of Europe."

Asmat appears displeased at this. "And what is this Europe that it sends you far from home like a common carrier to beg at our markets?"

"Madam, we hardly beg —"

"I feel sorry for you," and turning away, "that you should come from so wretched a place."

Her beauty is sumptuously petulant and I cannot help but feel a transgressive urgency. "I regret I'm not able to show you its riches. Besides," and shifting slightly from her, "I would not have had things otherwise. In so far as India conditions my destiny, I find myself at your hearth and the hospitality of your husband."

She flashes angry as if disadvantaged in a game she no longer takes pleasure in. "Be careful, then, not to overstep that hospitality!"

"I wouldn't dream of anything other than to press my gratitude."

This is disarming, her expression scarcely present as she screens some risk of thought. I've found such women easy flirts but tensely stoppered where passion is potential, their station rankling desire. "The food will have been laid," she demurs.

"Asmat."

"Come, he has trusted me to summon you."

More by way of assurance that there is nothing ill-toward, I reach out and catch a wisp of her shawl, its gossamer indescribable.

"He is liberal with outsiders," she hurries, and in no way anxious to free herself. "With those he finds interesting, whose manners are so foreign there is little call for the customary purdah. I – the others," and wincing, "we're permitted to partake of more intimate meals in the company of visitors."

"For that I value your husband's moderation all the more."

"Then, by God's grace and all that eschews dishonour, do not think to value mine!" she snatches.

"Have I ventured to offend you?"

In the consternation of this delicious privacy, and to my surprise, she takes my hand and caresses its knuckles, searching, perhaps, for more than ornamentation in the number of my rings. "Francisco, please. Should I drink from your cup, it will be the death of me."

I cannot deny that I wanted her. In all the world there is not a femininity to rival the beauty one finds in Hindustan. If an afflicted peasant can conjure an arresting portrait of poise and colour, how much more the arraignment of a noblewoman or princess? Though of my race and sorely dreamed of during the fever-sweating voyage back East, not even Lucretia Jansz could compare with Asmat Khanin. Stained and dishevelled as they were upon that fatal islet, the squalid rump of a survival purchased at such cost, I must confess to feelings of revulsion. Their sufferings touched me less than the judgement I felt. And as I gazed upon their ashamed and weary faces, I remembered that young Rajput widow who had lived close by, of whom there was no dissuading from custom as she bathed and dressed in her finest clothes, adorning herself with jewels as if it were her wedding day.

You are but a woman of tender years, argued the city governor. *It is a sin to end what you may mean to others.*

I already know the meaning of what I do.

Yet I would offer you five hundred rupees yearly should you venture otherwise.

It is not for lack of money or the fear of life that I wish this thing. Even if all the treasures of all the kings in this world were offered me, I should still mean to live with my husband.

He was laid out in readiness in the burning pit, her madness softly reso-lute. The governor, like Pilate, turned away.

On Batavia's Graveyard I savoured the sort of debacle that didn't lend itself to poetry.

He did not strike me as a priest, leastways not the sort whose bearing is inflated by the insistence that they act as God's temporal governor. A Jesuit certainly, his head closely cropped so as to look like a cannonball, his beard severely shaven in that style which resembles an unlove for whiskers. But we were each far from home, and in the transit of meeting, distance subdued an enmity which shouted loudest from the pulpits of Europe. War between our nations was semi-official and sanctioned the competitive capture of souls, yet along the frontiers of what was scarcely known to Europeans, facing strug-gles which prompted unlikely fellowships amidst the teeming foreignness of where we lived, we were quick to set aside our differences and seek an accom-modation that spoke more of man than God. I didn't warm to his sable code of dress, nor he to mine for that matter, and we both laughed for our recogni-tion that in ceremonial, at least, we each resembled some collar-tugging crow against the backdrop of Hindustan.

It was in Agra where we first met, then later at Delhi in a cross-path of travelling enterprise. The emperor had issued from his fortress, and the city, like a swarm of flies disturbed, bestirred itself to attend the royal host as it set forth on its incremental journey. I was one in that slow and human river unto Kashmir whilst he – Andrade – in smaller caravan and headed elsewhere, hailed me in the clamour of the street. Memory is a chimera. I can scarce dissemble a beginning or an end to our conversation, to a-portion that which belongs to Agra or to Delhi. I simply know that even if he wasn't the first of friends, his countenance was sufficiently constant and familiar to make him welcome. Indeed, who hasn't tolerated an unpopular classmate, someone outcast or near invisible, only to embrace them in later years and under altered circumstances when, no longer surrounded by the goads of one's youthful intemperance, chance breeds an alliance with such a rediscovered creature?

They were on donkeys, paused and pushed to one side as the imperial throng jostled its way through the city. I mightn't have recognised him were it not for his pale complexion.

"Antonio," I shouted, "what brings you here?"

He rolled his eyes, his present costume more akin to that of a Hindu merchant. I dismounted my mule, waving Salomon on, and threaded the procession to where he and his companion stood.

"I doubt, Francisco, you've forgotten our commission as men. Cloister or factory, we're each bound to stretch ourselves a little in the service of our work."

His companion looked at him with perhaps a whiff of subordinate disapproval. "I don't think you've met Brother Manuel," gestured Antonio. "He's to accompany me."

And this other eyed me with a wariness that was insinuating, his bow calculated to feign a companionableness dissembling of his true emotion. Such stepping from the shadows would remind me of Cornelisz, the civility of a villain.

I motioned Andrade aside. "Like me you leave Delhi to follow in Jahangir's wake?" and feeling a polite rancour at his Order's ability to debate in the presence of the emperor. And, indeed, we had first met one another in the precinct of Agra's Red Fort. I'd been returning to the factory, exasperated at yet another rebuff from the royal authorities, and not mindful of my footing. I'd stumbled on the cobbles and he, in passing (no doubt on his way to some more profitable exchange), had reached out to curtail my fall. In that stabilising gesture, the acrimony of what our respective costumes might have signalled was precluded by an instinct for fellowship. It would have been churlish not to have thanked him and he, in turn, surprised me in my native tongue by asking where I was from, perhaps calculating from my Flemish origins that I mightn't have strayed too distantly from the Faith. Neither would it have passed his reckoning that Hapsburg oppression had much to answer for in the pillage of my homeland, despoiling perhaps (but not entirely) an earlier piety.

"And you've come up from Goa?" I'd enquired.

"By stages, I imagine, we have each increased our distance from home." His tone was cordial and conceding. Then turning to resume his appointment, even though punctuality was rarely rewarded where Mogul authorities were concerned, he paused to add, "Watch your step, and in doing so may the true God likewise watch over you. Perhaps we shall meet again."

And so it was, from time to time and in the bazaar, as we each sought personable repose in the crowded anonymity of a world about its business. Vetting in what we mutually tendered, it wasn't difficult (provided certain stances remained tactfully unpushed) to converse in a neighbourly fashion, the humble lodging of the Jesuits not far from our factory. Not that we exchanged invitations to visit; no, the suspicious militancy of our respective communities would have rendered such engagements uncompanionable. Nonetheless, we continued to bump into one another to the extent that our easy familiarity was maintained. And here we were again, crossing paths, all of us astir at the outset of Jahangir's holidaying disposition.

"No," Andrade said, "others are assigned to follow where the emperor leads. My companion and I head north."

I gazed with perplexity at the rigour of his strapped animals. What lay to the north that was so expeditioning? "In search of other souls to snare?" I queried, wishing to appear light.

"We leave in search of a far and rumoured place."

"Which place?"

Andrade looked at me with the restrained amusement of a tutor whose rhetoric is sometimes silence. He was possessed of a vague yet imperturbable knowledge, a mission to self-enlighten as much as anything else. "There is a pilgrim trail to a land not yet China. They say the path rises steeply, the air sharp with the scent of snow, that a gigantic sky crowds the soul."

"Beyond India and the Mogul?" I asked, tempted to smile.

"'Tis a land-locked kingdom at the roof of the world whose tent is lifted by a mountain of such grandeur that the heathen allege its cardinal faces are made of crystal, ruby, gold and lapis lazuli." Andrade, my elder, was suddenly lost in a youth I found touching. "At the end of forty days' march, in a realm perhaps once Eden, 'tis said there is an unrivalled temple, venerated throughout the unknown world."

"And you would go there to put an end to this?"

"Would you not venture yourself to discover such a thing, to satisfy your vanity then appease the Lord in the salvation of those freshly minted in their ignorance? Besides, they may be Christians."

"Ha, you Portuguese are a credulous lot. After all these years, still searching for Prester John!"

The friendliness dimmed in Andrade's eyes. "What motivates you, Francisco? Why would you journey to a foreign hemisphere, to this heathen inverse of what you were born to, if merely to play the merchant?"

Brother Manuel had moved nearer and was studying me with a mercenary's eye, that seasoned unlove I find prevalent among sailors.

"We live," continued Andrade, "a long time in this country if spared, that is, an early summons to God. I was but a child in my homeland; like you, perhaps, I have lived my maturity in the Indies."

I didn't quite understand. Was this Jesuit the agent of another nation, an adventurer in quest of converts, or was he trying to attach his purpose to a place he could no longer escape? He appeared to read my confusion. "Francisco, I daily seek that I may remain here, that it has been worth the peril of my coming. We Portuguese are adept at cutting our ties and establishing new homes, of never looking back. Ours is a transportable soul; under Christ we belong everywhere."

"But you *are* of Portugal?"

"I am a Christian, first and foremost, and as a Jesuit brother the Holy See commands my presence here. No less has the blessed kingdom of my birth been chartered by God for His divine mission. And yes," he added, placing a hand on my shoulder and leaning close, "I am not without the frailty of having been born a man."

I shrugged, wanting to part on civil terms, Salomon and the others now out of sight. "I follow Jahangir because the Company wants it," I said. "Its motives are none too divine, though I should be less than honest were I to complain that the prospect of seeing Kashmir doesn't lure me."

"Well then, perhaps we shall journey not so very far apart. Perhaps little more than an eagle's wing." And embracing me, "May the angels guide you to the haven of eternal salvation. God's speed."

"Ah, but whose God?" I answered, unable to restrain myself. "There's no shortage of religion in this land."

"Don't mock your own redemption. When it comes to dying, summon me."

Strange. In him I gleaned a charity absent in the arid certainties of my brethren, a grace reminiscent of the martyrs of old Rome. I momentarily suspected the best of all that had existed prior to the Fall, before the world had lapsed into this present gloom of wars spiked on faith. If he seemed less extreme than was commonly imagined by our punctilious burghers, I felt less fixed in the militancy of my infant and adopted creed. Agra was beyond the practical jurisdiction of our chiefs; indeed, it was a city of cosmopolitan beliefs, the court enshawled in Islam, the streets awash with market life and Hindu spiritualists. A Christian might go unnoticed unless of the proselytising kind. Indeed, his death might go unrecorded altogether. Despite conflicts in Europe which pitted Rome against Reform and extended this antipathy along the seaways of empire, there were moments when, Catholic or non-Catholic, the remove from all kith begged the solacing witness of a Christian of whatever persuasion. Nearer to where our powers lay, the Fatherland had counselled the killing of the Portuguese – these crown-sharing cousins of our oppressor – at moments when to kill a man was no more than to besmirch his uniform. The opening of a battle was like a bright new day, especially if effected by a distancing gunnery, and we *were* in the business, after all, of overwhelming Portuguese interests. Little by way of compassion was expected to accompany the dying, and each man would turn from what he'd been a party to and seek refuge in the bravado of victory, the smear of blood trickling its ink in official reports to our glory.

But there were other deaths, deaths hidden from the lurid spectacle of history. Within the interior of untrammelled kingdoms, we merchants, clerks and misfits found ourselves alone and craving home during extremities of illness. And home was anything but abroad, here or in India. The cultivated prejudices of a man count for very little when a foe is the only friend to hand. I had on occasion (and as our unlikely paths crossed) watched Andrade rescue men — Armenians among them — not only from their fear of death but from that soreness of mind which might otherwise have cancelled their hope of an afterlife. If Jahangir styled himself Seizer of the World, Antonio was no less its Stealer of Souls. He tolerated little doctrinally other than the ritual of his church, yet his charity was a firman that respected few borders, his compassion, when what humanly remained was condensed at the threshold of the unknown, an earnest comfort to the dying.

Most Merciful Jesus,
lover of souls,
I pray You,
by the agony of Your most Sacred Heart,
and by the sorrows of Your Immaculate Mother,
to wash in Your Most Precious Blood
the sinners of the world who are now in their agony…

And who were we to stand between fear and conscience? Who were we to deny that the choices a man proclaims throughout his life might desert him in how he chooses to leave it? And by comparison with my randomly met Jesuit, who was Gijsbert to talk, that empty bucket of a man who continued to wring his hands and weep with impotent sorrow, too afraid to test the mettle of his faith? I'm certain Andrade would have confronted the tiger even though he, like the Christians of old, were to have had the flesh torn from him. Gijsbert's cloth was a passport to a better life, cruel though the journey for his family turned. Yes, a mouse of a man, looking for a place and an opportunity to hide away. By contrast, Antonio gave the impression of being ready to intercede in whatever prospered his conviction, even if the manner in which he fitted himself to that mission possessed a touch, too, of something less than holy.

⸻ᴄ⸻

"Tuan, the sick-sitter is here."

I'm like a schoolboy awaiting the result of a test I've doubtless failed. The details can only be painful. "Tell him to go away."

Hartanti regards me doubtfully. She understands the power of the Castle, understands that a man confined to bed is worth less to her than the good-will of another who occasionally comes a-calling. She knows we Dutch are inscrutable in our morals but that the sway of one person over another is universal. Despite the fact I find her insolent or indifferent by turns to my person, I remain loyal to what she affords me, those reduced comforts such as I yet command. Maartens, others like him, they have no need of me. He is an enemy, a citizen of that world which manoeuvres to outshine me in the outliving of me, a false well-wisher and would-be thief of legacy. The dead are always betrayed by the living. It's an unequal contest.

A sudden crack of thunder startles and deflects my thoughts. Air stirs and breath fills me. I will not die. Leastways, not before my sick-sitter is similarly pinioned by the effects of tropical life. The determination must show in my face because Hartanti now settles to negotiate my pleasure instead of his. She may despise me but I am her creature, after all; she understands my simple needs. In my contempt for an outcome all Batavia presently anticipates, I presently arch for the rhythmic dance of her fingers.

Let Maartens be turned away. Let him get caught in the rain. It will elicit the stench from his clothes and even up the discomfit. All is mildew here.

⸻ᴄ⸻

Would you so readily forsake me, Francisco, for the hand-love of a servant girl, some whore little better than a slave?

I – I have fallen on hard times.

You have fallen altogether.

Thunder once more troubles my disquiet. I become sensitive to an intrusion, the stealth of which would rob me in the fencelessness of my conscience. Nothing has deigned to travel with me, *I say aloud.* All is wreckage – human or otherwise.

This is not the man who dared to love.

We were younger, Asmat.

No, not so young. Nor so very long ago. You had a delicate beard and the eyes of a poet.

There was thunder, I remember. The solemness of the plain was intensified by the approaching storm, the yellow sky – never blue – now squeezed into a horizontal slit beneath thunderheads that coiled like serpents in hues of black and purple. We watched the rain, you and I, as it advanced like some translucent army, birds darting before it, the worldly of Fatehpur Sikri hurriedly securing their property and summoning unworried children.

You were travelling to Bayana.

You had whispered you might follow.

The old palace had been abandoned for years.

I'd spent nights in its crumbling caravanserai.

Hawkers peddled prayers to maternal yearning in the courtyard of the mosque.

Jahangir, no less, was born in the nearby house of the Christian wife.

The storm was near when I caught you up. My servant – he who brought me – would surely die were you and I to be discovered. There was no one I could trust.

And yet we stood for all the world –

That world abandoned –

In full display of what was coming, at the summit of that vast and public stairway...

Do you remember what was written in the arch above the gate?

I remember that I quivered as the rain thickened on our tongues.

He who hopes for an hour may hope for eternity.

I remember clasping you in the splendour of that illicit moment. I can smell, even now, the perfume of your sheltered hair, taste the perspiration of your forehead, feel the radiance of another life cradled within the assembly of your feminine intrigue. In the glare of what belonged to me by right of love, I felt a forbidden joy too unconscious of where we were or of what cruel witness might entail.

Something made you draw your face away.

I thought I saw…

Thunder rumbles overhead like a report of gunnery.

Who was it?

No one. Least…

Francisco?

Medari knows I travel this way. I've had to put up with his company more than once at the caravanserai.

Who? This person is here? He knows of us?

I coolly survey the red-stone recesses, once imperial and holy still, and become aware of men and women in this refuge of embrace, screened by shadows and the sound of rain. I glean their furtive and apologetic shine of eyes, and shudder before the mirror of risk and scruple.

All journeys are a distance of processional apprehension. Who hasn't embarked on a voyage without some niggling doubt, some wariness that the best laid plans are ever at the mercy of encounters unforeseen? As Commandeur of a squadron which was detached from the main fleet as early as Texel, then further separated from any other ship after rounding the Cape, this aloneness fomented an unease that could only be assuaged by our none-too-soon arrival at Batavia.

In the early years, when I was young in the business of the Company, the prospect of the unknown was at least abetted by counsellors and captains who shouldered responsibility for the success (or otherwise) of our ventures. I readily obeyed their orders in the surety that their decisions were not mine. Indeed, it is a comfort to play the lieutenant to another whose judgement you implicitly trust. Then, as I migrated from the edge of command towards its centre, I found myself the hub of others' trust. Yet no loyal lieutenant would I find in Cornelisz or Jacobsz. Instead, I was betrayed in what I would have expected of *Batavia*'s commonwealth, distanced from those dependent by agents unworthy of their nearness to me.

And so the Company – that august mechanism wherein I had sought advancement and begged indulgence, having spared little of myself in the enlargement of its power – was to fail in its witless greed to sieve the chaff from the grain. In the rush to man the Indies and manacle the natives, it had permitted messianics and murderers to infiltrate its distant adventure.

From the outset of that voyage, my high commission freshly notarised, my instructions clear and Governor Coen awaiting my return, I felt the unease of a man whose calculation of risk seemed no longer entirely counted. That I must share the Great Cabin with Ariaen Jacobsz was cause enough for concern. But there was something else, something that had broken loose and was knocking about in the stowage of my person. It possessed a smell as foetid as the orlop deck and a light as hurtful as a desert sun. In the privacy of my bunk-cramped quarters, a moment's contemplation was sufficient to intuit that my looking-glass had been replaced by an hourglass.

Death retreated before us like a wily foe, luring us deeper into its realm and mortifying our spirits. It was imperative that we find water for those left behind, yet the salted ocean mocked us.

We fell in with the continent on the afternoon of June 8, the fourth day after the disaster. I maintained a journal throughout the ordeal – strange, perhaps, given the press of matters. But there was much on my mind, and I was determined to keep account of the days and monitor the unpredictable behaviour of my companions. Indeed, there were none in whom I might safely confide my thoughts. Already I had an eye to my survival, something entailing more than the mere preservation of flesh.

Jacobsz glanced at me and then studied the shoreline, the surf running high as far as the eye could see in either direction. Behind a veil of spray the cliffs, red and unyielding like the fortress walls at Agra, diminished any hope of early sanctuary.

"Skipper," I shouted, "we must try to land. We must find water." But even I realised a landing wasn't possible, that we were detained within uncertainty by the certainty of ruin were our craft to risk the breakers. The noisy panic of apprehension was all silence in the boat.

"We'll hold off," responded Jacobsz, his words intended for his brother officers rather than myself. Whilst everyone was conscious of my Company rank, they worried lest any command of mine should interfere with the skipper's judgement.

"Well we can't just bob around in sight of shore," ventured Evertsz.

"What shore?" exploded Jacobsz. "Even if we managed to ride the surf — and do you see how laden we are? — where in God's kingdom is there any beach?"

"The skipper's right," I said, altering my course and seizing an opportunity to distance the treacherous boatswain. "We are no rescue to the others if we ourselves are lost."

If Jacobsz wasn't particularly concerned about the fate of those left behind near the wreck, he wasn't insensitive to the necessity of my support. "Dusk will be upon us within the hour," he judged. "This is no place to linger without eyes."

And so, between the sorcerer's evil islets and the edge of this unapproachable land, we spent our first night at sea without the security of our now-lost ship.

Night is the most exhausting of temporal latitudes, the most unnerving in its sustained interrogation of the soul. Alone — or in unspeaking company as I was that night upon the sea — one is detached from the hue and habit of noontide and paraded, as if before a true and populous Star Chamber, to account for one's deeds or lack of. If the blaze of day is tiresomely filled with actions becoming of a man, then night is the revealing ebb-tide of more exploratory misgivings.

For want of anyone I might speak to during such wakefulness, I have conversed with my doubtful double and attempted to interfere in the scripting of a biography which raises more questions than I can readily answer. Here, in my stultifying confinement, I see no stars and must listen, instead, through walls of sick-room silence for that immanent clockwork, the nightly rotation of God's soothing regulation. The most disagreeable ticking belongs to the bloated hammer of my heart — I find the sound almost suffocating and out of chorus with the unseen heavens. In any case, stars are rarely seen in this tropical broth, leastways not to the number and clarity observable from the slopes of Kashmir. Of my journey to that far-off place, I recall, now, that in halting for the night, and with one's back to the campfire, it was restfully defining to ponder the day's event and probabilities for the morrow. But douse the flames and the surrounding darkness suddenly glimmers with a distant mantle until then little apprehended and even less understood. Beneath the stellar vastness we are prone to lose ourselves in lonely shiver.

Mariners learn to read the nocturnal sky like a chart, its motions mapped within the circumference of human need. That is the plain utility of it. But there are other layers, other applications which speak as much to the spirit as of science. We know from books, as the ancients learned from the stars direct, that stories inhabited the night sky. Journeys were trials, the stellar compass a backdrop to wilful heroes and retributive justice, to careless impulse and implacable fate. When fable fell into senility and the one true God was revealed, the stars were stripped of their nursery falsehoods to become the decoration of a simpler truth, an angel host venerating the quotidian return of the sun, the Son of God, Light of the World...

Hmph — Nur Jahan, Jahangir's queen. *Light of the World*. The emperor's inspirations were no less self-flattering than those of other men in their moulding of the earth or domestication of the heavens. And what might Antonio have portrayed of the stars? Was there some lesson in their orchestration to impress upon the emperor a new insight? Indeed, how near did the Jesuits actually get to so powerful and worldly a throne? I wonder, in fact, whether that imperial despot ever contemplated a nightscape — even from his garden at Srinagar — or was the darkness simply banished by a musical torchlight of sycophants, opium and wine. Perhaps he was more fortunate in finding so little time for the dark, for I can admit to having felt no comfort in its speculative essay as we bobbed in orphanage upon the sea.

That first night was cold and imprisoning. We were whipped by winds from the landless west, the crowded constellations blinking at distances which defied me to imagine what such distances might imply. Indeed, it seemed as if every star in creation had ventured out to coolly appraise our dilemma, and in their multitude it struck me that I did not know where to look for God. In our tiny ark, with no guarantee that the waves wouldn't swallow us before dawn, the contention that we might be truly alone was unmanning. If I obliged myself to believe in Him, it was also true that in my prayerful need I was awed by the celestial oppression of an unlighted sea and moved to query whether anything in the heavens perceived us as we perceived ourselves.

Someone groaned in the darkness. The baby, almost forgotten, hiccupped a brief cry. Our predicament was as yet too novel for many to have hardened into bloated fatigue. As for me, I turned my thoughts from the inscrutable ministrations of the Lord and placed my trust in the tactical seamanship of Ariaen Jacobsz.

So you trusted my friend and accomplice.

I trusted his skill. We had no other choice.

Yet you trusted not me?

You were too fond of the lower decks. You courted favour recklessly.

And what might I have gained in dallying with the lower decks?

Men and arms. Power.

To what purpose?

You know full well; you admitted as much at the trial. To commandeer the ship.

Yes, well, you and Jacobsz did a polished job in demolishing the prize!

The disaster was not of my doing. Jacobsz was at the helm when I arrived on deck.

You don't like things going awry on your watch, do you? Perhaps if you'd been more solicitous of your responsibilities. But then you were a stay-in-bed sniveller to everyone on board. Oh Francisco, if only you'd been more a friend to me.

Friend? You were more a fiend!

There you go again, name-calling and abrogating your pastoral care.

You're confusing me with the predikant.

Now *there's* someone I should have killed, the useless waste of fear that he was.

You exterminated his family.

Really, would you have wanted more Gijsberts in the world? In any case, I had his daughter spared —

That she might be tethered in whoredom to one of your lieutenants?

Coenraat van Huyssen was as fine an officer as ever served me. *Your* lieutenant — that bumptious spoiler, Hayes — had him treacherously slain when we came to parley. I have to say, yours were an unimaginative lot when it came to the tactical possibilities of treaty.

Why would anyone trust a murderer?

Why would anyone trust a deserter?

Meaning?

You, Commandeur, abandoned us with little food and even less in the way of water. Harsh decisions were called for. The kingdom was in peril.

Your kingdom was a charnel house. You quenched your thirst with blood!

I can see we're never going to agree. But then you never attained the licence of absolute rule. Always a servant.

You flatter yourself.

You attached yourself to the train of the Mogul emperor. You were a camp-follower in the dust of another's greatness. No wonder we've all had difficulty fitting you to a garment of capital responsibility. You've not been much of a decision-maker.

I decided your fate.

Ha! And what a feeble magistrate you cut, searching all the while for answers where there was little call for them; branding me a fiend or a tiger for want of seeing me as a man.

How a man when you were so inhuman?

How anything else when the so-called righteous semi-drown a person to extort a confession, cut off his hands to appetise a hanging, or smash his body to pieces on a cartwheel?

You were accorded no less than you deserved.

And *you*, Francisco, have been accorded no less than the merited suspicion of others. Oh, I feel almost tender – how could you let *me* happen?

You mock me sir!

Ha, you mock yourself. You wriggle every which way to avoid knowing me. You grasp at any circumstance to excuse your dereliction.

The calamities were many and conflating!

You even blame the neglectful stars for not smiling with the light of God's mercy. As if *He* would even hear the begging of those too pathetic to be noticed! Only a mind grown stagnantly fearful would invent such a poppet. The night is endless, Francisco – surely you learned this in the open boat. Surely you learned that the stars were unreachable, that the only land within reach was unknowable.

God raised the sun each morning and so rekindled hope.

You say that because your expectation of death was daily postponed. Not so now.

Is your cynicism so impatient?

I was with the wreck until it sundered. I could not swim, and each night leading to that eventual disintegration closed around me with its rocking horror of invisible dangers, of sliding crates and splintered furniture, of startling ruptures that screeched of injuries indistinct yet mortal. It was like being in a dungeon as others, before me, were led out before a jeering crowd to lose their heads. You allege I was too fond of the lower decks? I'll tell you what I saw in the occasional flare of torchlight as I shadow crouched. I witnessed the very pillage of discipline, a swaggering and indulgent embrace of death for want of sobriety or the marrow to imagine otherwise. In that abandoning fume of wine and brine I glimpsed a flickering sodomy, of men reduced to boys in fevered lust, life's urgent practice reduced to straining members, to hand-fucking and arse-plugging when the ship's own chastity was in dire need of dressing. Yes, the very scum you would have me fornicate over was floated to the surface of your quarters, and I suspect your dick, Francisco, would have stiffened at this closeted spectacle were you not so lascivious a hypocrite. As for me, my appetites were of a different cast, calmer and more planned – and yes, I confess I was afraid. These people – and the others like them, marooned on that crust of terra firma – were not to be trusted. The slightest movement or apprehension might cause licentious panic. Like goats they needed tending, yet all of *Batavia*'s shepherds had fled.

All were taken off the ship who could be induced to leave! You crept like a spider in the shadow of opportunity. You were looters, all.

I stayed with the ship, its most senior remaining official, while the women, children and the sick were put into the boat. Believe me, it didn't go unnoticed that you and Ariaen ferried little more than your meagre courage vaunted.

The wind had risen, the surf was high.

I sent a plea for help with the carpenter; he swam through death to reach you.

We couldn't manoeuvre the yawl to come alongside; the sea by now was galloping. It was a great grief; anyone might have read it in my heart.

Two days passed and still we clung to the cartilage of that disaster. Ha, you label *me* a looter when, instead of more folk, you managed to have your precious jewels and personal effects rescued and deposited alongside those who shivered in the wind without sailcloth or covering! Little wonder they called it Traitors' Island.

The only treachery was your eating of the very folk we rescued.

Not so at the moment of my deliverance. My name was a sweet wine upon their lips. Their bedraggled camp had at last found itself a leader.

This is monstrous! What Nature omitted to destroy, you unnaturally disposed of!

Pff. You're deflecting. This is your nightmare. I merely did what I had to do.

And that was kill?

A man is many things by necessity. I had to steer a course between a cloying lack of enterprise in most and the hot-bloodedness of others. Those soldiers and cadets you remaindered me with were as passionate a challenge to restraint as ever any commander had to contend with. You had slept throughout the voyage, Francisco; yours was a less than durable authority. My physic was proper to the point of survival. I forged a utopia for those most fitted to live.

It wasn't a place wherein life thrived!

Why is it you reduce everything to these sorry platitudes? I swear you have no imagination for Nature's dark inverse, for the very humours that give your so-called light its contrast. Good is only so because evil is equally ill-defined, and your God only exists because you fear His absence. Tell me, is day any the more sacred than night? Is the sun a more honest broker than the moon? I'm sure you've found your nocturnal hours more than serviceable in the arms of some whore or another's wife. As I suffered them in the madness of that semi-abandoned wreck, surrounded by deserters deserted and presently drunk to a pitch of delirium, the water surged through the lower decks with a thudding that sounded like some rhinoceros broken from its crate. There was no friendship in the stars, no kindling of hope in the risen sun. The huddled on Traitors' Island were obscured by spray as the surf pounded us within that clutching reef. Yes *Batavia*, day and night, was my unravelling coffin.

More the pity, then, that you were permitted to escape its grave!

Hindsight is a formidable juror, no? What were you thinking in concluding your business with the islands before you'd even concluded your rescue of those still trapped on the ship? It was a doubly-damned desertion.

You were a malign star; the fate of others was in God's keeping. I was presently compelled, under His guidance, to serve the greater number, those whose foremost need was water.

And so you turned to Ariaen Jacobsz.

He possessed the loyalty of his officers and men. This was a watery mishap that only a sailor might redeem.

Let me tell you, then, a greater scoundrel you could not have found. The minute the ship was breached, his dream of stealing her was lost in the emergency of that greater theft, our confederacy scuttled in the scuttling of his courage. While it's proverbial that there be no honour among thieves, he was certainly the first of rats to abandon a sinking ship. Would he return to revive our piratical dreams? Not likely. Not with you in tow. Shipwreck, my dear Commandeur, cools the ardour.

Yet you continued in your devilry as if expecting liberty to prey upon the world.

I simply ruled what chance and opportunity had delivered into my keeping.

Your tyranny was without design?

My so-called tyranny was the result of my scandalised abandonment. I did not pray to God to be a better man should He grant me my wish to live. There were no answers, no comforts to sustain me during that endless night which counted itself out over eleven days. The meridian glare was but another snatched breath such as you granted me under torture, an intermittent stay of execution during the progressive annihilation of anything that suggested you and I were of the same mould. I died with fear out there, and what survived was numb to consequence in the absence of anything as fearsome as the casting of the waves or toothy creatures of the reef. Maybe I did believe in a providence more closely aligned with the spirit of who I was. I remember glancing up at faces, the stupid, bovine faces of those who would raise me from the shallows then fall upon their knees for the great good fortune of having found someone to rule over them. Only they knew not of my secret, nor of my need to repress them in its keeping.

⸎

You never spoke as such when confronted aboard the *Sardam*. I saw no evidence of your existential fears, your soul refracted from black to grey in alleviations of doubt. All I gleaned was a creature determined to save its skin, twisting and writhing as if to shift itself of that telling membrane which proclaimed it for the serpent that you were.

⸎

Jeronimus testified that he was with the wreck for eleven days. In fact two of these were spent clinging to a spar which, as fate would chance, drifted to the shoreline of that acre upon which the majority of folk were stranded. Reflecting on our own precariousness in the longboat during those self-same days, searching for water at a necessary risk to ourselves, I do now wonder what it must have been like for him to bob and turn in that winter sea, sodden and exhausted, the night a bitterness of stars, the fear of drowning all too consuming a companion.

Eleven days after the wrecking — and as Jeronimus, the last man to escape *Batavia*, was rinsed into the unsuspecting arms of the purgatorially isolated survivors — we finally made a landing on the Great South Land. Just as Cornelisz would doom the hopes of those who succoured him, so the continent doomed all hope of providential aid. From that twinned and fateful moment our stories were as divergent as night and day, good and evil. In the weeks to follow, my enterprise to redeem that which was interimly lost was mirrored by a satanic intent to amplify that loss and scoff at redemption. I was the most senior Company man in the prosecution of rescue; he was its most senior representative in the persecution of innocents. I commanded *Batavia*'s longboat; he commanded Batavia's Graveyard. I had to deal with Jacobsz and Evertsz; he had to deal with Hayes and his loyal handful. And in these parallel times a gulf of such enormity opened up that it scarce seemed possible our worlds should meet again. Yet we each were intent on accommodating the possibility of the other's survival, of dealing with a resumption of ties should any of us cheat death in those first weeks. The shipwreck had shifted the ballast of enmity but had not dispensed with enmity itself. I was anxious to return, to see what the calendar might permit me to recover. Thirst and hunger were the trials I imagined most to have paralysed the survivors on Batavia's Graveyard.

On the day our wretched boat fell in with Company ships in the Sundra Straits, Jeronimus began his reign of terror. During that hastening period in which we sailed on to Batavia (and with what exhausted trepidation!) to meet with Coen and explain the situation, Jeronimus exceeded conscience to instigate the first in a series of silent murders. Even as Evertsz was dangling cold on a rope for his outrage against Lucretia, Jeronimus was arranging for the throats of the sick to be cut by night. On the day I departed Batavia, provisioned to rescue the castaways and salvage the Company's goods, Jeronimus dispatched his henchmen to nearby Seals' Island to annihilate the men and boys he had quarantined there. As the Indies sank beneath the northern horizon and the *Sardam* entered the latitudes of an ocean that stretched from Timor to the alien south, Jeronimus was organising a second massacre, this time of the women. And as the days ticked by, so did the initial horde of folk diminish, those surviving the night now numbed in unspeaking wonder as to where their neighbours might have vanished during the hours of darkness.

In my ignorance of how things fared and in his unknowing of my fate, Jeronimus must nonetheless have possessed some premonition of my return. The spiteful killing was almost done, and it should have left them little to do but enjoy the desiccated fruit of their despoiled Eden. But Jeronimus was preparing for war, first against Wiebbe Hayes and his chancily escaped company, then against the possibility of my advent. I had little inkling of who Hayes was, but together we would form an alliance that would crush the crimson mutiny on Batavia's Graveyard.

But that was at the end and of a time when the injury was beyond all remedy. Throughout those countless hours of meantime, and at moments when I was replete with my own emergency and gave little thought to anything beyond its margin, terrible happenings were liable to erupt at the Abrolhos, happenings as random as an unbidden thought and as completed as the ending of life itself. Those who were sacrificed would die more permanently than Jeronimus himself, his ghost tormenting me with its insinuating legacy of what-ifs. In my fevered weakness, night has become this terrible theatre in which the audience – obscured in the half-light; known, yet only vaguely – sits in deceased witness of whatever I might act. Their critical murmur plies an expectation; they know the play better than I do. I'm too embarrassed to admit that I don't command my lines.

The day our longboat was sighted – yes, the day I felt an incipient reinstatement of the Dutch world and Cornelisz began his killing – yes, weak and careworn though I was, I experienced the emotion and gratitude of a man who has been spared a summary fate for further interrogation. There were too many questions and unknowns at that stage to permit anything other than the story to further unfold. Despite Van Diemen's spitefulness, I was given my commission to direct how the drama might end. Little could I have anticipated that my assistant had taken it into his head to script a story that would beggar me and mine.

—ᴄ

"Tuan, there is someone to see you."

"If it's Maartens, tell him I'm already dead!"

"No Tuan, it is another of the dark coats."

Hmph. I sweat in cottons stained like a sewer and still the respectable insist on jackets that must cook the innards of a man! "Who? Did he say who he was?"

"Tuan, only that you've met before."

Any visitor is dangerous. They'll enlist anyone in an effort to unearth something that doesn't exist. By all that Christ suffered, Lord it's painful to have your remains picked over before you've had a proper chance to expire! That we may have met only engenders a suspicious boredom.

Perhaps remembering my hunger the last time someone called and was turned away, Hartanti quickly disappears to usher in this strange acquaintance. And strange he is; old enough – or so he appears by the weather of his face and greying whiskers – to beckon a connection that defies more recent memory. And yet he's not unfamiliar. Indeed, something in the adjustment of his scrutiny reminds me that I'm not so recognisable myself.

"It's been the better part of ten years," he announces as if to interpret what we each confront, yet still I cannot piece where those years lead back.

"We only crossed paths the once," he says, and removing his hat, an act which further distances recognition. Yes, he must have worn a hat; he looks wrong without a hat. "You were boastful in your fondness to get ahead. You'd not long arrived in the East."

"You were with the fleet – no? – when we stormed and made good Jacatra?"

He laughs as if to admit he'd been spared that smouldering moment. "I was never the guts and glory type – although I stood my youth in the ranks, pike in hand. No, I came out here to escape the pillages of home-grown war. And a good thing too. That old guard – Coen and the like – I see they're piling up in the cemetery." He pauses apologetically, remembering where he is and what I contemplate.

"There were so many faces," I say, "so many strange sights."

"Yes, the world must seem strange to men who define it from the climate of their birthplace." He unbuttons his coat, the brim of his hat pinched between his fingers, and turns to position the chair.

"You had a child," I say. And now I recognise him – at least I think I do, my distorted recollection one of a seemingly more confident man.

Meyer appears momentarily vulnerable. "I'm pleased you recall of me something other than the Company."

"At least I supposed you had a child. There was a woman, a native – young, I think. She bore a swollen belly. The Company flag was draped like a bed sheet."

"You were observant."

"I was new to the settings of my employment, their novelty. Wherever we went, I suppose I expected a little bit of Amsterdam to follow."

"Save that for Batavia. The canals here are as foetid, I imagine, as the ones back home."

"Have you been there?"

"The Fatherland, you mean?"

I nod, if only for the craving of an unloved fragrance I'll not meet with again.

"We're never free of where we're born," he says. "Such is our first love. But be warned, she's a fishwife, all right, jealous of anything that tempts us abroad. You find love elsewhere and she follows, loud and carping and disruptive of your discovered paradise."

"Was it yours, then – that village?"

He inhales sharply as if only now remembering to breathe. "Paradise is rarely savoured long. It's mostly anticipated or lost. The woman who mothered my boy – and the lad who followed – they were the heartening of me. That outpost, while it lasted, was like a pocket hidden from the jealousies of those too preoccupied to notice."

"While it lasted?"

"Come, Heer Pelsaert, a man doesn't rise to your station without knowing how things fare across the business."

"I was in India all those years, land-locked and in a thwarted paradise of my own. Then there was the return to Holland."

"Ah," he sighs. And because I pause awhile in reverie, he adds, "You need not be guarded with me. I've not come here to spy."

"Strange, that's exactly what I suspected when we met; that you were involved in some sort of espionage."

He smiles. "Back then we were Company men – at least that's what I admitted to in front of Gillis, God rest his soul."

"He's dead?"

"We're all taking turns," and looking away. "He was a good sort, the one Dutch face I was regularly pleased to see. And not just because of the gin he brought."

"How did he…"

"Die? Drank himself to death."

My mouth gapes with surprise. "But he was so sober. So sober in his opinions."

Meyer shrugs. "When you can no longer sleep with who you are in the sight of others, you lie endlessly awake. Or drink. But I see I'm tiring you. You're not well –"

"No no, stay!" He's watching me with the sympathy of one who seems accustomed to vigils. "You've not sickened, yourself?" I ask, and before I might receive an answer which either shames or disinterests me, he avoids the subject by replying, "What was Holland like? Are there still such things as ice and snow?"

"I returned for the summer only."

"Oh," and disappointed, as if having come here to prise some information about a mutual acquaintance.

"It was humid," I tell him, "only a little less so than here — and more crowded than I remembered. Except for an absence of Asian faces it was not unlike this place, the savour of the wharves no different to Batavia's waterfront." After a moment I ask, "You've not tried to go back yourself?"

He shakes his head curtly like a teetotaller before a proffered cup. Then I remember his woman and their children. If Jacques Specx, Governor of all the Indies, was constrained to separate business from his personal life and leave a half-blood daughter to the tender mercies of his predecessor whilst visiting the Fatherland, how much more improbable would it be for a man like Meyer to flaunt the taboo and think of shipping his family to Holland. In any case, his relatives on the other side of the world are surely dead. He's been here longer than I.

"What then have you been doing in all these years?" I enquire.

"Back then I tried to keep on the right side of custom, to poach something of a living among those whose company I shared."

"But you were wholly a Company man?"

"I was wholly my own man and, like any other, an opportunist."

I think about this, the divergence of the personal from what is sanctioned.

"What *were* you doing at that outpost?" I ask.

"How much do you remember?"

"I remember you were shoeless and bare-chested. You had a sword and a tattoo."

"Ha, I must have resembled a pirate!"

"And I have lived among would-be pirates. But no, you remind me of a man I scarcely knew — leastways not at first, not at a time when I might have expected loyalty in others nearer my station. He was just a minion in the service, anonymous in the general head count. I was to discover he was someone you could depend on, yet I wasn't to know of this until the damage to myself was done. Now he's been promoted and accorded the admiration of Batavia."

"You mean that soldier, Hayes?"

I close my eyes and exhale. There's a silence; a hum of silence.

"I was once a beginner like you," I hear him say. "But then I quickly discovered that I enjoyed the local life. An outsider is only as acceptable as his ability to converse, and I had a gift for language. The Company needed men on the ground. There were Portuguese interests to supplant, English interests to forestall." He pauses momentarily as if to order something in his mind. "The English I have no time for; they're scavengers who skulk in the wake of wherever we go. But the Portuguese, they have a mind to settle — much as if their motherland is of so poor a soil it scarcely warrants any thought of return. And maybe I, too, was a Lusitanian of sorts. I saw no need to leave that village once wedded to its life."

I'm reminded of what Andrade alluded to. "Weren't you lonely?" I ask, opening my eyes.

"I wasn't whilst the Company was interested in trade only."

"Meaning?"

"Heer Pelsaert, you're a man of considerable standing —"

"I'm dying," I interject, boastful of its authority yet abhorrent of the truth.

"The death of an individual alters nothing," waves Meyer. "You've climbed high enough to know that the Company has a readiness for violence, that we're hostile to anything that gets in our way. It's not just other whites we fear, it's the very physic of these cultures we ingress."

The natives must be ridden with a sharp spur.

"Coen is dead," I say. "The English are no longer a threat to the island trade."

"Not before time. My wife and children are gone. The village I called home is razed to the ground."

I lift myself to attend him closely. Is this another thing for which I'm to be held accountable?

"Batavia was under siege — the sultan was convinced we kafirs were about to be driven into the sea. Throughout the archipelago local scores were being settled. What is deemed treaty one moment is collaboration the next."

"How? I mean, could you not...?"

"I wasn't there when they came. I was in Aceh, getting close to the Portuguese. There were rumours, even then, of the threat to Jambi. A trader trades in more than cloves and pepper; every local market is a wash-day of gossip and innuendo. Only I didn't hear of *this* until it was too late. Even the ashes were cold when we tied up. Nothing stirred, nor was there any sound. Except for the flies. In the compound they placed the heads on stakes —"

I gasp.

"She was not among them. Of the boys, too, I never discovered."

It's the moment wherein I perceive him for the ghost that he is.

"We pay a heavy price for our presumption, Heer Pelsaert. The Bandanese, they were relatively easy to exterminate. But here, on the greater islands..." He is no longer looking at me. My room is a stage on which he rattles his soliloquy. "I hate Batavia, it's pretence to commerce when everything is exaction. We sham friendship among those we meet whilst eyeing what we hope to steal."

"But we *do* trade, Meyer; we exchange —"

"Only on terms that make us unloved. Believe me, we're not a generous race – even among ourselves. What did you start out at – twenty-four guilders a month? A man doesn't go far on that. And you, Heer Pelsaert, have travelled very far indeed."

"I remained a loyal servant," I defend, suspecting that he may have been sent here after all.

"That's not the same as an honest servant. But, look, I've not come to disclose or discuss your secrets. We've all done a little on the side. Gillis was more honourable than most. He was aware of his contradiction and didn't try to hide from the fact – at least not when he was alone or drank with those he trusted, men who in their weakness hadn't abandoned a sense of what their slavery had done to honour. Do you drink Heer Pelsaert? You don't strike me as much of a drinker."

I wince with the humour of one who knows too well what drink may accomplish. I was just returned from the Abrolhos and had not fêted myself in months. Indeed, I'd not felt as well for over a year and was momentarily beguiled into thinking that the curse had been lifted. With the remaining mutineers turned over to the Fiscaal, I sought a rare draught of normality. Batavia is a small town. Everybody knows everyone to some degree. It isn't difficult to enlist a drinking companion or arouse the interest of a woman in this endless ménage of availability. An innocent cup would have been the least of it. But even the obliviating necessity of wine, its medicinal fog, now pollutes my palate when, with memorial horror, I see Asmat take the cup (as if stealing a sweet) and drain it at a gulp, wholly ignorant that the mixture which consoles me will kill her.

Pity I wasn't with you then, that you only had that liverish Deschamps to lean on. I might have concocted a restorative to steer you free of manslaughter. But then to have buried her in the factory, where rumour may have found you out and dug her up! I mean, really. At least we drowned ours and left them to the economy of the sharks —

"Tiger! Get out!"

"Pardon?"

"No. Meyer. Not you. *He...*" And I shiver in that recognition. "I am endlessly pursued by ghosts."

He is staring with the detachment of one who is yet to make up his mind about me. Why should I care what he thinks? Yet I do care. He wouldn't be here if not for the stories that are circulating, stories designed to erode the respect I've spent a lifetime earning. It's crude enough having to experience the withdrawal of one's vigour and become this senile and powdery *katel*, but to suffer an accompanying and unjust erosion of esteem is altogether too mortifying. Surely something must survive a man other than his soul? "Why *did* you return to Batavia?" I compose myself.

"Where else was I to go? We're all marooned here. Only Governors and Councillors earn the right to return. Their dreams never really migrate from the hope of a villa on the Herengracht."

"You are still a servant of the Company, then?"

"It's aware of my talents. We don't exchange much business at present."

I exhale, more a sigh, and cast my thoughts at the ceiling. Despite a perpetual shortage of manpower, there's this perpetual surfeit of those dislocated or unfit for service. Batavia is a lean ship with too much useless cargo. I'd smile with self-including humour if not for the truth that only vigour prospers. I loll my head and focus once more on Meyer. "Why have you come? What importance might I bear you?"

"Forgive me, Heer Pelsaert, but scarcely any at all. You were some distant and newfound star, your rotation through the heavens only touching me that once and long ago. But just as you followed Gillis to my home, I now followed that man they called Stone-Cutter to your sick-bed, here."

"You knew Pietersz?" My heart races at the unspecified import of this.

"We all came to know him, up to a point. The day they ended his life. In the sounds that gurgled from him, we all cradled our innards with a self-touching fear."

"You were there?"

"Where else was I expected to be? We were all there — even you."

There are no words. In my mind I'm searching the crowd, my eyes averted from the scaffold. "How did Pietersz's death bring you to me?" I finally ask.

"I wanted to see a Dutchman die. I wanted to see someone pay for the loss of my family. And I wanted them to know that it *was* a family, that she wasn't some blackamoor I'd knocked up and was happy to pass over for the sister. And the boys, too, were a bridge to whatever I'd hoped of the future. Out there, on the fringes, death goes unremarked. The loss of an outpost is a for-feit of opportunity, a loss of trade. The Company keeps strict records which are only wanting in what we privately smuggle. We are all just functionaries. The High and Mighty don't know the names of people they can't put a face to. The cemetery beyond the walls is a common grave. But then I remembered you, and learning that you might soon be snatched to the Devil for whatever crimes you'd committed, I was curious to observe whether death had a dif-ferent perfume."

"Is it my death, then, that you also seek? Look how rank a thing I am. Look how filthy a man becomes when he can no longer maintain his covenant with what he was. You need not drink like Gillis to remind yourself of how far you've strayed from the very soul of hope!"

"Calm yourself, I'm not here to gloat. To the contrary, you may yet have soothed me in such a manner as you may soothe yourself."

I glare at him suspiciously, my heart bottled, and feel that I'm about to be asked a favour I'll be reluctant to grant. Meyer slumps back in his borrowed chair and the room appears to swell before me, absorbing him in its Spartan detail. There's a breathlessness of still-life, and were anyone to enter they might not, at first, discern our human presence. It's then that I observe the door ajar, Hartanti's eyes glimmering in the gloom beyond. It's impossible to gauge how much she understands.

"I said I wanted to watch a Dutchman die, but that enthusiasm, never very real, quickly waned with the first half-dozen strikes of the crowbar. I began to look around, anywhere but at the destruction of a man I did not know, whose cries were like the wheeze of a bellows. I was watching the crowd, its reflexive shudder every time the iron bit, the glaze of excited spectacle turning to horror. If the art of such punishment is to keep a man alive for as long as possible, I'm sure many were soon hoping for the mishap of a rapid death. The justices sat impassive throughout, as central to the performance as Stone-Cutter himself in a match of stamina and stomach.

"But you were not among them, Heer Pelsaert. You were not up there on the bench. And as I, in crumbling desire to see a scapegoat die, sought refuge in the crowd, I glimpsed you, richly dressed but pale, stationed at a level of assumed anonymity. It took but little memory to recognise you. Besides, you were a much spoken-of actor in this drama that was now drawing to its close. In all good tragedies the wicked are punished and the fair inherit the peace. Peace didn't sit well with those fierce-faced lords behind the scaffold, nor did it seem to belong to you. You were not with them — why was that? Were you, even then — as I find you now — too reduced to brandish your vengeance? In any case you did something which singled you out, something that alluded to your wounding yet also to a defection of sorts. You turned and walked away."

"I had seen enough."

"But these men, they had scattered your reputation."

They'd no more than killed the folk on Batavia's Graveyard."

"But were there none from there with cause enough to see that chapter close?"

"Hayes — perhaps you wouldn't have known him by sight — he commanded the guard that morning. It was a final reward."

God yes, I had seen more than enough of judicial killing. Wiebbe had headed the detachment, too, the morning we rowed Cornelisz and the others across to Seals' Island, the freshness of the sea little mitigating a crawling sense of dread. No one imagined himself as anything other than a spoke in the wheel of justice, helpless now to decide fate otherwise. It sickened me to contemplate what I must do, my apprehension only by fact less mortal than that which subdued the prisoners in the boat. Once ashore, it became a business, rowdy and messy. Hayes showed the same fortitude and dispatch as when he'd killed the first of the mutineers and seized Cornelisz. Yes, the Company had been right to invest its faith in him. But of that duty I assigned myself, its responsibility became all the more odious with Pelgrom's incessant weeping and wailing and begging for grace. He was unnerving the others about to die, and became writhing and hysterical as his turn beckoned. I glanced at the heap of hands beside the block, the gulls standing vigilant nearby, and could stomach it no more. I allowed that bastard boy to live, his swooning gratitude as disgusting as his unmannish craving to be spared.

Though none savoured the business of that morning, as it hastened to its conclusion there were few who wouldn't have wanted it concluded altogether. My unexpected leniency cheated them of the strangled silence they craved. When we rowed back to Batavia's Graveyard with still a prisoner in our midst, perplexity and annoyance was engraved on the faces of the survivors. *What, is it not ended?*

The others, too, those whose fate was yet to be decided, they looked for omens in the return of Pelgrom, for hope of life against all Godly expectation. Rescuers and rescued combined, we were still outnumbered by those indeterminately accused, whose hands were hidden. And yes, we were still communally dependent upon one another as the salvage continued by day and investigation exhausted us by night. I scrutinised Salomon, my trusted assistant down the years, his quill recording each day's uncovering, and shuddered to realise his complicity, this dutiful clerk of courts making no effort to refute the accusations that would include and condemn him. He was like an innocent younger brother to me, his hands stained with unwanted blood. I would have spared him had it been in my power – and, indeed, I did prescribe the lesser penalty of keelhauling and flogging. But in the end my preclusive sentencing was of little consequence. Those who petitioned me to have themselves punished before our imminent arrival in Batavia – the interrupted voyage of its lost namesake now drawing to an end — presumed me to be of less violent temperament than the Lord Councillors to come.

My re-arrival in Coen's capital proved anything but congenial to my wishes. To be surprised in crime is to be merciless in its extirpation, and in the eyes of surprised authority there was little tolerance for what might argue mitigation. When I submitted my report to the Fiscaal Advocate, those matters which had persecuted my dreams and taunted conscience were no longer matters in which my advocacy was sought. Of course I wanted to put the entire episode behind me, but not before I was satisfied that my actions to resolve the demands of justice had been approved. But no, the nightmare, like a tragedy whose popularity is inextinguishable, was compelled to play itself on yet another stage. All of Batavia, this small and friendless port, was astir with excitement and given an opportunity to chorus the finale in a saga it had no involvement with. Those I returned never stood a chance, not that I cared for any other than Salomon — and I wish to God I'd marooned him with the other two on the Great South Land. The intensification of sentences was a judgement upon my judgement, a slur on my sense of proportion. On the one hand I was attacked by Van Diemen for not bringing the ringleaders back to corroborate the testimony of those still imprisoned; then, if I spared anyone, I was accused of unseemly leniency! The high Lord Councillors whose ranks I was nominated to join would have their blood, their language unequivocal with respect to the fate of those I'd spared. They were delinquents — all — who, on account of the abominable and gruesome cruelties and unheard-of murders, would now be punished with the cord until dead. All except Piet-ersz, the stone-cutter and Cornelisz's fallen lieutenant, who was to be broken on the wheel. In my experience of who he was, I couldn't sanction Salomon to be included among those who would suffer on that day. You may have seen me in the crowd but all I saw was that elevated circus of death. At the foot of the scaffold there was an unspeakable shuffle of players.

Too many gibbets; I'd had a brace of them erected on Seals' Island and had stood at the foot of their terrible execution, watching the tiger and its cubs dangle in expiry, their deaths doubtless hastened in the loss of hands. I had no desire to stand before another such spectacle, to endure this lurid and self-righteous crowd which had no connection with the Abrolhos. Still, I was there because I was near-appointed to a place alongside those ashen-faced lords. I was there because I have always had this fidgety inclination to see a thing through to its end. But there are limits, and I turned away as the last of those condemned, Salomon foremost among them, climbed those undecendable steps in the wake of a now unconscious Pietersz. I had needed to be there for my former assistant, although I'd not wanted to catch his eye for fear of misunderstanding. As it was, I no longer recognised him in his dungeon clothes and unshaven fear. I no longer recognised the world I once thought myself to have been in possession of. I had become a spectator, the outsider in a story that was fast relinquishing its need of me. I had to escape that place, the crowd which gossiped *I hear Pelsaert has been censured* without recognising me at all. I had to flee what was fast becoming my diminished self...

I open my eyes in a fit of blinking.

"Meyer?"

The room is empty.

"Meyer?" I call, and wondering whether his presence was but dreamed. The door closes stealthily, shutting out the life beyond.

Specx:

Every man is the circumference of his point of view, the captain of his own resolve. From where I sat, in Coen's vacated chair, the ledger needed squaring.

I have never known such silence for its traffic of voices.

You think there wasn't anything to add to what you assumed was done? Allow me to inform you that the responsibility of governorship is not so different from the management of a hospice when it comes to the colony's physical and moral delicacy. The *Batavia* case was a suppurating wound in need of cauterising. You had bound it as best you thought, but with bindings soaked in the original injury. It seems strange to us that you imagined any healing might ensue when there was still the malignancy of contamination. The *Sardam* carried miscreants; you had not cut deeply enough.

How else might I have proceeded? I had already extinguished the principal nest of vipers. I had brought the others back for further examination.

You, sir, presumed to forestall what *we* might judge of the affair. Your interpretation of justice done was generous to a fault.

With respect, I've been accused of not bringing enough of them back!

The vilest should have died, whether in the Abrolhos or here. But did you imagine yourself sufficiently placed to have acquitted the matter of any further dissection or decision? We were duty-driven to pick up where you'd left off.

I defy any to have managed their actions with as clear a purpose. Even Coen was sensible enough to appreciate that an uncharted reef can, in an instant, turn the world upside down. Had he not nearly met with wreck himself when, returning to the East like me, those unheralded outposts of the Great South Land suddenly manifested themselves to affirm its hostile reputation? Had he not witnessed the nocturnal disturbance of the sea as the ship's company rushed to alter course? Coen didn't stoop to judge in matters as inscrutable as the will of God. He simply ordered me to do what I must to retrieve the situation, and sent me on my way to come across the Abrolhos a second time.

Coen is dead. I now fill his shoes. The transition was not without incident. Further to the injury inflicted on my daughter, his expiry bequeathed me a city under siege, our ships the only surety of retreat should Batavia fall to the Mataramese. Even then the fleet was diminished, your flagship lost and the *Sardam* withdrawn in the recovery of survivors. You imagine you had a uniquely difficult time of it, restoring order in one rebellious ship's company? I stepped into the august responsibility of defending our interests in the East, of staring down a military calamity!

I've remained more than fair in my dealings with you, but we've not seen one another since parting at Texel. When you eventually caught us up with your flotsam of miscreants and tales to bristle the hair, I wasn't given to a tolerance of mind. Batavia's civility is tenuous, its replication of what exists in the Fatherland merely a veneer. Yes, persons of strange opinion come here, and it is my duty to limit the enjoyment of uncustomary behaviours. The light of what is acceptable is made luminous by the shadow of the gallows. By God, the dungeons were simply a welcome!

Is your daughter mended?

Not nearly enough not to inflict a little pain myself.

Into the menace of perpetual darkness, a clanking of chains and the squeal and grate of hinges. All dungeons are alike in the simplicity of their terror. *I have been brought here for a purpose beyond my control or contrary to my reasoning.* But at the end of the day a dungeon is not a place of reason.

Jacobsz hears the commotion of their arrival, feels some relief in the swell of numbers, then fear for the latent incrimination of who they might be. He listens intently for clues, for some intelligence in this departure from what has become his life: a mildewed nocturne in the wake of pain.

That Pelsaert had proven a squealing prick, this much was to be expected. No sooner had they been picked up in the Sundra Straits than he'd gone like a whining beggar to each and every uppermerchant, accusing the very seamen who had saved his hide of crimes a lesser dignitary had little chance of refuting under torture. As it was, they hanged Evertsz, almost on arrival. Jacobsz had felt squeamish for the bastard, the incriminating clatter of his urgency as he shouted, "Hey skipper, you fuck! You've knifed me! You think that flowery cunt'll save you?" *Come on, come on,* struggled the guards. And Evertsz's voice rising on a scream. "Don't think I didn't see what you were up to — licking the fucker's arse! You stabbed me! You stabbed *me* instead of him!" *For Christ's sake shut up!* And Jacobsz anxiously thinking the same thing. *Don't worry, the rope'll soon stifle that tongue of his.* Jacobsz watched him being dragged up the shadowy steps in his desperation to shout the truth. Yes, he had glimpsed the preliminaries of that last act, Evertsz's imminent death a shuddersome prophecy.

Then there was nothing, nothing for weeks on end. Nothing arising from his routine torture to decide anything in the minds of those who held sway over life and death. The skipper knew he'd have been accused of plotting mutiny. He knew Pelsaert was a slimy behind-your-back sort of cunt. The authorities needed a quick kill to convince themselves they were onto it. The attack on that stuck-up bitch Lucretia was just the excuse they needed to throttle Evertsz. Still, it wasn't mutiny – fuck, no. And Jacobsz wasn't sorry to have seen him off. It was one less enemy of life.

Nonetheless the situation was scarcely solacing. He sensed that the weeks fast bleeding into months were in dangerous abeyance, that the keys to his cell, once turned, might announce a development whose only certainty was its threat to his survival. He knew that Pelsaert had sailed south to recover the survivors. Luckily no mutiny had been sprung. Despite a clandestine recruitment of those bored and hungering for piratical adventure, *Batavia*'s wrecking had pre-empted that pipedream. They could all stay silent now and ignore what they were on the eve of doing. Their boastful world had dissembled overnight into an adult check of the consequences.

But there's never any sense among the senseless. A plan, however bad, is still a thing to own. Someone would have spilled his guts, bragged about what he might have become had disaster not intervened. Cornelisz was a coward, this much Jacobsz knew. But if there were loose tongues and rumour was naming names, then the undermerchant would have to act, either to silence those who spoke of what never was or purge those who remained loyal to the simplicity of the voyage as intended. Then again if Evertsz was gone, how fortunate might it also be for Cornelisz to have perished with the stricken vessel? The skipper had been with Pelsaert in the yawl as it bobbed helplessly alongside the dying Indiaman, Cornelisz and the last of them marooned on its disintegrating timbers. Yes, he had left the undermerchant to his fate, and the drowning of this most slippery of confederates would not have been a bad thing. But then Ariaen's luck was never unalloyed; he spent his dungeon hours mulling over the permutations of chance, every eventuality seeming to tar him in some way.

What if Cornelisz *had* survived to seize power? Not everyone could be expected to join the mutiny. If those loyal were not already disposed of, any imminent rescue would intensify the need to resolve that issue, to preclude an atmosphere of claim and counterclaim in which even the most hardened conspirator would fear the noose and soften his involvement. No, to be rescued along with a lot of saintly loyalists was no rescue at all. Cornelisz would have to have them killed. All of them. Pelsaert must walk into a trap.

Ariaen sweated in the belief that Cornelisz didn't possess the mettle to command. An arse-lick diplomat, to be sure, but not hardened like a sailor. Still, there were dangerous opportunists who were tempted by the temper of their steel. And hadn't Cornelisz seduced even his own rancour to enlist him in a suggestion of piracy? Ariaen partly sighed, partly groaned, to contemplate what he couldn't yet know. And ironically, he knew more concerning the inevitability of his fate than those who were yet to condemn him.

But suppose Cornelisz *had* survived. Suppose he'd gathered their now ship-less companions and dared them to imagine a future which, as Ariaen presently stared at the chains and masonry and the vengeful power of Batavia, was best not thought of at all. The die would then have been cast. To have killed those who might tell would be to have killed Pelsaert as well. Supposing the undermerchant had overwhelmed the uppermerchant and seized whatever rescue craft to turn pirate, what then? Jacobsz would be lost in a subterranean limbo of withering muscle and dimming eyesight. It wasn't as if the mutiny's success could lead to his rescue, here, from Batavia Castle. The unknowing of how or when he might die would simply be prolonged in the enquiry: *Whatever happened to Pelsaert?* He, Jacobsz, would remain the one glued to this spot, unable to wriggle away, unable to be judged with any certainty, hostage to a life of detention.

He thought of Zwaantie and longed for her company. It would have incurred no sacrifice of lodging on her part since she, too, had been assigned a cell upon pain of further examination. At first he was unnerved by her cries, then reassured by their pitch of insolence. Ah, she was a game one, and sure to buy herself favour with her saucy knowing of what men delight in. But the walls below ground, foundation of the barracks above, were thick and airless and he soon lost all whisper of where she was. Released, he hoped, but jealous at the thought of her enterprise with others less restrained.

Fuck Cornelisz! Fuck that Devil's slippered tongue!

It was dangerous enough to have captained the loss of a ship, but in company with the likes of that pampered arsehole, Pelsaert, the responsibility could be watered down among the many who would vouch the shipwreck unforeseeable, the reef and those desolate outcrops uncharted. His conduct in the wake of the disaster had been exemplary. Even the uppermerchant couldn't have faulted his leading seamanship. Upon a charge of recklessness his examination would be severe but not necessarily fatal. Time would release him. Pelsaert couldn't substantiate anything. Yes, all he had to do was remain strong and endure. But Cornelisz, might he have succeeded in an audacity which imperilled his — Ariaen's — future? Might the Abrolhos be no distance at all when it came to consequences that were set like a slow-burning fuse?

No, it was unlikely Cornelisz would be roving the eastern seas, fitted out with stolen garments and plundering Spanish galleons off Manila. In the first place Jacobsz had seen to it that *Batavia*'s most senior officers were with him in the longboat. Those left behind were the infirm, the unruly and mostly useless. Even if Pelsaert were overwhelmed, it would be a motley crew, little capable of navigating the lonely tracts of ocean. It lightened the skipper's heart to visualise this, the rescue ship itself without rescue as discipline broke down and dissension drifted her off to oblivion. Yes, all he had to do was remain calm, to control that explosive temper of his (which, in any case, was denied the intoxicants that unleashed his tongue) and bear it out. Without hard evidence to incriminate him it would simply be a matter of time before the Company, anxious to salvage something from its loss, availed itself of his services once more. After all, the VOC was a pragmatic beast.

In the elongating darkness whose only timepiece is the twice-daily visit of the turnkey, whose only vapour is the spice of his now rancid uniform, Ariaen dozes away his fearful imaginings and lives like mould in the humidity of his cot. The absence of resolution has its softer side, an aspect of almost convalescent controllessness. It startles, then, his somnolent routine when the clank of keys heralds an untoward disturbance. Jacobsz springs to his feet, surprised at his vigour and alarmed at heart, as if knowingly reconnected with the immediacy of where he left off months before. Loud cajoling shoves them in their shuffle, the swaying lamp casting fresh shadows against the wall. Someone stumbles on the descending steps, the chains yanking and the whelp cowered.

"Get up you piece of shit!" A thwack and a groan. "Get up I say!"

Ariaen squeezes his face against the grille. A number of figures crowd the passage, and heavy doors are being forced ajar. He can't rightly recognise any of them. Then he sees Deschamps, or at least someone who reminds him of Pelsaert's womanly favourite, his hair now long and matted, his costume fouled and countenance dishevelled. "Where from?" he hears himself shout.

"Ah, Ariaen," a guard cries, "you're reunited with your lost friends."

"Friends? I see no sailor I recognise."

"Come, skipper, that's ungenerous. These tender villains have come home from the sea – those that are left of them. Hah!"

"*Batavia?*"

"Aye, *Batavia* all."

"You men," shouts Ariaen, "there's been a rescue? Guards, hear me! Heer Pelsaert, he was successful?"

"That rather depends on what he hoped to find," laughs a gaoler in a manner bereft of mirth.

"Ah skipper, you left behind a tidy brood of vipers."

"Deschamps, I see you! What news of the undermerchant and the folk we landed?"

But Salomon is numbed by circumstances which are all too clearly foreclosing on his life. Like a chastened schoolboy, almost as if sleepwalking, he permits himself to be rough-handled into the nearest cell.

"Skipper, all Batavia is abuzz with the story –"

"Heer Pelsaert – ah, *there's* a man who knows how to step into shit – he has brought us back not one but *two* tales of mayhem and disaster!"

"Pietersz, you're here too?" shouts Jacobsz.

But Stone-Cutter appears even more subdued than Deschamps. Whatever pertained in the open prison of the Abrolhos has been countered by the judicial reality of these dungeons. If back there, beneath cloudless skies by day or glittering stars at night, it had been a place to kill, this now, most certainly, is a place to *be* killed.

"Ah skipper, I shouldn't drink with this lot if I were you."

"He mightn't have much choice. Their eyes will all a-bubble when they tie and ladle the collar."

"Too true. Hey, skipper, the undermerchant is hanged!"

"This lot will be next for the gallows, mark my word!"

And laughter jostles the prisoners. One is whimpering; it's almost the gurgle of a child.

"What took place?" croaks Jacobsz, sensing all but without any detail.

"A mutiny without a ship —"

"And murder without motive."

"Heer Pelsaert, a right and proper sort," and there's malice in the tribute, "got there but not before time —"

"Most as were first saved were slaughtered."

"They say Pelsaert condemned the undermerchant 'cause he managed to screw the wench who'd held out on him on the voyage —"

"Hey skipper, wasn't your strumpet the lady's maid?"

Jacobsz doesn't succumb to anger. It's too important to learn what went on, to know exactly what it is he must distance himself from. Murder? Christ, if they could throttle a man for daubing a woman with shit, what in the Devil's name might they not do to a man who is linked to murder? Fuck! Pelsaert first has Evertsz hanged, then it looks as if the powdered cunt has had the wherewithal to finish off Cornelisz as well. Not a man for an open fight; no, more an assassin, the very thief of life!

And recognising that earlier misgivings about him are likely to be compounded by the incontinent fears of these lesser men, Jacobsz steadies himself to shun all knowledge of who they are, to refute any connection other than concede that *Batavia*'s manifest proves they were passengers aboard his ship. They're all neighbours in the Castle's dungeons, but he will remain aloof in his scruple not to die with them.

I know all this about the skipper. I know what his cell smells like, what his fear of death entails. Whether through bloody flux or by knotted flax, the end appears all too likely, awaiting just beyond the door. I breathe for the moment, and so does he. What I hope to inhale afresh, he too prays for on my behalf — if only so that he and I might remain shackled like unlovely brothers. It is said abroad that the wrecking of the ship and magnitude of the mutiny was cultured by discords at the highest level. Yet I would ask what position of command doesn't attract envy, which agent of authority doesn't invite slander?

I remember how his eyes adjusted to the sight of me in the bucking gloom of those first minutes, the cruising calm now shattered by a loud surf and dismal spray. Everything slipped and caught its breath. He doubtless saw – short of any fear of drowning, a concern he never displayed – where we would inevitably end up. "Skipper," I'd shouted, "what have you done to have drawn a noose around our necks?" Perhaps I had said too much. Perhaps in the risk of punishment to myself he saw his reprieve from negligence and whatever else in a reclaiming union of interests. He knew I needed him to stabilise the situation, to save us all from being utterly lost in the hours ahead. There was no telling what daybreak might reveal – indeed, whether the scenario of our predicament was at all endurable. I knew, too, that he needed me, that there were two thresholds of survival to be negotiated. Without ever visiting his cell, I knew what Jacobsz would be like in the bowels of Batavia Castle. I knew because of his behaviour during those days on the Timor Sea when he hoped his leadership might paint him in a different light.

But I am no fool. I was aware of what he really thought, aware of what he had cost me in terms of *Batavia*'s loss; that from here on I would be daily reminded to plead my worth to a displeasured Company. Even before Cornelisz did his worst, Jacobsz had injured my reputation. And I am not a man to overlook a slight.

I am alone yet ghosted, doubled as if in scrutiny of my bed-ridden self. My eyes are polished curvatures, twin moons of light. I can see them as clearly as if I were seated in the corner darkness, unannounced yet vigilant. It's difficult to tell whether these, my eyes and whatever they illumine, are aware, as it were, of this harbouring other presence – in fact, whether I might know myself! Like two nightwatchmen they convey a sentience that eschews repose, yet they seem unaffected by my corner trespass. I know that as I dream I am reduced to these outposts of sleepless conjecture, eyes lustrous and at odds with my prone and weakened state. For the present I can do nothing but beguile myself with thoughts.

Boredom and loneliness, ill-health and its compensating appetite for pleasure, any man might spend his time – agreeable or otherwise – in the company of women and wine. Didn't I witness the mogul harem, if witness be not too forceful a claim for so jealously guarded a possession? Life for many – even emperors, I suppose – necessitates some allowance for the anxiety that living, of itself, is never enough. Indeed, each man seems a tribe in contest with his neighbour, despite the sharing of cups. Yet how hamstrung any celebration of success. A man no sooner acquires property than he must employ servants to guard it; he no sooner takes a wife than feels the need to take another, and another – all because there is little permanence to be milked from that initial satisfaction, nothing to savour but an insensate memory of taste. We covet what we have not, even if it's like was formerly in our keeping but allowed to fade with familiarity. Boredom's disaffection is a spur to most enterprise.

I've always contended something rickety and uncertain in the way a harem was supposed to gratify a man's esteem or announce his arrival. Yet you could still play the child – at heart, if not in fact – as the women were all so young, leastways those who were added to the roll. While there were many fine houses in Agra, there were, of course, others – shelters crude and impecunious – where one wondered why a man would so burden himself with a retinue of women who appeared no more than utensils to his kitchen and little inclined to pleasure. Still, in the homes of the wealthy, never was a man more lasciviously sated than in the power he exercised within his zenana. It was the gilded cage, a place of perfumes, ointments and intrigue, of secluded women ripening into petulance and gossip.

It was on the occasion of my first summons to his house that I received Wasim's gift – the livery of green and lavender I would later wear on subsequent visits – and was presently abashed in arriving, his invited guest, emptyhanded. I ought to have known better; after all, I'd resided here long enough to be familiar with the rituals of graft and gratitude. To plead that I was not long returned from Bayana and dusty, still, with crop concerns was simply to make excuses.

That aside, at first it had all seemed straightforward. A servant called at the outer gate of the factory, the very same who, later, would shield and accompany Asmat to Fatehpur Sikri. He possessed the bluest of eyes, eyes that startled in their contrast to his dusky skin – an unlikely companion, one would have thought, to recruit to so clandestine an undertaking. He studied me, only ever this once, with the swift and assimilative curiosity of one who was above being surprised by his master's inclinations. Indeed, having taken me in at a glance, he reverted to something unseeing, his obedience bent on direction and escort. When we arrived at our destination, this leg of his commission now ended, he disappeared without my notice, and it was only later, when I was to be conveyed back to the Dutch enclave, that his reappearance gave profile to his absence.

"I'm afraid you will find my house but a trinket of the paradise enjoyed by others," smiled Wasim, his golden tooth an idol amidst its betel-stained neighbours.

He was steering me across a small courtyard that murmured with watery decantations, a fountain sprinkling the surface of its tank so lightly that unhurried fish were clearly visible.

"The emperor is inclined to thread the noses of the salmon he encounters with pearls," observed my host, and raising one eyebrow. "Mine are simply fortunate not to be destined for the table."

And to Wasim's table we appeared headed, my curiosity everywhere competing with the restraint of good manners. Although I had been admitted to many houses during my sojourn at Agra, the spacious if somewhat Spartan aspect of our factory – a small fort, really – was the most extensive of the buildings experienced. Of course the imperial splendour of the Mogul residence was altogether more elevated, but it was neither private nor likely to secrete an invitation to come dine with the emperor himself. No, my dealings until then had been transacted in the business quarters of brokers and lesser merchants or on the premises of shopkeepers, creatures scarcely better off than humble workers due to the rapacious demands of officials who, in the emperor's name, might rob them in an hour of an entire month's profit. Now here I was, in the private mahal of a nobleman at the centre of empire. As I passed through the garden's cultivated symmetries, its air moistened with scents of soothing peach and almond, I was admiringly conscious that water and plants are both a refreshment and recreation unknown in our cold country. At the edge of the garden was an open pavilion which I took to be the sitting place intended, spread as it was with handsome carpets, and with two servants and their trays hovering close by. But no, Wasim clapped and spoke sharply, whereupon they removed themselves to a passage that reached deeper into the cloistered mystery of this unknown house.

There is nothing like a first visitation to illicit a sense of marvel and seduction. As if holding a mirror to my thoughts, the lime-plastered walls, polished with agates so that they shone like alabaster, were indeed a looking-glass wherein I perceived of myself the apparent motion of another. As the passage narrowed, the sugary walls forwarded the light as a river does the sky. We presently arrived at a second and much smaller court, marble-paved and without cultivation except for a potted row of limes. It seemed to serve no purpose other than compel an appreciative pause before what I surmised was the domestic hearth of Wasim's compound, a single-storeyed building that gleamed beneath the sky's lantern, its loggia permitting the indoors to borrow from a light which exceeded the compass of its walls. Unlike the defensiveness of our own weather-strapped habitations (and even accounting for the necessity of parapets to disincline robbers), the interiors of these local mansions breathed with an openness that was self-certain and fanciful. Rich was the inlay that trimmed the doorway I passed through, its chain-like patterns of green, orange and blue shimmering against the predominant white. Such flourishes were a necklace to the garment of the floor itself, the carpets richly patterned and overlaid as if thrown to captivate the wonder and delight of a buyer. This shop-like impression of cleared display was augmented by the fact that there was no furniture of the kind we delight in such as tables, stools and cupboards. Instead, the furnishings were soft, their timbered frames light yet lavishly ornamented in gold and silver. And as if in legacy of their nomadic past, everything of most value, while reminding them daily of how prosperous they had become, appeared portable, their wealth embossed in plates and salvers and ready – like the harem itself – of being whisked away. Yes, if the houses of these grandees appeared very grand indeed, there loitered, too, a sense of impermanence as shifting as the curtains affixed to hooks that created screens as insubstantial to what was solid as their owner's misplaced piety in Mahomet.

Having left my boots at the portal, I was gestured to a cushion which faced the entrance, my back to a wooden screen which portioned off this section of the building. The servants with trays now stood to either side of the door like sphinxes until Wasim snapped his fingers and they drew near, kneeling to proffer what I thought was some refreshment but, instead, proved to be dishes of lime-scented water with which to wash our hands. Wasim even cupped the water to his face, his eyes blinking as if aroused from slumber, his smile shedding droplets from his neatly trimmed beard.

"This is most measured and serene," I commented, also smiling, and inhaling a spicy alchemy more delicate than the aromas which permeated the factory.

"Perhaps not as serene as you imagine. Ah, here is my cousin, Hussain..."

And a man of less refined appearance, of dark and unkempt whiskers, entered the room, fending with an open palm our stirring to rise. Touching his breast he intoned, "May the fruits of Allah always grace your table." His embroidered cap – indeed, the plainness of his smock and trousered costume – gave him the aspect of a divine, a supposition of office that appeared well fed. Then breaking into a playful grin, his teeth unevenly broken, he tugged upon one bat-like ear and seated himself on a cushion that appeared accustomed to his weight. I was still eyeing him when, from another doorway, yet another man emerged, this time a hurried and apologetic boyishness about him.

"And this is my wife's brother, Muzaffir."

Likewise, this gentleman touched his heart in salutation then hastened to a cushion on the far side of me. Wasim leaned close, "He has no gift for punctuality. It's well for him I married his sister."

"Ha," and a youthful laugh. "It's as well for you, my lord, that I eased the match." Muzaffir, his teeth yellow but intact, flashed me a smile and whispered aloud, "It was Hussain, there, who knew of my family and its feminine riches. My father was redoubtable but Hussain, like me, has a notion for how a thing might work."

"Might is not the same as make," waved Wasim, then reaching for my shoulder, "and I have been making for them all so as none might much feel the need to work."

"Pithily put, cousin! Your words would no doubt echo like counsel in the pearl-pinned ears of the emperor. I hear he has quite a fetish for language!"

Wasim shrugged and smiled ruefully as if to say: *Welcome to my household; do you, too, have relatives such as these?* "Cousin, brother – whatever you would take from me in addition to the food I provide, let this not detract from our greeting of the Dutch factor, Francisco Pelsaert."

I inclined my head, amused by the accented sound of my name and delighted to find myself privy to this bantering introduction. Then realising the prelude to have been staged for my benefit, I responded with thanks for their hospitality.

Muzaffir nodded gravely. "Your Turkish is not bad."

Sniffing like a rabbit in anticipation of food, Hussain addressed me also, saying, "There was an Englisher here some years ago –"

At that moment a cloth was brought by two young girls and spread upon the carpet before us. Thereupon precious dishes, irradiant with leafy inlays and emerald-eyed peacocks, were entered and set down with their steaming cargoes upon hunting scenes of gambolling deer and javelin-wielding cavaliers. Despite my presence in the heart of Agra, I couldn't help but feel as if being fêted at some country lodge.

Postponing what he had a mind to say, Hussain hovered over the dishes with an appreciative murmur. There were artful bowls of dressed rice, spiced meat and wheaten cakes. I was, by this time, well accustomed to al-shalla, pulao and zueyla, but these and other delectables were served with perhaps too little butter and too much spice for the usual Dutch palate. Walter never really adjusted to the cuisine; his strength, once imperilled, found insufficient nourishment in what he would allow himself.

A male servant – clearly a butler of some self-dignity – now arrived as the girls departed. Kneeling, he proceeded to apportion a combination of scented delicacies and presented me, as the honoured guest, with the first plate. Hussain greedily studied this transfer as if worried there mightn't be enough to go around, while Muzaffir glanced in my direction and nodded approvingly. "This is very good. You like our food?"

"I should scarcely have survived had I not adapted."

"That is scarcely a compliment," brooded Hussain, still focused on the ladling of dishes.

Wasim gestured impatiently. "Forgive my cousin," he sighed. "The indulged are liable to exceed themselves."

"To the contrary," I replied, "I meant only that I've taken to the appetites of this country like a native and should, doubtless, find myself searching and bereft, were I at home, for favourites non-existent in the Netherlands."

"Is there a national dish?"

"Bread and herring," I answered lightly.

"Herring?"

"The food of affliction."

And a knitting of brows compelled me to be serious a moment and elaborate. "There was a time when our country was invaded and our cities under siege. There was little to feast on but the sea and our defiance. We remember those hungry years."

"And the invader?" queried Muzaffir, leaning forward like a child at story time.

"Defeated with all his host. And with the help of God."

"Yet I would understand you are not entirely free," challenged Wasim. He was contemplating his food, preparing to dip his fingers.

I considered a moment. "We are not free," I responded, "of an arrogance which, though sorely troubled in these times, would still dare to rule us as their power permits."

"And are they powerful?" enquired my host.

"In Europe and the Americas they are a bullying race."

"And your countrymen fear them?"

"We have been pushed to fury more than fear. We now muscle them everywhere, especially their cousins here in the East."

"The Franks, you mean?"

"Yes, the Franks, as you call them; the Portuguese to us. But they're the Devil's own and as scheming a crew as ever profaned the goodness of God or conscience of man."

There was silence, during which I realised I may have overplayed what we trumpeted to strangers. In our virtuous energy we were ever vigilant to discredit a rival and unholy them before those who little shared our grievances. Conscious that I may have bemused – if not amused – my hosts with such trenchancy, I was mindful, too, that not all Mahometans share an orthodoxy of belief, that there were sects which might cheerfully turn to murder to prove that theirs was the truer gospel.

I smiled to acknowledge that my own passions could, when loosened, run to a certain colour. "All I will say," I added, "since I wish not to sully your generosity with my complaint of those who would injure Dutch interests, is that a priest is no priest when he would steal the ear of a king, and that Jesuits are rather inclined to exclusivity in their counsel."

"I think we understand," grinned Wasim, dipping his fingers at last and stirring his plate into a paste. "The emperor has but two ears and his circle of advisors is more than crowded. The Franks would seduce him from the faith as they would move to control our shipping. To many of us they are an affront. They goad us with their unarmed piety, their serpentine words and haughty ways."

My host deftly scooped a morsel to his lips, and I followed suit. He was chewing in keep with his thoughts, then to me he said, "I see little in the manner of your infidelity to provoke us. Indeed, I see little in the spirit of godliness – true *or* false – among you Hollanders. I mean no disrespect; you are my honoured guest. And a man of business always makes better company than a man of God."

Hussain grunted his concurrence and jabbed at his plate, besmearing his fingers to the knuckle, soldier-fashion. The only spoon visible was reserved for the ladling servant who, like some eunuch to our conversation, appeared oblivious to what was spoken.

"The English," Hussain smacked his lips, "they are different, no?"

"They are our cousins by conviction," I conceded, "but like the Portuguese, they would pursue a rough trade with us."

"And you play rough in turn?"

The question sounded like an accusation. Mindful as I was of our growing might, my own enterprise had always seemed peaceable. Certainly, I'd been with Coen at the subjugation of Jacatra, and I'd heard grim tales from the Banda Islands. But I had never stood with those, sword in hand, at the apex of assault. Despite the sweat and weariness of the road, mine was a life of merchant guile and negotiation, of procurement and safe return. "I intend to play no one false," I replied.

"Hm," shrugged Hussain, knowing it bad manners to lick his fingers but sorely tempted. "As I was about to say when we first sat down, there was an Englisher here some years ago. His name – ah, what was his name?"

"Roe?" I prompted. "The English ambassador who was here before my time."

"No no, the first one. He who spoke Turkish – perhaps even better than you."

"Hussain!"

"What?" he objected. "I doubt our friend here minds."

"Please excuse him, Francisco. His father – may God clasp his soul in peace – was his brother's younger. I'll say no more." Then returning to Hussain, Wasim announced, "It was that chameleon creature called Hawkins; he's the one you're thinking of."

"That's him!"

And Muzaffir nodded, too, for a memory he didn't possess.

The recapture of a fact was too much for Hussain; he licked his fingers and went on. "Now this fellow Hawkins, he quite impressed the emperor with his knowledge of our tongue. He was like some rare oracle who could give voice to other worlds."

"Yes, the emperor became very hospitable," added Wasim.

"He did more than that," smirked Hussain. "He honoured him as if he'd not come from some Englisher king but were an amir from within his own household."

"The emperor – may Allah prolong his reign over us – is lavish to those who are loyal," added Muzaffir.

"He was promoted to rank and salary at court –"

"I hasten to add that the court was little moved to share the emperor's enthusiasm."

"Bah, cousin, you yourself are a courtier! You know that few who surround the emperor favour anything but their own reward."

"As you witness, Francisco, conversation here is not likely to translate happily beyond these walls."

"I savour such candour, this chance to better understand."

"That's not all a man might savour!"

Wasim was looking a shade put out by Hussain's ardour for revelation. "Come cousin, surely –"

"Our honoured guest, how long have you been among us?"

"The years, now, are beginning to mount."

"And you have taken a wife?"

Muzaffir's eyes lit up.

I assumed no one mistook me for a virgin – at least I felt compelled to trust it so – yet neither could I boast a live-in woman.

"Ignore his impertinence," Wasim shook his head, setting his plate down to be replenished.

"Ah, but I mean no disrespect, only that the emperor – like his father before him, may his greatness be remembered – can be generous to foreigners."

"How so?" I entreated, my ear pricked for any advantage.

"Why, a wife, of course!" And turning to the others, "Didn't that Hawkins receive a woman, courtesy of his majesty?"

"Yes, it was so. I recall there was some delicacy..."

"The Englisher, being an infidel, would consent to none but a maid of his own misguided creed."

"But a Christian they did find, and at court, no less."

"Yes, the daughter of an Armenian, a favourite of the late Akbar."

"Both master and servant, by this time, having travelled the road of non-existence-—"

"She'd become a ward of the state. The emperor had only to snap his fingers—"

"Or keep his fingers to himself," ventured Muzaffir, grinning.

"And the lady was produced," twirled his lord and brother-in-law.

"Whereupon the Englisher, it is said, could no longer withstand his fortune!"

And we all laughed for our knowing of what a man might allow himself.

"But permit me," whispered Hussain, and drawing near, "to give you a piece of advice. If you wish to advantage yourself and sample the fruits of this land, convert to Islam."

"Cousin," warned Wasim, "I fear you stray towards blasphemy!"

"Not so," and likewise setting down his plate and gesturing to our impassive waiter. "The Englisher was finicky; he'd only lie with another infidel. These Franks, the ones who come dressed in black and smell of donkeys, they who would profane the Prophet to his face – may Allah boil their souls – they take no woman at all. But we," and now leaning back and patting his sides, "we – my cousin and I – we each maintain a stable of beauties as sanctioned by the Prophet."

Muzaffir snorted. "Since when was Farida ever considered a beauty?"

"You, Muzaffir – dog boy," retorted Hussain, and coarsening his speech, thinking perhaps I mightn't comprehend, "your stable-life is a disappointment to the memory of your sister's father!"

"It makes him angry I'm so choosy," Muzaffir turned to me, grinning. "Why harness yourself to four donkeys when all you crave is an Arabian mare?"

"Ha, he lives like a guest among us, turning up for meals, and begging our women to darn his laundry. He styles himself a brother yet flits among us like some mendicant sparrow!"

Wasim presently cleared his throat to remind them that a stranger was present. "Cousin, brother, I beseech you."

I couldn't help but want to return them to their playfulness. "But to take a wife," I said, "how might I choose?"

Hussain, his bat-like ears flaring, glared at Muzaffir as if daring him to boast a response beyond his experience. But the slighter man merely ground the heels of his palms, the fingers of his right hand sticky with sauce, and made a noise approving of my question.

"A man chooses as he would choose his livestock," waved Hussain, "and need not seek a camel in a horse or a goat in a deer. Haven't you heard?" and grinning, now, as he leaned back on his cushion. "A man should marry a Persian for companionship, a Khurasani to do his housework, and an Indian for sex."

There was a ripple of knowing laughter and I, too, smiled for the neatness of this formula before asking complicitly, "Isn't a man of your faith permitted a fourth wife as well?"

"Cousin," Hussain's eyes flashed, "your guest is quickly divining the advantage of becoming one of us!" Then turning to me, he added, "Yes, my friend, a woman from Transoxiana – to whip so that the others may take heed and keep the peace!"

Muzaffir was a merriment of teeth, his lips curling like rolls of dough, and even Wasim allowed himself to forgo that mask which oft concealed what he was thinking. We were four men in the contemplation of four wives, a huddle of giggling schoolboys whose joke was assumed to be beyond the literacy of our still-kneeling waiter.

And then I saw you.

Wasim immediately rose to his feet. I couldn't tell whether he was pleased or annoyed, whether you'd been summoned to arrive at this moment or if you'd decided to interrupt our prurient feast. I was entranced, unable to grasp you in any detail, and so embarrassed by what you may have overheard that I scarce knew how to act or to excuse myself of what I seemed. Each of us has an instinct for what is beautiful, a magnetism that doesn't necessarily transport in the opinion of others, but for me something shifted at the core of my being, made my chamber flutter to sounds of disturbed recognition. It was as if I had never known myself, never known how lost I was within some played-to and unchallenged expectation. Now suddenly I was in this unforeseen yet all too real a world and wondering what it might be like to be in Wasim's shoes, to possess you as he did. My host turned to me, having raised your hand in stately consort, to announce, "Agha-ye Pelsaert, let me present my wife, the begum Asmat."

I caught myself wondering which of the four, as defined by Hussain, might best have described you.

"It is an honour to meet so important a lady," I murmured, "when…" I wasn't sure of my bearings in so conventionally guarded a world and could feel my reaction, my manners being tested.

"Yes," continued Wasim, and with so subtle a smile I again felt as on that day when we'd first encountered each other, our uncounselled impulse to connect infringing, perhaps, on some more measured motivation. "As you see," he said, "our women may appear without the veil, or as they choose in circumstances where privacy and trust are assured."

Then gesturing you to a nearby cushion, I saw that two other women – maybe older; certainly less comely from the outline of their eyes, for they had chosen to retain their masks – had joined us from what I now perceived had been their lurking observation behind the wooden screen.

Misreading, perhaps, my restrained formality, Wasim added, "Waheeda, my most recent, she is with child and presently indisposed. It is a blessing from God to find oneself, at last, in possession of the future. Do you have children, Francisco? – no, of course not; forgive me."

I couldn't tell to what extent I was being measured and found lacking.

"As a guest," he continued, "– and one might even venture to say, your being so far from home, as a kind of orphan – you are welcomed as a brother in this house."

I bowed as calmly as I could, no longer preoccupied with brotherhood alone but moved, instead, to snatch glimpses of you, to decipher that which so animated my distraction, this flash in which I imagined myself wedded to your body as if I were, in fact, the master of this house. For certain it was those jade-green eyes, startling in their contrast to the blood-shot duskiness common in these parts. And the extravagance of your husband's gold, settled in proud ownership upon your throat and arms; you might have resembled some eastern Cleopatra. Your clothes, too, begged scrutiny, their detail so richly patterned as to be impossible to take in at a glance, their coverage of your skin concealing little of your form. Yes, it was these things and doubtless more – so exotic and unexpectedly presented to a foreigner – that made me coy in my insurgent desire to stare, and unleashed in my mind a compensating fantasy of possession. In what I drew from your uncovered face, I willed your eyes to look at mine – as indeed they did, just long enough to smuggle an enquiry, to admit of yourself some independence of desire and expose, in me, my infatuated soul.

I returned to Wasim with difficulty, my concentration focused on an impermissible musing, the topic of which dishonoured all of us. Yes, I felt deceitful in my receipt of his gifted livery, its green and lavender prompting that I should come again now sheathing a surreptitious motive.

And you would dare say this to me now? You would dare unthink the unkindness you besmeared yourself to the knuckles with, soldier-fashion?

You have every right to be angry –

Don't think to soften me! It was cruel what you wrote. And to foreigners – infidels – as well.

I was angry with what had passed...

'Some of the nobles have chaste wives,' you said.

So ill-disposed towards myself with what had happened, and at the prospect of giving up India, that...

'But they are too few to be worth mentioning.' Where do I lie in all of this? Was I a paragon, too little worthy of your attention? Or merely one of a dozen you enjoyed, a harlot among the rest?

Asmat, you were different.

How so when 'most of the ladies are tarred with the same brush, that when the husband is away, even though he thinks them safely guarded by his eunuchs, his wives are too clever for Argus himself with his hundred eyes.'

It was not for your ears. You were already dead.

As if that counts for anything! Words have a tendency to live on, to settle accounts beyond any protest from the grave.

I only meant…

You meant to protect your reputation by slandering me.

It was not like that.

The eunuch, my servant, kept us — you — alive. And yet you would defile us, we who risked everything in the gamble of your vanity.

Asmat, my words were harsh and cowardly, I confess. Their cleverness concealed a pain that wasn't at liberty to express itself.

Tut. You were right about one thing, Francisco, and she shakes her head with sad contempt, *'A woman might procure for herself all the pleasure she can, though not as much as she desires.' You were indeed a thief who fluttered my heart with your novelty. But in the end it was that childlike Rajput widow who captured your imagination, who filled your heart with a mortal sorrow that ached like love.*

I was horrified.

You were moved by the chastity of her madness.

I was afraid before the imminence of death.

It's strange to recount how we end up. None of us live for the manner or moment of our end. How should we when the end can be so unexpected or farcical? You were slashed of glamour when I took that draught, our fragile romance shattered into something even more fugitive than its fugitive self. Imagine, a woman compromising more than just her-self in the comedy of her demise!

It was not like that.

No? Then you tell me, tell me my death wasn't a shocking embarrassment, that your concern wasn't the fear of being discovered or a feeling of touch-sore inconvenience in the presence of my perturbed and suspicious husband. Tell me I wasn't any less worthy of love or esteem just because I wasn't destined for the burning pit.

I can scarce breathe for the stories that rush upon me, remembrances which, like importunate debtors, refuse to be turned from the door and hover at the windows. I feel stifled in this heat by what heat alone could never achieve, tortured to continue living as if already dead. They are my harpies, these imaginings. They are the crows that would pluck out my sight. Yet the darkened place which ought to ensue is ever painted in lurid hues that dance like fire-light against the furtive cavity of my skull. Yes, my life, its peace of mind, is endlessly rattled by sordid grotesqueries, a grubby carnival intent on starving me of dignity. It's as if I've walked into a public square without clothing, those who would *psst* or whisper warning drowned out by the mocking jeer of the crowd.

❧

They brought him from where he'd been kept the past two weeks, a limestone pit removed from the shore of their island and close to the tiny fort erected for their defence. He'd been made to pluck the birds they'd tossed him, to help prepare, in a smother of guts and feathers, the meals of those he would have exterminated. Yes, Hayes had trained himself a formidable little militia.

Cornelisz was still attired in the garments he'd been captured in, the gold-trimmed laken of his preposterous rule now torn and filthy. There was the odour of a serpent about him and, despite his misfortune, a lively and cunning eye. I almost expected him to embrace me, to shake himself free of his captors and exclaim, "Thank God you've arrived!" But in that recon-nected moment, any pretence that what had happened had occurred without his knowing was obliterated in the insolubility of what lay between us. There was too keen a memory of his rivalry and assertion, of a disposition gratuitous in manipulation and innuendo.

For sure, I had always believed Jacobsz to be the instigator of all calumny. But in the confession extracted from Jan Hendricxsz who, with others, had sought to seize the *Sardam*, the lie was given to Cornelisz's pretence of inno-cence. "You have murdered *how* many?" I'd gazed at Hendricxsz, stupefied.

"I don't rightly know," swallowed the soldier. "Between seventeen and twenty… It was all done on the orders of the undermerchant."

"And you never paused to query the villainy of what you were about?"

Hendricxsz stared at me without seeing, as if looting his thoughts for anything that might interpret the moment. Despite a large frame, he appeared vulnerable and childlike in his captured reasoning. "We'd been together a long time," he answered. "It wasn't just here, on the island. There was the voyage, too, the months at sea. Bonds were formed."

"Did you not think mutiny a crime?"

"All the men most upper were involved – the skipper, the undermerchant, the boatswain..."

"And I – did I not constitute the ship's most senior authority?"

"Sir, you scarcely existed," he answered sheepishly. "You'd taken to your bunk and were unseen for weeks at a stretch. It was to have been no great trouble to smuggle you overboard."

There's nothing quite like the sensation of being rendered supernumerary in the matter of one's fate. "And the others?"

"We were to arm those who were loyal and get rid of the rest."

"Loyal to *whom*?"

Hendricxsz didn't follow. He knew only that their dream of pirating was at an end. It seemed to him unfair that shipwreck should have wrecked their enterprise as well. He was a soldier, used to killing, and therefore not a child. Yet I was unable to fathom whether he realised he must surely hang for this.

"Bring Jeronimus."

It was towards evening when they lugged him aboard the *Sardam*. The others who had threatened were by this time securely bound, tethered to the main mast. Already their number – with yet more to subdue – posed a logistical question in the minds of the righteous. The mutiny still smouldered on Batavia's Graveyard (as I now learned that islet named), and though we had won the first battle, there was still our cause to effect. Fortunately, I could rely on Wiebbe's tutored troops.

I had summoned the ship's council; had the chart table cleared and benches set up. Apart from the cunning of his unsmiling eye, Jeronimus's caked and unruly appearance in so ordered a circle more than hinted at the level of depravity that had opened up in our absence. The very environment into which he was ushered, its lantern glare and judicial hygiene, likewise seemed to measure in his mind the gap he needed to close. I looked at him with great sorrow – at least that's what I wrote in my record of this meeting, although my emotion was more an admixture of astonishment and suppressed fury. Such a scoundrel and the author of so many disasters! Even after shedding all that blood, he still intended to go on. Fortunately, God intervened – although I've scarcely slept without wondering how He could have permitted such atrocity in the first place. I can only presume to thank Him for the presence of the Devil, for how else might a man make sense of the apparent shortcomings of His all-powerful sway? If not for the abbreviation of virtue, wherein might there be any need for mercy? And might Jeronimus qualify? It was tempting to wish the best in men, to redeem them in their weakness and punish them as a sign of forgiveness. I asked Cornelisz why he had allowed the Devil to lead him so astray from all human feeling, and without any real thirst or hunger.

"It wasn't me," he flatly replied.

"We have a confession that implicates you," I countered. "It's alleged you were the leader of a cause whose wicked ends were scripted in blood."

"It wasn't me," he repeated. "It was David Zevanck, Coenraat van Huyssen and the others – they who *that* man there," and pointing at Hayes, "killed."

Wiebbe had already described to me the circumstances of their deaths, their capture turned to slaughter as their fellows manoeuvred to rescue. Hayes had signalled the arrival of a new and spirited resistance, the depleted ranks of the mutineers now forcibly challenged.

I wonder that we only have your testimony to go on. Van Diemen haunts me with the supercilious opportunism of a jealous man made all the more power-ful for the declaration of his spite. *Those at the core of the mutiny are conveniently dead. If not killed before your return, you certainly curtailed any verification of who was responsible for what by your hasty execution of the alleged ringleaders.*

They were all confessed!

I think, Heer Pelsaert, too many witnesses have been summarily dealt with. It was premature to presume what Batavia might need to know.

Despite the horrors of the Abrolhos, there have been times when I have longed for the saline openness of that lost and lonely place, when I have craved the authority of my own court.

I looked at Jeronimus with anger, then with a sudden squalor of fatigue. My fellow officers were stripped bare with suspense, greedy to uncover the story of what had passed in our absence.

"How might we believe you," I asked, "when you conceal yourself in the deaths of others?"

"I exercised no command over what you find. I can only say I'm relieved the evil doers are gone, even though Hayes has served me roughly and murdered those who, brought before your justice, would have vouchsafed my innocence."

"You deny you were set to steal the ship?"

"I knew nothing until such time as we were ruptured and you'd abandoned us, along with the skipper. I learned then that Ariaen had plotted to throw us – you and I, the good Company men – overboard to go a-pirating off Malacca. I knew not whether you were dead, and prayed daily for your deliverance and return."

Jeronimus lowers his gaze as if having shyly confessed his love for some great lady. The lie is as palpable as it is breathtaking.

"And these others, the felons killed by Hayes?"

"They were scoundrels, all. They pressed me, as undermerchant, to authorise their behaviours. One had to do a great deal to save oneself."

"How is it I find you all attired in this pomposity of plunder, these tawdry uniforms trimmed with braid? If your filth describes the poverty of what has taken place here, the fact that you set about to dress alike hints at something darker and more boastful."

Hayes interposes: "The red may have concealed the blood they shed but it doesn't conceal the shit they're in."

I glance across at the soldier. It would be churlish to censure him, given his steadfastness, but there can only be one commander now.

"Take him below," I say, scarce able to look at Jeronimus for fear of appearing less than the authority I impose.

Ginger-bearded Wiebbe snaps his fingers and Cornelisz is rudely shoved.

"Heer Pelsaert," winces the prisoner, "have I not suffered enough at the hands of these ruffians who would seduce your credulity?"

"And make sure he's observed at all hours of the watch."

The ship's council rises from its bench to exhale a speculative whistle. There is evidently much to be gotten to the bottom of, but first there is the rump of the mutiny to crush. What with the number of the God-forsaken already crowding our decks, the prospect of tomorrow's confrontation brings little relish. Surrounding myself with the *Sardam*'s officers, I delay Hayes to skim him to our purpose. "We must act while the rebellion is in disarray. No doubt they'll be planning a reception for us."

"Sir, dangerous though these monsters have been, their star is on the wane."

"Well, equip ten of your men from the ship's armoury. Before dawn we'll approach the island where the remainder are encamped."

This captain of militia nods with appreciation for the cadence of command. I then turn to my companions of these discovery-thwarted weeks at sea. "Increase the guard," I say. "The prisoners at mast will whisper nothing. The lagoon should be closely monitored for any disturbance, our guns primed and a wick left burning throughout the night."

And for the first time in more than three months, Jeronimus and I share the soothing bobble of a ship like an old married couple long out of sympathy with the origin of their affection. Not that I ever felt entirely at ease with my subordinate. His glib tongue, increasing as the voyage continued, polluted my trust and made me regard him as if some devious suitor of my estate, impatient to supplant me should the opportunity arrive. During the fatigue which befell me after leaving the Cape, never once did he attend to see how I fared. It was as if that maritime interlude had conspired to ignore me, the noises of the ship – and yes, there was laughter – a declaration that I no longer existed. One day the seal on my cabin would be broken, my dust discovered and swept overboard.

And to think, now, that he was an apothecary, that he possessed the skills and bore a duty of care to me as his superior. The Company ought to have bonded us, and yet he would play my murderer! I wonder why he didn't attend me sooner. After all, a simple drug might have produced a most lethal effect. Just look at Asmat and that potion mistaken for wine. What heals may also kill, and Jeronimus could easily have screened his crime, his assumption of command deemed necessary and legitimate. But no, I was to learn – if I not already knew it – that he was a coward, passive to the extent of possessing a maniacal trust in fate. He fed off the consequences of what festered around him, consumed the carrion of a surrounding rage. If he were central to any plan at all it was to acquire a mastery of others in the language of their vicious instincts, of fuelling passions in the hope that he, too, might feel their reflected heat. Jeronimus was a spider who sidled into Ariaen's void.

Am I make-believing this? Am I seeking to justify my early dislike of my benighted understudy? If I longed to sleep in the reconciliation of all that I feared might go awry, I instead found my soul in thrall to what most soul's dread, the betrayal of an innocent faith and the disappointment of hopes we suspect, all along, to have been vain. Whatever ambition I had of retrieving the situation, it was gone. The horror, the imagining of what had taken place was bad enough, but to live with its subdued yet insinuating aftermath, this was the unremarked canker now at prey upon my mind.

My sleep is always burdened with curiosities, with visions that play the cousin among themselves and resemble steady thought. At other times I no longer know of what it is I dream or think. My inactive body becomes a couch of unsolicited imaginings, and the looting impulse of nightmare is never far away. I am forever confounded, twisting to confront a presence that so appals my rest but whose heckle avoids easy recognition. Something lurks in the shadow of my soul, something which is neither the illness I weaken from nor the mask of Jeronimus.

Jahangir suddenly alights from his throne with the facility of an acrobat, his slippered feet padding plumply across the marble floor. His amirs squeeze themselves between the columns of the audience hall, their citrus robes and downcast moustaches, coloured sashes and sea-shell turbans loaning an air of festivity to the bazaar-like atmosphere. Marvelling, still, at how the emperor has descended from his balconied preserve, my sight lingers on that vacated dais and, to its rear, a screen carved in the whitest alabaster and a cipher of harem curiosities. I'm both startled and unsurprised to imagine I glimpse Coen in the shadow of its forbidden portal. Even the nobles of the court seem

to alter with my every blink, their visages yielding to those of the good burghers of Batavia, men dressed in pigments contrary to their solemn character.
My kind might have considered themselves unduly harlequined, their bearing
compromised, if not for a saturnine manliness which displays a certain cannibal tendency.

"Pelsaert, are you attending?"

The emperor's humour is not to be kept waiting. "Majesty," I bow, and
on the way down, perceive the Seizer of the World to be somewhat shorter
than myself.

"Come man, after all your disappointing efforts to impress me I'm eager,
now, to see what you've come up with."

The audience hall is open to a cloister, something between a garden and
a parade ground. I see a breeze of countless heads, an emptiness of fountains.
To tell the truth, I don't know what I rightly perceive beyond the sun-bounced
stream of marble that flows against the hour. The emperor has waddled ahead,
knowing I must follow. There's a thing like darkness, a debility in the midst of
this creamy glare. Jahangir pauses; has apprised himself of something before I
can catch him up to explain. He turns to me with the prerogative confidence
of a first impression. "A turd doth not a tulip make. Don't you agree?"

"Your Majesty —"

But the turbaned ruler has resumed his examination of this cloth-torn
pollutant, constrained as it is to a single tile like some life-sized chess piece in
a game such as his father might have played with harem girls at Fatehpur Sikri.
I would fear for the emperor's life except that this thing of rags and sweat and
sullied flesh is securely chained. Only its eyes rove unfettered. They sport
with Jahangir, chancing. They dissemble from mine, knowing.

"Does it have a name?"

My heart beats for what is done yet not extinguished. I steer from the
amber light in Jeronimus's eyes and seek an ally in the diaphanous and pearl-
choked emperor. "None worthy of a man. More a beast."

"You're intriguing me, Pelsaert. Come, to business!"

Perhaps I can enlighten you.

"Ah, it speaks!"

And before I can intrude, a blow is delivered to the side of Cornelisz's face by a guard who, genie-like, materialises from nowhere then vanishes.

"It is not customary, however, to address me until invited to do so."

Jeronimus raises his head, by now habituated to pain, and smiles to conciliate the emperor. He gleans opportunity in the very risk of interview and, given half a chance, will insert himself into the delicate relationship I have with Jahangir to unsettle the emperor's faith in my judgement.

Jahangir steps slowly around Cornelisz's imprisoned form, their two minds withholding in the contrast of appearance. The emperor knows he cannot come unstuck. It is with the playfulness of one of his cheetahs that he allows himself an indulgence which can never harm him. He needn't draw close to be able to graze. "He – for yes, Pelsaert, this is surely a man – he smells like the abode of bats and owls. Have you kept him in some lightless Hindu temple?"

"Your Majesty, it was Hayes who captured the tiger. It was he who confined him to a hole in the ground."

The amirs, their oriental countenance momentarily recovered, are standing on a beach with their backs to the sea, the fluted arches shading them from the sun. The ruby in Jahangir's turban emits a piercing light. "This is no tiger, Pelsaert. A tiger is a game piece, forged of God. It is deployed to test the mettle of rulers. Its fur is not as this stench here. A tiger is what a king might slay to assert his kingliness, to demonstrate to Allah the worthiness of his human estate. And I am that state."

Standing behind Jeronimus now, he regards me in the amused surety of his rank. "This, Pelsaert," he spits, "is a sickness within the fold, an infirmity of the human herd. This," and pointing with his jewel-dusted finger, "is a rebel!"

Jeronimus's eyes lock on mine without the least surrender. He has no option but to endure the Great Mogul whilst attending to what I might next think.

"You would boast yourself a king," whispers Jahangir in Jeronimus's ear, "yet you deport yourself in rags. Your realm was but a sandbank in a moment of time, your palace no more than a hole in the ground."

"Ample for him who has to die."

Jahangir flinches as if inner stabbed, the genie unsummoned in chastisement of Jeronimus's unsubmissive tongue. "There was a sage, beloved of my father and myself, a Sufi of unusual grace and lofty understanding, whose heart was free from the attachments of this world, whose hermit needs were so reduced that others jeered at his thimble of prosperity."

"What became of him?" I ask, unbidden.

"Oh he died, as sages do. It is a grief in growing that those who teach us are the first to leave us. But tell me – you, thing – Pelsaert's nightmare – how came you by these words of a saint?"

"Am I any less of sovereign thought for having been captured by my enemies? Am I any less the chemistry of what I absorbed and might have proven if not for the spoliation of others?"

"Pelsaert, we have a philosopher in our keep!"

"Sire, his silvered tongue is but base metal."

"Then I'll ask again: rebel or mystic, how dare you so upright an opinion of yourself when others claim of you the worst of crimes?"

I presently notice that Lucretia stands with Coen in the shadow of the throne. She is wearing a white dress, somewhat soiled, and is without a jacket. I sense the press of harem women against the nearby alabaster screen.

"A man – a true man – must riot against the condition of his birth if it be inferior to the condition of his imagination. Only the supine would affect not to improve themselves."

I confess myself a little in awe of Jeronimus's spoken courage.

"You were born of nothing," remonstrates the emperor.

"You were born of greatness," shrugs the prisoner.

"You gambled to increase your estate."

"You gambled on changing little."

Jahangir's mind twitches, its impulse to strike the villain tempered by the novelty of this defiance. Most men – at least those brought before him in their passage from this world – are simpering before the imminence of death. The monarch now stands squarely before Jeronimus. "Why should I have entertained a change when my father bequeathed me all there was to have? My fate was dawned at birth. I was an emperor's son, God-allotted to the maintenance of that grandeur." And as if not quite satisfied with his response, he adds, "Mine has been a path difficult to improve on."

Jeronimus snorts and Jahangir – Lucretia flinching – strikes him with the back of his hand, his ruby ring opening the prisoner's cheek. Coen wonders why the emperor bothers to converse with Cornelisz at all. Just hang the pervert.

Jahangir recovers himself; seems a little abashed to have been unleashed in weakness by so bedraggled a creature. It's more seemly – and impressive, always – to strike the great.

Raising the un-guilty hand to the pearls at his throat, he says, "I am not ignorant of the workings of the Christian mind. My father and I entertained Jesuits for years, and the great Akbar – may his memory be sanctified – even created a mahal for religious debate. Yes, I don't mind a Jesuit; he's no more scheming or polemical than any mullah. And in doctrine I rather fancy the notion of redemption in death, that the renunciation of an evil life might open the gates of paradise. As a man who has travelled widely within his empire, I rather admire that freedom of destination. But you," and addressing both Jeronimus and myself, "you Dutch, you're altogether blinded to remain one thing, to be the excuse of what you are by the dictum of your faith. Of all the heresies, the notion that the fate of every soul is fixed at birth? Little wonder I prefer the company of the English, arrogant and petty though they be. At least when they drink they don't moralise unprofitably."

"But your Majesty," I cry, "I too have travelled your empire and seen little other than men fated to the condition of their birth, servile and accepting unto death."

Asmat Khanin now eclipses Lucretia at the pedestalled throne. Her lips are pursed and she is shaking her head.

"Pelsaert, I've a good mind to have you on your knees and next to this one. This is my realm, opinion is my prerogative. As for matters of faith, I do not interfere in their social consequence. Hindus are altogether beyond my reckoning when it comes to the slaveries they perpetuate among themselves. And I won't deny it isn't inconvenient having subjects who subject themselves to servitudes that serve the crown. But as for those who would be king, it is a little trite to rely on predestination. Fact of birth is one thing, belief in the unalterable is altogether something else."

"Why then would you consult an astrologer if not to sneak a peek at what is already written?" Jeronimus is grinning with the pomposity of one who deems himself wiser than his captor.

Jahangir is again more inclined to answer the question than punish its insolence. "It is customary to interrogate a moment of decision. Choice is not something you leave to chance."

"And of what substance is a stargazer?"

"A creature more ponderously elevated than he who deciphers messages in another's shit."

"Yet you, too, would have your stools examined."

"Ha, you smell as if you daily bathe in my corruption! But tell me, aren't you a dabbler in baser stuff yourself?"

"Ah my lord, we would have made fine drinking companions in the Abrolhos. As an apothecary, I would have fed your addictions."

"And plotted, in my addled state, your theft of what further belonged to me."

"My lord, you injure me."

"Not nearly so much as is about to happen. Pelsaert's trinket — the cameo — you stole it, hid it in your tent."

"I removed it to my safe keeping. Until such a time as we would be rescued."

"Except that you intended to destroy your rescuers."

"Quite right!" I interject.

"What then?" continues Jahangir, waving me aside.

"Yes, what then?" I echo.

"Ah!" barks Cornelisz, and glaring at me, "what credibility has that coward? He would unwrap Constantine's jewel in the nocturnal role of the ship and caress it as if it were his dick!"

"Is he not afraid to die?" enquires the emperor, turning to face me.

I cannot answer, knowing Cornelisz to be craven in his mortal fear yet bold in strategies to survive. He would prick the very conscience of his executioner and paralyse his arm with a mirror of doubt. I cannot speak for him because I, too, am afraid of the spectacle that awaits me. Yes, I am afraid of death.

"Pelsaert," interrupts Jahangir, "I say this kindly – you must learn to be cruel. You must learn to alienate that fellow-feeling which animates your scruples."

"Your Majesty, I bear this man no love."

"Ah, yes, but you need to explain him."

"He is beyond all reason."

"No one – and mark me, Heer merchant – no one is beyond a charge of reason. Only the savour of individual logic varies. He is no more like us than you or I resemble one another, yet we three have arrived through the womb and will share an inevitable parting from this life. He is not too distant an animal, and in that allowance I will grant you your voice to speak unkindly or otherwise. But actions are seldom sympathetic where more than one interest is concerned. You pride yourself on being a loyal servant of the Company yet I sniff secrets that you trade on the side. The Company has seen fit to promote you, yet its reward has proven a lean banquet. Look over there; see those in the farthest row, the turbans which crown no face?"

I behold a silhouette of onion-headed men against a sun-blinding sea.

"They, Pelsaert, are like you, fallen from grace, imperfectly in possession of what it is they've done to earn my enmity. But rulers are an indulgent lot. I'll redeem most in time – send some on a barefoot pilgrimage to China to purchase a plate, assign others the governorship of some ungovernable frontier fort. There are individuals, though, whose reason runs counter to the security of one's estate, whose ambitions imperil the docility of what I would have of them. The law of the hunt is but a refinement of the law of the jungle. A competitor is merely a controlled predator. Where there is no control there is rebellion. And rebels are possessed of all the reason on earth; they covet what another has. They would turn the world upside down in the attempt to steal what they didn't have the wherewithal to possess in the first place. They would displace you of your property and displace you of your life."

Jahangir turns to Cornelisz.

"This, Pelsaert, is not a mystery. This is the wrath of envy." And signalling his executioner, "*This* is a rebel."

"No!"

The headsman freezes in the steadying up-swing of his blade. Jahangir, his forehead wrinkling, turns to face the audience hall with its forest of lotus-fluted columns. The saline glare of the nearby ocean affects the penetration of his sight. He raises his hand like a visor to his turban. "Who, there, challenges my authority?"

"Have mercy, father."

Jahangir spins about to see Khusrav, his rebellious son, chained and kneeling upon the flagstone next to Cornelisz. "Confound you!" And then to the assembly: "Did I not spare his life, I who proclaimed a sovereign should deem no one his relative, not even his son?"

There's a scuffling noise, a suppressed cry from behind. As if annexed to Jahangir's celerity I witness, in his about-face, that the eyes of the prince have been thrust with needles. Cornelisz flinches, and even I marvel at the savagery of life enjoined here.

"No more!" That same voice – distinctly a woman's – issues from beyond the alabaster screen, its palpitating precinct. The courtly multitude holds its breath.

"And wherefore would I not destroy all enemies of the throne?" shouts the Seizer of the World.

"Rebellion is a rite of passage."

"Not in my house, it isn't!"

"In the ruling planet of our house, more than most!"

"I tell you, Pelsaert," he mutters, "these women of the zenana are not to be unattended."

I see with senses other than my eyes. The screen to either side of the throne is fluid with the glimmering opinion of those who are like players in the wings, a chorus of senior queens and dowager aunts. Even the great Nur

Jahan, empress above all others, disapproves of the dishes to be consumed at this cannibal feast. She has her eye on her husband's other son, Shah Jahan, that all-pervasive prince forever *not* at court, his sanguine loyalty harbouring an appetite for his brothers and his brothers' brood. I should have fancied myself in ancient Rome were I not in modern India.

"So," summons the emperor aloud, "what would you have me do?"

"Majesty empowers magnanimity," answer the women.

"What, free them?" And unbelieving, though ready to submit to the collective will of what no man other than he is permitted to cherish.

"Your eldest, my Lord, is punished, his confederates impaled in a lingering whisper of regret."

Jahangir turns to Khusrav, his needled eyes precluding a more terminal providence. The emperor is even inclined to sentiment. "'Tis a hard fate, Pelsaert, to become a father. And I must be a father to so many. But *this*," and pointing to Cornelisz, "this other?"

"He must confess his crime!" It is a fresh voice, and Asmat stands on the royal podium, fixing me with her stare for it is not *she* who speaks. The voice wears a fairer complexion, if also a more public note of accusation. Lucretia is ushered forward by the empress. Unlike the elaborately attired begums, her arms are bare, her flaxen hair like the bone-bleached Abrolhos. She stands proudly above a gathering unlikely to appreciate her distinction. Indeed, to have been tarnished, even against one's will, is to have lost one's lustre among this heathen lot. And yet she stands in contrast to the multi-dyed crowd like a jewel of the most precious simplicity, her eyes a clarity of rain. I am reminded of something a man departs home to find, his leave-taking forever a journey in nostalgia, of sought return to something that never really was. I sample the image of my kinswoman and am filled with admiration for her modest nobility. Surely this is a language we share. Surely this must beggar the preening rainbows of Hindustan.

I forget that Cornelisz makes this an unwelcome and unwholesome Dutch threesome. And Asmat, herself, continues to fix me with a stare that demands some explanation.

Who is she?

A woman from the ship.

Which ship? When?

She was aboard *Batavia*. It was during my return to the East.

You had already abandoned India — and me?

It was because of you, in the first instance, that I had to leave…

You loved her?

I loved the thought, perhaps, of loving her.

Don't toy with words!

I sigh, forever refining my approaches to the truth. Asmat, you were dead. She sat at table with me in the Great Cabin. There were always others, others who precluded any overture of affection. Besides, I was ill. Hindustan had loosened its fevers upon me.

Tut. But for the opportunity, you would have possessed her!

Asmat, I did not betray you aboard *Batavia*. It's hard enough admitting to sensuous thoughts, that frailty blinded me to the evil brewing. If I betrayed anyone, it was the folk I failed to protect. If you must know who I've slept with, her name is Guilt.

"Pelsaert," interrupts Jahangir, "I confess to finding the notion entirely foreign."

I see now that Coen is standing slightly to the rear of the emperor and near enough to Cornelisz to grasp him like a truculent schoolboy. Although I cannot read the Governor's expression, I sense his displeasure in having Dutch affairs paraded before this oriental circus, no matter how imperial its elevation. Any formal aspect he shows Lucretia is tempered by the desire to have her speak no more. Nur Jahan, not knowing who Coen is, despises him. His self-discipline appears friendless, and she pats Lucretia's shoulders. "Let the girl reclaim what was taken from her. Let him confess."

Cornelisz squints at the sun. This forced development makes him scowl. He shifts on his knees, his chains like overweighted jewellery. Khusrav is nowhere to be seen — no, there he is: Shah Jahan is escorting him towards a door in the courtyard wall, one arm thrown across his brother's shoulders in a gesture of comfort, the other concealing of a dagger.

"I have lived none other than as God ordained." The voice is whining, insinuating.

"You acknowledge then that there is a God?"

"You make me laugh, Commandeur. If I did it would make a sorry joke of your belief. What, He ordained all this?"

"You mock me as you mock God."

"You mock yourself! If God exists, He is not the creature of your faint imagining. If God exists, I am the very breath of what He allows. There is nothing I have done that God hasn't put into my heart. If God is perfect in virtue and goodness, then I am one of His angels upon this earth."

Coen yanks violently at the chain. The yowl subsides, the air smells of salt and blood.

Recovering, his eyes swollen with pain, Jeronimus slowly surveys the crowd, the distance between himself and Lucretia abbreviated in a tension of recognition.

"If God is unafraid of His handiwork," she says, "He will sanction you to speak the truth."

The audience nods approvingly and turns to the prisoner.

"I was kind to you," he whispers. "I wrote you sonnets and decanted Spanish wines. I touched you with the tenderness of a trembling youth. And still you were cold to me."

"You would purchase me to your loins – I who was married and in search of my husband – with stolen goods and threats of death."

"I never threatened you."

"Then what of what was said to me? *I hear complaints from the Captain-General that you do not comply with his wishes in kindness.*"

"That is true. I did complain to Zevanck."

"And he threatened me with the fate of the others unless I did what you wanted!"

"It wasn't meant to be like that. The women – all the women spared – they had a duty..."

"What duty was it mine to be raped?!"

Jeronimus winces as if seized in an irregularity he'd not contemplated. More than mutiny and murder, this monster had craved a queen equal to the possession of his delusional kingdom. For once he appears rueful and apologetic. He looks around and perceives the judgement of men, their preclusive opinion once a thing is done. "It is true," he says, "you are not to blame." Then, with an integrity I find nauseating as it is startling, "You were in my tent twelve days before I could succeed."

And with that declared, Lucretia stares at me with the contempt of a woman for whom a criminal has had to prove her worth when I, by my silence, have seemed to condemn her. Yet how might I declare my faith in her or understanding when little separates me in desire from Cornelisz?

The prisoner senses this. The old sneer returns as he twists his head to appraise me. "So I am to die for this? The fact that I possessed her and *you* did not?"

Impotence hinders the impulse to strike him.

"Neither of you have ever possessed me!" shouts Lucretia.

Nur Jahan shakes her head and glances at her husband as if to say, "Such infidels!" Asmat, in turn, swallows a humiliation more poisonous than the draft which killed her.

"It is not true," I quietly reply.

She retires beyond the alabaster screen.

"Asmat, wait!" I cry.

"Come, my friend," says Jahangir, tapping Cornelisz on the shoulder. "The time has come, and even the mighty may show compassion in the hour of another's death."

Jeronimus rises to his feet, now fetterless, and steps into the boat. As if genie-like, Jahangir's silent executioner is suddenly transformed into Wiebbe Hayes. This chesty and uncomplicated hero possesses the sanguine habit of officiating at the doom of men. I do not follow. Clouds deepen the shadows of the audience hall, and all the courtiers disappear. Even Coen and Their Majesties are no more. Only Lucretia remains, perched defiantly above the emptiness of the throne. And in the sculpture of that upswept balcony, it's as if she stands at the sternpost of *Batavia* herself, as if the ship were ploughing into the royal quarters of a dimension now vanished to me.

—ᴄ—

He sits as others have done at the edge of my bed:

"Brother Manuel and I travelled for weeks on end, the roads dusty with endless chapters of village life and the fatiguing company of strangers. Then, when the sameness of God's creation seemed unyielding, a moment would strike wherein its mantle would be shot with colours of such wondrous and intriguing hue that something was added to what a man might be disposed to know, even as it left him bereft of what it might likewise mean. I saw three cows standing guard over a sleeping dog at the juncture of a busy crossroads, a perverse nativity that cohabited with the indifference of a thousand heathen lives. Yet who was to say that it wasn't a shadow play, a sign perhaps that within the fabric of such commonplace, idolatry was never distant from the alphabet of Christ?"

Andrade is toying with notions that run counter to his schooling, his curiosity inclined to generosity where conception is not so Jesuit-closeted. I, too, have witnessed minute wonders, things I'd never thought to see and whose detail described departures from a bonded life.

"We were thirsty and took the opportunity to drink from a nearby well. The strangeness of our appearance – indeed, the strangeness of who we were – drew a crowd of giggling children. And still the dog slept on."

Does he really attend my bedside? Everything shifts with a seamlessness that has me seated opposite his narrative, the table between us polished, Andrade semi-silhouetted against the cloister's green flowering. I have never travelled to Goa, yet where else might I be? I'm his visitor, to be sure, yet given to the most peculiar sensation of attending a ghost.

"I was brought up to see Satan in everything that wasn't Christian, that wasn't of the true church. The many Dutch, like all separatists, were heretics in league with Lucifer."

I realise Andrade has no face. What I hear issues from the darkened obscurity of his cowl.

"Yet as a man I have widely loved as Christ once sought to love his fellows. I have found my neighbour more than companionable when all uniform was left at the door. You and I, Francisco, we have respected one another – there's more to our affable dog than dogma, eh?"

I smile to consider this fated man a friend. But why fated, and in what way a friend?

"And so even as I travelled among the heathen," he continues, "it wasn't difficult to contend that their vegetable sellers were no more than ignorant of where their prayers ought to have been directed, their families accosted by no greater evil than poverty, their routines no less daily than the lives of honest Christians. If the fume and tocsin of their sacrilegious temples were pollutants to the nose and ear, those rosaries of marigold were, by contrast, sweetening to the eye. Other than the diabolic sacrifice of animals, their compounds appeared no more harmful to the thoughtful traveller than a child's sandpit."

His hidden self pauses. I can tell he would like to believe in what he paints, but I have the feeling he's been censured. A judgement of sorts has been passed upon his encounters.

"What happened to you?" I ask.

"They were without the meaning of God..."

"Meaning what?"

There's a chewing sort of pause.

"We drank from the well and prepared to move on."

"And?"

"Our servants took umbrage at the delinquency of boys who fingered our saddle bags."

"The locals can be testing, I'll grant you."

Silence.

"Go on," I say.

"It could have ended badly. As it is, I'm reminded that the world is ill-tailored to the very enthusiasms that direct me in God's path."

"You're more an explorer than a priest. Your cloth allows you to travel where many are not permitted."

"My cloth marks me as a target."

"Your strangeness is your passport. There's nothing like playing God's ambassador to arouse the curiosity of a heathen prince, especially where that divine is unknown, its power untested. Believe me, the greatest danger comes from kith. Van Diemen is merely the most obvious of my would-be assassins. Surely you, too, have enemies within the militancy of your order?"

If a sigh can reach into the future, assuredly I hear it.

"Tell me," I beg, "what happened?"

"One of our companions – the layman who commanded our baggage – he reached for his blade. There was a reluctance, at first, among the natives to understand what was happening. A woman cried out. She was robed in white as if in mourning or destined for the pyre herself. Whether she had a son or a grandson among them, I wouldn't know; only that a murmur of fear presently rippled the community, that they now saw us for what we were, strangers of a dangerous complexion. The men began to shout and cluster, although the only weapon drawn was that of our compatriot. I hastened to him, hissed that this was no place to assert we were Heaven-sent. *What about our luggage?* he remonstrated. *The bags are secure*, I replied, *we are not!* Brother Manuel stood there open-mouthed and trembling. Because of the sneerful forwardness he oft displayed, I'd always imagined he would watch my back. Instead – and though not shirking in his love of God – he reacted to the unbidden with the fluster of a startled hen."

"Would that not be true of any man surprised?"

"Forgive me, my judgement is terse. Our advent was poorly done. We had turned the smooth into rough."

I nod more in sympathy than understanding. "What next?"

"Nothing. The community stood in sullen witness as we gathered ourselves and moved on. We were a danger to them – as we were a danger to ourselves – and best allowed, like a serpent, to slither away. Only the old woman maintained her harangue, whether in anger at us or the inaction of the villagers, I couldn't tell. It was then that I saw a white cow bucking and rearing and chasing others, its horns lowered. The dog opened its eyes and raised its head for the first time. The omens for what we might accomplish were not good."

"But you arrived at your destination?"

"We journeyed on through a now back-turned land. Its population, like the trees themselves, grew sparse, the tiny wooden houses all bolted door and shutter. It was as if we had become invisible. Men chewed and spat in the shadows; women adjusted their shawls and passed without acknowledgement, their ambulations steady and as casual as the cattle nearby. Despite the increasing cold, the sun overhead burned our faces and dimmed our vision. Against the stony backdrop we often heard, before seeing, the agitation of trotting goats, the herders – invariably children – cracking their animals along with sticks. We were in constant thirst despite the endless ravines whose streams cut a starchy taste from the rock. Such waters, when crossed and gulped by man and mule alike, troubled us with their disconsolate ice, our cramping bowels a sudden and inopportune gruel.

"Whenever we paused to enquire of the path ahead, the intelligence was chattering and baffled. When we asked after Shambhala (as several of the geographers at Goa had labelled this rumoured kingdom) we were greeted with a silencing withdrawal or confused ignorance that made us wonder of the mountains ahead, that distant and frosted wall in the rarefied air. I believe, Francisco – as I believe you know this, too – that there is a hunger to fulfil what we choose to imagine. I had seen the waste of Agra, its unattending multitudes and jostling nationalities, and had felt the place too fraught with worship and too pompous of rule to reflect on the true Lamb of God. I had imagined a place unaffected, a kingdom worthy and awaiting Christ's teaching – yes, a temporal chalice in which to pour His Holy Blood. But of the local guides we enlisted to convey us from valley to valley, their knowledge was constrained to the domain of a two-day's march, their appetite to assist diminishing when, instead of silver or whatever it was they anticipated, we presented them with copies of God's Holy Writ."

The cowl grows silent.

We are ill prepared for so much in life, and I'm reminded of Jahangir's careful scrutiny of gifts, the weighing of their worth in a fashion bereft of sentiment. Only paintings – including, of all things, portraits of the Holy Family – cultured any feeling in him. Like Andrade with his bibles, who did I really think I was going to satisfy with my toys and Nuremberg clocks? And Loos and Pelgrom, had I merely abandoned them, empty handed, to barter for their lives with empty trinkets? What commerce existed in that vast and empty land where neither God nor civility dreamed of residing? And in my recollection of that continent, despite the contrast of its arid skies and reddened earth, I think I can empathise with Andrade's disappointment. Every cove and depression of its shoreline which promised safe landing would have been matched by mountain passes that led to yet further grandeurs of indifference. Where human life was glimpsed, it remained remote or fleeting. Yes, as adventurers both, our journeys were fraught with isolating difficulties.

And so the memory of who he was is once more interrupted. In fact the chronology of my thoughts is altogether baffled by intrusions of unsummoned accent and embarrassment. How galling is it to find the gallery erupt with catcalls that disrupt my recitation. As a writer of facts I was attentive to an order of telling. Wasn't my history of the Great Moguls testament to this, even though its pages were smuggled into the reputation of another? I realise, Pieter, we weren't literary rivals; nonetheless you owe me a great debt. Indeed, so irksome was my stolen self that I prepared, in private and with consummate care, that *Remonstrantie* which was so well received by the High and Mighty back home.

Yet as I lie here now, the story I endure seems all a-muddle. The fear of being misunderstood or judged has loosened my control on expression. To entertain a thought is to entertain its theft. I find myself chasing demons who jeer at me from the safety of a forgotten moment. The measure of my once assumed success now blooms in lurid episodes I fail to repress, scenes of such mocking intensity I find myself shouting, as if into the wind, for all the world to pause and hear me out. But no one attends; leastways none who would not want to do me harm or remind me of a supposed injury. I am losing my grip on my narrative.

—ᴕ

"Here, sip this," she whispers.

My eyelids crocodile-part with the heaviness of one still drugged.

It should be Hartanti — who else? She's been my nurse, slave and companion now for how long? Of course I might wish it Asmat. But Asmat is dead. At the very least I still know this. The face before me is difficult to recognise, its eyes brim moistly in the gloom like a camel's. There's the smell, too, of a camel blanket, its mustiness oiled with perspiration.

"Come, drink," she says again. "It will keep up your strength. We still have a long way to go."

"Lucretia?"

She doesn't answer. The cup is at my lips, but it's as if she has turned to begin tidying up my chamber. For a moment I fancy we are both aboard *Batavia* and alone in the Great Cabin. "Where are the others?" I query.

"About their business," drifts a voice as unconnected to where she stands as the cup now pressed to my lips. The taste is sharp and colic, and for a moment I imagine Jeronimus works in a room beyond the door, grinding pastes and philtres with a duty that is polite rather than charitable. Lucretia and he have been talking, negotiating what must be contributed to my comfort. They don't particularly like one another, nor do they particularly care for me, but we're all constrained to the roles we play.

"Where do you go from here?" I ask her.

"My husband is in Arakan." Her hair gleams fair, and her apron ties describe a bow about her waist.

"He wasn't here when we arrived?"

"None remained when we arrived."

I make an effort to sit up straight, and find myself on a cold bench in the chequerboard hallway of my mother's house. Lucretia is a servant, the sort that mistresses fault and masters favour. She is indeed comely. "Where's Maria?" I ask, my voice childlike.

"Your mother disapproved of her. We all knew how sick you were. We all wanted what was best. But your mother was adamant: *Come Maria, the child must be dressed and breakfasted and ready for his grandfather. Quick now, Francisco, out of bed!*

"But you're no servant," I object. "I've seen you — you've servants of your own."

"Zwaantie, you mean?"

I'm not certain of what I mean.

"Francisco, things have changed. Whatever the life I once possessed..." She pauses, wistful. "My husband was ambitious and, as a good wife, I was ambitious for him. But the lure of the Indies has proven fatal. Boudewijn remains in Arakan; he's buried there."

She then studies me harshly. "But you knew that, didn't you. Even before you returned to the Abrolhos. You knew that my marriage was as ruined as my dignity, that my servant had become another's queen and I another's slave. It's a topsy-turvy world. Even your veiled lust was an insult to what ought to have prospered. Or maybe you were just a symptom of the truth out here, that one can't be too squeamish in the scramble for a different kind of decency. Did you know my husband was once a diamond polisher? He used to purr that I was his most precious jewel. Do you know what he was doing in Arakan?"

Her question makes me uneasy.

"We've all deluded ourselves," she continues. "At an opportunity of my choosing I'll be returning to Holland."

"You wouldn't dream of staying here — as my companion?"

"Something less than your wife, you mean? A servant still?"

"No, I only meant... Forgive me. Everything has been so compromised. I daren't have hoped —"

"Do not hope, Francisco, even though your journey is yet to finish. Drink of that which eases you but is deathly to others; you'll need all your strength to meet what comes. And though you're surely done for, yet I and those who populate your dreams will watch with curiosity as you choose the humour of your passing. It's not so terrible a thing to die; it's nothing any can escape. And when I can stomach, again, the notion of being marooned at sea for months on end, I will return to the Fatherland in the very ship, perhaps, which conveys your will and testament. I know it's a thing you've already composed. Your mother will be needy of its consolation."

"You know this — this which was entertained during a brief despair?"

"You're a practical man, a man of furtive preparations."

"But I want to be inspired, to be impetuous!"

"Haven't you lived impetuously?"

"It feels like so much failure."

"Between how you live and what you'd have others perceive of you, there resides the contradiction you fear before God. It is the inheritance of Adam."

"And yet you proved no Eve to tempt me."

"I was married, Heer Pelsaert. I counted on you as my protector during those long months at sea."

"Didn't it cross your mind? Didn't we share an intimacy of sorts?"

"I never permitted you to unfasten me. Boudewijn — unknowingly dead — awaited."

I think a moment, consigned to the stew of my sick-bed. And to think is to wriggle in recognition of what an embarrassment *Batavia* was. Not so much the loss of the ship itself; no, that was almost excusable in its unforeseen rendezvous with an invisible reef. Rather, I'm ashamed of the existence that was lived aboard; moreover, an existence dreamed in all its sordid imagining. In the drift towards calamity, even I lost sight of how encompassing the universe of blame might be. The ledger of accountability permits no private trade, yet how often did I succumb to reveries that concerned none but myself and those with whom I might have chosen to effect some dangerous congress. To think that I could have so forgotten myself, to have so allowed my member to stiffen — paralysed though I was for much of the time — in lustful conceit of a woman who didn't belong to me! But when has that ever been an obstacle? Someone's wife, perhaps someone's pimped or procured daughter — have I never sought any who I might legitimately call my own? Lucretia – oh yes, quite beautiful to me as the days accrued and our world shrivelled on its axis! We were all so far from home and in circumstances which suspended the usual commerce of manners. Indeed, as I review my days before their threatening closure, I see that everything deemed politely normal was subsumed in an improvising allegiance to adventure. I have pursued my adult majority like a mercenary in the employ of a mercenary enterprise. The caution accorded children to grow into respected citizens of the Republic has scarcely found expression in the morals of the Company. 'Tis all hypocrisy and blind eye except when something goes spectacularly wrong. Then all is obloquy for what might otherwise have been privately overlooked if not for a public need of distancing censure.

And if I strove to apply myself to some fraternal value of responsibility, how do I plead in what I failed to protect? How might I admit to my shortcomings in the first place? To be ambitious is to countenance little in the way of obstacle. To have succeeded in ambition may give pause, perhaps, to some estimate of the cost. As it is, my legacy has been abetted by a chronicle of cover-ups. Yet am I any the less honest for that? Have I inflicted harms I'm not already rueful of? Lucretia, yes, I did want her. Like many a man I was bound to be captivated by the sky-rinse of her eyes. Her scent was the entertained opportunity of another bed, her couch a raft of life rather than this mortal cot. Lust is not rape. To sensualise in one's mind is not the equivalence of capture and enslaved concubinage.

"Have you quite finished?" she asks, her arms folded. I fear she's been spying my thoughts. But no, she's impatient to effect what is required and be gone. "Come Maria, Heer Pelsaert must be dressed and ready for his grandfather."

"But Opa is dead," I cry.

"Don't be silly. He's coming to collect you."

"Madam," interrupts Maria, presently the very image of Hartanti but with an accent of the North Sea, "the Commandeur is too ill to move. See how the blood sweats from his pores!"

"Nonsense." Lucretia is staring through rain-streaked panes onto the pallid light of winter. Cornelisz stands outside amidst the breeze-snapped washing, the courtyard famished of colour. "How do I look?" she turns, and pinching her cheeks. "Opa must think well of me if I'm to restore my fortunes."

"Madam, I cannot tell," and this gentle woman, once my nurse, wrings her hands. "I was a fragment of his boyhood."

The light dims a little — a winter cloud, the hour, I do not know. Only that Lucretia attends my dreaming, here, in Batavia. Can it be she really *has* come to say goodbye? "Lucretia, don't go."

"Francisco," and she makes an unhappy face, "I can't be expected to stay when you, too, are preparing to leave." Then, more soothingly, "I shall accompany your papers to Europe. I promise. I shall trouble your aged mother with news of your departure. I shall watch as she catches at memories I do not share and suffers a grief that, perhaps, neither of us feels. And as a widow myself, I shall marry Opa."

"But Opa *is* married!"

"One minute he is dead, the next he's married — which would you have it?"

"There was a wagon. The morning was cold. Jeronimus was standing in the courtyard — no, that can't be. There was mama, to be sure, and Maria too — she'd raised me from my bed. I can still taste the heat that fouled my breath, the chill that stove my ribs. But my sisters were nowhere to be seen."

"Your mother was newly re-wedded. It's the fashion of widows in a life so fettered with death."

"But surely your beginnings were more steady than mine?"

"My dear Commandeur, don't you consider it strange that anyone should venture East unless compelled? I never knew my father. My mother remarried when I was two but died when I, like you, was still a child. I stayed on with my stepfather — a sea captain, somewhat like Jacobsz — until he, too, died. Then there was nothing for it but a husband. Yet even he disappeared. I don't rightly know where Arakan is. All I'm given to understand is that he was dealing in slaves. For the Company."

You could do worse than marry Marta van Luyck. They were Opa's words as we left my undernourished infancy behind and sat side by side in the stumbling wagon. My grandfather had an eye for opportunity's purse. I was but a boy; he was a veteran of life's vagaries and danger.

"Your grandfather has forged a career out of widows; I, too, intend to distance fate and find another husband."

"And I?"

"I'm afraid, Francisco, your capital is spent."

"But I've no wife, no children to endure."

"Don't speak to me of children," she stiffens. "My three babies were surrendered, all, to God before I quit Amsterdam in search of Boudewijn. And to think that the lot of you lusted after my death-spawning womb!"

I swallow, humiliated by an offence it would be dissembling to disown.

"Pray for the salvation of your soul, Francisco, and give thanks to God you were spared that infant calamity." And as if to wither any objection, she adds, "Orphaned as a child, I was orphaned as a parent! Widowed before I knew of it, I was next assaulted then kept in a state of rape. In the justice of what followed, there was little by way of apology or understanding. Not even *you* could look at me on the Abrolhos without a sense of silent shame."

"I'm sorry – truly."

"What does it matter now?" she sighs, and calming a little. "I'm thinking of my future, Francisco, and that is something we cannot share."

I sense a sadness that is not unkind. "Was there not a moment of affection between us?" I ask.

She looks at me with an autumnal resolve that betokens my winter more than hers. "It was altogether too sorrowful and menacing an interlude to play at love. Everything I had known was receding in the wake of *Batavia*, the bluster of the North Sea giving over to an unimaginable calendar of distance. Yes, I did feel for the loneliness of my station. And I did find your company warming in my too-starved circumstances. But even flirtation lost its savour in the rancour of souls too long imposed upon. *Batavia* was too tiny a conveyance for too vast a fortitude. When something went wrong, everything went wrong. To deny another's appetite was to feed another's wrath. Far from any thought of sex, you became a bedridden sort of ally. Even now I must tend your lips with medicine and remind you of how weak you are. Yes, whatever we might have entertained was an aberration, a moment's fancy before the world recalled us to who we were at the approach of that impending storm."

As I lie here, looking up at her, is it simply true that I've little wanted to be thought ill of? Did I properly consider Lucretia other than to imagine myself between her legs? That she was equal born, this would only have enhanced my self-respect in a conceit that was less than respectful.

Then everything became filth: the dangerous innuendoes, the nocturnal assault in which she was smeared with shit — that entire stench-of-a-ship now unwashed in sinew and in wit. Even *I* was an abomination to myself, sweated and unbathed, my breath a stink of deliriums and abandoned caring. How might dalliance have prospered in that putrescence which led to rape and murder?

"Your story is no longer mine, Francisco," and she reaches for my brow. "Yours is a life already lived."

"Must we part?" I hunger, and knowing that what I seek is the salvation of all my failed enterprise, that in this white-fleshed cousin, whose race is no barrier, I might redeem what I failed to protect in Asmat.

"Perhaps a student of these times will one day chronicle your tale. In the meantime I must pursue my struggle, just as you must prepare for the road ahead."

"But Ma'am, look how he stews — he's unfit to travel!"

"Nonsense Maria," and Lucretia turns away. "His grandfather will soon be here. I've a new husband to think of, and Francisco must attend to his whores."

"Mother?" I cry. "Maria?"

"Mother Maria and by all the saints in Heaven, this one has a fine arse!"

The other women laugh.

"Hey Croock, your language!"

"Hey Croock, yourself. Since when have you become squeamish?"

"We'll have no popish recitals here, right, Heer Pelsaert?"

"Ah, the Commandeur's a man of the world. It's even likely he was conceived in the Roman faith."

"Take care," remonstrates Sambrix and I, too, find my breathing stifle.

"Oh come off it, you simpleton. Half of Amsterdam was born south of the border. You're from Antwerp, isn't that right, y'r honour?"

"In a place like this we're all from some place else," I laugh, and Pieterge tickles my ear.

Croock slams his palm down on the bench and hollers for another jug. In the pipe-fume of evening it's impossible not to feel a little fuddled and dry of mouth. Yet my blood stirs at the proximity of Willem Jansz's wife. She's been slow to judge and quick to court me. Having just this fortnight returned from the Abrolhos, the flattery of lust is a sweet antidote to the tribulation of recent months.

Sambrix, despite his Calvinist disdain of Catholic speech and manners, has his hand beneath the bodice of a woman whose name I can't retain, whose skin is oily (not that this is unexpected in Batavia's Christmas stew) and whose leer betrays an absence of several teeth. Still, it's the thighs that count, and the lass is satisfactorily proportioned. Croock's woman is altogether more restrained and shadowy. There's a hint of age, a maturity faintly mocking even as he surreptitiously fingers her sex. We're like boys at a bordello except that the tavern is more public, a circumstance that makes me uneasy. Myself, I'm like a widower who's discovered a taste for its liberating advantage and looks nervously askant to see whether others have discerned this appetite. Pieterge has been well and truly tried, but it's not hard to see why anyone wouldn't have wanted her at the earliest. In her thirty years upon this earth she's been married a good proportion of that time. Jansz, her current husband, is away in Ambon. He's what I've been, a respected Company merchant. But now — after the delays and hardship caused by *Batavia* — I'm about to present my credentials to the Council. Yes, I'm about to become an Extraordinary Member of that august body! This will shit Van Diemen — to have to sit at table with me, to be denied the opportunity to strangle my voice before it enters the room. And Pieterge Jansz no doubt sides with my suit; is forging a connection. In a business where husbands regularly die, she sees the virtue of a Councillor in the wings. And I? I too play this game. Another's wife is the freedom to make one's excuses and move on. Yes, life becomes secretive and episodic…

"Come on, y'r honour, no gloomy meditations, eh? Let's toast!" And Croock seizes the jug and sloshes gin into a round of cups. "To the eternal anatomy of women! Now there's something to praise God for."

"Hey, in the name of that very God, keep your voice down," hastens Sambrix, just as keen to fuck but looking to see who else might spy his craving. I'm reminded of the watchful shadows at Fatehpur Sikri and feel cheapened in the contrast.

Pieterge yawns as if signalling it's time she and I departed. But Croock is having none of that. It's he who's introduced us. It's he who introduced himself to me as I stepped ashore with my cargo of villains and spoiled goods. *Commandeur — sir — I've been commissioned to help billet the rescued, but I see…* His eyes had been readied for a spectacle of privation; he wasn't prepared, though, for the manacled troop that filed from the *Sardam*. His mind was capable of assuming that someone might be charged with negligence concerning the shipwreck — as a Company man himself, he was not unfamiliar with its custom of declared crime and selected victim — but so many? *Sir, is everything alright?* he'd whispered, and I found the tone of his superfluous query a comfort. It wasn't long before he'd provided me with refreshment — and a woman. It was almost two years since I'd had the pleasure, and the weight of recent misery had become so habitual that this manifestation had seemed, at first, an insult. But older habits die harder still. I need only converse with myself on the subject to reawaken a denied lust. Pieterge had a lovely bosom and openness of thigh, her bed was heaped with freshly laundered linen. At first I was ashamed of my appearance, the scabbiness of my maligned body and its weathered lesions. But she was generous, a traveller also of life's unpredictability. And despite the craftiness I concluded of her willingness to bed me, I felt her impulse to overlook my damaged form momentarily heal me — and perhaps something in herself as well — of an ailment which, like tears, could be wiped away in the press of love. My most vivid memory of Jansz's wife is linked to that bedchamber of soothing contact, its afternoon light a syrup of forgotten initiations. It calms me, even now, to think of the gratitude I felt. Only it couldn't last.

Sambrix was still fondling his girl on the sly. Croock knew how the night would end and was in no hurry to unbuckle himself. "Honestly, y'r honour, Sambrix is the biggest squib I've ever met, a man with his eye all too fixed on the door."

"Bugger you, Croock, I just don't trumpet what others might get snitchy about."

"*He-he*, I take him everywhere. He's the perfect stooge. Too stupid not to tag along, too squeamish not to keep an eye out. Fun without fear, that's me! Fear without fun – ah my dear Sambrix…"

Amidst this good-natured bicker I feel almost adolescent, and in the gap which has opened up between who I was and who I am, I'm beginning to sympathise with Sambrix. To play the youth as one grows old, 'tis best to play the game in private. And again I glance at Croock's woman. She's experiencing nothing new or replenishing in this, and I suspect she may be a purchased whore. *But aren't we all?* the question seats itself at our table.

"I'll tell you, y'r honour, there's not enough pleasure in Batavia."

"Come, the place is awash with gin shops. It smells like a juniper forest –"

"Yes, when it doesn't smell like a dung heap! But you're a simpleton, Sambrix."

Pieterge laughs and Sambrix's strumpet stirs as if unsure whether she's to be called upon to speak.

"All I'm saying is, Batavia has too few advantages for so many rules. If it's not the Company it's the fucking Church Council – oh *do* keep your hat on, Sambrix; you can't be burned for heresies here. But y'r honour, that hardly makes us any freer. I don't know what they think human enterprise is, but any man who exerts himself to journey half way round the globe is entitled to complain a little and drink a lot. Hey, isn't that so? And as for companionship, we're all on tight rations here. We might bully the natives and trade in everything from spices to slaves, but when the sun goes down there's bugger all to keep us at home. And what home? What sort of place is this? Jewel of the East, my arse!"

"Careful who you speak in front of," smiles Sambrix stickily.

"The Guv'nor here," whispers Croock, leaning close and referring to me, "he knows what sort of place Batavia is, don't you y'r honour?"

"To speak plain, I don't really know the town anymore. I was in Hindustan for several years, then back in Holland before the recent voyage…"

The table falls silent. No one wants to touch on a subject that may offend. I rather feel for them in their embarrassment and rashly add, "Whether township or shipwreck, Batavia seems destined to play into the hands of the Devil!"

"There, you hear, Sambrix? From the mouth of the Guv'nor 'imself! 'Tis an unnatural place, and all the more bitter in pretending otherwise. Pretence is never pleasurable. And those fucking predikants, sticking their noses into other people's business and peddling an Almighty who's got no time for the likes of you and me. Why should I bind myself in the service of an end I can never enjoy? I tell you, this shitty outpost is more a penal colony than some new Amsterdam – don't do this, don't do that – and its punishments don't fit the clime!"

Croock laughs at his own joke and the others glance at me to determine whether they are safe or not. But how can I indemnify them when I, myself, feel a current of censure in the manoeuvring of unseen enemies? "Drink up," I say, and finish my own cup at a swallow. I give Pieterge's hand a squeeze and wish us invisible to the scrutiny of this cooped-up port. Then the toothless wench pipes up, "I hear Zwaantie Hendricx has been released from the Castle."

Croock leers at her. "Now why the fuck would you mention her?" I can't tell if he wants to protect me or hide something.

"I don't know," she giggles nervously, "it was just something to say."

"Come on Croock, leave her be," and Sambrix wraps his arm around her shoulders. "Let's all have another drink."

Croock's woman yawns but in signal of little more than boredom. As for me, I'm nettled by the mention of Zwaantie, not that I don't daily think of everything connected with *Batavia*. But to have been released without telling me, what does that imply?

"Well Guv'nor, you're out of all that now. The rescue's done, the wicked punished or soon to be, and the likes of that whore of no account or future."

"Unless she marries the likes of one of you gentleman," announces Croock's woman.

"What, after hearing she's serviced 'alf the felons aboard the Guv'nor's lost transport? Christ almighty, she'd fairly crawl with the pox!"

Even Sambrix grins, abashed to think that a man could become that desperate, and resuming an absent fondle of his companion.

But Croock's woman is not to be deflected. She knows – as we all know – that life's elementary principle, especially at this distance, is to propagate alliances with whomever comes to hand. "What, you think you're any better? Fie! – a gentleman will take up with a whore and a lady a fishmonger for all the permanence a wedding in these parts affords. And it's not just that Hendricx woman. There's she as was once her mistress, and the predikant's daughter as well. Widow or child, a female needs a protector, but the market's a rough trade. Even *with* a husband," and she eyes Pieterge, "there's scarce little of the comfort we'd like to imagine."

"Upon my word, I come out for a bit of fun and find myself sullied!"

"Tut, I'm permitting you liberties, aren't I?"

Even I smile at Croock's mock wounding, aware of the advantage to be had in the possession of another's wife. Indeed, it's Pieterge this time who says, "As if it's not chancy enough coming all this way in search of a better life, your husband then scampers off, wriggling with apology – for it's the Company's fault, don't you know – to some other posting where I've little doubt he's screwing some blackamoor."

And we all laugh for the frailties that define reality. Ours are make-do sorts of family, circumstantial and opportunistic.

"There are none who are sacred, that's for certain."

"What are we to do?"

"Eat, drink and make merry, eh, for in this accursed stew we will surely die."

"That's the spirit, speaking of which – hey, we need another pitcher over here!"

And we fold back like petals to the sun, uncaring for the moment of anything but the moment itself. *Do not speak to me of love*, Lucretia might have said. Well I don't speak of love. I don't speak of anything. It's best I remain silent, fixed on nothing and on no one. I feel for Pieterge's hand without looking at her. The tavern is a gloom of other presences, of folk congregated in abstinence of anything worthy. The wet season simmers the pulse, and the imminence of Christmas – this oft forgotten token of who we are – is bizarre and disorienting. Thunder rumbles overhead like the report of gunnery, and I draw my face away.

Who is it?

I see myself as I often do these days, a player caught in scenes I've not properly rehearsed, whose habit of lingering in the moment un-guards me against that which I do not see coming. *No one. Least...*

Francisco?

Medari knows I travel this way. I've had to bear with his company more than once.

This person, he is here? He follows you even here?

I am ever followed. I am ever being watched.

It was Maartens. I can see it now. It was Maartens all along, his simpery face like an apple in that orchard of sterner fruit. On the road to Kashmir, in places of the most arid vacuum, the tedium of march was often startled by milestones of such shocking spectacle that you couldn't help but pause to study what the eyes discerned but one's soul reviled to witness. Mortised into their conical structure, with faces that no longer saw and whose expressions were anything but at peace, the severed heads of enemies – whether criminal or rebellious, I was never sure.

How is it so many die, and so easily, beyond the domain of my own struggle? Whilst I daily seek some personal ratification, others daily lose their heads, the violence of which deprives them of all voice. For thirty years a man may live like any other, then at a blow that ordinariness is cut short and he contributes his grimace to that unholy tower. It's the ultimate and strangely anonymous pagoda erected to impotence. Yes Maartens, a severed little visage, a bit player in the imperium of a machine that only notices an individual when it has a notion to repress him. And mark me, the Church is every bit as castigating as the Company or State.

"Heer Pelsaert, you have been summoned to account for your behaviour with the wife of one, Willem Jansz."

I'm certain Batavia's Church Council busies itself out of boredom.

"What do you have to say?"

"I have nothing *to* say," I reply, peeved that I should have to answer at all to the accusation of some snide predikant who happened to be skulking in the shadows of a place his sanctimony ought never to have lured him.

"Do you deny improper congress with Willem Jansz's wife?"

"I deny doing anything that isn't sanctioned by the custom of this place."

"I must warn you, sir, God takes a dim view of local custom. Likewise the Company, as God's agent, is unsmiling in what its servants fail to observe." And I realise now, because I didn't know of him then, that I'd failed to perceive Maartens seated behind the others in clerkish attendance. Yes, much like Salomon, he was writing it all down, learning to know me before I'd had a chance to perceive him.

"You need not lecture me in what the Company expects," I say. "I've been schooled in its nursery. I have been obedient to the extent that I now command obedience –"

"Steady, Heer Pelsaert. Your pride ought not command ill-usage."

"And what ill-usage might I affect? Look at me, look at my eroded spectacle! It's difficult to discipline my wits when I don't possess the strength to restore or discipline my body."

"It should not prove difficult, then, for you to end your unchaste relations with the woman, Pieterge."

Even I don't see the difficulty, other than I despise being lectured to as if some misdemeanant schoolboy. In any case I detest this sort of publicity. I've spent a lifetime trying to make a name for myself – now I find myself spoken of in the same breath with the likes of Cornelisz, my fame now linked to the infamy of *Batavia*, and my every recreation spied upon. Where was the censure, made good, of these moralising humbugs when real crimes were being perpetrated? Where was the levelling hammer of Church law when Cornelisz ran amok? Gijsbert was of little sway, a hand-wringing ball-lessness of a man who, the minute he is saved and conveyed here, infers to anyone with a will to listen that I was somehow complicit in the disaster! Predikants are a base metal which tarnishes the Word. Little wonder the Whore of Rome thrives when our good Protestant burghers content themselves with the significance of crumbs at carnage's banquet.

But enough of why they riled me, these unctuous fools. I was anxious lest my enemies manipulate a censorious Church Council to undermine my admission to the very highest ranks of the Company. I was anxious, too, not to have Lucretia learn of my dalliance. Not that I was ashamed of Pieterge — far from it. No, it was something other, something rooted to the moment when, with Wiebbe and his troops, I first stepped ashore on Batavia's Grave-yard to liberate those who were left. I could scarce bring myself to look at Lucretia, such was the change her ordeal had wreaked. I could scarce look upon any who'd been pressed to whoredom, such was the shame I felt in hav-ing been unable to protect them. I was to remain officiously aloof or ill by turns, and that is how I passed those purgatorial weeks of salvage. Now here I was, in Batavia, and in danger of being pettily scandalised, of being seen to appear callow and self-serving.

I don't think I shall ever see Lucretia again, and I think it best our fates conspire at that.

Dutifully I surrendered Pieterge and dutifully she surrendered me. Her hus-band was returning from Ambon, an island where the ghosts of murdered Englishmen and of Bandanese enslaved were the repercussion of our merciless quest for nutmeg. Perhaps that's why I favoured India over the island trade. It was too big and too land-locked in its self-importance to be bullied by the likes of us. All the atrocity I witnessed there was oriental in its origin. I was a merchant on a mission, not a conqueror.

In any case the time had come for me to present my credentials. The Governor and his Council were my compass and reward. I presently forgot how perilous my near approach had been, how afraid I'd felt of being wrecked by the accursed shipwreck itself. Yes, time to starch the collar and dust my coat, to bear myself with a carriage that refuted illness and catastrophe. This was my day!

Although I counted Specx a friend and had been ill at ease, like everyone, in the presence of Coen, I nonetheless wished the dead Governor here to witness how far I had risen in his service. Although we'd met but rarely — and not at all since my assignment to India, save for that ravaged interlude as I stepped ashore from the privations of the Timor Sea — the man possessed an aura which commanded grateful obedience. I'll always picture him in his breastplate, his demeanour as curt as its blue steel before the rising smoke of Jacatra, that native pyre essential to his reinvention of the world. He had plans that were more audacious and lasting than the un-picturing gamesmanship of the many who surrounded him. And if I, too, had had early dreams, I confess they were of a youthfulness that conjured no certainty other than that I must leave home to realise their shape. Still, through the resolve of many challenges and my toil in strange and remote places, I wanted to convey the weight of this to Coen and say: *Yes, I too have breathed and felt such things! And while my passage to this moment may have been less exalted than yours, truly have I attained the wisdom of what experience may afford and earned the right to join your Council.*

But when I fronted that hemispheric mirror of the High and Mighty, the oriental reality of an occidental dream, its atmosphere was heavy with the spice of something overripe. Specx seemed like a friend I had inexplicably offended. Indeed, in that cramping darkness I would no sooner have presumed to have called him Jacques than enquire of the now-departed Coen whether he had a room to put me up for the night. The affinity I'd felt, the assumption that we shared some brotherhood of ambition, vanished in the chancel gloom of the Council chamber. Furthermore, Van Diemen was too profusely there, a spoiler to whatever extremity his jealousy might direct. "While Heer Pelsaert finds himself nominated to our Government, we pray his judgement remunerates the trust conferred by our counterparts in Amsterdam."

"Their confidence, sir, is supported by my long experience in the East."

"It would appear they are more apprised of your virtues than we, here."

"The path to the Fatherland is shorter from India."

"Gentlemen," interrupts Specx, perhaps none too pleased with either of us, "our interests are fastened to the security of our sea routes, the body we would closet vaster than the territories of old Rome. If Batavia lies at the heart of our operation in these parts, let us remain mindful of just how reaching our ambitions are. Surat, my dear Antonio, like Japan, remains at an exceptional distance from ourselves. Yet we would labour to know of and control everything that passes."

The chamber falls silent amidst a downpour which drums on the tiles overhead, and I am drawn to the thought that we are beset by water from every which way, our flesh ever damp, our garments ever limp.

"My predecessor was unflinching in his conviction of our national destiny," resumes the Governor. "And I, too, am of a mind to seize any opportunity that abets our momentum. The Company's brilliance has been brilliantly dared by men of valour and intuition. All of us have travelled far – and not without danger or tribulation – to sit at this table."

A satisfied smile lightens the mood of those who have already made it, who presently sit with felt upon their brows instead of steel. Only the cloying atmospherics betray the fact that we are not at home.

"I had the honour of being introduced to Heer Pelsaert when we were both returned to the Fatherland. If not for the early misfortune of storm and separation, our fleet might have anchored here intact. The losses of that voyage we all know." And a wincing concurrence around the table discomforts me. "But we must give thanks to God that from such disasters something was redeemed – not least, one of the Company's brightest sons."

A pity about the ship, its guns and those sorely needed settlers.

Yes, and did you know that Pelsaert was scarcely ashore before he'd gratified himself with another's wife.

You don't say? I would have thought he'd have had other things on his mind.

Absolutely!

After all, there's still this Batavia *business to conclude.*

Hmm, I dare say he was relieved to discover Coen dead and unable to enforce an explanation, if you know what I mean.

For sure, Specx is firm, but the previous Governor was downright frightening —
He'd sooner have died than permit himself an untimely pleasure.

"Your Excellency," speaks Van Diemen, not a man to be denied the last say, "since you bring notice to the matter of *Batavia*, it is imperative that we expunge its stain from our business in the East. The Fiscaal Advocate has examined the prisoners Heer Pelsaert sought to keep alive and concludes — as I do — that their continued breath only serves to pollute the dungeons."

"Antonio, I think all of us are heartily sickened by the stench of what remains. And Francisco, I'm relieving you of your attendance upon these matters, something I imagine you would welcome."

But I'm uncertain of the implication of what Specx says and momentarily prickle with sweat. "My Lord, with the exception of Pietersz — the one they call Stone-Cutter — and the skipper who was imprisoned when I first arrived, did I not serve the Company in the sentences I imposed?"

"Keelhauling, flogging, a confiscation of wages!" tuts Van Diemen, "do you call that just punishment for rapine and murder?"

The honourable lords nod in sober wonder.

"Antonio is right, Francisco. These crimes are without parallel. That they were permitted to fester aboard a Dutch ship, then be carried out among Dutch castaways, this is an infamy whose surviving miscreants we cannot indulge. Nor is it a knowledge we want circulated abroad. The English already hold us to be without God for the killing of their people at Ambon. This latest incident is an evil we can ill afford to have viewed as somehow natural among us. Gentlemen," and he addresses the others, "the Advocate has verified the guilt of those who have perpetrated these most gruesome atrocities. I have seen the report, and the sentences of those brought back will be revised."

Jacques doesn't look at me but there is a chorus of agreement among those seated. The Governor snaps his finger, a door opens, and in walks his secretary, a specimen as meek and as inconsequential as Salomon in a duty I'm certain is about to snatch away the life of my former assistant.

"Gentlemen," continues the Governor, "I've had this resolution drafted for your endorsement. Read!"

And the young man, preoccupied with not tangling his lines and in getting the tone just right, delivers that august inventory of doom with scarcely an ear for its obscenity. As he nears the end of his recital, his confidence grows with the shrinking responsibility of speech. Indeed, his pleasure in performance is abetted by the concluding acclamation of what he now hears from his own lips. The Councillors of the Indies will gratify those persons who have shown themselves faithful and who piously resisted evil. Yes, Wiebbe Hayes, who sailed out as a common soldier yet allowed himself to be used as a leader for want of any other, is to be promoted to the rank of Standard-bearer and given wages of forty guilders per month.

Again, and on what should be my day of days, I feel myself too abstracted from the script of righteous outcome. It is messy and conflicting, I know. I have wanted to put as much distance between myself and the Abrolhos as possible, to disconnect in the minds of others any link I have with the terrible events of the mutiny. There are already those who would call me Piss-weak Pelsaert. Yet the Council now deliberates as if I were altogether invisible. Their oversight of what I was compelled to improvise is perfumed with a spice of judgement. Hayes, Hayes, Hayes – of course he was a worthy leader and combatant! He was our agent on the ground, our soldier in the field. But who, in God's name, orchestrated the rescue? Who clinched the victory when Hayes, in battle alone, might have succumbed to the oppressor? These people! Ugh, I want no further involvement. Yet neither do I want what I suffered, nor the intelligence of my actions, diminished. Surely there is room enough among this ruling presence to have them say: *Heer Pelsaert, by your actions in responding to the emergency, the tiger and its cubs have been exterminated; allow us to attend the jackals that trotted in their wake. We welcome you as an equal — nay, as a leader all the more worthy for having survived shipwreck and dealt with the monstrosities of mutiny, to have been tested in a crisis and not found lacking in resolve.*

My truant thinking is reclaimed by a shuffling murmur of assent. The Council has decided and Specx leans over the parchment, quill in hand. "The executions will take place on Thursday," he says.

"Heer Pelsaert," Van Diemen turns to me and, in a voice none too private, enquires (as if I were being given a choice), "you'll no doubt join us before the scaffold?"

—⚬—

Although it had been an ambition to become a Councillor and, perhaps, even one day Governor, I had little stomach for Batavia in the aftermath of its namesake's loss and the judicial killings which were no less calculated or appalling than the crimes of the mutineers themselves. Despite a barber's surgical approach to the canker, an odour of foulness still infected the conversation and thoughts of those who, in whispered malice or over a mug of gin, shook their heads and stared at me in passing as if I were spattered with the blood of innocents. I was both a prestigious casualty and one of the strangest of survivors – not a survivor at all, in one sense.

For a man who had much to prove (and in the eyes of some, everything to redeem), I may have appeared shiftless, something of an internal exile with enforced time on my hands. Yet nothing could have been further from the truth. I was extraordinarily diligent in the recovery of my intended path. The *Batavia* episode had no more than detracted from the immediacy of support I required to relay me back to India. Yes, I needed to complete the mission which disaster had occluded. Only then might I settle in this "Diamond City" as the natives jest of our hard-edged colony, and for such a time as my work might apprentice me for the return to Europe and a permanent seat among the High and Mighty. But, first, to India and my unfinished business. Jahangir was dead, I now knew, but the jewels and plate had been salvaged from the wreck, and Hindustan had a new monarch. What oriental despot wouldn't thirst for the novelties I brought?

I confess there was more to it than this. India had been my life, my forging for better or for ill as a man. My reaction to its jostling opportunity and its splendid indifference had refined my ambition. Yet all that governed the personal was now vanished. Those who had chaperoned me on my journey, as well as those who had partnered me in the cultivation of my tale, were gone. What would I be returning to? To whom might I address myself? The factory at Agra would only furnish subordinates now loyal to that usurper, Vapoer. There was no one in whom I might confer who possessed the educating peerage of Van den Broecke. And of long-gone Van Heuten, his grave — like Asmat's plot of undisclosed repose — would simply beckon its unwelcome alternative.

Yet in the curiously unfamiliar world I now breathed, with Batavia scarcely a comfort, I felt a sudden nostalgia for the anchorage at Surat, that untidy port and gateway onto the Mogul world. And for distant Agra, too, that untidier metropolis, its imperial lusts strictly segregated from the town-camp squalor of its populace. Yes, I found myself wistful for that unfulfillable destination, wanting to gamble myself once more upon the road of an earlier but less-articulated ambition. And if I felt less bodily robust, not so my commitment to seeing the matter through. I had made a case to the Chamber in Amsterdam; I was leading our nation in the seduction of a foreign prince. The toys and trinkets themselves were worth a king's ransom, and with these I hoped to beguile Jahangir's successor into granting firmans that might strengthen our hand over the English and the Portuguese. And if, in the scripting of this final chapter, I were to perish as other Dutchmen before me, would it be too terrible an ending to slumber, at length, in the latitude of Asmat's dust?

But before I could fulfil my promise, Jambi intervened.

The season hadn't yet arrived wherein I might speedily sail to India. In the meantime the Portuguese were manoeuvring to displace our priority at that upstream river port.

Specx had risen from the table and was standing by the window, his hands clasped behind his back. "Gentlemen, those bastard sons of the Vicar of Rome have strayed in our direction." Outside, the sun was shining with a soupy humour. "Such trespass is intolerable. The trade is ours, and Jambi is too near the Straits to consent to anything but war."

"The sooner, I say, we make up our minds to take Malacca and eject them from these parts altogether, the smoother it will be," replied Pieter Vlack, the dead Coen's brother-in-law, and not unlike that other Pieter — Van den Broecke — in temperament.

Hear, hear!

Specx was eyeing him, his factional self-assurance. A man like that — his predecessor's protégé — could easily shift opinion. As with Van Diemen, the Governor knew only too well that he was served by hungry men, men who might readily step into his shoes given half a chance. Perhaps it was that which prompted Specx to make up his mind. Or perhaps Pieter's fearless talk accommodated a decision already made. In any case it was best to put the talents of such a man to use. "Reports received only this morning indicate the extent of Portuguese meddling. Jambi is under siege, the river blockaded by Catholic galleys."

Those present let their outrage thump the table.

The Governor, nodding, returned to his chair. "I have in mind a demonstration of force."

The chamber fell silent.

"My predecessor was not a man to call a halt — nor am I. Councillor Vlack, I want you to take command of the expedition. You'll have ships, troops and guns. And Heer Pelsaert," he turned to me, "I believe you're sufficiently recovered. I want you to accompany Vlack as his second-in-command."

As unexpected as the operation was, I felt honoured before my peers to be given this commission. And not a little apprehensive. I was a merchant after all, not a soldier, and whilst not unacquainted with organised violence, in matters pertaining to critical generalship I felt not a little intimidated.

"My word, Pelsaert," Vlack got to his feet, "we'll have some sport with these monkeys, eh?"

I smiled with the humourless determination of a leader in the calling. Yet I needn't have worried. Even as Van Diemen grumbled about our diminished strength due to losses in the Abrolhos, a formidable fleet — *Batavia*'s absence notwithstanding — had gathered in the roadstead beyond the Castle walls, its pennants streaming in the breeze and its armament in need of martial employ.

"Francisco," Jacques drew me aside as the meeting broke up, "I trust you're up for this?" It was kindly meant.

"I," I swallowed, "a young man then, was with Coen when this very place was put to the sword," and anxious for no one to think me a weakling.

Jacques laid a hand on my shoulder. "Misfortune has unfairly reproached many a man," he said. "I never doubted your ability when you were summoned to lead the fleet from Texel. A man can be cursed in the companionships he's forced to bear." Then leaning close, "Use this experience well. Recover who you were. Learn from Vlack."

It was my turn to nod, to convey what words couldn't promise. "I should hope to have this business concluded before the September monsoon," I murmured.

"Ah yes, India."

Its chimerical promise floated between us like a language whose syntax was difficult to grasp. Even as I contemplated the resumption of my end there, the place itself, like some vast ant nest — and in this, a place no less arid to my searching than the reddish hinterland of that unyielding southern continent — yes, India teemed with a vehemence unmoved by who I was.

"Any news of Van den Broecke?" I politely asked.

"Pieter, why yes. He departed Surat not long after you, but instead of Europe, he came here. Carried Coen's spurs at the funeral. Carried off Coen's widow as well, as the wags would have it. He's escorting her to the Fatherland, and when he arrives will doubtless make some capital for himself."

What suddenly frightened me was the theft he might make of my share in what we'd written. I was always being solicited to contribute to this or that, to reports which were aggregated at Surat to be shipped here or home. *Francisco, you have a sensitivity for the realities of life in this heathen land… My friend, you're an astute observer of local custom… Francisco, why not a chronicle of the emperors!* My words, running into thousands, were as bound to the estate of my superior as a wife's dowry to the disposal of her husband. How could I trust him?

"He was a good friend to me," I replied, not untruthfully but with little warmth.

"He'll be back. He's been granted substantial perks in the Banda Islands." And pursing his lips, "Nutmeg has grown lonesome for the want of any to tend it. My predecessor's methods" — and I could sense he was thinking of his daughter's ordeal — "have created a labour shortage. We've been compelled to restock the islands with slaves."

Lucretia's husband, bartering at Arakan, crossed my mind. I nodded, knowing that we've all allowed ourselves to undertake things which oppose sleep. And let's face it, the trade in slaves is as lucrative as it is necessary. But to enter into that backwater business and its crude receipt of stolen goods, I wonder that Lucretia's husband could have been such a man. Perhaps in death his soul was relieved to have found so unsavoury an exile brought to a close.

Look at you, ruminating with equanimity upon another's extinction!

"Yes," continued the Governor, "we've rather dealt with the English in this part of the globe and condemned their island allies to near destruction. It's up to the likes of Van den Broecke to manage the lands we've cleared. But the Portuguese, they're still to learn that there's no place for them on our doorstep either. That's why I'm sending you with Vlack. Trade is our lifeblood and business is often war. We all need to return to the basics from time to time. The airing will do you good."

That night I slept fitfully, wondering whether I might ever complete my journey. Or would Jambi itself prove the reality I had unforeseen? Might I never sidestep the intrusions of circumstance and amended order? Indeed – and as in our relation to God – might I ever remain a servant of the Company in a servitude that was unnegotiable?

The following morning I met with Vlack. He was in a buoyant mood, his breakfast eggs inhabiting the greasy crust of his moustache.

"This is only the beginning, Pelsaert," and he opened a folio from which he pulled a chart of the archipelago. "Jambi lies between us and Malacca. We chase these monkeys out of Sumatra and their reason for being here is diminished. They'll be holed up across the straits and it'll only be a matter of time before Malacca falls."

Although less austere in appearance than Coen, Vlack was cheerfully a warlord in the cast of his deceased brother-in-law. It was presently gratifying to be harnessed to the charm of another's aggression, and if our expansion meant an assertion of strength, so be it. There were plenty in this world who might yet be made to kneel, the weak a banquet of the strong, although it was by no means clear to me that the Portuguese were lining up to be butchered. Our ships had previously failed in their effrontery on Malacca, and the Lusitanian soldier, though generally ill-disciplined, had a reputation for the fanatical. Despite his bravura, Vlack was aware that rashness was more in the instinct of a gambler than a Captain-General, and that of those generals whose rashness had been crowned with victory, their impetus had benefited from the fickleness of fate. There were any number of loose commanders whose lives, and that of their men, had ended in folly.

And so the provisioning of the expedition began, the ships gradually subsiding at anchor as the stores and armaments were loaded, the decks below scrubbed with vinegar in preparation for the embarkation of our men. Even the *Sardam*, my trusty workhorse of the year just gone, was made ready to join the fleet. When all was completed and the day of sailing arrived, the trumpet of each ship blared in martial annunciation, the drums a steady rattle and in counterpoint with the slow-furling pennants of the VOC. The guns of Batavia Castle began firing and each ship took up the salute, loud cheering filling the void between reports. While the sailors went unsmiling about their business, those who claimed any rung in the hierarchy, from the lowliest corporal to Vlack himself, began to hum with the licence of those entered upon some glorious enterprise. Indeed, we senior officers shared a pre-congratulatory cup, toasted the Fatherland and glowed with a kind of paternity for what had been assembled under our command. Very soon the roadstead was reduced to mere drifts of visibility, the pungency of ignited powder our departing perfume. Those who had flocked to the shoreline grew indistinct and increasingly distant as the world we entertained now closed around our mission. With anchors weighed and our momentum listing to starboard, any contemplation of what had led us to this course was subsumed in the minutiae of an operation whose most doubtful element was the constancy of its human parts.

The mouth of the Hari River was not overly distant, not like the near infinity that separates Holland from Java with its vanished year of time. Yet as soon as we were at sea, the coastline but a smudge in the turbulent palette of atmospherics, I began to feel nauseous in my return to shipboard life. Little matter that Vlack and our experienced officers ought to have reassured me; little matter that our mission was curtly defined and strictly ordered. The fact of having put to sea – and *I* in command of a ship not unlike *Batavia* – immediately made me suspicious of surrounding behaviours. The stilling of a conversation at my near approach, the merest impression of slight in a servant or hostility in a sailor, these things rankled with their portent for conspiracy. I looked for treachery in every response to an order that was not received with enthusiasm, and had little taste for the men recruited to our cause. I saw myself as an unwilling master of mercenaries, men here for reasons none other than the lure of their meagre wage and the salutary contrast of vagabondage back home. Despite the blood-sport afforded by a rival Portuguese presence, there was little love of national destiny. There was little love of me.

In Vlack, who bore overall responsibility for the success of our mission, I placed the greatest confidence. Indeed, he was a confident man, unperturbed by setbacks which were never more to him than delays, and he never failed to slap me on the back or relish the prospect of banging a few foreign heads together. As for the various skippers (Jacobsz, of course, was of no concern to me, his hide still dungeon-locked at Batavia), the expedition gave them an opportunity to manoeuvre in splendid symmetries and engage in competitive seamanship. Rival vanities were allowed so long as they collectively spurred the Company on.

If I were motivated by a superior subtlety, it was a nicety of scant value in a world whose powers and goals were blunt. I had long ago learned to disguise myself, having traded all my life in anomalies which might have tarnished the eventual portrait of a man in cumulative possession of success. The public man is a marble man, a substance wrought with sharp and concussive tooling into an object of cool perfection, its form bereft of the ardour of its making. I had been passed over for promotion. I had learned to trade on the side. I had loved women I oughtn't to have touched. I had felt the timbers beneath my feet rise and swell with an unbidden power. And all the while I had sought to remain an exterior of judicious predictability. In everything that has troubled the conscience of he whom I should like to have been, I have buried that shame, time and again, in secrecy.

When we reached the mouth of the Hari there was little latitude for speculative reflection. Jambi was several leagues upstream and there was not a Portuguese ship to be seen. Were we to plug the river and advance towards the besieged town; sooner or later we would encounter an enemy for whom no route of escape had been devised. That contact, when it came, could only be savage.

Our ships advanced in cautious file, jachts such as the *Sardam* feeling the way and taking soundings. Each bend in the river was suspenseful, a slow unwinding of enemy-planned surprise. Vlack grew less jovial, less epicurean in the licence of his humour. Responsible for the lives of hundreds, he had withdrawn into a listening intensity. The enemy was unknowingly near; the fight, when it came, would offer a blessed relief.

Troops were landed on either side of the river, there to probe the banks for Portuguese machinations or ambuscade. First the skirmishers with their cloth hats, muskets and cutlasses. Then larger companies of men, some whose preference for helmets afforded little shade or comfort in the tropical heat. Although we'd not come to make war on the natives, the villages that drew their sustenance from the cultivated fields nearby were deserted. We knew the locals were in hiding at the edge of the forest. We knew that the visibility of our masts and striped banner of our militant republic signalled a warlike approach. And I was reminded of the abandoned ashes upon the clifftops of that unknown land, of glancing rapidly this way and that for evidence of homemakers who had such impoverished materials to work with. Almost unnoticed in the final vestiges of flight, there they were, their black and sticklike figures scampering into rockeries resembling the foundation of an antiquity long forgotten. I remember the place smelt of flies, that a pestilential cloud clung to our sweat-stiff bodies. As presently we closed in likely battle, the war of another latitude transported to these regions, I wondered momentarily at the fate of Loos and Pelgrom, yielded up to wander a continent of flies, to nightly camp (if indeed they were permitted the luxury of survival) in ignorance of how the world truly fared in their absence.

As if it mattered, the great silence of unknowing stretching between us. How might whatever I did — apart from spare their lives — be important to them? And how might I be tempted to remember them other than at times when I doubted my capacity to live in the moment?

A signal cannon startled me, its unsubtlety of communication. For all the caution we would exercise to dampen the intelligence of our arrival, we persisted in trumpet calls and gunfire.

"Commandeur, over there!"

Smoke was rising from a village where our soldiers pressed. I marked the inhabitants by their coloured sarongs, their naked torsos spirited in protest. At water's edge were the telltale signs of a barrier: heavy chains and a rudimentary capstan. It seems the Portuguese had been of a mind to obstruct the river but that their customary indiscipline had permitted the device to remain untried. In any case, it didn't sit well with our men for the natives to have permitted a foreign power to devise so unfriendly a welcome. I couldn't tell which of the buildings was ablaze, only that figures flocked to an open space that sloped towards the river. Armed with halberd and pike, our men looked like giants and of a mind not to be disputed. I could hear shouting — more a gaggle really, the clatter of animated pleadings — then the carriage of a voice I recognised. Surely it was Hayes. It took but a moment to single him out. The company was shepherding the villagers like goats to a remove beyond what needed to be done. I witnessed one protester brusquely knocked to the ground; saw what I took to be the village headman dragged to the fore. Hayes, his head uncovered, was pointing in the direction of the chains. My heart leapt to mouth as I summoned up a vision of Meyer's lost utopia: its chickens and its women and its cooking fires protected by a delicate truce of uncertainty. I, too, had travelled rivers such as this, praying for welcome and hoping to ingratiate myself to the extent that the Company's maxim of trade at any cost mightn't prove so. I heard the skipper behind me give the order for the culverins to be primed, saw Hayes strike the headman, his troops crowding like a collective fist, and foresaw the near and abysmal tragedy only too clearly.

Without reference to my fellow officers, I turned and ordered the trumpeter to signal our shore company, to direct them to advance upstream at once. Accustomed to the imperia of Company lords, the skipper spat an oyster of tobacco and pocketed the option of not firing the village as if that, equally, were an operational possibility. At the sound of the trumpet, Hayes glanced across the water in our direction and pushed the headman away. And then he did something which surprised and not a little startled me. For at a distance which made me marvel that I should have known him in the first place, *he* appeared to recognise *me* and raised a hand. It was less a salute; more some comprehension of the moment. It were as if, in our catching of the other's eye, a conjoined potency had resiled from an iniquity not unlike rape, the village coming close to disaster but disaster luckily averted. A building torched, a few bruises here and there, what did it matter? In life, as in its unspeakable impulse to self-annihilate, we had each learned that things might fare far worse.

I'd not known that Hayes was with the expedition. It should have come as no surprise; he was a soldier after all, and we were here to counsel the Portuguese at point of sword to abandon any pretence to the pepper trade. It turned out he was with a transport attached to Vlack's flagship. Nonetheless this continued sighting of the man was like running into someone who had done you the sort of favour you'd rather the world not learn of. There was something about his previous heroics that ought not to have counted as a deposit on everything to follow. After all, one laudable deed in a moment of crisis doth not an angel make. And yet, in fairness, I was comforted by the notion of his presence, by the surety that at any hour during the darkness of this campaign I need only hail him to know that all would turn out for the best. As a man, too, who sought favourable witness from one who knew that I had done my all, I wanted to summon Wiebbe to my cabin, to resurrect the conscience of what I had hoped, as his brother-in-arms, to deliver. Yet as a man jealous of his good standing and unwilling to entertain odious comparison, I wished him back into the ranks – loyal, yes, and ever serviceable, but also invisible. In the tie of what we'd gone through I might have loved Wiebbe, but I wanted no one else to know.

Our progression up the Hari was made unnecessarily tortuous. The continual landing of scouts and skirmishers, the intimidation of villagers, the constant alerts, these were all to little purpose in probing an enemy who seemed to have vanished.

"I tell you, Francisco, nothing would give me greater satisfaction than to catch these monkeys basking in the damned siestas they're so fond of."

The suspense was spoiling Vlack's patience, tarnishing his sporting humour and turning him into something altogether blunter and more dangerous. Word was about that a Portuguese fleet was sailing from Malacca to relieve the forces already committed at Jambi. If true, we ran the risk of being caught between the two, our intended rescue of Jambi captured by the relief of the besiegers themselves. Vlack and I decided to divide the expedition, to maintain a minor pressure in the advance but withdraw the bulk of our armament to the open sea, there to better manoeuvre in the face of danger. It should come as no surprise, though, to learn that sea battles are far and few between. Upon the unmarked cloth of ocean, scanning for one's adversary is like searching for the proverbial needle in a haystack.

In the meantime our original quarry, all too aware of our superior determination, was making ready to lift its siege and retire, as best it might, downstream. I later learned that several companies had marched overland to the coast to avoid capture. The Portuguese transports at Jambi signalled their intention to leave at the arrival of our advance party, among whom was Wiebbe. The monkeys, as Pieter constantly referred to them, preferred to slip away without so much as firing a defiant shot, anxious no doubt to conserve their strength for whatever awaited them at the mouth of the Hari. Even then we scarcely saw them as they scraped away, their sails a squalid yellow against the sweat of an unlaundered sky. There was some discussion as to whether we should attempt to block and destroy them. For want of mortal provocation our skippers, in this instance, were of a mind to preserve the varnish of their ships. Our mission had been accomplished, the Portuguese investiture of Jambi had collapsed and their power was in recoil. Besides, it was judged best to save our shot for the rumoured fleet that we ourselves had re-entered the Straits to challenge.

But there was no fleet, and when the truth of this was made plain to Vlack he grew furious. "We should have cornered, killed and eaten the bastards! If a Chinaman can sup on the brains of an ape, I could readily drink from the skulls of a dozen of these monkeys!"

A smile of indulgent agreement passed from face to face. True, we might have assailed them at sea, but the cost may well have exceeded what Batavia deemed prudent. After all, the Portuguese on water were not to be taken lightly.

"I tell you, Pelsaert, we won't be unencumbered in this part of the world until the buggers are put back in their box. And even then the job won't be finished until we take Malacca. The day can't come quick enough, and believe me it'll happen in our lifetime!"

But I wasn't certain I had the life to spare; the old tremors had returned. My mind began to slip in fragment-picturing, the episodes of the past few weeks adding their layer to a story which was cloyed into no particular shape or priority. I would summon myself to focus as the moment dictated, then excuse myself to go below and fawn upon my bunk, victim of that shivering illness that so plagued my captaincy aboard *Batavia*. At least I'd become less suspicious of my companions. We were well-provisioned, successful, and in no want whatsoever of the dangerous compensations of mutiny. Vlack had proven himself a robust leader.

With a contingent of soldiers left at Jambi — and I never saw or heard of Wiebbe Hayes again — we set our course for home. And yes, it was with an accommodating gratitude that I presently considered Batavia just that, a place firmly charted on our map and the foundation of our search for whatever might succour an unfixed want, this limitless hunger.

As my strength permitted, I viewed the coastline to the south glide peacefully by and wasn't sorry for the success of our operation *not* to have tasted blood. I was contemplating my onward leg to Hindustan and felt weary at the prospect of another foray into its thorny realm. Curiously, I found myself thinking of Antonio Andrade. Had he returned to that thoroughfare in Delhi where we last crossed paths and wondered, too, what had become of me? What tales of adventure might we have traded, what places foreign to our eyes? I never saw him in the train of Jahangir; I never heard of his return to Goa, not that I would have been privy to such intelligence. There'd surely been priests among the Lusitanians at Jambi, but of that encampment all trace had dissolved at our approach. The Portuguese may have been derided as monkeys but privately I was pleased to have beheld none destroyed, to have been spared the discovery of Antonio's body or, if captured, my witness of his distress before the reduction of his compatriots. Yes, I was relieved they'd taken the hint and run. Yet I was aware, too, that in my unknowing of other destinies, I felt that a part of me had disappeared with the unheralded vanishing of Antonio.

As the fleet neared Batavia I grew more miserably abandoned to fever, the frozen heat of its aching chatter. There was not water enough in all the oceans to quench the thirst that raged in me, nor the sense to care that its brine might curry madness. Indeed, I was talon-gripped by a delirium that shrivelled me into a cowering schoolboy. This was not the first time I'd been giddied into uncaring, feeling once more the leaden smother that had so deprived me of self-command aboard *Batavia*.

"Don't die on me, Pelsaert," summoned Vlack. Then, with an impatience that made me wince, "Christ, look at him. Our only casualty may well be him!"

And so I was stretchered from the ship, apologetic or apathetic by turn. I remember the sun needling my eyes, their jelly swollen by the torments of my bodily demon. Like awaking from the stupor of a night's carousing, the light unbearable, and knowing that the only remedy is to not move at all. Except that I *was* being moved – not against my wishes, or those of the Company, but without the consent of hope. Where to? *Wherever...*

"Heer Pelsaert." The familiarity of an unfamiliar voice. My eyes swivel at their peril. I shiver at the scorch of this shadeless noon. The circle of a hat eclipses the sun, a face embedded in its silhouette. "Sir, it seems I'm once more at your service."

"Croock?" I whisper, more in thought than utterance.

"I've found you a place. It's outside the walls but comfortable enough. The Chinese are the other side of the canal. Plenty of colour, eh? I know you enjoy a spot of local colour, that you're not one to be put out by these foreign devils, ha ha."

Croock is no longer looking at me and my litter sways. I haven't the strength of curiosity to see who bears me, only a sense that all has been arranged, and not necessarily with my interests at heart. The graveyard is beyond the walls, close to the Chinese quarter.

"Bear up Guv'nor, we'll soon have you rested and back on your feet."

In the familiar procession, I suppose, of another dying Dutchman, I feel the stares of those in the street. Soon the hum of public life gives over to a shadier and much cooler tempo, to the truculent bark of a woman and squall of a baby. It's as if the music of some collective orchestration has been fractured into its component sounds, that what we hear as the whole is, in this place, reduced to backroom privacies of solo practice.

These sounds would become my neighbours, introducing me to a hearing whose silences had just as much to say as sudden eruptions of family clamour. The timing of my day would be measured by the ebb and flow of noises whose authors I never saw, whose age and gender were but a clue to lives I might never know. Hartanti had been sourced from within this neighbourhood. I remember Croock commending, "Careful there," as they squeezed me through the entrance of a house still bearing the scars of last year's Mataramese incursion. The simple wooden structures nearby testified to the resilient immediacy of Chinese market gardeners. But these observations were something my vagrant eye took in without recourse to instant comprehension. A man may die through a multitude of images, a refraction of countless sightings which comprise the memory of a life in disarray. Even then, despite the heat and shiver of my flesh, I glimpsed in bitter alienation the needed succour of my mother and, more importantly, Maria. *Ma'am, see how the child stews, the blood sweats from his skin...* "Guv'nor, this girl is Hartanti. She's to attend your needs."

And through a glaze of dazed understanding, I perceive a duskiness of face ill at ease with the burden she's been assigned. "Hartanti?" I mumble, and for a moment I imagine myself back in India. The world is filled with lost faces.

Thus was I settled into my cot, this bed I never leave.

Thoughts of India slowly dissolved in the vapid atmosphere, never again to be moistened by anything approaching the possibility of return. Jahangir, dead, was an implication I was slow to absorb, Shah Jahan a reality I would never know.

Strange, is it not, that for all our knowing that we must surely die, one rarely apprehends the approach of Death. I had been assigned, as it were, a test of reclamation and had set out on the expedition to Jambi, its exercise but a prelude to my onward voyage to Surat and, in turn, the dusty overland to wherever the Mogul capital resided these days. But I understood now – and momentarily without a care – that my return to the land wherein I had shaped myself was lost in the humidity of decay itself, that my dreams of future were now little more than memory. Yes, I realised that the voyage to Jambi was the last I would ever make.

The distance is a blueness that fades to white. Indeed, whiteness defines the border of what I see, the breeze sombre in its cooing. In every direction the mountains stand back to clear a space in which any man must perceive how puny and alone he is. Ice marbles the grey-blue slopes and ascends in thickening branches to purities of frozen pasture higher up. And despite my advent, the jagged and imprisoning peaks belie any confidence that the threading path continues.

I see him – at least what I take to be him – at the outreach of my voice. "Antonio?"

The hooded figure is turned from me, and for a moment I'm not certain it's a man I summon. He – or it – is perched at the end of a little promontory whose stones may have been arranged by human hands but are more likely to have been sculpted by the elements to suggest a withered kingdom. Close by, and little bigger than some open-air altar, is a pagoda from whose iron crown stretch strings of coloured flags, torn and faded. An ancient eye unsettles me despite its flaking fresco; it seems to condense the strangeness of this place, to monitor my movements on behalf of a world I trespass. In the flutter of pennants with their calligraphies unknown, I wonder of those who have raised such a church and of the demon lore they practise. If ever anyone needed reminding of how small he is in relation to God's purpose, then here is ample affirmation in the rarefied ether of these unyielding mountain-folds. To listen to the silence is to attend the borders of one's soul.

Although nothing visibly saunters in this untouchable landscape, I grow uneasy, as if alert to something that has recently taken place and may reoccur at a moment's notice. Perhaps it is that unmoving figure which alarms me. "Antonio?" I call again.

Is it he? And why would anyone tarry at this comfortless spot? In wariness I look around and guard myself.

The breeze is of ice itself, and no amount of sunlight can lessen the anxiety one feels for the frailty of one's skin. Anything might happen to a man in this inexplicable emptiness. I can see that the air paws at the fabric of his hood, that his outline is of cloth and that he is no trick of stone. I stumble a few paces closer, pebbles kicked a-skitter, and still he does not acknowledge me.

Walter lies upon his cot, his eyes luminously famished. The fear which grips him is not the fear of fever; no, it is the unnerving motion of others which defines his inability to move. He is whispering. I lean close, a handkerchief to my nose.

I always knew that God would punish you for leaving me to die.

You sickened. There was nothing I could do.

I look away, uneasy and stare through an opened door into the extreme light. And there they are, the imploring and the angry, the shallows kicked and splashing in a panic of stampede. *Don't leave us! No, come back!*

No, I can't think of this! Surely I dream; surely this happened only the once? Walter – and I turn to realise that his cot is mine – Walter, are you there?

But all is silent. We are variously positioned in that airless room at Surat. I've just arrived. There's Walter over by the shutters, eyeing me with suspicion. His hair is lank and I can tell, even now, that the climate has its grip on him. There's Pieter, too – yes, my mentor in the making. And Salomon as well – no it can't be; I heard the crowd jeering as his turn approached.

I motion to Walter to open the shutters. It's stuffy in here, and more disconcertingly there's a smell which emanates from my person. I'm afraid the others will scent my humiliation. *My God, man, your conscience raises a stink! Come, we have no secrets here.*

But I don't know what to offer. I'm uncertain of what it is I hide. I look to the floor to check that I've not fouled myself but it is Salomon whose thighs are stained. He's wearing sackcloth, his eyes as bug-bright as the stare of Death itself. Pieter blows his nose, impatient for me to speak.

Is it Batavia, *then? Does nothing else count?*

Of course it's Batavia*! You don't come away from something like that with your reputation intact.*

But the mission to Jambi was a success! Ask Pieter.

The ensuing silence is mindful.

Which Pieter — Van den Broecke or Vlack?

Vlack, of course! I was his second.

The silence, this time, is pawing.

Indeed, Van den Broecke didn't think you up to the responsibility of full command.

And I detect the spite of another. *Antonio?*

He had little choice but to appoint someone else, someone with greater — shall we say — diplomatic gifts. Especially after your empty-handed return from Kashmir.

Walter, can't you vouch for me?

I discern the evaporative rattle of his breathing and glance into his eyes as if into the dimming of my own. In their shrivelled light I perceive no fellow-ship or consolation. In fact, I no longer know at whom I stare. *Antonio?*

Which one — Van Diemen or Andrade?

The question merely shapes a hiss of laughter. Aware that my nemesis lurks close, I again wonder at the fate of that unheard-from other. Was it too treacherous a comfort *not* to have fired on the Portuguese? Can Van Diemen know this? Indeed, is it futile to feel in the uncertainty of what one feels for?

⸂

The cameo! My God, where is it? And the plate? Cornelisz possesses them! No, Cornelisz is dead. Yes, they were retrieved, marked by the imprint of his polluted hands but retrieved nonetheless, a fortune wrapped in rags. But if no longer stolen, where have I placed them? This room hasn't the furniture to store all that I'm responsible for. Its neatness is impoverished, its care pinching. Has Hartanti smuggled them away? I must find them, otherwise my mission is incomplete! But then I can never complete myself; from one deceased emperor to another, I'm the ferryman of what no longer matters. Yet to steal from a corpse?

Cheer up, Pelsaert, you over-rehearse yourself. You're not dead yet, and it's infinitely more profitable to squeeze the fear of what lives.

You would further injure me in my weakened state?

And you would accuse Hartanti? Indeed, it is a dying man who weaves most fugitive, and in your case it's a moot point as to who's been stealing from whom.

How so?

Reports are filtering through of certain irregularities at Agra. The factory hasn't been maintained in a manner befitting Company regulations.

My heart leaps at the thought of what they may uncover. My conscience is clear, *I bluster.* Whatever we did we did to exact an influence in that heathen kingdom.

It strikes us, sir, that there were two levels of commerce operating in Hindustan, and that one was pursued to the detriment of the other.

Local businessmen were eager to avail themselves of our opportunity.

It's difficult to discern how private money-lending might have benefited the prosecution of legitimate Company business.

Private trade cultivated close relations.

Too close a relationship, it would seem.

I blink, startled, and would know of what I am accused, all too aware of the dangers that lie along a path best un-trod.

You were in India to perform a certain task, a commission you greatly exceeded.

And I see now that Maartens is seated close in the manner of his first visit. Zealotry is usually applauded in officials, *I challenge, insulted that this pasty poltroon should become my inquisitor.*

Exactitude and obedience to God's commandments are applauded more, *he answers.*

There are no Ten Commandments south of the equator, *I spit with uncharacteristic insubordination.* Who are you to challenge me with what you can never hope to understand?

Heer Pelsaert, it gives me no pleasure to press you with the concerns expressed by others.

And who might these others be? Name the authority by which you would come here to diminish the achievements of a dying man?

I come here because I am requested to do so –

For God's sake, Maartens, stop hiding behind your collar. We both know you're a mouthpiece of interests that would as readily place the knife in your hand as do the deed themselves. *He is still pretending the righteous youth, playing the go-between in a defence of rules he would willingly transgress if ordered to do so. His presence nauseates me more than I already feel.* You're neither a cleric nor a man, Maartens. You're a grovel of a thing in the stoop of another's cowardice.

And rather than take offence, he smiles – a wan and weary smile as if for all the sorrow a man might bedevil himself with.

When we hear of what's rumoured to have taken place at Agra, *he says*, it contributes to our unhappy understanding of what may have occurred aboard *Batavia.*

I see no connection between the two.

A man – especially a man charged with shepherding others – may attend too closely his own affairs.

If you would accuse me of anything, speak plain.

Your private dealings set a bad example. I hear the recorded commerce at Agra is less than what the lifestyles of its factors might suggest.

And I remembered Meyer saying to me all those years ago: How much do you earn? Twenty-four guilders a month? *God, to think of it now, such a lowly rung on which to have begun my climb. I turn to Maartens and would parry him his ignorance:* You hear nothing, then, of anything you might understand.

Is it so difficult to form a picture?

Let me ask you, since you deign to be an authority on the workings of our business, what was Bastiaensz up to in the Abrolhos, tending to the skiffs of murderers, pretending to play the intermediary between Cornelisz and those he would slay? Let me meddle a moment in *your* hypocrisies.

Heer Pelsaert, if I may make so bold as to assume a love of what we both hold dear, I represent the ship of state, its unalienable right to prosper under God. Its captains are entrusted with the preservation of its timbers, our merchants the brimming of its holds. God may protect us but only if we enter into His covenant and protect ourselves from sin.

Maartens, the only thing that surprises me is that you bother, still, to come dressed as a sick-visitor.

He reflects a moment, his tongue roving the inside of his shaven cheek. It would be best if you, too, spoke plain.

In what way are you a more loyal servant than I – a better man, perhaps?

I honour my instructions to the letter.

You serve, then, nothing of the imagination?

I imagine no more than what I know to be the truth.

And that is?

Whether you intended harm or not, you compromised our ship of state. You edged it into currents liable to disaster.

You overstate my influence.

Ha – you who would be Governor!

And I realise it's no longer Maartens with whom I speak. "Hartanti!" *I call, and coughing as if to dislodge a fishbone.* If I took, it was only because I needed to – the pay poor, the expectations great. "You don't know what it was like – to have lived among them!" I shout aloud. "You sit here in the unsullied collar of the colony. Slaves put milk on your table and you never once consider how it's paid for! Well the entire business is chancing and it's personal! Of course I traded privately – we all do! There are no rules south of the equator. But I never stole."

The silence is moist, and there's an echo like the dripping of water in some subterranean chamber.

"Are you there?" I challenge, knowing that my enemies shift from foot to foot, unseen. "Hartanti?" And still the silence remains unquiet.

She died.

Yes, she died.

The wife of another.

Yes, just one among many.

Yet you would love her to within peril of your life.

I would love her, yes, yet not nearly enough. And I scent now what I have always known: the exasperation of self-loathing.

How is it, Francisco, a man might pity you?

No one pities me. Therein lies your answer.

Yet you would weep for this frailty that has befallen you.

I weep for the cock-up of a life half-lived.

A measure somewhat fuller for you than the emptied chalices of your acquaintance.

No one lives unencumbered. But look, peace be with you – I lie not here to nibble at whatever bait you sport.

This is no sport.

No, dying never is…

I had been to the house of her husband on several occasions. Wasim Khanin was of that golden dust that haloed the emperor and illumined those in service. As an indication of how far he needed to advance himself, his orbit was sufficiently distanced from the throne to allow him the luxury to look around and sample both the machinations of his peers (his world) and the oddity of foreign embassies (mine). Knowing the emperor extreme in his power and indulgent in his curiosities, Wasim perceived merit, not to mention a cultivation of interest, in befriending me as I stood at the outer edge of this opulent and competitive savagery. It is true that a foreigner is never without a press of natives eager to peddle some service, usually those unwanted and unwarranted. It goes without saying that there is no end to business as charity in this land. But in this instance I was more than willing to ally myself to the unstated attention of a courtier, a man who, in the end, might mirror me in the privilege of discovering something both foreign and intelligent. At first I wondered whether he, too, was an ambassador of some description, such was the fairness of his skin, the pale light of his eye. A handsome face with an aquiline nose, his beard was trimmed in a fashion I would hasten to adopt while his costume mocked the sable of our ways and was festive in overlays of citrus hue. Indeed, it was in the greeting of this man that I ceased to make comparisons and look no further than with appreciation upon such variegation. Only the women were more gorgeous, still, in their apparelling, more gilded if only glimpsed, for in the countenance of the court they remained largely unseen. Theirs was a privacy requiring special access, and in an atmosphere of studied courtesy, what with my stumbling Persian and a traveller's delight in finding oneself at the threshold of all this lordly governance, Khanin and I began a conversation which set the door ajar onto realms removed from the indigo plantations, traders and haggling of my merchant ways.

I pause, my breathing thick with the creaminess of memory, my heart beating faster than temperature ought to permit.

And what did you do with this opportunity?

Do? Why I lived in greater sympathy within the complexity of that alien kingdom. *"We can't behave like Coen, you know. We can't just come here and bang a few heads together..."*

Yet of your ambitions your greatest accomplishment was to bed the wife of a local lord.

It wasn't like that!

No? Then you tell me how it was.

"Your Persian does you honour," he smiled, and I felt instantly that I might be intimate with this man.

"I find it a challenge," I replied. "The shuffle of so many tongues in Hindustan might easily consume a linguist."

"Ha! We speak only what we need to." Then, with a broadening smile affected by one golden tooth and the stain of betel, he asked, "And of what caste of infidel might you be?"

I laughed aloud, shushed by those nearby and amusing Khanin who nonetheless kept an eye on the throne. And in truth my laughter masked some confusion as to how to answer. "I am a Hollander," I said, but that didn't explain my origins in Antwerp or my years of undertaking in the Spiceries. It was long since I'd smelled or tasted anything of the Netherlands, and it occurred to me that a return to my adopted nation might prove as strange a meeting as my presence here among these privileged Moors.

"I see you think before you speak." And as if shepherding my thoughts, "Don't concern yourself, we are all foreigners here."

It was difficult to credit that anyone might appear more out of place than a representative of one of Europe's warring factions, but then the entire Mogul edifice itself was a foreign implantation, the martial efflorescence of a tribal invader. Fury had attended its disciplined arrival from a place rumoured to be the cradle of conquerors, and the vigilant hope of follower-reward now sustained its ascendance, the plains which stretched as far as the oceans, east and west, turned into one vast treasury. Nothing belonged except in the person of the emperor, his acolytes living by his favour. And such favours, as bestowed, were not insubstantial. Because a son, too, might not inherit the chattels of his father, that which enriched a noble household was indeed richly lived. The society of these people remained a ritual of gift-giving and receipt, a refinement of that mercenary instinct which had impelled them into Hindustan, there to impose their customary circulation of its spoils.

Thus with the magnanimity of a conqueror out of harness, secure in the belief that his sword had done its work, Khanin invited me to cross the threshold into his domain, to behold the wonder of his household, its organisation a scaled mirror of the imperial abode. And as if I'd been summoned before the sovereign himself, my host snapped his fingers and presented me with a sumptuous costume of silk, its emerald and lavender vibrancy sewn with pearls.

"You Hollanders don't strike me as particularly colourful," he smiled. "These hues are a little tame, yet a good departure for you, I think."

"But my dear sir, I visit you empty-handed!"

He raised a palm to my shoulder – to sample, perhaps, the meagre simplicity of my fabric. "I can see, then, that you are doubly blessed, for Allah rewards those who are grateful." It was my turn to smile, uncertain of what I might in turn surprise him with. Maybe I shouldn't have perturbed myself;

after all, he was as curious as I to see what might materially unfold in the twinning of our interests, neither of us suspecting that the interest most shared would be his wife.

And so, my dearest Asmat, I entered your home – an invited guest – and you, by a passage I ought to have discretion-locked, quietly entered my excited soul. What gift bore I for your husband? None but the theft of his mistress. And what did I bring you? Only death. Wouldst that I had never have met you – except that life would have remained bereft of that which so amplifies its marvel. The insistence of your possibility was like the shivering of some frozen deep, a revelation that beneath its ice-cast plain our planet's blood ran warm with a current of unfathomable spirit. Despite the wonders I had seen, I'd rarely travelled in exultation of the moment or lived for any-thing other than its material advantage. In your unexpected advent, however, I derived more than a carnal passing; in what you disturbed of my spirit, I felt magnetised to an excess not previously entertained.

I wish now that I might have possessed for you Constantine's jewel, the cameo a precious talisman bridging West and East, past and present, its rarity too precious for the likes of an emperor who commanded everything, who trophied everything. Even your husband, despite his civility, seemed more preoccupied with the inventory of his wealth to count you as anything other than a possession. After all, you were one of how many wives?

Perhaps I seek to mask my theft. God knows I acted with little dignity in the circumstance of your death. Like so many things I regret, I'm penitent for the disservice of your unsung grave, your whereabouts unknown to those who may have wondered. I know that Mahometans are guarded of nothing so much as the chastity of their harems. But by the time Wasim Khanin's spies – not to mention Medari – may have aroused his suspicions, the demands and turbulent happenings at court would have blunted his violence. There are few things less important to an ambitious man than the sensitivities of his wife; at the same time there is nothing more irritable to his complacency than those sensitivities made public. Did he know that you and I sported dan-ger? The imagination of a Moor who keeps more than his share of women is ever imprisoned by what he fears to lose whereas a merchant, by profession, remains always a trader. In either case, Asmat, you suffered by our neglect. You died because neither Wasim nor I foresaw your jeopardy; you were too much the adornment of our separate necessities.

And now that necessity leaves me picked; my every action has consumed me. The affection I might have lavished was snatched by panic. The day was already stifling with a heady mix of sweat and incense when that young widow appeared at her doorway. I had hoped it to be some play-act, a ritual borne of token tribute. But there were others, women whose arms resembled sticks, whose fingers were splayed like a scream, their costume smeared with ashes, their chorus as wailing as anything from old Greece. The widow seemed not of their kind – indeed, she was robed in her finest garments and gold glittered in her face. So like a bride in her measured calm. My heart thudded with incredulity at the spectacle unfolding, knowing all too well the custom of this country. When the City Governor approached her, I felt my spirit lift at the purchase of his authority. "Madam, you need not do this…" And she smiled like a flower, her beauty unconscious of the devil at play within the treasury of her mind. *He was my husband and I must go to him.* "Lady, let me restore your field of hope, let me restock your youth with riches." *I have been more than favoured by wealth. I want for nothing but the breath of my husband.*

"The cameo!" I cry out. "Here, give her the cameo!"

And the throng swivels to face me, incensed that I might lure her from the burning pit.

She smiles. Asmat smiles. "My dear Francisco, it is for love that I must die."

"But you are not a Hindu!" I shout, further dividing the crowd. "Your husband keeps many. Might I not reclaim just you?" And Constantine's jewel, its ancient thunderhead, weighs like an embarrassing trinket in my hand.

"That's no trinket," Medari hisses in my ear. I stare at its chariot, the imperial family swathed in jade and myth. "You have kept this from the emperor," he spits. "You have stolen it for your own profit!"

But my hands are empty, my mind distracted. As she threads the jostling spectators she distributes gifts of rice, the clamour of hands uncaring, and I know, even before the final act, that I am about to lose everything.

"Shall we not share one last drink?" she asks, holding the Venetian glass. It's as if I'm standing both before her and to the rear of that pitiless crowd, my presence imprecise and powerless to intervene in what threatens. Yet what would I have myself do? How is it I'm all optic and no aggression? Why can I not pirate the steerage of another's soul? "You need not do this," I hear myself say as Medari sifts my pockets for everything I've denied him, grubby little turd that he is. The City Governor shakes his head for the folly of my repetition. Asmat sparkles in her apprehension of what her death will mean to me. "Remember what was inscribed upon the arch at Fatehpur Sikri, above the torment of our daring?"

"It was raining. I hardly saw."

"But *I* saw," jabs Medari. "I saw you there!"

I shove him aside; he's of no consequence. All I see is her. The living memory of her. "The world is a bridge," I catechise, "pass over it but build no house."

And as if I have granted her my leave, Asmat smiles and leans close to kiss my cheek. "You and I," she says, "we shared no house. We ventured nothing but an hour of passion."

And although I cannot dissuade her, yet am I compelled to utter that aphorismic desire: "He who hopes for an hour may hope for eternity."

"Until then, our eternal meeting," and she raises the glass to her lips.

A great jeer goes up, a kind of horrified satisfaction. The sky smoulders with ash, the sun ripples behind its furnace curtain. She lies before me, in need of being snatched from so public an abuse. "Salomon," I urge, my voice low so as to conceal what we're up to. "Quick, hurry! We must get her out of here!"

And we become invisible to the crowd although the crowd has not forgotten its mission. As we carry her down the steps an arm suddenly plucks Salomon away. He's being pitched towards the scaffold, lost in a tide of hands. The heat of the killing place outside Batavia Castle is lurid with anticipation. I try to raise my voice but my throat is airless. I watch, jaw-swallowing, as he joins the others – puppets stripped of mind – there on that stage of death. Can I not scream: He was not to blame!?

But the very danger I would summon to myself, the very protest by which I might trumpet my complicity, falls on deaf ears. I am not spared but I am spared for the moment. I scoop Asmat to my breast, her substance again transformed and incorporeal, her ashes flowing like a waterfall from my arms. Her irreclaimable dust stains the green and lavender silks I wear, the pearls soiled yet gleaming in their ruin like a reminder of my theft. Yes, all that remains is the gifted livery of her husband. And the cameo?

Were any of their deaths more terrible than mine, their sudden violence more harrowing for cutting short the breath where breath remained? I'm shitting blood. My breath is foul and I taste of shit. I *am* shit.

O NE LINGERS IN a state of contemplative exhaustion. I scarcely move for
fear of signalling the poverty of what strength remains.

What I long for is a re-beginning, the normalcy of an unscripted yet not
unselfless hope. Such a place (for we ever conjure these things as if viewed
from the casement of intimate perspective) has a savour of adolescent summer. If I close my eyes and straw the air between my lips, I can picture myself
as a child, seated atop a wall and tracing the manoeuvre of other boys as they
shout to one another, their orchard ambuscades not altogether playful. I don't
leave my place. I never come down from my narrow vantage. The rush and
tumble of others tantalises my spirit yet I remain ever threshold, my backside
numbing in this perpetual abeyance. Surely I, too, am a part of the game?

No, this can only be a false imagining for such recollections are unmemo-
rable, the truth stoppered and reversed and presently masquerading in mead-
owy sentiment. If, like a child helping to gather in the harvest, I would have
myself belong in a fashion which summons attention to itself, I retain no
memory of being cheered on or accepted by others. Of those country lanes
and orchards outside Antwerp, I recall only the stone walls, damp and looking more of winter, and of my belonging to others – elders – who bore with
or traded me as concern affected. I was loved, I suppose, after a fashion.
Indeed, I was never permitted to go hungry. But even play seemed like theft,
an embarrassing lapse of concentration within the family's makeshift determination to survive.

I learned early what it was to be earnest, and it pained me to lack the
wherewithal to help defend the family. I didn't even understand what it was
we were struggling against. An imposed frugality had something to do with
it – at least that's what the pinched expression on my mother's face hinted at,
although initially I thought it may have been guilt she felt in no longer possessing for me a father. Then when she married again, I was no longer needed.
And Opa didn't seem poor. Yet throughout those early years I always had this
feeling that we were being hunted, not so much by men in arms – the Spanish, perhaps – as by an unspecified doubt that questioned our right to the very
clothes which never entirely foiled the chill. I think I grew impatient to come
of age. I think my grandfather was of a similar mind. Our games, if you could

call them that, were more in the nature of a nod and a wink, of playing the defender and acquiring the discipline to receive whatever others were of a mind to deliver.

I was about twelve when I first accompanied him to Amsterdam. He had dealings with a banker on behalf of some monastery whose love of God was dearly nourished by a passion for His worldly munificence. The Dutch East India Company was but recently formed and its fleet made everyone — the godly and uncharitable alike — feel portent in what we were still to possess. If Opa entertained ventures surplus to Marta van Luyck, there were seas other than the North and horizons farther than Dunkirk. As we travelled from a nation unbecoming to another in the making, the low-lying farmlands on either side of the border as indistinguishable as the weather overhead, I felt tethered to a journey whose ramifications remained unclear. It was also exciting.

Amsterdam. It was on the lips of the entire world. I heard her mentioned whenever the victuallers made their deliveries, whenever Opa's servants paused in their chores, their faces bright as burnished copper. More than Marta van Luyck might ever attract in speculation, Amsterdam was the queen of all our marvels, the temptress of fortune. I was anxious to glimpse her swelling magnitude, this rumour of a world like none other within the planetary cradle of God's kingdom. The only other time I've been intrigued by the reputation of a great city — indeed, a foreign city — was when I set out with Walter and our tiny entourage for the much-spoken-of capital of the Great Mogul. And in both instances it was difficult to dissimulate where and how expectation shaded into disappointment or disappointment graduated into awe. The outskirts of anything can present uncertainty in arrival, and the centre may proffer a grandeur whose story is not your own. But if Jahangir owned Agra and Coen, like Pericles in the makeover of Athens, had seeded Batavia, it was less easy to identify any personal signature in the shaping of Amsterdam — except for the nickname *Jan* which I and everyone else would soon become familiar with. Yes, the *Jan* Company.

So it was that after a journey of two days we arrived at a thickening in the mist, the autumn light tinted with wood-smoke and comparable to the tainting dust of Hindustan before the monsoon. There was a quiet humming, a sound distantly studded with the bark of dogs and an overcast of traffic. The steeples of the city were the first shapes to resolve themselves, and so I began to listen out for bells and, indeed, detect their discordant competition. Before I realised that the city was upon us, those first ramshackle habitations had suddenly congealed into suburbs of working life this side of the moat. If, like Antwerp, Amsterdam was succoured by the sea, its artery of marine life was for the moment concealed, the fortress ramparts and impressive ditch coolly staring down our approach from the landed south and that which had witnessed siege and sack elsewhere.

I had never seen anything like Amsterdam. It was truly a universe, close and crowded in comparison with the pasture of everything I had known. Indeed, my childhood at point of entry through the city gates grew more innocent and spare, and the only reference to what I knew, my anchor in this surge of novelty, was Opa. He touched my shoulder as our wagon was drawn into the thicket of life. "Once upon a time," he said, "this was Antwerp."

I couldn't believe that Antwerp was ever this. It presented as no more than a village compared with such endless clamour and bustle. Inside the city itself more moats appeared, each district framed by water, and there were barges brimming with fruit and vegetables where roads and carts ought to have been. I felt increasingly belittled as we followed avenues whose narrowness was accentuated by the rise of houses on all sides. Never did I see such building, such confusion of assemblage. Amsterdam appeared to be in a perpetual state of construction, a place arrived too soon at what it would only one day become.

Then I began to sniff the sea, a brininess that couldn't quite disguise the fact that it smelt none too clean. I didn't know where we were headed, only that Opa was cloaked in a kind of speculative calm as if recounting what he needed to remember. The houses began to take on an appearance of something less refined; there was less paint and finish, more in the substance of undressed beam and brick. The streets themselves grew burdened with goods: bales and boxes and all sorts of conveyance stacked along walls with an abandoned air. The people, too, seemed tethered to a diffidence that didn't lift with the light. I have seen such monotony and mistrust, such lopped-off existence in the backstreets of India.

We suddenly passed a lane that revealed the harbour, my breath catching at the sight of its intense scaffolding. But before I could properly take it in, we had rolled on. "Eh?" queried my grandfather, noting my excitement and perhaps thinking I'd had my first glimpse of Amsterdam's lascivious whores. Another side street intervened and there they were again, great spires without solidity, open to the sky yet restrained and given outline by a thousand ties. Their base was a confusion of odd and conflicting shapes – like a tumble of houses – only the effect was exquisite and appealed to my boyish wonder. We were within shouting of the wharves, and the city's claustrophobia abruptly ended before an expanse of water that was neither sea nor river. Upon this watery plain, near and distant, were ships such as I had never beheld, so densely flocked and of such variety that their masts were like a forest in win-ter. The rocking stillness gave the impression of some auspicious preparation, and I could tell that even Opa was staggered to re-witness this redoubtable maritime.

"Where do they all come from?" I asked, excited.

"Some are from the Baltic – the older, smaller ones. But these," and ges-turing to the great hulls that rose in tiers of elaborate castling, "these are Indiamen."

It was like seeing for the first time a rumoured creature, of being intro-duced, perhaps, to a king, the revelation all the more disclosing for its unex-pectedness. A banner such as I had never seen so openly displayed presently billowed in vast sheets from the masthead of all, and smaller craft plied between the larger ships and what I would learn was the Pepper Wharf, its commerce pungent to the nose and mixed to less savoury appeal with tar and fermented bilge. Although not affixed on war, the spectacle harboured a militant aspect – cannon being craned into barges preparing to push off. Only there was little evidence of soldiery; indeed, our wagon was surrounded by a throng which compressed those elegantly attired with others of the most beggarly outfit in a business which rewarded them, perhaps, in different ways yet doubtless rewarded all. Even now, I can picture him as I failed to picture him at the time, a newcomer to this mercantile theatre of chance. *Heer Pelsaert, let me introduce you to Jeronimus Cornelisz. He's new to the Company...* Yes, he was clean shaven and hungry of eye. He was somewhere in the mean of what was then too widespread for me to take in as a child, a species of opportunist too nuanced for me to apprehend. As it was, my grandfather shrewdly eyed my excitement and either pondered the progress of what he had in mind or quickly formulated a proposition hitherto unthought. "Would you like to become a sailor?" he smiled.

I had no idea what I wanted to be. The question seemed another of his games, a jeopardy of capture in reply. Perhaps he took my silence for a negative. Certainly the men who tended the lighters appeared coarse and unlaundered. They wore a confidence, too, that was alarming, their language making me glad it was only Opa and I who were present and not my mother. In fact there *were* other women but these in no way resembled her. To begin with, they sported an appeal that was unsettling; indeed, they were quite willing to loiter in the street trading familiarities and whatever else. Despite being somewhat soiled in the invitation of their dress, I wanted to know more but was afraid of where it might lead. I felt as if I had tripped upon a set-up in which everyone was in on some joke that I, alone, was unschooled in reading.

My grandfather likewise observed my shy fascination. "Sailors rarely make a profitable marriage," he said. Then assessing my narrowness of shoulder, added, "To become a skipper is about as much as you might aspire to."

Polite in uncertainty, I answered nothing.

"To truly command an Indiaman, however," and we turned now into a strand whose warehouses commanded an uninterrupted view of the anchorage, "you must become one of *them*." He indicated a building whose gabled front was squarely pocked with windows that admitted nothing of the life within.

"Who?"

"A lord of the Company."

We trundled on to where he had business to transact, but there was little doubting I was expected to keep in mind all that I'd seen that day, especially the proud and unyielding edifice near the waterfront. I had seen the ships and glimpsed the whores. It only remained for me to learn that the most powerful figure in this new and unholy trinity was the Company itself.

I was, of course, eager to explore an Indiaman – what lad wouldn't? And as a boy along the path to manhood, I was bound to be intrigued by specimens of the opposite sex who weren't the least timid in their overtures. But as for what I might do with my life, it seemed Opa had taken the matter in hand and was making enquiries to have me apprenticed to the fastest growing business hereabout. No, nothing to do with mortgages and property management and the like of what he obtained his living from but, rather, a whole new game of speculative trading. I would become a soldier of commerce with all that attached to its uniform: the command of ships, women, and respect. Yes, although I didn't realise it at the time, Opa was fitting me to a new life.

This was not my only journey north with Opa. His cousin Hans also lived across the border, at Middelburg; a warty-nosed fellow, kind enough but a little too fond of his wine and cheese not to glisten unpredictably at supper. The merrier he got, the more likely he was to dish up a camaraderie that seasoned the kitchen with his loud opinion on almost anything. At times it was a thankless listening on my part, an attendance for the sake of manners. As he and Opa traded news, I often found myself overlooked and weary in what little involved me, or so I thought. Hans, I imagine, was like uncles everywhere, creatures whose lesser blood incites them to tickles of mischief and occasional interference in the upbringing of their nephews. And if he snored loudly as he slept, he was no less in the habit of farting when he drank. My grandfather would sigh at this and proffer me one of his enigmatic smiles.

"The boy, have you found him employment yet?" enquired Hans.

"As you can see, he's still a stripling. My daughter would grieve to have him too removed."

Hans cut a potato and impaled one hemisphere on his knife. "Dirick, Barbara has proven herself quite adept at adapting. How many husbands is it?"

Opa shook his head, inclined not to take offence. "It's scarcely her fault Death stalks her hearth. Besides, young Francisco has been a first-rate companion. Haven't you lad?"

I could only nod, feeling shrivelled in what I might intuit but was too junior to voice.

"In any case," continued Opa, "I intend to marry, myself."

Hans stared across the table. "Don't tell me: she's pretty, rich and widowed."

The other laughed. "What's the point of business if you can't milk it for that little extra?"

"Your grandfather," said his cousin and leaning close, the two hairs on his wart like the ears of an ant, "you want to follow his example. Marry money. Either an heiress or the widow of some important captain." Then shifting himself to fart, "It's those damn bacon and apple pancakes I had for breakfast."

"But sailors aren't rich. They don't make good marriages," I piped up proudly. That Opa had broached the subject of marriage was of no surprise since its innuendo had echoed throughout his house ever since my arrival.

"Not a sea captain, laddie. They leave little but the debt of their everlasting absence. Why, a woman may as well be a widow from the outset. And a poor one at that!"

My grandfather stretched in his chair. It was good to hear from another mouth that which mightn't chime as delicately from his own.

"Young man," continued Hans, "a *real* captain rarely smells the sweat of those who accumulate his wealth. He's rarely in the same place. A *real* captain," and drawing so close I almost swooned at his frothy breath, "can flip the lid of a magic money chest and not bother with the detail of how it got there."

I clearly looked confused.

"My word, Dirick, you're evidently none too prodding a guardian," and Hans raised his tankard to douse a laugh.

"Francisco will learn soon enough. For the moment, though, I keep him at his letters and in the pocket of my visits here and to Amsterdam."

"You should apprentice him to the Company."

Opa looked at me with the thought already measured. "I'll probably marry in the autumn," he said. "It'll be a simple affair; I won't distract you from your business." Then yawning as if to make ready for bed, he casually asked, "Middelburg – the VOC?"

"Booming," replied his cousin and affecting to stand, his well-fed frame bubbling a belch. "Hey," he turned to me, "my pardon, lad, for sounding so rude, it wasn't me, 'twas just the food!"

As with Hans, I grew increasingly attached to my grandfather. It wasn't as if I hadn't known him all my life; rather, it was simply that when I went to live in his house, my mother became a rare treat and I felt the natural order of things put back-to-front. The manners one assumes for a visit had become a vigilance I might never forgo.

Still, we arrived at an understanding without that understanding ever being discussed. And despite a boy's awkwardness in being introduced to the world, I rather enjoyed our excursions and grew bolder in my appreciation of its unfurling horizons. A sense of promise began to qualify the mystery I'd earlier felt when confronted with silences that were like speech suspended at my near approach. As I accompanied Opa on his rounds, initial feelings of trespass began to alchemise into observant curiosity. I was admitted to variants of his own fastidiousness, the exhibited standard of darkened rooms and polished floors, of box-like furniture and handsome globes. Like heirlooms placed high on a shelf, the comforts of possession felt curiously cold and distant. The wealth managed by my grandfather seemed inert, faintly dead, even as the paintings, common enough, of ships gathered at Texel were a reminder of that brisk trade which underpinned this hourglass tranquillity.

As one stepped in departure from the vestry of some house or monastic compound (I was always entreated to perch in waiting whilst my grandfather was ushered into the business sanctum), the resumed sunlight or rain or wind would buoy a sense of motion within the stock of how I lived, the roads travelled turning to good account some detail of enlightenment. Yes, it wasn't solely of business, of conveyance 'twixt one appointment and the next, and I believe Opa chose the occasions I might accompany him with a view to impressing on me the variety of what abounded in this world. In permitting me the last vestiges of boyhood, I was likewise being encouraged to acquire habits of discernment that would stand me a lifetime.

Once – it was in the very heart of winter – we ventured north of Amsterdam. Opa's appointment afforded me my first sighting of Lake Ijsselmeer, a phenomenon resembling a frozen desert, its surface crowded with skaters. I was filled with awe and remember turning to my grandfather who, likewise, was inhaling the chill marvel of something almost overlooked in the displacement of years. I had an instinct for wonders to come, for all the unimaginable chapters in which life's splendour would be crafted from the unexpected. I think I even imagined what love might be.

Strange, is it not, to think that, as a youth and fêted to behold this icy recreation, perhaps one among the hundreds who bobbed in playful velocity was a childish Cornelisz, our futures unwittingly set in drawn convergence. All that I appreciated at the time, however, was this startling image of winter, its clarity and unlikely vigour.

Only in Kashmir, at the lake beneath Jahangir's summer palace and at a time when the emperor and his retinue were well advanced in their withdrawal to Lahore, only then did I again sniff that distilled rawness, my lungs chilled and a little ticklish at first. The lake, there, was beginning to sharpen with ice, its marbled acreage crisping in its clasp of Srinagar. I couldn't help but stare at those strings of men – black on white – who shuffled mistrustfully across the water's winter crust. Despite my trailing mission and frustration in dealing with self-serving lords, these interludes of becalmed spectacle made up for the weariness of disappointment. An unusual light or mood not typically entertained, these unbidden moments were enough to stir a solacing reflection and replenish a sense of who I was as distinct from what I had come to represent. As I ponder, now, this oscillation between innocence and lethargy, I wonder at the likes of Coen and Cornelisz and whether they were ever detained by such pauses; whether they, too, endured the stillness, the inhalation of a certain grace. Or was it all blood and power with them, their acts of conquest and murder a flight from humility?

—❧

No, I would not become a sailor, though the sea would indeed claim me.

When Opa died I was not yet eighteen. I realise now, as I probably suspected all along, that despite the blood-tie of affection, I'd been little more than a lodger under his roof. With him gone, I was an embarrassment to his estate, a mouth without an income. If Marta was in no unseemliness to have done with me, neither was she very accommodating. The property had been left to her, and as I had grown into a young man and she was yet a young woman, there loitered a potential for misunderstanding, for a rivalry which, from her point of view at least, might lead me to claim something of my grandfather's will *or* make unwanted advances. As it was, Opa had made his instructions very clear. I was prized as a child of his daughter, but little more. I would not be suffered to starve but neither would I be permitted to profit.

With my schooling at an end, I was doing odd jobs of a fiscal nature, mostly derived from the charity of my grandfather's acquaintances. I visited my mother and she was pleased to see that I had grown into what she deemed a fine young man, a blush of whiskers upon my chin. Yet welcomed and fed for a few days, treated courteously but at a distance by my stepfather who calculated the cost of what my return might imply, I was forever on the move.

It was at Middelburg, at the house of my dead grandfather's cousin, that I ended spending most of this transient period. Despite his years, Hans had always seemed younger and scruffier than Opa, less a burgher than a tavern-keeper. He traded locally in the re-conveyancing of all sorts of cargo and owned a warehouse into which the VOC decanted its transferable treasures. Everyone seemed to know him, to seek his opinion on how various markets might ride the ripple of events overseas. There was talk of a foray into Hindustan, of rivalling our protestant cousins, the English, who, in any case, were not above stealing a march on us, even as we were supposed to act cooperatively against the Catholic league. If Java, to my ears, was a rumour of middling kingdoms and the island-studded East a harvest of spices for the mere dropping of an anchor, all talk of India was of a fabled power as vast and as godless as the pagan Chinaman himself.

"Ever hear of Pieter van den Broecke?" tested Hans one October evening as we dined on Leiden's commemorative dish of bread and herrings. I couldn't say that I had. "The family, like yours, are from Antwerp. I'm sure Dirick had something to do with 'em at one time. Anyways," and sucking a dribble of oil from his thumb, "Pieter — it was through him — when I'd gotten the warehouse — that I negotiated my deal with the Company. Lord, he was just a young blood, little older than you, now," and wiping the grease from his moustache with his sleeve. "Well, anyways, he's shot up in the world, earned 'imself the respect of his betters and the scraping of lesser men. There isn't much choice, you know, as makes sense for a young man starting out — least-ways not as I see it. 'Tis either beggary or the Company."

And with a grimace of concentration, his eyes shiny in the candlelight, Hans belched as if surprised, perhaps expecting something else. "So much for the food of affliction," he waved. "Anyways, where was I? Ah yes, the Company. And when I say Company, I mean *real* Company work — not wasting about on wharves and counting the wealth of others. Making a wealth of *yourself*, that's the play."

I wasn't stupid. I knew it wouldn't upset anyone for me to say: *Ah, the Company. Now there's an idea...* But I'd been brought up, first and foremost, to listen, and I could tell my relative thought me slow. Hans breathed with an impatience that bordered on indigestion. He was right. I couldn't sit around here all day listening to him fart his opinion on this or that. I did want a hand in shaping things to come, to be something other than a poor cousin at the table of another's bread — ha, the food of affliction! And curiously, despite the itinerancy of my childhood, I wanted to undertake something that would please my mother.

"Van den Broecke, was it?"

"No more than ten years your elder."

"From Antwerp?"

"To Middelburg and Amsterdam."

I considered this, a moment. "And then what?"

"They're saying India is the next big thing."

"He's already there?"

"They're all out there somewhere – them as would make 'emselves captains of the commerce!"

My uncle's conversation was ever leading and attached to the benefit, material or otherwise, of his opinion.

"But how might I be any more than a servant?" I asked.

Hans's face lit up. "You're right to be thinking ahead. Mere clerks are no more than water bearers with inky thumbs. I've employed the same crew now for a couple of years and they'll have to smell my corpse before they realise anything has changed." He was grinning without the least intent of dying. "There's *us*," he leaned close, "and then there's *them*. And the *them* are best served if they serve *us*."

I was staring at his plump and polished wart. I hadn't been aware of my inclusion in anything until surprised in this complicity.

"As a family we're not too badly off. Things could be better, mind you, but the times have not undone us." He leaned back on his stool, rotated his shoulders to loosen the tightness of years, then shrewdly stripped me of my adolescent sanctuary. "Middelburg's a quarter to Amsterdam's half. I'm talking about VOC power. This temporary peace with Spain has freed up our port. We're a gateway to the future. *Your* future, if you choose wisely."

The world was open to me, the ships here and at Amsterdam a beckoning conveyance to adventures whose shape in temperament or time could not be envisaged. I was aware, only, that a populous number sailed and returned – or so I imagined – with such proof of wealth that I never much thought of how they went about it.

Uncle could see that I was amenable to I knew not what, that I needed a little caressing. "As a family," he repeated, "we're not too badly off. And as a family we're obliged to assist one another."

I continued to sit, uneating.

"Francisco, you're not yet twenty and the Company – if it's to take you seriously and tutor you in its ways – will require a sizable surety."

I nodded as if following his drift.

"I was fond of your grandfather. He was like a brother to me," and Hans pinched his nose. "I've made enquiries; the deed is settled. That's why I'm putting up a thousand guilders to have you drafted. That kind of money buys a powerful start."

I was dumbstruck, whether from the frightening amount mentioned or the settling of my future, I couldn't say. I was to report the following morning to an acquaintance of my uncle's at the Middelburg Chamber and proffer his respects. Then do as instructed.

At first I thought the thousand guilders wasted and experienced a forlorn guilt in the costly purchase of so lowly a post. I was a mere assistant to an assistant (though sheepishly grateful to be so invisible whilst I acquired a sense of how things worked) and, at sixteen guilders a month, assigned the most tedious of clerical duties. It alarmed me to find myself among those who happily tolerated an unvarying habit – Opa's routines had always been so leading. My willingness to query that which made little sense and to inspirit the fashion in which things were done did not go unnoticed, and before long I was drawn aside and congratulated on passing an assessment of which I was altogether unaware.

"You are well-fitted," I was told, "to abet our machinery in the East. You're under contract, and we need reliable men. Young, healthy men."

I was lodging with Hans, handing him my salary. I returned that evening to let him know that I had been advised to put my affairs in order. In the wavering light, the hearth imparting its lustre to this unsentimental room that bore his sweat, it was perhaps the closest I ever came to experiencing another's fatherly tenderness towards me.

"Put your affairs in order, eh?" he repeated thoughtfully, and pouring me a cup as if I were a seasoned drinking companion. "Well here's to your health," and he drained his own with a sniff. "I can't say I'll ever see you again."

The candle flame wobbled on its stalk between us.

"Five years is a long contract, a long time to be absent in this mortal life. And mortal I feel, Francisco, although I've not suffered as others, nor am I about to give up the ghost."

His eyes were rheumy in reflection. "When Dirick died, what else was I to calculate but that my time, too, was fast approaching? I didn't journey to see him interred at Antwerp. Why should I? He and I will soon share enough of the hereafter to grow weary of one another. No, die by yourself, I said, I still have business to attend. And you know what? He laughed. *Don't expect me, either, to go out of my way to see you boxed and buried.* But you know, a day or two apart isn't the same as the separation of a year or five."

I was young enough not to appreciate what such an absence might mean. I was young enough not to realise that a person's life falls into chapters, and that these inevitably leave unfinished or deflected the story of previous hopes and intent. "Uncle, I'll return," I said, "and with the money to pay you back."

"Pff. 'Tis of no matter, seeing how you see me old. When you go, I'll make myself another thousand, sure enough. After all, your employer is not above throwing custom in my direction." And then reflectively, "No, it's more the reminder that things have a habit of circling in ways that never quite tally with what you set out to do. I say to you, Francisco, let the Company be your maker and don't be stubborn in how you think. Take advantage of everything. Learn from the likes of Van den Broecke and Coen and these others whose names are on the lips of the Chamber. And forget us here; you won't have time to remember, in any case. No, no," he raised a hand to my objection, "we're now to muddle through in different worlds, you and I. And when it's your turn to die, think *then* of where you sprang from, of what you accomplished. And if there's room enough in your suffering, pray for us, we who will long have vanished in your ignorance."

At that theatrical juncture our supper candle, low of wick, sputtered and went out.

"Christ almighty!" he banged the table.

The hearth flames kept the room alive and, following his lead, I too chuckled. Hans even managed to belch. "Pff. So much for that."

With my future assigned and Hans detained by business during our last days together, I no longer felt so supernumerary. Indeed, in my unmolested soul I felt a great surge of promise, of undertaking beyond the staging of a life scarce yet begun. The only troubling hint of exile came when it was time to leave. I'd not seen Hans the night before; he'd not returned from matters requiring his attention in Amsterdam. Nor did he turn up in the morning. And though I had made the effort to cross the border and visit my mother and sisters a week earlier, I'd found them preoccupied with matters that effectively precluded anything but a brief acknowledgement of my imminent departure.

Don't expect me to overturn what I need to do, just to see you off, Hans had warned. But I hadn't expected to be so alone at that moment of embarkation. I kept glancing over my shoulder, even as I tossed my canvas bag into the yawl. As we pulled away in preliminary voyage to the awaiting ship, the local oarsmen unperturbed by the emotion of those signatured for overseas, I scoured the wharves and their teeming concourse for a paused and waving figure, too needy in farewell to realise that the substance of my homeland was presently a thing of the past. It welled in me like a faceless grief to intuit that I would never see Opa's cousin again, that any distant return would be to a place made strange through absence, whose shaping familiarities were already strained by the undemonstrative fact of their fragility.

As we drew alongside the mighty retourship that would be my berth during the unimaginable months ahead, my pining valediction was abruptly clipped in the delicacy of transferring from the yawl to that immense and shifting broadside. The unsynchronised rhythms of these large and minor planets tested my leap of faith, and clambering with unsteady legs to the main deck, I next looked up into a concocted wonder that was never entirely still, whose structure was makeshift and changing. The rigging and canvases were as fitting a shrine as any Greek might have dedicated to Aeolus, the ship's shrill harp, when under sail, delivering a music that grew boisterous with speed and was valued, because of this, over all else. Indeed, it wouldn't be long before I discovered my inconsequence regarding the vessel's handling, my constitution variously chilled to the marrow in those early days or heaving with sickness.

Presently, and amidst the deck confusion of making ready to weigh anchor, I was pressed to find my place and report to the supercargo.

I contrast that initiation, now, with the arrival of Jeronimus aboard *Batavia* and try to re-imagine something of the trepidation he must have similarly felt. But who am I fooling? He was ten years older when he entered the service, already a man shrewd of observation and imbued with secrecies. I can see, now, that he was less in awe of his new surroundings than assessing of their potential to gratify his lusts. By that time the Company was taking on men from whatever quarter, the quest to inhabit the colonies desperately short of recruits. Few questions were asked so long as there were few answers to be expected later on. And as for a thousand-guilder surety...

And so, in innocence of what I was to find and take up in the Indies, I sailed from one life to the next in the *Weapon of Zeeland*.

A sailor, no. I didn't care for the protracted quarantine of a long voyage. Quarters were cramped and, despite the immensities of weather, there was always an airlessness below deck. Whatever one might admire in our maritime architecture (and there are countless things to marvel at), the ingenuity that goes into piecing and provisioning an East Indiaman tends to illuminate the obvious by way of trying to mitigate its miseries. There is never enough room or privacy. And unless one is a sailor – this dubious occupation providing a somewhat invidious respite from boredom – there is never enough employment for so large and confined an assemblage of men. The food, too, calculated as it is to avoid starvation, grows unpalatable in its paucity of array.

A voyage is the greatest test of endurance – to be more precise, it's an incisive challenge to what one supposes of oneself. From the lowliest cadet to the highest official, all are equally fated to suffer the suspension of that which governs his habit and desires. A voyage conspires to bridge that which is unbridgeable, to detach a man from familiar continuities and induce a trance-like forbearance akin to sleep. Much is made of the sea's romance; it's usually the talk of fishermen and coastal traders, men untouched by distances that outstrip the measure of an eye and who sing of freedoms contained within the russet of a single sundown. An ocean voyage is far more dogged, its initial novelty, like a false promise, soon imprisoning in its unchangeability.

Yes, we were too tightly crammed.

It was difficult to credit so small a craft as having delivered so many to this moment of decision. Our numbers outweighed our general confidence to continue, yet there was no going back. Jacobsz was insistent. But even he knew that, having swayed my mind, the responsibility for survival was now vested in his skill. It seemed that everyone trusted the skipper yet the skipper himself was in need of confirmation. Having presumed against my doubts, he most definitely, now, wanted me on board.

We gathered on the beach that morning, stepping from the vacuum of a night which had delivered nothing. All were ragged and exhausted and disappointed that not more had come of our success in landing. The wind, as usual, was in perfect accompaniment with the surf, the sand scouring our ankles and sores. The young mother wanted, perhaps, to culture a distance from the others and swaddle her newborn in some fantasy of protected space; to pretend, as it were, that our emergency wasn't far removed from what was normal. But Zwaantie wouldn't permit her to stray and kept an eye on the men who clustered close to the longboat. She understood all too well that nothing here was normal.

"Well," he said, and unable to utter my name or rank, "are we agreed?"

I glanced wearily at the skipper, at his hunger to have done with this form of starvation, and felt a cross-current of envy and guilt. Acceptable or not, his ability to arrive at conclusions within a moment's deliberation left me feeling derelict. "Let me summon someone to notarise the decision," I replied, casting an eye among those who sat dejected on the sand nearby. Salomon wasn't with me; indeed, I couldn't recall when I'd last seen him, whether it was aboard the ship or among the folk we'd deposited on that shell-grit crust. "Never mind, I'll script it."

I took a sheet of paper from my box and prepared the ink. I felt myself at the mercy of sailors, a hostage in Jacobsz's camp, yet no one – apart from Evertsz – displayed the least hostility. It entered my head that Jahangir, too, had been briefly the hostage of his chief general before that seditious gentleman, wondering what next, had seen fit to decamp from his own presumption. Like Jahangir, I was nominally viewed as the law in this place without name or fixture, and it was imperative that my actions not be misconstrued as desertion. When I had finished, I read aloud:

> *I, Francisco Pelsaert, Supercargo and Commandeur of the VOC Ship Batavia and in Council with the Ship's captain and senior officers, hereby declare that having rescued a majority of the Ship's people and securing them on a nearby Island, and having searched without favour for water with which to succour those so misfortuned, our luckless endeavours having removed us to so great a distance from the Shipwreck as to make our return both profitless and impractical, it is resolved by the present Council to forthwith cross the Timor Sea with God's guidance in the hope of arriving at the Port of Batavia and alerting the authorities to the plight of our stricken countrymen. Witnessed this Day, June 16, Anno Domini 1629.*

> *Francisco Pelsaert, Commandeur*

I handed the stylus to Jacobsz and he added his signature. It was then passed to those instructed to line up and witness their approval of the decision to abandon the Great South Land.

Jacobsz was already inspecting the boat, ensuring that the raised boards which had abetted our crossing to this disappointing continent were now secure enough to rebuff a continent of ocean. If there had been a moment's relief in electing to call off our fruitless search, the immensity of what we were now preparing to undertake gave pause to even the stoutest of hearts. The skipper whistled a summons and the aching figures of those who, after months at sea, had spent their first lean day on terra firma presently filed towards the boat with a resignation bred of haplessness. Before stepping into the shallows, each man pocketed himself a small stone. When it came to Zwaantie she asked of the skipper, "What's this?"

"'Tis to suck on as the need arises," he replied, his eyes marshalling the others, and with a gruffness that was almost tender. Then looking at her as if they were alone, "'Twill ease the thirst."

Zwaantie nodded, then turning to the mother who seemed oblivious of everything shaping her fate, stooped to pick up a second pebble.

Only Evertsz hung back. Perhaps he realised that in stepping into the boat he was almost certainly giving himself up to death. As if the threat of drowning wasn't enough, the very prospect of salvation, that for which we all prepared to venture ourselves, could only diminish his chances of survival. Either I must die or he must pay.

Jacobsz said something and the two of them fell to arguing. It was a hissed exchange which had less to do with the madness we were about to embark on than the polity of who was in the boat. The skipper glanced at me, seemed frozen in a moment of prophetic insight, then turned to slap Evertsz with demonstrative violence. "Listen to me, and listen to me good..." was all that I managed to hear as I stooped, also, to collect a pebble.

"You promise?" whined Evertsz. "You promise 'twill be done?"

"Come on. Get into the boat!"

And so we forwent that which was firm but without feast for the heaving risk of whatever lay ahead. Having kept to the ambiguous security of that coastline, we were now committing ourselves to days – possibly weeks – in excess of any expectation of help should the waves upset our boat and deliver us to the sharks.

It occurred to me that lately I had spent a lot of time crossing from one responsible situation to another. Their rapid sequence gave me little time to collect my thoughts, little time to acquire the mastery needed to avert consequences that hourly threatened. Yet hourly we drifted through the making of our story, the end too uncertain to imagine it as history also. All was a-grapple with what most imminently threatened, a juggle of contingencies scarcely reasoned.

"Come, balance the boat!" shouted Jacobsz as we levered ourselves through the first broken surges of foam. Everyone sat upright in a clutch of panic, the oars flung wide like the wings of a dragonfly.

Beyond the spray, beyond the swell and menacing breaks that threatened to swamp this new beginning, our sudden and regained stability was accompanied by a release of breath that permitted each to look back with desolate relief – and no less a feeling of betrayal that relief itself had not been discovered in that desolate land.

For me it was yet another leave-taking, another before I'd had a chance to take proper stock of what was being left behind. Those in the Abrolhos were now at a double remove, the impellency of the moment leaving in its wake an accruing bill of unfinished business. So heavy was my heart that it seemed the very edifice of life was one of unforeseen flight, of stepping into situations only to realise they were neither new nor entirely accidental but had festered from earlier wounds of disaffection or impermanence.

No, I was no sailor, and in recent weeks, when the flux was upon me, I had gagged in the belly of *Batavia*. But with the ship now crippled and our party reduced in prayer to this shoulder-squeezing ark, the sea continued to dominate the very issue of life itself, to moisten us in shivers as it salted our tongues.

My lips, even now they taste of blood. I scrape them with my teeth and am disgusted at the scum, soft and jelly-like. To swallow is to feel as if drowning in the brine of one's fever. It's as though the body's outer city has fallen to an invader, the defenders (such as yet breathe) having retreated into the citadel of the skull. There the thatch burns but the walls, although baking, are not yet sundered.

Batavia's walls were not breached, even though the surrounding districts were burned to the ground. It was fortunate, you might say, that I left the gate at the bottom of the sea.

How's that? asks Coen, inclined to sound out a military angle.

The Mataramese may have picked its lock – ha ha. Then where would you have been?

We have men. We have arms.

Jahangir's army was two hundred thousand strong.

You, Pelsaert, hisses Van Diemen, you have left both men and arms back at the wreck.

We couldn't cram everyone into the longboat.

Instead of Hayes you brought a woman and her baby.

Hayes was needed in the islands. There was a war there, too.

Francisco's right, intercedes Coen. We can manage without him.

The entire world will manage without him!

By the soul of Christ you're a malicious prick, I stab.

Antonio – Andrade, not Van Diemen – winces. His is two presences: the first, a surpliced priest, bible in hand and standing beneath an enormous arch; the second, hooded and seated close to where I lie. Except that I am no longer lying. I seem a vapour among them, an ether of feeble connection.

They were indeed an alien lot, murmurs Andrade, and I'm unsure of whom he refers. Suddenly I see his caravan in the frozen shadow of a gorge. Wiebbe is standing in a blade of sunlight, the sea sparkling behind him. There's a sudden stench of bat shit, and Cornelisz's face rears into view to eclipse Wiebbe's silhouette. His grin becomes a leer before his head is struck from its body.

That, *Pelsaert, is what you do with competitors.*

Don't you mean conspirators?

No, I mean competitors. Jahangir cackles drily and turns away. His army is two hundred thousand strong, and they ride on winged camels and clouds of horse.

God's angels await you, intones Andrade, taking a step closer.

You know I cannot return.

Once a Catholic...

Even more so a Calvinist... Besides, you know the Company hates Jesuits most of all.

But when I look at Bastiaensz I have my doubts. He's perched on a cot — confined not like Jacobsz who is in a dungeon deep, but detained for want of spirit. *They mocked me and my God*, he says. *If I would so much as pray, they flapped in mimicry of my goodness, those seal fins the serpent wings of their demonic masque.*

Andrade looks at me and shrugs. *Where were your Christian martyrs in this new Rome of yours? Only righteous sacrifice can atone for the breaking of God's covenant.*

"God, my arse!" jeers Cornelisz's head, spittling blood.

I look away, horrified. Even Andrade flinches.

"I can tell you now, from within this discarded casing wherein my lusts were tutored, God is a poppet of your imagination, the fruit of a delinquent craving. Believe me, I have found – as I knew when living – neither God nor Satan."

Yet you speak to us now, I gasp. From where?

His nostrils snort. "Your conscience is the very prick to this little theatre."

And of that which you boasted during the voyage?

"Purely the tabled puffery of an unadorned truth: that you only live the once so you'd better make the most of it."

Don't listen to him Francisco, cries the priest.

"Don't listen to him Francisco," repeats the head, prissily.

I command you, unclean spirit, whoever you are...

Cornelisz grins and is whole once more.

I command you to obey me, I who am a minister of God despite my unworthiness...

"By the Whore of Rome herself, who is this costumed milksop?"

Even Coen and Van Diemen are spellbound by a spectacle such as seldom infects their sleep. Jahangir is tending to his nails. *You Christians*, he shakes his head and not looking up, *you're as dangerous to yourselves in your childish beliefs as the Hindus over whom I rule. Don't you agree, Medari?*

I told Pelsaert, your Majesty, not to trust those infidels, Pagoo Singh and Nagar Bai.

Medari's right, Pelsaert, you simply can't afford to get in thick with these people.

Francisco, please, cries Antonio, *don't listen to them.*

"I tell you what, Francisco," swings Cornelisz, now dressed in red laken and wearing my broad hat at a rakish angle, "let's test this priest of yours."

Test?

"Yes. Let's scratch the surface of his faith."

Andrade has now fallen to his knees and is incanting a prayer of banishment. *Depart transgressor. Depart seducer, full of lies and cunning...*

"O sticks and stones..." prances the tiger, twirling a sword uncommonly jewelled and therefore pilfered. "But let's return to what he defends: this pious partnership which pretends to a foot in this world and another in the next."

There's a logic of merit and reward, I say, a connection between goodness here and godliness throughout eternity.

"And you believe in God's absolute power to order His creation?"

Absolutely.

"Tut, Francisco. You know you tell yourself a mischief. How else might you judge me in God's name?"

Be gone foe of virtue, persecutor of the innocent...

"Be still you pampered imposter! I tell you, Francisco this meddlesome priest is no more than a spy, the word of God his cloak and God himself but a feint. All this talk of the Almighty merely serves to purify the most dubious of your self-justifications."

Jeronimus, you blaspheme appallingly. If God's vengeance were suddenly to manifest itself —

"What, a lightning bolt in the here and now? Don't concern yourself. Such a divinity, were He to exist, must necessarily enjoy a malicious humour given the number of so-called innocents He permits to be eaten."

You're their murderer!

"No, more the instrument of His will, if you would permit Him to be absolute."

He has gifted us a *free* will, I say, wherein we might prove our worthiness.

"Like the free will expressed under torture whereby I was pained to confess to crimes I didn't commit."

You still deny?

"I deny you!" And his face becomes a fierce grotesquery. "I deny you the comfort of this fantasy that justice should exist!"

I had you punished.

"You had me no more than killed. And as you can see, I'm none the worse for it."

You're a ghost, proof of an afterlife. And suddenly I'm confounded, not wanting to credit that he might in any way be saved.

And he is laughing, now. "Francisco, there *is* no afterlife." And he disarms my objection, adding, "What you see is the very doubt *you* have always harboured, the doubt that there is a divinely sanctioned encampment called paradise."

Holy warriors enjoy its fruits, I assure you, enjoins Jahangir.

Don't believe him, hisses Andrade, breaking off his prayer. *These Moors are savage infidels.*

"And the followers of Christ are meek?" heckles Cornelisz. "Since I am the very devil of Pelsaert's conscience, let me enquire of your purpose in setting out for that rumoured mountain kingdom?"

Andrade steals a glance at me. *To discover Christians*, he answers hesitantly, then cloaking himself against Satan's imperious stealth, adds, *to spread the word of God, the teachings of Christ.*

"What need of discovery if Christians were already there? Why spread a word already spread?"

The Church of Rome required confirmation. Besides, and looking peevish now, *they were not Christians we discovered.*

"Tut. Like me, you were just an adventurer. Like me, your actions were fitted to dominance."

Their king received us kindly enough, even though the place was cold and the people reduced for want of comforts.

"Fertile grounds for a missionary, I should have thought."

We did what we could. I became an advisor to the king...

"See, Francisco," shrugs Jeronimus, his head none too securely attached to his shoulders, "religion, it's about the man who would play the king on earth."

I found myself quite suited to governing, interrupts Coen, and religion scarce had anything to do with it.

"Same here," rejoins Cornelisz, "until overwhelmed by godless men who pretended their brutal luck was Heaven-sent."

You were a tiger, I say.

No Pelsaert, he is a rebel who would seize what you left without, first, properly securing.

I turned only briefly. It was little more than three months!

Jahangir shakes his head, the pendant on his turban and his earrings dancing. *Throughout my reign I have learned that it entails but the inattention of a moment to procure the death of something — whether life, friendship, hope, trust. You trusted this man?*

I trusted the high office to which he was beholden.

I trusted my sons, my amirs, my generals. The emperor grows solemn. *Your rebel — the lowly born and impotent miscreant that he was — he's onto something here. Nothing of glory is done for the glory of Allah alone. Why would a man slit the throat of his brother to steal his wife or covet the riches of his neighbour when none of what is gained may pass with him into the afterworld? Even the Prophet we share has declared that a rich man is no more able to enter Paradise than a camel to pass through the eye of a needle. And why? Because of some perceived misvirtue? No, I'll tell you the truth. The Epicurean is right. There is no afterlife. You may as well take as many wives as you like — oh come now, Pelsaert, don't be looking so chary; we know you're not above slipping between the sheets of another man's bed. And while you're at it, amassing in coin and IOUs whatever you imagine you're entitled to. All that private trading. Dealing in undeclared goods and loans of stern percentage. Who's to know? As long as you approach your deathbed in the swaddling certainty of having captured as much as you dreamed of, then you've won against life's odds. Not cheated death; no, not that. But made the best of a cornered contest.*

I am frightened now of what is beginning to sound like a conspiracy of shades. Van Diemen and Bastiaensz are no longer present. But these others — the dead — appear to see something I fail to comprehend. Where do you issue from? I cry. Are you all in league?

Hardly, answers Coen, polishing his breastplate.

But where is my bounty? Where are my riches? Am I to die short of what I might have attained?

"Ha, don't complain to me of a life cut short!" retorts Cornelisz.

Coen and Jahangir exchange a look.

I might have seized Malacca, whimsies the governor.

I might have recaptured Kandahar, sighs the emperor.

Then they each turn to stare at me. *No, what we imagined, what we set out to accomplish, these things have mostly come to pass.*

And Medari (can he also be dead?) brings a golden tray bearing two cups encrusted in rubies and sapphires. The royal blood and merchant warlord, each with an empire to sustain, toast one another's glory, an emerald laughter staining their teeth.

Medari catches my eye and pokes his tongue.

You're an insolent fuck! I shout.

Sticks and stones...

I rub fire into my eyes, hoping to abridge a realm which, even as I suffer its phantoms, I find uncompassing and devoid of the constancies that surely hallmark truth. Its territory is not terra firma, and blinking, I again see Wiebbe standing in a blade of sunlight, the sea sparkling behind him. Again, too, Cornelisz's face rears into view, eclipsing the soldier's silhouette, his grin the very leer of Satan. Andrade bends down to comfort me. *Give place, abominable creature, give way, you monster, give way to Christ in whom you found none of your works.* I am lying on my back, the arch rising heavenward beyond the eyes-closed priest. In the pattern of its inlay, in the calligraphy which scrolls the message of a shared prophet, I read what at first seems difficult to reconcile: that this life is but a bridge to the next, therefore build no house upon it.

For he has already stripped you of your powers...

Antonio, it is me.

...and laid waste your kingdom.

Batavia's arched gateway lies at the bottom of the sea. I see fishes in its waters green and am startled by the swollen passage of a serpent. Cornelisz eases into view behind the priest.

You! I choke.

He extends an arm — laterally, so that my eyes are swivel drawn — and Asmat reaches for his hand.

My swallowing is violent. I can't control my throat.

He has cast you forth into the outer darkness where everlasting ruin awaits you.

There's water, poured. And even pieces of biscuit on a plate. It's been set out as if for something larger than a mouse, something less than a man. The stillness of the room is expectant, even though I no longer anticipate a visitor — leastways none who might retrieve what lately seemed more important than the unexpired fact of life itself. Might I have grown too weary for vanity? In a sweat of thanksgiving, my laboured breath does not detract from the relief of finding myself alone in this quiet room with its biscuit on a plate, a thoughtfulness I've not the strength to avail myself of. Instead, I lie here, mapping the ceiling with a crowdedness of mind and feel something tickle my ear. It's wet, and I realise my charting eyes have sourced a stream unfelt along creased and greasy riverbeds of flesh. And I can only say that it is sadness I feel, not regret. Or if regret, then with a penitence that is comforting. Yes, the provision of water and a biscuit, this orderliness of confinement which verges on respect, for this I feel meekly grateful.

I allow the tears to dry where they flow and add their stain to the crystallisation of what I am becoming. If Hartanti were present I would reach for her hand, mine grasping like a child's in its weakness. But Hartanti isn't here, and were she to re-enter the room she would doubtless mistake the sincerity of anything I tendered.

"We are not your foes," smiles Medari. "To the contrary, our rivalry breeds character, it earns you a respected name."

He has not let go of my hand, is sampling my fingers in turn, feeling for the knuckles in each. I'm reminded of the butcher who wields the crowbar, only this is a more innocent time — innocent for me, at least, whose adventure is youthful and without blemish. *Look here,* nauti *is like a growing lad who is still to come into his prime and vigour...* It was Medari who first explained to me, in this fashion, the varying grades of indigo.

"Indeed, a merchant is a nomad. We possess no habitat other than our livelihood; we share no tribe other than this roving fellowship."

"You regard not India your home?"

"Pff," the breath escapes. "India is full of Indians," and he spits a stream of betel. It glistens, dark as blood, in the flickering torchlight, and the walls of the room we share are stained with the mucus of other lives, much as if the chamber had once been a dungeon, its floor awash with suffering. Yet the caravanserai has been constructed to an honourable end, although less than honourable men have undoubtedly embraced its sanctuary with nary a sheltering thought for others.

The first time I visited the place was with Walter and our two Hindu servants. Fatehpur Sikri had long been a backwater, its imposing stones drained of life and courtly intrigue by the imperial resurgence of Agra. There was a funereal air to this manufactured capital now out of season. Because it was no one's tomb — excepting that Sufi saint's whose benevolence of prophecy, once fulfilled, had spurred the great Akbar to confect this short-lived capital — a certain indifference attached itself to the relic of an emperor's conceit. Akbar was not Allah, whispered critics of the late monarch, and the populous veneration which protected Hindu and Mahometan temples did not attach itself to the remainder of the royal complex, although it was unclear as to what might construe trespass.

The once busy city beneath the palace walls with all its attendant necessities and services — yes, its artisans who toiled daily to hew and shape great blocks of russet sandstone and inlay these with strips of marble; those, too, who jewelled the earthly ceilings with a counterfeit night; yes, the engineers who squeezed a thirsty land to assure the palace that its terraced geographies would always feature representative rivers and ornate pools; the wives, likewise, who lived for the nurture of their own creations: children who shrieked and somersaulted or begged as children the world over are wont to do; the whores, too, who seduced the lonely or massaged the disappointment of men whose reward never tallied with what was taken from them daily; yes, the goatherds and the butchers and the peddlers with their monkeys, the carpet weavers and the merchants who stroked their beards in assessment of what might turn a profit in the invention of another's need; the folk who bickered for a bargain at the morning markets, such venues the very glue and transaction of life itself — yes, all of this evaporated with the vanishing of the royal presence, the metropolis shrinking to a village as its muscle withered. The *nauti*, as Medari had so elegantly put it, had become the *katel* without having savoured the intermediate vigour of the *ziarie*. Parks were ploughed and goats explored the abandoned courtyards. Overhead, vultures circled in patient majesty of this over-ripened and discarded fruit.

Walter and I were on our first tour to the indigo fields, and the caravanserai would ordinarily have beckoned a welcome haven. Its quadrant, however, was overshadowed by the looming edifice of the abandoned royal quarters, the domes floating like follies in the gathering dusk. Our conversation in approach, too, had been unsettled at the passing of a sentinel minaret whose appearance suggested an unholy marriage of pagan superstitions. Beneath the cupola at its top, the column was a daggery of stone tusks, the very hedgehog of a thing. Perhaps Akbar had been mad. The expression "going native" might apply as much to conquerors as to any citizen of those lands subdued. Only later, when I chanced upon a roadside tower of heads (itself a Mogul flourish), was I confronted by a more sinister stamp of how this country chooses, at times, to adorn itself.

The foreignness of everything, arriving as we did just short of night-fall, only oppressed Walter the more. Passing beneath an arched gateway, we entered a theatre of flambeaux and settling livestock, of boys in long white robes jogging barefoot at the beck and call of their masters, the clash of tongues, shrill and metallic like swordplay. Already our servants were locked in fierce negotiation with dubious-looking villains, most no more than boys whose missing teeth and knockabout appearance underscored their worldly confidence in procuring lodgings to our undoubted satisfaction. Walter and I drifted through this carnival scene, past the central well where copper pots were handed to one side and oxen led to drink at the other, and on to a row of cells which faced the courtyard. Beneath each darkened arch, atop steps that raised a view across this sanctuary of pilgrims and commercial travellers, braziers cultured cooking smells familiar and now hungrily savoured. With only half a mind to concentrate, we were being shown an alcove – *Oh yes, a most superior. You from Englisher, no?* – which was indistinguishable from its neighbours other than that the fumigant of an impromptu kitchen had not as yet had a chance to dispel the reek of piss and armpits.

"A right shithole, this," judged Walter.

"It's only for the night," I countered, not wanting my senses bludgeoned by his languishing morale.

It was only natural that the eyes of the many should be drawn to the novelty of two conspicuous foreigners. But as we deposited our belongings and our servants attended to the donkeys, I felt from within that ogling crowd the focused stare of one who was weighing the merit of insinuating his acquaintance. Indeed, so intense was this sensation that I had little difficulty in espying he who would know us better. He was squatted over a pineapple-shaped huqqa, pipe in hand, his smile more a surmise. It was as if he already knew us, was just waiting for us to settle in before coming over to say: *Well who would have thought to have found you two here!*

And venture over he did. "Hollanders, no?" and bowing in the style of *I most humbly welcome you to my shop.* "I have had occasion – several times over – to travel to Surat. I only pray to Allah – may His goodness magnify compassion – that one day that port which so prospers foreigners becomes an unlocked gateway to Mecca." His more than serviceable Dutch startled me. "I think you," and turning to Walter, "are not unfamiliar. My name is Abdul Khabir Medari. My father was a barber in Kabul."

Walter withdrew a moment in calculating inventory, as if trying to think of what it was he'd forgotten to pack, before looking up and replying, "Yes, we know you. You were to have been of service." His tone suggested that nothing of the sort had been the case, and even I vaguely recalled mention of Medari, the day I'd first met with Van den Broecke and the others.

Medari grinned, his engagement undermined by a broken tooth and assemblage of unhandsome features. He was wearing an embroidered skullcap that gave resemblance to the pilgrims I'd seen en route to the coast – although, as I would soon learn, there was more of the usurer about him than anything pious. Indeed, he was of a type whose cunning was garbed in diplomacy. He shifted his gaze from Walter to myself, perhaps to assure himself that he didn't know me, before dealing with the allusion of my companion. "Forgive me, but had we settled on some business?"

Walter caught my eye. *Watch and learn.* "How was it you sought us out at Surat, Medari, promising to broker a lucrative cut of the indigo harvest, yet you delivered so little?"

The Moor reached for Walter's hand but Walter was having none of it. "I can see," shrugged Medari, "there has been some misunderstanding."

"I can see," retorted Walter, "that a promise is not a bargain and a bargain, in some quarters, not worth the promise of a whore."

I breathed deeply at this, and perhaps the Mahometan sensed the apology of a deputy. There was no doubting Walter could be brusque, and even I, of late, had begun to suffer the humidity of fatigue and irritability.

"The crop was no good," Medari stood his ground.

"Yet we heard the Armenians grew rich on the profits," persisted Van Heuten.

"Ah, my dear merchant – those greedy Armenians would gorge themselves on their right hand if they thought there was money to be made. They pay too much."

"A payment you're more than happy to receive and fob us off into the bargain!"

Again Medari glanced at me, his bland smile masking the calculation that it was I, not Van Heuten, whom he needed to befriend. Could he perceive, even then, the Reaper's impatience to redeem my companion? Returning to his antagonist, "I repeat, the crop was no good. These idolaters who sow what they would cheat of you, they refuse to open their eyes to the one true God – may Allah be exalted throughout the world – and for this He has sought to visit them with pestilence."

"Yet the Armenians – not of your creed – are permitted to prosper from it?"

Medari grinned once more as if to indulge too literal a child. "You, my dear merchant, are likewise an infidel, even if we share the prophets." And he laughed at this unexpected pun before drawing near. "You see, to learn something of your speech is to learn that Hollanders, like English, are infidels among Christians. No?"

Walter winced at the proximity of his breath, the toothy stain of betel. "I've not come here to debate religion. I leave that distraction to the Portuguese. If you must know, we've been compelled to set up shop in Agra because there are none in these parts who might broker for us."

Medari raised both hands as if to rebuff the imputation or gesture reassurance.

"None," continued Walter, "in these God-forsaken parts who can be trusted to keep his word."

In this foreign encampment I felt somewhat admonished by the assertiveness of my countryman and looked away, the square teeming with end-of-day folk unlike ourselves in costume yet all too similar in the squabbling commerce of a shared ordinariness. What might a donkey or a camel infer of any difference among us? A whip will savage flesh in whichever language, and baggage is a burden under whatever sun.

As the sun, itself, subsided and the faithful were called to prayer, Medari touched his heart and excused himself with a grace that was nothing if not refined.

"I tell you, Pelsaert, the sooner we conclude this little tour and return to Agra, the better."

I watched as lines of prayer mat were hastily laid and the acolytes of Mahomet arranged themselves without marshal or instruction. Few pikemen would have so formed up without the brandishing of their sergeants. Every man knew his drill, and I momentarily felt at one with this human mosaic which, despite exclusions bred of creed or custom, conveyed a universal petition to be granted sanction in this world and salvation in the next. Even as I looked on, many Hindus, too, attended with an idle curiosity that belied the intolerance of the Moors for the incense and painted satyrs which so crowded the native pantheon.

"Fucking heathens," muttered Walter, struggling to breathe.

Near the well and in corners of the square, oxen were lowing on twisted necks, goats skittered in packs, and camels sat at anchor. Someone spilt a pitcher of water and words were traded, the exchange prompting a belligerent shoving. The scuffle kicked up a cloud of dust, sticks becoming weapons, and the edge of prayer dissolved into an all-too-earthly fracas over who had offended whom.

"The lot of 'em would no less think of slitting the throat of another as of taking a shit," added Walter, beset by something peevish which moistured his brow.

Mogul guards — never obvious due to their lack of uniform — hurried to break up the melee. Men drew shawls around their affronted dignity and drifted off in sullen twos and threes. High above the caravanserai, the sky was mottling into a soothing transformation of colour: from nectar to coral, an irreversible deepening like blood in tainting saturation of a bath.

Walter turned and withdrew into the comfortless shadow of our lodging. An oil lamp was procured but still the night weighed premature and oppressive. The servants snored in a corner; Walter tossed restlessly and coughed as if acquiring the habit. And me? I struggled to becalm myself, to free myself from the shackling discontent of others. My compatriot was proving a poor companion. His contempt for everything around us made me wonder what it was that had induced him to play the merchant in the first place. Surely the certainty of foreign parts ought to have been a caution. And in fairness, he wouldn't have been the first to have had his business sensibilities rankled by the environment in which he found himself. Still, there was something broken or breaking about him, a marked withdrawal that bespoke some realisation that the life before us — or at least for him — was no life at all. Had he glimpsed or intuited a danger I was too undecided to see? Certainly he would die before me, his example of little warning in what would one day stew my strength. *The sooner we conclude this little tour and return to Agra, the better...* That was just to give himself courage, to medicine himself with the hope that the best of all things past might be reclaimed. But Agra wouldn't offer the sanctuary he craved, and to rewind himself further — to return, perhaps, to the Fatherland itself – would have been, in the circumstances, the ultimate ignominy, a confession that he hadn't made it, that his promise had faltered. As I see it now – and even if it meant death to him – there was no going back.

"Pelsaert," he'd whispered, his scalp threadbare, his flesh sallow on the skull. "You will take over."

I nodded solemnly, a spectator in this overture to another's extinction. I'd never warmed to him; couldn't summon the loss or love so ingredient to disaster. If anything, I felt a tugging promise of responsibility. Yes mine was a dispassionate compassion.

Walter must have gleaned my truant thoughts, that calculation behind the eyes which was investing in a future he no longer shared. "You needn't strip me before I'm dead."

"Forgive me, Heer Factor, but I think you overtire yourself." My formality said it all.

Even if Death's ledger reflected unkindly on the stamina of Europeans, I found it impossible to put myself in Walter's situation, to believe that I, too, might be snatched by an invisible miasma. In the midst of death the fury of life was teeming.

"You remember this, Pelsaert: I died in service. You tell 'em. *Tell 'em!* I abandoned no one."

I found myself drawn from that room, my thoughts beckoned outside by sounds of being which, like the passage of a stream, skimmed my imagination to more sanguine possibilities. Water was direction, an unstoppable presage into the future. And hadn't we, as a nation, chosen to fit ourselves to its elemental temper, to harness its power in the wager of ourselves upon the world? Whatever its scale, its fluidity was the motion, the very lifeblood of existence. Except when drowning. That sudden contradiction made me blink, made me look away.

It is said that drowning has a softer edge. Frankly, I've known none who have died thus and returned – even briefly – to deliver their verdict. If we trust in God, why must the ordeal of dying so terrify? For sure there are terrible ways to cease, moments of calculated pain and humiliation. And even without war or judicial dispatch, nature itself seems unnaturally violent. Irrespective of how you pray, the Horsemen of the Apocalypse shudder the soul of man. And yet we believe in the mercy of an afterlife. While Mahometans cling to their fable of paradise and Hindus, in creeds without number, devise cycles of reincarnation that defy life's wastage, wherein do the souls of those *truly* saved reside? In the surety that there is a life after this, Heaven's kingdom must be as populous as India itself with all the righteously departed, its mortal immigration stretching back to the pages of Genesis! Yet despite the assurances of men both learned and theological, not to mention the inspired trust that teeming multitudes surely dwell in unison with Christ, there remains this startling silence from beyond the grave. Is it too childish a fear to cherish hope in ways that concede to the misconception of other faiths, to fairytale gardens of milk and honey and eternal bliss? I examine the purity of our own church, its austere and republican sentiment, and find myself wishing, perhaps, for a little of the nursery colour which so adorns the papist fantasy. Maybe in moments of doubt I'm reminded I was born a Catholic – though only just, and without nurture in its doctrine for our family was pragmatic in what it worshipped, my grandfather all too aware of the advantage in attaching us to the Reformed Church. I sometimes wonder whether, if not for the violence we visit among ourselves to prove a point, religion itself might be permitted to become a private affair and trouble none aloud. After all – and unlike the papists who insist that God can never be communed with except through the intermediary of a priest – our belief is one of equal countenance before the Almighty. Yes, I am not some schoolboy to be lectured to by a Jesuit. God is in direct speech with my conscience.

And yet how confused my certainties become... The puritan form I observe qualifies its mercy and reserves salvation. If I think about it as Calvin is supposed to have done, its superiority garners little love. For all that God is powerful, man – his creature, surely – remains a loathsome and embarrassed thing. If His will governs the actions of all men, wherefore do evil men practise? And if virtue holds a candle to the door of salvation, is this no guarantee of admission? Was the sin of Adam so terrible that God grew stern and selective in His choice of who might live eternally and who was left behind? And if life is predestined and the salvation or damnation of souls determined before birth, what value does virtue serve? Can an evil man effect to thread the eye of a needle, his entry into Heaven contingent on nothing more than Fortune's wheel, a reward in circumstances wherein reward is not the object of the game? Might Cornelisz, for all his murderous profanity and rage against the power of the Almighty, find himself, despite himself, saved? Those damned beyond their understanding are damned to live in a servitude of longing for what they can never hope to know while God's elect, those whose cause for celebration is likewise imprecise, are granted perpetual life. As with Noah in his rescue of creatures before the flood, what sort of choices does God make? And what choice had I?

They sat silently and with an air of entitlement, rows of faces I was not altogether certain of, their expression fugitive and cutthroat. If I was supposed to have captained that state in its emergency, there was little to suggest that I was any more to them than a solitary voice amidst the muted fervour of self-preservation. There was shelter, of sorts, in being a part of the mob, of feeling that a neighbour's death might spare one this time around. While it was expected that someone take charge, the effect of my recent illness – not to mention my absence from the quarterdeck when Jacobsz and his whore had themselves rowed about the anchored fleet in a loose and drunken state – these matters had eroded my standing. My authority had been too long confined to its cabin, too slighted by others during its non-appearance, and those now castaway were uncertain in whom to turn.

Jacobsz was standing on the shingle with Gerritsz, the uppersteersman, and Evertsz. It was then that I noticed Zwaantie seated in the boat, and realised that decisions had been made as to who would come and who would be left behind.

"Skipper," I hailed, "why do we burden the longboat with so many?"

It was not a challenge likely to endear me to those already settled in this first division of fate.

Jacobsz ignored my presence and raised a hand to Gerritsz's shoulder, their talk maritime and pressing. Evertsz eyed me with a peevishness that suggested I was perhaps one more thing the skipper should attend to before we set off.

I drew close. There was scarce room for the water cask we had yesterday failed to deliver. Items discarded were piled above the tidal stain which demonstrated how low and desolate these islets were, how vulnerable to heavy weather. The wind continued to drive from out of the northwest, and although we were marginally sheltered in the huddle of our kind, there was no escaping the gloom which spared us just enough to reveal how hopeless our predicament appeared. To one side, perhaps no more than half a mile distant, *Batavia* groaned in uncomprehending agonies like a faithful dog that would leap to our presence but for its mortal tethering to the reef. Her larboard bow was facing, the ship untrimmed in a tangle of self-fettering chaos where the skipper's gamble to lighten the load had resulted in the on-board collapse of the main mast. If it was a miracle none were killed then and there, that is where all miracles ended. The folk still trapped aboard were difficult to dissemble; no doubt hopelessness begat inertia. In any case the wind and spray would have cowered them into seeking shelter, even if there was no safe place to withdraw to. The reef itself, delineated by a waxing surf as far as the eye could see, boomed like cannon fire. Beyond a foreground of coral meadows, the Indiaman, now cannon-less, resembled an exhausted stick insect trapped within its seething filigree.

In the other direction, and at roughly an equal distance, lay the larger of these two islets so unhappily colonised. The people there were clearly visible, their number larger but ungoverned. At least the sailcloth had been put to use, several crude shelters having been formed from props and barrels. I couldn't bear to look at them, to think of them. Not after yesterday. And if I could see them, they most certainly could see us. Did they hope I might yet return?

"Commandeur," the skipper summoned, "the time has come to quit this place."

He knew my objection to be perfunctory, that the reality of situation demanded our removal. To imagine that we might go back to the stricken ship and take off water, this was as fatally delaying as to hope that the casks themselves might float ashore in the event of her breaking up. Since dawn on the second day of our island captivity, people had been murmuring, asking why we didn't venture to the land scraps hereabouts in search of water, for whether here or on the wreck or on the islet across the way we should surely perish. Jacobsz had warned me that the restive might take matters into their own hands and seize the boat. I know 'twas said to bully me, to force my hand and dishonour a reluctance to abandon the one hundred and eighty souls stranded upon that other crumb.

To leave the others, I'd said – not to mention the goods of the Company – I'd be responsible before God and the high authorities at Batavia.

But we can't just sit here —

Praying for a miracle —

Waiting for the weather to abate —

Waiting for the end!

"You see," the skipper said, knowing he had the support of those he'd gathered together whilst I, by contrast, afforded them no more than a momentary prick of conscience, "the counsel of the majority is that we can best help the others by first helping ourselves."

I was beginning to observe of Jacobsz, too, that he was best served by crisis. Idleness or boredom played to his vulgarity, but in the distemper of the moment he exhibited a cool if ruthless sense of purpose.

Evertsz muttered none too discreetly, "Let him stay if he wants."

But none wanted to sacrifice my critical sanction, and the skipper turned roughly to the high boatswain and, thinking himself beyond my hearing, hissed, "You had the chance yesterday; you kept him in the boat! The others are not agreed that we can leave him behind!"

Evertsz scowled like a schoolboy trying to save face. "They would have seized us all – *and* the boat!"

"Precisely. But that was there," Jacobsz pointed to the other island, "and this is now! We're in it together."

"He'll still have to be silenced," the tone even lower, more fitful.

"And I say stow it!"

I pretended not to overhear, knowing enough not to argue for the moment with what I wasn't certain of in the lead-up to the wreck. Suffice, I could tell that Jacobsz was having second thoughts concerning whatever he was mired in.

I thought of Lucretia, tarred with shit, a shivering victim in what I sensed was a broader move against me. *Evertsz's voice*, her own quaking with the import of what her testimony might unleash, *it was he who led the others*. And because it was Lucretia, because it was *she* who had spurned the skipper's advances, *she* whose maid now filled the void in his affections (each, now, with an axe to grind), there was little doubt in my mind that Jacobsz had devised the assault. But was Cornelisz, too, involved as Salomon had intimated? I searched our shipboard past for origins of an unholy alliance. Was that ill-judged boating party at the Cape – Jacobsz with his soiled queen and Jeronimus, in attendance, as his chief minister – was that the source of their confederacy? Had the berating they received antagonised their petulance and turned them from malcontents into something altogether more vengeful? There was too much presently going on, too much which demanded my immediate attention, to luxuriate in the wherefores of conspiracy. If it was a lukewarm trail I followed, at least my foe was not sufficiently skilled in subterfuge or certain of his next move to be able to discount my dogged authority.

"Skipper, I'll first leave a note for the others." And I wrote on a leaf from my table-book that we were going with the longboat to the other islands, narrowly visible, and if failing to find water there would proceed to the main South Land, gauged to be but a little distance beyond the eastern horizon. With the benefit of God's mercy we should return before long. This I placed beneath a bread barrel to be left behind. And left, too, was the smearing panic of those faces, the rudely upended contents of a human chest now spilled and vulnerable. If the jumbling moment oppressed me with its disorder – for Zwaantie was now seated in the boat, Jeronimus was trapped on the wreck, and Lucretia with Bastiaensz, his family, and all manner of community stood castaway on that island prison – I would nonetheless return to save them all, to restore each to his life's trajectory. I would make right what had gone so dreadfully wrong and limit the breakage to the loss of the ship alone. This was the only way I could calm my trembling. We would push off without further word.

The wind was snowless winter and I was grateful for the hedge of numbers. The oarsmen coordinated their sweeps and we fell into a lurching rhythm, the waves shallow across the lagoon, the swell more testing as we ferried ourselves over a deep channel towards those larger scraps of terra firma to be explored.

I didn't look to the islet where the others undoubtedly drew together and wondered. Perhaps it was the baffle of the breeze but, unlike yesterday, I heard nothing from that quarter, no shout of fellowship. I remained focused on our present intent; behind me, Jacobsz and Gerritsz standing to either side of the tiller. Yes, everything would be redeemed, I told myself. We would find water. It was unimaginable that this quarter of the globe – the mainland, certainly – should be bereft of streams. The very grip of June at this latitude south, the lowering skies and bitter westerlies, suggested that rain, some-where, was certain to have fallen, that failing the discovery of anything in the Abrolhos, as the skipper reckoned us to be, there must surely exist rivers flowing back into the sea along the Great South Land. Yes water, the finding of which would answer for any misunderstanding and reunite our scattered tribe.

But nothing in the immediacy of what we scouted delivered any result. The larger of the two islands investigated, that which afforded a hill no higher than the acrobatic perching of ten men, and which would henceforth become known as High Island, here, after struggling in the sucking ooze and being razor-nicked by coral, here among the rocks along its shore, we found only brackish pools, the lapping sea having poisoned their freshness.

Our investigation of this and the neighbouring island was conducted in broad sweeps but nothing of sustenance was gleaned except the presence of strange, hopping cats. Surely where such creatures thrived there resided drink of some kind. But no, not unless there were cisterns hidden amidst the spiny vegetation that cowered close to the unnourished soil.

That night we rested in the shelter of low, limestone outcrops. Beyond the hiss of waves close by, a deeper booming could be heard from the far-thest edge of the reef. I couldn't help but brood upon those still stranded on the wreck. I almost thought I heard the plaintive calling of *Batavia*, herself a spectral reminder that the dead are never quite so. I couldn't help but wonder whether the undermerchant were still alive and, if so, how awful and alone it would be to confront Death throughout the unwitnessing hours of darkness. As I conjectured thus, might calamity have already chosen its moment?

I heard someone weeping. Zwaantie? No, there was that other woman, so cloaked I hadn't at first noticed the child. But then I heard the baby mew from a different quarter and realised that another of our company was moved to grief during these shivering hours of respite. I found the orphanage of that sound unmanning and wanted to weep, as well, for what was to be endured at first light.

"Shut that brat up or take it down wind."

"Shut the fuck up, yerself," growled another. No one much stirred. It was merely a form of rollcall.

If I slept, I slept as I ever do these days in a tangle of dreams which, if benign, played false my heart upon waking, their disorienting nursery – a mother's warmth or the caressing domesticity of a hope too removed from what I've lived – curling like parchment at the touch of a flame. And if released from nightmare, then the sour realisation that I was detained within too truthful and harrowing a situation to elicit any comfort. I felt no longer the captain of my being but, rather, a part of the wreckage, powerless to assure myself, let alone others. Again I pondered God's purpose, the nature of this test – indeed, His reasoning for tests at all. I tried to fathom what it was that had so qualified our company to undergo this baptism of extreme exposure, what we each possessed that should converge us thus in prayer. And in the chill desert of that night, freed for an hour or two from having to exercise any responsibility other than maintain my morale, I wondered why God would choose to invent so desolate a place, and whispered in summons of myself that this wasn't the time to doubt Him. But my thoughts were confused and running, our discomfort too primitive a challenge. We had been grateful, yes, in the first instance to have been granted ground on which to stave off drowning, but that reprieve now seemed to me a play such as a cat would make with a cornered mouse. If I prayed at all, I prayed for the dawn to come and rescue me from such morbid conceits and reflected, once more, that these troubled hours may have coincided with Death's snatch of others now transfigured in eternal night.

A right shithole, this, Walter had said.

At least God had resided at the caravanserai in plural manifestation.

It's only for the night, I'd countered, and wincing now at the irony of what I wouldn't have given to exchange the strangeness of that place for the remote untelling of this. Back then we had settled into the unfragrant darkness, seeing with our thoughts as blindness strove to give some form to sound. Our first concern, perhaps, was for robbers. But who within that dormitory of merchants would have glanced at us with anything other than make-room curiosity? Were we not a profession of brothers whose nation, first, was trade? There was little to take from us in any case, travelling as we were to appraise the quality and volume of indigo produced. Medari was right, we hailed from no identifiable place, defended no patch of ground. Unless insistfully pompous in our arrival among these people, such people, too, had converged at this camp whose frontier was tomorrow's nomadic anticipation of profit. The only theft, when it came to it, was in unfair advantage. Yes, we would willingly steal another's business.

Something flapped close by, a bat perhaps.

In spite of the unfamiliarity of place, there was nothing for it but to deny such brooding wakefulness and snatch a moment's rest, to shelter beneath my cloak and preserve what agilities remained. From the crawl of constellations I calculated that daylight was still some hours off.

The distance is a blueness that fades to white. I know I sleep for what I see is unharnessed of sound, yet I am entranced into believing.

He stirs at last, the unheard breeze tugging at the fringe of his hood. The low and jagged limestone is our only protection. It's been sculpted by the elements to suggest a withered kingdom, perhaps an exhausted or misguided enterprise. As if in mirror of the question I am about to put, Antonio – for I take it to be him – asks me, "What happened next?"

Suddenly my ears are unstoppered and the wind scalds my cheeks and nostrils. The sea sizzles like fat in a pan; it sighs like a combing of leaves. Except that there are no trees.

I stare at the swelling light. Its blueness fades through all the colours of breakfast to an unyielding glare of realisation. It's dawn once more, and the skipper is up and moving among his most senior officers.

What happened next?

Very little, at first, by what I was able to contribute. The experience of recent days, slow to resurrect an authority presently as levelled as these wind-flattened cays, had turned me into a follower of events.

Not that Jacobsz ruled. Not entirely. While his practical abilities were much counted on, it was only of the moment that others deigned to follow. Outside necessity, he was a tainted vessel. It was under his stewardship, after all, that *Batavia* had been lost.

It seemed we were each limited in what we might command, any decision affected by the fearful braying of those herded under us. And if the skipper had momentarily seized the initiative and was eager to abandon those castaway, then bearing what I knew and held against him, I couldn't afford to let Jacobsz out of my sight. I couldn't trust him to return with succour when all along he'd been little inclined to believe we might find water. And even if we did, what next? *We might slake their thirst for an hour*, he'd said, *but we can never ferry the amount needed. They'll be chicks to the exhaustion and death of the parent*, he'd added, somewhat poetically, and even I knew them to have become unruly in their yammer. For better or worse we knew we would abandon the Abrolhos; all that day the carpenters set about building the boat up with planks, for we saw that it would not be possible otherwise to reach the continent.

Those unskilled were put to digging wells, and throughout the long hours the beach grew pitted with failed shafts. Even Zwaantie took to the spade determinedly, cutting with a fierceness that proclaimed she dug for two, the limpid mother and her child stowed to one side. Across the sawing and hammer and the thrust and grunts, a purposeful silence permitted the wind to embroider our thoughts.

Against nightfall we saw the ship's second and much smaller boat approach. I had left this in the neighbourhood of the wreck, and it now brought Gillis Fransz, the understeersman, and maybe ten others in search of water. One look at our empty wells and the heightened gunwale of the longboat alerted them to the fact that our plans had matured beyond any lingering stay.

"You intend to leave?"

"There's nothing here to drink," I replied. "The continent is our best hope."

The two parties stared mistrustfully at one another. Fransz turned to Gerritsz, his close superior, and then the skipper. "Take us with you."

"But the others, they'll need the yawl," I objected.

Jacobsz, his arms folded, turned his head to spit. "The others are going nowhere and are a danger to themselves."

I ignored the implication of this and asked of Fransz, "How fare they?"

The understeersman grew evasive. "They're none too pleased your camp is abandoned."

"They want to know why *you* are not among them," added another of the newcomers.

Fransz stared at his feet a moment then glanced up at the skipper and myself. "They've already named it Traitors' Island."

I swallowed, visibly stung. "But that's preposterous!" And everyone was staring at me as if *I* were to blame for the slur that blackened their names.

Jacobsz inhaled deeply, satisfied he'd been proven right and bracing himself for whatever was to come. "The yawl may prove a lifeboat to our cause," he said. "It would be easier to negotiate the surf with in the search for water."

Fransz fixed his expression hard on me. "Commandeur, none of us are prepared to go back to where the others are – or to the wreck."

Even I could see that there was nothing to be gained by redividing the party and endowing those chosen with the animosity of those selected to remain behind.

"All right, then," I assented, "we shall leave together."

⸻ᴄ⸻

What I proposed was not in keeping with what transpired. I had thought to secure water early within the prospect of that immensity, for who could have imagined a land so barren and moistless? I even invoked the Almighty, certain that if we placed our trust in Him a logic of mercy would prevail. I had seen men die before — seen women, too — but was determined not to apply that witness to any scenario in which I might affect the outcome. "If we find water on the mainland, we shall make as many trips as are needed to secure those we leave behind."

So you agree, the separation is necessary?

Someone must bring news of our sad happenings to the Honourable Lord Governor.

So you agree.

Before we departed, I had a resolution notarised that we would do our utmost to relieve our poor companions in distress. Although I didn't confess it at the time, I no doubt lived in dual intent, self-deceiving. Even as we edged further and further from the disaster, I remained most public in my desire to return and succour those left optionless upon the beach of what was christened, in our absence, *Batavia*'s Graveyard. Could I possibly have imagined that I might bring them rescue without any real rescue at all, that we might have shuttled back and forth with what amounted to buckets of water? They would have drunk themselves dry before we'd even dipped beneath the horizon to replenish them.

As it stood, fate would seduce that other self in me, that part which too easily tired in the exercise of what might have been expected. I may have wanted, at first (and in all ignorance of what was to come), to have staunched the bleeding, to have constrained a runaway injury, yet I was now a runaway myself. And the character of my escape was so arduous that this newfound adventure in survival gradually paupered any notion of return. Even as we found ourselves physically banded in the longboat and without summons of a moment's privacy, I'm sure that in the increasing stupefaction of our thoughts, we each were of an instinct to get as far away as possible from what had happened.

At noon the skipper took a reading of our position, no small feat given the imbalance of our boat. I dutifully recorded a latitude of 28 degrees, 13 minutes south. It wasn't long afterwards that we sighted the continent, the westerly breeze in solid backing of our transit. After the blur of crisis and hapless probing, we looked to land with the yearning of those who think nothing of the flames as they escape the discomforts of the pan. That smudge of destination was as yet without form, and hope populated the unseen shore with, if not exactly confidence in Nature's bounty, then certainly some apprehension of her mercy. It was an idle dream to help fill the hours, a brief interlude of enterprising thought.

At our bobbing approach, however, that continental promise stretched itself north and south in a monstrous embrace which undermined our feigned courage. It was as if some curiosity, plucked by chance or studied through recommendation, had suddenly and without warning transformed itself into something leering and malevolent. One would have imagined that the onset of such a vastness might have promised succour, yet our nearing cautioned us to be less expectant, especially as evening fast approached and the land, throbbing like a scar at sunset, grew solemn and indistinct as purple night fell.

Evertsz cast the lead, and we had ground at seven fathoms. But it was too dark and too dangerous to draw any nearer the surf, and the skipper headed us away from shore and into the wind, its flush stirring us to shiver and cloak ourselves tightly against the unseen elements. Having lost *Batavia* in darkness, we keenly felt our vulnerability before the presence of this unknown shore. If our mighty ship, whose quarters were such that the sea might be overlooked and intrigue fester, could be ruined upon the merest coral outcrop, then how much more the vigilance required to keep our tiny ark from being dashed upon this unchartered immensity which had spawned the Abrolhos. There was no turning from the sea now, no opportunity to retire below and wring, in sleep, any respite from its ceaseless importunity. We were tightly wedged, suspended in a cramp that was impossible to ease, except that our anxious thoughts accommodated discomfort as something secondary. That we were all, quite literally, in the same boat, this too absolved us of that deepening fear of dying alone. In fact – and despite simmering animosities – not for some time had the captaincy of purpose enjoyed such unanimous support or concentration.

It was after midnight when Jacobsz, having taken us away from land, issued an order to turn about. As if in chary stalking of a wild beast, this stitching close but never closing with the shore would be repeated in the days ahead as we vainly sought a place to land but were driven back by the hostile surf and insistent isolation of this demolished-looking country.

So began our journey north, a journey unwittingly destined and separating itself from all that had gone before. We were no longer at one with the thirst of those left behind, their inert camp not forgotten but forgotten enough in what we, more confined and at the mercy of the waves, had hourly to contend with.

At first light the continent was slow to disassemble from the sea itself, its barren silhouette unbroken by either forest or mountain. With the maturing dawn, land and water grew distinct, the former slipping into an armour of perpetual rebuff. Yes, a bad and rocky place, the cliffs as high as those of England's Dover.

There *was* one place on that first day's exploration where we toyed with the intent of landing, the success of which might have altered the course of what ensued. It was a small inlet, sheltered by low dunes but removed from us by the treacherous surf. When a stout westerly sprang up, it was all we could do to ensure that we weren't forced to gauntlet-run the breakers. If the two women cried out and the baby shrieked, the distemper of others was no less an expression of the peril we all felt. Only Jacobsz and the men attached to his every command appeared too preoccupied to show much fear. They were in constant balancing, the scarce-canvassed mast of our longboat trimmed to wean us off the threatening shore. Such was the difficulty in maintaining a safe position, however, that Fransz's sloop, that lifeboat to our little expedition, had to be cut adrift. If all had been mindful of their thirst, such was the hazard, now, of sinking in the wind and hollow seas that we threw a portion of our bread overboard and anything else that was in the way. Throughout the night we bailed a flood that sloshed about our ankles, the rain adding its weight to our endangered buoyancy. The only comfort I took was the hope that those on Batavia's Graveyard had, likewise, received the storm and harvested its downpour.

As day approached, the wind abated and we bobbed, bedraggled, in the colourless pallor of dawn, chilled but survived. Despite our best endeavour to hold our position, we were not where we had been, the inlet vanished and the cliff wall gloomy and impenetrable. The breeze was now running from the southwest and the skipper steered us north, the continent on our right as we slowly unspooled distance, looking to pick the lock to this undiscovered land. Thus we left the past behind in a gathering of miles, a past once bound to the governances of our former ship and presently diverging into a different tale, a different trial.

How might things have otherwise fared had we managed to land at the inlet on that first day, sure of finding (as detection would later prove) fresh-running water? But by then – several months later, our rescue having revealed the magnitude of ruin – the story was done, or so I thought. The tiger and its cubs had been extirpated, and it only remained for me to seize an opportunity to cast off those spared delinquents, Loos and Pelgrom. But it wasn't the end, not really. More another compromised moment, another matter settled to the detriment of something else. Yes, it was a cruel postscript when, after so much blood and folly, Fortuna might have relented a little to sanction a more tranquil aftermath. I was certainly thirsty for signs of life, and it was the smoke which gave me hope, smoke where, months before (and screened from land in our overcrowded ark by the booming surf), nothing had tokened welcome. With the *Sardam* standing within cannon shot of the Great South Land, I presently commanded the yawl to negotiate the breakers and land where, doubtless, our recently stranded mariners awaited. I would swap the wicked for the fair.

The boat's company disappeared beyond the beach into the sweep of a watercourse. I was afterwards informed that a fresh cascade was indeed present, but of that drawing signal smoke it was none other than a fire of the blacks themselves. Our men traced their footsteps in the sand – evidence of a scurrying departure – but as on prior occasions when we'd tried to make contact, they persisted in hiding themselves as only frightened savages might before the proffer of a civilised hand.

"No luck, then?" I cried as the yawl returned.

"No sign," the leading seaman answered, scarcely able to look at me for the disappointment we all felt in not recovering our vanished friends.

I stared at the beach as if untrusting of what was reported, half fancying the lost *Sardam* crewmen to come running to the shore, waving and shouting: *Stop! Wait! Here we are!* "But I thought," I murmured. "I was convinced..."

None could bring themselves to comfort me. Not even Salomon, my assistant all these years and one who had sat as secretary to the ship's council during its investigations, adding his signature to the sentences imposed — even his own. He stood by, pale and voiceless, like the ghost he would soon become. It seemed we could never salvage enough, that there was little to congratulate in the very notion of recovery. Despite a heartfelt gladness to be rid of this place, there lingered aboard the *Sardam* a dismal air of failure.

"It's been more than a month," said Claas Gerritsz, the uppersteersman and now senior surviving officer.

"But we *had* seen smoke. Not these two weeks gone! It was surely them. They merely had to await their rescue."

No one questioned what I said. Not aloud. But there was no escaping the inference that perhaps we should have investigated at the time, that I should have ordered a boat.

"Waiting for rescue is not as easy as it seems."

"Who said that?" I spun around.

But all were of the same expressionless mien. Their very attitude was one of solidarity and withholding.

"We couldn't be in all places at once," I added. "We were needed near the wreck. For the salvage. Besides..."

A breeze resembling silence motioned our small ship, that unintelligible land rising and falling beyond the bulwark like a thing escaped and leering.

Do you think not now, in hindsight...?

Of course I think it! I think of nothing else — those men as lost as I in the futility of it all!

But you gave — or failed to give — the order.

What order? I came to rescue the folk, to refute a charge of desertion —

Who so accused you?

It was what they thought. All of them!

Perhaps you imagined it.

Does it matter? None could look at me but feel ashamed for the state they were in. To re-find them was to discover something altogether different from what had been misplaced. That which should have redeemed me in the eyes of God turned bitter in the unholiness of what a man might become. I was forced to be a gaoler and a hangman when all along I was meant to be the guardian of thrift and order.

So there was no order?

Ha, amusing… And I sigh like one cornered into revelation, of having to admit that things had gone badly.

The principal malcontents were dead — all but that fretting youth, Pelgrom, he whom I'd spared against the inclination of harsher counsel. No sooner were they hanged than a violent gale sprang up. The sky was an anvil of wrath, a bruised load beneath which the cutthroat ghosts of those justly executed were denied ascendancy. Across the surface of what was temporal, the elements were squeezed into a storm of such violence that I prayed we not, likewise, be banished from Heaven's kingdom. Detained in a purgatory of concurrent and unresolved matters, the exemplary punishment of certain mutineers had left a cloud of complicity over others, while the salvage of Company property was slow and weather-dependent. Neither could fully displace the other in my mind; neither seemed hopeful of a conclusion that would wipe the slate.

Having forfeited enough of human life, I was determined that as much of *Batavia* as possible be recovered. The heaving seas and shift of wind from west to south made diving hazardous, the Gujaratis, with no more than the practised bellows of their lungs, timing themselves to go under as the swell permitted. It was dangerous work, our small boats — including those fashioned from debris washed up on Batavia's Graveyard — manoeuvring at the edge of the reef wherein our ship was scraped. The poop was an island castle, an object of conjectural folly and as impervious, now, to function as the ruins I'd seen in India. And further ruin was promised as the wind once more rose to a gale. The *Sardam* strained at anchor and the encampment on

Batavia's Graveyard was a desolate flapping of canvas. When conditions at last quietened, renewed hunger and thirst approached and I ordered the thickets burned on High Island, all the better to hunt the hopping cats and search for fresh cisterns such as those which had sustained Hayes and his loyalists. It was a venture better rewarded, now, than when the longboat had first set out in quest for water all those months ago. While the casks were being filled, others fished in the smallest yawl and discovered a barrel of vinegar – too large for them to handle – lying on a reef.

So much had been lost. So much needed to be accounted for.

The following morning I sent Jacob, the *Sardam*'s skipper, together with four others, in the larger boat to retrieve the barrel. To make it worth their while, I instructed them to venture to distant islands lying further west, there to see if other Company goods had been washed ashore. Of course I was anxious for their safety and indicated that they should try to be back by nightfall. Yet we were all accustomed to existence within this watery hemisphere and skilled at plying our tiny craft between one insubstantial outcrop and the next. Conditioned by the sea, the trickeries of fate were more likely to spring from the villainies of man. After all, had I not seen our kind adapt to the stringencies of this almost landless desert? Had I not crossed the Timor Sea, myself, in an open boat? *If you must stay out overnight in the recovery of what you find*, I'd said, *so be it.*

As things transpired, my orders proved inconvenient. Before noon the weather grew somewhat calmer, the seas smooth. I went in the smallest yawl to the wreck where a full money chest was spied, pinned by a jettisoned cannon. When the wind resumed its afternoon bluster and the balance of the yawl was troubled, we were forced to abandon the day's effort with heart's regret. I needed Jacob's larger boat.

That night the skipper and his men did not return.

Next morning, a hard southerly was upon us, and venturing on deck, I enquired, "Any sign of the skipper?" Beneath the loud and tuneless hum of rigging, I felt the others withdraw from the conscience of my thoughts into a stillness both silent and judgemental. I nodded as if concurring with a shared hope. "Let me know when they're sighted," I said, and returned below.

But there was no summoning knock at the door, and towards evening it began to blow harder still. I lay awake all that night within the *Sardam*'s relative security, listening to the rising wind and wondering what may have happened to those caught out on the open sea. The jacht creaked and rocked and bobbled on the chain like an animal lithe but spooked. At sun-up, a full storm was upon us, the lagoon a haze of foam and salt spray. At the edge of the reef where *Batavia*'s carcass was daily belittled, the surf thudded with a ferocity pertaining to the change of empires. I expected her spectacle to dissolve in a smothered crash of timbers, her fragment masts to snap and disappear. But perhaps the world, for all its violent excess, was made of sturdier stuff and that it was I, alone, who shivered in the implication of what stood to be lost. To say that I feared for the skipper and our un-appearing boat was only the half of it.

Have I lost these men? Have I lost them for a meagre purchase of vinegar?

All that day and the next, the wind continued to strike from the south, from regions so speculative as to confound philosophers and cartographers alike. There seemed no let up to its spitting denial of what I penitently prayed for. I could no more imagine the preservation of those unhappy men than I could credit the recent carnival of mutiny. I had thought the sky uppermost, the ocean glued in sullen servitude to the planet, but all was topsy-turvy. Out on Seals' Island, God's ignoble handwork swayed in an oblivion of bloodied stumps and stretched necks. I couldn't see their salt-hardened corpses and was grateful to the storm for that solitary advantage. It seemed, however, that everything I commanded was thwarted by a malevolence in league with this grim and unpredictable hemisphere. The enforced inertia distorted my imaginings and made Nature appear the most villainous of chaperones. How might we here, at the tail-end of this sorry affair, continue to survive such closing days if not firmly bound against a still snatching fate? Yes, one miscounsel was all it took to subtract further from this fragile convalescence, our recovery subject to fresh attritions the longer we stayed.

Yet when the wind abated and the weather cleared, I did feel that purpose had been restored to our enterprise. My thoughts became a little calmer.

But they were not for the five men disappeared?

I couldn't wait for the skipper. Conditions were too favourable not to act upon. I went to the wreck, again to see whether we couldn't raise the pinioned money chest. But the swell was unpredictable, breaking dangerously at the edges of the reef. Much of what had been was no longer, the storm having washed away all that wasn't sinuously tethered. It was disappointing.

After noon had passed, I decided that the yawl should be provisioned with bread, water and wine, and ordered Gerritsz and his mate to voyage across to the nearest islands and see whether they might find the skipper and his companions.

You waited until then?

The salvaging proved impossible. Conditions presently allowed me to direct my attention to the lost boat.

You put Company goods before Company lives?

We were all Company men. We — those of us not turned by the Devil — we stood to our duty. Perhaps it was harder (the waiting, I mean, until everything of value was retrieved) for the women, those who had survived. In any case, the yawl continued to search at some distance from the wreck. I watched as it disappeared from view like the boat it sought, and grew momentarily timid before the prospect of a second disappearance. Gerritsz allowed himself to be commanded but not without a degree of censure in his acquiescence. He had proven himself a reliable mariner and stalwart of the rescue, but he was also a witness of my shame. I couldn't help thinking my subordinates doubted my appreciation of what I tasked them to do. As it was, I instructed Gerritsz and his companion not to risk themselves, and to lie close to any scrap of land should the weather blow foul. That I should lose him *and* the *Sardam*'s skipper would be too calamitous an accident and deprive us of our most experienced seamen.

Then why have sent anyone, let alone so many, to retrieve one paltry barrel of vinegar?

My sense exactly!

Van Diemen, the distance between us annihilated so that he stands at the edge of conscience, is unmoved by the difficulties I faced, the expectations I was chartered to accomplish.

Every salvageable item was to be accounted for. They were my orders.

But surely, to rescue the people —

And the cash.

Francisco's right, intervenes Coen. I expected nothing other than a full recovery. And I spared him nothing that might assist, least of all time.

He appears as I imagine from the tone of his written instructions, direct yet counselling, much as if he'd appointed me a first-time governor to some newly acquired territory:

In case of storm and hard winds, do not be precipitate in abandoning your commission and departing lightly because there seemed no means of salvaging the money. Keep in mind that the sun comes round to the south, that summer will draw and beautiful weather is to be expected. You should remain near the wreck until the waters calm and all the cash is saved... And Francisco, we expect no less, even if it means you must stay three, four or more months out.

What about the Mataramese? We'll need him and the others back, quick smart, to help fight those bastards.

Antonio, we've sufficient means to deal with them, whatever their number. Other ships have arrived. Our force is more than replenished – for the moment, at least.

Then returning to me: Francisco, if you find our people in desperate thirst and must remove them, strike for the continent, either south or to the north. There, find a suitable anchorage and shelter the jacht until the sun has drawn south of the line. Then, as circumstances prove opportune, contrive to cross back to the wreck and salvage the cash. This is your obligation to the Company and a matter upon which your honour depends. Inspire the divers to do their duty. Promise them they shall be well rewarded, that they must recover, if possible, all the money so that the Company may receive some recompense for its great loss.

Antonio *pffs* as if to deny that anything might weigh against the imbalance of such ruin. I can tell that Coen agrees with him but is determined, nonetheless, to mentor me in what I must carry out: Remember, too, to bring the casket of jewels which was saved at the time the people were deposited on that island. And if the people are no longer there, follow in search of them; save everything you can lay your hands on...

And they wonder why I sent after an unsecured barrel of vinegar! Antonio, you were as ravenous for me to fail as you were to succeed my Lord Governor.

Don't you worry, Pelsaert, I *will* be governor one day.

Gentlemen, your ambition to serve the Company and allow it, likewise, to empower you is of no account. There is a gap to close, not a rivalry to entertain. Francisco, in making good this voyage you shall keep a detailed journal and note shallows, reefs, inlets, bays, capes and anything else for the future knowledge and benefit of the Company. Make sure you fix the latitude and longitude of everything correctly.

Then turning to Van Diemen: We need to learn more of what lies to the south. Our capital, here, is but the axis of what I would further reap. And then laughing, something he rarely did: Don't look so chary, my lord. One day a new discovery may even bear your name!

And so it was that I was put under no obligation to hurry back if our return should short-change the Company. And after the disappearance of the *Sardam*'s skipper and companions, that subsidiary injunction to make discoveries gave me heart when, three weeks later and November, now, we noted columns of smoke to the northeast. Not only that, but as if revealed by God, the continent came into view in conditions which exalted the height of even the dimmest land scrap. Never had we seen the mainland from the vicinity of the wreck, and if this mirage seemed strange and wonderful, then surely those fires were a signal that we, too, could be observed. I firmly believed that Jacob and the others, after fading from our view and being in our prayers, had been skewed to that distant shore rather than capsized and consumed.

It gives me pause, now, to admit that I proceeded to little think of those presumed stranded on the mainland. If anything, I found myself relieved to be able to concentrate on that which was expected of me, and had already breathed more easily when Gerritsz had returned from his investigation to report that, though he'd found no trace of the *Sardam* five, there was still another island further north. Yet as if I needed reminding, I found, once more, that to launch anything in these parts was to invite a malice of southerlies. No sooner was the yawl dispatched to that distant prospect than we found ourselves beset by gales which verified how fragment and insecure our existence was. Like a child who fails to absorb a prior lesson, I presently regretted sending the boat out again. For five days I was confined to Batavia's Graveyard, unable to communicate with the *Sardam*, and deprived of bread and other necessities. Deprivation, however, scarcely affected the humour of those who had not stepped from this island-raft turned charnel-house – in particular, the women. They continued to huddle beneath the bleached and tattered canvas, the hours strumming with insufferable repetition. As governor of this detached and interim colony, I felt an incumbent heaviness in trying to keep everyone busy, of distracting them from too sour a contemplation of what it meant to be here.

When the winds eventually lightened and the yawl returned, I gave thanks and learned from those who had braved a landing at that unvisited place that there was nothing of value, only sand and gulls.

Nearly two weeks later, our solemn ways were suddenly buoyed when distant smoke was again sighted. I told myself it was the skipper; that he sought to remind us that they were still alive and shouldn't be forgotten. But I had thrice risked a small boat to venture, first, in search of flotsam and, then, lost sailors. Men who had survived shipwreck the once – not to mention some who had fought alongside Wiebbe against the Devil – were, in the event of a second stranding, more than capable of maintaining themselves whilst awaiting rescue. I saw no advantage in further tempting fate, of dispatching the yawl across that formidable stretch of water. Not when our work in the Abrolhos was almost done and I might shortly bring the *Sardam* over to the mainland itself. Besides, I'd spared that wretch Pelgrom with the stated intent of marooning him on the continent, and in the final adjudication of sentences I similarly condemned Wouter Loos. I prayed that the skipper and his spirited crewmates would pardon me in the delayed exchange, that in their rejoining of our number we would rejoice and share a wondrous intelligence. It was a musing I consoled myself with as, each day, the carcass of *Batavia* yielded less and less and the mood among the folk grew more unspeaking. *Who knows*, I deigned to smile, *they may even have recovered that unruptured vinegar and be, even now, sporting some diversion upon its circular table!*

As it was, the divers fished up a box of tinsel and four Moorish dishes. Nothing more. I could scarcely credit it was coming to an end. The salvage had been stored alongside the living dead on Batavia's Graveyard, the quantity of goods seemingly small compared with the aspiration to convey a full ship-load back to Java.

"Commandeur, in manly truth there is nothing more to be gained by remaining." It was the summons to forgo this irksome present for the unpredictable but necessary resumption of life.

There was just one more matter that needed settling before I could give a full account to the Governor. The prisoners.

In war it is not unknown but less common to massacre the entirety of a defeated foe. Hayes, with my timely arrival, had crushed the mutiny but not before its Satanic energies had tempted or coerced a great many folk. This shiftless population now stood stooped and unkempt in the debris of its guttered kingdom. The wicked cabal had already been half-exterminated by Wiebbe on the shores of his island, yet Cornelisz and a ring of evil-doers had survived to give slippery token of what had taken place in our absence. It wasn't difficult, in the betraying evidence each gave against the other, to arrive at a verdict of guilt for the most heinous of these villains. But in the solemn ministration of justice, as the eight condemned gave final word of themselves, one – Allert Jansz, still Godless and unrepentant – bawled: "I may be called on to die but you," and his eyes raking us wildly, his feet unsteady yet clinging to the ladder, "you'd do well to watch out. There are many traitors who live, and they'd happily seize the ship and carry out what we are punished for."

"Name the bastards!" shouted one of the *Sardam*'s council as the soldier at the foot of the gallows, his shoulder stained with the dripping wounds of those who had gone before, casually awaited my order.

Perhaps the agony throbbed in Jansz to the extent that he no longer cared to barter for another moment of life. "You think – atop everything else – I'd turn myself informer?" And he spluttered a gurgling laugh.

I nodded to the soldier who presently yanked the ladder away.

Having watched — awaiting his turn — the deathly struggle of those now dangling, Pelgrom couldn't compose himself to die, even though he'd been spared the painful loss of a hand. It was sickening to see and hear him weeping and begging. Sickening, too, the spectacle of justice already meted out. There were those who would happily have excused my presence for a few minutes, allowing me, perhaps, to retire along the beach to vomit, thereby enabling them to finish this business in my absence. It would have silenced the hysteria. Pelgrom was all the more detested because of his youth, the raw swagger of his violence. But in my leniency I permitted Cornelisz's cabin servant to live whilst my own assistant these many years would ultimately be granted no such mercy.

Jansz was right, there *were* self-concealing traitors among us, those whose complicity sought cover in the punishments visited upon the tiger and its cubs. Pelgrom aside — and also Wouter Loos who, for the moment, I kept alive, seeing in his monster a captive not dissimilar to Wiebbe's uncaptured self — yes, these two aside, I was aware that there were others tainted to less evident degree.

Having decided we should sail for Java in two days' time, Batavia's Grave-yard began to be stripped of its recovered stores in their transfer to the *Sardam*. It was not without feelings of incredulity that as I watched the dismantling of this island hell it seemed so puny and banal a space for so grandiose a madness. Perpetrator and victim alike seemed diminished by the impermanence of that camp as it hourly faded before my eyes. Indeed, what came to the fore was the uneven quality of that human salvage and my need to sift the penitent from those irreclaimable. I would advantage those who might readily be judged and swiftly punished with a mercy I was inclined to bestow, thereby bonding them in grateful loyalty. The others — those slow to reveal themselves and whose crimes required further investigation — of these there was now little time for the ship's council to enquire. They would be closely watched during the voyage to come, then quarantined in the roadstead before Batavia Castle.

That night, in prelude to our departure and with orders not to be disturbed, I began to write up my summaries, concluding that while death might ordinarily follow such crimes, circumstances in the Abrolhos were far from ordinary. How else might I save Salomon?

> *Not without guilt have such persons behaved themselves,*
> *and in all too great a fear of death. They did nothing to*
> *restrain the murdering scoundrels; instead, closing their eyes*
> *and dissimulating rather than fight for justice, their honour,*
> *God and salvation. They have smirched their hands with the*
> *shedding of human blood, although they were forced to it...*

I remember inhaling deeply, my stylus poised on an upturned wrist. One doesn't undertake these things lightly.

> *– To wit, Salomon Deschamps, senior assistant, is to be three*
> *times keel-hauled then flogged with one hundred strokes.*

And as if to deny any charge of favouritism, I smuggled him in among a batch similarly sentenced.

Even now I see him. I always see him when that particular wound of conscience opens up. His eyes are large and sorrowful, his perfect stillness enshrines a contradiction which neither permits him accusation or defence. It's as if he's aware of his own shortcomings, so trusting of the censure others feel that he cannot lift a finger or raise a sound to protect himself. I want to pity him yet end up pitying myself. I know he would not betray me in anything, that he knows I have ever showed him favour. We have known one another long and by choice have spliced our fortunes. That which damages one necessarily afflicts the other, even be it a misfortune that absolves either of any further loyalty. I know *he* knows that he deserves to be punished. Pain is not something he would willingly endure – indeed, he would sooner strangle a baby than suffer death at the hands of those who coerced him. And yet he would atone, having added his signature (like the dutiful and diligent clerk he always was) to that paper which condemned him and described his fate. I hate – as in what I fear reflected – the courage of the weak.

You hid from what you might have done. Such cowardice was unseemly.

You hid, too, from what had happened, undertaking to bury her in the garden, and hoping no one would find out.

I didn't kill her! It was an accident. My back was turned.

Yet what you would bind me to was, likewise, unseemly. I aided you in what ought never to have been countenanced, your illicit pleasure turned to dissimulation and concealment, the very thing you would fault in me.

Salomon, Asmat was dead. That woman, Mayken Cardoes — her child still breathed.

I tried to hide from the others, to avoid their dreadful caprices. But Stone-Cutter Pietersz sought me out, just as you summoned me to help dispose of the body of another man's wife. They were standing in a circle — Cornelisz, Zevanck, Hendricxsz and others — the tent's solitary lamp magnifying their shadows so that light itself was diminished and the insinuation of their voices made deeper and more monstrous. "Deschamps, there is a half-dead child. We can see you're not a fighting man. Here's a little noose. Go and fix it so that we on the island don't have to put up with its wailing all night."

I blink as if to refocus myself on Salomon. If I expect to see (in concert with what I hear) a less amenable countenance, I am mistaken. His eyes remain large and sorrowful, his being utterly surrendered in its capture.

I'm sorry, I say. You have always been loyal. Haven't we travelled great distances together? But murder is murder, even if it appears to you that there are deaths of a different colouring. I must hurt you now to prevent you from being further harmed.

I am frightened, and he looks away. *I wish you'd put me ashore with the others — Loos and Pelgrom.*

They would have eaten you.

And he hiccups a tearful laugh for the fearful irony of what awaits. *At least I might have died as I'd lived, timid and subservient in the conscience of my soul. Or had I survived, I might have lived accidentally and adapted. Instead, I was forced to atone before that unholy crowd in shitting fright and humiliation. They had thrust a noose into my hands that night on the Abrolhos, and for the folly of being afraid they would now thrust my head into a noose at Batavia. I have been a poor player, doubly punished, and you have seen me off, your secret still your own.*

Yes, in what I would forestall I staved off little. It is a persecuting irony to realise, now, that the undoubtedly guilty Loos and that miserable cabin boy were granted, by me, a better than even chance of surviving whilst those whose evil-doing was goaded must now step into the breach and absorb the shock of justice. Coen was dead, and though he had been the most feared of men, I was confident of my ability to reach into his fortress understanding — a returned son to his stern yet not unrelenting father. His orders in dispatching me to rescue were not without an assignment of trust; he would expect me to do my duty, and upon my return to Java with what I was able to discover and reclaim, I stood ready to give a full account of my actions. If not exactly gloved to the countenance of his own, I was nonetheless certain I could explain that what had happened in the Abrolhos had been dealt with to the executive satisfaction of his most obedient servant.

The moment we marooned those two delinquents and set that ungiving environment astern, I felt — in spite of the calumnies I'd been aggrieved to discover and the sorrowful disappearance of Jacob and his men — yes, I felt as if *Batavia*'s shattered weight were no longer pinning me. Those sea-scourged fragments, formerly unknown to any footprint, were now as unlovingly shunned as once, just months earlier, I had desperately sought to reacquaint myself with their elusive mirage. The air was inflated with a tonic of restored momentum. Of Cornelisz and his malcontents, we left them rotting at a distance, the clean and hungry sea ahead.

In the course of our journey towards Sumatra and the straits that would signal a resumption of normalcy, I experienced interludes of deferential passivity which, in the recent extremities of conspiracy and disaster, I'd rallied against. Indeed, I found myself possessed of a holidaying inclination to view the Cocos Islands, the beckoning skies by turn either dark or blistering, our daily reckoning diminishing the equatorial distance.

Within the *Sardam*'s refugee manifest, Lucretia and the surviving women kept to themselves and constrained their airings to solemn moments when sea and sky merged into an indivisibility of murdered dreaming. It was as if the apothecary had poisoned the lightness of lust and weighted its springtime to the very depths of the ocean, the women who'd been left behind as I went in search of help now stripped of their formerness and breathing a semblance of ashes. It stung me all the more for what I'd idly entertained during the earlier stages of our voyage. Yet if man, by nature, is destined to forfeit his innocence, then how much more would I have presently settled for any of those ordinary sins which, in light of the monstrosities that cast those tigers beyond God's forgiveness, seemed slight and not as removed from Eden's intrigue as perhaps imagined. There are degrees of sinning – or so I told myself, and swallowing.

In the hours that passed, the weather blew up shrill, the easterly running to a topgallant gale which prevented any carriage of sail. Throughout that rain-scoring night we rolled in heavy seas, and at noon, for a second day running, had no latitude, the sky sour with a hue that matched many a stomach, the horizon unreliable. The nearest we gleaned of the unseen Cocos were the vast rafts of weed that bobbed and buckled like shaken carpets. By comparison, our longboat crossing of the Timor Sea had passed remarkably well, our triangular sail evenly filled upon even seas. Doubtless God approved of what we would redeem. But in this scooped-together conclusion to everything that had taken place, it was as if He presently reserved the right to argue and withhold salvation. We drifted at His mercy and were driven by His breath until, spared in the knowing that our mortal kind would prove quite vengeful enough, the days grew calm and the water smooth.

With the now skin-scarred Salomon adding his signature to the completed trial log, we hove in sight of Java and the smouldering island of Krakatoa, the shoreline an endless jungle greenery. This was in stark contrast to the ungiving land, vast and spectral, that lay in intercepting disservice to the south. We were no longer ragged as we had once been – though morally there were those who, completing this voyage for the first time, were yet to answer for the raggedness of their behaviour. Drifting past Bantam and the sleeping English that early December morning – and yes, exactly six months after the loss of our precious flagship – we finally drew abreast of Man Eaters Island and arrived – God be praised for our safe and concluding passage! – in the roads before Batavia.

However, when we dropped anchor before the Castle and I discovered the great lord dead, the world I'd sought to master grew even more remote. I realised, then, that in the subtraction of that one man, everything which had been kept in check – and I don't mean governance or order but, rather, rivalry and ambition – had fermented in his absence to permit new and grasping alignments. It was as if his estate had been plundered by my jealous siblings as I wasted time and life attempting to retrieve a barrel of vinegar.

It was hot, unbearably so, the monsoon arriving to defeat the festive starch of Christmas. Defeated, too, were the Mataramese, their host, like the legions of Spain in the Low Countries, melting once more through curtains of rain into the surrounding jungle, hungry and bedraggled.

"Ho ho, so you've finally returned – and not before time."

I could always count on Van Diemen to welcome me sourly. And despite my satisfaction in having made it here at last, I was instantly put to no illusion as to what my arrival might contend.

"So few, Pelsaert? Tut."

I needed to see the Governor before I was tilted from my own telling.

Yet even as I was advised that Jacques Specx was now in charge, so, too, the new incumbent appeared well-informed when it came to the meaning of the *Sardam*'s manifest. Not even Van Diemen could marshal his ill-will as speedily as the faceless democracy of rumour. It stripped me of the pride I might have garnered in having rescued what was left to save. It made me feel as if all jurisdiction had passed from my hands. The *Sardam* itself seemed possessed of a disembarking instinct that was quite independent of any direction I might give. Like an aficionado mesmerised by the twists and connotations of a play just ended, I found myself seated and alone as other theatre-goers shuffled for the exit. How were they moved to disappear, I wondered, without my comment or command? How was Batavia able to recognise (*"You to the left. You there, step to the right..."*) – yes, how was it that this starched presumption of a place knew whom to manacle and whom to asylum? I don't remember their leave-taking, those who'd sailed with me the interrupted once and others, twice, in an aggregate of risk. I don't recall their faces in departure, nor any mood of fellowship in farewell. The only visage I see is my own, a searching expression given to lamenting that of all who had vanished I, now, accounted for what survived.

Yet wicked word would bounce and comport itself like some Chinese whisper. *Did you hear? Can you believe? He's surely jinxed...*

Jinxed, my arse!

Hmph, I can count on you, Antonio.

Don't look to me as though I were the author of your embarrassment.

And how might you have handled matters in a situation such as you never found yourself?

Not like some master's apprentice, left in charge to play the fool and expecting to be petted for not setting fire to the premises.

I loathe you.

Loathing is a poor substitute for leadership. So is servility in judgement.

I would that you spoke plainly.

I would that you knew when not to throw good money after bad. A barrel of vinegar? For chrissakes Pelsaert, 'twas little more than the mouthwash of the Lord.

I've never much cared for the pious aroma of vinegar. I'm grateful for it, of course, but it's too much associated with what is wrong in the world, its need of sanitation. I am swabbed with the stuff – when I am bathed at all – and its fumant medicinal stings my sores. I scarce believe that Helen of Troy would have chosen so pungent a substance in which to soak, or that Cleopatra thought a wagered pearl no mean sacrifice to its acid as Neptune's gem slowly dissolved before Mark Antony's disbelieving eyes. Spiced with apple or herb, I've never tasted its attraction. Presenting less than the suppleness of wine, I regard it more like some infirmary nurse, stout in care but without any attribute of sensuous love. I've been informed by dyers that vinegar can be used to fix the chemistry of indigo. Such utility, as I lie here peeved and prostrate, elicits a belligerent acceptance rather than admiration.

Yet there was once a time, and not that long ago, when I looked on it as a blessing to bestow upon travelling folk swaddled in vapours emanating from the bowels of the ship. At supper in the Great Cabin, a certain odour was already attaching to some whose company was sly and mephitic. That aside, the ship's atmosphere was growing tainted with the fume of too airless a carriage. Once we hit the doldrums, a lack of breeze and the brassy sun made *Batavia* stink like a sour shoe. And in what issued from the orlop deck, a shoe which had trodden deeply in the muck.

At first it was all so unimaginable, that which was to come. Our business at Texel was committed to departure, our preoccupation one of checking and rechecking the inventory of all that was necessary for the voyage. The North Sea bade cool and gusty; there was little anticipating that our environs might shortly be transformed into something hot and stifling. On that first day out, and with the Dutch coast still in view, we were visited by a storm of such malevolence that the women wept and a majority of our number — unseasoned recruits to the sail as well as soldiers and cadets destined for the colonies — withdrew into themselves to steady their private ships and balance the content of their stomachs.

Things had not gone well. On the first day of *Batavia*'s voyage (as would presage her last) there was a fearful and unexpected gripping as the ship's momentum was seized by some devil of the deep. We were all thrown to a stagger, Cornelisz nearby tumbling to the deck. Everyone instantly forgot his private ill in the alarm of this unspecified peril. Only Ariaen Jacobsz — he whom I was resolved to get along with — only he and his closest officers appeared resilient to superstition. Singling one another out, they clustered with curses on their lips, their rivalry of opinion marshalled by hierarchy and command. Turning quickly to enlist an abeyant crew, they set about their counselled duties as if under cannon fire.

"Skipper," I shouted, a wind of rain in my face, "what is this that threatens?"
Eerie that summons, now, don't you think?
Cornelisz struggled to his feet, his eyes shining, his fear attentive and excited. Overhead, clouds of canvas were shortened, the ship no longer listing as it had on grinding to a halt. I could tell from the skipper's face, from his cajoling voice — a tone which implied, simply, that there was work to be done — that the matter wasn't critical. Unlike our situation eight months later, he appeared more embarrassed (and therefore more inclined to bully) than the stunned and calculating captain of that emergency to come.

We were grounded on the Walcheren sandbanks. In rehearsal of what would prove the final gambit of *Batavia*'s short life, boats were lowered on a turbulent sea and chains fed out in measure of whether we might winch ourselves afloat. Men were everywhere dispersed, some aloft and others, now soaked to the skin, a ship's length astern our rigid fixture. The skipper, himself, had descended the poop to command amidships, his orders bawled from the foot of the main mast. It were as if, stationed thus, he might better scent what it was he was given to work with, that he might eyeball a man more directly. I always thought him ignorant of distinctions that would have made him less amenable to vulgarity and more worthy of his rank.

As our stuck but buffeted hours wore on, the decks grew crowded in penned escape with those who could no longer bear to stay below. If nothing else, the stench had grown intolerable, the biliousness of folk more than matched by seasickness among the pigs and other livestock. The pumps had been set to lighten the bilge and combat any unseaming of our fabric, the drainage spewing out on deck and sluiced through the scuppers. It was a sobering introduction to life at sea, one that had many suddenly mindful, perhaps for the first time, of the discomforting months ahead.

By dusk *Batavia* was free. "What damage?" I asked.

"None," answered the skipper, guarded." We shaved a few hides from the keel. That's all."

It seemed that in the mortification of stranding, he was determined not to launch this voyage (as he had when last we sailed together) with a display of rancour that cooled my respect for his person if not his seamanship. Despite this day's bad omen, he was anxious to get us underway, to regain the flotilla which was my presidential command. When we did, it was with an embarrassment that undermined the pageantry of our departure. While it was a relief to have *Batavia* intact and rejoin our sailing companions, one of the latter had been so badly damaged by storm that there was nothing for it but to condone its limping return to Holland. Yes, right at the outset, we were all a little worse for the weather.

A ship is necessarily the most controlled of worlds, a nation-state reduced to its hard-pressed miniature. Within the grievous lack of space there is a reliance on collared purpose quite unimaginable to landed folk who may wander as they please. In the mechanic of cooperative governance, my task was to ensure that the laws of the Company were observed to the letter. Everyone was to contribute to that essential through generous obedience. Like a country magnetised around its overlord, there was a court of sorts and protocol of hierarchies that glued our floating commonwealth, just as in war there is a higher ordinance which has the capacity to suspend a people from internal enmity and galvanise a more selfless patriotism.

Not that we were united in nationality. Sailors being a mongrel lot, their service to the Company was presently abetted by the fact that most were sons of the Fatherland. The soldiers, however, were a mixed bag, a mercenary cast that well reflected the purchasing ambition of foreign princes and borderless opportunism. In addition to those native born and expected to stand to the defence of their country, there were others from as varied estates as Scotland, France and Germany – all of them blooded in the miseries of the continental conflict. When I think of what is mired in the religious wars that bedevil Europe, why wouldn't a soldier volunteer for service abroad and put an ocean 'twixt him and all that was formerly loved and now devastated? Among the ship's number, too, were novices in the profession of arms, cadets whose bravery was as untested as their understanding of what was due and proper before the prospect of unleashing themselves. I think about this now in light of the approaching drama which feasted on the defenceless among these three hundred closely gathered souls. My investigations into what took place in the Abrolhos revealed much, but at the time of sailing I was only conscious of those nearest me in rank and civility. I didn't appreciate how airless – and therefore how fomenting of viciousness – were the transit lives of troops confined to the orlop deck. The sailors were only marginally better off, stationed a deck higher amidst the guns and frigid hatch-drafts, their number – more than half the ship's complement – impossibly crowded. It was a policy born of ruinous experience not to quarter soldiers with sailors. In any case, the rotating watches of the latter would have tripped and grumbled over the enforced idleness of the troops. Yes, it was best to segregate such dangerous twins.

Yet when danger came, it was not at the instigation of those before the mast – though like most with little to lose, many were readily recruited to a bad cause. Rather, it was from within the circle that cushioned me that a multiplying disaffection was born. That cabin boy, Pelgrom, he at first merely witnessed the insolence, gloved or otherwise, of his superiors before being granted notions above his station. Cornelisz saw to it that he was corrupted, doubtless mocking me behind my back and schooling the impressionable youth in the alphabet of disrespect, mutiny, and eventually murder. Yes, it was the undermerchant and the skipper who each possessed a hungerful pride such as would induce them to risk what they could ill afford to lose. Yet Cornelisz had experienced no deprivation in berth or table such as that endured below by the bored and irritable young bloods who would become his henchmen. There was nothing they shared other than the stiffening pretence, once aroused to temerity, that they should have it all. And of all the lowly men most curiously destined, he whose ladder would climb as Cornelisz, his neck finally noosed, was shoved from his, it was Hayes, a common soldier and resident of that rocking and sulphurous dark, who would emerge into the light to defend that which had been of little comfort to him, to uphold an order in which he was but modestly rewarded. Perhaps Wiebbe was grateful for the shipwreck. Perhaps it gave him the opportunity to get out and stretch his legs. It certainly afforded him an opportunity to display his martial talents. And in that, as with Cornelisz himself, I wonder where he came from, what he perhaps was running from. A man with that much fighting gravitas was surely no common soldier. Yes Wiebbe, always too good to be true, his loyalty negating the material excuse of others who thought themselves ill-served and, like Cornelisz, would entitle themselves to a kingdom when the inheritance of a house might have done. Stone-Cutter Pietersz befouled his position as the soldiers' second in command, a man of minor rank but of rank all the same. He was another who would desert his post, not realising that to act as Jeronimus's second in illegal and unholy commission was to follow his master to an exemplary death.

But all of this was a revelation to come, when the story had played itself to an end and the improvising cast had received its critical review. In the beginning, in the unrealistic hope, perhaps, that we might find the experience more than tolerable, we were largely unknown to one another.

—ᘒ—

Ah, vinegar… That's right. How my thoughts wander.

The sailors used garlic as a personal fumigant and safeguard against creatures vile and demonic, or so the superstitious murmured, their eyes furtive with this unwished-for knowledge. Not even the bracing winds that ushered us south could launder the pungency from men grown stale with the chewing of that root.

The ladies might have been expected to find their shipboard quarantine repugnant but it was Jeronimus, initially, who seemed most offended, a cloth daubed with camphor (or whatever he kept in that medicinal chest beneath his bunk) and pinched to his nose, his eyes tearing in the grandeur of everything that played about us. Even I felt my collar salt and soil, my ruff early put away for such a time as I might meet with the Governor at Batavia.

There was little to do in those early days for the likes of Jeronimus and myself. Indeed, we were as little occupied as the one hundred soldiers below, men whose service would not be summonable for another fifteen thousand miles. The security of our precious cargo, of course, was to be maintained, and deferring to my most tried and trustworthy lieutenant, I assigned the task to Salomon, my bookish scrivener in India and travelling companion these past eighteen months. The money chests were deposited in the Great Cabin, and the most precious jewels – including Constantine's cameo – were under lock in my quarters. I never thought *not* to call Salomon aside and press him with any matter that came to mind. I never thought to share a confidence or serious professional concern with Jeronimus. From the first day we met, I felt that the latter's near appointment had been done as a favour for someone, that the man assumed his position not out of love for the Company but as a means of escaping something unstated. But what, if anything, was he running from?

And given his supercilious hauteur, that air of superiority common to men whose business successes are such that ordinarily they're never compelled to leave home, what did he hope to discover or achieve in the colonies? He was not like me – or even Salomon. Whatever spurred his careful ingratiation, there was something more serpentine than servile in the way he probed our vanity. The new man, just wanting to learn the ropes and fit in, yet ever giving the impression that he didn't really care, that he busied himself with only what was necessary to avoid a charge of dereliction.

Jeronimus cut a presence at table in the Great Cabin. He loitered at the edges of its conversation before making it his own with some challenge or observation that permitted him to monopolise thought and occasionally unsettle his fellow diners.

"Well, I have no idea about that," dismissed the skipper with a contemptuous snort. "What good does that sort of thinking turn a profit to? Too many idle arses back home, I say."

"Skipper!" I remonstrated, and acting as a kind of chaperone where ladies were present.

The predikant and his family swallowed as if oblivious, Bastiaensz perhaps hoping that their eldest, Judith, hadn't heard. I noticed a subtle smile on Lucretia's lips. The skipper noticed, too, and was well pleased.

"Ariaen, you judge too hastily," replied Jeronimus. "Even a worm has its worth."

And Jacobsz did seem little inclined to squash this one. It was obvious he cared nothing for the substance of the man; the undermerchant struck him as too self-pampering, too superfluous to any usefulness other than his rumoured ability to cure toothache. But in loving me not, the gruff mariner perceived an irritant, perhaps, in Cornelisz which was of small consequence to him but might trifle with the jealous etiquette of Company officials. What did it matter that Jeronimus fielded notions as remote and unintelligible as God's nightly lanterns? With next to nothing in common, the undermerchant might proxy him in annoyances that would never come back to bite.

There *was* something, however, that would bind us in an unhappy chain of events, something unforeseen yet not unforeseeable in the danger such companionships had lately effected at sea. Little wonder seasoned sailors were troubled, as if stalked by the evil eye, when a ship's manifest included women. And as Helen of Troy, bathing in vinegar, would unwittingly unleash all the brutish misunderstanding of a conflict whose infernal genie was lustful pride, so too Lucretia, in the starved intimacy of life at sea, would beget a rivalry that was little tailored to her liking. Neither she nor I would disturb the morals of the ship (not that I would have been averse to an overture of intimacy, such was the attraction we all felt for this paragon), but if her presence on *Batavia* was a much discussed cargo, her dispatch was intended for her husband in the East. Irrespective of the pull she might have enjoined on any man's loins, we were duty-bound never to give licence to an unspoken lust. Yet her companionship was keenly sought, its conferral an emblem of society in a cloister too narrow to represent any mirror of society at all.

It was Cornelisz who first used her presence to signal his status as a man of pedigree and learning. Once free of sickness and the unwelcome compromise of his quarters, my chief lieutenant began to cast about and fit the ingredient of what he found to the potential of what he might become. The vast number of men, those below deck and invisible to him, were of slight consequence. A servant was always a servant and without influence. But in Lucretia he discovered a table companion through whom he might direct and dominate the discourse of others.

"I too, lady, am at a novelty of what we undertake."

"But surely you're not as tender as I who now finds herself entirely at sea? You have your work; you answer to Heer Pelsaert." And snatching a glance at me.

"I assure you, I'm quite green – never more so," and laughing, "as when we embarked on storm and stranding."

"We were never stranded," interjected Ariaen flatly.

Jeronimus ignored the skipper. "My life has been anything but *this*."

"How, then, did you come to sign up for the ends of the earth?"

Before he could reply, Lucretia hastily enquired, "Is it really so, captain?"

"The skipper measures time in miles. Both are great."

None were moved by my answer.

"Men see opportunity where opportunity leads," reclaimed Jeronimus. "The Indies are our new world, a frontier of reinvention."

"Sounds like you're avoiding something at home."

"Forgive me, skipper, but *where* exactly might home be for *you*?"

Ariaen scowled. "I've little time for a place of my own, what with ferrying you lot to your destinies, God help us."

"Skipper, may I remind you..."

But no one was perturbed, least of all the Bastiaensz family which, gathered at the end of our squeezed table, resembled one of those stolid household portraits.

"You have no wife then?" asked Lucretia, and immediately regretting the impertinence as Ariaen held her gaze. He was calculating his response by choosing not to respond at all.

Jeronimus, running his tongue over his teeth, slumped back in his chair as the cabin boy, Pelgrom, replenished our tankards. In recollection, now, have I just spotted him? A pimply youth, his cheeks flushed. Was it that he was so young, or beneath us, or intimidated by the predikant's daughter, or afraid of the skipper? Surely not me? My rank may have been lordly but my manner was fatherly, my authority more counselling than despotic.

The skipper was licking grease from his fingertips, an act that wrinkled Lucretia's nose.

Jeronimus feigned to yawn. "None of us are afforded anything other than the hope that we might nourish what lies in our innermost heart."

"I don't follow," turned Lucretia."

"We angle to get what we would have, once the notion of its desirability is planted."

"Whether it be right or wrong?"

"My dear lady," he laughed, "let me not alarm you. There's no greater a conscience aboard this ship than mine," and casting a mocking glance in my direction.

Lucretia was of tidy conceit herself and in no way inclined to permit Jeronimus his glib superiority. "I still don't follow what you stand for," she said, "whether it be honour or opportunity, in this world or the next."

Gijsbert intruded a little cough. "It may be a matter of conjecture to some – and of no bearing whatsoever to the Godless fornicators and cannibals we're destined to meet..."

Mrs Bastiaensz paused in her eating as if to query the necessity of associating with cannibals.

"...but as a man of the cloth," continued her husband, "our hopes for what transpires in the next life have already been settled. There are those of us who are saved and those consigned to its direful alternative."

"But who can distinguish?" retorted Lucretia, no doubt thinking (as I later learned) of the little ones lost, and resiling at the stumpish image of the predikant's family.

"My dear lady..."

It was ever the prefacing civility of those who would tender their worth in the anticipatory esteem of her company. "The finest minds have uncluttered the mysteries of our faith. We pray to be numbered among those destined for the Lord's ark, yet who can say that his place has been reserved? As the Lord would have it, He has fashioned a lean and clean ship."

"Ships are neither lean nor clean. They're fat with filth," goaded the skipper.

Even I considered Bastiaensz a provocation, his starchness an archness that didn't tally with the experience of we who had sailed the world or spent time in the East.

"I've already noted," he defended primly, "that the lowliest sailors express beliefs in sparse keeping with any possibility of salvation."

"The only belief a sailor shares – if he chooses to share anything at all – is the hope that he might duck the Devil's injury and be spared long enough to enjoy his time ashore with another man's wife!"

"So you've no family you're sufficiently fond of to want to think the better?" challenged Lucretia.

"Madam," rounded the skipper, wanting her to respect the unapologetic pragmatist that he was, "I *have* no shore life to speak of." His command of the months to come, their conveyance and their safety, was a compelling responsibility which brooked little in the way of questioning. Few, he would have us understand, knew the realities of a displacing survival as well as he.

"Whether I choose or not, the Company is my compass, the boatswain of what I'm spared a blessing to do. I speak plainly — I must so since I daily deal with the scum of the earth. I am *Batavia*'s beast-keeper," he grunted, "beggin' the pardon of the uppermerchant 'ere."

I disliked Ariaen's tone of irreverent complaint, his air of superiority.

"Let's hope, then, you keep her tigers caged," smiled Jeronimus.

Jacobsz turned sharply in his seat. "Let's see you, witling, manage the equivalent of a regiment in the field these months on end!"

This time Lucretia didn't smile, nor did I caution.

"Skipper, forgive me," soothed Jeronimus. "I meant no disrespect. Only that, as Noah to our enterprise, you have a curious zoo to tend."

"Father," piped Gijsbert's son, "is Noah a citizen of Calvin's godly republic? And might the Heaven prepared for us be not already filled?"

"Nicely put!" twisted the undermerchant. "Well Gijsbert, have you anything to assure young Giblet here that life won't end at some padlocked gate?"

"Jeronimus," I remonstrated, "neither of us are schooled in the detail of theology."

"To the contrary, it requires little logic to imagine God less than just if all a man need do to enter Paradise is be born under the accident of one star rather than the next."

Lucretia grew thoughtful. Even the skipper was mindfully pricked to challenge a doctrine foreign to his sense of discipline. In the ensuing pause we were each aware of the concussing waves, the creak and muffled shudder of the ship. Halos of light slid up and down the table, the oil lamps swaying in their gimbals. Everyone was waiting for Gijsbert to speak.

The predikant raised a napkin to his lips, realising that something other than eating was expected of him. "Heaven is reserved," he decided, "for God's true band of brothers."

"But who, sir, is granted the right to choose his relative in this?"

Cornelisz's challenge echoed the discomfort I sometimes felt when the certainties of our human mission are shadowed by misgiving. Was everyone denied the grace of God who wasn't one of us? Surely there were too many of us to begin with.

We were too numerous, he'd argued. *There wasn't enough water or meat.*

Who gave you the authority to decide?

Why, everything I did, God breathed into me...

Gijsbert was a simple man. An imposter, if truth be told. Anyone could see he was recent to the collar, just as Cornelisz was new to his Company station. Each was cut to the cloth of a different origin, yet here was the undermerchant, nudging the predikant to expose himself.

"I take it, sir, you're not convinced by our faith," ventured the cleric, hoping perhaps to curtail the subject in a polite variance of views.

"I am more – how might I express it? – open to a variety of opinion."

"You'd be in good company," tabled the skipper. "An East Indiaman – Christ, it's the very idea of purgatory as the old preachers would paint it. You never quite know how a voyage'll end, who'll come out ahead. And then what does it matter? Jews and Franks and Blackamoors – I've sailed with the lot of 'em, and those as didn't die on the voyage seemed downright pleased and lusty as land hove into sight. I doubt a man can know more than what's shoved in front of his nose."

"Hear hear, skipper," and Jeronimus raised his cup. "Why pretend to know so paltry a thing when there's so much more we might profit from in our searching ignorance." Then holding my eye, "Why ship to the Indies if only to cling to the prejudices that impelled one in the first place?"

"Am I to understand, then, that you *have* left something behind?" played Lucretia.

"My word, you're as forward as a wife in what you'd prise from me!"

"And as you know that I travel to Batavia to rejoin my husband, have you no wife of your own?"

The undermerchant's eyes flickered as if he were momentarily absent from himself. I don't recall his precise turn of answer, only that it struck me how little I knew him. Later, after he had admitted to his crimes yet was of a mind to recant, I myself had fisted the table, shouting, "Why do you mock us when you've freely confessed?" And he looked at no one on the *Sardam*'s council, reaching into himself as if some private drawer to reply, "It was to delay the verdict, to cheat those who would wrongly cheat me of my life and to speak, once more, to my dear wife in Batavia."

It was inconceivable that Jeronimus should have a wife already in the Indies. Yet, by that stage, I no longer knew the measure of what was true or false. In Jeronimus I was forced to abandon that often comforting deference to plausibility.

"No babes, then?" I heard Lucretia enquire.

Again Jeronimus hesitated. "I'm looking forward to a life in the bosom of the Company. I'm sure Deschamps, in the corner there, will aid me."

My long-time assistant smiled unwillingly, and I realised that of these two who were nearest me in matters pertaining to the Company, I knew next to nothing of what they dreamed. It worried me in relation to Jeronimus; it shamed me with respect to Salomon. It was easier to construe a story around Bastiaensz and his family, the lot present and accounted for in the decision to depart the Fatherland. Except that therein lay its mystery.

"Gijsbert," I said, reaching with my knife for the unscarred cheese, "how come you by a posting in the East for the succour of your family?"

"We are hopeful," hastened his wife, Maria, "– just as you've been gracious to our boy – that the colony will support the virtue we import."

Gijsbert junior, their eldest, grinned with the bashfulness of an obedient son granted licence to become a man.

"The Directors are desirous of fortifying our overseas missions with goodly Christian teaching. The Governor, too, is adamant that our outposts conduct their business with merit."

"Best of luck," muttered Jacobsz.

Jeronimus snorted and pushed his plate away.

"Skipper," I turned, and ignoring the undermerchant, "Surely you'd agree that in these lands a little of God's Word might go a long way."

Jeronimus was eyeing me as if a player who had too readily betrayed a weak hand.

"I speak nothing," announced Ariaen, "of those lands wherein a Christian is a form of stew. As far as I'm concerned, there's little place for preaching where there's little risk of drowning."

"Of the men at sea, then," I persisted. "Surely virtuous commanders stand to benefit from their sailors' fear of God?"

"They fear no more than me, the sharks and an unsavoury death."

"In any case," snatched Jeronimus, "what need of fear if they're already saved? And what need of good conduct if they're already damned? If Heaven's full, Hell must be more crowded still!"

"'Tis true," entered Gijsbert, not wanting his provenance addressed as if he were not present, "that the people on this ship are little inclined to savour God's comfort. Many is the man I'm unable to represent for such is his reserve, whenever I draw near, that I cannot dissemble the atheists and mockers from the men of faith."

"You refer to our services at sea?" I tried to help.

"The men look as if cajoled to attend. They listen without attention and pray without devotion. My exhortations are as spray upon the indifference of their reef."

"Tellingly put," smiled Jeronimus. "But was your flock at home any more amenable to your messages of goodness?"

"I was a church elder," answered Gijsbert, somewhat abashed. "Ours was a hardworking community."

"We had a mill," added Maria. "They were the sweetest of years; the birth and rearing of our children." Then her features grew arch. "We were prosperous then."

Gijsbert patted his wife's hand while their brood glanced anywhere but at their parents, embarrassed perhaps by their inability to leave.

"How does a miller become a minister?" enquired Cornelisz, feigning interest.

"What turns an apothecary into a merchant?" asked Lucretia, pointedly.

"Business fell on bedevilling times," conceded Gijsbert, addressing himself to the lady. "Our horse-drawn operation was no match for the wind-driven technologies of the new," he sighed.

"It's an age of sail," shrugged the skipper, "and it's high time we harnessed all that we'd command."

"Better us than others, eh?"

"Too right! I wouldn't trust the English not to round on us in a thrice."

"Please go on," encouraged Lucretia, returning to the predikant.

"Things went from bad to lost. None wishes to see his neighbour fall but there was little the community could do. We are a large family, as you see. There were simply too many of us to exist where there was little to exist upon. All the more cruel, don't you think, in a nation gone mad with wealth."

"The Company," I responded, "is the engine of our independence, its wealth our destiny."

Everyone around the crowded table looked at me as if to say: *Yes yes, we understand all that, but that's not to say the justice we entertain isn't, at times, entirely just.* I felt a need to redirect the conversation and turned to Cornelisz: "Jeronimus, had you always a desire to put to sea and seek your fortune in the Spiceries?"

"I would put it to you, sir, that only those most secure in God's bounty could have dreamed up such a gamble by which we, in proxy and at their bidding, venture to risk ourselves."

"You are not wedded, I gather, to the ambition of what you might amass?" queried Lucretia, her discreetly mocking smile doubtless impressing itself on Cornelisz's secrecy and furtive anger. When he didn't answer, she thought to prod by way of conciliation. "Everyone, of course, bows to your skills as an apothecary."

"Madam, I am no more than Heer Pelsaert's humble second."

The skipper glanced at the undermerchant. Perhaps it scuffed him to witness how close to the wind this land-lubbered sop managed to sail in matters affecting the fairer sex.

"Did you not practise of your own accord?" persisted Lucretia. "Was there not a shop window with a pestle and mortar and the sign of a crocodile above the door?"

"Such a cosy picture. No, I'm afraid one's creditors respect neither talent nor belief. Isn't that so, Bastiaensz?"

The predikant inclined his head, cautious.

"What use to the Company is a man who can't manage his money?" tested the skipper.

The undermerchant smiled. "Aren't all sailors brothel bankrupts?" he riposted.

It was Ariaen's turn to leer as I cleared my throat: "Ahem. May I remind you, gentlemen, that there are women and children present."

"Quite right!" Cornelisz sat up straight. "It would appear we are all, in various ways, indebted to the Company." Then raising his tankard, "May its purpose reward ours!"

If I was at peace — albeit cramped and assailed from time to time by spells of indisposition — yes, if I was at peace with the notion that my Company endeavours defined me, I grew aware that the majority of this circle over whom I presided were not just green to the rigours of a protracted voyage but had suspended, perhaps forever, the occupations once assumed to define them. They — these migrants, these folk betwixt lives — they appeared feeble and unfocused to the point of vulnerability. Even Cornelisz, I could scarce imagine what he might make or take of Batavia when we arrived. Having been appointed undermerchant with nary an apprenticeship in the business, I could little other than conceive of him disdaining what he found and decamping into some archipelago backwater, there, perhaps, to set himself up in a state of petty wilfulness, to become an ungenerous version of Meyer with a servile child-wife.

How had I become so suspicious? Has it been that in the aftermath of what transpired I have sought to make up stories about people, to attribute to each the character of their undoing? Have I unwittingly sought to censure others for their particular misfortune? And yet, did Bastiaensz's brood deserve to perish like that?

Their eldest, Gijsbert Bastiaen, the name all too redolent with assumptions of legacy, was a fine young man, eager not to sit out the journey. In taking him on as a clerk, it was as if Salomon had acquired a younger sibling, the two of them giggling like girls in exchanges that were not of my rank and, therefore, privilege to share. Gijsbert senior, of course, was also an employee of the Company — I suppose the family felt itself sufficiently contracted to entitle its journey east. But to what purpose? While any man might shield his vulnerability in the anticipation of God's mercy, there was little enthusiasm for piety during the usual course of business. Predikants were only valued when things got tricky, and even then it was preferred that their summons come with the ability to wield a sword or shoulder an arquebus. For the most part Coen thought them a waste on the Company purse, the lesser lay-readers an even greater idiocy. Yet here they were, this petty burgher tribe now turned family of faith, looking to reclaim themselves in a new life lacking parish or prediction. Certainly, who could have foreseen that Gijsbert might be so sorely tested and compelled to bear so heavy a cross well short of Java?

From the tenuous beginnings of those dinner conversations, Cornelisz had snatched at Bastiaensz and drawn him into a masque the latter was incapable of appreciating. *This merchant, in the beginning, had behaved himself very well...* It's poison to think he could even utter that qualification in the wake of what happened to his family. It's hateful to hear that he coupled the undermerchant's name with mine, that he linked us in dispute to Lucretia, and would have it that this was the origin of all our disasters. Would that he had better served his daughter than slander me! Specx was right – a more forthright man of God might have tilted matters differently.

But by then his family – all save Judith, that is – were buried in a pit above the only beach which gave easy access to Batavia's Graveyard. As Gijsbert would have it, he was spared to be mocked: the island's body-weakened boatman, launching rafts by morning and hauling them in at day's end, his only comfort his knowledge that Judith was now the fondled possession of one of Cornelisz's lieutenants. That and his bible.

Is it an interesting book? *scoffs Cornelisz, standing over him on a crust above the shingle.*

Why don't you kill me now and have done with it?

That's not what you said. That's not what you really think.

Surely I'm permitted to grieve.

You're not permitted to disturb the peace. "Be silent or you go the same way." Wasn't that what Wouter said to you, having holed young Giblet's head with an adze?

Gijsbert swallows a knot of spittle. My daughter and I have been like oxen before the axe, hoping to see in the morrow but ever in the readiness of meeting God.

God God God! God can't *hear you!*

Silence.

I know you're in there – *hi-ding!*

I don't know what else I can give you, having yielded all.

Oh don't be so miserable; you're practically family. Your daughter's now hoisted on Coenraat's yard. Indeed, you're like a provincial uncle to us.

I am the plaything of those I fear, creatures so inflamed with a belief in their impunity that I am, at one moment, to be decapitated, the next, poisoned, then after all such menace, reprieved that they may find some use for me, knowing my only purpose is to be tortured by what they threaten.

Oh Gijsbert, they're just boys. A bit boisterous, I'll admit, but they've been cooped up on this island – and after all those months at sea – with scant entertainment other than the killing of your family. And the rest. I'll tell you what, I have an idea! There are those, the ones on the High Island across the way. They don't see us for what we are, men who have had to make the hard decisions. After so much blood, don't you think it's time we bury the hatchet? Ha ha, did I say that? My apologies, Gijsbert. It was a night of bitter discomposure, the tent dark and crowded. The boys couldn't have been expected to use anything else. Besides, you and your daughter, you *did* dine well at my table that fatal hour. Real cask meat. Wine, even. Not the shitty seal skins you've been chewing on lately. I know, I know, you've had neither bread nor rice, oil nor vinegar. But Gijsbert, your hungry superfluity of kin has been eliminated – a timely preclusion of suffering, I should have thought, since death is widely practised in the colonies – and your daughter has become a whore, and here you are, thinking about what you've *not* been given to eat. Honestly, you need to reclaim a little perspective. So instead of moping about, wondering whether we're going to kill you, I'm going to give you a little task – a promotion, if you like. After all, you signed the oath of allegiance; you're one of us. Now, you're to cross to that island over there. You're to parley with that soldier, Hayes, and invite him and the others back. Say it's been a misunderstanding, that our distemper was driven by thirst. Tell him, what with the wells they've discovered, there's no warrant for discord. You can do this, Gijsbert. You're a man accustomed to getting up before others, of uttering the Word of the Lamb.

You have slaughtered my lambs.

Not all.

Gijsbert stands there with closed eyes, the tiny congregation, such as braves to attend him, scoured by the iodine scent of salt and blood. God, I beseech you, *his hands unclasp, his arms outstretch,* to take the frightened and oppressed under Your wing —

Oh bravo! *cries Jeronimus. His boys — Pelgrom chief among them — are flapping the severed wings of battered seals in a dance of such lewd impiety, it seems that Satan's crabs are feasting on fallen angels.*

Gijsbert awakes as if oblivious. The others, kneeling, shuffle closer to one another.

Cornelisz turns to Van Huyssen, Zevanck, Hendricxsz and Loos. This is why they live. For the moment, at least.

And their laughter, he knows, is a torture to the predikant.

Gijsbert senses my presence, steals a reproachful look in my direction. You could stop this.

I'm not here, I reply. *I was never here.* And contemplating the kneeling martyrs and all that mixed race of survivors above the shingle, I'm reminded once more of what I daily live with. *Save just the once...*

So as you abandoned us, so did we welcome *him...*

I was not the only one who left that day. I was detained in the boat against my will.

Gijsbert drops on his haunches. I don't know about that. Only that I'm blamed by those who've never known what purgatory is for being more alive than dead.

None was more 'twixt worlds than I, I say. I know all about purgatory.

Just listen to the pair of you, dismisses Jeronimus, licking and comparing your wounds. If either of you had been more forthright, do you imagine it would have made any difference? The power to seduce is in neither of you. You've not the gall to seize what opportunity affords, what the imagination might flatter. You merely trail in the wake of what's yielded, hoping to make a meal of another's bounty, while I —

Steal, then seal the deed with murder!

Those who would have themselves killed are easily disposed of. My dear Francisco, you really do need to get the hang of this —

I'll see you hanged, alright!

Stop it, the lot of you! Lucretia is seated like a queen in the Great Cabin, her high collar a scallop-shell of pearls, her hair a periwinkle of diamonds.

I am arrested by the vision she presents. You are the very image of Helen or Cleopatra, I say.

Then I am her Paris, purrs Cornelisz.

A thief and a coward.

And I her Antony, ogles Jacobsz.

A braggart and a loser.

Oh you men, rails Zwaantie, stepping from the shadow where the money chests are stored. She's no more than what you want the world to think your members worthy of. I can tell you now, she ain't no lady —

Really?

And I ain't no lady's maid.

Hmm...

The undermerchant and skipper exchange a glance as if already divvying up the spoils. Lamplight sways to the motion of the ship, the table both passive and restive, a landscape over which cloud and sunlight chase one another. Then all is dark save for the taper I bear into the corner of this now deeply nocturnal moment.

My God, I whisper, smelling her before actually mapping the injured contour she presents. I turn to the officer of the watch. They did this?

Lucretia is numb, looking at no one and shivering in shit. The fact that she is half-naked strikes none of us as immodest. We are too shocked by a lurking menace within the ship.

Who has done this to you? I ask deliberately, as if doubting her ability to hear or understand. She looks up with the timidity of one who no longer trusts in the protection of my authority.

There were many, she swallows, and perhaps still disbelieving. Their hands were well-rehearsed. My lips were cupped by such rancid flesh I cannot, even now, spit the taste from my mouth.

Has her maid been summoned? I turn to the officer.

I ain't no maid. And there's a gurgle of laughter.

No, please! And Lucretia hugs herself, the ribbon still tightly haltered around her neck, her eyes half a-bulge.

I can't doubt that half the ship isn't aware of what's taken place, that the darkness isn't silent with a straining of ears. But who? Which half? The smell is disgusting.

I saw no one distinctly, she cowers.

The skipper?

No.

And then in a surge of ashamed anger: But I recognised that other's voice.

Which other?

Evertsz. The boatswain. The one in whom the skipper confides. They murmur viciously in my hearing.

She's piecing it together, the ruinous logic. Go on, I say.

The skipper would malign me. Ever since I spurned his advances.

In spite of the calm with which she imparts this intelligence, and having given me something to go on, Lucretia presently resumes the morbidity in which she was found: a quivering wreck, her fingers gooed in filth, her garments ripped and hoisted to besmirch her privities.

She must be attended to. If not the maid, then the predikant's wife.

No one wants to touch her. No one, in all proprietary, knows what to do with her. As Zwaantie, doubtless, wiggles her arse for Jacobsz in his cabin, I survey my feelings for the ruined mistress and discover that I've lost my lust. Indeed, in the conspiracy of this variant rape, I feel like a pimply youth suddenly rescued from his intemperate daydream by a concussion that knocks some seriousness into his behaviour.

Judith attends with her mother. I see she is shaken by what confronts her, yet she also appears contemptuous of *Batavia*'s princess. If Zwaantie thinks Lucretia has had it coming, Bastiaensz's daughter appears to have made up her mind that she would have handled things differently. Certainly, she would never have permitted events to deteriorate to this tarring with shit. I sense a conciliating adjustment among those who would fear their neighbour and seek to accommodate an unpredictable situation.

I turn to the officer of the watch, unable to communicate my musings. Evertsz, eh? But I'll wager Jacobsz is behind all this.

It's at this moment that I'm reminded I've not kept a lookout for what Jeronimus might be up to. I've never felt easy about him, and even less so after that episode at the Cape: he with Jacobsz and Zwaantie in the ship's boat during that un-sanctioned tour of the fleet; all parasols and gin whilst I was ashore, bartering with Hottentots for stores to secure our passage into the emptiness of that Indian sea. Subsequent illness had laid me low, made me unaware of who was in league with whom.

Have this place cleaned up, I order. Have the deck scrubbed with vinegar.

Lucretia was not seen again. Not outside her cabin. The days were blue and raw with the approach of winter, the season at odds with what now passed in the Fatherland. Many were hugging themselves in the bitter fall of temperature – the women, the idlers, the human cargo which only fleetingly came up on deck to gulp such air as might preserve them for another day below. Little wonder the gambling troops were kept in a separate dark beneath the mariners, the latter – as surly a lot as one might ever fear to meet – rising and retiring at the turn of each watch to alternate scenarios of discomfort. In the briny dampness, ceaseless duty made them harsh critics, their inclination to brood at perceived injustices as dangerous a volatility as the boredom that fogged the orlop deck.

It was difficult to tell what effect Lucretia's assault had had on the ship's company. Perhaps all were waiting for me to act with inquisitorial swiftness, to establish a court in which they were all to be held accountable. To know what they were being accused of, to know in what way they might be punished, this would give them something to rise against. Already Evertsz was putting it about that the entire crew would be disciplined because of the whores we'd shipped — at least this was what was reported to me, for the boatswain himself took care to be dutiful, if sullen, in my presence. But I had Lucretia's word. And I could tell that the boatswain was uneasy with what I might or might not know. I was only too happy to abet his uneasiness since I, myself, was uncertain of who — and how many — were in on the plot to violate the lady. Jacobsz was not pulling his man into line, and Cornelisz seemed unconcerned that I might trouble myself over what to think. Indeed, he and the skipper were spending much time together at the taffrail, conversing with a publicness that appeared to have put behind them any differences of taste or background. The content of what they spoke could not be overheard, and this did nothing to belie suspicion.

Now that I had recovered a little from my illness — indeed, had emerged like Lazarus from my cabin tomb — I couldn't help but feel that the eyes of all were watching me, awaiting my next move. If the ship's polity would manoeuvre at my earliest shift, I was inclined to oblige them nothing.

Bastards. Bastards, all!

The venom I feel at times is more potent than the poisons which keep me steady. I know I will not recover — recover enough to live without this thinning that no appetite can restore — but it's not in what I bodily fray that so discomforts. It's the rage — this exasperating impotence, if you like — that I feel before an orchestration which insists on resisting me. It's directed at this story which is not my own yet all too plainly what the world would interpret. Yes, mine is fast becoming the legacy of what others would make of me. I can feel my heat, even now, stewing a sweat that does nothing to assuage my fever, my pulse kicking like a horse improperly stabled. To be stalked in body is one thing; to be stalked in soul is altogether something else. I fear I will die the more for what is fast slipping beyond my persuasion to remedy.

That stupid Bastiaensz and his daring to opine that there was trouble between myself and the skipper over two women. He used me as a sheet to his conscience, pretending it wasn't his fault that he was forced to join the mutineers, blaming me in common with Jacobsz for a falling out which sired that Golgotha. Neither I nor the skipper – much as I detest and censure him – were at the Abrolhos when its famine aspect became a jungle. In any case, the predikant would better have spoken God's truth had he observed what was going on between Jacobsz and Cornelisz. There were two women, to be sure – Lucretia and Zwaantie, the mistress and her spiteful maid – but they were ingredient to a dereliction hosted by the skipper and undermerchant in a tale that played to vanities not my own. Yes, even Gijsbert and his daughter, Judith, might be said to have added their performance to that theatre of jealousy and submission. But no, the bastard would run with the fox and hunt with the hounds, then absolve himself in the scandalising inference that the entire debacle stemmed from my failure as protector of *Batavia*'s folk.

"Skipper, there has been an assault." It wasn't possible that he hadn't already heard.

Jacobsz didn't meet my eye. Instead, he focused on my waistcoat as if pondering what it might take to unstitch my guts. "Who?"

"Lucretia Jansz."

His mouth wrinkled and he nodded meditatively as if to say, *I'm not surprised*.

I was on the verge of accusing the boatswain by way of provocation when it occurred to me that such a charge might well be expected. The skipper's antipathy towards Lucretia was no secret. He'd made much of the maid after his overtures to the mistress had been successively rebuffed – on the last occasion with a firmness that exchanged entreaty for anger. Jacobsz was too smart not to know I'd suspect his involvement, too smart not to parry it with the unspoken challenge: *Well go on, then, prove it.* To prove anything, of course, would be to reveal that they were all in it together, a situation I'd be unable to remedy since it would galvanise the ship's company against me.

"We must investigate," I said, more to measure his reaction.

"As you will," his eyelids drowsy. It flittingly crossed my mind that he was spending too much time below with Zwaantie instead of rest. It was clear he didn't share my sense of outrage. It was also clear that I'd been too laid up in my cabin. The voyage, with all its condensing prejudice, had progressed without me.

When it came to asking questions, there were few intrepid enough to venture an opinion or report what was rumoured. Already Evertsz had drawn attention to his guilt by swinging to the offensive, persuading men in darkened companionways that those who had no business interfering with the work of God-fearing seamen were hell-bent on punishing them for the bleating upset of those who had no right to be at sea in the first place. Well let me tell you, the skipper won't stand for it! 'Pon my oath, he'll stand up to that watery prick!

I looked around me, took stock of those whose loyalty I might rely upon, and was not encouraged. The sailors, hard men all, were disciplined as a company to obey none but their officers. On my account I could number Salomon and Gijsbert's son and an assortment of clerks, and no doubt the emigrating families, but what we purported seemed more moral than robust. As for the soldiers and cadets, they were a cause whose scruple I could not determine, whose ranks may have blended already with the skipper's renegades to stew a swollen malcontent. In the assault upon Lucretia it was as if some experiment had been initiated wherein all were in silent thrall, waiting and watching to see what my next move might be.

No, I would not arouse them. I was too newly reprieved from that accursed and recurrent sickness to test the solidity of my command.

It was Salomon who further piloted my thoughts, his timid intelligences perceptive. Jacobsz had never cared for him – *Pelsaert's bum boy* I'd heard him called. My assistant was altogether too bookish for the likes of that boorish sailor. And chaste. It was this combination, perhaps, which attracted Lucretia. As my second in so many things (and it is telling how rarely I thought so of Cornelisz, my actual lieutenant), Salomon exhibited a delicacy which doubtless led to a candour of sympathies. In the aftermath of what had befallen her, Lucretia confided her fears to him, warned him – and therefore me – 'twixt tears and anger of what the assault might portend. I imagine her humiliation had made her shy of my presence. The undermerchant, too, was scarcely seen, and only then at mess times where he practised not to notice Lucretia's absence or the tension which sullened table conversation.

"The undermerchant and the skipper have become great friends," whispered Salomon.

"It's not possible that the skipper didn't know of the move against Lucretia," I whispered back, declaring my suspicion for the first time.

Salomon blinks in the gloom in which we behave like conspirators ourselves. "The skipper and the lady's maid – he has openly made her queen of the ship." He pauses, only half-way there, and knowing that what he has to say may have to be repeated publicly. "And the undermerchant is his confidante."

"Pff," I breathe contemptuously. "Such a small ambition to play the jester to that even greater fool."

"No, Heer Pelsaert, you mistake the skipper's power."

"I observe he plays it loud and recklessly."

"Forgive me, but the skipper is a sailor only."

This time the pause between us is teasing. Salomon is already privy to that which cannot be spoken of; privy, again, to my renewed vulnerability.

A silhouette looms in passing. It is Evertsz, less inclined to some plausible destination, I think, than to check on how our worries fester.

"You cannot mean," I hiss, after the boatswain is gone, "that *he –*"

"No, of course not. That man, like me, is under order and obligation."

"Then what?"

"That man is the tool of an instrument which is in the hands of another."

"Stop speaking in riddles, Deschamps!"

Salomon swallows. Then checking to see that Evertsz is truly vanished, he reaches close in a manner unaccustomed and speaks into my ear, "Jeronimus."

I breathe hard, unconvinced but prone to wonder. I mean, what are we talking about here? "The undermerchant controls the ship?"

More nervous still since he of whom we speak is capable of materialising like a phantom, smiling, while at other times remaining invisible when needed, Salomon explains, "He panders to the skipper's vanity so that the skipper readily consults him."

"So if Jacobsz was behind the assault on Lucretia – and let's face it, the misguided wretch believes himself ill-served in his handling by the lady – do you mean to suggest that the undermerchant was behind the skipper's audacity?"

"Heer Pelsaert, the skipper bears you no love and the undermerchant bears you no loyalty."

I can see it pains him to betray a senior official. "Jeronimus was behind the assault on Lucretia?" I ask. "Impossible! Why, he chided the skipper – told me so himself – when that miserable brute persisted in making a nuisance of himself. We all knew that Jacobsz smouldered, that he was like a volcano in the ferment of too great a heat."

Salomon raises an eyebrow.

"What possible motive could he have in bringing harm to the lady?" I ask.

"Madam van der Mijlen," and citing her married name, "has become brittle in their company."

"But the skipper has snared the maid in lusty compensation."

"That still leaves the lady," he replies like a schoolmaster indulging my unwillingness to apprehend the problem.

"Meaning?"

He takes a deep breath, glancing furtively about. "The undermerchant has always thought the skipper less than worthy of what he boasted. He believes himself better manicured, both in style and breeding, to whatever the lady might find choice."

"That's preposterous. Lucretia – Madam van der Mijlen – is not to be tempted," I say, and back-tracking the landscape of my every illicit thought, strangling the snigger of secret desire to ensure that I remain undisclosed. Yes, had I not played a solitaire of what-ifs, speechlessly inferring, were our friendship to grow warm, that an arrangement of sorts might be tolerated?

"The undermerchant is not above using his powers of persuasion," my assistant struggles hoarsely, as if something is lodged in his throat. "He is convinced of his charm."

"Why then would Cornelisz wish to see the lady harmed?"

"It's more in the way of hurting you."

I stare at him, astonished, waiting for him to go on.

"He tires of pretending he's in any way second to you." And knowing that this isn't quite what he means, adds, "He has no appetite for the years you've served, for your..." and he looks aside, embarrassed by the implied criticism, "your token health."

I inhale sharply.

"He would have things sooner rather than later. They – a great many – well, we all thought you might die."

"Was that a thought devoutly wished?" I ask icily.

"Your recovery, if you'll forgive me, has not been without its disappointment to some. What they might have picked over must now – if they would have it – be seized."

"They?"

Salomon again glances left and right as if just being spotted with me might warrant his destruction. "The corners of this ship are dark with speculation," he hurries. "Batavia is assumed by most, but it's not the only destination rumoured."

"What, some other country?"

He shrugs.

"But who," and fingering my lips, "who would dare utter so loose a thought?"

"I hear the lower desks heed it from above. But they know not who, exactly, commands these excitements. Only that the supercargo – you, sir – wants them flogged for what happened to the lady."

"Have they no mouthpiece?"

"They say the skipper will stand firm."

Good Lord, my magistracy is alleged tyrannical without having been put to any test. "And the skipper is a creature of the undermerchant, you say?"

Salomon nods.

"So nothing can occur without his complicity?"

Salomon's mouth wrinkles as if to indicate *I suppose so.*

"And if I've proven myself obdurate by not dying in my bunk, how might they persist in whatever scheme they dream of?"

Salomon sighs; he's tried to warn me. Lucretia. Of course. It's a provocation. And Cornelisz will make up to her later by making her queen, not just of *Batavia* as the skipper would have done but of Batavia's Graveyard itself.

—⁓—

Jeronimus eyes him with a lustre bred of darkness. I can't tell whether we're still below in that furtive companionway or some other lightless abode. There's no moon, nothing to go by. Then slowly my eyes adjust and I hear, as much as feel, the chillness within my ear, my cheeks burnished with exposure. Somewhere in the getting to this place we've passed beneath a frost of stars, their silence jostling. The crying of the baby is enough to fill God's allowance of just one sound at a time. Except that there is no God. Not here.

"Your master can't protect you now," he says, glancing in my direction, my phantom witness. "In fact, you've had it rather easy," and taking a step towards Salomon.

The clerk, like some nest-fallen chick hiding in the grass, doesn't move.

"The boys and I," continues Cornelisz, "we've had to decide everything, make all the arrangements."

Hendricxsz, Zevanck and Stone-Cutter gather to complete the circle.

"There's so little here, so much misery. We've been racking our brains as to how to even the equation."

"Racking someone's brains!" sniggers Hendricxsz.

Cornelisz waves aside the interruption.

And it is clear to me that we stand within the undermerchant's shelter. Except that I can't possibly be there, can I? My voiceless witness would construe that I have become one of *them*, for Salomon is surrounded and alone.

"Even *I* have tried to alleviate suffering," admits Cornelisz. "With what medicines remain, I've tried to administer comfort."

There is the slightest pause, a hiatus in which Salomon yet clings to wilful innocence. It's a vanishing hope. Jeronimus may as well have been about to explain the facts of life to him.

"Mayken Cardoes' baby," he sighs, "what more could I have done? The tonic I gave it..."

And Salomon glances sharply in my direction as if to accuse upper and undermerchants alike of being wayward with their drugs and potions.

But the baby lives! I interject, *I hear its fitfulness.* And in truth, throughout the voyage to Timor we could scarce escape the insistence of its struggling life. But no one heeds me, no one sees me except, perhaps, my forsaken assistant – here, where God does not exist.

Cornelisz is now focused on a new experiment. His apothecarial trial has proven inconclusive. That which pretended relief has fallen short of death. "Deschamps," he says (and all the while his henchmen, aware of what their master is about to ask, never take their eyes from Salomon), "there is a half-dead child. Now we all agree you're not a fighting man. Here's a little noose," and he produces a length of cord with a slipknot. "Go and fix it so that the rest of us on the island are not troubled by so much wailing." And he steps forward to garland the clerk with this injudicious halter.

The message is inescapable. Salomon has seen enough to know that this is not a request.

"Go on then. What are you waiting for?"

He will do anything to escape their murderous presence, to flee the violence they would option on him, even if it means becoming one of them. And as he steps from Cornelisz's tent in search of innocence, he finds himself once more an unwilling accomplice to circumstances not of his doing, to crimes not of his invention. Laughter behind him, crying before – where he is is a darkness of silent hiding, an imminence which can never be resolved. In what I imagine must feel like the loneliness of Gethsemane, it's as if I kiss the infant with death myself, although I can scarce conceive of the depravity that Salomon now chooses to enjoin. Still, in its aftermath I find myself helping him to conceal the body. We're carrying her down the steps, the dogs in the compound snarling. *Quickly, before the night is out...Medari mustn't know!* The island twitches in its slumbers, knowing that each night another of its castaways goes missing. *Quickly, here by the sea...* We scoop a hurried pit above the tidemark. Salomon momentarily looks up, his eyes haunted and unreaching like a soul adrift in the emptying horror of what he's become. Then eclipsing that which the stars would faintly witness, Cornelisz's silhouette hovers over us. His boys are back at the tent, drinking and devising torments for the morrow. But the apothecary come merchant come Captain-General has slipped away from their enjoyments to ensure that his will has been done in this place where God does not exist.

It was only a dream yet the horror of it lingers like an unpurgable foulness. I chew my thoughts, my lips as much torn in restless meditation as in symptom of this wasting which will ultimately consume me. Yet what is it I would most defend? My life – ha! – this overheated flesh which pants in shallow draught? Or perhaps my conscience to the justifying extent that I might calmly meet my maker? I think I little think of God – leastways, not of a divine examiner who would have observed my every mortification and known me for the faithfulness I've coveted.

And in truth, we only value what we live. A man rarely enters into the spirit of death, not while he yet draws breath. One may know the end is only moments away but the extremity of mind is focused on those remaining drops of life.

Cornelisz gave vicious pre-eminence to what he was in this world. With the others looking on, awaiting their turn, he writhed unreconciled, the closing drama not to his liking, his story commandeered by an unsympathetic justice, and screaming, "Revenge! Revenge!" What did he mean by that? What power to avenge or intend anything did he possess with that noose around his neck? He wasn't thinking of his crimes, that much is for certain. And had he been given half a chance, he would have massacred the rest of us and become as one with Beelzebub, our Lord and Saviour never figuring in his pantheon.

And yet...

I sigh in frightful recognition that I'm not at peace, that in my gradual disappearance I'm no more at ease with my ambitious well-meaning than had I lived in pursuit of evil. It is because of what I can no longer retrieve of myself that I feel so abject, that I long to shout in the face of Van Diemen and everyone who would diminish me: *Revenge! Revenge!* I am *not* Cornelisz – God knows we inhabited opposite diurnals! Yet there are those who would couple his name with mine as if pairing us in some unlovely matrimony.

Damn them! He was a monster!

And clever.

I cannot help but chew these thoughts. There is a foulness that lingers on the tongue, an injustice I would sorely injure. And as if the prospect of death isn't daunting enough, this whispering denial of the life I've lived, the censorious rumours amounting to a story I don't recognise as mine, such counterfeit goads my anxiety. How might I be judged in the next world if I'm not permitted to authenticate who I am in this? Will the saints, in council, seek a letter of recommendation from Van Diemen? Shall my referees know me little or, worse still, number among my enemies? Why is my conscience so unsteady?

Such is the chill that fingers my heart in the fading of this world. God may not know me if I do not know myself.

⸗

If I close my eyes; try not to think...

No, it's no good. The darkness is a shuttered room filled with paintings: portraits I don't need to see in order to know that they exist, their countenances rigid. How crowded this silent and inert world.

⸗

Clean it out! my lungs hiccup.

It's like choking on a bone; like being dragged from the sea to splutter in a reclamation of air.

Clean it all out! the bubble inside me pops.

It stinks worse than a stable – worse than *Batavia*'s orlop and the bilge beneath.

Hartanti is changing the water I never touch in the basin on a chest I cannot reach. She turns, surprised, this spasm more kicking than what has passed for life in recent days. Does she imagine I would have her handle me?

All hands on deck! I shout. Fetch the buckets! Of course, fool – get rid of the hands. Tip them overboard! There's that vinegar we retrieved. Tap the barrel. Be liberal, there. I want the decks scrubbed like bone. Lucretia, tidy yourself up. You too, Cornelisz. Your hose are in a deplorable state. Ah, that smell. It's little wonder they riot. Open everything that closes. Burn frankincense. The stench of the stable must be perfumed, its filth mucked out!

Oh how it possesses me: the smothering fragrance, those bluish coils of smoulder. And at the centre of everything, an idolatry greased in ghee and wax. I was poised, observant, but not wanting to be seen by any who might query my presence in the Devil's warren. Yet I needn't have worried. To be caught in this promiscuity of adventure would have been to challenge, likewise, the presence of those who spied me, all of us tempted to journey among the heathen. Yes, to have traversed half the globe was not to stop short at unfamiliar custom, no matter how misguided or offensive to God.

The Hindus tolerated my curiosity as if shruggingly convinced that every shade of Christian, Moor or infidel was embraced, whether appreciative of the conceit or not, in a single chain of being. At times I felt as if jostled by entranced children, the alcoves of their saints musty, dark and unadorned. Cave entrances beckoned like bloodied lips with friezes of crudely daubed colour, and in the craze-eyed sanctuaries of the gods themselves, their unblinking patience was accorded unnerving animation in the wreathing incense. Indeed, this sickly-sweet miasma raised a sweat upon the skin, and on occasions when I delved too deeply, either disoriented in the cavernous gloom or pressed by the shuffling crowd, a stifling suffocation came upon me and I grew desperate to escape the airlessness. At other times such dwellings seemed almost abandoned, their colossal remnant testament to a haunted majesty which had long been supplanted by Moor and Mogul. In the near impenetrable darkness, one's eyes adjusted more slowly than one's nose and ears, the mildew of dung, its insufferable stench, in sensory correspondence with the squeak and twitter overhead. *No, don't disturb them*, I cried – but too late! — my guide, his torch aloft, illuminating a vault not unlike the upturned hull of a ship. And that monstrous revelation, a crawling barnaclism of unseeing eyes. The tempest, when it broke, was a fury of bat-sound. Disoriented and tripping towards a rectangular throttle of life, its beckon from the tomb.

Quick, that last gagging exhalation.

Suddenly it's like being flung into another dimension; *like being dragged from the depths of the sea to splutter in a reclamation of air...*

If it were up to me, says Medari, picking his nose, I'd demolish all these idolatrous cesspits.

For once I'm in agreement with the Moor.

Walter is dusting his sleeve. Whether carved from caves or crudely cobbled from blocks of stone, these are diabolical abodes.

But Walter, you never came with me. You never saw.

Did I need to? You've seen for yourself what suffocating mysteries they are.

Infidels and thieves, spits Medari. That's what I told him. Idolaters, all, who worship painted whores and would deny Allah, may His name be glorified and exalted.

Your imperial masters seem tolerant enough, I say.

Pff, they are in the habit of treating with the Devil.

And I laugh for the irony that as merchants Medari and Walter show little humour for the rewards of accommodation. Or is it that two is company, three's a crowd? Would they have the Hindus eliminated from their land, all the better to contest a rivalry un-smeared by ash and face paint and this plethora of gods that would equal old Greece for absurd behaviours? Perhaps a man simply wants to feel at home wherever he strays, that there is too much here which is alien to the habit of a more congenial competition. Personally (and at times when religion fails to separate us), if I ask not what a man believes in I find him more than reasonable.

Medari draws nearer, perhaps wanting to travel with us for greater security. He has a tether of laden donkeys.

We take the imperial highway, I say. Nothing will befall us where the emperor passes.

That's a joke, slaps Walter mirthlessly. We're as likely to die — wrong place at the wrong time — in some ambush of royal factions as be murdered by bandits.

You overstate the danger, I laugh dismissively. After all, I'm a man of the country. A man who has made it his business to know such things. The road from Agra to Lahore is one of the safest in the world.

Walter's right, Francisco. Jahangir is not as firm upon his throne as he once was.

Van den Broecke is standing by a window, looking out on the street where the animals gather, looking out through the entrance of the cave into a dazzling heat. Then turning to me: Remember what we once told you? The emperor is a creature of his affection for Nur Jahan. And with his health so — how shall we put it? — so inopportune, his wife is planning for the succession.

Surely she — a woman — doesn't intend to rule?

She already rules!

And they are all laughing at me: Walter, Van den Broecke, Medari. Even Jahangir is shaking his head.

Pelsaert, he says, I know you mean well. How could he not (and turning to the others) when he wears his innocence so publicly? No, my friend, my wife and her brother would make mischief in my house. Already my sons are as divided among themselves as they are derelict in their obedience to what I would command. Yet Nur Jahan soothes me in my frailty, prevents me from consuming too much opium. And Kashmir. That, too, soothes me. The hot dry, Pelsaert, it sweats an agitation in my blood. And blood tends to flow too freely in the heat. The plains are no place to be when the monsoon's long passed. Ah, but Kashmir...

He becomes dreamy. Then addressing me once more: Look, I'm headed there this summer. To see the gardens in bloom. We have tulips now — it's a family thing. I think you Hollanders would find them enchanting; so colourful against so drab a backdrop as your country presents. You'd appreciate what we've done with water, too. As you flush it from your land, we raise it into fountains. Really, Pelsaert, we ought to get to know one another better. What do you say? Indeed, why not pop up for the summer?

THUS WE MARCHED unto Kashmir, the army two hundred thousand strong, dust rising from the trampled fields which spread to either side of the highway. There was a splendid savagery to the self-importance of the troops, those especially who formed the corps of cavalry. All along the column and in complete disharmony, kettledrums and blaring horns raised a din that suggested a succession of makeshift rehearsals on the way to some village festival. Interwoven with the martial panoply were throngs of people – men and women of every vintage, children who scampered in sullen acquiescence, babes held tightly in their mother's arms – all ambling and wheeling carts, the more nimble or irritantly determined selling food-snacks and trinkets on the trot. It was as if an entire city had been emptied, its population tethered to the messianic whim of an emperor rarely seen amidst the commonplace of this grand migration. Indeed, the imperial household was strictly off-limits; there were already newly minted cripples whose curiosity, slowness or diminished sense of self-preservation had earned them a caning from guards who cleared the route of march. The palanquins of the harem moved like a convoy at sea in the untroubled hiatus of a wider disturbance, the roadside beaten aback to give the impression that they passed through uninhabited country. What was swept aside in prostrated remnant was then drawn into the vortex of this walking republic. Indeed, there was something sticky or magnetic about the choking exodus, a clamour bred of order from above and opportunism from below. It was altogether different from any spirit of retreat, the spooked and herded shuffle of a dwindling army. And if this spectacle of massed itinerancy brought to mind such countervailing impressions, any perception of rootlessness was disabused in the fairytale creation of the imperial camp. It was as if the palace at Agra had been carved up and carted in the wake of wherever the emperor so whimsied. Indeed, an army of builders rightly anticipated his daily destination so that all was in readiness by the time of his arrival. Mimicking the royal mahals of the citadel departed, tents were erected for the continuance of every ruling business inside a wooden palisade which, itself, was adorned with gates and towers. It was a gigantic theatre prop, a caravanning forgery erected for nightly performance – except that it was guarded with all too real and lethal a zeal by soldiers who knew that the heart of empire was within their keeping. Mahabat Khan, the monarch's boyhood friend and chief general, saw to it that the camp was properly defended — although against what or whom it was difficult to say.

Initially I'd marvelled at how Jahangir's enclosure might be dismantled after the leisurely departure of his entourage, only to be re-erected and awaiting a few hours hence. To be sure, there was no shortage of manpower, and the transporting elephants and camels numbered in their hundreds. But there was a sleight of hand, a magic which eluded me until I realised there were *two* suits of accommodation, that they overhauled one another to be ready, in turn, for the emperor's arrival. If, to me, each day was an adventure, a step into what was unknown and therefore unpredictable, for Jahangir nothing much changed but the scouted scenery, his ability to distance and control it abetted by the familiarity of his wandering home.

In spite of all the sandstone and monumentalism that weighted down this ruling clan, the Moguls, as Wasim pointed out on the day we met, were foreigners to this country, observant only of those habits which served to preserve their opulent banditry. No amount of building or settled wealth could banish that roving instinct. Indeed, their possessions were entirely portable: carpets, robes and jewels — not to mention their women who were the most guarded of articles. That others not of family might accidentally view them, this could lead to dire consequences.

So the emperor travelled as if perpetually at home. Which he was, all things belonging to the man who possessed everything. Except filial loyalty. It was no secret that Shah Jahan was banished from the imperial presence, his own camp one of wretched exile. Yet harried as he was, he would not surrender to the mercy of his father (as had his brother, Khusrav), and was doubtless maintained in sedition by the intrigues of those who would play the king.

Was it so very different from the misadventure that befell *Batavia*, a rebellion of sorts from within the leadership? And did not women, great and small, influence the judgement of men who were fallible in the blind-sidedness of their supremacy? Were not the wiles of Jahangir's meddling queen matched by insinuations of female desire aboard the ship?

You would have the blame shifted from where it clearly lay?

I hold my breath. Interrupted. Waiting to hear more. I'm quick in discovering none applaud a justification. "Speak!" I summon.

The darkness is unavailing.

"Is there nothing? Nothing at all to light the way?"

But there *was* a light, one rising above the bivouac. As the last of the camp followers trudged in and the mobile capital assumed its load of noble sycophant, pedlar and prostitute, this kingdom for a night – some twenty miles in circumference, I heard tell – presently drew its compass from the hoisted lamp that transfixed the royal enclosure. Whatever played there was not for our ears. The suburbs of this transient city nuzzled down (the dust settling like drizzle, the light bronzed and meditative), its residents trying not to over-jostle their neighbours in the tending of an animal multitude. Everything smelt of grain and ordure, of the kitchen and the stable. Only the elephants gave strange trumpet to what might otherwise have proved an ordinary nocturne.

"So how do you like your excursion thus far?"

"'Tis strange to number among so many. I find I scarce exist."

"Hm," he nods, the ruby in his turban winking.

"Have you ever been at sea by night?" I enquire.

"I've had no occasion to trouble myself. For the pilgrims, of course, I worry that the hajj might be traduced by pirates. The Franks, too, and their crow-caped priests can be a vicious and demanding lot."

"Perhaps you should allow us to convey your people to the Red Sea."

"Ha, Pelsaert, you're incorrigible. On a beautiful night such as this and you're angling for a deal."

"I'm here to serve."

"Serve yourself," he laughs, not unkindly. "Listen," and drawing close, the smell of spirits on his breath, "I *have* mostly everything I want. What need of some empty sea when this is all the ocean I desire? And I the ocean's jewel."

"How so?" I ask, beguiled by the night haze, the dusky firmament reflected in a lake of lotus campfires.

"It was written at the time of my birth."

I turn to him as if a cherished companion of the cups, my sentimental friend. "Go on."

Like an actor he clears his throat:

> *"A priceless pearl from the empire's sea,*
> *A lamp of brightness from the light Divine."*

"What, all that," I rib, "in your honour?"

"No, wait — there's more. How does it go? Ah yes:

> *A pure pearl from the ocean of justice has come to the shore,*
> *A bird from the nest of pomp and bounty has alighted,*
> *A star from the pinnacle of glory and beauty is manifested,*
> *A rose of this kind they have not seen in the circle of the garden."*

I laugh good-naturedly.

"It is so," he touches my sleeve. "What need *I* of some vacant marine when oysters flip and unyoke themselves at my crib?"

"Who wrote that?"

"Some panegyric. Possibly Abul Fazl. You know, he and I never really saw eye to eye. My revered father — may his tomb be the sanctuary of pilgrim prayer — accounted him indispensable. *Pff.* When people favour another, they favour not you. When a father attends a slave above his son, there's sure to come some reckoning before the filial contract is restored."

"How did you renew your father's love?"

"By surviving as my brothers drank themselves to death."

"And the slave?"

"I had him taken when my father wasn't looking. I had the head of that unsightly fawner cast into the privy. Then had a shit." And to forestall my query as to how the mighty Akbar might have absorbed that affront, Jahangir elucidates: "A father is a short-term proposition. An heir, however, is his legacy. An heir is his life beyond the grave." He raises one pencil-thin eyebrow. "My father was angered. Perhaps even aggrieved. But there was never any doubting our rapprochement. Therein lay the future."

"You're not a man to cross," I smile nervously.

"I do only what is necessary. And necessity is my business. But look, I am a generous host," he brightens, "and you and I, I believe we're destined to arrive together at something quite auspicious. Can I offer you a cup, find you a wife perhaps? Ah, but that's right, you're soon to lift the veil of a lady who would profane the sanctity of her marriage bed. I tell you, in our ancestral lands they have a penchant for disfigurement and stoning. But here in Hindustan, you see, it's almost a duty to practise new civilities, to turn a blind eye to what is local in the seduction of beauty. Did I tell you, Pelsaert, that my wife was once married to an Afghan and that she had a daughter? They say I orchestrated her husband's death, that mine was the wanton hunger of the prophet-king, David, and she my Bathsheba. But the Afghan had it coming. My emissary was my foster-brother, sent to summon the wretch in assay of his loyalty. But that wolf, perhaps scenting the telltale of his own scat, unseamed my man at a blow, whereupon those loyal to the royal standard dispatched the villain along the road of non-existence."

There is a pause – time, perhaps, to reflect on actions that decide the fate of men – before I realise that Jahangir is merely savouring his turn of phrase. Mindful that he is a sovereign, and a somewhat dangerous one at that, I duly await his thoughts.

"I had the wife and daughter brought to court. And do you know what she said to me?" He laughs and becomes as misty as the thickening night itself. "It was the New Year festival. I'd already had myself weighed on golden scales, the balance of coin and jewels distributed to those thirsty in merit, and among the ladies I discerned her standing shyly but with a firm hand upon the shoulder of the little girl. I tell you, Pelsaert, I was moved. It's hard to lose a parent, even if he be a traitor or a king who bears you little love. *I will be a father to this child*, I said, stepping from that coterie which had, until then, contained my lusts. And do you know what that demure maid replied? *Who am I that I should be numbered among the emperor's wives? I'm but a poor widow — only, take pity on my daughter and show her kindness.* How do you like that! I tell you, Pelsaert, I was smitten."

And he glances towards the lofted torch that stands sentinel over the quarters where Nur Jahan sleeps.

"And the little girl?" I prompt.

The emperor's expression becomes turbid. "She married a prince, of course." Then more soberly: "One of my sons." And more quietly still: "From the period when I thought nothing of bedding a slave girl."

"At least you have the wherewithal to provide handsomely for your children," I try to cheer.

"Do I? A family can have too much. Its appetites can become insatiable."

We warned you, tuts Walter.

She — the queen — is of dangerous stock, sighs Van den Broecke, and adding, *She and her brother, they're fated to play a dangerous game.*

Asaf Khan has married his daughter to Shah Jahan —

"The Wretch?" I cry.

"That selfsame ingrate, thank you Pelsaert, who would rise against me!" spits the emperor.

And the queen has yoked her daughter to Shahryar.

"I'm running out of sons worthy of the succession," moans Jahangir, his eyes as drooping as that rat-tail moustache which seems niggardly cruel.

And now that the father —

The Persian adventurer —

"Itimad-ud-daulah. Ah there, Pelsaert, was a vizier whose counsel one could savour."

— has died —

The queen has presumed upon her access to the king —

To limit His Majesty's access to her brother —

While Asaf Khan, in turn, makes of himself a small target —

By keeping his politics discreet and his son-in-law informed.

"What, does he plot behind my back?" Jahangir appears genuinely surprised.

Pieter looks to Salomon who flicks back through the ledger to see what's recorded.

I expect you'll find little to incriminate him, drawls Walter. *They're all crafty buggers hereabouts.*

Here, pipes Salomon, *there's an entry here.*

"What does it say?" hovers the monarch.

Ah, corrects my assistant. *I'm afraid it's a different Khan.*

It makes no difference, they're all the same, hastens Walter.

No, this one was a general...

"Mahabat?" brightens the emperor, "the companion of my youth? I tell you, Pelsaert, a loyal and talented soldier is worth more than a dozen shiftless princes. He would serve me against my own, pursue 'The Wretch' to the very limits of his insurrection —"

Compel rivals to rethink their differences?

"Who is this noisy cynic?"

"Majesty, forgive him. He's not in possession of himself."

Too right! If I was in possession of who I'd planned to be, I wouldn't be in this shithole of a place!

But Walter, by now, has been a long time dead. Still, it's as if my presence in Jahangir's camp were a continuation of that journey which had sheltered us for the night at Akbar's caravanserai, that in waking next day to find my compatriot vanished and myself more or less alone, I am poised, should courage not desert me, to enter a rapture of possibilities in this endlessly surprising land. After all, my presence here is not without some expectation. As I settle amidst the jostling sleepers in contemplation of the stars, I wonder how Antonio Andrade and his companions have fared this day, their journey without crowd or fanfare yet no less ambitious, I suppose, in what impels a man to test the frontiers of his soul. I had a mission, so to speak: to keep track of the capricious lords who reigned over this portion of the globe and to avail our interests by appealing to their avarice. In truth, I was enjoying something of a holiday, Salomon's subordinate witness notwithstanding. But Antonio, could he ever admit to anything as indulgent as this? Was he never at ease where duties of the robe prevailed? Or was being a priest a disguise for being something else?

'Tis a landlocked kingdom whose mountains are of such grandeur that their principal is said to be made of crystal, ruby, gold and lapis lazuli...

It is treasure, then, you seek.

'Tis said there is an unrivalled temple, venerated throughout the unknown world...

Or the temptation, perhaps, of some shadowy god?

It would seem, Francisco, that the spirit of trade among you does not enrich your communion with the Creator. Even allowing for your fallibility, would you not venture yourself in His name to discover such a place as Shambhala, to satisfy your curiosity as well as appease the Lord in the salvation of those unredeemed in their ignorance?

I'm not sure, Antonio. I only know that I find myself in prayerful hope of God; that He might forgive me those transgressions so unwittingly compassed.

Andrade stares with a concern that little comprehends the sorrow I feel.

We begin our journey as babes of blank intent, he says, *our inception rooted in the lust of others and unchosen in time. Then we who reach our majority come to the realisation that between birth and the day we first intuit death, Eden is as lost to us as the blinking of our childhood. Nothing remains as it was or how we might have mapped it.*

Unless, of course, you think to recover Eden in the discovery of whatever resides at the top of the world.

He waves me aside.

And if there be a people already there, I continue, then surely they've not broken their covenant with God to have been blessed with such splendid quarantine. Perhaps it is we who are isolated, you Jesuits the more lamentably so in your scruple to abide by none who do not share your doctrine.

Ha, spoken like the child of a renegade faith he's unsure will admit him to salvation! Listen to what I say, Francisco, and listen carefully. We pass but once through this world. Its opportunity is too fleeting to represent anything other than a preparation for the eternal life to come. Among us, God is sifting the righteous from the wicked, the propitious from the uncontrite. Yet all possess the opportunity to dwell within His metropolis.

Even the evil ones?

Even the evil — here on earth — if they repent and believe in Him.

Cornelisz died stubborn, I murmur.

Then he burns in a lake of fire.

Upon that we agree, I say. But if, where you travel, you discover it pristine and its folk unchristian?

Then it is not the paradise of which we dream. Yet we may make it so.

"For Heaven's sake," interjects the emperor, "if there is a paradise, then surely it is Kashmir! The Frank tires me, Pelsaert. Look, I don't mind their theological subtlety, but when it comes to governance they're devious mischief-makers. Whatever that frozen territory to the north amounts to, I can predict one thing: Andrade and his companions will sow doubt and consternation among those who rule there. And uncertainty in a kingdom doesn't augur well."

Hands on thighs, he levers himself wearily to his feet.

"Goodnight Pelsaert, I'm calling it a day. You know where I am if you need anything. Just be wary of the guards. They're liable to kill you if you give them cause to think you're no one."

"Are we ever likely to meet?" I ask haltingly.

Jahangir turns at a distance, his outline already dissolving in the darkness. "We've spoken of this before. Isn't it enough that I am the reason you follow? Go to sleep. Tomorrow I will show you wonders."

There's a swelling grumble of sound, a vibration that startles the animals. Dust rises and obscures the outskirts of the camp. People bestir themselves, curious but not alarmed. The horsemen surge towards the imperial heart like a current of blood, their turbans scarlet poppies.

The light overhead is dazzling, inert. Something jars. Something is not quite right.

"Go back!" shouts a figure on the beach, and all the while determined to catch us up. Any impulse to thank God is presently revoked by an instinct for danger.

"What do you make of this?" I utter, my lips scarcely moving.

Jacob, the *Sardam*'s skipper, stands at my shoulder. "This place has gone to the Devil," he answers, sensing more than I.

"Have the men stand to arms," and knowing not what it is we stand to face.

All the while that figure draws closer, waving its arms, determined to cleave us to its universe even as it would strive to liberate the many from its prison. It was one of those moments wherein, dreading what I might presently learn, I felt called on to juggle a correction. I didn't know who that lonely figure was. I didn't know there were people working on my – the Company's – behalf to salvage hope from nightmare. And in coming face to face with Wiebbe Hayes, I attempted to place him among the many who had taken their

turn on deck, sucking air into lungs begrimed with the filth below, or relieving their boredom by scrubbing the decks. It has troubled me since – as if I'd
overlooked some obvious and vital clue – that I didn't spot Hayes at the outset,
that our months cooped up together didn't furnish recognition.

I tell you, Pelsaert, a loyal and talented soldier is worth more than a dozen shiftless
princes.

Yet I never entirely trusted him for his honour which so impeached my own.

You're a fool to have worn your jealousy so. He was none other than the servant of
your cause.

Mahabat Khan was your friend and servant, too.

Mahabat?

The general you thought more highly of than others. The man you
instructed with bringing your rebellious son to heel.

Shah Jahan had become wretched in my eyes. I needed someone who well understood
not to involve himself in family matters other than to deliver up what belonged to me.

Those who serve us have motives, too, and they are not always sympathetic.

Your crypticisms are beginning to weary.

Who do you think rode with his legions into your camp that morning?

He burns in a lake of fire? Even now? With the vanishing of the sun it isn't
difficult to imagine such radiance, its yellow flicker against a backdrop of oily
night.

So it was the evening we sheltered on land, the longboat dragged high
above the waves. We used a hearth already seasoned with the ash of former
fires, the natives doubtless watching at a distance made unfathomable by the
lack of all other lantern. Our world was contained within that nimbus of
wobbling firelight, our unknowing of what lay beyond its circle a corrosive
to courage. It was not just the night air that chilled our backs as we faced the
flames; a creeping incertitude made one turn from time to time to stand sentry against that unrelenting immensity.

"Do you think they're nearby?"

"Of course they're near! We're the only glimmer of light 'twixt the stars and damnation."

A ruminative pause.

"What d'you think they're of a mind to do?"

"How would I know what blackens the heart of some black bastard?"

Neither Jacobsz nor I were inclined to join the talk; least, not yet.

"I wonder if they're cold?" murmured the young mother, cradling her infant and staring into the flames.

"Them as are naked are like beasts and without feeling."

"At the Cape the Hottentots greased themselves in cow fat."

"Fuck, no!"

"Exactly!"

And there was a gurgle of laughter. Zwaantie's polished eyes caught those of the skipper, an element of impatience – of superiority, perhaps – in their lustre.

"But if they're cold and we possess their fire…"

The infant sputtered awake and disturbed the crackling hush with a tight-throated wail. Its pitch unnerved the camp and made us feel that, despite the glow which signalled our presence, we'd just drawn loud attention to ourselves. Everyone propped themselves upright and peered into the darkness.

"Hush," she soothed, as much afraid of the company in which she found herself as the unseen blacks. "Shhh."

"At least they'll have their choice of meat," remarked Evertsz.

The mother looked up, startled. Zwaantie shook her head, contemptuous but unsure.

"They say," continued the boatswain, "they eat their youngest – that all share in the crime – that the savages hereabouts be the children of Cain."

He was grinning in the firelight, well pleased with his frightening inference of a cannibal attack.

"Nonsense!" I intervened. The skipper spat into the flames. "None has ever treated with these people," I tried to reassure. "Their customs are unknown, their attitude timid and their needs undernourished."

"My point," smirked Evertsz. "A hungry man will stop at nothing."

"Stow it," ordered the skipper. "We keep a look out and we get some rest."

❧

Keep a look out. Get some rest. The command and counsel were as comforting as a watch without eyes, sleep without oblivion. To dream – if one did and it not be creatured by things that licked with a predatory humour – was to add to that exhausted disappointment which came with the ashen reality of sunrise. What strange world was this?

To cross beyond the sand and surmount the nearest bluff was to abruptly baffle any hint of ocean. What had been wind and waves was now a climate of inert presence, the drone of flies giving scent to something that lived as I could not imagine. It was as if we'd stepped into an empty crypt, a darkened place soiled by scavenger beings that scurried at our approach into the splintery landscape beyond. All that retraced us to the shore was the dull thud, that husk of an echo which put the sea at a distance of stone.

As the hours once more gathered and the sun wearily dissolved into a burnished liquid, night loomed from the land. The flies fell silent and bird scraps cawed their final note, our heaping of twigs (for nothing grew into so much as a tree) clattering like a rattle of bones. And then it got cold, in spite of the fire; cold in a way that left one faintly crawling with an absence of resolve. Is every night like this, I wondered, far from home, far from any acceptance that home might option many things so long as some accommodation is struck? This, here, was a void between harbours, a predicament of transit that was no place at all. Like being caught in a snowstorm on a winter's night.

I closed my eyes in the fevered chill and tried to revisit the experience of other occasions in which hope had seemed a shrivelled thing. How one laughed about those moments now, the bravado slyly admitting to a chastening terror. But in what we presently encountered I could discern little in the way of encouragement. Perhaps it was the cramp which brought to mind the frozen icing of Lake Ijsselmeer – that silver desert beneath the winter grey. And all those skaters, too, in their slip-staggering glide. I almost smiled — *Opa, look!* When the cloud parted and the sunshine fused with ice, those human weevils were consumed in so searing an incandescence that the plain truly ached with fire. Cornelisz — yes, even he threaded that fierce illumination.

I listen to the thudding surf and feel the entrapped mettle of another world. I hear scratchings that live by night and a squawking of things disturbed and afraid of the dark. Time here has no meaning. Or motion. It is ill-defined and without diurnal replenishment. If Jeronimus suffers in unending death, it is surely in a place such as this, a void bereft of destiny.

The next day was much like those to follow. The camp stirred with the bleating of animals and smell of frying foods. Our servants prepared our breakfast, having already taken their repast in the pre-dawn gloom. Voices clamoured at a thousand cross-purposes, and depending on one's youth and the obligations of burden, a spirit of carnival continued to infect the march.

Between the domesticities of morning and sundown, of departure and arrival, we rode a highway flanked with plane and mulberry trees. Having made it my task to learn and memorise the history of this kingdom, it didn't escape reflection that Jahangir had once had such trees cut and sharpened into stakes, whereupon the unhappy confederates of Khusrav's rebellion were impaled. Even as we advanced along this avenue such as any great ruler might construe for the benefit of travellers, so too had that captive prince, mocked and shackled to his elephant, entered Lahore with his father's servant drawing his gaze to the fallen friends thus featured in this grisly honour guard. I swiftly banished the unsavoury image and took pleasure in what now bore healthy fruit, even though our march passed for a locust-plague in what was left stripped and wilted in our wake.

Beyond the road, in the fields and open country, trees were scarce, each cluster of four or five usually marking the site of a village. Nonetheless, the region between Agra and Lahore is well cultivated and, I daresay, the most fertile in all Hindustan. At every span of miles equivalent to a day's travel there was a caravanserai, although the shelter offered was in sparse proportion to the enormity of numbers now ascending on Kashmir.

Just when the habit of daily progress seemed assured, the imperial retinue would unexpectedly stay put, the mobile suburbs wary and waiting until news was conveyed that the emperor was inclined to seek out and hunt the local game. *More likely nurse a hangover*, it was smartly joked.

A vast troop of lords and soldiery on horseback, matched by an equal number of foot-trotting beaters, departed camp for the sporting pleasures of His Majesty, this interruption to our journey of no consequence to one whose will and presence were the *prima facie* of every destination. Where travelled the emperor, there did his reason lie, and every vista was presumed to be turned towards him. Although a backdrop to his existence, we countless individuals fell outside the radius of his concern. At his whim we could become as objects consigned to the sun-withdrawn shadows of night, objects dropped into a fathomless sea.

For days, mounting into weeks, the imperial presence remained in the field, his camp an excursion away from where the rest of us milled in impermanent quarters, trying to anticipate the trajectory of his desires. There were rumours of the gamebag, the phenomenal slaughter. But all I could see around me was the depletion of our supplies and an increase in neighbourhood tensions as our stalled economy sought to sustain itself at the hearth of dubious welcome. If local traders were quick to appraise an opportunity – and I, too, took advantage to meet with such as might advance our Company interests or, if truthful, my personal needs – there were others, including head men and local governors, who were less enthusiastic in their reception and accommodation of Jahangir's nobility, let alone the vast army of camp followers. Still, what worry they who owed everything to the caprices of the emperor? To guide him to a forest kill was to risk being promoted to a rank of six hundred personnel and five hundred horse! I could only marvel at the appropriation, in one man, of so much wealth and the example of its distribution in so narrow and perfunctory a service.

My God, Pelsaert, you're a beggarly begrudger!

Majesty?

Ah, don't try to fob me off with your respectful civility. You'd have my ear, soon enough, yet you speak rudely of me out of earshot. No, don't deny it; it little matters. You're no worse than those I permit to kiss the threshold.

And I can tell he isn't angry. He's handing the reins of his horse to a materialising groom. His colour is up. There's a trickle of sweat upon those decorative ringlets that sentry his ears. His eyes are polished with excitement.

What sport! he claps, then stretches out his muslined arms.

Pelsaert, your merchant's vocation lacks the spice of danger.

Deer and antelope? I'm sure I've faced greater dangers in the service of the Company.

But a tiger?

Yes, I've faced one of those, too.

He isn't listening. The animals — thousands of them — are being laid out at his feet, the horses snorting and stamping at the never-safe scent of blood. It's a veritable reliquary of destruction: so many partridges and fowl that I look up at the sky to see whether any birdlife still exists. Everything is beginning to turn at the altar of surfeit, this stupendous poaching so pointless if for the sake of counting alone.

I tell you, Pelsaert, I got this close — and he narrows thumb to forefinger — to shooting a nilgai when an idiot groom and two bearers suddenly appeared. I was furious — and frowning boyishly, now — and ordered the groom immediately put to death.

I startle at this.

Oh don't worry, Pelsaert. I spared the bearers and merely had them hamstrung. Then smiling, he adds: In a manner befitting those who had less than capitally offended, I had them mounted on asses — after all, they could no longer walk — and paraded through the camp so that none might be so bold as to spoil my gunnery.

But surely it was an inadvertence, an accident?

Tut. As soon as my orders were carried out, I continued hunting with hawks and falcons.

This rather silences the matter with a severity that bears little challenge. Even Jahangir grows sensible to my sober digestion – my fear, I suppose, of causing offence. He taps his moustache then turns to me:

They say the milk of an antelope is of great benefit to those who suffer asthma.

I look up, and he smiles like a parent dispensing treats.

And I saw a spider, once, the size of a crab. It had seized a snake by the throat and half strangled it.

My lips prise in wonder.

There, you see! And squeezing my shoulder. The world is filled with marvels, each to its purpose, and those which confound the natural order are an intrigue to soothsayers and the like.

I once came across a cat that hopped on its hind legs, I reply.

'Twas a mongoose, I assure you.

And a whale, too. No longer of the waves but washed up, its penis like a giant serpent burrowing into its slack immensity. The flies and stench were snatched by the wind that blew off the North Sea.

And in the pause that ensues, as this lord of sun-baked plains and airy mountains struggles to conjure what a beached whale might look like, I recall the courting parties of that blustery day, the women lewd in what they mockingly compared to the virility of their suitors. A couple of wenches even conspired to waddle – to the hoot and laughter of their companions – as if freshly plucked from horseback, their legs bowed in moulded straddle. If the lads felt at all diminished, they didn't show it, instead hoisting the girls aloft and carrying them, squealing and wriggling, into the waves. There seemed to me no good omen in the life-abandoned carcass of that naked beast. But then I, unlike the others who were bawdy in daring, was without a woman to test the vigour of what was, lately, always on the rise.

Well, Pelsaert, you've made up for it now, lightens the emperor. And among the women of the world! From maids without a mind to wives whose ill-advised husbands would have you mind your step. I see you hunt in quite another part of the forest!

It occurs to me I have never seen him without his jewelled turban.

Mind you watch your back, he warns.

An audible *hmph* escapes my nostrils.

Tomorrow the royal standards move on. The game, hereabouts, is all taken.

Do we hasten now to Kashmir? I ask excitedly.

It may take months and the summary of a hundred marches to reach such paradise.

Can nothing be achieved more expeditiously?

Why the hurry? To get there any the sooner is to blemish the lustre of its novelty all the more quickly. You'd have me trembling to return before I'd scarce had the pleasure to arrive.

It's only that I'm running out of time.

What might time matter to one who has so little influence over anything?

With respect, Majesty, I think the imputation slanders.

Nonsense. Enquiry travels with me. If I choose to meander through Bayana and its indigo plantations – a commodity, by the way, I fail to comprehend can mean so much to a nation's self-respect – then the detour is no detour at all. Inclination and curiosity are their own virtue. In me they are the circumference of life.

Would you accompany me to the indigo fields?

Jahangir wrinkles his nose. When I was but a child, he says, my revered father – the very manifestation of kindness and grace – wanted to discover the source of the Ganges. He had an expedition fitted out, the party journeying for months along the river as its banks steadily narrowed. At length they disappeared into a rising forest, struggling over escarpments by day and shivering in the dustless air by night. Eventually they came to a rock that was, by nature, sculpted in the profile of a cow's head. From its mouth spewed a torrent of tremendous force. None spoke, for such was the thunder of water, and they contemplated that accidental form as visionaries or children might construe a likeness in the evolving physiognomy of a cloud.

Momentarily we two are seated as if on opposite sides of a campfire, his anecdote scarcely keeping the darkness at bay.

Was it the source? I ask. Was it the end of their search and the beginning –
the issue, if you like – of all life here on the plains?

There was no telling what lay beyond that socket of stone. The expedition moved on and upwards, teetering with their animals on the cusp of
catastrophe as they threaded canyons and crossed passes amidst the foothills
of God's eternity. But the river was not rejoined. A famine loneliness scarred
the essence of that crystalline atmosphere. Even as it burned, there was no
warmth to the sun. There was no further penetration.

I was thinking of Andrade, of his separate journey into the Himalaya.
Were his swelling ridgelines, as Jahangir alluded, the fringes of God's eternity? Was his mission, all along, to draw nearer his Creator? Did he hope
to ascribe some human outpost to that most remote and unaccompanied of
aspirations?

Did you ever venture to find out for yourself? I ask.

What need? I never doubted my father's enquiry, only his love. He inhales
deeply, judgementally, before adding: That elevated region is a temptation to
none but shepherds and hermits.

But the rumoured kingdoms?

I know of China. I've received gifts from there. I know of nothing in
between.

But –

If there *is* anything, Pelsaert, its impoverished incivility will be of scant
concern.

Yet the Jesuits –

I know, I know. You Dutch – the English, too – you never tire of reminding me they're a spent force. Because the Franks are weak, perhaps they seek
some primitive cousin with whom to spar and squabble. I've given them permission to travel to the edge of the empire. Beyond that allowance and protection, they become a curiosity and irritant to those unworthy of my greatness.
Why should I bother myself when they may readily be killed by tribesmen
who roam the territories they trespass? And if they *do* thread a path, it's an
intelligence my captains will store to our advantage.

He is staring into the flames that wriggle between us.

I tell you, Pelsaert, I have no need of empty spaces, of perpetual winter when spring alone entices.

And he glances at me, smiling: Kashmir. You will see.

To close with something is to cauterise that which animates its attraction. Like cutting flowers from a garden, believing Eden's essence captured and made convenient within the chalice of a vase. With such initial perfume there is little inkling that death already stills life's nutrient, the beheaded blooms like thirsting trophies. Thus in our hunger to possess we little realise that what we would cleave to is fated to disabuse our fondling anticipation, our dreams shortly to become a nostalgia bred of shortfall. I'm reminded of what Medari said about indigo, that the *nauti* is like a growing lad still short of his prime, a thing unconscious of decline. And that the *ziarie* is its state of potent majority – an awareness, perhaps, that whatever would be savoured is of the instant. Perhaps that was Jahangir. Perhaps that was the many of us – men who were determined *not* to acknowledge that what was possible was already delineated and destined to shrink.

I accept, now, that I am the *katel*, decrepit and weighed down by misfortunes that have assailed me in health and human bondage. And yet the mountains, metaphorically, which so oppress me were once a fact of liberating grandeur and release from the heat-choked plains.

The march proceeded with a purpose that was carefree in the mind of he who ordained it. The people simply followed, their trading multitude thriving on endless barters of service and reward. No one questioned the inconveniences of transit, and I observed a bitch and her pups walking doggedly in the shade between the wheels of a trundling cart. The entire migration glinted beneath the Gangetic sun like a casket of jewels upturned and strewn in the dust.

At last a far-off haze began to resolve itself into washes of grey and blue. Before long, the distance grew outlined, and a copper-white shone through in chips that resembled masonries of stone. As there is no limit to the number of hilltop fortresses in this land, I imagined some unknown citadel or acropolis. Pointing it out to one of my servants, I was advised it was the snow that never melts.

Despite the gradual drawing of this high country, we remained yet in the grip of hot weather, the tail of our column a haemorrhaging sack of sick and discarded humanity. Everything in Hindustan is of immense quantity, especially its people, and the subjugation of an individual to exhaustion or death is likely to go unnoticed. Even large families are but tiny grains, the poorer they are, the more invisible to any duty of fellow feeling. I, too, succumbed to a day or so of fever, my strength sapped and my appetites vanquished. If I possessed no family assurance, I was at least accompanied by Salomon and attended by servants who proved quite loyal to the Company's pay. As I lay in a welter of flushed indifference, Walter's sanguinary visage intruded upon my conscience, mocking the surety I had once felt for the open-endedness of our grand adventure.

Don't be troubled by his embittered ghost.

Someone is sponging my brow. You're here, *I say*, in my tent?

Wasim is standing behind him, a shadow in the service of his emperor. I wonder if he knows his wife is dead.

You know, Pelsaert, I once paid a visit to the port of Cambay. This was years before your advent. In fact, it was at a time when I was rather besieged by Englishmen – first Hawkins, then Roe. I had never, before then, beheld the salted ocean, the seas you Europeans find so compelling.

Wasim says nothing, his eyes two chinks of light in the dusk behind his master. Jahangir's forehead looks massive in the glare of a lantern, his skin yellow and waxen. The ruby of his birth resembles a lozenge of blood in his sarpich.

During those few days I was encamped on the shore, merchants, traders and other indigents were summoned to partake – in accordance with their condition and humility – of such gifts wherein a master might reward his servants, a father his sons. A dress of honour here, a horse there, some travelling money — and there's nothing like a vacation, eh? In fact I'm quite accustomed to playing the tourist within the borders of my kingdom. Indeed, to holiday locally is to locally thwart temptation. Besides, my rebellious sons were not averse to seeking confederates in the sandy country of Gujarat.

He pauses, but still my brow is sponged.

It is hot, terribly hot before the rainy season. It is a land oppressed by stagnancy. I understand the inhabitants — those living close to the sea, at least — think of themselves as fishermen and sailors only. By the way, how found you those Gujarati divers?

They glistened with the sudsing of each wave, their skins saturated to a hue which made them resemble darkened seals in the billowing turbulence.

I agree, *responds the emperor*, they're not of textures I detect among my own countrymen. But were they any good?

They excelled, *I reply*, in raising several chests from the deep. To draw sufficient breath was to thread an opacity of death.

I grant you, the people thereabouts are given to devotions that folly the natural course of things. Having extended the skirt of magnanimity, I visited the tomb of a local saint, a venerable to whom is ascribed this wondrous belief. In his season of experimental youth, his gifts were such that he had little difficulty in restoring life and turning grief to joy. Having raised several men from the dead, his father became aware of these miraculous intercessions and sent him a prohibition, declaring it was presumption to meddle in God's workshop.

Jahangir studies me closely to glean my humour. In my current state, it's a story I could take a fancy to. I'm in need of a miracle, *I smile wanly*. But dead, you say, his shrine a tomb?

It's not difficult to lie dead in this place, *replies the emperor, and his smile becomes a grimace*. At that time of year the heat was very great, and we marched by night to avoid the sun. And like you, I fell into a fever, my weakness such that it appeared to others I had long been confined to bed. Imagine — I had no appetite, no taste for anything!

Then glancing over his shoulder at the shadowy attendance of Wasim, he continues:
The water was unpalatable, the streams which gave scant promise to villages were nearly always dry. The wells, too, were mostly salt, and the neighbourhood tanks had become like buttermilk from the washermen's soap.

Wasim nods the once as his eyes resume their fix on mine. A creamy thirst embitters my breath. And still my brow is sponged. But by whom, I cannot tell, I cannot see. Only a slender forearm, dusky like those of the divers at the wreck. And feminine, too, for the golden bracelets that jangle in the lamplight.

This is not where I'd choose to be, *I hear Jahangir say.* But then we would never have met had we not stepped from home to seek our fortune in the plunder of another's.

And suddenly he is no longer there. The companionable consolation of his audience is at an end, and a waft of air suggests both vacancy and a swap of phantoms. My forehead sweats (that sponging hand is gone) and I ache within a glare that is darkness. Only Wasim remains, valet to his imperial master, and now master of his own affronted dignity. He steps forward from the shadows, from that imposed and decorous restraint, to hover close. His eyes glow like shards of Roman glass. And his face, drawing closer still and unyielding, is the very mirror of my conscience.

Where have you hidden her?

As if freed from darkness and the stench of bats, the plain shrills with a shimmering light. It is morning, the travelling mild. Last night's deluge – unusual for this season and potentially damaging were the indigo not already cut – has found its discharge in dikes which remind me of home, the fields fragrant with a moisture soon to dry. The atmospheric clarity overhead, however, becomes adulterated as one's eyes descend to the horizon. Indeed, there *is* no horizon, only a hazy thickening which veils distance in conjecture. Field workers congregate, their miniscule communities set apart and unknown. It yields me pleasure to travel among places whose routine is untouched by my passage, whose localness remains unmoved so long as I do not pose a danger.

Live and let live, the credo of a fruitful anonymity. Except that I now have good reason not to draw attention.

Our party consists of five, an uneasy balance inasmuch as two are unknown to the other two, and even I am unsure of whom to trust. I don't mean Asmat, of course. She is the fledgling in my keep.

We set out from Fatehpur before sunrise, the flagstones bearing puddles from the thunderstorm passed. It was agreed that she and her servant would accompany us to Bayana. Having already caught me up in illicit rendezvous was an act so intractable that, in a passion of aroused daring, to venture further was to risk little more. I'm sure her eunuch didn't think so. He doubtless regarded me as this dangerous article that might cost him his life, yet was obliged to handle with discretion for the love his mistress bore me. I was mindful of his circumspection and arranged for his complicity to be diluted by having one of my own servants suggestively exhibit the tendencies of a husband. My man was likewise none too pleased – especially as he was a Hindu – but all I bade of him was that he ride a little in advance of Asmat, and that she at all times keep herself closely shawled. Where manliness might have winked and grinned, collaboration filled them with fears of consequence. My orders were sharply, if sullenly, obeyed.

Our night together had been fondling but chaste. The massive gateway proved too open a shelter from the rain or public prying, while the caravanserai compelled in us a play-act of companionable convoy, a suggested chaperoning, perhaps, of some headman's sister to her family village. I kept a razored eye for the likes of travellers I might recognise, especially Medari who possessed the annoying habit of showing up when one's billet was firmly anchored and boots removed. He'd make himself at home, fending off all unwelcome with the most ingratiating civilities. It was impossible to make the man speak plain, and he only revealed something of his truer character when alluding to others he felt at ease to slander. Even as he took it upon himself to explain the grades of indigo, one felt as if obliged to reward a shallow regard, to wave him off with a gesture of baksheesh.

Bayana lay at a distance of two days, and the mounting hours warmed with fatigue. Our mood grew brittle in the hardening light, and there seemed insufficient bounty for so great a risk until, thrusting aside the monotony of our forced appearance, I entertained an image of Asmat in all the splendour of her unfastened self. We were like children in the hide-and-seek of some unrestrained moment, wilfully unknowing or simply dismissive of the fact that what we played at would trouble or infuriate others. I found it difficult to credit that the intimacy we practised was, likewise, the purview of her husband. Our passion may have been illicit but, in my favour, I argued that I sought the embrace of none other. I was hers and hers alone for the duration of the journey. Contemptuously, I considered it would be some time before Wasim noticed her missing from his stable of wives.

Of course it was all make-believe. What had I undertaken other than have her join me on a business trip? Still, as I dropped back on that dusty road to insert myself between my servant (her suggested guardian) and the donkey which bore her like the Virgin, I searched the fissures of Asmat's shawl for that which beat with an erotic anticipation, her concealed flesh no doubt perspiring and her stamina tested, yet hoping for an endurant smile that discounted such discomforts and understood that all would be refreshened when we stopped.

That night we took shelter at a small saray which the late King Akbar had ordered built for the comfort of lady travellers. Asmat's eunuch saw to her apartment and the laying of her bedroll. My two servants, without prompting, attended to their duties and began preparing supper. The eunuch deposited a cloth-wrapped parcel which, once undone, greatly augmented our ration with delicacies that provoked the only appreciative comment I heard from my men. Otherwise the conversation was wary and pocketed and nearly always silenced if I drew near. As far as I could tell, Asmat's servant and mine shared nothing but an unwilling sense of accomplice. Even she and I found ourselves reduced to whispers in this atmosphere of unspeaking tension. Their judgement was less than moral; after all, too many things were readily exploited in this land to countenance shock or any sense of unfathomable wrongdoing. No, it had more to do with the well-known guardedness of men in relation to their wives, and of their dangerous wrath, their vengefulness all the more indiscriminate the higher they stood in society. And if my men were unsure of who the lady was, the fact that she travelled with a eunuch gave some indication that I was playing with fire. Put simply, none cared to be scorched.

Next morning our conjoined service had the caravan assembled and ready to depart before Asmat and I had so much as stretched our limbs. It was as if they were anxious to smuggle us on our way before anyone else should greet us over breakfast. Cloaked against the early chill, we ate with fingers the cold fritters offered, then found ourselves beckoned with respectful haste to the animals saddled and waiting. I prayed that Asmat wasn't feeling too compressed and wearied and therefore out of humour with the necessary fashion of our desire. She only smiled and said little as if to reduce the audible footprint of our trespass. That she squeezed my hand as I steadied her upon her saddle, that was enough.

The journey proceeded as the day before, only I now began to feel a proprietary responsibility and, I daresay, a satisfaction that exceeded all other consideration. It were as if Wasim, without his knowing or consent but in light, nonetheless, of his dereliction to apprehend such things, had forfeited the right to call himself her lord and protector. Let us meet with whomever along the way, it mattered little. In an environment where she was unlikely to have known a soul, I was swollen in my pride at possessing so beautiful a woman, even if her appearance was cloaked and indeterminate to those who idly stared at our passing retinue. Was any man more enamoured with transgression, believing himself to have purchased a perfect liberty? As the miles mounted between ourselves and Agra, I came to believe, too, in the fairytale of our domesticity, in the naturalness of our travelling union.

Indeed, travel was the least demonstrative of collusions as far as witness entailed. Our servants may have felt none too easy but it wasn't as if Asmat and I overlooked their sensitivities and were pettish in behaviour. Still, I'd not thought readily ahead and had presumed, without first seeking their permission (for how was one to ask?), to take shelter with one or other of the local indigo traders. Perhaps I sought recognition, a kind of prize-gathering legitimacy. If I had discovered something of myself in Asmat's seductive availability, I wanted others, also, to apprehend (and perhaps approve of) the licence I so felt.

Towards late afternoon on that second day we came in sight of the indigo fields, the plantations stretching as far as sight could reach. Already the bushes had been cut, and thatched shelters designated the distilling vats in which their leaves were steeped. The visible intensity of cultivation lifted my spirits, especially as this renewed promise was in contrast to recent blights of almost biblical proportion when the crop had been rotted by rain or consumed by locust. Little wonder scarcities and hardship had led to an adulteration of produce and ferocity of competition among buyers. The Armenians, I must say, they are the least discriminating – acting like hungry dogs, tearing at the refuse of a once grand banquet. Their greed would have growers believe that even their *katel* is entitled, and that time and opportunity are fast running out for the rest of us. But like all scavengers, their appetite is finicky and restless, their bark greater than their ability to bite. That's why I deal with select and established merchants, men who sow what they would reap and who know us to be quantiful and honest in our dealings. Customers like us are worth conciliating; customers who don't fail to command the lion's share of the crop for Europe.

Thus did my mind stray momentarily from Asmat (as, doubtless, Wasim's did when balancing his boat in the current of palace intrigue), the fields mentally transposed into soap-like cakes of cobalt. It revived me, in one sense, to reflect that business was the ruling planet of any escapade I might enter into. And of course it was enchanting to arrive at so lustrous an hour, the sun stout with a focus that intensified every observable fibre. In the glow of what was reassuring, my humour restored to the extent that doubts entertained along the road were suddenly resolved in a perfect splicing of interests, Asmat had become the supercargo of my impetuous return to the district.

Bayana had once been a large and beautiful town but since the floods, a few years back, and a correspondent shrivelling of the indigo crop, it too had begun to decay. Its one long street was one long bazaar, and a saray was located at either end. In the early days I'd lodged in testing rotation of their less than salubrious offering, and found myself latterly cheered and grateful to men like Mirza Sadiq and Ghazi Fazil, rich merchants with whom I established a solid trade and who, upon my arrival in Bayana, would insist on my lodging with them for several days at a stretch. So much as I wanted to dare the world to approve of my illicit good fortune, I understood that the reveries of a long day's journey were of little counsel when meeting up again with men whose behaviours were forthright and whose wives were loyal. None, locally, had ever sought to sweeten my sojourn among them with gratuities other than an invitation to partake of supper or to shelter with their respected families. If I wanted to revere Asmat with pleasures such as my poor lot might offer, the very character of our flight, even if limited to this peripatetic smatter of days, was an adventure that stood us apart from life's uneventful respectability. To assert ourselves in any way was to assert our presence over grudging secrecy. As things transpired, I deliberately unheralded our arrival and sought accommodation at the saray least likely to offend romance.

Water was drawn, and as Asmat and I sponged our limbs, our combined service fitted out the chosen rooms. Indeed, once settled, I allowed them to go and divert themselves in the town, all the better to give the two of us a chance to breathe some privacy. Asmat looked at me, looked at our somewhat soiled surroundings, and appeared to ask: what now? In previous visits I had sought out Sadiq or Fazil, or if less inclined to Mahometan courtesies (for falling in with Medari along the journey sometimes made me crave a Hindu household), then Pagoo Singh or Nagar Bai. But my advent was as yet unannounced, and if our lodgings were less than auspicious, the hour was still ours to make of it what we might.

"Come," I said, "there's a place I want to show you." I was smiling, lit up, perhaps, like a boy now bribed by self-suggesting promises.

I led Asmat back outside and into the supposed anonymity of strangers. I summoned a nearby cart, its driver pointing to his chest, bemused but conditioned to obey. I addressed a few words to him in Hindi; he rolled his head in understanding. Then turning, I handed Asmat up into the vehicle, her identity screened in the brisk readjustment of her head-shawl. Seated side by side, and at a pace determined by the mule, we proceeded out of town in the direction of a low range which hedged what had seemed a featureless odyssey these past two days.

As the hills drew near and more delineate, so too did signs of human preoccupation. Upon craggy ridgelines, nature's crenellations became visibly ambiguous with an infill of man-made structures, the rise and pause of land employed in fanciful foundation for walls and other dwellings. In these regions, palaces and forts assume a fairytale whimsy, the seriousness of defence abetted by difficulties of terrain. And within such sheltered worlds, yet further privacies are devised and screened.

I had the cart pull up at the foot of the nearest inclination and indicated, with a purse that amply alerted him to his good fortune, that the driver was to wait without question or impatience. Within an eroded gateway a narrow path, steep and paved with stone, led to the ruin of a once splendid mahal. Asmat and I soon found ourselves panting, the exertion quickening the pulse. In the absence of other wanderers, she allowed her shawl to fall, the russet afternoon deepening her colour and illumining her eyes. She leaned heavily on my arm, even though I was scarce the more sturdy for lack of breath. At length we arrived at a portal and, beyond, a vista overlooking Bayana and the plains stretching back towards unseen Fatehpur and Agra. The haze below was beginning to thicken into a sediment of copper-grey, even as the sky overhead remained starched and cerulean. At the very edge of the cliff was a most beautiful shrine and, within, a great many of its monuments stood undamaged. Though I had visited the place before, my curiosity had been ambient rather than precise. Back then, mine had been the reverie of an alien, the indiscriminating optic of a foreigner. Now I was accompanied by one who was no stranger to these lands, yet her comfort in or appreciation of where we ventured was difficult to tell. I looked about me at the statues and the ornamentation and realised I'd not given much thought as to whether they indicated a Hindu or Mahometan reverence, so intermingled was the script of custom in this place. I only know that I spoke softly in my lust, that I prayed the spirit of sanctity might not proscribe Asmat's sense of licence. To me she appeared intrigued and sampling, stilled yet wandering. She reached out to stroke the spine of Nandi, the carved bull a seated miniature wherein all that was rampant in the Vedic pantheon had been exiled to leave but this rustic and reposeful expression.

"Do you not think it profane," she challenged, "that such people should venerate an animal as if it were a god?"

Her tone was not entirely malicious, her movement among the columns of the portico measured and enquiring. She might have been deftly fingering the artefacts of another's bedchamber, inviting me to participate in her interloping survey. The relics of a defeated rival, perhaps, the abandoned toys of a childish perversity. Yet the Nandi was undeniably beautiful, the antiquity of this semi-collapsed environment in which fig and mulberry wriggled their roots momentarily transfigured by our intense and present togetherness. Yes, other chapters and lives, these swirled at an outreach connected to our fragrant opportunity.

"I feel no rankling at all," I replied. "Nothing that deflects me from the joy I feel in being here with you."

She smiled idly, knowing herself already entered into the exchange to come.

Leaving the abode of the rarely visited consecrate, we ascended into the nested gardens of the forgotten palace. Stifling our surprise in glimpsing Gujar shepherds and their strayful goats, we were now hurried to seek a sequestered spot, some corner in which to seize occasion and unburden a shared and sensual disquiet. The day was not yet dusk, and in that peach and turquoise gloaming, the sky was full of birds.

Her skin was a varnish of honey, each bead of perspiration shaped like some translucent ladybird to magnify the perfection of her chemistry. The gold that adorned her limbs bestowed a kind of conjugal glory to our stolen necessity. Nonetheless, and as if to minimise the tinkling of our presence, she removed her bangles and set them upon a font-shaped stone that was suddenly the furniture of our open boudoir. As I trembled to get the unfastening of her right, any embarrassment on my part was allayed by the inwardness of her smile, her expression of complicit pleasure enough to slow me in my fumblings and command a more conscious savour of what was granted. I was touched – betrayed into a moment's belief of authenticity after so long a wandering – and enchanted by the coral beauty of her teeth, luminous between the pouter of her lips, a taste of cinnamon rising on her breath.

In the languid satisfaction that followed our lovemaking, our fingers interlaced in tender assurance, I ignored what was obvious and, instead, drank fully of a rapture in which everything – and meaning nothing in particular – seemed poised and perfect. The quiet rustle of surrounding life, like the shiver of leaves in a warm breeze, appeared accepting of who we were and of what we were doing. In a conceit of imaginary privilege, I propped myself on one elbow to admire Asmat's form and this empathy of environment which had couched us in the pursuit of affection. And in the declining warmth of that loitering sky, the birds I most remember – probably because of their collared plumage – were the vultures that landed out of sight beyond the shadow of the trees.

In all the regret and sentiment of hindsight, that private hour was to prove the high-water mark of our illicit adventure. From thereon a preoccupation with the clandestine schooling of our time detracted from its momentary luxuries.

We remained two more days in Bayana as I had business to attend. With promises of hasty return, I left Asmat each morning to pay a call on the crop buyers I was acquainted with. The unusual accompaniment of my arrival in the district had not gone unobserved, and I was greeted with a smiling enquiry which suggested that I, for once, might not enjoy as vigorous a bargaining position as before.

"She is a lady known to the Company in Agra," I lied. "Her brother trades in cotton and has a fleet of boats he plies along the Jumna." And then, as if to forge some connection: "She's here to visit relatives."

My untruth was seen immediately for what it was, my lie graciously untested by those who might have asked after such relatives – their neighbours, after all. Ghazi Fazil was even brotherly enough to invite me to bring the lady – a resident of the capital, no less – to dinner that evening if her family might spare or choose someone to accompany her. He said he was soon to make the journey to Agra, himself, and that there were several questions he might put to her.

Despite the pride I felt in being linked to so beautiful a woman (not to mention that dangerous and self-betraying desire to expose my illicit good fortune to select strangers), Asmat, the prisoner of her own escape, now steadfastly refused to risk such a meeting. Her husband was her husband still; already her concerns were focused on her seamless reappearance at home, her absence hopefully unremarked. She was not inclined to venture, once more, to the hilltop ruins.

My negotiations complete (at which the price of indigo was settled at a rupee per maund more than the going rate at Ghanowa or other nearby villages), arrangements were made for a caravan to transport the purchased consignment to Surat.

Surat, how it momentarily beckoned! In an ardent instant I thought nothing of seizing Asmat and relinquishing Hindustan altogether, of effecting our escape into a dream of home that was suddenly Flemish and of watered fields and blue-grey skies. It took the confusions of an intimate excitement to remind me that I was only sojourning in these eccentric lands with their volatile melding of race and creed, that I was only here to make what was needed to secure what I wanted. And in a mental rush to extricate myself from details which conspired to detain, I beheld the promise of a completed circle, a return to origins in which I might presently be reborn a lucky man. With so exotic a lady, so ravishing a beauty upon my arm, what cloaked and buckled masonry wouldn't find itself transfixed and nodding its approval?

We gave you a gem of great antiquity to convey to the East, to purchase the conciliation and love of its heathen prince. Now you return with this living jewel, this signet of success...

Except that Jacques Specx stands among them. A man I am yet to meet. A man whose Asiatic wife and half-breed daughter are no fawned-over creatures of acknowledgeable family. Because they are not permitted to step foot in the Netherlands. Because they do not exist except to evidence the sorts of behaviour separately borne out in the colonies and their farthest outposts. Our loves, as our lives, are distant and outcast.

My ardour cools as my anger swells at the thought that all escape (my theft of that which would make my hearth complete) must stop at Surat, our ships unlicensed to carry a contraband such as I would smuggle, the Company unsmiling on any venture it may not profit from.

And in that contemplation I realised I was trapped. My youthful enthusiasm had jumped at the opportunity of serving in some faraway place, and the summons of the Company had been ornamented with the sights and scents of an orientalism undreamed of until encountered — and even then, never stripped of its hypnotic peculiarities. So long as one fulfilled the script of one's mission and sent back precious consignments of indigo and cloth, it was possible — nay, it was necessary — to immerse oneself in the wonder of its ways. Work and rivalry sought reward in the calm indulgences of an Indian night, and one grew accustomed to tolerances that prevailed in this part of the world. Not Walter, of course. But then he should never have ventured beyond Surat. He didn't have it in him — the imagination, that is — to experiment with absenting himself for a while to enter into the grain of a foreign life. To turn and look at our ships in the River Tapti was to be tethered to the climatic behaviours of our kind, to be abridged by an invisible causeway that nourished our national conceit. To loiter at Surat was to draw no line in the sand, to know not what it was to even envisage going native.

I presently didn't know what to do or where to turn other than prolong the moment and fall back on Agra. Salomon, the others — all of them as detached as I from the Fatherland — they each depended on me. The mission — our factory and the contacts we'd made, the steady accumulation and conveyance of expected produce — these things would have withered in my complete absence. Conversely — and perversely — the factory had become the only home I knew, its precious construction and tedious habitation robbing me of years of life. Little wonder I went to Bayana on buying forays or travelled in the wake of the imperial camp — indeed, took every opportunity to get out of the house. Little wonder I sought to divert myself in recording the customs and history of this country through instalments dispatched to Van den Broecke in the necessary belief that I was making a difference, that with a knowledge of these parts we would somehow make it our own. But sometimes it was like trying to analyse the water in which one was drowning.

It was all right for Pieter. He had only to sail away, from time to time, to relieve a sense of imprisonment which sometimes darkened the mind, especially during periods of illness when the prospect of death — never far from the heels of apparent wellbeing — sweated greedily within a mildew of rooms fumigated with incense. How quickly a mood might swing from excitement in novelty to gloom in revelation. And as if the prejudices of the Jesuits and machinations of the English weren't enough, our own society was limited and given to fractiousness when work alone was insufficient to distract it. Not Salomon, of course. I never saw anything but mildness in him — at times an almost nervous subordination, as if trusting me to see him through. Through what, I couldn't say. Perhaps our tenure in this place. Walter's, after all, had not been an edifying death, and the thinning of our ranks somewhat checked the enthusiasm with which we'd set out on our mercantile adventure. There were moments when we couldn't face one another, when civility or duty was too threadbare a garment to cloak the warp which separated us from the everyday familiarities of our fast-fading homeland. And the longer we resided here, the less the Company seemed of a mind to understand the constraints by which we lived. We were no longer working, like pupils on a bench, within the immediacy and oversight of one of its counting houses. We were operating, now, at levels of emissary and commercial espionage in the heart of another and more uncontrollable world. Coen had set too simplistic an example in his conquest of the Spiceries. In the wake of that enslavement, the High and Mighty at home were swift to assume that what made sense around a boardroom table in Amsterdam was readily communicable to our doings half a world away.

I'd once heard said of the Portuguese Governor at Goa — an intelligence which, at the time, seemed to confirm my belief in our right to prosper at their expense — that he had responded to endless edicts from Lisbon with the words, *I obey, but I do not carry out*. I felt a present empathy for his exasperation in the rancour that assailed me. The lust which had given sway to an illusion of love felt cut off from whatever might have sustained it. My affection was compelled to fly a pirate's ensign, my precarious liaison denied safe harbour. I grew querulous and contradictory, thwarted without being able to betray the full measure of my malcontent.

I diverted myself by responding to the repeated propositions of several whom we'd partnered in — how shall I put it? — diversifying the business. Our forthright appearance and early civility had paid a dividend, and the trust of local merchants had given them the confidence to borrow from us rather than those usurious moneylenders at the bazaar. The interest I charged – as we all did; even Salomon, who quietly followed my pattern – was contrary to Company law. But the active hand of that august institution was so distant and delegated that, with truth and impunity, I could well echo that Lusitanian to declare, *I obey, but I do not carry out.*

Until the day...

～6

The attentions of the emperor seemed more distant than ever. Indeed, actual leagues now separated the factory at Agra from His Majesty's mounting pre-occupation with Lahore.

Wasim Khanin had followed in his master's wake but, like so many courtiers, and uncertain of events within that deadly inner sanctum, had not removed his own household to the apparent new capital. He lodged with or imposed himself on others who clubbed together to make themselves visible and, thereby, memorable to the emperor. To declare their presence was to publicise their willingness to serve and be rewarded. It was all a bit wait-and-see, and I relished Wasim's absence not only for the obvious opportunity it afforded but to limit, also, the embarrassment I silently suffered whenever treated to his hospitality. If his wife's willingness helped sanction our carnal discourse, equally I took no pleasure in making him a cuckold or faking virtue to his face.

But Khanin's removal to Lahore was not the only movement in that direction.

He – this other – arrived one day without warning, a carefully manicured addition to a cargo of spices that had been landed at Surat then caravanned overland for sale in the bazaars of the now dowager capital. He exuded an easy (if concealing) confidence, a flair for being at one with what was ambiently necessary. I might have warmed to what I saw – indeed, there was, about him, an eagerness and demeanour that put me in mind of myself.

Except that he wasn't me.

"Heer Pelsaert, I take it," and appraising me with the studied eye of one who made few concessions to what others might read in his own appearance. I felt my dress to have grown too florid, myself to have blended too visibly with the fabric of local ways.

"Let me introduce myself," he said, and removing what was almost a gauntlet. "Hendrick Vapoer. At your service." Then casting about for someone to receive his cloak and accessories. Salomon obliged.

"Perhaps you were aware of my coming. No? Pieter – ahem, Heer van den Broecke – speaks glowingly of what you have achieved here."

"Strange," I replied, "I've heard him speak nothing of you."

Vapoer grinned shrewdly as if having tested the calibre of my ordnance. "I have a letter which explains everything. I only arrived at Surat at the beginning of the month. He and I had much to discuss. He was anxious to learn how Governor Coen and our interests fared in the wake of diplomacies unsettled by the English incident."

"You mean Ambon?"

Vapoer inclined his head as if deigning to overlook a profanity. "We bear the English no obligation, especially where they dare to trespass." And ignoring the inflexibility of our justice, added, "They're inclined to want to profit from where we first endeavour."

"Still, at this distance from the Fatherland – and with the exception of the Portuguese in whom no sentiment of sharing might be expected – they are our nearest neighbours. As Christian folk, I mean."

"Heer Pelsaert," and he stared at me with queer appraisal, "we've not ventured this far to settle down and accommodate our rivals. This is not a colony. And this is not your home, no matter how many years you may have resided here." Then, having betrayed too much, perhaps, of what he already knew, he flushed a warmth of perfect camaraderie, of shared professionalism. "We're here – you and I – to test our wits against the vanity of the Great Moor. To seduce in him a craving for toys and beneficent trade."

It made me giddy to consider this stranger's use of the plural. Having herded the pack-animals into the stockyard where Salomon, now, removed himself to oversee their unloading, three or four stewards gathered to await my instructions. It presently dawned on me that I had a guest to accommodate. Grudgingly, I accepted that these were not my private quarters but the property – albeit developed by myself – of the Honourable Company. "I'll have an apartment prepared for you," I said. "I well know how tiring travel can be in this seemingly endless country."

Vapoer nodded his concurrence. "I won't incommode you long," he replied.

"Nonsense." I'd made up my mind. "A fresh face from home is a tonic to us all." And it further occurred to me that our adaption to what was local had formed a habit of perverse suspicion when it came to unannounced manifestations of our own kind.

"Here, let me settle this on you," and withdrawing a canvas envelope from his waistcoat. "I'm sure Heer van den Broecke has plenty to say. I know he esteems your reports, the observations which so render a sense of this region." Then glancing away as if to take stock of his surroundings, he added, "You'll find he gives notice of why I'm here."

"You've read this letter?"

"No, of course not," and laughing, somewhat hollow. "But he has a notion; one that I share."

I would press him no more beneath a sun that had already bleached the courtyard. By the time we dined that evening, I'd had the opportunity to digest Pieter's correspondence and, after an initial and private fury, settle my distemper sufficiently to become agreeably inquisitive and partnering by turns.

It transpired that Van den Broecke had calculated our interests at Agra too removed from the relocated throne; that in spite of the indigo locally collected and a populous market for our spices, our access to the emperor had lessened. Vapoer was merely passing through. Pieter had ordered a second mission to leap-frog all that I had sweated and sickened over to build these past years, and to travel to Lahore, there to persuade an avaricious government of the rewards to be had in favouring Dutch interests. Hendrick, he wrote, was very much one of us, a man uninhibited by risk or foreignness.

He and his team were anxious to parley with us, to absorb the wisdom of our experience with Mogul officialdom before moving on. It was in a sugary style that Pieter praised our Agra operation, describing it as the jewel of the Western Quarters. I knew also that Batavia Castle was styled the Diamond City in jest of its grim and gem-named bastions. Language could be used to colour and disguise anything. So when Pieter explained that our factory was to offer a leg-up to Vapoer and his men, that our solid gains were to prime his sortie, it was clear that I was being told we hadn't done enough to ensnare Jahangir's cupidity. The inference was curt. I had failed in the eyes of those who knew nothing of what it had taken to forge our presence out of nothing, who believed that a road, once built, had always existed and was therefore nothing to marvel at as further inroads were sought. Yes, I had failed where Vapoer was commissioned to succeed!

The professed enthusiasm for like-minded men is overstated. To invest in like company is to risk invisibility. In other circumstances I might have warmed to Vapoer. Unlike Walter who, even when living, had tended to cast a funereal pallor over things, Hendrick possessed an appraising energy and daintiness which put him in mind of me. We might have been two theatre-goers in reach of accord concerning the merits of a play; two epicureans in happy suit concerning the quality of a fowl just eaten, the Madeira drunk. It occurred to me, however, that this sampling appreciation for things in which one might expect to become an expert would not extend, in Vapoer's case, to any hands-on knowledge of indigo. Not for him the repeated assignment of assessing whether the crop on offer was in its youth, prime or decrepitude. One could immediately tell – by that manner, for instance, in which he warmly addressed you whilst his eyes roved elsewhere – that he was in pursuit of bigger things, that his conversation was structured towards gleaning information. That sense of ongoing momentum made me question what I was doing, myself, at Agra – whether, in consolidating our outpost, I hadn't betrayed myself into habits of repetition and make-good. The fact that Vapoer was destined for Lahore – and Andrade, come to think of it, for some rumoured kingdom of the mountains – made me feel rooted to something I might never exceed. Indeed, what had I grown of our business lately, above what was rightly expected by the Company, other than that which the Company must never hear of, namely our use of its funds to loan to reliable merchants — Mahometans and Hindus, alike — who repaid with an interest that greatly augmented our never-get-ahead salaries? What had Meyer said all those years ago? *How much do you earn? Twenty-four guilders a month?*

It had seemed such a long way from the top, and even now I earned little more than eighty.

You can breathe the world's hypocrisies and learn to cultivate an unblinking heedlessness, or...

Or?

Never mind. You shall surely rise. I see it in your eyes.

— You had the eyes of a poet. A woman's voice. Asmat's. Her husband has followed the court to Lahore.

As will Vapoer. His eyes take in everything. "Who's that buried over there?" he asks.

I am startled, uncertain of chronology and aware, only, that the present is a scavenger which thinks nothing of gnawing at the bones of the past.

"Walter van Heuten," I reply. Then, as Vapoer waits for more (and untrusting of Van den Broecke not to have briefed him to the extent that he knows more than I've forgotten), I add, "He was our leader when we first arrived. There was precious little for it but our wits and industry." And I feel a pride and compassion for my predecessor such as I'd not much tendered before or after his death. The advent of this newcomer makes me feel that my season, too, has advanced beyond my ken or mastery.

"You buried him in the grounds of the factory?"

"There was no place else — leastways, no place for a Christian."

Even the Jesuits were inclined to embalm their corpses and transport them back to Goa. I was thinking again of Andrade, of the extreme unction I'd witnessed him perform. Even Walter was desirous of receiving the sacrament from a Catholic rather than insist on dogmas denying him any comfort of Christian semblance. It was no heresy as death approached.

"It is not to say that a burial ground hasn't evolved," I say, choosing to voice the banality rather than admit to myself that in all likelihood it beckons.

The ground is generally unvisited and unflowered. It's as if it is held by Christians and heathens alike to be poisoned by the interment of such thwarted arrival.

My own health has been compromised by this robber climate. There are days on end when I lie prone, too weak to even contemplate escape from all that aligns with a not so distant vanishing point. My end. Perhaps the advent of Vapoer is a call for me to declare I've done my bit among aliens who, likewise, consider me an alien among them. I speak Hindi and a serviceable Persian — I would like to think that my presence here has been more than tolerated — yet it irks to imagine that Vapoer may hasten to Lahore with scarcely any understanding of who these people are (or any need to), secure a deal, then hasten back to the applause of Van den Broecke and an awaiting ship for the next posting in his stellar ascent. Some people have the Midas touch, an almost effortless facility for attracting gratitude or approval in everything they do.

Of course I was jealous. And without any proper knowledge of what it was I feared. My insecurity was driven, perhaps, by an awareness that I had succumbed to habits that were not as selfless in their service to the Company as they had once been. In any case, I doubted Vapoer was as goodly as Pieter had implied in his letter of assigned mission. He no doubt knew how to please his masters by way of feathering his own nest.

Hendrick stayed with us a fortnight as he prepared his onward expedition. There was a constant traffic along the Grand Trunk Road: merchants and messengers affiliated with our business, such being the network we'd already established, a living map of contacts which matted together our ability to make way in this realm. Indeed, we had provided Vapoer with a bridge to Lahore.

During these days of preparation, I was of the utmost service and agreeability. I even offered to send Salomon with him to help smooth the way. But Hendrick politely declined in favour of his own men and enlisted, of what I offered, only porters and the most menial of stewards. A number of crates which had, earlier, been deposited in the stockyard with instructions that they remain undisturbed were now mounted on mules for the final trek to the capital.

"And these?" I lightly asked.

"Novelties," he replied. And realising it was incumbent on him to sustain the cordiality we practised, he added, "Nothing of worth – other than they might bribe an eye, unlock a door." He smiled shrewdly for the games we were led to play with children whose tantrums, if soothed, might prove compliant in the distribution of their valuables.

At the end of the fortnight I bade him good luck and farewell and watched, with Salomon at my side, as his party passed through the factory gate and into the teeming neighbourhood that was much like a roving bazaar itself. Vapoer had resumed his travelling attire: a broad hat which screened the sun even as its darkness absorbed the heat, a similarly heavy shirt whose lace collar would, before long, be used as a neckerchief to mop the sweat, and a pair of breeches already uncomfortably stretched in the saddle. The European abroad, I might have smiled, and imagining the disenchantments to come. Except that I was in little doubt Vapoer had it in him to succeed.

"I wish you'd gone as well, just to keep an eye on him," I murmured to Salomon, and turning for my apartment, its retreat from the glare.

Novelties, eh? What had I been saying all along? I trust they had the foresight not to package seahorse teeth!

It was quiet in the wake of Vapoer's departure. Too quiet, the light excessively vacant for so harsh a sun. The unavoidable time spent with my Company counterpart had curtailed a routine of rendezvous with Asmat, and his departure was as disorienting as waking from a dream and suspecting, groggily, that some appointment had been overslept. News reached me that the indigo purchased in Bayana had arrived at Surat in good time for the mustering fleet, and that the price for this commodity was now second only to nutmeg. Because everything appeared under control, I grew uneasy in what leisure afforded me to think.

I desisted from my labour in chronicling the succession of Mogul monarchs. It seemed an indulgence, now, in light of Vapoer's advent and commission to pursue what was evidently a shortcoming in our relations with Jahangir. That in which Pieter and I had cooperated – me assembling a history of these parts, he incorporating my words into his official dispatches – yes, from here on my contribution would cease.

Whilst Vapoer was away and beyond all easy reliance on Van den Broecke, I would insert myself between the two to document the possibilities, as I saw them, pertaining to India. My knowledge of the region – its geographies, peoples, customs and administration – would form the backdrop to a description of our business as it might become, my thoughts on how best to employ our speedier ships to circumvent long overland journeys (and their reliance on costly rights of passage) an advantage till now unreckoned. Simply cut out the middle men who inflated our expenses with their sought bribes and threatened harms. After all, we ruled the waves in these parts, the Portuguese assurance now scuttled and the English wary of our fleets. And what I would essay was for the ears of the Company Board itself. Let Van den Broecke and Vapoer discourse all they liked, I would save my argument for the High and Mighty. It was time to overleap that which constrained me, to accomplish myself, not like Vapoer, in the direction of Lahore, but at the very table of those who tillered the VOC. I would permit none to cipher my voice or rob of me my authorship of thought. I would speak for myself!

Thus did I work in the evenings on my *Remonstrantie*, the candlelight a-wobble in the near breathlessness, the city's river-scent provocatively fecund and discharging of thought. My lines, their glistening quillmanship, began to hoard themselves in rigid inscription like the statutes of another time, their recovery illuminated in the torchlight of a struck adventurer. I had the distinct impression I was being ushered in my writing, that my words were ordained to portrait more than what we might exploit if we but steadied to define the opportunity. Indeed, like Hammurabi's laws, I felt I was compositing a work which would long survive me and my struggles to become a pillar of the Company's maturity.

I was glad of the distraction, its focus on something solid, for after Vapoer's departure I lapsed, once more, into feverishness, the delirium of which affected my ability to recite any outline or command of self. There were no physicians of our kind, and even had there been a European doctor, I doubt whether he would have had the skill or experience needed to countenance the maladies indigenous to these parts. Only the Jesuits — and I refer here to Andrade — entertained some knowledge of medicine, and in what I observed, much of their learning was applied on bended knee and in prayerful petition to God. Bloodletting was the remedy I particularly dreaded. If the practice sought to purge an evil curdling and help cool distemper, it nonetheless induced a giddy nausea that left me further weakened. Still, to faint whilst a-bed was of little consequence.

When sufficient strength and clarity returned, I summoned pen and ink to resume what was necessarily observable of India. And document a warning: *This would be a desirable country if men might indulge their appetites as they do in our own cold lands. But the excessive heat makes a man powerless, takes away his desire for food and limits him to water, the drinking of which weakens the body.*

It was not just of water, though, that I drank. There was a replenished reserve of gin which, at certain hours of the day, beckoned all too companionably. And of course there were my medicines, the draughts locally procured or imported from home. At times when I felt low and lonely in convalescence, it was soothing to imagine some apothecary politely doffing his hat to my mother as, in meeting, they each contributed to the other's business: she to purchase the medicines that might succour me; he to prepare the philtres that would restore everything to what it was before the Fall. It was a dream as craved as the nostalgic certainties of one's childhood, a reverie all the more poignant as one succumbed to a weakening that felt like abandonment.

Where is she? I idly thought, and wanting comfort, now, where all before had been excitement. And when she came, one evening, it was with a sullen toyfulness that no longer ascribed to any purity of lust. Indeed, she made no effort to conceal her unsolicited arrival at the factory. It was as if, in the afternoon of our passion, there was less cause for her to hide of herself what, before, might have incurred complete ruin. Despite the gossip aroused by her husband's absence, Asmat may have been a visiting relative – one's sister, even – for all the piquant nonchalance she displayed.

"Your countryman has departed," she said, "and still you did not imagine me enough to send word."

"Asmat, I've been indisposed this past fortnight."

She glared at me questioningly, and I felt my fervour rekindled. "With sickness," I added.

Seeing me somewhat recovered yet sombre as a child, she softened a little. "I might have played the nurse."

"And I have wished you here as we were in Bayana," I answered, as if speaking the entire truth.

"I don't know, Francisco," and moving slowly, her finger outstretched and tracing the walls of this chamber which served as my reception and personal abode. Spread across the table were my notes for the *Remonstrantie*, my tell-all of what I'd seen of India. I'd not even summoned Salomon to make a fair copy of these thoughts, such was the privacy I felt for so unconsultative an undertaking. Any alarm concerning what I'd written of local wives – that harshness borne, perhaps, of frustrated unbelonging – was buried in a fathom of words beyond her native literacy.

"These boats," she said, her face drawing close to a small painting which had begun to moulder, "is it of these that you came here?"

I nodded the once.

"And by which you will one day leave?"

Perceiving her freedom, she likewise sported with my embarrassment. "Who said anything about my leaving?" I replied.

She smiled with a knowing that was little short of bitterness, despite the fact that she *and* I had contracted as much of one another as we were each liable to permit. She wouldn't – *couldn't* – come with me, and my intentions were as much unclearly stated as the notion of being totally honest with her. She knew my loyalty to be both passionate and idle, my tenderness grateful yet easily distracted. She knew her husband and, therefore, would deign to know me when what she wanted for herself no longer sprang from any humour of lust. "I don't believe you when you say you have no wife," she prodded. "Surely, in your country, you have a family to go back to."

"Only married sisters. And a mother I may never see again."

"How can a man live so barrenly?"

Breathing sharply, I responded, "Is that all I was to you – a man devoid of situation?"

Despite the latitude granted by her unwitting husband, Asmat was too honed in the combative rituals of married life to appreciate that I mightn't feel honour-bound to refute her slur. My anxieties – professional and physical – only added to a sentimental indignation. I knew she was here for little other than an unrelished vindication, to see for herself how effectively I'd forgotten her. And to justify her resistance.

And I, too – despite a longing to feel again that caress of forbidden splendour – I, too, knew it best to search for what was fractious in her demeanour, to wave in evidence her retreat from love and turn to a profit of disengagement. But in the justice we each imagined for ourselves, there was also a desire to encompass that which was not yet fully tempted or explored, whose harvest was not the time-stewed yield of the lowly *katel*.

"I'm here, no? – even though it would cost me dearly should my household discover where I am."

"And you trust your eunuch?"

She snorted incredulously as if to say: *Do you not remember Bayana? Do you not know that nobody knows?* "Do you trust your own servants?" is what she said.

I looked away, abashed. "Forgive me. I've prayed for you to come."

"Good. Because this satisfies me also."

Once more she turned to survey the contents of my room, to finger the limited ornament of a bachelor's lodging. Attracted, perhaps, by the blue opaqueness of a Venetian decanter, she took a pace towards the chest on which it sat, together with a matching glass. The richness of its hue, its hint of heaven, helped gloss the bitterness of what I swallowed in diluted droplet. Her ears, I noted, sparkled with sapphires of the same deep colour. Despite my reliance on that tonic during bouts of sweat-soaked depredation, I was presently restored enough to think myself clear of any danger. There was a glitter in her bearing which stirred the embers of what had burned without reflection. I felt soiled in my work clothes, unprepared in dress and toilet for what she offered – perhaps for the last time. I needed to cleanse myself of excuses that had kept us distant these past few weeks.

"Let me go and wash," I said.

Even now I recall my uneasiness in leaving her unattended. Was it that I didn't trust her? Perhaps. Our liaison was a fickle creature and I didn't credit her not to yield to boredom in my absence, not to dishevel the pages she couldn't read or trace a critical eye over the simple objects that pleased me. Yes, I didn't trust her not to judge me.

I had left her for no more than five minutes. I never dreamed she would mistakenly sample (and in such full measure, as if it were wine) a privacy so singular (*No! It's not what you think!*) that its medicinal fortune might elsewhere kill.

Quick, Salomon! Lend a hand!

His face is a shock of involuntary obedience. Something murky spills from the corner of her mouth.

Outside, the night is dark. As it should be. As it needs to be.

Except that suddenly a nuisance moon is released from its cloudy mother-of-pearl. Lighting the steps. Illuminating the stockyard. The walled-off garden. The shadowless walls. The moonlight is a frosted sea.

Concealment is risky, success accidental. Success is limiting the damage, playing for time.

It's fortunate I'd not aroused a servant to bring us food. Yet the hour is not late, the compound not likely to feel deserted. Retired, only, to its lamp-lit quarters, its bailiff casual. Nothing stirs but what we ourselves bestir. Like thieves within the store of our own accounting.

The garden – my garden – offers the only obscurity, its shrubbery disruptive of all that is swept and ordered and clearly visible.

It is only later – after we have done what was needed to be done and stand back, dazed, in a telltale of sweat – that I begin to listen to the noises that were with us all along, to sense the life that was a door or curtain distant yet never sought to peek during our preoccupied desperation. It's only later, much later – and as my mind whirs in plausible lie and counterfeit – that I wonder of her eunuch, left standing outside the gate. I daren't return downstairs, to test once more the silence of my feet and spy if he waits for her, to meet his eye with the unspeaking truth that I have doomed him also. It's best to pretend nothing, to carry on as if she never existed. He waits for what was inadmissible to wait for in the first place, his covenant with his master corrupted. I would send Salomon to see except that I don't want our anxiety betrayed.

In the morning the servants treat me warily. I would challenge their humour were it not for the fact that I must conceal myself. Ignore anything and everything which dares not shape itself in words. No, nothing out of the ordinary has occurred to ruffle the calm of our sober industry.

As customary, the gate is closed and I cannot see beyond. I don't wish to see.

Despite what must have been rumoured – that the lady, in the absence of her husband and like so many of her harem sisters, had become addicted to the manipulative pleasures of her body servant and absconded with him and her jewels – I received no word of hearsay. And to my never-sure relief, I never saw Asmat's eunuch again.

In love, as in death, there is no going back. And yet we would spend a lifetime entranced with what preoccupied a single season, its story all the more real for what we re-imagine of it. And tyrannical, too, in the loss or forfeit suggested.

As free of certain encumbrances as I now appeared, there was no denying the overcast which afflicted my former simplicities, just as fever and fatigue had increasingly disrupted my ability to direct the factory during bouts of illness. My appetite for ambitious learning, the optimism once entertained when setting out for unknown shores, had turned lethargic, my captaincy now despondent and subject to terrors of self-inquiry. Yes, my spirit was beginning to manifest visible stains of guilt.

How I longed for the onset of a storm not of my making. How I prayed for its delivery from this becalming rot. Yes, any event, any excuse to set in motion a command of action through which I might renew myself.

⟶ᢈ

"Go back!"

It didn't make any sense. I had come to rescue.

His hurried approach, his brandishing wave, it was an immeasurable relief to discover that spring did indeed follow winter, even in this inverted hemisphere. But as if warning of a nettle or some poisonous bloom, my near approach was challenged not to harvest what I thought to delight in.

"God be praised, but go back!"

I turned to my companions on the beach but they, like me, were astounded. Those with swords deftly tapped their pommels.

"There's a party of killers," he gasped, "on the islands near the wreck." And pointing. "They have two sloops and mean to seize the jacht."

I quickly glanced at the *Sardam*, its anchored isolation, then scanned the lagoon in the vicinity of where we'd left the majority of folk. A soft breeze ruffled the ultramarine and baffled any sound from that quarter. The only thing visibly stirring was smoke rising from a location much nearer, and I had thought, there, to find and be reunited with the survivor camp.

"All is treachery and war. Go back to the jacht — you must secure it!" And looking over his shoulder in the direction he knew the danger to lie.

I followed his gaze beyond his makeshift yawl, two of his companions leaning on their oars, the other two standing ragged but expectant as if momentarily plucked from battle to receive further orders. In the digestion of his intelligence I failed, at first, to appreciate that this was other than that long-anticipated day of cheering re-acquaintance — the clothes of the castaways somewhat tatty, of course, and their bodies lean, but convinced their relief would be as generously received and forgiving as the joy expressed at any wedding feast. Only slowly (and as my foreboding mounted) did I glean at a foreshortening distance the movement of a larger boat bearing a greater number of occupants. Despite an expectation of wear after all these months, they appeared curiously uniformed in red. The oars dipped with a hunger that didn't smack of starvation.

"Quick, back to the *Sardam*!" I shouted, and now scuttling to our tethered boat. Hayes, likewise, signalled his men to shove off. We pulled a rapid stroke for the jacht, its onboard crewmen ceasing to shift about and no doubt marvelling at our hurried return. I was standing, steadying myself against the tiller-man, all the better to raise my voice above a sluggishness of time. "Break out the weapons!" I cried. "Arm yourselves!"

~⟡~

Go back.

Those words echoed like a drumbeat throughout our steadying preparation. In what Hayes had quickly intimated, I was uncertain of the forces arrayed against us. The shock of insurrection, its volume yet to be tested but its menace all too closing, had invoked in me a silent rage of cheated purpose. For once I appeared calm – decisive, even. I had come to retrieve what I imagined I'd left behind, only to discover that treasure robbed, and I was in no mood to philosophise while thieves still roamed and sought to plunder. Even before I knew precisely who he was, I realised I needed to assert myself, not only over the dissident force but within this alliance I now shared with Hayes. Did I suspect of matters, even then – and before the disaster was revealed fully to my disbelieving senses – that Wiebbe's hard-fought survival might judge me?

Go back? No further retreat was possible. Come hell or high water, whether just in time or too late, I had returned. I had fulfilled my promise.

~⟡~

Except that I hear no applause, no utterance of *Well done!* All is silent as I lie here in the moulder of this tomb-like representation, Death's vestibule. They have thought to secure me, to hide me from the living. I'm firmly shuttered from the moon and stars. Only cracks of sound filter through: the bark of a dog, the whelp of a child.

The survivors – yes, the survivors were praised or pitied. And those who sought to destroy them? Well the scoundrels were branded in the sight of God and man alike. Yet I, a victim too, am neither accorded sympathy nor spared censure. What kind of survivor am I?

Gagging on what clags my throat, my breath short and struggling, I fear I might not long remain a survivor of any description at all. Worse than abandoned, I feel already forgotten.

"Is there anybody there?" I say aloud, more to register an echo as proof of self.

Hmph. As expected.

But as I lie here, the nothingness becomes charged, the atmosphere pregnant with some back-stage tension steadying to reveal itself. I grow icily afraid. Am I alone, am I truly alone?

In the darkness it is others I see: a crowd whose face is not explicitly familiar but imploring nonetheless, whose clamour would petition me in their prayers. My heart is light and racing, not in heated anticipation but with dread. There is something shouted, a yammer more imprinted on the conscience than properly heard, the gulls rising and screeching over the outcry.

Come back!

⟿

I thought you said it was *Batavia*.

Well of course it was *Batavia*. That was the loud bang which made us all sit up.

Loud, you say? I was there, jolted from my bunk. That grinding squeal like a howling animal. All that was thought connected was suddenly rent, objects and persons – indeed, their very character – all tossed hither in the unfastening of our world. God and salvation seemed conspicuously absent in that moment's vortex. The situation was no more heartening as I arrived on deck, the shocked spars juddering against a night sky, cold and distant, as whatever that evil which lurked within the deep tightened its vice-like jaws on our ship.

I admit you were unfortunately placed. But that calamity only confirmed the rumour circulating that you were an accident waiting to happen.

Whence this slander?

Admit it Francisco, you were living too curtly by your threadbare conceits.

Of what then, other than *Batavia*?

Perhaps the woman you buried like a stolen treasure.

That, too, was resolved.

And those prohibited lending practices which bestowed on us a reputation for usury and irregular dealings.

That was of minor account.

Like your success with the emperor.

I feel fit to strike him. Before Walter and I travelled to Agra, *I say*, there was no regular commerce.

Even conceding that which was true but no longer true enough, we think you may have overstayed your initial mission. You've been too distantly your own master, too willing to obey but not strictly carry out.

That's a lie!

Too much the libertine and tourist.

By all that is holy, what a hypocrite!

Vapoer has returned from Lahore, *continues Van den Broecke.*

That was quick.

And proven himself adept at negotiating with Mogul authorities.

There is silence as I contemplate the strength of a wave fast approaching.

I've instructed him to head back there. Of course, we don't want to duplicate our operations...

I'm still waiting.

So I'm giving him overall charge of the Hindustan mission. You'll oversee Agra while he's at court, but the old capital is now the foundation of our drive on Lahore.

You're giving him my job?

Well, your contract was coming up for renewal. Don't get me wrong, you've been an absolute asset to the Company. What you've done here, what you've learned and reported, it's set the stage for our next incursion. Still, time for a change, eh?

And I now know that I was right to have retrenched my energies to essay, elsewhere, all that I'd discerned of India. I'm not about to play second to a man who's the very mirror of my ambition. My suspicion at his unheralded advent is more than confirmed.

I'm of a mind to return to the Fatherland, *I say.* It's years since I've seen my family, and my mother's not getting any younger.

I trust you'll not forsake us altogether. Hendrick will need you. *I rely on you.*

Then why replace me?

He looks away, searching for something to examine. Everything tarnishes with time, even our best endeavours.

Yet we are all alike, I muse, living on our wits and stratagems. The only discernible difference may be the ability, in some, to alchemise their personal avarice into some semblance of Company appetite. Many are begrudged their salary by those who would manipulate the greatest theft.

Meyer, I recall, had known more than I was capable of appreciating at the time. "How much do you earn?" he'd leaned close. "Twenty-four guilders a month?" I was forced to swallow. It seemed such a long way from the top.

What are you paying him? *I ask.*

Van den Broecke is still casting for something to deflect the wounding of what's taken place.

Vapoer. What is he getting?

And at once he stares at me with a truthfulness that would dispatch a brother to the gallows. One hundred and sixty guilders.

Even though I'd steadied myself for betrayal, the unearned magnitude of twice my salary makes me grin with disgust. You fuck!

Pieter doesn't flinch. I'm doing you a favour, *he says.* You were stuck. That turd Medari was hinting at the inadmissible, his innuendoes travelling along that barely subjugated road between us. It's a miracle her husband didn't march a company of soldiers against the factory. No one would have stood to protect you then. The English would have looked askance and quietly rubbed their hands. Don't mistake their drinking love. Their hate is second only to – and nourished by – their fear of what we did to them in Ambon. A Dutchman caught out in the hinterland, here, is ripe for crucifixion. And there's not a Jesuit who wouldn't supply the natives with the recipe for how it's properly done.

Even if my distaste is visceral, I cannot deny his speech. And what angers me more is the feeling that his righteous back-room words simply mask an agenda to replace me as opportunity presents. Vapoer is indeed the incarnation of an earlier self, and Van den Broecke, with his easy access to a ship and a world I've not visited in years, knows that our enterprise is built upon the skeletal remains of those who first entered the forest. He believes I've done as much as I might accomplish, that my capital as a scout and scavenger is exhausted. Over the corpse of my deceased labour he would have another raise the VOC banner, its swirling trio of red, white and blue an anthem of ongoing invincibility.

~6

All is treachery and war. Go back?

~6

I don't know what Salomon made of these shifting circumstances. I had fallen foul of a mentor and friend and, oblivious to the sentiments of he who had served as my scrivener, felt myself sorely betrayed. I was determined, in countersuit, to capitalise on the genius of my argument as to how we might conquer India. Not by sword, fire and pillage but by gentler persuasions that appealed to the fickleness of local honour. Gifts and inducements, such was the currency of a productive friendship. That's what friendship had been reduced to: the insinuation of advantage.

"Come on," I said, "we're leaving." My flourish was purely theatrical.

"Leaving? But to where?"

"As soon as you've completed a fair copy of the *Remonstrantie*, we're returning home."

I never enquired of Salomon whether he had a home to return to. And until that time when I embarked from the Abrolhos in search of water, jostling to keep my authority alive in a boat that Jacobsz had filled with those more suited to his purpose, Salomon had never been distant from my service. I don't know how he spent his time in the Fatherland whilst I visited my mother and sisters. He simply materialised as I needed him and shadowed my every inclination like an extension of self. It was unwelcome to realise I'd overlooked him, that I'd not conscripted my faithful retainer into the longboat. In fact, I'd not recognised him among the surging crowd on that forlorn scrap of beach, the soon-to-be-unattended who beseeched me not to leave them, even if that absence was declared only temporary. Indeed, I never saw him again until we rounded up the last of the mutineers. And the murderers.

Yes, I suppose I trace my declining belief in the Company – and with it, a sense of fixture – to the advent of Vapoer, not that he was wilfully to blame. But I no longer knew in whom to trust. The injustices I'd witnessed and thought little of because they'd not much affected me (other than play to my advancement) now revealed a world of factions and favourites. To survive in what I merited, I too must push my suit to an unsentimental degree, favouring none but the opinion of those who had access to the High and Mighty. If I'd had occasion to love Pieter like an elder brother, I understood, now, that I was an instrument in his self-making, that there was scant regard for my work and sacrifice. It perhaps chastened him a little to have forfeited my support. He may even have regretted, albeit momentarily, his decision not to press for the renewal of my contract. Perhaps the delicacy of certain matters, not least of which was the rumoured body in the garden, had made it necessary for him to attest a change of plan which reduced my exposure.

"Francisco, if I can't persuade you to stay, allow me to entrust you with this," and handing me a sealed envelope.

"What is it?" and wondering whether Vapoer was privy to its content. It was marked to the attention of the Directors of the Company.

"A commendation. Among other things it states that I should gladly have retained your services because of your excellent work and experience." Pieter raised a hand to his throat. "I also paid tribute to your knowledge of the languages spoken at court."

A moment's silence opened between us.

"There is the usual chest of correspondence," he recovered. "You'll safe-keep it on the *Dordrecht*. Present yourself to Brouwer when you dock at Amsterdam. Make sure that letter supports whatever you purpose."

I stared at the envelope as if ambushed, and reached within myself for the argument most telling as to why I was now departing. My un-recuperated health, perhaps; the desire to further bury my stolen and mis-starred love for Asmat? Despite an angry sense of dislocation, there were tears in my eyes. But it was too late.

It's ironic, now that I lie here in the dark — and believe me, the unfetching light of day is no more illuminating — yes, I find it ironic that I should have imagined myself escaping the limits imposed on me by quitting India. I suppose I thought it *was* the end of my sojourn there, that the make-good I envisaged for myself was derived from the portability of what I knew. I would take back to the Netherlands a first-hand account of how matters stood in the populous Western Quarters, a knowledge as valuable as indigo or nutmeg and just as one-way. My service would be lauded, and although I had little idea as to where or for how long I might reside, I was sure to be pensioned among the powerful. Who knew what opportunities at home awaited a man who had proven himself abroad!

Long before I stepped onto Amsterdam's Pepper Wharf, those who had attempted to rule or ruin me had become distant and belittled, tied to an environment they were likely to sicken in or die. And here would I be, in the land of my birth — or nearly so, for Amsterdam had long played to the ambition of my countrymen.

Francisco — you and I — we're both sons of Antwerp...

Not anymore. Not either of us.

As things transpired, more's the luck I might have chosen *there* to live out my days. In this reduced state I cannot tell if it's acrid Batavia or my person that stinks. I can state one thing, though, and without contradiction: if I ever get out of here a second time, I'm not coming back. Perhaps I'll find a rich widow as Opa once teased. A Marta van Luyck, eh?

Hmph. A not-to-be-sniffed-at ambition, perhaps, but a little too late, I fear.

No, it was Pieter, as the wags would have it, who carried off a widow — Coen's. It was he who returned to Europe to so trusting a reception that the concessions heaped upon him might more satisfactorily be managed by a local overseer in the Banda Islands. Indeed, there was little reason for him to go back East. Unless, of course, to succeed to the governorship itself. As it was, I presently had an impression of my own to make:

You mean to say you would have us dispense with the overland route altogether?

The volume and superiority of our shipping is now such that its traffic sails unimpeded.

Short of shipwreck, pipes a voice, and there's an exchange of cautious jest in the chamber.

Quite, I say aloud, determined not to be scuttled by some untoward technicality.

We hear reports that the Great Moor is dead —

That Hindustan is likely to be torn by civil strife.

Nothing was known for certain at the time of my departure. Jahangir has become frail with addictions peculiar to his family — indeed, most rulers of those regions possess a fondness for indulgence.

Opium and intoxication is the vice of princes everywhere, opines one sober judge.

Such families are so sinfully intermarried that anyone with half a mind might profit from their madness, seconds a more republican and, dare I say, calculating sentiment.

I clear my throat in qualified agreement and give them time to work their questions.

Our investment in that realm, then, is fragile?

Our mission liable to assault?

Everyone cranes forward to scrutinise, in me, the least hint of uncertainty or disquiet.

Not at all, I say. Only those with a claim to the throne – and in some instances, those perceived to have a claim but who would rather run a mile – only they are likely to suffer any violence.

But there are armies –

And we all know how indiscriminate troops can be –

Let me assure you, my lords, any war of succession will be fought in the vicinity of Lahore and the royal treasury.

Isn't that where we sanctioned the dispatch of what's his name? You know, Van den Broecke's man, asks one starched collar, and turning to his High and Mighty brethren. *Never mind, isn't that where we sent a mission?*

Quite, I affirm coldly. And fighting could, of course, disrupt our communications.

I thought you said our interests weren't imperilled?

True, but there's no avoiding the necessity of conveyance overland between Agra and Surat. It's reason enough to be on good terms with the Great Mogul, whomever he may be. But I was referring, more, to the rest of the country. Its difficulty of terrain and lawless practice, its tolls and bandit lords, such impediments alone should give us cause to rely more heavily on our maritime.

Ships cost money, I hear them thinking. And I'm momentarily struck by the contrast, in appearance, of our commercial government with the gem-studded colour and opulent gesture of the Mogul court. Never did power sparkle more like a summer sea than in the high-stakes theatre of that shimmering edifice.

The power of this Mogul, then, is not absolute?

He need must fear his clansmen and his neighbours?

The emperor reigns supreme when at home but is not above coveting his neighbour's property.

Including ours?

No, we possess little to unsettle his sense of majesty. Indeed, like his father, he has often entertained Europeans with meat and shelter.

But the calm of Hindustan is no longer to be trusted?

And even if we suffer no violence ourselves, our embassy will be with someone new?

Let me assure you, my lords, I have followed the political peregrinations of the Moguls closely.

And what can you tell us?

Yes, how does that oligarchy Heer van den Broecke referred to shape events?

The "gang of four", as we styled them — Jahangir and his closest advisers: the father-in-law, wife and her brother? It no longer exists. The father — by all accounts an able vizier — is now dead, and the queen and her brother competitively promote their favourites with an intrigue that may prove lethal. What was once defined by blood and marriage and centred on the throne has, with the emperor's frailties, come unstuck. If Jahangir is indeed dead, any vestige of the old alliance will have turned to rivalry.

There is no planned succession?

Any usurper might prevail?

One of the emperor's sons, Shah Jahan, has been in a state of insurrection for some years. He's married to the daughter of the queen's brother. Now there's *one* faction — one abetted, ironically, by the man the emperor commissioned to suppress his son's misbehaviour.

They are eager to hear my interpretation of events, and I feel my star rising.

Rebellion in this country, I continue, is as common as its princely avarice. The empire is tormented by intestine disorders, and sons can scarcely wait for a parent's death to luxuriate in the power, wealth and autocracy of their every whim. Small jealousies which merely kick up the dust in a village become fully-armed uprisings among the eager-spirited magnates. And where none may share in the government, its tyranny leads to a revolutionary demeanour where alliances within this patchwork kingdom are forged or broken as opportunity and insult decide.

The High and Mighty eye one another with the confirmed view that in India they must deal with the likes of mad men, albeit wealthy ones. One of the lords would probe further: *Queens are not unknown to rule as men where their blood runs hot.*

True, I answer, but the queen of Hindustan has manipulated a poor outcome.

How so?

I said before that the emperor had commissioned someone to suppress his son's rebellion. Well, things began to fall out among the ruling clique when Jahangir's childhood friend – and the empire's most formidable general – was accused of presumption and dishonest practice by the lady Nur Jahan –

The queen?

Quite. It was her first step in removing a powerful tool from the reach of any, not to mention a rival influence over her husband. The court was on its way to Kashmir, Jahangir's summer retreat, when this general, Mahabat Khan, overtook its progress with five thousand of his soldiery. He had come to plead his case, and having ridden into what proved to be an unarmed camp, unexpectedly found himself a royal hostage-taker. Pieties were avowed and the emperor encouraged to remain seated on his elephant, so to speak, but this Rajput warrior now controlled the imperial caravan and directed it to Lahore.

What are we getting at here?

Yes, this is all very interesting but –

Your indulgence, my lords. The queen encouraged her husband to go along with the Khan's unplanned chancellorship, at the same time plotting through secret messages to muster a loyal counterforce. Even the general perceived his days were numbered, that he favoured no talent for the intrigues of government. When a number of his men were set upon, he knew the game was up and fled into the borderlands where fugitives perpetually evade Mogul capture.

So the king was restored to his throne –

The queen to her power behind it?

Not quite. Her brother, don't forget, is father-in-law to Jahangir's disgraced son, and Shah Jahan – or 'The Wretch' as he was now officially titled – is as practised at turning former enemies to account as any in his illustrious family. The man who had served his father faithfully, only to be abandoned, now sought rehabilitation in the service of the son.

These intrigues are as interminable as they are unfathomable!

Nearly so. The point here being that while Nur Jahan was manipulating the demise of any who compromised her influence with the emperor, her brother, Asaf Khan, was likewise manipulating the assured succession of his son-in-law. The queen's camp had alienated a powerful servant; her brother now picked up the disgraced soldier. He has an eye to the future, and would have his daughter queen rather than his sister. Nur Jahan fancies herself in the favouring of a royal grandson, a creature kept close to an ailing and sentimental monarch. But the cause of the thus-far ineffectual Shah Jahan has received considerable turnaround with the support, now, of Mahabat Khan.

Heer Pelsaert, who then rules the country?

If Jahangir is dead, then my guess is Shah Jahan — with or without the wading of a river of blood. Of those who abet his seizure of the crown — for unlike Europe where firstborns are commonly accorded rights of property, the death of a ruler among the Mahometan empires often entails a fratricidal squabble — yes, those who helped him to the throne will constitute the new cabal of viziers and favourites.

And the consequence to ourselves?

Yes, will the change of government bode ill?

Among them as would rule over Hindustan, the imagined shedding of so much blood can only herald an accumulation of resentments and give precedent to those who would further kill for the sake of power. But as we don't aspire to rule there, our witness of the local danger prepares us, in business, to anticipate the character of those with whom we must deal.

I'm certainly beginning to appreciate the challenges you've had to contend with, Heer Pelsaert.

But tell us, the proposition of your Remonstrantie, *it still applies?*

Rulers change but the system is unlikely to reform itself. The Moguls make war to serve an opulent peace. All is theft and redistribution within the empire, and those who rule do so through a combination of carrot and the stick. Service — especially if one loses a limb in the good fight or sustains a tiger mauling — is rewarded. Favours, by contrast, are purchased. And bribery with gemstones, novelties and toys is never out of fashion. To solicit the goodwill of the monarch and his cronies is to open a discussion as to what best serves their interest — and ours.

How, then, fares the practice of our rivals?

Yes, what of Spain's cousin might we yet extinguish?

The Portuguese strive to maintain their audience with the emperor, ostensibly to insinuate a papist attitude and castigate the ungodliness of others. Still, they're only too happy to profit from the transport of heathen pilgrims from the port of Cambay to the Arab lands. In former times, when their trade was prosperous and spices saturated India, I've heard tell that village women wore necklaces made of cloves. Alas, they no longer predominate as they once did, although priests and adventurers are still dispatched from Goa on expeditions which garnish their hunger to possess with a missionary zeal.

And the English?

They slavishly distort, to their favour, the lesser tiers of trade. They fill the markets with quantities of raw coral and heavy woollen cloth, with swords and knives and sabres that quickly rust. For the temptation of the royal camp they bring tapestries worked with Old Testament stories as well as precious inlays, pearls and balas-rubies. Above all, they've seized on the emperor's interest in new inventions, in curiosities rare or never seen in Hindustan.

What might interest a Mahometan prince who has everything?

Guns. Always guns. And horses. Also jewels — perhaps an antique box or casket with various ingenious locks. They love mechanical workmanship — a Nuremberg clock springs to mind.

My enthusiasm is palpable. I tug at my collar, its constraint having grown casual to the point of unfamiliarity during my long years away.

The English, I say (and feeling a rush of patriotism), they mock us as only self-serving cousins might. Prompted by what they hear, Agra's nobles ask whether precious stones are known in our country, whether there are craftsmen as skilled as those found in England, Venice and other European lands. I feel strongly, sirs, we should make it clear to them that our nation is not merely on a level with others but that it surpasses the entire world for skill. Every year we should send rarities to the value of one hundred thousand guilders to Agra!

There is a shocked intake of breath. Then:

We note from your paper the items you suggest —

The quantities you recommend —

The venerable lords look from one to the other then back to me.

How might we profit from such an indulgence?

Most of the goods could be sold within the palace to the profit and honour of the Company.

How?

Through an agent familiar with the language and customs of the country. Someone who can deal with the difficulties and improper procedures arising from the greed of local governors.

There! I have rolled the die. All eyes are upon me.

Pieter van den Broecke writes you are a clever fellow.

Pause.

It appears he was loath to forgo your services...

It's all right, I think, and aware of my beating heart. I have presented them with what they need to know to consolidate our commercial presence in India. It's detailed there in the *Remonstrantie*. Now give me my reward.

Seven years is a long time...

I suppose you're not as connected to the Fatherland, these days, as you once were...

No wife. Perhaps no family...

No doubt the Company has become your foster-parent...

You must be missing the familiarities you have made your own...

Back East.

NO!

I don't know whether I uttered any sound or they simply read the alarm in my eyes. But I am standing in the chamber, and each of the Lord Directors would appear to have me do one last thing before I die. I feel the heat rising in my veins, a keepsake of the fever that follows me yet to this cold place.

You have proven yourself most eloquent in persuasion.

Yes, and in what we've read of yours, our appreciation of how matters stand out there has been widened.

Absolutely. As for here, of course, we understand that you may need to attend certain matters —

And in any case, it would take some time to commission the items you particularise —

Hm, perhaps we ought to seek the advice of Rubens or another who specialises in antiquities.

That's an idea. An informed opinion —

Yes, before we sign off —

And prepare shipment —

For the autumn sailing.

The High and Mighty presently conduct themselves as if the meeting is concluded, turning to chatter like a murder of crows over the entrails of a fresh kill. Their beak-like noses, their winter eyes. Amidst a creaking of chairs there's a congratulatory obliviousness that smells of camphor. I am still standing when they remember that I am standing, still.

Of course your work cannot go unacknowledged, Heer Pelsaert.

All murmur in agreement. Hendrick Brouwer is smiling as if to assure me of good tidings.

We should consider it a favour —

And we understand from what you tell us that a favour must be purchased!

There is general laughter.

Yes we, the Board, consider it necessary for you to return to the East Indies and oversee —

As only you, an agent familiar with the language and customs of India might ensure —

The sale of this specialist consignment.

An agent? I reply vacantly.

Brouwer's smile disappears. *Francisco,* he says, and revealing our close relation, *Batavia is to our overseas possessions what Amsterdam is to the Fatherland. The Company is the government, both here and abroad, and for the Council of the Indies we require men who understand as much of what determines us at home as, indeed, they can judge of how best to advance our interests elsewhere. Most of us have lived our professional lives in segments, and I would suggest*, glancing around at his fellow Directors, *that India will not end up your destiny.*

Their concurrence is nodded, not unappreciatively.

Just don't risk so valuable a cargo on the voyage out —

Yes, no shipwrecks, eh?

And so this starchy and concluding jest before trays of Madeira and spiced biscuit are entered.

"**Y**ou have made a good impression, Francisco."

Brouwer must sense my hesitancy for he quickly adds, "What you've written in that report of yours is stamped with the authority of one who's been there. Listen," and drawing close, his breath a staleness of sweetened things, "those of us who have ventured East understand one another. Many of these others, they've never so much as stepped aboard a coal barge. But if counting houses are the things that rule us, then your arguments certainly added up."

I stare at his collar, sewn with pearls. It's only when his hand clasps my shoulder that I look up. "We each have work to do," he smiles, "work that will earn us our reward and respite in the end."

And I find myself nodding. Wordlessly. Like a man under sentence of death.

Just at that moment a figure pauses on the step above. "Why, Hendrick," floats the voice, "it *is* you. I see, then, you've finished your meeting."

"Abraham, hallo there! Come — come, let me introduce you to Francisco Pelsaert."

And a man at first indistinguishable from any other sable-dressed burgher descends and reaches for my hand. "Sir," he grins, his face genial but flaccid, his vintage roughly my own, "I see you have the complexion of one who's not much in these parts." Then turning to Brouwer, "Doubtless, a man of the world!"

"In truth, Francisco's not long returned from India." And brokering the introductions, Hendrick informs me that the Town Clerk (for such is his office) has been instrumental in managing Amsterdam's burgeoning transformation.

"Ha, I merely do what I can. Still, there's no denying that the daily swell of populace has made the city a nation in itself." He shakes his head as if yet marvelling at the honour bestowed on him for its administration. "The new Rome, eh?"

"Only the empire's roads, these days, are more sea-like," adds Brouwer.

"Of course I feel so stay-at-home," shrugs the other, "so inexperienced whenever I pass the wharves and slip-yards."

"Nonsense, we need good men at home!"

And am I not good enough? I think.

But the Town Clerk, a man too disingenuously humble to be anything other than assured, continues. "I'm busy — and content, of course. But the adventure of it, eh, the horizon of what we seek? Still, I'll leave it to the young — my nephew, for instance."

"Where is he?" asks Brouwer. I presume he's intimate with the family.

"Batavia. And doing all right for himself, according to his father."

"His name?" I ask, pretending interest.

"Pieter Cortenhoeff. A lad not fifteen yet already a standard-bearer."

"Francisco is soon to sail for Batavia and the Governor's table. Let's hope your nephew is as fortunately destined."

I had wanted to revive my standing within the Company, to be highly valued for my counsel. I'd envisaged a future in which others were now sanctioned to do the bleeding. And yet my journey was to repeat itself, to reprise the departure of a former time. I was again being consigned to an operation in the field. Even with the balm of promotion and hint of greater things to come, I was going back.

I no longer possessed the naive energies of callow youth. I didn't recall or correlate Cortenhoeff's name with anything until I'd had a chance, at last, to draw breath at the Governor's table. By that time the redoubtable Coen was dead and it was Specx I submitted to, dragging across his floors, like some haemorrhaging deformity of which I was ashamed, the moral wreckage of my absent year at sea. Patient and awaiting, seated in a carved chair that was more a teak throne, the former fleet president was installed with such belonging that it seemed the Governor's quarters had always been his residence. Except that there was something chastened about its atmosphere, something more scrubbed and teetotal than even Coen's spotless violence might have merited. In the candle-worried gloom that cornered those chambers by night, I thought I detected a presence, a shift of lightlessness that was both frightened and elusive. Imagining it a trick of the senses, the phantom, perhaps, of my own uneasy tale, I was startled to hear weeping, the echo of a broken soul.

Tilting his head to one side, the table servants already dismissed for the evening, Specx drew a tight and thoughtful breath. "Sara. My daughter."

It was only then — and in sudden imagining of what Batavia had witnessed, the talk all too lurid and unfeeling — that I recognised who the young standard-bearer had been.

I didn't know at the time of my departure from the Fatherland that Pieter van den Broecke had similarly quit India. But then he worked within official channels and knew closely how to trim his sails. As far as the Western Quarters were concerned, he *was* the official channel, his correspondence with Coen more than leapfrogging any intelligence I might receive. As with the arrival of Vapoer, I could count on being among the last to know. Little wonder I took matters into my own hands to present myself at the headquarters of the VOC itself. Yet in spite of the favourable impression I'd made, I still felt excluded from those circles which decided my servility with a confidence conserving of their unperturbed sleep. It concerned me that I might be awkward with Pieter. It concerned me, even more, that I might have to reside in Agra awhile, the billeted guest of Vapoer in the very factory I had more than built.

An unheralded and revolting image assailed my mind as I pictured the Company dogs – great brutes of criminal deterrence and forever hungry – pawing at the garden I had created in the likeness of what I'd observed at court and of wealthier houses visited. Give a dog a bone.

Truth be told, I didn't rightly know what I was returning to. In spite of everything I'd described to the High and Mighty, there was no telling how a struggle for the throne may have affected my contacts, or where the new emperor – presuming it was Shah Jahan – might have established himself. The Moguls were a roving lot, and Lahore, Delhi or Agra – even some place new – might each prove passing capitals for the imperial pillow. The camp was as real as the palace; one had only to follow the crowd.

The thought of all that travel – on top of a lengthy sea voyage to Java, and from there to Surat – made me reel. At least I should again meet Coen, if indeed he remembered me. It was a career lifetime since I'd stood nearby at the battle for Jacatra, and even then he'd permitted himself to be attended by little more than the universe of his will. No doubt he was aware of my name; Van den Broecke's correspondence would have kept him up to date as to how things stood in Hindustan. Perhaps it was Coen himself who had forwarded a plucky Vapoer (as he'd done with me, all those years ago) to instil a bit of energy into the Indian mission.

Well, things had matured somewhat since then, and despite the usurpation I'd suffered locally, my professional standing had been more than refreshened through Brouwer and the Lord Directors. I was returning to Batavia to make good my promise that the Company would make good of me. And I learned, just before we sailed, that I'd been provisionally appointed a Councillor of the Indies, a satisfaction which restored my energy and enthusiasm. It surely meant that I was destined for Batavia Castle, little matter what digressions my second and executive apprenticeship in the East might bring. I was all the more appeased when the ship for this voyage, newly minted, was likewise christened *Batavia*, her ballast including the dressed stone for a new gateway into that colonial capital. Despite my reservations, I felt myself the custodian of an enterprise that had nominated me among its captains. I was returning to a Batavia that had outgrown my memories of it, a Batavia I mightn't recognise but whose solidifying structure I should surely one day inherit. In such headiness I smiled to consider that while Shah Jahan may have seized Hindustan, I had retaken my future.

"Sahib. Rise up."

My eyes ache but that, perhaps, is more in keeping with what I drank last night. I've a dryness of mouth, the taste of which is not unrelated to the nose of a cesspit. Melons are being cut. Juice is what I need. A pitcher of cold water, too, with which to wash.

"Salomon," I call, yawning to stretch myself awake.

He appears in the doorway of our solitary room, the building an inn or house, perhaps, its rooms accommodating whatever the communal need. I'm not sure where our servants bedded themselves down, only that our belongings have been deposited close by with an expectation that they should be readied for the animals.

Salomon, too, is yawning. "It looks like Fakkad Khan was right. The entire camp is stirring."

"Sahib, it is true," and my man hands me a beaker. "Today we go to Kashmir."

I inhale and smile at the prospect of once more being on the move. "How many days?"

"Yes sir, we will go directly."

"But how many marches?"

I receive no intelligence other than a most dutiful grin, and turn to Salomon. "Think of it as a holiday."

He, too, grins before wincing at the pulsing in his temple which reminds him of last night's revelry.

We find ourselves among others in the tail of Jahangir's comet. Randasingh and Fakkad Khan, travelling together for purposes not altogether clear, have befriended our little party in a pause commanded by the emperor's inclination to hunt during this stop-start migration.

"More than a comet, sahib," had counselled Randasingh the night before, and passing me a drinking bowl which proved more stimulant than supposed. "The emperor is the planet of all riches, the landlord of our wellbeing. In his prayed-for wisdom he mediates with the gods to safeguard us against —"

"'Tis a wonder Allah doesn't lightning-strike you here and now!" interjected Fakkad Khan, and signalling me to pass him the bowl. "If it weren't for the fact that these infidels," and gesturing to his companion, "are like children in their superstition, they'd be damned to eternal hellfire for such blasphemy."

"Listen not to him," pleaded Randasingh, his expression largely concealed behind an ox-horn moustache. "He is without the grace of compassion."

"And when have I ever beseeched God to have you whipped for your improper devotions?" returned his friend, his eyes hooded in the supper light above a nibbled chin of whiskers. Facial hair was all that distinguished them as, with heavily ringed fingers, one passed the bowl to the other and received a dish of almonds and dried figs in return.

"I tell you," spoke the Hindu, "the emperor has the blood of *all* his subjects running in his veins."

"The emperor is a Mahometan," declaimed the other.

"Well then, he is of a kind with his father."

"Do you think so?" I asked.

"But of course!" replied Fakkad Khan, surprised, and for once I'm stared at simultaneously. "The Moguls are a benediction to these lands —"

"There's not a drop of their blood which isn't mixed with the valour of the old families," added Randasingh. "By my word, Hindustan has proffered more than a strong hand!"

And there was laughter all around before Fakkad Khan thought to remonstrate. "See how he forsakes truth for exaggeration?"

"Not at all, my friend. We Rajputs have been residing in the palaces of the Moguls since the day our manhood was tested and our valour not found wanting."

"Or your vigour, by the number of snotty children you sire!"

"Ha! Now who utters a dangerous foolishness? Just remember who the emperor is; who his mother was — who his *father* was, for that matter. We Rajputs have been the staple of empire, a party to its nursery as well as its armour."

"Well put, Sir Rajput," I cheered, tossing back the circulated beverage.

"Tsk," waved Fakkad. "My father was an officer in the imperial cavalry, befriended in trust by the great Akbar himself. There were so many horses in his stable that it took a day to count them all. And the stable itself — you never saw the like of it. It stretched from beyond the horizons of the north to a place out of view in the extreme south!"

Randasingh and I exchanged a glance, our lips parted with uncertainty as to whether Fakkad was being boastful or becoming intoxicated. The Hindu winked then said, "You are quite right, my friend. My father — being a warrior from Mewar — was as fond of swords and weapons as your father was of horses. He had a lance so great that one end touched the earth whilst the other pierced the sky."

"That can't be," slapped Fakkad, and sizing me into his protest. "Where on earth did he keep it?"

"In your father's stable."

Our laughter did nothing to coddle Fakkad's soreness, and it was time to retire. Salomon, who had been yawning for some time and whose mastery of local speech was limited to courtesies and the ability to count, had followed our conversation like a man who glimpses a distant mountain through cloud breaks. While it had been warming to share additional company, his trailing comprehension compelled a vigilant civility which was wearisome. Yes, we were all drowsy, whether from our cups or the conversation, and sleep was welcome.

Now, as drums and trumpets were distantly heard, we knew the rumours to be true: that Jahangir's dalliance had exhausted the numbers of live game hereabouts, and that his calendar summoned Kashmir were he to continue enjoying the timed perfections of an impeccable life.

Where the emperor took route, so did the rest of us — for reasons, perhaps, that were daily reassessed in the novelty of where (and in what condition) we found ourselves. Well might I enquire of Salomon out of Company hearing (and smiling to acknowledge that I was its captain and arbiter at so distant a remove): *How do you think your holiday, thus far?*

Beyond Lahore and the fording of the Ravi — a spectacle no less epic than Moses and the sea-crossing children of Israel — the terrain grew more forested and difficult. While the tidemark of our human flood was everywhere evident (the roads pulverised and fray, the trees stripped and adjacent meadows trampled), our exodus could no longer be glimpsed in whole but was strung out over pass, valley and river crossing.

"The emperor has a fondness for the first budding of spring," alighted Randasingh, gasping as if he'd been carrying his small pony and not the other way around.

"You might say he has a necromancer's fastidiousness," added Fakkad Khan, catching up.

"It's said the court astrologers do a splendid business –"

"That the emperor would scarce so much as pluck an eyebrow without their auspicious say-so."

"So the advent of spring, what might it mean to us?" I asked.

"No less than Srinagar where he first tasted love."

My expression must have begged an explanation.

"Not a woman, sir merchant," Randasingh shakes his head, "but an ideal. An ideal of place removed –"

"Of a perfection set apart."

And in what they said I was prompted to think of Andrade, of his journey to some fabled Eden, perhaps, wherein the gulf between innocence and our sinful descent might be narrowed through an act of missionary contrition. The zeal with which he had spoken of his impending journey to the mountains was one with an elder brother who presumes to have learned the better of his ways and seeks, now, to dominate his untouched siblings with that headstrong reformation. He would make them doubt their innocence, goad them into accepting that their ignorance is depraved, then save them through deflection from all that had animated his desire to seek experience in the first place.

I too, momentarily, felt that our coming may have eaten unquestioningly into the substance of foreign lands, that the despotisms we displaced within the Spiceries, for instance, had nonetheless subtracted something else as well. Might Jahangir be strangling Kashmir with his love? Might this place I was extraordinarily eager to see have its blush blighted by too intent and grasping a suitor?

"Believe us," said Randasingh, and mopping the perspiration from his brow below a discoloured turban, "your emotion will soar when you glimpse the valley."

"'Tis a perfumed garden of countless fruit trees and flowers," added Fakkad, stroking his whiskers. "My father took me with him when his cavalry first escorted Akbar here."

"That must have been some procession," mocked the Rajput.

"Pff," waved the other and resuming, "Like the father, so too the son. Kashmir's enchantment is so seductive that it has long remained the destination of contemplative and pleasure-seeking monarchs."

"I do not disagree with my friend, boastful though he is."

"If not the allure of a woman," I said, "then you certainly make it sound as such."

"Psst, come close. Ever since he discovered her, Kashmir has ever been the emperor's mistress. When Agra proves too aggravating a wife, the plains too hot and the politics too suffocating, the emperor makes up his mind to visit this regenerating beauty."

"Already Lahore – much closer to the hill country – is foreshortening the distance of his impatience."

"For whatever the emperor pleases –"

"So must the emperor be pleased with."

"He will not miss a moment of his love's embrace."

And as we recovered ourselves and reviewed the passing column, Fakkad fondled his chin in a sunlight that felt discernibly cooler than when we first stopped and pointed to the rigours ahead. "That means chasing winter from his path."

Winter. I had quite forgotten there might be such a thing as was once this stern and unsmiling visitor of my childhood. Those mornings when fingers ached in an exposure of chores, when one's chest shrivelled within its cuirass of bone.

Of course there were delights, too. The evaporation of dampness, for one, as moisture turned to ice. Yes, the magical and once-a-year inversion of water, of ponds frozen over. As a boy I had skated with the circling throng, party to a masque so uniquely of its season that its recreation was inseparable from the feast of Christmas. Throughout those light-famished days I snatched at stark and revealed beauties: the stencil everywhere of black against white, the intimacy of a pallid radiance that throbbed, perhaps, to protract some greater insight. Yet for all its mystical presence, I suppose that what I sought of the atmosphere was some hint of homecoming, the return of spring and un-studding of my rib-clenched suspension. Yes, throughout those crystalline and leafless seasons I impatiently awaited a coming of spirit which tolerated hopes of warmth and, as I grew older, something more amorously speculative. But then, later on and far from home, I forgot all this in the sweat of the archipelago and heated plains of Hindustan. The quickening shivers I soon developed were unrelated to any icy blast or snow. There was simply the dry season and the wet — an acrobat's tumble, back and forth, from dust to mould and then dust again.

If, at first, the warmth had been welcome, the insistence of that moistless sun soon diminished one's tolerance for endless summer. The alleys of Agra grew offensive in their stink: plant scraps and offal, cess and putrefying animal remnants in gagging contest with the suppressant scents of incense and the crowded exhalation of a populous capital. Over a succession of days, sometimes weeks, great thunderheads would build in what was now a colourless sky, the morning haze yielding to portent shapes as afternoon drifted into evening and still the genie failed to unleash itself. In the lethargy which drought effected, the senses grew blunt and unseeing. The shadows and doorways of this alley-crazed city became congested with a torpor that resembled Death's rigour. Nothing was lithe. All was desiccated and brittle.

When the rains came, there was blinking celebration. Children and old men ran into the streets to see if what clattered overhead and hissed throughout the neighbourhood was true. The young clowned and shoved each other with an immersing enthusiasm, their elders relieved and recalling, perhaps, an expectation of what was now to come. As the dust turned to mud and filth began to float, it was moot, the advantage of one season over its opposite.

Now here we were, entering into something meet with that elemental quartering of the calendar, the rotation of which had already witnessed leaves drop and hunger strip the land, whose almanac had lately conceived of snow and now dared to re-imagine spring.

But before the budding of that season, there was still the wretched straggling of winter to contend with.

$$\sim$$

So that the passage of laden beasts over difficult hilltops might be more easily accomplished, I dispatched a large number of stone-cutters and spadesmen to smooth the way. I value the comfort of travellers. I am a great traveller myself.

I smile grimly. It is dim, a little too dim to feature him distinctly.

I see no point in bearing with inconvenience when, with a snap of my fingers and the muscle of a thousand servants, a road might be trimmed as a garden is cultivated.

It was no easy path to follow, I say, and perceiving enough to tell that he takes mute offence.

It was no easy industry to undertake, he replies, *what with the Afghans, nearby, stirring trouble at the ancestral hearth. And to think that my great-grandfather was once the King of Kabul! Never mind. Mahabat harvested a great many of those black-hearted ingrates with his blood-drinking sword.*

I knew next to nothing of this at the time. Only that the kingdom, regionally, was in a perpetual state of insurrection wherever the Mogul hammer was absent and jealous men manufactured claims. What I was all too aware of was that a capricious ruler might little care for the wellbeing of his subjects. Snow was still falling on the mountain passes leading to Kashmir, and the slowing column appeared insufficiently cloaked to fend the icy winds, the animals, likewise, pitiful or rebellious in their exposure to temperatures unaccustomed. Whatever the discomfort of the sun-baked plains, there were few who wouldn't have wished themselves turned around. But then their lives and livelihood were not theirs to decide.

The Jhelum was running high and fast, and it was there that Salomon and I, in company with Fakkad Khan, Randasingh and countless others, caught up with the imperial advance. In something more akin to the crowded apprehension of an army in disarrayed retreat, thousands pressed towards the obstacle of the river. A striped tent had been erected on a rocky outcrop, its sides pressed like the sails of an Indiaman to screen Jahangir and his retinue from the wind and eyes of his people. Already a number of sappers, eager to prove their worth, had attempted to swim across and been swept away by the current.

Believe me, Pelsaert, my potency as the people's lord and protector was being tested. I was obliged to effect a solution in keeping with vigilant authority.

Scouts were surveying the Jhelum upstream and down, and after several hours there was a decided movement towards a discovered ford.

I ordered two hundred elephants to help cart the effects of the people — as well as those too feeble to make it on their own — over to the opposite bank.

As for our own crossing, I had our most precious items and scrivening supplies tightly bound in leather satchels and strapped atop other stores that might well survive a brief dunking. The water clenched like a bear trap, and we felt warm, if not dry, just being out of it again. And so the march continued.

I had thought myself then cold, but the discomfort of wading from that river into a windiness of snow was small compared with the saturating uncertainty of those days and nights in the longboat. The sea was a dampness we never escaped. In the loss of *Batavia* we were bereft of shelter, mocked and marrow-chilled in our exposed survival. A river might be inconvenient, even precarious in its crossing, but the edgeless advent of the sea was too great a leviathan to contemplate alone. In that unshielding desert each turned to his neighbour, hoping that he mightn't discern the mirror of his fear. It was this dispiriting privacy, this never distant want of optimism that snuffed the spark of warmth. 'Twere as if that which had previously worked were now proved witless, one's untested trust swallowed in not knowing where to turn or how to behave. Yes, I had thought myself cold in the pre-thaw of those mountain passes, but such discomforts were amply shared, the ceaseless crowd a security that misfortune would select only the careless or the weakened.

Pelsaert, the people hereabouts speak of this moistless tension — a magnetism, if you will — wherein there is neither cloud in the sky nor flash of lightning, yet for all that is unapparent, a crackling voice rolls down from the hills.

What does it say?

You know, I never thought to enquire.

We mull this over. And since he is an emperor, it is inevitable that his thoughts will impose themselves on mine.

It's not easy divining God's will, he says, especially as others — blind of sight and deaf of hearing — would clamour to have you interpret His justice and His missives. I am my people's defender, defender of their faith. But Allah is as testing of my judgement as I who devolve the governance of Bengal to my friend Mahabat. I, alone, cannot illumine the mysterious certainties of God.

I think it is the volume of this place in which we find ourselves, I answer, that has made God seem so tentative, so detached or missing from what we might seek in prayer. Like the mantle of stars over a darkened sea — too many and too distant to be familiar, too gelid and unilluminating to banish one's apprehension of what the world may or may not harbour.

And thinking to myself: I had trusted Ariaen as Jahangir had trusted his astrologers, each in their way pilots of regions unknown and, perhaps, best untouched. But in spurning risk, risk was always present.

In the end, what good were my soothsayers? he asks. What did they promise that could cheat the inevitable?

You were hunting...

Yes, Pelsaert, that day will come —

When one of the bearers fell to his death from a precipice...

Yes, a day when the omens are not propitious, and what has been forestalled can be forestalled no longer —

He was chasing a deer. The sun was hot...

Not like today, eh? And musing. Still, is any day a good day to die?

Did it speak to you then?

Who? What?

The thunder from the hills.

———

The hierarchical civilisation of the plains grew tawdry and disordered as we slowly threaded the mountain passes. Companies of noblemen roughly pressed their mounts through pedlars and tradesmen and lowly camp-followers. I thought I glimpsed Wasim Khanin. It was difficult to tell. The group of riders may have been official; they may simply have been officious. There was no overlooking who *we* were, however, our novelty as European travellers remarked with stares that questioned the meaning of our presence and its chosen severity. If it *had* been Wasim, he was clearly not in a mood to dally or even acknowledge that we were acquainted. Rumours everyday beset the column, and men of station and swagger pushed themselves to keep within optic of the imperial standard. What conjoined lord with beggar, and every rank in between, was the suspension of his usual shelter.

"I thought the Moguls a nomadic lot," I sighed, responding to a shivering Randasingh, the vibrancy of his costume despoiled by travel and a necessary overlay of sackcloth, "but, surely, can this be how they holiday?"

The Rajput was less than caring.

"Don't mind him," said Fakkad Khan, "he's not toughened to a life in the field. Now, when my father commanded the emperor's cavalry –"

"Oh to hell with your father's cavalry; it's just so much horse shit!"

Salomon, himself grown sullen, raised an eyebrow in agreement with the Rajput. Our threadbare journey – these protracted stages of march without proper safeguard from the elements – was enough to jade anyone's forbearing.

———

In the morning it began to snow heavily. The road grew slippery and the weaker animals began to stumble and fall, further slowing our progress and adding a piteous dimension to the misery of those whose beasts could not rise again. Just when the emperor was being cursed for his relentless drive on Kashmir, it transpired he was not above the suffering of his subjects and sent twenty-five of his own elephants to assist in the recovery of their baggage and drag donkeys from the mire.

It's true, *he says*. I halted two days on account of the snow. It was all very annoying, of course, but what could I do? I summoned three astrologers – one after the other and under separate escort so that they mightn't confer – and asked of each his insightful opinion. And do you know what? They unanimously predicted a break in the weather! Incredible, don't you think, that I should pay good coinage for assurances such as this? They must have severally seen that they'd strained my belief in their efficacy for, without a word of a lie, they each went on to assure me that Kashmir would manifest itself upon the first day of spring. Now *that* was risky.

Not that it mattered, for I was determined to fulfil their prediction. The ladies were beginning to grumble – not Nur Jahan, though; she's long been my rock – and our provisions didn't look like feeding the entire company of servants unless we got a move on. I tell you, Pelsaert, I was seized by this idea: to bear my torch in advance so that others might see its light and rouse themselves to follow. I was determined to lead, to rally their courage. What is a monarch, after all, but the parent of his people's wellbeing?

I gave the order that we should take only those most attendant upon the royal stirrup. I assured the ladies it would be an adventure; I appealed to their sense of escapade. But you know what women can be like. Their notion of adventure was to secure the satisfactions of Srinagar as quickly as possible. Apart from Nur Jahan – who, my friend, once slew five tigers with five bullets and is not averse to the rigours of campaign – yes, apart from the queen, they all grizzled and would not be parted from their creature comforts. Ah, *he sighs*. In spite of my injunctions, it was still found necessary to have seven hundred elephants convey the advance camp.

I smile without sympathy and feel the saga of Hannibal's warlike crossing of the Alps cheapened by this baggage train of fripperies. And yet the spectacle is not without summons. The hazy light and cultivated greenery of the lowlands has been stripped and replaced with solemn buttresses and wind-carved shards of ice. Against this stark and colourless backdrop, the silken curtains of the howdahs are reduced as tinsel, the

decorative harness of each elephant now muddied and the animals, themselves, discon-
certed by the foot-pad chill of earth. Plaintive trumpetings screech and grate in the
brittle air as mahouts clip and cajole and soothe and whisper in the parchment-ears of
their charges, each beast willing to cooperate yet driven to service in an environment
unfamiliar and threatening.

And so you left the others behind, *I say.* For the solace of your women and their comfort.

He doesn't immediately reply. A convoy of emotions ripples across his face before he resumes his narrative calm. You're not an easy one to befriend, Pelsaert. Too much the critic by way of deflecting from your own example. Let me remind you — since you complain that others fail in their courtesy to loan you justice — that our way grew hard. And, indeed, I strove to ensure that our party's spirits remained dignified, though there was little to console us in that shadowing emptiness. Just when enough was almost enough and the womenfolk found themselves fatigued with cold, we came upon the advance tents as if a gift from the hidden world. I and the ladies alighted and took shelter from the sleet and rain. Yes, we were together, *his face dimpling in recollection of that good fortune. Then he turns to me:* How many did you leave behind? *And sneering:* How many women?

I swallow, unable to utter a word, and inclining his head, he continues:
The land grew increasingly barren. Shepherd boys roamed at a distance, wary in the protection of their animals, although there was little clue as to what such flocks subsisted on since all was stone and gravel where it wasn't blanketed with snow. 'Tis strange to relate but I glimpsed peacocks and black partridges — as well as monkeys such as those to be found in Afghanistan — proof, all, that such creatures can survive in a climate like this. Yes, it was a grand and scoured landscape of blue-greys and salmon-jade. River ice floated like foam in boding of the thaw to come. At one particular crossing where the flow was swift and deep, our path was raised upon so slender a trestle that we had to unload the elephants and coax them through the icy torrent. The footmen and horses surmounted the bridge, and the stores, likewise, were conveyed as ants would crumbs to where the elephants were herded on the other side. My father, years before, had had a saray erected on the ridge overlooking

the river, but I never much cared to stay there due to the echoing rush below. The sound was ceaseless and without quiet at night; I was enamoured, more, with the promise of Srinagar's cloud-mirroring lakes.

—⸜

Yes, I too would fall in love with the tranquillity of Kashmir's sheltered valley, its verdant pastures and its lakes. Was this akin to what Antonio hoped to discover, a kingdom of such sensuous delight that its luxury was all the more pronounced for the hardship endured in getting there? Had *I* inadvertently arrived at *his* rumoured Shambhala? Indeed, might I stumble across him in the local marketplace as we each explored the ingredient of life at such a distance? And laughing with incredulity at our mutual discovery – at the discovery, in fact, that God, king and commerce might meet in this same place.

To begin with, that which was glimpsed at a distance (a perfection bred of perception after so arduous a journey) swiftly wrought in us sensations of bodily relief. Blossom was in shimmering abundance and roses, violets and narcissus grew without prompt or cultivation. The emperor had been correct in the timing of his arrival. After the etched immobility of those territories devoid of tree or verdure, Kashmir seemed the very incarnation of welcome spring, its carpet not unlike the tendrils of design and colour which decorated the floors and walls of grandee houses farther south. As for the hunger endured by many, one need only extend a hand to procure a ready supply of apple, pear or walnut.

To me, at that moment, everything was wondrous. Even Salomon smiled wanly like an invalid prevailed upon to receive the salutation of this belated fairyland. After the rigours of the march (and despite being warned that our destination was nothing short of paradise), our release from wind-scraped passes and fast-flowing river ravines into so lush a calm seemed little less than miraculous. Perhaps the miracle lay in our surprise that the valley might exist at all, ringed as it was by forbidding alpine overlords.

"See that peak," pointed Fakkad Khan, "that which hovers above the city?"

I nodded, uncertain of the singularity amid so grand a spectacle.

"That's Solomon's Throne," he said with a pride that was almost hushed. "There are ancient writings proving that the Wise One built it with his own hands."

"A namesake, eh Salomon?" and turning in my saddle, my lips tasting of blood in the effort to smile.

Randasingh presently joined us as the column straggled without regimen, many dragging their feet in the sludge of an already arrived and pleasure-pursuing crown. "There are the royal apartments," he pointed, the castle rising beyond the city like one of those impregnable Rhenish fortresses.

"The emperor is fond of poetry," spoke Fakkad. "I've heard the valley described as a garden of perpetual spring, that clover surrounds his citadel which is terraced to the skies, that in this soul-enchanting season the gates and walls and courtyards are lighted by torches of banquet-adorning tulips!"

"My friend," laughed Randasingh, "I believe you fancy yourself a voice already in the sovereign's chorus. He'd certainly approve of your servile panegyrics!"

"Tut. You'd be the first to avail yourself of any favour shown me."

"And is some such favour likely?" I asked, reminded once more that I know next to nothing of their purpose.

"We're here for reasons as wishful as your own," responded Randasingh.

"We're here because you never know your fortune," added Fakkad.

"This is where the emperor prefers to be when the heat in India increases. 'Tis said his body burns like a furnace owing to his consumption of excessively strong drink and opium."

"The legacy more so of his youth —"

"For the queen now manages his intake of pleasures."

And we three pause to reflect on how our calculation in bettering ourselves is studded to the garment of a largely unseen, unknown (and of us, unknowing) prince whose appetite is for whatever is placed beneath his nose and pleases. Our motive in having undertaken this arduous journey is to have ourselves sewn to the livery of his largesse, to elicit a curiosity which, while not elevating us to his princely brotherhood, might nonetheless see us handsomely rewarded should we visit upon him some interest or other.

"Well, whatever pleasures are to be had, they won't be found here at this blistered arse of the march."

And we turned our animals, all in need of rest and grooming, into that sluggish current of souls which must shortly exchange one trial for another as it sought shelter in the overburdened environs. Come what may, the sensation of having arrived at this farthest of places buoyed me, and I was anxious to discover the secrets of the city once I, too, had procured lodging.

Unlike the plains a world away where stone and brick comprise the substance of larger towns, the houses here were built of pine, their interstices filled with clay. Even the mosques resembled churches of the Baltic, and there wasn't a dwelling that didn't exalt the use of timber, which wasn't ventilated with handsome openwork instead of glass or windows. If I did wonder, momentarily, how the inhabitants coped with draft, I soon put it from my mind. Like Jahangir, I was here for the season only. And that, too, which made Srinagar seem garden-like – indeed, less a metropolis than it actually was – were its roofs which, for the most part flat, were covered with earth and sown with grasses and onions. People didn't so much as live in the fields; the fields invaded and mantled their homes with a cloak that softened the sound of rain and fended off rude cold.

But such beauty was at a remove and on closer inspection the people appeared poor, with little to distinguish them from labourers. The men, I could see, were exceedingly strong in the loads they carried, a feat all the more remarkable given how little food, as I soon discovered, there was to go around. And if the children were handsome and spritely, such enchantments were left at the doorstep of maturity for the adults who ensued seemed not of a kind with that vanished juvenility. The women, in particular, proved small and lousy, and in contrast with those who chanced my eye in Agra's bazaars, it initially made my flesh wriggle to contemplate their nudity. Doubtless the season just ending had conditioned their appearance, their coarse woollens open from neck to waist, their foreheads strapped with a reddish band, and a sooty-looking clout spread to cover the legs. Yes, as Srinagar widened at our approach, so too grew my impression that all was not as one might have sought.

I warned you, Pelsaert.

Did you?

There's always something in the leaf-litter to compromise an aspect of perfection, something disagreeable to the unsuspecting touch.

I pause in staring contemplation of where I have arrived.

Don't misconstrue me. Kashmir is the very satisfaction I crave. Why else put the harem to such inconvenience, risk its humour in such prolonged portability?

Short of war and spectacle, how else might you fill your time?

Oh, away with your prudish and judgemental commentary! Let's just stick to factual observation, eh? The men, for instance, shave their heads and the women, as you've doubtless noted, do not launder what they wear. Nor does any drop of water freshen the bodies of these people.

I almost smell that self-shielding sweat. And unto this you've brought us?

I've brought no more than my retinue — and the army, of course.

And the rest of us?

The ambition of your own imaginings.

Fakkad Khan taps me on the shoulder. "All the nobles curse this place, for upon the emperor's impulse — and at a burden of such travel and deprivation — it makes the rich poor —"

"While the poor cannot fill their stomachs," adds Randasingh. "Look around you. With the coming of our multitude, commodities will grow scarce and their prices soar."

"Nonetheless, the emperor is secure within the plenitude of his citadel..."

"Hm. He cares little for his people's welfare where the health of his conceit is concerned."

And so to this new but ambiguous reality I found myself arrived.

⸺⸱⸴

Thus have you found yourself in many a similar situation, eager to control yet unsparing of how your dictates might chasten others. Your comfort and your pleasures.

'Tis a strange pleasure when your every thought is furtive.

A sign, surely, that something was not quite right.

Not everything amiss confers a stain upon my reputation. Jahangir had his fortress. It, too, was a lifeboat of sorts. Mine, when it came, afforded little protection.

Yet those denied a place on its benches were as resentful of your privilege as that burdened populace its duty to the emperor.

There were many who took advantage of the opportunity. *I'm slurring, feeling slightly intoxicated and hence careless.* Jahangir may have had his harem, *I say*, but the women of the city sold themselves in great number to the baggage train. It was like unto like. There were base pleasures to be peddled in the coming of so many, a sowing in the thaw.

And did you, likewise, abase yourself, even though the women were of filth?

It was at a time and place of easy appetite. Wasim was distant and, perhaps, purposefully unrecognising of me. But then he was preoccupied, one of a thousand mounted gentlemen vying for the emperor's notice. We few Europeans who accompanied the march were as burrs upon an ox, insignificant and incidental to the purpose of the beast. Besides, I'd not lain with his wife, though such was my attraction and conceit (not to mention the flirtation of our words) that I imagined Asmat, too, to have become aroused in the contemplation of a lover other than her husband. The thought of knowing her obscured the repugnance I felt in satisfying the urge which overtook me in the alleys of Srinagar. I never came away from those shadows without a searching sense of shame, nor did I fail to avail myself of their opportunity as renewed hunger compelled. The eyes of those women shone with the pleased indifference of creatures diverted from other drudgeries, for the needs of men were swiftly dispensed with, the coinage of a few invasive minutes worth more than a day's labour. With a man's appreciation for the satisfaction of his lust, my cooling aversion had less to do with scruple than rancidity. Whores were not outcast in my thinking, and certainly not in the heat of engagement. In the sweated aftermath, however, it was deflating to recognise that the face beneath your own was foreign to the ambition of your esteem. I would smuggle such experiences into a privacy whose Pandora was only unlocked in contemplative or accusative moments. I grimace, even now, to reflect that Hartanti considers me a predator, even though my demand of her was little more than hand play.

You are without a wife, even in your native land? And then: *Are you always without a woman?*

If I be honest, there are certain transactions I'd not willingly speak of with Asmat. Nor Lucretia for that matter. That which *is* requires little comment; that which would voice an indulgent fantasy requires greater guarding. For in truth there was a time, Lucretia, when, prior to the onset of all our disasters, and confined to intemperate slumber in the cradle of the ship, I dreamed of you and stroked myself.

Instead of which, Francisco, you forsook both of us for the hand-love of servant girls, whores little better than slaves.

They were all whores, my dear, in the slavery of that island jungle. Serpents flourished and tigers freely roamed. A man can dream one thing within the constraint of its improbability; the notion of guilt remains unsummoned. But in what I returned to find – nay, even before that; in the very shipboard assault upon Lucretia – my fancies were made repugnant in circumstances of factual rape. What I entertained in hypothesis (Lucretia's scented thighs wrapped in capture of my own) was enough to have me indicted among those detained to answer for their actions in the Abrolhos. I had been saved from myself by the transgression of others, my sobriety reinforced by their forestalling crime.

Yet they were distasteful to you. The women.

What I discovered there was distasteful – the death of any pretence to decency.

So your daydreams were without censure whilst our marriages were condemned.

They were no marriages.

No? Let me explain a fact of life: a woman will gravitate to whomever offers surety. You abandoned us at a precarious time. The men couldn't be controlled, not without appeasement.

It's a lie.

You weren't there, *he counters.*

Cornelisz always shelters in the conscience of my authority. He's like some parasite feeding off my scruple, his manipulativeness in keeping with Van Diemen's. Worse, he exploits my hesitancy of mind.

If you had only stayed behind, Lucretia could have been yours, *he tempts.*

There were rather more important things to think of than concubinage!

The island was desolate, its people yammering and divided, *he continues.* The women were too few and too visible not to seek shelter as upheaval mellowed into something more drawn and revealing. Indeed, I wonder how you would have played your hand had you, instead of I, remained behind.

You dare draw a parallel? You dare suggest such atrocities were inevitable?

I dare only to remind you that you weren't there, that the press of men put the women at risk. We took the most vulnerable into our care. Lucretia, Judith —

You set up a brothel!

From which those two were spared —

To become your and Van Huyssen's personal property.

They were attended with a courtesy as fastidious as the keep of any Mahometan princess.

They were little more than creatures of your harem.

A household protection you have little compunction in violating.

Such women are not free —

To satisfy the freedom of your lust? *His husking laughter is contemptuous.* Let me tell you something, Francisco, there was a hunger in those women to have what came at a price. If Lucretia felt at all soiled, she certainly didn't show it, pampered as she was with silks and damasks. If she didn't much put herself about the camp, it was because of her fear of the other women, their jealous spite. And the predikant's daughter, she too found the attentions of her plumy paramour very much to her elevation, if you know what I mean. *And laughing harder still.*

Believe me, we who established order on Batavia's Graveyard, we who maintained a humour of treaty among its brutish residents, yes, we afforded sanctuary to the most precious of the women. And you know what, Pelsaert? — well of course you do! Let's face it, you've hobnobbed with the heathen, broken bread with him, admired his stable of women. You were even low enough to lessen your cuckolding of the man by telling yourself you had a perfect right to liberate a wayward wife –

Time to give the Prince an outing! shouts Evertsz, patting the front of his breeches.

Cornelisz smirks. You see what I've had to contend with? You may have caused that one to be hanged but you left me plenty of other villains. No, I saved Lucretia from the rabble. I made her queen of Batavia's Graveyard. And as with Jahangir's consort, she was screened from the unseemliness of what went on here. The others were debauched; she alone was mine.

Your prisoner, you mean.

I'll let you in on a little secret, something bred of fear – or is it shame? The dilemma of those who enjoy less than what they imagine they're entitled to helps stiffen the persuasion of any benefit you possess. Lucretia and Judith were not slow to appreciate the advantage of our patronage, our – how do princes express it? – yes, *of our great love.* Ah, and love it was, for I sorely doted on the lady and would have drugged her disavowing senses with pliant philtres had my apothecary's mortar – with its tender inscription, *Amor Vincit Omnia* – not gone to the bottom of the sea. "Love conquers all," *he shakes his head, with a wistfulness that sports a serpent's eye.*

And you'd have me believe that Lucretia loved you?

Power is aphrodisiacal. Even Lucretia would succumb. Of the predikant's daughter, she would have made a good apothecary, concocting in herself a blend of youthful infatuation, tolerance for sibling annihilation and appetite for self-delusion. I tell you, Pelsaert, I was envious of Coenraat in possessing so accommodating a wench. While the seduction of a child was, perhaps, too easy a sport, Lucretia's initial scruple – she had a husband, as you know; ah, but that wouldn't have suggested an obstacle to you – anyway, her reluctance proved too galling a modesty. I, too, had my honour to uphold. My trusted councillors –

Henchmen and assassins!

And ignoring the outburst – my councillors were not beyond perceiving the anomaly as they each retired to their allotted women after the day's business was done. Washing the blood from their forearms. Seal for supper.

"What do you mean you haven't had her yet?" Zevanck was a little crude, I confess. "Fuck me if I wouldn't fuck her dead," I overheard him remark to Hendricxsz. Of course I wanted to woo her, to win her to a glorious sense of self reborn. Subtlety takes time. But then it didn't seem right that I, the senior surviving and un-deserting officer, should be denied the exercise of his loins. Circumstance had entrusted me with the safe-keep of your jewels. Circumstance had called on me to decide how best to palliate the sick. Circumstance had promoted me God's angel among the Devil's own. Any sign of weakness or undue challenge would be fatal to the recovery of our spirit. "I've been busy," I demurred. "The welfare of you all has been my prime concern."

"Right, then. Since you've been too taken to weary yourself with what a man ought to expire of in the fucking, I'll have a word to her."

Such a loveable lad. Do anything for you.

"Hey, bitch! I hear you resist the Captain-General..."

Oh dear, oh dear. Believe me, Pelsaert, I'm not a man to trespass where uninvited.

"Now unless you want to go the way of that serving girl Wybrecht Claasen..."

You see, some of the women were... Well, you're a choosy man. And not one to suffer the wastage of superfluity.

"You'll comply with his wishes..."

Yes, I was running a fit-for-purpose community. Survival had its price.

"You'll fuck or you'll die."

There's no doubt about it, Zevanck's little interview wrought an immediate change in the lady. *Come, my dear, why so glum?* I encouraged. *Here, take a little wine-moistened biscuit*, I dunked.

She looked at me as if from a hole, furtive yet comprehending. I tell you, Pelsaert, your cock would have shuddered at a possibility now made certain. *Such timidity doesn't become you*, I softly wagered. *Come, remember our table talk at sea, the spirited fencing of attitudes? There's much in me you might find assuring. And of course I'd prefer to converse with you at night than grouse in sleeplessness with the likes of David, loyal as he is to the persuasion of my every comfort.*

There's a lot to be said for a man who can straddle the contradictions of a situation. In that castaway kingdom I found myself able to assimilate their unruly desires, to weave from necessity a single and coherent strategy. I was not free of Zevanck's hovering shadow, yet neither was the soft dough of sanction unsummoning of my touch. I couldn't stop the killing – oh I know you don't believe me – but I *could* deflect their blood lust. And so Lucretia, you see – well, her eyes were suddenly opened. I was her best hope in a universe of unpredictable outcome – unpredictable, at least, for those too tepid to risk an element of risk itself. Even death seemed less dangerous once entertained. But just as the job of hangman may appear unsavoury to some, someone has to do it. And who more unlikely to hang than the hangman himself, eh?

Certainly that wasn't my impression of how matters played. The impatient gulls closely gathered, intrigued by the still twitching hands, the bloody dribble that was nutrient enough. But then all of that was not before the world had toppled topsy-turvy. I returned to Cornelisz and his seizure of what eluded me:

You know, once they begin to understand that martyrdom is a less than pensionable option, those formerly wedded to a certain self-esteem find themselves suddenly receptive to new and unimagined alternatives. In fear of being harmed and finding me harmless, an adjustment, shall we say, unclouded the mind of the lady to her privileged condition. I was constantly enjoined by council; our tent was the seat of government. In addition to my adjudicating voice, she couldn't help but observe the respect with which I was treated, the subservience of petitioners who scarce would raise an eye to mine. Or hers. Having asked for or expecting little, Lucretia found herself coupled to a deference that worked its charm. She might even find herself whispering in my ear, seeking to counsel against the tenor of what others said. I tell you, Pelsaert, to imagine that you might wield an influence is to submit to another's power. *"More wine, my dear?"* And if at first she held her cup out tentatively, it soon became an unquestioning reflex. I know you know the harems of the Moor. I know that Eastern sensualists keep their women closely guarded. Yet do these women not tempt themselves to liberties which push at boundaries? Do they not creep in rebellious excess to the very edge of what others would restrain in them? You think Lucretia my prisoner? What prisoner settles for so conclusive a surrender without conspiring to make the most of it? She may have been uncertain of herself at first, but as the possibilities of what was on offer impressed themselves upon her imagination, I tell you, she – and Judith, too – derived a surging satisfaction from their status as queen and lady-in-waiting of Batavia's Graveyard.

Yet not a tear was shed when you and Coenraat died.

That's what you choose to believe. But they were suddenly without their protectors, exposed to a violence of enemies the likes of whom would tear a man to pieces in their envy, who'd suffer any revolution to guarantee that all sank to their level of muck. I had weeded without prejudice to ensure that this garden, of which I was its elected caretaker, should prosper against the very test of want. And in that mission she grew to see the order of my ways. She warmed to a love of sorts.

It is my belief that the lady was prevailed upon to do whatever aided the sparing of her life.

Then why are you not wholly convinced that she isn't tainted?

I didn't know how to speak to a creature so hollowed out. They were like ghosts in the aftermath, perched with unseeing eyes as the sun emerged like a bloodspot from the sanguinary lagoon. Each dawn ushered a chill reminder that there were things which could scarcely be believed, let alone understood. Lucretia, then, was an experience I might never know.

You construed enough to imagine wrongly of the woman I loved –

Ha, the woman you wronged yourself!

Tut, Francisco. Even I was honest enough to pardon her in the peril to which she was subsequently exposed. As in how you now find yourself, my love looked around her, at the bitterness of those who considered themselves ill-handled, and realised that to shortly become my widow would garner little sympathy. Truly, how I admired her timing, her sense of the opportune! She was a perfect soul mate, her aptitudes as considered as my own. As I was being dragged to the boat – I don't know where you were; probably off puking at scenes already playing in your head – she stepped from the crowd. Not much of a crowd. And not that animated either. Rather solemn before the prospect that our doom was not so much an end as yet another incomprehensible ghastliness. Still, there was something to be gained from that travesty of justice, and Lucretia — actress that she is — raised her voice against the shackling silence to reproach me for the sins I'd visited upon her against her will. Her eyes were hard, their intelligence desperate to intuit that I, too, read her meaning. I tell you, Pelsaert — since you've never known the humid pleasure of her thighs — one couldn't help but admire one's own good taste. So delicious her accusation, so private an airing in so public an assembly, I was momentarily lost for words. Then I saw the others. First Hayes, that bastard of a killer. Then Judith, standing a little to one side, a shawl wrapped about her famished shoulders. Her father had already settled himself in the boat, grateful perhaps to assume the role of what a predikant was sometimes called upon to do — you know, administer the last rites. I tell you, I don't think vengeance even crossed his mind. His was more the discomforted pity that men such as I should exist to trouble his platitudinous conscience. No, it was the daughter who touched me with that image of what it was to become a widow, cut adrift without warning or goodbye, unable to make her peace or affirm her love, an outcast in the speculative mistrust of others. No, I would not allow this to become the garment of my own dear love. And so I turned to Lucretia and answered before all, "It is true, you are not to blame. You were in my tent twelve days before I was able to have my way with you." The gratitude in her eyes, their signal of understanding. If only to die for that. It was the only concession I ever made.

But then my binding was tugged and I stumbled, returned to that convoy of death, my companions a feeble and faltering lot for whom there was no excuse. The best of them — my boys — were already gone. The noble young Coenraat. And David, my trusted lieutenant. What remained were fawning self-apologists, vermin who'd as readily blame another for their villainies as stab or bludgeon an innocent out of sight. It made Hayes appear insufferably judicial to hear their frantic bleating. It made us all look worthy of death. I hated Hayes, and I hated them. But most of all, and for that sanctimonious avoidance with which you parried any apprehension of your own culpability, I hated you.

They were none of them friends to Cornelisz. Not when his sovereignty was ended. Not when they were each bustled before our tribunal.

For a moment I thought I might weaken, that the sickness was again upon me. But it proved no more than a palpitating confoundedness as we lolled within the eye of that storm.

Everything had been so giddying. First, the lazy smoke drifts and my initial conceit that we had found their domesticity intact. Then relief unsettled as that gesturing figure on the beach shouted, "God be praised but go back!" It was as if I had inadvertently trodden in muck. I felt a sudden stickiness of heart as I glimpsed the cannibal demeanour of that fast approaching boat, something akin to purposeful panic. "Wherefore would you come aboard armed?" I'd demanded, having hastily put the *Sardam* into rigid defence. And that caging reply, "We'll answer when we're on the ship."

It was astonishing to watch that boatload of monsters shrivel with uncertainty. They were young, all of them, and beneath the paternal stricture of our guns they became as children once more, schoolboys presently to account for their playground savagery. First one sword, then another, each was tossed into the sea as if to deny all evidence of what had been intended. And with a passivity that spoke, perhaps, of some gambling hope that in surrender their punishment might be lessened, they mounted, one after the other, the rope ladder which delivered them into the binding of their captors. Perhaps they imagined themselves prisoners of war; after all, we had blundered into this inter-island conflict, alerted by one side to the treachery of the other. And prisoners always attract a ransom. Provided their repatriation is viable. Provided their worth is bankable.

But we were a long way from anywhere. And there could be no trading where the Devil had so clearly stamped his work. Clustered on their arses around the main mast, already too sizeable a crowd for too small a craft, and knowing that there were more to come. It wasn't long before I learned how Hayes had dealt with his prisoners. *Worry not on that score, there'll be plenty more villains to replace those killed.* And in the long run that was true. There seemed no end to this battalion of iniquity.

It's curious, now, to reflect that that boatload of felons was more or less the same as that which was rowed across to Seals' Island a fortnight later.

Their piratical intent had marked them as the most dangerous. Their crimes were the most cumulative. They and Cornelisz. An unedifying spectacle. Pelgrom managing to survive for a third turn in the boat, this time cut adrift with Loos to suffer an imponderable exile upon an alien shore.

But the decision to execute or maroon anyone had, first, to lawfully emerge from evidence which seemed, quite frankly, unbelievable. And so, with our mood jolted from joy to consternation, we commenced our interrogation, the tribunal set up in the *Sardam*'s cabin. Jacob and Claas and other of the ship's officers sat to either side of me, the charts cleared from the table as the first of the prisoners – Jan Hendricxsz – was brought before us. Like the others seized, the menace of what he may have been was ridiculed by his costume of red laken and tattered braid. He appeared as if some ceremonial guardsman dragged through the campaign mire. One had to focus on the eyes and unshaven hollow of his cheeks to discern the intentliness that lurked behind such dress-up.

"State your name and rank," I began.

His voice was clear and respectful.

"A soldier?"

"Yes, Heer Commandeur. From Bremen."

Perhaps a good man to have close by in a scrape.

"And what have you to say for yourself?"

His eyes shifted from mine to other members of the council, and perceiving us to be of the one edge, his face dropped in untidy scuttle. It was clear he required prompting, some recall to that underworld which was connected with how he presently found himself, shackled in the creaking stuffiness of the *Sardam*'s cabin.

"I've been warned to entertain the worst," I said. "How is it there was such a lust for killing?"

He glanced up in survey of something I couldn't see. "Once it starts, it never stops."

"Go on," and feeling soiled in having to caress from him his confession.

"I'd been in Mansfeld's army," he tried to gesture, as if that somehow made of him a victim also. "A number of us – us as were on the ship – we saw service beyond the Rhine. It's a blunt thing, a soldier's life." Then eyeing each of us with an air of calculation, "They do that sort of thing in Germany."

I'm momentarily distracted by memories of Jacatra, the pikemen forming up and steadying before their disappearance into the battle haze, the pomp of assemblage vanished in a despoiling uproar. It was the screams of the women that alerted one to the onset of the beast. But women, too – doubtless unnaturalised yet not without courage – they also laboured in the fields of Mars, the haggard defence of Leiden a family affair of militiamen and housewives, of young and old alike, all entrapped in that tempest of time and place, the loss of soldiers ill-affordable but the destruction of hearth a catastrophe not to be countenanced. Yes, lying in the streets, the dead no longer of their nightmare, the starved survivors stubborn in their wager of outraged solidarity. It was a tale every schoolboy was obliged to heroicise: the breaking of the siege, the feast of bread and herring like a second Easter. That such poverties of scenario should lend themselves to desperate measures, it is little to be wondered that terrible things mightn't seem what they are, the bodies... how many?

Someone spoke. Hendricxsz. It was in response to a question; Jacob's, I think. There was a sharp intake of breath among my fellows. Then the figure caught in my consciousness like a leaf on the wind.

"You have murdered how many?" I gazed at him, stupefied.

He was once more staring without sight, looting his thoughts for anything that might explain what had happened. Despite a brutish muscularity, he appeared vulnerable and childlike in the seizure of his appetites. Perhaps it seemed to him an unfairness that, having survived war and wrack (not to mention the instrument of his own malice), he should find himself suddenly captured in so forward a surrender. Surely he realised he must hang for this.

The others, too, they opted for a truth of sorts as, one by one, they were hauled before our stern review. None denied what his accomplice had alleged, adding only that it was Cornelisz who had incited them to act with such murderous dispassion. The fact that little torture was applied, that their evidence was corroborating, this pointed to a dereliction of authority scarcely credible. And like schoolboys seeking exculpation, they each placed Cornelisz at the centre of their riot. I had never cared for the undermerchant; had always felt the reptilian coolness of his disdain. His Company skills were, at best, perfunctory, his ambition inscrutable and fawning. Even when summoned, his attentiveness was bereft of application. A lazy bastard, the sort who wouldn't lift a finger if he could weasel another to do his bidding. And ever dainty at table: that gentlemanly pretence, his tongue the most active muscle in an otherwise recumbent posture. To presently credit him with everything indicted was to imagine more than what his ingredient suggested. Yet it confirmed, too, his dangerous possibility, the misuse of an intellect concealed in indolence. The lazy man had indeed enlisted others to do his dirty work, unsuited as he was to performing tasks that might ruffle his collar or abrade his delicate fingers. His violent touch was conveyed through the hands of others, hands which, a fortnight later, were gathered like so much shark bait at the foot of the gallows. Indeed, and for all his satanic instruction, such was Cornelisz's squeamishness that I don't think he'd ever witnessed as much blood as attended his own execution.

"Bring him to me," I'd said, Hayes promptly turning on the heel to retrieve, from that territory he had made his own, his captive and the accompanying enigma as to how and why such things had occurred. Fallen in fortune as he visibly was, Cornelisz was alert as any sailor to the shifting breeze. He trimmed what he was with a calculating intelligence that sought inclusion in our government, flatly denying he'd had any part in the crimes committed. Everyone – even an undermerchant – had been pressed to accord with the wishes of the most menacing scoundrels. The oath they'd signed was forced. Which was perhaps true for the many – and in this regard I recognised Salomon's signature with unsettling dismay. But the oath – and it transpired there was more than one of these as the mutineers reconciled themselves in deepening alarm to new watersheds of atrocity – yes, the oath bonded them to the direction of their Captain-General. So, Jeronimus, how could you be compelled through fear for your life to *initiate* the very terror that was hitherto unknown? How could one be the architect of disaster yet deny all knowledge when its very plan was dedicated to your genius?

"Van Huyssen fancied himself a great man," he said. "It was he who played the lord." And with a smile of deflective insight, "I think his noble blood ran a little thin, his inferiority too urgent to countermand itself."

"You allege it was he who ruled?"

"Heer Uppermerchant, there were several. The spirit of the beast inhabited these dangerous youths."

"And you?"

"I was a fettered observer. Like the predikant."

"You lie. You're sinuously threaded throughout these horrors."

"My honour and my loyalty, these are sorely wronged by those who would now conceal themselves from what was conspired. It was the skipper who thought to seize *Batavia*, Zevanck who proposed to capture whatever came to rescue us. Besides," and staring at me with an accusatory eye, "I never thought to see you again. What with Jacobsz commandeering the longboat, I imagined you tossed into the sea, your own witness swallowed beneath the waves."

"And how would you know that the skipper had designs upon my life if you were not privy to the plot?"

Again that rapid calculation behind a vacancy of eye before blinking to declare, "Those who literally missed the boat were forthcoming in their anger. There was little need of secrecy in the entrapped emptiness that confronted all. What they would have had aboard the ship they now visited upon the island."

"And yet there was another island – Hayes's. You never thought of casting yourself as a refugee in that direction?"

He snorts laughter, the kind that embarrasses one's self-belief. "Unlike you, Heer Pelsaert, I had no boat in which to make good my escape."

It seemed he had an answer to everything. Perhaps he'd long meditated on what he'd report during his captivity under Wiebbe. Perhaps the humiliation of so ineffectual an outcome had given him pause to refine his distance. And so, as presented – and contrary to the incrimination of his accomplices – he tried to talk himself clean, his glib tongue telling the most palpable lies, and making out that he'd not had a hand in any of it.

I slept little that night in the wonder of it all, no longer so much shocked and disbelieving as troubled by what appeared to have retreated from my presence. I was unable to touch the world I had known, its custom torn from my grasp with a violence so sudden that it was unaccompanied by any cry of pain. Indeed, it was with scrambling curiosity that I surveyed the injury, this amputating withdrawal of a former certainty, the effect of which would doubtless throb its displeasure before long. It wasn't merely a question of right or wrong. Rather, a tremor had so disturbed the earth's solidity that I no longer trusted matters to reside in stone instead of glass. All was tentative and fragile, all was bathed in a colour dim and distant. I had drawn to an end of self which had ever been the cipher of everything supposed, and the instinct to be sensibly appalled found itself outweighed by something more personal and sinister. Yes, in the banality of what was possible, I found myself presently disconnected from righteous outrage by this feeling that I was altogether missing from the fancies of that atmosphere, that like fishes out of water I was bereft of the means to breathe belief or comprehension.

The light of day came as sweet relief. With sword and musket we descended on Batavia's Graveyard, capital of the unimaginable, only to find Loos and Mattys Beer and the last half dozen already surrendered in sullen recognition of a cause irretrievably lost. The poverty of their number – their poverty of stature and wellbeing – again disturbed my expectation of what we should find ourselves up against. There was no Satanic legion, no darkened host cornered by the light of God's army. They were but few and grubby and therein did my understanding fail me – was left begging, perhaps, for too furnished an explanation. What struck me most about that reunion was how the wicked and the fair did not attempt to segregate. Just as there had been nowhere to run to during the height of the mutiny, so now, in its exhaustion, was there nothing for it but this mute and toppled immovability. The innocent – if any truly were – must have looked on us with an awakening sense of confusion, our voices the music of some remote and nursery time. Lucretia – I hardly recognised her – emerged from a tent I soon discovered had been Wouter Loos'. A spoil of war. Her expression said it all. We had come too late. The news I bore of her deceased husband, it withered on my lips. This was not the moment to speak of ordinary bereavement.

With the fight-less villains apprehended and the rescued too maimed of spirit to stir from the ashes, I sought immediacy in the recovery of what was looted, the casket of jewels – including Constantine's cameo – a welcome find that brooked no criticism. And as it was a calm day and I found the atmosphere of this soiled camp too degrading, I set out to visit the wreck, its bulk greatly diminished since last I saw it but remnant enough to promise some binding of riches lost. As we rowed atop that subaqueous ruin, my sentiment for the loss of everything swelled in my throat like a sob. So beautiful a ship now shattered, the sea rising and falling in drowning possession.

"There! Commandeur, do you see?"

At first I could see nothing but the memory of what had once pigeonholed our lives: the vanished familiarity of my quarters, the minutely wrought grandeur of the Great Cabin. And also the nooks and places I might never have known except that their cavities were now asunder; yes, the lower decks upon which had slept two hundred men, and those narrow companionways in whose darkness conspiracy had scurried. It was the story of what had been — or what might have been had we passed that reef unwitting and things remained unruptured — that consumed my sight until summoned once more to look. And there it was: first one, then another. The money chests in varnished ripple, strewn amidst the fragment confusion of planking and distorted cannon. The expression on the faces of my companions heartened me.

"All is not lost," I nodded, and imagining the season, with its clammy sun, to have rotated in our favour. "If the weather continues to abate, we may recover more than first thought."

But all *was* as good as lost. There was an irreducible boundary that couldn't be recrossed. If the material world — the Company world — might proffer its consolations, those fruits, even in their damaged reclamation, were not enough to assuage a darkening sobriety which little concerned itself with the accounting habits of public life. The privacy of my soul grew more haunted as, returning daily from the wreck, there was yet another night to be negotiated, another interrogation to be endured.

At first, and like the salvage itself, the challenge was appreciable but not without its measured process. And though our horror was great, we were mostly spared the employ of more exemplary forms of extraction. 'Twas truly marvellous to witness each villain follow his fellow in freely confessing to his crimes. What was as chilling as their murders, and invoked in me a suspicion that all was not finished, was their indifference to any human feeling or remorse. Only one in the initial batch seized had cried out that he'd been very willing to murder, that he didn't know how he'd strayed so far from God. All of them, they gave no reason for their actions. Except, after skulking hesitation in which each failed to adequately explain himself, that they were in thrall of the undermerchant.

It was time to interrogate him closely.

Already I'd had those prisoners who were aboard the jacht removed to the grit and tatter of their former kingdom. I couldn't bear to sleep on Batavia's Graveyard, to be chastened by its ghosts or contaminated by its shackled miscreants. The nightly rocking of the *Sardam* – my small but painted berth – soothed me with its sanctuary. Likewise, the ship's council conducted its business ashore but returned each evening to the buoyant hygiene of our vessel. In that vast expanse it was the only place we quarantined, the only space we jealously protected.

In what had been Jeronimus's tent, two barrels were set upright with planks laid athwart to serve as our judicial bench. Nearby stood a third barrel, filled with water, and, beside it, a crate and canvas collar. Such measures hadn't been necessary until now, but when it came to Cornelisz, his indignant denial of any leadership or involvement was so contrary to the evidence gathered that there was little choice but to put him to the torture. Fear ignited in his eyes as the collar was fastened, his head pushing hard against its inescapable tank. With his arms already tied, his bucking was further constrained by men who secured him to the crate.

"You leave me no choice when your lies are so palpable." And I nodded them begin.

The ladle was carefully swivelled so as to waste nothing, the water plastering his hair to his face. I beheld the very likeness of baptism and, before our investigations were over, would be confirmed in my suspicion that Jeronimus belonged to some heretical sect when, once condemned, he begged bathing in the comfort of the Lord so that he might die in repentance and peace. Trial by water, it was our penance and our providence. Surely Noah's flood was what called us to account. Surely the raising of the Fatherland was proof of our reclamation. And before returning to the prisoner, I recalled mention of that which I'd never seen but had wondered of its meaning. Yes, dated to the time of my birth, the drowning cell at Amsterdam's House of Corrections, its inmates working its pumps for salvation. I suppose that to fail in one's amendment was to justly perish. Yet there is an irony in the timing of any punishment, an anachrony which fails to preclude disaster even when conditions may have been favourable to the abortion of all misdeed. There was no doubting Cornelisz's evil incivility. There was not a man among us who, watching him squirm and wriggle from the truth, didn't think he deserved to have his head pushed under as had been the fate of so many at his direction. Yet survive he had when Divine intervention might have foreclosed on the crimes to come. Yes, here we were, testing his stamina when, right from the beginning, Fate cruelly skipped the opportunity. Coward that he was, Jeronimus had simply floated, undetected, past the snores of Death, the last man to be washed ashore alive. He had passed the test of water once; I was determined he not so easily cheat the examiner a second time.

"I tell you it wasn't me!" he spat, his head twisting on a stretch of neck as the ladled pool rose to his lips. Then there were no words, only a sozzling indignation, a sputter of frantic protest.

And if a man be untainted?

I looked away, certain of Cornelisz's guilt yet uncomfortable with the efficacy of our method. While there were those already spared the rigour, those whose confessions had precluded the necessity, might others less talkative strive in silence or denial to elude the confirmation we sought? Returning to Cornelisz's ordeal with just revulsion, I suddenly queried what expiry might prove if truth were always stalwart. Drinking one's innocence, drowning in immaculacy.

"Enough!"

The puddle which obstructed speech was lowered. Cornelisz coughed and rasped. I looked at him without seeing who he was. Just the body of a man, the bellows of his life pushed to its limit... They'd employed water at Ambon. On the English. On those who confessed. On misdemeanours I've since had pause to question in these hours of sleeplessness, knowing that failure to live with pain and survive its bite is not to live at all. The yielding of a solitary admission at that distant place had been enough to train an axe upon the necks of everyone. Coen even charged the English for the cloth employed to wrap their shattered bodies. We had smiled with wary satisfaction upon the hearing of it, comforted to know that we were feared – and most of us privately relieved that we'd had no hand in it. And now here I was in my own judicial nightmare.

"Jeronimus Cornelisz, do you still deny the outrages in which others allege you were their captain?"

"I've done nothing but suffer that injustice. They're liars, liars all!"

"Again," I nodded to the torturer.

And again that bonded thrashing, the splutter and gurgle. Then catching his breath, the dignity of having once been potent now bedraggled in the humiliation of that canvas bib.

"Their confessions were freely given," I said. "Their truth already condemns them. Yet you say they lie?"

"Why don't you put them to the torture?" and snarling. "See if their truth is all you trumpet it to be."

"And why would they deceive us?"

"To spare themselves greater infamy for the crimes they alone committed!"

"And you had no hand in this?"

"My hands were as tied as they now are," he mocked me back.

"Again," I nodded to the figure who stood behind him. And again that spluttering protest. Busily did he negotiate his fate, drinking down as much as his distended stomach could consume. Whether out of friendless panic or the guzzled bloating of his body, Jeronimus was soon pissing himself.

"Have you anything to tell?" I asked when he recovered a little.

"Only – only that you have the wrong man."

"Can there be a right man? A leader?"

"There were no leaders." And still snatching at his breath. "Only men who, once orphaned, played like wolves."

"Yet you enrobed yourself in apparent government."

"I sought only to moderate their ungovernable passions."

And ignoring so glib a statement, I added, "'Tis said you advocated seizing the jacht."

And he laughed with incredulous contempt. "And how, pray tell, might I have affected to capture the jacht when that brute, Hayes, had me trussed and shitholed? God, I hate the injustice of what you would believe of me. I loathe the very debacle of what others have made of my life!"

"What, then, would you have had?"

My fellow councillors prop themselves in attentiveness, the air rank with the sweat of canvas. The tent drums and slaps in the breeze, and conversations outside are patchy on the ear. It seems everything is fragment, the very fluid of this reluctant story, though terrible, now dried for the day like those gullies on the continent which speak through silence of some vanished time.

⌐o

How would I have had it? For a start, I would have had my efforts crowned with gravity and gratitude. But then it has always been my lot to suffer afflictions of circumstance, to find myself robbed, my destiny made destitute. I had a wife, you know. And a babe.

His smile is wistful.

Belijtgen – my life, before all of this – ah, well... The pregnancy was difficult. It seems I was snared in misadventure from the very beginning. Do you know what that's like, Heer Pelsaert? I can see you're aggrieved but, believe me, some lives are more thwarted than others. There was this bitch of a wet nurse – indeed, this witch in search of a purse. I don't know how she managed it but she poxed the boy. My infant son, *he grimaces.*

Her skill was such, her art so concealed, that I would gladly have employed her at another time. A time, by then, precluded from idle speculation by so dark a treachery. Hmph, you imagine me a monster but I couldn't even poison that infant whom Deschamps later dispatched. It wasn't in me, you see. It wasn't in me to procure the massacre of innocence.

Something now autumnal, his glass grown opaque.

My wife never fully recovered from her confinement. My son not at all. They were the most solemn hours of my life as I sat in a kind of noiselessness that disowned me. Despite the disconsolation we shared, I was of small comfort to Belijtgen. It was as if she had awoken to the misplacement of her love, that she no longer recognised, in me, her bulwark against foul outrage. For that deranged bitch, you see, was proclaiming to anyone of a mind to listen that our nest was polluted, that my darling was an ulcerated whore and that my loins wriggled with vermin. People grew reluctant to salute me in the street for fear of catching something – first, some physical contagion; soon enough, a moral one. The shop bell ceased to ring. The stuffed crocodile above the door no longer advertised hope to those whose limbs and intestinals ailed. Instead, it winked a more insidious treachery. My pestle and my mortar, the nostrum that in remedy an apothecary's love might conquer all, now sat idle and unfragrant.

It had been trial enough to make of myself what Haarlem had seen fit to reward. I was not of privileged birth – no. Not like those who sailed with discontented coronets, boys determined to avenge themselves for having been sired a prince when they each imagined themselves a king. They keened their swords with an indolence bred of acrimony. And I? I, by contrast, was too busy learning Latin and Greek to concern myself I wasn't born of title. In what I acquired by way of knowledge I felt myself more genuinely a gentleman. After all, they each bowed to me, those bastard boys and junior sons denied inheritance. Even you, Francisco. Yes, even you. I felt a faint contempt – a lilt of the heart, even – for the posturing which so cloaked your uncertainty. Your anxious envy amplified my ease of mind, grew me calm and calculating in what I might achieve as you, by contrast, bewailed the enormity of what you stood to lose. To have little is to risk nothing. And where Hell does not exist –

Who told you it doesn't?

Why, Heer Pelsaert, *and smirking at the interruption,* it rather surprises me to see you pounce on such shadow play. I know for a fact that you believe in hell on earth, but this? *And twirling a finger in the dark.*

Torrentius. Now there was a man to spike the guns of superstition; a pigeon, of sorts, to crap on cowering belief. He came into the shop a couple of times. The pastes and spirits so beloved of painters – even your precious indigo! – it was all there for the purchase. His wit was as nimble as my hunger for distraction. And as we got to know one another better, so did I become acquainted with his circle. They called it a fencing club, but it was more in wit than with rapiers we sported. There were others; not just painters and their patrons but men of indistinct profession and loud ideas. At night his salon shone with a chandeliered brilliance, its splintery light as variable as the certainty of what was spoken. I tell you, Pelsaert, the world became a less wicked place. Yes, the logic in living seemed irrefutable. To have and to hold.

For the first time, I see him happy.

And so I held that fabled jewel, the cameo of Constantine. It delighted the others, its talismanic magic a surety of better things to come. The light in the tent was giddying, the smoke of blubber no less fragrant of dreaming than the fume which spiralled from the pipes at Torrentius's gatherings. And if a gentleman be at liberty to toast both Christ and the Prince of Darkness, if his talent elicit admiration and his Epicurean manner the indulgence of those less primed to outrage, why not then a brother of his inclination? I know you judge me a disciple of his libertine ways, that my evil, as you and others so contend, was the product of his teaching. But that is to deny me the attribute of having given others hope, of implanting within their meagre expectation an ambition for so much more. They loved me, my bastard boys – those denied and without the script to make more of their lives than what the Company might entitle. I clothed them with permission, I released in them a spring that allowed the mind to soar in excess of what was dubiously ordained. Once inured to the habit of killing, I smoothed away all doubt with the truth that there was nothing to curtail such freedom, that necessity was indeed its own imperative. The consciences of my boys grew easy as, with each washing of blood, there reverberated nothing to check them or condemn. Their only lord was my sanction, and I had long been given sovereignty to determine, in the absence of God, what was best to redress the insults which had befallen me.

His pride is all too briefly firesome and bright. A furrowing shadow descends to settle on his thoughts.

The divine has always been inopportune, *he sniffs*, its intervention as wrecking as the moment *Batavia*'s splintering destroyed your dreams. Yes God, if he exists, is a skulking bully, a furtive spoiler. If I were bound to give Him semblance I would say He dons the mask of Hayes, just as I appear the visage of His retribution upon your vanity. But let's not blame anyone for a significance which does not exist. Torrentius was playful when he spoke the truth: that there is no Hell to constrain us, no fiery eternity beyond the grave. He meant us not to play our desires false or modest, not to shy as maidens from what we would possess as men.

And yet you said to me that all that you did had been put into your heart by God. You yourself summoned God as your witness.

If God is omnipotent, I cannot have acted without His collusion. If He doesn't exist, you cannot invoke Him to judge me. But consider this: if He *does* exist, then He is *not* the creature you so righteously imagine.

You mock me in what you say to get away with such abhorrence.

I merely elucidate the truth. All men are free to become more than what most allow themselves. I would have had myself swell to fulfil what opportunity presented –

That ambition was to go a-pirating after killing those who didn't fit your purpose!

Instead of which *you* would have my potency choked off at the end of a rope.

God or no God, you deserved to die.

You don't get it, do you? There *are* no just deserts. The circumstance, so galling to me, merely allowed you to return at a moment conducive to the sway of others. Chance deflected you to Hayes and allowed him to whisper in your ear before my boys were able to capture the *Sardam*.

So you freely confess it after all.

Yes, yes – I know I told you I had no intention of seizing the jacht. And in many ways that island kingdom was the high tide of my happiness. Nothing ran counter to my inclination; in the end, not even Lucretia. But you, of all people, know that an outsider can rob you of your destiny. It was only a question of time before rescue arrived, and of what comfort might that be? Hayes didn't believe in me – in fact, he'd do anything to affirm that shuffle in which you all bowed and scraped to morals rarely rewarded. He would have me in chains then scamper around you like a puppy, excited at the prospect of being tossed a bone for having kept the world so unexceptional. Yes, that man had me imprisoned long before he actually had me in hand. He was as wretched to the experiment of what I may have become as that bitch of a wet nurse, both of them hysterics who would raise the rabble against all that was mine. So I had little choice but to plan on seizing the jacht. A bit like you, I was trying to make the best of an unravelling situation.

Ha, you say one thing then scurry aside in cowardly contradiction.

I contradict nothing but your presumption to know everything.

I scarcely know why you behaved so contrary to human decency.

It's my turn to be surprised that so senior and experienced a Company official should imagine humanity so constrained by decency. Look around you! Look at what has taken place, here, in the East. The great Coen himself was not above civilian slaughter. Yes, my friend, look at what you've turned a blind eye to.

But murder for the sheer pleasure of it?

I took no pleasure in that ungovernable excrescence. One merely rides the storm. One breathes as best one can in an atmosphere of such ruthlessness. Believe me – and despite the fact that you would have me killed – I was a survivor. I outgrew the garment of my youth to become a businessman and a husband, and when that advantage was destroyed by cruel event, I strove for renaissance in the promise of the Company. Only, *and he regards me with an expression of such cynicism*, its promise possessed all the morality of a bawdy house, its manner all the swagger and innate danger of a mercenary.

I am momentarily at a loss for reply. Appalled though I am, yet do I find myself fascinated by the unholy lustre of this evil that would debate me. I fear being tainted, of understanding the motive which impelled him, yet I've little choice but to lift the covers in search of that which might reassuringly divide us.

If you must know, *he continues, aware that I attend him closely*, it was Jacobsz who planned to seize the ship. I had observed you both throughout the voyage, the wrangling jealousy bred of boredom. I could see that you were weak, not just in constitution but in your inability to match the skipper's temperament. Jacobsz was grumbly and impetuous – and many a time I counselled him to master his passions – but you were limpid. To converse with you was to garner the impression you were always checking to see whether one's words hadn't spittled on your sleeve. I was the salve between the two of you; a shipboard diplomat. But war was brewing. Your manner was too precise and withholding for so long a quarantine, especially as the skipper laboured whilst you, at table, reminded him of his manners. You should have gotten along, you two – the ship's master and its supercargo. You ought to have shared some respect, your complementary authorities. Instead, you permitted the skipper to rankle and imagine himself unfriended where preening merchants were concerned.

I, too, was a merchant. But a man, first. A man who could sympathise with another's thirst for friendship. And so I grew friendly towards him. Though clearly roughened around the edges, he was easy to talk to. After all, there was little dalliance in your conversation, scarcely anything to suggest you were worthy of intimacy. Of Ariaen, though, his fervours were as bold and as rampant as the feline figurehead of our ship. The skipper's uniform was too stretched a garment for so mercurial a disposition. His tone could be decidedly unofficial.

He smiles sadly – perhaps with painful irony – for the beginnings of the end.

I'd chided him and asked what he intended with that woman. *He looks up at me.* Strange, is it not, to think that even then I considered myself her protector. Anyway, Ariaen answered that because she was fair, he was desirous of tempting her to his will.

"And how would you manage that?" I'd tried to make light.

"With gold or by other means."

And later, after we'd departed the Cape – yes, after you'd affronted his dignity with that public dressing down and thoughts of Lucretia were already an embarrassment to him – I chided Ariaen for his sulks which were so self-pitying.

"Such a sow's cunt," he'd rumbled, referring to you. "President of a fleet he can't keep together, Commandeur of a ship he can't sail!"

And I'd have to admit there was justice in the complaint, especially as you'd taken to your bunk, your command – whatever that entailed – void of any summons.

"I tell you, Cornelisz," and fisting the taffrail, the scroll of ocean fretfully abandoned to the imminence of another night, "I can't stomach the fuck much longer. I have a mind to make myself master of this ship."

"And how would you manage that?"

These visitations, these snatches of interrogation, I can scarce tell whether they be real or the embellishment of a fevered imagining. There are things told me I've found difficult to credit.

Now sit nicely. 'Tis but a joke.

And Pelgrom bawling at a distance for being ordered to stand down, Mattys Beer snatching up the blade whose edge has been keened on coral.

The boy, seated and blindfolded, is all too aware of what a lark might amount to in this place and, because of that, all the more afraid to disobey, straining his ears to apprehend what's afoot and hearing only a teeter above the distant surf.

I am reminded of something Meyer said of soldiering – at least I think it was him, such are the uncertainties that so populate my mind. For those wounded and abandoned in retreat, there is an interval, a silence in which the clamour of familiarity fades and something sinister arrives. The authority of that moment is without justice. Only power presides. As it was with Cornelisz, so it was with Coen as he presided over the fate of young Cortenhoeff. The awful waiting, the pregnant hush. Imagining to see, something heaving on a breath...

Shit – look out!

Christ, I don't want it on me!

The masking laughter and assurances sought in a complicity of glances; then turning from the divided body, the realisation that what they've done is quite public, those still left (but by no means spared) sorely numbed in their witness. There's no pretending that they, the perpetrators, can be other than what their deeds proclaim. There is no magistracy, no decency of appeal to doubt. All is consumed in the violence of this evil banditry.

And still, for the coward that he was, it is nigh impossible to understand the loyalty he stirred. His treachery was so manicured, the apery of his followers so crude. It's a wonder he wasn't eaten by them for the weakliness that was there for anyone to see. Perhaps he merely afforded even the dimmest amongst them a mantle of permission. *We took our orders from the undermerchant,* wasn't that their constant refrain? If it had been the skipper, I might almost have understood the seduction of his cajoling authority. After all, it was Jacobsz I'd fingered as the one intemperate and powerful enough to seize the ship, a brute of violent passions. Hadn't I seen him cuff and bludgeon insubordination throughout the voyage? But Cornelisz?

Yes, perhaps it was the air of legality he remitted to what others desired themselves believe. After all, they swore an oath of brotherly love and bondage — not once but twice — to the community of his thoughts. It was as if a father had licensed his sons to acquit themselves in ways no mother could condone. *Now boys, it'll just be our little secret...*

Yet among the many who signed, there were those who never loved him, those whom fear betrayed into despoiling their souls. Salomon. Even Gijsbert. How did so shirking a villain as Cornelisz manage to shrink the entire manhood of Batavia's Graveyard?

Breathing hard; wondering... *Unless he merely crested the peak of a more universal villainy...*

Could it be that virtue is as exceptional as evil and that most men lead lives of placid uncalamity, collared only to decide upon what is righteous in the splintering of what is usual?

"Come, Pelsaert. It's time for us to go."

I look up. "Your Majesty?"

"The flame leaf of the chinar – that efflorescence which so stirred in me dreams of vigour – has begun to brittle. They say snow is falling beyond the valley."

"But I have little more than arrived. I'm still searching for a place to stay."

And not listening to me: "I weary of he who is uninvited, the one who shadows and curtails my every pleasure."

"It is the lack of someone, perhaps, that keeps me restless."

"Methinks 'tis more your sickly metaphysic. Come, the phantom is upon us."

"Phantom?"

"Neither of us is long for this world."

"You mean Death?"

His tongue, unseen, plies the enclosure of his pursed lips. His expression is thoughtful. "The servant of that great summons, eh? The herald of our grave reunion."

"But a reunion with whom?" I probe, wanting to gauge whether his conceit is in the fashion of my own.

"Those who have crossed the winter pass before us." And he's already on the trail and ahead of me, saddled on a donkey rather than a stallion, seated like the humbled son he couldn't love. "Those lost to us."

I sense a crowded absence rather than any, in particular, by face. It's as if, still unawares, I'm becoming the last to arrive at my own destiny. Most of the sand has passed through the glass, yet I am not of those grains. "Wait!" I shout as he begins the journey south, retracing steps which will elicit nothing new. "What about Antonio?" and glancing in the opposite direction, beyond the citadel and lake to where the mountains hoard themselves in terrains I will never know. I can scarce bear the bitterness that comes of having no business here. My journey to the valley of the king has proven no more than a shadowing of his presence. I know my excuse was to follow where he went, to tail whatever fortune might occasion, but to turn back now is to inescape this leash I've made of duty, this servitude that binds desire. I am deadly keen to learn what lies beyond the horizon, to witness what has become of another's life — and therefore this strand of my own.

"Do not unduly concern yourself," summons the emperor. "Your priest will attend you, for we are never without Jesuits. They're like flies in their insistence, impervious to how close they come to goading my hand. Believe me, that frocked acquaintance of yours, should he attempt to advise too closely whomever is the petty lord of his uncovering, shall find himself swiftly hated by those whose influence he seeks to usurp. There are rebels enough who would seize a crown without needing to create mischief among those who would honour themselves in defending it. And so we must depart, I to deal with a confrontation I thought never to mar my autumn, you to prepare for the trial which, even now, nourishes itself in blind abeyance of the circum-stances in which you will one day meet."

"Cornelisz, you mean?" And exerting myself to catch him up.

"If you must settle on him to deputise for everything else." His brow furrows. "For me it's Mahabat. It's 'The Wretch'. It's the absence of those I trusted to be always there and true." Then looking at me with a harshness that springs from some honesty of disgust, "I am too old for this."

"Mahabat seizes but an opportunity. His rule will be brief and sputtering."

"It is undignified."

"What, to be surrounded in your own camp? Come," I try to soothe, "none expect to be surprised by a burglar."

"Yet I loved him like a brother, showered him with responsibilities —"

"Then listened to the evil of those you loved and trusted more."

He glares at me. "You're a harsh critic, Pelsaert."

"I scarce know what to make of the circle with which I was entrusted."

"Are we really — any of us — the innocents we imagine ourselves to be?"

"How do you sleep at night?"

"Opium helps. My dreams return to Kashmir, and all is as it was the day I first arrived. Then I awake, dawn soon follows, and I'm expected to reveal myself to a populace which feeds off that certainty. And you?"

"The habit of sleep, you mean? I don't. Leastwise I find no rest, no dreamy consolation of paradise unfettered. Yet in everything that passes through my mind, such constituencies cannot reside in wakefulness alone. These night sweats of unsummoned visitation are too frightful and unnerving to concede entirely that they may be factual. My darkness is crowded with the aloneness of being summoned to account. And I cannot account for much of it. Those who would partner me in sleep are the very ones I fear may partner me in death. I'm unnerved, scooped from within by the prospect of remaining trapped in this rehearsal of nightmarish association."

"You snare yourself in the haunting of your fears."

By now his troops are in clanking counter-march, the warming plains to the south in need of rebel weeding.

"Come, Pelsaert," his voice thins, "let's get this business over with."

The rising dust mingles, in effect, with Coen's firing of Jacatra and Mahabat's transgressive cavalry. The moment is obscured in the condition of its making: the sea-spray high in its pre-dawn masking of disaster; the waterless sun griddling at not so great a distance those blacks who, in conceit of imagined perils and impervious to our summons of despair, flee beyond our reach.

"Come back!" I shout.

The imperial camp was some time gone from Srinagar before I, too, made up my mind to leave. The quiet, at first, had seduced me; the settling calm of a place returning to its more mundane existence. Was Kashmir really thus, I wondered, a commonness invaded seasonally and compelled to play the whore, to pander to the court and then, its springtime blush exhausted, find itself abandoned? In the resumption of what was small and permanent, there now seemed little urgency to rise in the morning. I was curious (confident I could catch up with the emperor's train) to explore one final time the streets and timbered alleys so recently obscured by crowds. Where all before had been pollens and the smell of stewing meats, the now cooler mornings were possessed of a haze that was slow to burn off in the sunshine. Where puddles overnight collected, they little dried, and of the inhabitants who went about their business, they likewise seemed the residual of something ingloriously permanent and marsh-like.

This was not without its charm. Autumn transformed the valley into colours reminiscent of my youth, this seeming of Europe quite at odds with India's wet and dry or the verdant perpetuity of coastlines that trimmed our seaborne highways. In the rarefied stillness, the lake inverted the surrounding mountains within a girdle of topaz efflorescence.

Slow to draw myself away from the relic of this season fast turning, I visited the now loosely guarded terraces of the Shalimar Bagh, my intrusion as exotic as many of the plants which had been collected to gratify His Majesty's delight. The sweepers who raked the fallen leaves into mattress heaps barely acknowledged my passing. So this was where the most frivolous of pleasures had been pursued, I thought; here was where the intrigue and torch-lit splendour of that great privacy had displayed itself for the world to see. Except that I wasn't of that world. Below the slopes of that populous resort, I remained as one with the invisible crowd. I assume Wasim and his ilk strolled what was cordoned in permission, their lowered voices and wary eyes little concerned with the gardener's artifice. And thinking of him now and the season passed, I wonder whether he considered his wife with any empathy for what the Shalimar and its vistas may have stirred in her bosom.

I never learned of where he and his companions lodged. I only know, for certain, that he glimpsed me on one occasion. I'd been in the custom, as usual, of following as others did. Many were the skiffs – sikharas as the Kashmiri style them – which plied the lake, conveying all manner of person and chattel. Goods-laden families conducted a gratifying commerce along nearby waterways where things were procurable long after Srinagar's vendors had been stripped of all consumables by the emperor's host. Indeed, it seemed as if the most vulnerable of inhabitants had retired to the lake's backwaters, there to preserve a domesticity at risk of being trampled by Jahangir's horde. Nonetheless the world sought them out, the surface of the water daily crawling with paddled craft that alternately disappeared into or emerged from small canals. I, too, followed in their wake – a tourist of this mountain-ringed Amsterdam or Venice – to uncover discrete communities of various kind and commerce.

Along the most sequestered of reaches, in houses scarcely worthy of the title and more like shelters erected for the summer only, it was pointed out by my cheerful boatman that I might procure, there, any pleasure I desired.

And so it was, one evening, that Wasim and I found ourselves insufficiently mantled by darkness, our common path too narrowly squeezed to allow either to slip past unrecognised. Not a word was spoken, and I realise now that I cannot occasion the last time we ever freely conversed. The revelation of that instant among women who, come to think of it, were little more than children, construed a barrier which never quite established or redressed the meaning of our trespass.

Knowing it was time to settle my affairs, that the evacuation of Srinagar had made things more transparent, I ventured one last time upon the lake with a purse intended for the girl who had served me without complaint. The citizens of the valley had made me tolerably welcome, and I felt notionally inclined to a farewelling courtesy. But as my sikhara neared the spot where men nightly alighted, all was shuttered with a silence that spoke of desertion, the dwelling of such humid press little more than an embarrassed theatre prop.

"No. Go back. Take me away," I bade the paddle wallah.

As we eased into the wider expanse of morning, the sun glancing off the surface of the lake, I was bemused to hear a cracking as if of glass which had been carefully wrapped. To my surprise I saw that the water was beginning to ice, that crystals were forming like the flare-spangled monstrances so favoured by papists. It was true, my boatman was cloaked against a chill I'd been slow to feel. He laughed and slapped the skinning crust with his oar. As we tied up at the town landing, I realised Salomon had been waiting all along, shivering with an impatience too polite to announce itself. His forlorn appearance reminded me of my responsibility. Reminded me, in fact, that I'd largely overlooked his existence in recent weeks. It was time to go.

Our small party made rapid progress. The passes were still short of being wintered over and our march, unencumbered as it was of the thousands who had departed some weeks earlier, seemed to abridge the dimension of that former hardship. Even Salomon found the going easier than dreaded, and we fell to musing about what may have happened to our former travelling companions, Randasingh and Fakkad Khan.

It was also highly speculative as to what awaited us at home – and yes, that is how I imagined Agra at that moment – having absented ourselves from the factory these several months. I was not to appreciate, then, how complicated my life would become, how queried my every move. Within Saturn's foreclosing horology, the ageing emperor's circle was manoeuvring to make the most of a life without him, causing old favourites to fall and raking instability into, as yet, an unignited pyre. Asmat still awaited my touch and her catastrophe, and from some far-off foothold of ambition, Vapoer (as yet unmet) was snaking in my direction to usurp me.

The *Batavia* incident – this thing, the story of which appears destined to become my entombing eulogy – seems such a jack-in-the-box, an event wholly unexpected and, therefore, unrelated to the general campaign of my existence. Off to so promising a start, I never thought to be brought unfairly low by an accident. After all, India had wreaked enough by way of compromises, its highs and lows the making and unmaking of me in equal parts. The mortification of Asmat's death notwithstanding, I could even appreciate the Company's new-broom gamble in appointing Vapoer in my place, and had retorted by stealing my own march against those who hoped my acquiescence would confirm their actions. But in all the doings and cover-ups I'd been involved with, it was, in Jeronimus Cornelisz, a strange and terrible angel that the Lord visited upon me in summary punishment of my sins.

⟳

"Tuan?"

I open my eyes.

"Tuan, they are waiting."

I must have been sleeping after all.

"It is time." Her voice is low, her tone tentative yet levering.

My lips are like an infant's groping, my tongue a helpless partner in the mastication of sound. "What?" I struggle. And struggling, too, to see beyond her. For a moment I confuse her with the nameless girl of that shanty by the lake.

"Ssh," and now cradling my head.

I'm inhabited by the disagreeable sensation of knowing I can never repay her for the kindness she exhibits. I know she doesn't like me. I know she does it for the credit of her soul, and because servitude is her privilege. I know she knows that I will soon be dead.

"You need to be strong," she whispers, and looking towards the window which, for once, is not shuttered.

"I am worn out," I gurgle. *My consciousness is like the membrane of a squalid eye, my bones incarcerated in a jelly of gore.* And seizing on a breath, "There isn't the strength."

"They are waiting, Tuan."

"Who?"

Again she looks away, her eel-dark hair no longer that cable of insolence, her forbearing less contemptuous. There is something almost solicitous about her detachment, a sobriety akin to that of a gaoler who relinquishes a condemned man from his custody into the circus glare of those final minutes.

Without, I fancy, having risen from my bed, I find myself in a darkened passage, the companionway where Salomon warns me, with whispered urgency, of a congealing evil I can scarcely credit.

"There will be more to it, mark me, than the rape of a single woman," he hisses, a fleck of spittle alighting on my sleeve.

"But Jacobsz, surely, is the engine of this disquiet?"

"We have him dungeoned," sings the reply in a voice not at all Deschamps'. It is Maartens, the sick-visitor. He straightens, pushing away from a ladder which leads I know not where, his eyes not at all timid. He ushers me forward. Hartanti likewise attends, but in whose service it is, as ever, difficult to gauge.

A gallery of windows to the right frames the scaffold beneath Batavia's walls; to the left, the Chinese vegetable gardens and cemetery.

Maartens must sense my hesitancy. "They're waiting," he says.

"Who?"

He pares the upper lip from his teeth with a spatulant tongue, weighing what I might find palatable. "All of us, really."

"Specx?"

"Of that I'm not certain."

"Surely you're not escorting me to Van Diemen?"

"The Councillor begs your indulgence —"

"He begs for nothing."

"Some paperwork has arrived from India. Vapoer is at a loss to explain it. We had thought the mission profitable," he looks away with that apple of a head I remember, now, lodging at the back of Batavia's Church Council, his smuggled presence recording each of my piqued replies.

"I won't answer to some understudy of greatness. Take me to Coen. My fear of him lacks nothing in respect."

Maartens withdraws behind piscine eyes, then inclines his head and gestures to an oblong of radiant light. A shape — a silhouette without firm edge — wavers into definition, the figure cloaked and tasselled.

"Francisco, you've returned from Kashmir."

"And you, your lonely north?" I answer, recognising Andrade as he dances me a turn so that we briefly share the crepuscular light.

"I imagine there is much we might speak of, our journeys a shared leap into that unknown, eh? I pray there is yet time to compare and align our compasses, to purpose ourselves in the undertaking of God's will."

I smile, my sensibilities not as one with my visible ruin, this phantom self in progress towards its grave. In Antonio I live to sanction and to contradict, to love and deny. Such is the competition of my spirit that I would have him fail in his search for Shambhala, yet such, too, is the wonder of my better self that I would applaud, as if borne in the baggage of his adventure, the things we might discover together. The frontier is a faraway place, the thinning of humankind all too pronounced in fastnesses that have no conception of our birth or rivalry. I find his eyes as searching as mine, his face so near as to distract me from the rancidity of my own breath. "Was it as you might have hoped?"

His hesitancy swiftly defers to an excited reinvention of the difficulties. "Like you, we were forced to travel disguised as traders."

"Ours was no disguise."

"No?"

The glowing oblong beckons and I'm impatient to move on. Antonio is attentive to the darkness whence I've come. "Are you still an apostate?" he asks, not looking at me.

"Can you dare separate Christians at so un-Christian a distance?"

And it's his turn to smile. "You're not long, I perceive, from appearing before God's seat. You were born a Catholic."

"My family's countenance was numbed by atrocity."

He inhales deeply. "'Tis no time to quibble. They are waiting."

"Who?"

The rustle of his skirts the only reply, I find myself alone. Behind me, all is sealed into an obscurity as baffling as forgotten thoughts. There's nothing for it but to step into the light, its vivid uncertainty.

As if emerging from a cave, the sky pulses with a green intensity, and all is vast around me.

"We need to make a decision," says Jacobsz, the tiller crutching a stained armpit.

Before I can query his release from captivity, I perceive the others, their orderly cuddy of heads uplifted and expectant. Everyone except Evertsz, that is, who looks away fiercely, contemplating, perhaps, the chimerical liberation of the sea. Is he destined to die a second time? I wonder. At a distance, and all the more arresting for its stalking of our silence, an unbroken thunder trembles on the breeze. The surf.

"Well?" the skipper asks, his tone devoid of hate, his bearing that of a man who is relieved, now, not to have to make the final decision. And it seems to me there is only one thing we *can* do. In the clarity of that moment, freed from a future that has otherwise consumed me, I glance at that un-giving shore, its beach screened by the rolling swell and breaking filigree, and know that its temptation bears no fruit. I will no longer seek where succour is withheld.

"If they are there," I say, "it is of no importance," and referring to the charred figures who, stick-like, scatter at our approach. Yes, I have stared at the smoulder of their fires, the ashes without hearth. Even Hottentot squalor didn't preclude a useful commerce, their cattle our provision, our silver their reward. But in this place beyond the Cape, distanced in time and separated by ocean, these fragments of mankind with their edgy fear are of no service to us. Tapping the replenished water casks, "We go back," I order.

The skipper grunts and is satisfied. Evertsz stands with one foot on the gunwale to summon the yawl which bobs close by. Its two occupants are not easy to identify – they seem at all places in a story whose calendar is falling into disorder. Loos – yes, I can stomach him – and that flush-fleshed youth, Pelgrom. Christ, I'll be relieved to see the last of him!

"Ahoy," shouts Evertsz, cupping his mouth, "Where are you headed?"

"To that unknown shore," answers Loos. "Pelsaert lets us live so that we may die an uncertain death." He is standing over his unsavoury companion and the trinkets given to barter for their survival.

Evertsz sees his chance. "Wait, I'll come with you!"

But the yawl has passed into the dusk which encroaches from the east, even as the sun blazes like a brass cymbal overhead and the sky, there, is bleached. All too clearly a gibbet is visible on the island headland that heralds our approach.

And there they stand in crescent flock, wavelets lapping at their feet as they invest the shingle of Batavia's Graveyard. Their outstretched arms, their expressions of misconstruing fear are as I remember. *Come back. Don't leave us!* The shallows kick and hiss with their stampede, the water unsteadying and strangely foreign to all who have dwelt within its boundless compass this past year. Splash splash splash, faces clawed askew, the yammer of a disuniting panic. Only this time I'm not pulled back into the boat by disavowing hands intent on saving themselves. "I will deliver the water," I say, turning to the crew who rest placidly on their oars. To my surprise I find it is Jacob and his brother seamen. He taps the cask. "It took some doing but we retrieved the vinegar."

The beelike drone from the shingle suddenly dies like a last report of gunfire. Coen is standing beside me, his breastplate steely blue, a red sash completing the appearance of a great condottieri.

"So, it's now yours," he says, surveying the coral archipelago which smokes in the ruin of its crushed rebellion.

"Was this how it felt when you took Jacatra?" I ask.

He wrinkles his nose. "I rather think I had more to build upon. Still, let's go ashore and investigate." And a page hands us each a helmet.

The crowd has reformed at the water's edge, a silent honour guard dressed in rags and bereft of shoes. The cask struggles like a piglet beneath my arm. Coen deigns not to notice; he's no connoisseur of vulgar comedy. Bodies lie strewn about, the slaughter random but intense. Nearer the tents the pikemen cluster. A drum rattles its curt staccato and the VOC banner with its embroidered lettering is draped across the entry of what were Cornelisz's quarters. No one much bothers to note my approach. Wiebbe is regaling his companions with an account of how it was: "When it came to fighting, there was little enough in them. It was an embarrassment, I say, verging on murder to have spilt their blood so easily." And chuckles of a knowing kind. "Some declared they'd fought in Germany. My arse. Just a lot of would-be looters. Not even proper pirates. Ah, Commandeur..." And he rises to his feet upon seeing me, his fellows turning to assess what next.

"Who's in charge?" I enquire, my voice reedy and uncertain.

The Company's ensign – brilliant in its red, white and blue – is drawn aside, and a slender young woman – more a child – reveals herself to the hungry stares of the troop. No man strays further than his thoughts, her uncovered shoulders feast enough. Then from the shadow behind her emerges a man of solid build, naked to the waist and skirted in a sarong.

"Meyer?" I say, more in whisper to myself. "You? Here?"

"Pelsaert," he waves. "It was only a matter of time." And stepping briskly to embrace me. Wiebbe sits observant within his circle, his men eating cheese with open mouths and rolling dice upon a drum as they cleanse the blood from their weapons. It doesn't hurt for Hayes to see that there are others I know, men of confident muscularity with whom I might align myself.

"But your family?" I say, and peeping over Meyer's shoulder to determine whether the girl now glimpsed is the girl once lost.

"Quite recovered," he smiles, and squeezing my shoulder. She ducks into the tent to re-emerge with a little boy on either hand.

"But I would have thought..." and not knowing what to think. "I mean, shouldn't they be grown by now?"

He turns to his child-wife with a fondness that appears almost some trick of memory. I want them to touch, to prove that they inhabit the same ether.

"You're a man of figures, weights and ledgers," he returns to me, "an accountant of deed and misdeed. It advantages no one to dwell exclusively upon a loss when the premise of all life is its brevity."

And seeing them there, I derive some comfort from the hope that I may have mistaken many things.

"You wish us restored and as one," he says. "I see it in your eyes." And he hoists the larger boy upon his shoulders, the other onto his hip. "We each live for what will pass, and in death may find ourselves rejoined with what was forsaken or misplaced."

"Then why am I haunted?"

Looking towards a perimeter of trees, the forest within which his domesticity draws its sustenance, he replies, "You've taken to answering for the Devil's play."

Wiebbe draws near to breathe into my ear: "Admit it, Commandeur, you envy me my hygiene of action, the fact that I sleep undisturbed by the ghosts of those who deserved to die."

"Do you believe in original sin?"

"I'm a simple soldier. It's you as was born a Catholic." And his expression is leering.

Perhaps I *am* envious of a simplicity that counsels sleep, that would soften and obliviate nightmare. *If only I might cut the guilt from this phantom self.* And aloud I say, "I've no desire to be cast by God as the Devil's stooge."

Cornelisz's menacing acoustic is heard at the edge of the forest; his guttural purr encircles the innocence of those who suddenly cleave to one another in the expectation of harm. I'm alarmed that Meyer's family, my sisters and their husbands, my mother and Opa – yes, all may be clawed to pieces in their unwitting separateness. Standing at a little distance and unaware of the danger, Gijsbert and Maartens, their collars neatly starched, their jackets more suited to the sobriety of a counting house than this dishevelling wilderness, are debating the number of angels that can dance upon a pin-head.

"Clownish and uncircumcised idiots," reproves Coen, and wanting to brandish his gauntlet.

"Aye, your Excellency," chimes Hayes. "They were of little comfort to the dying and of even smaller mettle in the prosecution of felons."

"*I'll* oversee the bloody prosecution," murmurs the merchant warlord under his deceased breath.

Then turning to me as he had that evening at Batavia Castle, his quarters as austere as a lonely sea at night, he is of a mind to give me this one last chance, to admit that in death he no longer commands the presence or vigour he once possessed. "You are to reclaim yourself for such a future as I, through diligence, have never failed to master or fulfil."

"Do you mean that I'm one day to become Governor?"

"I mean nothing of the sort. You're as good as dead and that talented arse-wipe, Van Diemen, has time on his side. Still, I don't care for a disaster on my watch, even less to having the afterlife haunted by another's failure."

"What more might I have done?"

Hayes and Coen exchange a sidelong glance. "I told you not to come back," says the great man, "– this was my express order – not to show your face until the job was completed."

My look of incomprehension further exasperates them.

"Look here," says Hayes, "His Excellency is giving you the chance to tidy yourself up. You're none too good to him cheerless."

"Tell me what to do."

"Now that's the spirit," and leering again in a way that makes him indistinguishable from the mutineers and cutthroats. "Kill him," he whispers, and reaching up to tap at my temple. "Kill him once and for all," and touching my breast.

The morning of the disaster crowds around me. They stand there in their hundreds, awaiting, from me, some expression of confidence that will fill them with hope. I look to the skipper for whom there is no question that the voyage must continue. Sailors are not settlers, and the settlers in their notional care are beginning to jostle like cattle freshly arrived at an abattoir. "You will not leave us," they bleat, and scenting in themselves the unpredictability of what they might become. There are more than I ever returned to.

"It is required that the Company's most senior official remain with the castaways of any shipwreck." Van Diemen hands me a scrolled parchment waxed with the Company seal.

I turn to interrogate Coen's ever stern visage but he's nowhere to be seen. Specx is being shown the chamber wherein his daughter was caught *in flagrante delicto.* He pauses to remember me before casting an eye over the women gathered by the shoreline.

"Do you understand me?" the voice of no one in particular. "You're not to leave the field of battle — not even to rally help."

Hendricxsz stares without seeing through bloodshot eyes. "The towns and villages — everything became so muddied. They do things different in Germany."

At the edge of the encampment a tattoo of hoof-beats raises a dust which obscures the sun. The horsemen shout and heckle, their red turbans a flowing field of poppies, their sabres shards of fire. The spellbinding of that encircling motion deftly unlocks caution, makes fear drowsy before such spectacle.

Jahangir grips my shoulder and I experience the autumnal love of a sunset shared. "I never imagined that one so near might so betray me," he mutters.

"He was a servant, after all," I reply. "They're paid to appear what they must seem, not what they are."

"And you — you've not thus found yourself undone?" He's too regal to permit himself an easy mockery.

Before I can answer, a sudden cry fetches our attention and those gathered on the beach splash into the shallows. Despite the emptying sensation of revisiting something that has unhappily taken place — indeed, I scan the crowd for my image — I find that I am not, this time, the object of their excited clamour. There is no boat. Jacobsz shrugs and looks away, embarrassed. I can tell there's a matter coming he'd rather not know of, a complication he's stoked but would now retreat from.

"Quick, lend a hand!" I hear them shout. "Help him! Raise him up!"

And a great crucifix of flotsam rises above their heads, the water cascading from a shroud of canvas.

"God be praised if it isn't the undermerchant!"

"At last, someone of authority..."

"Listen – all of you," I cry, "I've returned. I am here!"

But no one hears. Leastways none bother to turn in my direction.

Yet Jeronimus hears. In this insufferable pantomime he raises his head, his soaked and matted hair swept uncannily into a crown, and rolls his eyes as if resurrected from the dead. His grin is anything but grateful, his survival anything but unexpected. These fools – like the fools of Troy – will salvage him from his false abandonment! "Greetings Francisco," his expression seeks me out.

The die is cast, the sky bruised and purple as the soldiers play on, oblivious to that which will divide them and brew civil war where momentarily there was accord.

"Here! Here is the water you need!" I shout. "Here, too, the bread." And I deftly snatch the note I'd earlier left beneath its cask. "There's no need to fall out among yourselves."

But how can we presume to know what is not yet forged?

Yes, yes – at first this undermerchant behaved himself very well...

Without warning, a head rolls into their midst. A solitary scream sucks up the horror felt by all. Mattys Beer steps away from the now toppled chair, stooping to retrieve the blindfold and wipe his blade. A second head rolls among them, their panic gagging as they stagger backwards. Specx's daughter throws herself upon it, her heart no less scored than the flesh of her back. "Murderer!" she shrieks. "My father will make you pay for this!"

"And with Coen dead I'll pay even less for the widow," jests Van den Broecke, slapping my back in the presumption of our former camaraderie.

Thunder trembles, the clouds roiling like ashen thumbprints. I feel a quickening excitement, something akin to the adolescence of not knowing what next. The approach of a summer storm: its grassy perfume, the light dimming in a stew of magnetic calm. I'm untouched by the fear of others, too favoured by some singularity of grace that would bid me witness the unmasking of my soul. Rain stands at a distance like some paused and translucent army, shearwaters spiralling close as unworried children weave their game of chase in the palpable warmth. Yes, we stand for all the world to see and in full view of what is coming, clasped in a splendour of illicit moment. I scent your sheltered hair, taste the perspiration of your forehead, and gather to my breast the radiant miracle of another's life. I'm not at all self-conscious – not until something, someone, makes me draw away.

Who is it?

"No one. Least…"

Francisco?

"Van den Broecke, Vapoer – even Cornelisz – they all know I travel this way."

But then you're vanished from my arms, and I struggle to make sense of what evades me.

"A pity, Francisco, I wasn't around to administer to her need," says Jeronimus. "I'm something of a supernaturalist myself, always defying the silence Death is reckoned to impose." Then closely in my ear, "I could have potion-made her perky in no time. That Medari," he waves, but without a hand, "– such a snitch."

As the rain hisses in arrival and the surgent waves becalm, a clap of thanksgiving echoes through the camp. "We've no need of your water, now," they shout as sailors hurry to stretch canvases and funnel Heaven's bounty. The women toil with buckets in sodden relay towards the casks. No one minds. No one is of a mind to notice that the thunder speaks of something other than their salvation. One by one they begin to disappear, the water carriers struggling over swelling distances until, finally, they no longer connect with their fellows. Each is alone. Then it is that they attend the thunder.

Whatever I have loved, whatever I have tasted or been moved by in sight or hearing, there is not a moment to lose in the fight for its salvation.

Whatever I must do must be done of cold necessity. For the sake of others. For the sake of all our selves.

I seek out Wiebbe; alert him that he may be summoned. He surveys me coolly, knowing well my dependence upon his sword. "Be prepared to act at a moment's notice," I say. He weighs my words in the chewing of his thoughts then curtly nods, seizing the drum-roll of dice in a closing fist. There will be no more games.

There's a scuffle and a squeal, an oscillation of day and night in which the concealed is all too plainly presumed. Gijsbert breaks from his idleness with Maartens to turn to me for explanation. A muffle of overturning sounds issues from the predikant's tent, the light within fractured and elbowing. A gurgle drains on the ear as the sharpness of breath is throttled. "Not all of them, surely..." Gijsbert wears the startled expression of a man who discovers some gigantic and ruinous theft.

"Now!" I shout.

It's too late for them – the predikant's family. Indeed, it's too late for most who now crowd the open cloister before the Hall of Public Audience. There's a very public fracas on the beach – a dozen men in the act of reducing their number to six. Gulls flap themselves from harm's way, expecting nonetheless to savour what harm may bring. It's done so quickly, so neatly. Wiebbe approaches me with the swagger of a promise kept, his whiskers long and tangled, his face burned in its exposure to the sun. His eyes exhibit a lustre that is anything but faded, their blue as intent as moments of the sky above which continually reforms itself, is ever agile. "There, 'tis done," he salutes, and holding out his hand in a gesture of settled alliance.

"Ah, and prettily so," sings the emperor, alighting from his throne and stepping from the shaded Hall into the saline glare. "It raises an old tyrant's spirit to see the affections of those who should selflessly serve so reconciled in proper duty. Now let's examine what Hayes has secured. Let's see, Pelsaert, whether you possess the magistracy essential to your vice-regal aspiration."

His mother would be so proud of him.

My mother must never know of this!

"Come, come." Jahangir leads the way along a colonnade of fluted arches, his amirs – Wasim among them, with Meyer's wife and babe – lined up in respectful silence with their backs to the sea. Behind them stand the good burghers of Batavia, buttoned stiffly like crows in contrast to the citrus feather which ascribes the emperor's aviary. My shoes clack upon the marble with an insistence that makes me cringe inside my collar, all eyes trained on me with malicious curiosity.

"Hurry up, Pelsaert, the time has come."

He's a dissolving silhouette, swallowed in the creamy glare of a light without refuge, the sky no longer of any colour – simply unending. And this immensity seems to know me, seems to have awaited my coming or return. I am not afraid. Rather, I find myself intrigued, heartened by the caustic freshness of salt which pervades the air. It's then that I hear it – the surf, measured and immeasurable. It's as if I'm marooned and unaccompanied at the edge of time.

Except that I am not alone.

He's seated, one boot propped on the trestle table before him. The pull of buttons on his red laken testifies to an ill-fitted indulgence, its stitching of gold brocade unstuck in several places. He pushes back his hat, its ostrich feather bobbing in the breeze, and stifles a yawn.

"You seem unconcerned," I say.

He doesn't answer.

I approach the table cautiously, glancing this way and that as I collect my thoughts. He's studying his nails, the hygiene of his disdain.

"Where are the others?" I ask, and sensing their invisible host, watching.

He looks up, savouring, perhaps, the pretence of an inability to understand. His smile is of such wan contempt that it seems he has little stomach to feast on so cheaply wrought a superiority.

"What have you done with them?" I stand firm.

He shrugs. "I have nothing to answer."

"Not even for your mortal soul?"

And his laughter is growling.

"To hell with your devilry," I cry, "I'll no more tolerate its stamp here!"

He snatches himself to his feet but is unarmed, save for his venomous blood. And should its spilling sow the teeth of a thousand serpents, yet must I trust in God to armour my crusade against such snakeliness and aid me in the suppression of that terrible harvest.

The other senses my resistance, the fragility of his bravado. His expression becomes less assured, more vicious. "You'll never catch me," he says. "You're too squeamish to venture where I go." And pressing with both hands the table between us.

"I know where you will finish."

"Bah, it'll never be over. Not for you!" And pushing away, surly. "Trailing after the skipper, blaming him for what took place, unable to figure out there was a greater intelligence at work." His pride incriminates him. "Look around you!" he shouts. "Look at the fundamentals of what reigned here! While Jacobsz was fawning over you, masking his true nature to ensure that he reached Batavia in your good opinion, I reached into the very heart of that necessity which is so a mystery to you. To know that life bears us no scruple is to be freed of false modesties. There are the *haves* and *have nots*, and the rape of one is but meat to the other. It's an inescapable law where laws do not exist."

"Now *I* am the law. And whatever mistakes I've made, I shall not mistake you this time. Seize him!"

There's a blunt cry and a flurry of feathers. The colourless light of that empty day deepens into crowded twilight, a circle forming. At its centre a campfire flickers, skeletal driftwood fed into its embers to keep the water simmering. Despite my wanting to treat with them, the natives have not returned to their hearth.

"Do you think they're close by?" asks the young mother, and glancing over her shoulder at the approaching dark.

"Of course they are," spits Evertsz. "The Commandeur here is the only glimmer of light 'twixt the stars and damnation."

But the moment is too solemn for pardon. Evertsz knows it. Knows that his flattery ill-disguises his dislike; that it comes too late. Lowering his head he joins the line-up of those condemned.

Everyone settles into a silent suspension, this moment in which the clock is stopped and judgement presently ascribes the fate of those for whom there is no more time. Such is the smothering sensation in my chest, it's as if I'm about to read my own death sentence.

A chair is rushed me, forestalling any faint, and my papers (in Salomon's hand) are unscrolled on the bench at which I sit. Candelabra light my written words, Constantine's cameo a paperweight. Then clearing the anxiety from my throat, I begin:

"Because Jeronimus Cornelisz of Haarlem, aged about thirty, apothecary and later undermerchant of the ship *Batavia*, has behaved himself so gruesomely…"

Pretty words my petty lord.

"and been denuded of all humanity as if changed into a tiger…"

You try living in this cage of a place without deigning to rattle its bars a little.

"and because, even under the Moors and Turks, such unheard-of and abominable misdeeds would not have happened…"

Come now!

"we, the undersigned persons of the ship's council, in order to turn us from the wrath of God and cleanse the name of Christianity of such an unheard-of villain…"

Yes yes, get on with it!

"have sentenced the prisoner to be taken to a place prepared to execute justice, and there, first, to have both his hands cut off…"

What? My hands did nothing but procure a medicine for that whelping infant!

"and after that, to be punished on the gallows until death follows…"

And wriggling: *You're rather certain about that, my mortally fevered lord.*

"and with the confiscation of all his goods, wages and anything he may have claim to here, in the Indies, against the VOC, our Lord Masters."

"Ha, you would serve as thief to an even greater thief!" And struggling to free his arms. "Mark me, Francisco, your shitty salary and your shitty savings will likewise be stolen from you!"

"Prepare him," I command.

"Wait!" shouts Cornelisz, his eyes wild, his cunning panicky. "Let me first be baptised."

"So you admit, then, to living these years without God's light."

"Yes, yes. Leave me time to bewail my sins so that I might die in peace and repentance."

Wiebbe rolls his eyes whilst Gijsbert nods approvingly.

Cornelisz cleaves to the predikant as if to the witness of an honest friend. "I kept this man alive," he says to everyone gathered.

That's of no commendation to us, murmur the dead.

"Bastiaensz, tell me," hisses Cornelisz, "how much time will this buy?"

"My son, I see you're anxious to reside in the bosom of the Lord. I can baptise you this very minute in waters bloated with those recently summoned to His judgement."

"Bah, you fool, I'm in no hurry." Then wresting himself from the predikant, he glares at me, saying, "I need some warning; I need to know."

"What, how long you have to live?"

"How else might I prepare for what you have in store?" he scowls.

"In such a manner as you your victims readied."

"Ha," he gurgles, its subterranean echo prickling my skin, "I see you'll settle for nothing less than my blood and my life."

"Your life is not worth wanting. You'll be missed by none."

"My wife," he retorts, "she awaits in Batavia. Let me live that I might greet her one last time."

I stare at him in amused amazement. "I thought your family wrecked in Holland, your wife a cripple – doubtless dead – your babe withered in its prematurity." And before he can answer, I add, "I should have thought you anxious to be reunited with such infant innocence."

Such a howl as fills the sky; we're startled by the vigour of its mixed grief and rage. Wiebbe draws his sword but is uncertain wherein the danger. I resettle my composure and regard the prisoner with a harshness of eye. It's as if he is absent from himself – from his external features, at least – as the demon which animates his depravity withdraws him for a moment in bitter counsel. Then, to my unnerved disgust and the discomfort of all, he falls to his knees, his fetters chinking like pieces of silver, and begins to wail and beg like Pelgrom. "Please, please – maroon me with those two. I've sinned no more than they!"

Pelgrom, fidgeting, doesn't know what to think or say, and Loos fists the back of his head to make sure things stay that way. Cornelisz's successor then looks me in the eye and shakes his head almost imperceptibly.

"Get up," I say to the quivering hypocrite at my feet, adding contemptuously, "I would have thought you acquainted, well enough, with Death's bully-boys."

He razors a look that banishes all act. "Mark my word, Pelsaert, you'll not long survive me. I see the greyness of your flesh, the tarnish in your soul."

And in the weariness I feel, I remain unaffected by such prophecy. Indeed, I just want it finished. "Remove him," I say.

And yanking at his fetters, twisting this way and that at the touch of those who would bind him to my judgement, he shrieks, "God will not suffer me to die a shameful death! I know for certain – you'll see! He will perform a miracle this very night so that I'll not be hanged!"

There's a hole, a place of fragment bone and feathers, of filth and chill hopelessness. It's as shallow as a grave and as vast as the underworld. A stone is rolled across its opening to blot the sound of his foul unrepentance.

"Guard it carefully," I command. "I want nothing to befall him before we mean him just harm."

And turning, I'm startled to see Asmat, trembling like some shy and beauteous virgin, her eyes seeking communion, some privacy of trust. The scent of cinnamon accosts my breathing; the gold which encircles her wrists and ankles gleams like fire in the temptation of this moment. She shouldn't be here. It's difficult – dangerous for us both. Still, there's nothing for it, I decide, but to arrange our supper.

"No, don't leave me," she says. "Observe." And she reaches for the Venetian tumbler, my medicine glass.

I feel a compression in the chest, a sudden fall of temperature that shivers my fundament. Her eyes convey a glittering satisfaction as she raises the glass to her lips, and I cry out, "No!"

Whatever her boast, it is short-lived in the blunt and caustic transfiguration that follows. Her agonised face becomes an inhuman blur. Falling to the ground, she no longer inhabits any remnant of what remains. It's a wordless and groaning thing that coils at my feet.

Does he mean to kill himself? enquires one whisperer.

Does he believe that God will somehow deliver him? chimes another.

Personally, I think he wishes to spare himself the knife and strangulation. But before any of us can decide what to do, Jeronimus, in spasms that afflict his breathing, begs for Venetian theriac. He licks the last drop of syrup from Asmat's glass, his eyes and tongue alike as flickering as a serpent's.

"All better, prepared to die?"

He's suddenly down on all fours, retching and befouling his breeches so that his so-called miracle is working from below as well as above.

"What a spectacle you've become."

"Fuck off."

"Bastiaensz is a good man," I goad. "Prayer might launder you a little."

"If I'd known that spineless booby might outlive me by so much as a minute, I'd've had his throat cut for all that is unworthy of survival!"

"Submit you, then, to nothing?"

"I am what my flesh announces."

"Then let it be no more." And I draw my sword, the sun now overhead and intensely hot. There's a sound of hooves, the dust of horsemen. Wiebbe comes running up. "Go back," he gasps and doubling over, hands on knees. "He's escaped!" It's almost an apology.

I look at the circle of those now clinging to one another in a rumour of fear. A tiger's growl sets all their voice a-flutter like pigeons spooked.

Jahangir calls to me; is priming his gun. "Ah, Pelsaert, now it begins!" And the excitement of princely vigour animates his aged face.

Where I had thought the sea to be, I discern nothing of that linear clarity wherein a danger might be scanned. No enemy ship or mounting typhoon. Indeed, all is this territory of brush and nettle, of haze-reduced skies that obscure the pregnancy of distant clouds. I attend the emperor to enquire of what he's up to.

"It's simple. I've done this many a time. We'll have it flushed before our guns. By the way, you don't mind if Nur Jahan joins us? Such a marvellous shot! Did you know she once felled four tigers with just six bullets? Or was it five with five? Ah, no matter."

Beyond the line of beaters a colourful howdah wobbles into view.

But the register of something unnervingly near, a quaking almost subterranean, induces further panic among those unwilling to conceive that the world is other than they anticipate. Folk scatter every which way, the air filled with their yammer, our determined stance bustled aside in the frantic jettison of unity. It's not difficult to account for the many who will die where all is flight.

"Pelsaert, this is no time to stand about." And the line of beaters goes forward, their dusky limbs unprotected, their turbans more like unravelling bandages and revealing terrible wounds. The blaring horns and rattling drums intensify an awareness of inevitable confrontation, of imminent injury. Thunder ripples at a narrowing distance and a cry is heard, its piercing swiftly stifled. There's a commotion ahead, the path collapsed and a porter lost to the abyss. Men strain at tethers that connect with a cluster of dangling pack animals.

Jahangir grabs my sleeve, his demeanour shaken. "I saw this once. In a dream."

I turn from him towards the invisibility wherein a curdling growl now issues.

"He was in the act of chasing a deer..."

"A deer, you say?" and confused in what my ears claim otherwise.

"The sun was hot..."

"This is no slippered sport!" And wrenching my arm free.

"Wait!"

The sky trembles with a heatedness that smells of blood, and we both look heavenwards.

"If not God," I mutter, "then who?"

An explosion of arrival stops the heart, our poise briefly not of our command. The tiger is among us, having broken the line of beaters and pausing to jaw-crack the skull of one snared in the act. Its roar is ferociously triumphant, and unnerved formations of men break in flight, the emperor all but forgotten by those who now have something worse to fear.

It's only a matter of seconds before the tiger sees me – invites me, as it were, to contemplate oblivion in its crystal eyes. Despite my peril, I cannot feel but buoyed by its inability to divine my countersuit, to conceive of anything other than its craving to consume. As it paws aside the mangled corpse and the beaters distance themselves from the monster, I stand in focused spectacle, less girded for martyrdom than in gladiatorial readiness, though only possessed of a dagger.

Something makes a clicking noise behind me, an action too in haste and clumsily performed, and I glance across my shoulder. The leaping roar and detonation are as one and cancel my senses with their combined shock.

"There, Pelsaert," cries Jahangir as the gun smoke disperses, "I've ended your nightmare!" And a tray of opium is served, Randasingh with his father's lance and Fakkad Khan on his charger imbibing with a rewarded air.

But the emperor has not destroyed the beast, only shattered its teeth so that the ground grows spotted with their poison. The tiger tests its jaw – the wet reflex of pain – and howls so like a man that the sound is as unnerving for its unexpectedness as it is its anguished rage.

The tray is dropped, the celebration turns to alarm as the gun refuses to be hurriedly reloaded. "Pelsaert?" Jahangir stares at me with an unflinching that contrasts with the dispersal of his attendants. I would reach out if I could, but of my wish to seduce the emperor in friendship, the tiger's presence frustrates everything in a havoc of grave uncertainty. Then it leaps, its claws distended as if to spike whatever the wind might snatch away. Its bulk grows enormous, blotting out the sun as a second shot cracks loudly and the lead passes between us.

"Revenge!" shouts Cornelisz – "Revenge!" the monster all too human.

I topple beneath its weight like a sapling before an avalanche. So swift are its movements that I am unaware, at first, of the accruing damage its razored slashings inflict. Of its meaty breath, I consider *this* the most pressingly unwanted, and shift sufficiently to punch the brute in the face. The surprise elicits a savage snarl and I take advantage of its opened maw to strike with my dagger, to pierce its throat to the hilt. The recoil is sharp, the writhing frenzied, but in no wise is the danger ended. In maddened instinct it would kill that which has so inexplicably stung, and we grapple like wrestlers in wedded murder — I to my knuckles in its sinew, knowing that to draw away is to invite an annihilating swipe and choosing, instead, to cling to its garment like some mortal parasite, my knife fevered in its working at so close a quarter that it offers none.

At length the tiger hauls itself aside, dazed in the survey of its wounds and undecided as to what next. I likewise feel for, rather than dare survey, the ruin of my body. It's obvious we both must die, yet Death is a clumsy executioner. Hayes can stomach such unprofessional butchery no more and steps forward to lance the beast with a pike. The rush of sound is like a wind in combing seizure of a forest, the clouds inking angrily overhead. And accessory to this, I heed the reverberation, too, of something which at last un-hinges, a groan of agonised release as that which was snared now slips from its suspension to settle in merciful oblivion within the indigo deep.

"Pelsaert — oh my friend!" And Jahangir kneels beside me, snapping his fingers in summons of a beaker. "Here," and he holds the cup to my lips. The ruby in his turban is like a lozenge of blood, and I realise my fingers are sticky, that I besmear the hem of he who has bestowed its kissing upon the many who now form up behind him.

I try to speak, to reassure myself in the reassuring of this man that the storm is done, that his recognition is calming. But it's as if I am already parted from that which preoccupies his thoughts, a relic of the hunt now laid before his feet. My voice is no longer mine, the sound of what I would utter now distanced by a silence that envelops me in its warm pool. I am at once heavy and light, broken yet floating. Mouths gape and flap in mime, and the only thing I hear is this river-rush, a sort of cascading consciousness that stops my ears to the intrusion of everything I observe. I attend, instead, the march within me, its strident yet erratic stomp, and experience a wave of heat as if succumbing, short of sleep, to the effect of too rich a wine. I close my eyes and swallow heavily to survive this feeling, the nausea slowly ebbing from the shingle of my mouth. The carcass of a whale rolls towards the discharge of the sea, sandflies eating of its stench, and above an arid tumble of boats, houses cluster with a familiarity that has never beckoned. Girls are laughing, hoisted aloft by bawdy suitors who carry them into the twilight. I feel so tired – in spirit, all the more – and would fain rest but know not where to pause. Yet I no longer move.

"Come Francisco. Quick, out of bed!"

"But ma'am, the fever is upon him. Surely you see how it bleeds from his skin?"

"Nonsense," and drawing the covers aside only to flinch at the deep laceration of my soul. Somewhere close by, the spectre of a baby's mewling.

A table is set with a white cloth and a lighted candle. I want to drink of the water that stands beside the crucifix but I know it wouldn't be seemly, that the dead who crowd around and are upon their knees in prayer would shake their heads. When he arrives, their relief is palpable, the risk of having smuggled a papist among them now sublimated in the authenticity they feel for the solemness at hand. Yet he is anything but solemn, and in spite of the darkness which obscures this dimension wherein we meet, I see him smile, and with such comfort and assurance that I grow unafraid.

"Are you ready to return to Rome?" he asks.

"I passed you but a short time ago," I say, and trying to piece together the snippets of a friendship which has never had the wherewithal to be. And yet he is here for me now. "Antonio, you've allowed your hair to grow. There's ice in your beard."

The smile never leaves his face as he dons the chasuble. Someone hands him the water and a spoon, and I imagine myself about to sip when all is sprinkled in a fine mist. My eyes batten shut only to reopen on a sky that is clear. He is doubled over as if in weakness himself.

Go forth, O Christian soul, from this world...

"Did you ever attain your journey's end?" I ask.

Renew, O merciful Father, that which has been vitiated in him by human frailty, or by the frauds and deceits of enemies...

"Did you hear tell of what befell us? Were you among those astonished and dismayed?"

May you be a stranger to all that is punished with darkness...

"I am pleased you've come."

May Christ deliver you from your torments and eternal death, and place you in the ever-verdant lawns of His Paradise.

"Not a bad exchange," endorses Jahangir and grinning, the colour draining from his features, his torso ashen beneath its transparency of muslin.

"I'm so weary. I think I would rest awhile." And not for the first time a chill apprehension steals over me, this fear of being alone in an undecided moment. I close my eyes, only to realise they are unfastened once more, the archway rising heavenward, and in its patterned calligraphy the message: *He who hopes for an hour may hope for eternity.*

"The world is but a bridge," she continues, and nestling my head, "pass over it but build no house."

I'm unable to tell whether that is proper or sad. Still, I look up with such relief for her presence that tears begin to pool in my eyes. "Are you my angel of Death?"

She smiles and tenderly strokes my brow, then raises her face to look out over what I cannot see, her throat tight with emotion, the warmth of her limbs in wreath of mine. Beyond what her nearness eclipses of the sky, strange birds spiral at a distance against its cerulean expanse. My eyes follow them in unblinking trail until they vanish amidst the vegetation of a nearby outcrop and I realise, then, that we are in some elevated place.

"See," she whispers, and bending low to kiss my forehead before resuming her faraway vigil.

From this nested garden with its vine-clasped walls and crumbling memorials, overseeing a distance that stretches towards Fatehpur and the rising sun, the plain quickens with a miraculous alchemy as the haze-hidden fields, their dewy dawn, become as of the sea, the swelling radiance revealing a boundlessness of aquamarine. As I survey with awe the uncluttered infinitude before me, I notice something at first un-glimpsed, a distant object fixed to the almost imperceptible ocean ripple. Staring with speculative curiosity, I discern, in fact, that this object is slowly approaching, that a chevron opens in the wake of its casual progress. And as if apprised of a magnifier, I suddenly recognise her for what she is, her bow gracefully rising and subsiding, the water scooped and draining from the latticed beakhead as her gilded lion dares the way. With sails stretched and pennants gusting in the breeze, she ploughs towards me like a child's rocking horse, her rhythm reined to the rescue of my admiration, the temptation of my forgiveness. And so I wonder of what I've journeyed, my troubled heart now eased of pain as if awaking from some nightmare. I see *Batavia* in all the bloom of a destiny recovered, her promise mended and forever shrouded in the presence of eternity.

VAN DIEMEN STANDS at the casement of the Council chamber and gazes out on the parade ground. The apertures of the dungeons flank the shaded side of the quadrangle like grated mouse holes. He visited them, once, but the experience turned his stomach and he's never been back. Doesn't need to. The Fiscaal Advocate can oversee their purpose. All he wants are reports, documents to compare and use in evidence against anyone likely to deny him.

Maartens has put away his stylus and will gather up the minutes once the ink has dried. It was a good meeting, thinks Antonio, one in which his voice rang clearer and with singular authority. Who says Friday the thirteenth is unlucky? Even the resident cat whose duties are relaxed and whose dark coat underscores such superstition, threads his ankle with an acquiescent docility. He finds himself smiling without intending to, for to be caught smiling without admissible cause is to be caught in too suspect a privacy. As a junior himself, once, he knows what it is to serve ambitiously. And Maartens, despite an outward clericalism which makes him seem as if he wouldn't so much as nibble a crumb of cheese without the Governor's say-so, is no ingénue where advancement is concerned. It's not unusual to borrow men – especially those of a scrivening disposition – from the service of the Church. But harbour no illusion as to their principles, especially when they've been recruited to eavesdrop on the thoughts of rivals.

"Did you minute Pelsaert's death?"

Maartens nods the once. "In referencing our successful mission to Jambi, I recorded that the Councillor –"

"May I remind you," interrupts van Diemen, "that Heer Pelsaert was never duly confirmed in that position." And as if emphasising the improbability of it ever happening, he adds, "The *Batavia* incident alerted us to a number of questionable goings-on, matters incompatible with high Company office."

Maartens bends slightly, his face expressionless. "I've noted that the late *Commandeur* died here after a long illness."

Even that sounds too generous to Van Diemen's ears. But then he recalls his own epistle to Amsterdam's High and Mighty, and is soothed to imagine that his assessment must have made its impression by now. *It is certain that a completely Godless and evil life has been conducted on the mentioned ship of which both the skipper and Commandeur Pelsaert are greatly guilty. May the Almighty forgive their sin and make good the damage to the Company...*

It's of no small satisfaction to Antonio that the other is deceased and that he should find himself in possession of the final word. The unwanted dead are marooned from their salvation among the living. Yes, who would speak for Pelsaert if the man could no longer speak for himself? Even in the proxy of his voice, Van Diemen knows (as he similarly knows of what Bastiaensz had to say when Maartens conveyed the predikant's unopened letter to his desk prior to its despatch to the Fatherland) that Pelsaert's final correspondence to the Company is as incoherent as it is self-serving. Woe, woe, woe:

> *I can clearly see that a human being often finds that his worldly*
> *welfare has fallen into the hands of two or three perfidious men.*
> *At present the pack of all our disasters has moulded together*
> *and fallen on my neck, yes, not quite possible to express with*
> *the pen, and though I have cried my eyes, shall be able, by*
> *the Grace of God, to resume due service and Duty such as I*
> *have always endeavoured in service to the Company, as I did*
> *although I was exhausted due to serious illness into which I had*
> *fallen at the Cape until the ship happened to be wrecked that*
> *I had come to Batavia 400 miles with the boat in great misery*
> *with hunger, thirst and want...*

And so it goes, on and on until that grovelling sign-off:

> *Honourable, Brave, Wise, Provident, Very Discreet Honourable*
> *Lords, I shall pray God that according to my humble Wishes,*
> *He will safeguard Your Honours from further damage, and will*
> *bless you with a year of expansion and abundant trade and all*
> *that is necessary for your souls' salvation.*

You would have better served yourself to have invoked God to shepherd you from your own vices and shortcomings, thinks Antonio.

"And Heer Pelsaert's will?" enquires Maartens.

"What of it?"

"He leaves everything to his mother. Should we honour it by making the arrangements?"

Antonio considers. There's still that consignment of Pelsaert's — the jewels and the toys to dispose of, an indulgence which someone will have to pick up and deal with. Not to mention these reports of debauched living among those residing at Agra. He might be dead but it is far too soon to be putting him to rest. "Not yet," he answers. "The Company can't be rushing to the succour of every claim upon its servants." Then to underline the difficulty: "Especially as we're not fully apprised of whether the late uppermerchant doesn't, in fact, owe *us* something."

Maartens' expression grows even more inscrutable. It wouldn't do to be a friend of drink and seek unguarded release in the company of such watchful underlings, thinks Van Diemen. He doesn't much care for predikants, even less these laymen and sick-visitors who busy themselves without fit purpose. Yet the Church and its apprentices have their occasional use. Governor Specx certainly thinks so, although he remains less than enthusiastic about Bastiaensz, and admonishes the Church Council for its willingness to untaint that ineffectual cleric who'd sworn allegiance to the Devil's own. Well, I'll leave that to the Governor to anguish over, he thinks, having at least made use of this scribbler without a vocation for anything other than his nourishment.

Van Diemen has other things to mull over, ideas not as yet committed to any plan but worthy of consideration in one who may some day command this ship of state. He finds himself smiling once more and quickly returns his gaze to the window. A company of soldiers is marching across the quadrangle in prelude to a changing of the guard. The standard bearer, he sees, is that fellow who organised the resistance in the Abrolhos. Well at least the most reliable of them didn't die, he sniffs, and watching as their boots, to the tap of a solitary drum, stomp past the grated mouse holes on which he now permits his eyes to linger. With his back to Maartens he enquires, "Is the Fiscaal Advocate any nearer to concluding his investigations?"

The servant, uncertain of what is being asked, awaits elucidation.

"Oh never mind," and facing about, Antonio indicates with a snap of his fingers that the other should shuffle his paperwork together and be gone. Maartens bows respectfully in passing, leaving the Councillor alone.

Jacobsz is as guilty as sin, he thinks. But then he wasn't in the Abrolhos for all the killing that took place. I only had Pelsaert's accusation to go on, and now Pelsaert is dead. They're mostly gone, those who had something to answer for. All except the skipper and those two, out of sight, for whom an unwarranted mercy has set upon the Great South Land.

His concentration becomes intense, calculating, imagining the possibility when one day – and all of this is his to govern – he might push the boundaries of what is known; indeed, discover, perhaps, in the footprints of those exiled delinquents whether a white man might prosper in such regions to the south. It would require ships and men; men of particular resourcefulness. And hadn't Jacobsz demonstrated remarkable seamanship in bringing an open boat to Java? No one had perished on his watch. Furthermore, it isn't as if he can get up to any harm where he is. His release might even earn a fervent gratitude. And if the Fiscaal *does* conclude that there is something to answer for, then his hanging will be of no consequence.

Alone, Antonio permits himself to grin freely in this chamber wherein the mighty Coen rarely smiled. He reaches for the tray which bears the meeting's remnant sweets and coffee. He pours a little milk, crumbles a biscuit, and sets this down for the cat which purrs aloud in fond anticipation, his fingers caressing and kneading its scruff.

More will come, he thinks. Yes, in spite of disease and death, the colony will absorb and continue to fatten upon the hopes of an emigrating hunger. It's as if he can envisage its future, can appreciate in himself a talent for building up what force alone might only lay a foundation to. And shaking his head at the wonder of it, relieved, now, to have woken from the embarrassment of his own credulity; yes, to think that he had sorely imagined Pelsaert a rival for the affection of this empire destined.

AUTHOR'S NOTE

THIS IS NOT history; this is a work of historical fiction and one, at that, of the most speculative kind. In imagining the reveries of Francisco Pelsaert in the final days of his life, I have permitted myself to entertain a great many unknowables and distinct improbabilities. It is improbable, for instance, that he ever met Antonio Andrade, the Jesuit and first known European to venture into the Himalaya. One was an ambitious merchant of the Calvinistic VOC, the other an ardent Catholic missionary. That they resided in India at the same time, and were both adventurers according to their ends, simply excited my literary purpose.

Similarly – and despite the unflattering portrait he gave in his *Remonstrantie* – it is dubious whether Pelsaert was ever in a position to closely observe the Mogul emperor Jahangir, let alone meet this all-powerful ruler. Jahangir's presence in the novel characterises the dishevelled aspiration of an increasingly tangled and impressionistic consciousness.

What we *do* know of Pelsaert is derived, initially, from his own writings: first, the *Remonstrantie* (1626), a commercial essay intended for the VOC executive in Amsterdam and filled with observations concerning the people and customs of India; and second, his *Batavia Journal* (1629), a record of the shipwreck and its aftermath. In addition, much of Joannes De Laet's *Empire of the Great Mogol* (1630) was compiled from Pelsaert's reportage of the dynastic history and politics of the day.

Henrietta Drake-Brockman in her *Voyage to Disaster* (1963) drew attention to the biographical significance of Pelsaert's *Remonstrantie* and incorporated his shipwreck journal in her survey of one of the world's most infamous maritime episodes. It was her inclusion of Pelsaert's final letter to the VOC's "High and Mighty" which so haunted me, its tenor of nervous exhaustion dramatically at odds with his previously urbane literary manner.

The other key work I relied on was Mike Dash's *Batavia's Graveyard* (2002). This superbly researched history provides, in my opinion, the best contextual overview of the people and places associated with the brewing mutiny and its appalling narrative. Never absent from my desk, it was a major reference and source of ideas (the fascinating endnotes are not to be overlooked).

Other works which enriched my understanding of events and gave context to the Dutch encounter with Australia included Malcolm Uren's *Sailormen's Ghosts* (1945), Hugh Edwards' *Islands of Angry Ghosts* (1966), Rupert Gerritsen's *And Their Ghosts May be Heard* (1994), and Simon Leys' *The Wreck of the Batavia & Prosper* (2005). Of particular value, especially for its lavish illustrations and anatomy of the doomed ship (now replicated and docked in Holland), was Philippe Godard's *The First and Last Voyage of the Batavia* (1993).

As for literary fiction, the *Batavia* shipwreck and its consequences have spawned a formidable library of telling and retelling. The earliest of these date back to the 1890s, and Drake-Brockman herself had a novel published in 1957 (*The Wicked and the Fair*). Writers continue to be stimulated by the foreign ancestry of that distant time, its blunt and bloody drama, and a number of works (not to mention an Australian opera) have been produced in recent years – interestingly, several for young adult readers. *Pelsaert's Nightmare* is my contribution to a re-imagining of what it may have been like to have stood in afflicted witness of events that would change one's life and dispute its posthumous reputation.

For an overview of the Netherlands' mercantile activities, I am indebted to C. R. Boxer's *The Dutch Seaborne Empire 1600–1800* (1965). For a treatise on the Dutch mindset during its Golden Age, there can be no more informative a cultural history than Simon Schama's *The Embarrassment of Riches* (1991).

In my attempt to portray seventeenth century India (and further to those contemporary accounts given in the *Remonstrantie* and *Empire of the Great Mogol*), I made principal use of Bamber Gascoigne's *The Great Moghuls* (1971) and Abraham Eraly's *The Mughal Throne* (2003) and *The Mughal World* (2007).

The autobiographical *Memoirs of Jahangir* (1909 translation), of course, offered a singular insight into this ceaselessly indulged yet ever inquiring ruler. The panegyric lines composed on the occasion of the emperor's birth were sourced from Chob Singh Verma's *Mughal Romances* (1996). As for the small scene in which Randasingh and Fakkad Khan boastfully compare the status of their fathers, this tale was discovered in Ganeshji Jethabhai's *Indian Folklore* (1903).

In whatever loudly contravenes historical accuracy or offends credence in speculative verisimilitude, I alone am responsible.

About the Author

GREGORY WARWICK HANSEN lives in Melbourne, Australia, with his wife, Sherrie.

Having majored in literature and history at Monash University, *Pelsaert's Nightmare* is his debut novel.

An early manuscript was shortlisted for the inaugural 2016 First Novel Prize in the United Kingdom, and a later draft was a First Place Category Winner in the 2018 Chaucer Book Awards for Pre-1750s Historical Fiction.

Greg has also adapted the novel into a screenplay.

www.gregoryhansenwriter.com

ACKNOWLEDGEMENTS

PELSAERT'S NIGHTMARE HAD a lengthy gestation and I would like to acknowledge those who partnered its emergence, in particular its first readers. Offering one's offspring to the critical engagement of others is a daunting prospect, and the commentary and feedback received contributed greatly to the maturing of this work.

Notwithstanding my wife's sentinel presence throughout the writing process, Wayne Wescott's incisive enthusiasm for the novel's literary ingredient prompted the confidence to begin thinking of a wider audience. With a view to this engagement (and in full knowledge of the narrative and stylistic challenges inherent in *Pelsaert's Nightmare*), I am grateful to Duncan MacKinnon for applying a forensic eye to early and subsequent iterations of the text; similarly, to Christine and Ross Gibbs for suggestions which, I hope, rewarded their renewed encounters with the manuscript. Thanks also to Karen Stephens, June Graham and Erin Giles (as well as my mother, Shirley, and brother, Craig) for their patient reading of early drafts, and to my 11-year-old friend Callum Lam whose unwavering belief that 'this will be a good book!' must remain (for him, at least) untested for the best part of another decade. I also want to thank Hamish Fitzsimmons (well-versed in the *Batavia*/Pelsaert story) for his endorsement of this determinedly individual and sidelong approach to one of maritime history's most notorious chapters.

While not without their subjectivity in result, literary competitions offer a valuable testing ground, and I want to acknowledge the impetus derived from varying levels of recognition achieved through the Fellowship of Australian

Writers Jim Hamilton Award, the First Novel Prize (UK) and the Chaucer Awards for Pre-1750s Historical Fiction.

Of the physical artefact itself, I additionally want to thank Christine Gibbs for her cover art which so captures the sanguinary humour of Pelsaert's remembrances, as well as Jennifer Bullock for her complementary cover design and map drawings. Likewise, a big thanks to Julie-Ann Harper at Pickawoowoo Publishing Group for her guidance and contributive midwifery in helping to bring *Pelsaert's Nightmare* into the world. I also want to thank Doug Willis for affording me a digital existence and addressing my e-life concerns.

It goes without saying that the most generous and constant support has come from my wife, Sherrie. During these years of composition and promise, disappointment and eventual release, she has nourished my love, sustained my endeavours, and more than earned the dedication of this novel.

www.ingramcontent.com/pod-product-compliance
Lightning Source LLC
Chambersburg PA
CBHW020001120726
47903CB00004B/1083